OSCAR WILDE

OCEANS AND TIME BETWEEN US

Jolene McCall

OCEANS AND TIME BETWEEN US

Copyright © 2021 by Hori-Son Press

www.horisonpress.com

info@horisonpress.com

Hori-Son
PRESS

Cover Design by Lynn H. Pellerin

ISBNs: 978-1-938186-09-7 (paperback)
      978-1-938186-10-3 (hardback)

SAN 920-251X

Library of Congress TXu002246985

SPECIAL ACKNOWLEDGEMENTS AND MENTIONS:

The Berghoff Restaurant, Chicago Illinois, *Thank you Pete, 4th Generation Berghoff Family!*
The Clontarf Castle Hotel, Dublin, Ireland, *Thank you Sandra!*

Also, a special thanks to all who contributed in many ways. This has truly been a long rewarding journey, a vision that has taken many turns, leading to the final completion—

Josh & Kelly Carlson, Sandra Guillory, Kristin Hawkins, Matthew Rex Holland, Chase Manuel, Lynn Pellerin, Hannah Catherine Photography

DEDICATION:

A special dedication to Daniel... you are always in my thoughts, forever and a day—memories are made! Our song, *Somebody,* selected within the story, I chose for you. Always remember—our special moments in time. I love you eternally!

CHAPTER
1

It was a gloomy night in Chicago, February of 2000, as the rain mixed with snow flurries had continued for several days. Awakening in the night from my dreams, I walked into the kitchen to make a nice hot cup of tea, which always seemed to bring comfort on such lonely, dark, and cold nights like these. Climbing into the picturesque window in my living room, I sipped my tea as my thoughts drifted from deep within. My comfy nook had become my place of escape, my haven, as many nights I would cuddle up on the large fluffy pillows which lined the walls and seat. Often times, this was my place of tranquility before retiring for the night—a place to read a good book, as I had grown to love so many different genres over the years—history, various cultures, and art, even a good novel written by many of the greats from the seventeenth on into that of the nineteenth century. Lately, my nook had become my place of refuge and serenity, lined with many framed poems and famous quotes that I had collected over the years. They all seemed to bring comfort as I connected with the words deep within. This night like so many others, I would find myself—alone—yes, so alone. Yet, it was in the stillness that my thoughts would come from what some would claim to be merely our mind at work.

Nonetheless, as a writer, I knew my thoughts were from a deeper place, a place within, a place that must escape where it brings clarity and peace. Could I explain my thoughts? Was there meaning to my dreams? Does life seem to somehow get lost, and if so, where is it found? Can it be found, and what about thoughts and dreams? Do they live and breathe within us? Within a place deep inside, where one can live and breathe another life. Are we able to fathom their meanings? Is there something far superior in which each of us longs for but never seems to find? Is my life of purpose, and if so, where is purpose to be found? Oh, how the questions and the thoughts never seem to flee from me. Perhaps, they never will, nor are they ever meant to escape.

My life, oh Lord, my life—where do I find my purpose in this mere existence—where do I begin? For, I know it is near, and there must be meaning to my life somehow. The dreams come, and the dreams go. They seem to be more prominent and more often as the

1

days, years, and time continues. Oh, sleepless nights—awaken me to dream, even more.

~~~~~~~~~~

Her head was filled with thoughts once more as Cateline sat in her window seat, which overlooked the beautiful Chicago River and the skyline of the downtown area. She loved to view the moon with its reflection shining brightly over the river, with a gorgeous but lonesome type of tranquility of the city. Drifting back to the dreams that had begun again, Cateline commenced filtering through the book and assorted articles she had discovered only yesterday. The tears fell, cascading lightly over her face, as she knew no one would ever understand what she was feeling. She silently whispered some of her favorite quotes, *"As soon go kindle fire with snow, as seek to quench the fire of love with words."* [1] Awe, yes—Shakespeare had such a way with words, as I, too, feel lost—the fire burns within me desiring the love. Yes, the love that once was. My dear Mr. Wilde, if you only knew the depths of my heart— *'For a dreamer is one who can only find his way by moonlight, and his punishment is that he sees the dawn before the rest of the world.'* [2] The moonlight, how I love the blazing mirage as it shines upon the waters, with the glimmer of hope amongst the darkness beneath. Yes, help me find my way, my love. Let not the dawn bring forth my punishment, for my passion runs deep—oh, so deep—that I could touch you and feel your presence. Oh, such a world is this, but this is not my time, nor is this my century."

Knowing this would be another sleepless night, Cateline picked up the book and articles discovered the day prior at the library and filmed through the various pictures while reading the captions. Having read them numerous times since she had brought them home, tears still continued to flow, as if it had been the very first time they were viewed. Unsure exactly what it all meant nor what may lay ahead, she drifted back to the time when the dreams had first begun.

Cateline, being an only child, was born and raised in Boston, Massachusetts. Her parents were of Irish descent, coming to America in the 50s at a very young age from Ireland. America in those days was referred to as *the land of opportunity*. Yes, they had been very fortunate, opening an Irish pub in Boston's downtown district. Life had been good for them, the business prospered, and they eventually opened two other locations. Everything had seemed to be in their favor, except they had desired to have many children. This dream had washed away over time, as her mother never conceived in those first years. Despite everything, in their early forties, her mother was with child, a most unexpected pregnancy, and Cateline was born in 1975. How blessed they had finally felt; Cateline's arrival was often referred to as a miracle. She could still hear her father, as if it was yesterday, proclaim to others, "Yes, this is our little miracle baby blessed by God."

Cateline had grown up never knowing any hardship, as she was given the best education and opportunities for any child. However, she was very devoted and attached to her father due to her mother being ill and passing away before Cateline had yet to turn seven. Yes, she was a *daddy's girl* and loved him tremendously. It was in her early years, sometime after her mother's passing, the dreams had begun for the first time. They would awaken her in the night, producing much agony—screams and cries could be heard in those initial years after her mother's death, arousing her father as he would rush to her room to bring comfort. Cateline never quite understood their meanings in those days. Being consoled by her father, she would share each and every scene. With Cateline recalling detailed images and foresight, this always seemed to bring about a certain amount of pain to her dad. Even so, as time had evolved, Cateline was able to recognize the agony in which he felt. Growing older brought about the maturity to understand how excruciating it had been for him, where she began to conceal the occurrences.

Her dreams had always seemed to be born out of Ireland, for she could describe the various people and the locations in the most illustrative way to her father in those first years. As it was, Cateline had only been to Ireland one time when she was barely three years old and had no recollection of even being there due to her young age. In spite of everything, her father could recognize certain family members and others by Cateline's account. As for her descriptive surroundings, for the most part, her father was able to identify the locations in Ireland, with some being places they had been and others they had not. With her being just a child when they traveled to Ireland, her father knew Cateline would not have remembered. Still,

3

he assumed she must have seen pictures that were embedded in her mind, thus producing the exact portrayal of her depictions.

Nevertheless, as the dreams persisted, the insights shared with her father were of places in other areas of Europe. Ultimately, the dreams had always awakened her, as there would be a horrific death, but she never could visualize nor know who the person was that had perished. Her father had always assumed the nightmare of death resulted from her own loss of her mother, which would have been a normal part of grief. However, the reveries seemed to agonize her father extremely, as he had no understanding of how Cateline could describe those places in which she had never been nor seen. At some point, Cateline had decided to spare him the discomfort.

As time went on and Cateline grew older, the dreams had lessened. Cateline grew up a happy child, which maintained into adolescence. In the early years at Bradford College, the dreams returned and became more frequent. By the time graduation came, the dreams had become a part of her life, as it had been over a decade since they had first begun. During this timeframe, she recognized and knew who some people were as she had finally studied one, particularly in college—yet many were folks that her father had never known. Since early childhood, Mary, Cateline's closest friend, had become the only person to ever hear of these occurrences besides her dad.

Mary and Cateline had grown up together as small children, living in the same quaint neighborhood. They had been very close, as sisters, since Mary was also an only child. As it was, Cateline merely shared the visions with Mary but never went into the details of what she truly felt. What was embedded deep inside Cateline was lost within, held onto intimately—her thoughts and feelings solely buried in her heart. Her beliefs, she knew, could never be shared with anyone because no one would ever understand. Yet, her remembrances of all which she held within had become a part of her existence, for there was something much greater to the reasons for the dreams all these years. It was as if she lived and breathed in another period and knew that no one could even begin to understand her reasonings.

Drying her eyes, which were swollen after another night of tears, Cateline got down out of her nook and walked to the bedroom, taking down some old photo albums from her closet shelf. Walking back into her living room, she sat on the couch and sorted through the albums reminiscing over pictures of her childhood and both of her parents. Oh, how Cateline felt so alone. How she had loved sharing with her father, but once he had become up in age, it was more about protecting him from knowing her pain. With both of her parents gone, she would have given anything to have had one more day to share with them. One more day to have known her mother's past life. One more day to have asked many unanswered questions to her father. One more day to have had direction in her own life where perhaps, she would understand what the images were trying to show her. How Cateline knew that there was a meaning to all of this. Somehow, she knew that the dreams had been preparing her all these years for her mission, which lay ahead. So many thoughts filled her mind, contemplating to herself, "Oh, but what journey was this to proclaim? What direction should my passage be? And should it be that I would know what lay ahead? Where should I turn? Oh, Lord, should it be that You shall show me the way? Is there an answer to these questions, and so many more?" Cateline expressed loudly that particular night, "Lord, should my way be told to me? Should my answers be revealed? For, I cannot sleep; I feel as I cannot breathe. But, Lord, oh please that You show me my way. As I sit among darkness within my soul, I pray that You lead me—that You show me all where my journey shall go and for what purpose my life shall be."

Cateline felt alone—so alone. With her discovery, she knew and was determined that decisions had to be made. Arising from the couch, once again, she went to lie down in her bed with hopes of being able to acquire a few hours of sleep, but as the clock continued to tick, hearing each second pulse through her mind, the tossing and turning brought torment to her senses. Sitting up and flipping the switch to her bedside lamp, she looked at the time. Distraught, she proclaimed, "Three o'clock, there is no way I will be able to work today. I am not sure I can do this anymore. I must make a stern decision on where my journey in this life should lead me. I cannot make a wise decision without some amount of sleep." Getting out of bed once again, she decided to take an extensive hot soothing bath to soak up the effervescence and bring some solace to the distress felt within. As she lay immersed in the steaming water filled with lavender mineral salts, Cateline relaxed her mind and body in order

5

to think rationally. Breathing in the aroma, which filled the air from the bath salts, her thoughts drifted far away, absorbed in the dreams plaguing her mind. She must have relaxed in the infusion of the refreshing waters for at least an hour before deciding to get dressed.

Once dressed for the day, Cateline ate a quick breakfast before deciding to bundle up and take a long walk in Grant Park. It was a little after five, but there were always people up and about by that time of the morning. With the beautiful view of the moon descending from the dark, gloomy horizon, one could barely see the image of the sun as it ascended above the streaks of diverse shades of reds, oranges, and yellows. The various hues seemed to bring such a reflection over the river and the winter snows that capped the hills and trees within the park. There were men and women already up as they took their morning jogs dressed in running shoes and bundled up in winter gear—with white puffs of smoke on every breath from the cold morning air. She watched her own breath as it went forth gracefully through the early morning haze just before the birth of dawn. Cateline often spent much time walking through the park to clear away thoughts, to have clarity on what she was feeling deep within.

After some time, Cateline went back to her apartment and decided to leave a message with her boss that she would not be coming into the office. As it was Friday, Cateline felt the need for a long weekend to empty her mind of distant feelings and notions, where she could make a logical decision on the next stage of her life. Once she resolved to not go to work, there was a sense of relief that swept over her. Being extremely exhausted from lack of sleep, Cateline took a number of naps off and on that Friday. After sleeping several hours, she awakened while lying on her bed and began to think back over the day prior at the library and of her discovery.

Cateline having such a passion for reading, loved that the library was only a short distance from her apartment. In the evenings after work, she generally used the opportunity to take her routine walk to enlighten her day and then enjoy herself amongst the many books before heading back home. Cateline had been very solemn after getting off work on Thursday. The dreams had seemed to take a toll on her that week, and she felt as if there was something she was missing. Cateline had recently begun researching those periods—

centuries past in which she was drawn. On that particular evening, doing extensive research on those in her dreams from the nineteenth century, she had come across a book and then several articles which quite disturbed her. Yes—it was when she suddenly discovered a picture, which brought her to her knees. Reading the segment in the textbook under the image led her to search for other editorials, which she soon found. Cateline had swiftly walked to the area to make copies of the various sections while trying to fight back the tears. Being a regular at the library, everyone knew her and knew there was something wrong, as she was quite shaken and unable to speak. Presenting the book to the clerk, Maria, for check out, Cateline could clearly see by Maria's countenance that she knew something was wrong. Oh, how she had hoped that Maria would not ask, as she gave it all she had within to keep the tears from flowing. It was no sooner than her having that thought that Maria did ask, "Is everything okay?"

Nodding her head before speaking, she thought to herself, "No—oh, no, I am not alright, but I cannot begin to speak, as I would not even know how to explain why." Cateline put her head down, not to make eye contact when the words began to flow gravely from within, "Yes, I will be fine. I am just not feeling well."

On her walk home from the library, Cateline was in deep meditation about the pictures. Tears seemed to flow down her cheeks at the thoughts that were racing through her mind. She was at such a loss, knowing her heart belonged not to the century in which she lived but one from years past. Cateline was so distraught from everything thus discovered, not understanding exactly what she was feeling or what any of this meant. Arriving back in her apartment, Cateline collapsed onto the carpet in her living room, dropping everything from her arms, sobbing uncontrollably, knowing all along that what she had felt deep within was real. Still, she also knew that no one would ever believe her.

Lying on the floor, she cried out, "Oh God, I know this to be true but tell me why—why? I don't understand any of this. I know now why the dreams began so long ago, but now they are more compelling and oh, so very real. I know now why I am so drawn to that period. Yes, I know, but I don't understand what you want me to do. Lord, I cannot live like this, knowing what I know now. It is as though I cannot breathe—I cannot sleep—I have no appetite—oh

7

please, show me my destiny. Show me the way—yes, I trust you—yes, please let my life be in your hands." Her tears continued to flow hysterically on that Thursday evening, knowing her life would never be the same.

It was on that night when Cateline was awakened with one of her dreams, but this time it was so intense, so tangible, feeling as though she could touch that period, that timeframe, so long ago. This time, in her dreams, he had held her and called out her name, and she knew—yes, she knew that it was her—oh yes, it was her, and she was there for him. Awakening, she screamed, "No, no! Please don't leave me! Please, I know you are real—I know this is my life. I can feel your arms around me as you hold me. I can feel your touch as you touch me. I know your lips as they kiss me. I know your love as I have known no other."

Filled with tears and sorrow while sitting in the window seat in the wee hours of Friday morning, her mind had been in such turmoil. Now, reflecting on all that had transpired, with a long weekend ahead, there would be time to come to terms with her life. Having one assurance was the realization that what she had always believed was, in fact, reality. Contemplating to herself, "Reality, yes—but what does that mean? Reality—that I had another life?" With the new revelation, Cateline could no longer live as she had, for this new knowledge required a sacrifice and one that she would never regret.

Filming through the pictures repeatedly, Cateline smiled as she read the articles until they were almost memorized. "These pictures and these words are as much a part of my life as anything I know to be real," she thought to herself, "yes, all along, these dreams have been preparing me for my journey, my destiny in this life." But, then, tears flowed once more as she remembered the parting with such sweet sorrow,[3] for she had slipped away, vanished from his sight, forever and no more!

Cateline's weekend was spent catching up on lost sleep, with times in-between, consisting of either extensive walks or curled up in her little nook reading and dreaming while contemplating her next move. In the midst of tears, she realized that her life must take drastic measures in order to uncover the answers needed. At last, with a deep sigh, Cateline began drying up the tears, for she was finally relieved in her hopes on how to begin the journey—the next chapter of her life.

CHAPTER

2

Monday morning had arrived where presently, Cateline found herself up early and ready for the day. Having made some decisions on the course to take had seemed to soothe her mind where she had finally slept soundly. Checking her phone messages, the night prior, there were many that Mary had left over the weekend. Cateline knew she should have probably called her back but had decided that nothing or no one would take precedence over the time needed alone, for it was necessary to clear her thoughts in order to make a sound decision. In rationalizing all her possible choices, she had also decided to share everything with Mary after work. "Yes, I believe the time has come to share this with my long-time friend and show her the pictures," Cateline thought to herself while sipping the last of her coffee before leaving for work.

Even though Mary was the closest person Cateline had to family, one who was dear to her heart, she also knew that Mary would not be pleased with the final decisions which had been contemplated over the weekend and ultimately resolved to take. Choices were made which would soon change the path of her life and lead Cateline far away from Chicago—far away from what the two girls had always planned and dreamed of together. Cateline's resolution to her dilemma was rash—oh, how she knew, but there was also hope in explaining all which had transpired and how essential it was for her to go forward with her design. To Cateline, it was imperative for Mary to be at peace with her decision, knowing this was in Cateline's best interest. "Yes," she thought to herself, "Mary will just have to trust me."

Cateline and Mary, growing up together, were very protective of one another—loving each other as if they had really been true sisters. Over the years, one would seldom be found without the other. This had contributed to many who deemed them to have truly been related in some fashion. Yet, due to appearance, they were far from resembling each other in all aspects. Both girls were rather stunning in their own way, with Mary being noted by friends as the *cute adorable girl* and Cateline as the *tall attractive girl*. While Mary, at only four foot eleven, may have been petite, she was absolutely divine in all aspects, with her most prodigious coppery-brown hair, typically worn down—quite long, very thick, and straight. Mary was unquestionably a beauty with fair skin tone, slight freckles around the nose, and somewhat on her cheeks. Her freckles stood out to give her that sweet and charming look, while Cateline had the more ravishing appeal, with her hair also worn to its fullest length, relatively long with natural waves, a rich and warm, dark-brown color. Being five foot eight, Cateline was not only tall but slender. Her Irish fair skin tone with her large deep blue eyes set her apart from most. The two girls had many wonderful memories together, voguish events, where both being adorned beautifully, wore updos that were very prettily fashioned. Of course, there were also the off days—no school, summers, holidays, where if one wore a ponytail, the other did as well, to be sure. Regardless, when the two girls were out and about together, there were always many looks from those passing, as they both could turn heads.

As far as their differences, they were as diverse as night and day, yet they complemented each other. Mary was much more of the outgoing type who had many friends, with a bubbly personality and never a dull moment when she was in a room. Along with her fascinating stories, Mary could always entrance a crowd holding them spellbound for extended periods. On the other hand, Cateline was very kind and definitely not shy but much more reserved than Mary. Not that she didn't possess a dynamic personality; quite the reverse, Cateline was just much more selective on those who were allowed access to her personal space. She never seemed to feel the need for attention, even though plenty was received. All the same, Cateline had a way of turning the devotion around where the aim was more on gaining perspective on her associations, instead of allowing others the benefit of really knowing who she was inside—her passions and intimate secrets. Nevertheless, unless it was by her choice to be accessible, viz., Cateline lived a life much guarded, choosing not only whom but also when others were allowed access to unlock her hidden views, beliefs, and principles, revealing the truths behind all she dreamed of in this one life she was given, the secrets to her heart. Cateline was not one to have many close friends—no, her needs in this life were secure in having only a few intimate confidants to share the most cherished details of her life and thoughts. To Cateline, Mary had been that one person besides her father that she chose to share all the minutiae of her days if, in fact, there was anything worth sharing.

11

During her childhood and adolescence, Cateline's life had not been as full as Mary's. Cateline, in fact, loved staying home, spending time with her father, time at the pub, and with her closest friends. In comparison, Mary was very outgoing and loved being involved in any and everything. For the most part, the two girls had been inseparable from the time they were very young and on into adulthood. They both attended the same schools and even decided to go to Bradford in Haverhill, just outside of Boston. Bradford was a liberal arts college that had existed since 1803. Cateline loving just about everything to do with the arts and Mary being really interested in writing and literature, Bradford had seemed like the perfect fit. Besides, both girls were intrigued by Bradford due to all the history, which included the fictional tale by the famous author H.P. Lovecraft. Another noteworthy account that fascinated the girls about Bradford, it was also one of the few colleges that educated women in the 1800s, as institutions in those days leaned more towards men's education.

Once they had both graduated with honors, the plan had been to move to Chicago together. They loved Boston, as it had much history, but there was a certain charm about Chicago the girls seemed to be drawn to. The love for Chicago had occurred when Mary's father had to go there on business when the girls were around the age of fifteen. The whole family went along, and of course, Cateline was always included as part of their family. While Mary's father had been busy every day in meetings, her mother had taken the girls to explore the city. In this one trip, their love was sealed, for in the years which followed, they both continued to reminisce of their adoration for Chicago and their solemn promise to one day return and live in the *Windy City*, as it was often referred to.

Soon after graduation, Mary had interviewed with the Chicago Tribune and was almost immediately hired as an editor. Cateline had so wanted to join Mary, but with her father being up in age and his health declining, she knew that she could not follow at that time. Little did Cateline know, her father would only live not quite two more years. However, those last days together had been good ones for both her and her father, with more memories for her to hold on to forever. Even with her father's passing, it had been a tough decision for Cateline to walk away from the life her parents had dreamed of and spent years building. Nevertheless, Cateline knew that she needed a change and wasted no time taking care of all the particulars on her father's estate, as well as selling the businesses. Being in contact with Mary, Cateline had learned of a position at the Tribune, where she immediately made the arrangements to fly into the city for an interview. At the same time, she devoted a few days exploring various historical places with Mary.

The position in which she interviewed had not exactly been what Cateline had hoped for, but she was still willing to accept any offer with the Tribune and work her way up the ladder to a more desired position. One of her many dreams in life had been to have her own column, as she so loved writing articles and had become reasonably talented in her skills while winning a few awards during the college years. In addition, Cateline had grown up with such a love for learning and would absorb just about anything in books that had to do with history and the arts. On her final day in Chicago, the Tribune phoned to offer her the position in which she had applied. Cateline accepted and agreed that she could begin within two weeks. Flying back to Boston, she took care of all the remaining aspects to finalize her relocation to Chicago. Her car loaded with many of her personal items and movers in the process of transporting her furniture and other belongings, she was at last on her way to the *Windy City*.

Cateline worked very hard during the initial months at the Tribune, where she gave the position all that she had in hopes of securing a higher role. Soon, her hard work had paid off, and as her talents were noticed, the offer had ultimately come. Yes, Cateline had acquired a position as a columnist, and at that moment, she had felt as if her dreams for life had finally begun to come true.

With her own office and her own column, Cateline had been very content for quite some time. The only thing missing in her life was a steady boyfriend, but that had been something she had never acquired. It was definitely not because boys did not like her; on the contrary, Cateline scarcely seemed to connect. Unlike Mary, Cateline had always been more reserved, where some would have considered her shy. It was not that Cateline could not carry on a conversation; quite the reverse, it was just that her personality was rather different from Mary's. Cateline's number of close friends could be counted on one hand, whereas Mary's were limitless. Yes, there were many dates that Mary had arranged for Cateline, but she always seemed to shy away, and if, in fact, she did go on a date, there was usually never a second. Not that the boy never wanted the second date, but Cateline seemed to become disappointed and uninterested, feeling like something was missing. She would often tell Mary, "It's not that I don't want a boyfriend, Mary, it's merely that there are none that I really find appealing. I want it to be real, not where I date someone simply to be dating." Mary never seemed to understand; in fact, Cateline was not sure she even understood, and many times, she felt that maybe there was something wrong with her.

Eventually, Cateline made several friends from work and a few acquaintances through others that she knew. Often, her friends would all do things together in the city as a group, which she enjoyed immensely. She had gone on a few dates arranged by friends, but once again, there was never the desire for that second date. There were times that she felt the ideal guy would never come along, and perhaps, she was looking for someone to meet her father's standards. She knew that her father's shoes would be hard to fill, as he was the perfect man. He had charm and good looks in his younger days; he was very romantic and a complete gentleman. He had so loved her mother dearly, which was unmistakable in his demeanor when talking about her. It was also quite apparent, as he never desired to remarry and would often tell Cateline as she grew older that he had loved once, and he knew there would never be another. Cateline had always loved hearing the fairy-tale romance stories of their lives together from the first time they met and the years following. These stories of their life had become so embedded within, it was as if a part of her mother lived and breathed through her. She loved the notion of romance and the idea of having that one person out there that was meant to be solely for her—her one true love. Yes, she knew her mother had been very fortunate to have had such a wonderful man as her father, and Cateline desired that same kind of love—the fairy-tale romance that the two of them shared. All the same, as time remained, life had become a disappointment to Cateline, where men she had met never seemed to measure up to her expectations.

Perhaps, when one seems to find themselves in dismay, they may very well question, "Was it unrealistic to want that kind of romance? Are we drawn into that realm of chivalry as young girls that never seems to diminish? Do we settle for less than we deserve? Are our expectations far too great, and if so, are we not to look for that which is good? Should we then settle for seconds, or does God desire that we have firsts? Does His will, our Lord and Savior, look upon women as something to be cherished? And, if so, are we foolish to believe that our knights in shining armor do not exist? Can they exist? If they can, and they do, should we look for them, or will they find us? What is woman without an honorable man, and what is man without a virtuous woman? Should all be good to satisfy each other, which in turn satisfies self?" As Cateline thought about many of these questions, she was always drawn back into her passions, where her desires became more for spending time alone reading or researching instead of with other people.

A dreamer? Yes, anyone really knowing Cateline would have considered her a dreamer. The passions that were dear to her seemed to grasp her life and hold her in a sphere where none could ever enter. To Cateline, happiness was found in time spent in a world that lived inside of her. She could not escape, for it held her tight, and yet, there was no escape, for it was her life. A life lived within, where others would not and could not understand. Was she unhappy? On the contrary, Cateline was so very content and so very drawn into a world that none could enter, and none could ever take from her. She lived and breathed for everything within that only she could see, but what a life, it was a life; it was her life. She would not have traded it to be like the girl who seemed to have everything in the world, a life that was visible. No, she would not have exchanged it to be the person at the top of her career. She would not have swapped it for money nor for fame; she would not have traded it for any gain in the whole wide world. It was her life and her passion, and she felt it deep inside, and it was there where no one could disturb it, nor take it away, nor change its course. Cateline was caught up in a world of passion that no one knew, but she lived and breathed it, and it came to her many nights, as the dreams lingered and as she knew where her destiny would lie. She never could and never would have lived a life finding the pleasures in material things, but instead, her life desired to be filled within, with something far deeper and far greater. There were no pleasures in the material things when a world deep within held the key to her happiness. Her happiness was uncovered as she read and explored, seeking for what was meant to be found—and found it— she had. As she could not shake off what was felt deep inside, Cateline continued the journey to draw away from society, away from humanity and the cultures of her day. For she chose to live a life hidden within her very soul, one which drew her further away from what was real.

Monday morning, arriving at work, Cateline rode the elevator up to her office and had barely walked in to lay her purse down on her desk when Mary confronted her.

"Cateline, I called you all weekend. I was not sure if you were really ill since you called in sick on Friday. When I could not get a hold of you, I did not know what to think. I have been so worried about you. I even drove to your apartment, but either you were not home or chose not to answer the door," Mary stated firmly.

"I am so deeply sorry, Mary. I apologize for not returning your calls, but I never checked my messages until last night. Yes, I was home all weekend but went for many long walks in the park. You must have come by when I was out. Truthfully, I cannot talk about this at work; I believe it would be a very lengthy story to convey here. I would love for you to come by after work, for I do have something to share and will do it at that time."

"Are you okay? You know I love you like a sister. You are the one person I have truly been close to besides my parents. I have always shared everything with you and would expect you to do the same. I worry about you, Cateline, especially since your father passed away."

"I know and, I, too, love you as a sister. We will talk later today, okay?" Cateline replied solemnly as tears filled her eyes.

"Sure, I will come by after work. You know you haven't been yourself for some time now, and I cannot help you if I don't know what it is you are going through," Mary declared with a most sincere smile as she walked over and gave her friend a hug.

"Yes, I know you are worried about me, and yes, I have been going through a tough time. So, I have decided to tell you everything later today."

"I'm so glad to hear you say that, and yes, I will come to your apartment directly after work," she remarked strongly before leaving her office.

Once five o'clock came, Mary got in her car and drove to Cateline's. As she knocked, Cateline opened the door, and Mary walked in, reaching over to give Cateline a big hug, "You know I am here for you, and you can tell me anything, right?"

"Yes, I know I can, and I know you are concerned."

"Well, I have often wondered if you are still having a hard time since your father passed away."

"Well, I mean—yes, I do miss him, but it has almost been a year. I believe my job and being here with you has helped fill that void, but I think I will always miss my father; we were so very close," walking over to the couch, Cateline resumed, "before I sit down, would you like a cup of coffee or hot tea?"

"No, nothing at the moment, thank you," Mary noted while sitting down next to Cateline.

"Look, I merely want to say that I am sorry again for not talking to you about what I have been going through and not returning your calls."

"It's alright, as long as you are opening up to me now, all is good."

"I know you are going to find this strange, but you must listen to me and don't say anything until I am finished."

"Sure, Cateline," Mary assured her as she sat with her hands folded in her lap while Cateline commenced.

Taking a deep breath, she spoke most assertive, "For quite some time—well, to be exact, for years and years, I have had these dreams—you know the dreams I have shared with you over the years?"

"Yes, I do remember the dreams, but I haven't heard you mention them in a few years."

"Well, I have never stopped having the dreams; I simply stopped sharing them with you. In fact, I never even told you everything. I used to share them with my father when I was young, and then I saw the pain it caused him, so I stopped. I kept them to myself for years and then would share to some degree, most briefly with you. I suppose you were just an outlet for me to get them out to some extent, but I never really went into much detail. I guess I thought you—well, to be more precise, I knew you would try to reason with me on not putting too much emphasis on these reveries. I assume my dreams have been a part of my life since I was—well, a small child," Cateline paused as she looked down at the book and articles lying on the coffee table. Gazing back up at her friend, she resumed, "I have felt my whole life or at least as far back as I can remember, that I was born in a different time." Feeling relieved that she could get those words out, Cateline looked up at Mary as she sat there patiently for her to continue. "Mary, I can't explain it, but it began as a child. The

17

dreams would come, and the dreams would go. Nevertheless, over the last three or four years, probably about the time I started college or a little after, the dreams increased in duration and depth, along with the feelings that came with them. This past year—yes, since my father passed away, the feelings have grown stronger, and then for the last few weeks, I seldom sleep very well because they plague me over and over again." As Cateline sat there thinking about what she would disclose next, gathering her thoughts, she finally spoke most calmly, "My father knew that I often described people who were family members in Ireland, even though I was only three years old when I was there, but I also depicted others whom he could not recall. To conclude, there were locations, places that I had never seen, which I portrayed in my dreams. These exposés quite disturbed my father, for I was very young. To his knowledge, I had never seen many of the places I described most proficiently, not even in books. Yet, at some point in school, I saw pictures of various places that I had dreamed of for years, and eventually, I was able to recognize some of those in my dreams whom I have studied over the years, one in particular who is very well-known. Well, this one person, he has always been there in my aspirations, but it was a blur, and I could not tell who he was at first. This person is someone whom I have admired for some time, particularly his work from that period—to be precise, I have loved his contribution to art and literature for many years now. In these dreams, I am there as if I lived in that century—the Victorian era," she concluded.

"Cateline, that's natural. You are the only person I know that spends hours each week reading history and studying literature," Mary contemplated. She continued assuring her friend most reasonably, "I would think it perfectly natural that you are dreaming about it. Still, it doesn't mean it's real."

"Please, Mary, let me finish. I understand all of that, but there's more. I feel that I am being drawn back into the late nineteenth century. I have been going to the library almost daily, studying everything so that maybe I can discover those I have dreamt of from that timeframe, which I believe to be family. I have also been studying others of the social elite in that period to include this one particular man. As I was in the library several days ago, something happened that changed everything and has made me feel that I know I lived in that era." As she settled her thoughts, Cateline reached over and picked up the book that she had checked out from the library and opened it up to the marked page while handing it to Mary, "Look closely at the picture. The girl seated by Oscar Wilde."

Mary, holding the book, gazed upon the picture and proclaimed most earnestly, "Oh my gosh, the girl looks exactly like you," she perceived while regarding Cateline and examining the photo. "Perhaps the girl is Irish; she could have been an ancestor of yours from that period. I've heard of people looking just like someone from years ago, someone they never even knew."

"Yes, she is Irish, please read the inscription that I have highlighted at the bottom," Cateline added while Mary lifted the book and began to read the caption underneath— "Oscar Wilde among friends, 1881. The gentlemen sitting around Wilde were believed to have been acquaintances during his days at Oxford. The name of the young lady next to Wilde was Cateline. There were controversies among historians on who the woman was, with allegations that they may have been married for a short time. Still, others had claimed she was of Irish descent but had lived most of her life in America. It was told that the lady had vanished from Europe, where it was said that she went back to America, as it had been understood she was from Boston and had never been seen again. A number of historians had heard accounts of her marriage to Wilde, but no records were ever found to support such. There were claims that the couple had met in 1881 before Wilde toured America in 1882, where some had supposed he might have met up with her there, and they had decided to part ways. The picture was assumed to have been taken in Liverpool, but there were a few other photos which had also been discovered of the two of them at various locations in Europe during that same timeframe."

Mary paused for a few moments as she looked upon the picture before proclaiming, "This is unbelievable, but it still doesn't prove anything!"

Cateline reached over to pick up a folder to hand to Mary. "I did more research and have printed out these other articles from locations in Europe, which I found with photos."

Mary taking the folder pulled out several pictures of Oscar with the same girl. "I don't know what you want me to say. Yes, she looks exactly like you, and they seem to be very close based on their countenance in some of these photos; however, couldn't this simply be a coincidence?"

19

"As if it is not enough that her first name is the same as mine, she was from America and believed to have been from Boston, my hometown, did you fail to read where they thought her last name to have been McCarthy, my name?"

"Oh," Mary gently pondered, "No, I merely scanned through the articles, let me see."

Cateline pointed out where it stated that her name was believed to have been Cateline McCarthy. "Okay, but Cateline, this is absurd; I don't think that you could have lived in that period and then be born into this timeframe, do you?"

"Truthfully, I'm not sure what I believe anymore, Mary," Cateline earnestly remarked before continuing, "all I know is that there is nothing that you can say that will convince me that girl was not me. I don't understand it either, but I have felt that I belonged in that period for a long time. I am pretty much convinced of that now. I've been having dreams about being there for years, and some years ago of discovering the man in my dreams to be Oscar Wilde. I wake up crying and cannot go back to sleep. I know it sounds irrational, but it's as if I belong there, and everything I have ever wanted is right there! Please do not think I'm crazy when I say this, but it's as if I really knew Oscar. Not just personally knew him, but that we were in love at some point in time. I haven't shared these things with anyone, but now since the pictures, I must find out what all this means."

"Find out what it means? How exactly do you plan to do such a thing?"

"I put my notice in at work today. Over the weekend, I rented a storage building for what I wanted to keep and paid it up for one year. I also rented a storage place for my car, and I've bought a one-way ticket to Ireland," sharing her plans thus far, she maintained, "I also rented a room in this castle in Ireland to stay for a few weeks. I'm not sure what my plans will be once I get there, so I clearly planned for a few weeks at the castle, and from there, I will travel to other areas and just take one day at a time. Perhaps, after one year, I will have come to know what it is that I am supposed to do. I am not saying it will take me a year, but I will stay that long if I think that I need to."

With a slight laugh and bewildered expression, Mary elaborated, "I don't quite understand, what then—what will that prove? He died years ago, Cateline! You were not in that timeframe; how can you even consider that you loved him?"

"I get that, and I'm not sure what's next." With tears beginning to well up in her eyes, she continued most solemnly, "I'm sorry, Mary, but I feel that he is the one man I am to love and that I was there years ago. I know this all sounds foolish, but Mary, I love him and have always loved him. I can't explain it, but it's like my heart belongs to him and only him. I know that if I don't go back to my roots, I will regret this for the rest of my life. I must go and at least walk where I may have walked in another time, see things that maybe I have seen in another period, ask questions and research for who knows—perhaps, someone will remember something or maybe someone may have kept something—some relic of sorts, possibly in one of the places they may have visited. I must explore Dublin, Liverpool, London, and even Paris; after all, I am from Ireland, and these pictures were taken in locations I may have walked at one time. If nothing else, maybe there is a reason I am feeling all of this and something that God wants me to discover. All I know is that, in my heart, I trust this is the right thing to do. And I will not know why until I step out of my comfort zone and trust God. I know this sounds foolish, but all I know is that I feel it deep within my heart that I was there. And lately, I cry myself to sleep because I believe that I am supposed to be there. This is the best that I can explain how I feel. I know this all sounds so bizarre, but I am absolutely going crazy right here doing nothing. I have no idea if going to Europe will give me my answers, but I cannot stay here in America, where I will always wonder if I made the right choice. I must go!"

Mary listening to every word she spoke, replied, "I get it, and you know I'm here for you. Do you want me to take off work and come with you?"

"Oh no, I have to do this alone, and I'm not sure when or if I will ever come back."

"Please don't say that, Cateline. I agree, maybe you need to go where you can sort this out so that you can eventually get on with your life here, but I know you will be back. You will stay in touch with me, right?"

"You know, I will. Please don't worry about me and pray that I find whatever it is that I'm supposed to find. —Hey, my boss even told me that if I come back, I still have a job with the Tribune," Cateline said with a slight laugh.

With a somewhat wistful smile, Mary stood up from the sofa to leave. Upon Cateline standing, Mary put her arms around her friend before she resolved, "I love you, Cate, never forget that!" As tears flowed with Mary and Cateline both, they hugged and cried. Cateline walked Mary to the door as they said their *goodnights* with tears streaming down their cheeks.

CHAPTER
3

The following two weeks seemed to go by fast, as Cateline was very busy packing up her belongings for storage and deciding on what to take with her and what to leave behind. She was determined to take one large duffle-type bag, with convenient handles for carrying and a backpack to coordinate with the first, so her wardrobe would most assuredly be kept very slim. Besides, she would be visiting London, as well as Paris, and new clothes were sure to be a necessity at some point. Dreaming of a new wardrobe from Paris, the idea was pondered to actually purchase new clothes to bring back home. Her mind drifted with each thought, "How could I even think of bringing my whole wardrobe when I will be in the fashion capital of the world." So, without further ado, it was resolved, if need be, additional luggage would be purchased once there, but for now, the notion would not even cross her mind of dragging along any unwanted baggage into Europe. Keeping her wardrobe as simple as possible with the bare necessities, there would be no bulky, laborious suitcases. Furthermore, her guitar was a must, knowing she would never go anywhere without it, even if that meant it had to sit between her legs on the plane.

Cateline's guitar! Oh, the stories to be told! While packing it snugly within its case for protection, it brought a most flashing smile across her face—memories that went back quite some years. The disagreements that guitar had brought and such discord between her father and herself, but of course, it evolved in her favor, most beneficially, to be sure. Yes, being the only child, her father had certainly spoiled her, where it was so hard for him to say *no*. On the other hand, she had constantly been introduced to music from such a young age at her parent's pub, taking piano lessons for years, and was also rather gifted as her mother was in voice. Her mother had sung beautifully, and Cateline was clearly blessed to have acquired that most pleasing ability. The guitar years had begun sometime in her early teens, perhaps even at the age of twelve. Cateline was not entirely sure exactly when she had become so obsessed with acquiring the necessary skills and genius to master such an instrument. But, still, there was little doubt she had not determined to attain the talent demanded and do so very effectively. Her father at first tried to discourage her, feeling that the guitar wasn't proper for a young lady to play, but once Cateline made up her mind and was unyielding, it was a lost cause that anyone should try to persuade her differently. Nevertheless, Cateline took up playing it very well, indeed, where her father had been most pleased.

"Oh, but how I seem to remember all those arguments," she thought, reminiscing to herself. Yes, her father would state his opinion, and Cateline being so headstrong, always knew how to come back with a most brilliant reply until her dad realized he was not winning that dispute. And so, as it was, the guitar was purchased! Various musicians who played regularly at the pub taught Cateline different keys from week to week until she pretty much acquired what was necessary and blossomed from there, becoming reasonably cultured in her abilities. During those years, the guitar had become more prevalent than her desire for the piano, and in playing, her music, along with her voice, seemed to bring a certain peace into her father's life, as well as her own. In fact, it had brought both of them closer during those final years together, for her father had very much grown to love hearing her sing and play the guitar, which was relatively often during their quiet times together at home. It was this one instrument which she could not go without playing for very long. Music to Cateline seemed to harmonize with her inner-self in a way that was hard to describe, yet, for her to do without her music for any length of time would seem as if something inside had died. This, naturally, was reminiscent of the lyrics in Don McLean's song, *American Pie, The Day the Music Died.* [1] Cateline had always known her music abilities were gifts just as her writing, but they all seemed to be intertwined together. One thrived only joined with the other, and apart from music, it would be as if something was taken away, leaving her entirely empty inside.

Cateline continued packing her essential clothing, guitar, and not to forget her portable CD player—yes, her own sounds would definitely be a must since she was unsure what type of music they listened to in Europe. Sorting through her various CD collection, her favs consisted of much of the romantic sounds throughout the 50s and 60s, some of the upbeat music of the 70s—the Rolling Stones, the Eagles, Fleetwood Mac, Aerosmith, and the Bee Gees, to name a few. And then, of course, there were also her favorite tunes from her high-school years—yet, Cateline was more drawn to those days of romance, those years in which she had grown to love, brought on as it was from hearing the tales and stories from her parents. One could say that Cateline was well-rounded when it came to music since it was somewhat a part of her past. Yes, her greatest love of music was awakened as far back as could be remembered, not just by the influence of music alone but also by the classic novelist of times past. Her love for many of the celebrated novelists, such as Jean-Jacques Rousseau from the eighteenth century, impacted her life, where the songs of romance seemed to come alive to her like never before. He was one of her favorites of the Romantic era, along with many others who had deeply inspired her.

Cateline's immense love of music had always been there, but her parents' influence for the romantic era and the sounds of those times had, in fact, always been around; Cateline could not remember a time when they weren't. Both parents loved the music of romance, as the melodies could be heard flowing through their home, especially in the mornings. She even remembered how popular the jukebox at the pub had been, with one at each location. As time went on, her father still chose to keep some of the older music in the jukebox mixed with a variety of modern sounds, including many Irish tunes. The jukebox eventually had seemed to go out of style as Cateline had grown older, but her father had decided to build a small stage for entertainment at the main pub in downtown Boston. Besides the piano, he eventually had collected a range of diverse instruments, as he always invited any with talent to entertain on certain nights. As a result, the pub had acquired quite a reputation for the locals, and many grew to be like family to Cateline and her father.

Entertainment at the pub had become fairly popular over the years, where Cateline had joined in, playing the guitar or piano when needed. Of course, her ability to sing with such a beautiful voice was requested often, where nights with friends and acquaintances were deeply enjoyed. After all, singing was one of her best qualities. So, it could never have come as a surprise that love songs were her preference; those seemed to be the songs requested often and always were her choice if it were up to her. Still, songs from those days long gone seemed to capture something deep within—awakened something in her inner soul. When Cateline sang those songs of that timeframe, it was evident that she loved to perform. It wasn't about doing something to please someone else—no, it was doing the thing she cherished the most. The love for music, the arts, and times past were the things that brought much comfort. This heartfelt devotion somehow reminded her of her mother; it was a way of keeping her alive and close after all these years, but eventually, Cateline realized those songs, and that period was a part of who she was. A romantic—yes, she definitely loved everything about that timeframe, from hearing the tales to reading the books and listening to the songs. All these things were part of what kept that period of romance alive, awakening her inside—her inner self, her creativity where no other era could compete or breakthrough.

While packing, Cateline picked up an old photo of her parents from her dresser and dusted the frame. For the first time in so long, this picture actually stirred up a deep-felt pain inside. Even though the snapshot had always been in her room, it was like looking at it for the first time. Smiling in between a tear or two, she began to reminisce on those very early years, remembering her mother. Deciding this was a good moment for a tea break, she walked into the kitchen to heat up the pot and walked over to the stereo to play some of her favorite romance songs for the right touch to enlighten her day.

She settled in her tiny nook with a nice hot cup of herbal tea infused with orange peel, rosehips, lemongrass, and cinnamon while asserting, "Mmm—this is so divine!" Relaxing, lying back against her tousled fluffy pillows, she gazed out of the picturesque window at the beauty of Chicago. How soothing it was, so peaceful and scenic, while the words to the sounds of Brenda Lee gently filled the room, followed by The Duprees, and persisted while she took light sips of tea. Her mind lingered, drifting far away, dreaming of her days ahead—days in Europe, with absolutely incredible thoughts of her life beginning to change. Holding the photo of her mother and father once more, such memories of days gone by, a sullen look upon her face, somehow imagining them together in happier times, Cateline was relieved that the years they had together were joyful. Tears gently coursed down her cheeks, seeing their faces, bright and cheerful handsome faces—the two people who had come to America to have a better life. Yes, they had found that life—so young, so vibrant, so in love. Their house was always filled with words of love, romance, kindness, and gentleness. Even though Cateline was relatively young when her mother passed away, she could still visualize how her parents were always responsive and devoted to one another. Theirs was definitely a fairy-tale romance. It was Cateline's remembrance of their love, their passions, the romantic songs, and the romance novels which had shaped her to be who she was. Why would Cateline ever settle for anything less than what her own parents had? Because of those two beautiful beings, she was alive and desired what they had—no, she could never settle for less. They loved her and taught her so much about life, and Cateline had finally come to understand how valuable life was, how vital choices were. She knew that it was her time, time to step out and take that chance—a chance at life, a real-life, one that produced the same smile on her face, which was visible in her parents in the picture.

Further into her day, after much packing in this box and that, Cateline decided to relax and brush up a little on her French. Having taken a class in French for only one year, she definitely would not speak fluently but perhaps enough to make light conversation, if need be. Sorting through all her belongings with a stack that would be stored, another would be given away, and the last would be packed to go with her. Throughout the day, Cateline had continually added to her list of things to do over the following weeks. With many items being written on her *to-do list*, she jotted down to purchase a 110-volt adapter to convert to the European 220, a must for the CD player, along with many batteries, for sure, also making a note of the places she needed to go and business to settle before leaving. Then, speaking a bit of French to practice while working, Cateline proclaimed, "Appeler le fournisseur de téléphone portable, oui, I need to find out if there is anything else that I must do for my phone to work abroad." With that said, she wrote down to remember to pack the charger for her phone in the carry-on. Continuing her to-do list, she included all her essential documents to have in order—travel IDs, passport, traveler's checks, currency. Finishing, with her purse in hand, she walked out the door to take care of all her banking needs, including adding Mary to her bank account, just in case! The remainder of the day was devoted to shopping and taking care of many of the items at hand.

The days seemed to drift by very slowly, with Cateline spending most of her time after work cleaning up her apartment and other times were spent going to have dinner or drinks with friends. Her last weekend, much of Saturday, friends helped her move furniture and belongings to the storage place, unwanted items to Goodwill, and then surprised her with a fabulous going away party

27

to end the day. Of course, all but Mary thought she was merely leaving to travel Europe for an extended amount of time, with many desiring to leave all behind and go with her if, in fact, it was feasible. Yet, Cateline could not have ever left a job that early in her career if her father had not passed on, leaving her in pretty good shape financially.

The party that evening was quite the occasion where it was held at the home of one of her co-workers—a catered event and an unknown band. Although, the band played reasonably well, after being told of Cateline's talent, where after a few drinks, she was pressed to make an appearance! All in all, everyone had a great time, many tears and much laughter were exchanged. Leaving that night, Cateline went home with Mary since all her furniture was packed away.

The following morning, Cateline went back to her apartment to do a final sweep, ensuring all was clean before calling her landlord to come to inspect. Her landlord, who lived in the building, was very fond of Cateline and many times had told her that she wished all tenants were as good as she. Cateline had always been taught from a young age to take care of what did not belong to her and be respectful of others. She maintained the apartment well, and it was kept immaculate, as she lived alone and had always been one that kept everything in its place unless it was being used. This was a trait acquired from her father; with his business mind, he had continually reminded her that if one wanted to gain in this life, one must be disciplined, and to gain the respect of others, one had to give respect. He was a wise man, and Cateline knew she had been so blessed to have him as a father. Her landlord arrived and did a walkthrough, even though there was no need because she had been in Cateline's apartment many times and was most pleased with her neatness and demeanor.

Cateline desiring a few last minutes alone in her apartment, her landlady informed her to just stop by when leaving, and she would have her deposit ready. Standing at the door of her apartment for the last time, Cateline stepped back in and went over to the empty window seat to climb up in it one more time. "I really am going to miss this spot, but I believe that where I am going, I will never have any regrets." Closing the door, she dropped off the key to her landlady and took care of the last-minute business.

Climbing in her car, Cateline phoned Mary about meeting to get something to eat at The Berghoff Restaurant. The Berghoff was one of the oldest restaurants in Chicago and was known for its German cuisine. Feeling a bit nostalgic, Cateline wanted to go someplace that she loved for what might be the last time. The Berghoff had always reminded her of being in Boston, as her parents had emigrated from Ireland and opened up an Irish pub, in contrast, the original Berghoff family had emigrated from Germany back in the 1870s and opened up their restaurant, which served beer and sandwiches, later expanding their food menu where they became known for their authentic German fare.

Both girls arriving about the same time sat down at a table to enjoy a lovely evening together with great food and a beer, as they reminisced about all the times they had spent together growing up from childhood. Sharing in those moments brought such infectious laughter to the point of tears. They both knew that it could possibly be quite some time before they would see each other again, and neither of them had ever been apart for an extended period in their lives. "Mary, let's think about all the good times and remember each other always with a smile in our heart," Cateline mused most sincerely and added, "you know I will carry you with me for always and someday, we will see each other again."

"I know we will. It's just not knowing how long it will be and not having you right there, as I always have," Mary remarked vaguely, as she continued, "but I know that you will be fine and smart and not take any unnecessary chances, right Cateline?"

"Right! You know I have always been cautious. I admit, this is a bit crazy and not in my nature, but who knows, maybe this will be beneficial for me!"

"I'm really excited for you and, at the same time, sad that you are going. I wish I could be doing something exciting like this, but I suppose I'm merely content with my life for now."

"Someday, you will meet someone special, and that will all change, Mary. You will suddenly do things unexpected and unnatural to who you always thought you were. Not to mention, sometimes change is a good thing!"

The girls left the restaurant as Mary followed Cateline to the storage place to drop off her car. Locking up her vehicle, she jumped

29

into Mary's car and handed her the extra set of keys along with a slip that had the combinations to both storage buildings. "You do know, if you ever need my car for any reason, you do not have to ask, just go get it. Also, if I do not come back, the car is yours. I paid it in full once I sold the pubs, so I have no debt. Anything I have in both storage places is yours."

"I don't like it when you say it like that; it sounds like you are not coming back."

"Well, I do plan to come back, but I am unsure of where this journey will lead."

Once they arrived at Mary's place, the girls sat up until the wee hours of the night listening to music, talking, and reminiscing about the past and the present. Later on, Cateline had a hard time falling to sleep, as she had so many mixed emotions being filled with excitement and uncertainty. Remembering one of Oscar Wilde's quotes, *"The very essence of romance is uncertainty,"*[2] she thought about her whole adventure of the unknown being filled with the romance of cultures never experienced, at least not in her current life. Of course, leaving this life and traveling so far to other countries, which were unfamiliar, filled her with uncertainty, but she knew that was part of the excitement of not knowing what awaited her.

Both girls awakened early, swiftly dressing, they headed towards the airport. Unloading her guitar and large bag for check-in, Cateline slipped on her backpack and then turned to say her goodbyes to Mary. The girls hugged with tears in their eyes, as Cateline proclaimed most profusely, "A bientot, jamais dire au revoir."

"Yes, I will see you soon and will never say goodbye, as well," Mary responded, hugging her friend once more.

On departing, Mary turned to watch her friend again while she went through the line to turn in her sizeable baggage at American check-ins and then disappeared, walking towards security. Chicago O'Hare International was such a substantial airport with flights constantly coming and going. Luckily, Cateline would fly straight through to Ireland.

Once through security, Cateline located her gate and proceeded to buy a cup of coffee to enjoy while awaiting the time to board the plane. Relaxing, she sipped her Latté, reflecting on the long trip ahead. The journey she perceived was not the eight-hour flight to get to Ireland, but rather the weeks, months, and perhaps even years before she would decide to return to America, if in fact, that were the case. Everything was a bit uncertain, of course, but the excitement was building within as she contemplated what her life would be like for the near and far future.

After some time, boarding for her flight was finally called, and Cateline stood in line as they checked in every passenger. Finding her seat, she started to get comfy for the long flight, shuffling through her backpack for various items to suffice for the trip where she passed up the CD player, pulling out a good book to read instead. While the plane began to fill up with all the passengers, Cateline relaxed and commenced reading for the first segment of her trip. Once loaded, the announcements were given on the loudspeakers, and the plane was ready for take-off. All the same, Cateline had become very relaxed, where she truly was enjoying her choice of reading material—*The Warden,* one of Anthony Trollope's successful novels during the mid-nineteenth century. Quite enthralled, she was not in the least concerned of her surroundings nor of any other details concerning the flight. After a few hours, having a hard time trying to focus and stay awake, she decided it was time to put the book away, relax, and listen to some of her music with the headphones. Having already decided to stay awake during most of the flight, she knew her attention must be diverted to another pastime to keep from falling asleep. With the difference in time change from Chicago to Dublin, six hours with Dublin being ahead, the plane would arrive at 3:20 p.m. Chicago time, but it would actually be 9:20 p.m. in Dublin. Nonetheless, since there had been little sleep her last night in Chicago, Cateline thought it best to stay awake most of the trip, where she would undeniably be able to retire once settled in at the hotel. Plus, her plans were to retreat as soon as possible and awake early the following morning to begin her journey. No, her plans did not include wasting time sleeping all day in order to catch up with the time zones; instead, she desired to begin at dawn the following day, yearning to see many of the historical sites in Dublin before there would be any thoughts of traveling to other diverse locations of interest.

31

Several hours had passed before lunch was served, which wasn't too bad but was definitely not Boston nor Chicago cuisine. Cateline occupied her time reading again after lunch, finishing about half of the book. The remaining time was spent listening to her most cherished sounds—yet, it had become quite an effort, for sleep tried to overtake her on numerous occasions. However, when stewardesses came around, Cateline quickly asked for more coffee, which did the trick of keeping her awake for the long-drawn-out journey.

Hours later, the announcement was finally made; they were not far from Dublin. Cateline put away her book and CD player while most eager to start seeing land. The second awaited announcement suddenly came for all passengers to fasten their seat belts as they approached the Dublin Airport and would be landing soon.

Enthusiastic, she looked out the window to view the city beneath, as it was lit up vibrantly at night. The horizon shone with a gleam of light as the moonlight rose above and then inclined upon the waters. The coastline was aflame with the many lustrous lights from the buildings as they reached onward to the skyline with shades of reds and oranges mixed with dazzling greens bringing forward the city's breadth with the masses of suburbs that shown forth such life. The vast bridges as they crossed the various waterways beneath brought out the reflection of the many flickering stars and gallant streams of light with the richness of vehicles, as the people scattered about through the traces of highways, streets, and roads brilliantly ablaze. It was such an amazing sight, a city of enormous size, larger than anticipated. Cateline could hardly wait to arrive at her hotel and try to get a good night's sleep as she envisioned her dreams of what lay before her.

Once the plane had landed, putting on her backpack, she waited for routine procedures before passengers were able to get off the jet. She stepped out into the airport, walking swiftly with the other passengers as they hurried along towards the baggage area, where they would then wait for the belt to begin bringing all the luggage forth. Gathering up her hefty bag, Cateline began to wish that she had brought a suitcase with wheels but would make the best of it for now and perhaps purchase one sooner rather than later.

Several taxis were lined up outside the airport as she proceeded to one that had not been claimed, where the driver assisted Cateline with her bag. Thanking him, she then climbed into the back seat, stating, "Please take me to the Clontarf Castle Hotel."

"Yes, ma'am," the driver concurred as he pulled away from the curb.

Cateline loved the charm of the city as they drove block after block with so many points of history in view, she could barely wait to begin exploring Dublin, as well as many of the coastal towns. There were so many suburbs, with Clontarf being one, it was hard to tell when leaving one and entering another. Having read many interesting facts about Clontarf, Cateline looked forward to exploring this quaint inner suburb of Dublin as it stood in the 21st century. "Oh, the adventures which lay ahead," thinking to herself and thankful that much time had been spent before leaving in researching the history of all the various coastal communities. "All the outer suburbs, not just Clontarf, but Howth, Malahide, and so many others, how exciting this shall be," her thoughts continued. Yes, much planning had gone into her preparations to include many locations in Ireland before venturing into England. However, Cateline had decided that this trip was to take one day at a time to clarify who she was and what the dreams encountered really meant.

Cateline had chosen the castle hotel, as it was a short walk to the Irish Sea beaches, which lined the shores of Dublin. There was so much history of this great country, and she knew it was her history, where her roots began. Cateline knew that there would be plenty of time to take walks and have her quiet times of reflecting, reading, and writing with the scenic views along the coastline and the charm of the city's historical buildings. As she observed the surroundings from the taxi, her thoughts were to grab a bite to eat at one of the many restaurants at the hotel and then perhaps venture to the beach in the event there was a lighted pathway to get there. The hotel's brochure had noted that the beach was only a five-minute walk away, and with all the coffee drank on the plane, she was not quite sleepy yet. Other than perhaps a quick walk to the beach, her plans were to retire early, even if that meant taking one of the sleeping pills in her bag.

33

As the cab pulled into the luxurious Clontarf Castle Hotel drive, attendants came to take her large bag while she paid and tipped the driver. The outside of the hotel did, in fact, have the most glorious castle façade and was known for its twelfth-century architecture. The grounds were beautifully landscaped, with lighted walkways throughout. Cateline, entering the premises, was literally in awe of her surroundings, which were more in line with a classic look and a modern luxury flair. It was definitely breathtaking. Scrutinizing over all the exquisite furnishings, with such a delight, thoughts started to surface silently, "This is extremely impressive, and the service seems to be most exceptional." Cateline, checking in, inquired about the beach access at night and was then taken to her room, where she tipped the porter. Walking into the King Suite, it was elaborated in a diverse blend of contemporary and classic. The four-poster bed was draped with brilliantly flowered material as a canopy that flowed down each of the four posters and matched the drapes which encased both windows. The room was odd-shaped, where the ceiling slanted from the windows but was also inset with small areas similar to her picture window without the seat. The room was equipped with all the latest features of a sizeable TV system, telephone, and a most comfortable mattress on the bed with stylish bedding. Sitting down on the bed for a moment, it became pretty evident that she would, beyond a doubt, sleep very well after a brief walk to the beach and back.

Cateline decided to wait on unpacking her bag, knowing only a few of the restaurants were still open for a short time. Taking a quick glimpse of her hair and dress in the long-standing antique mirror, a light color of lipstick was applied before deciding she looked good enough as a tourist, but it would have to do for the moment. Hurriedly, Cateline left her room for one of the restaurants, heading back to the lobby area. She went into the Knights Bar, which remained open a bit later than the others. The room was enriched with handsomely polished wood floors, as well as an extravagant bar. Several tables were lined about, which sat four, embellished with oversized plush chairs, and besides the tables, there were also luxurious booths. Choosing a table, Cateline sat down on one of the lavish chairs, which was quite comfortable. As she looked around the room, she observed that many of the walls throughout were set in the original twelfth-century castle style, in which the brochure had noted—most exquisite, curved design, making an arch of sorts to walk through from one room to another. A server soon approached, bringing her a menu, and took her drink order. The menu was most delightful as Cateline quickly looked it over. Not desiring to eat anything heavy, she decided on the Knight's Seafood Chowder, which had Irish salmon and smoked haddock along with bacon and brioche crumb. The waiter came back with her water and took her order. It was not long until her food arrived, as it was almost time for the restaurant to close. Eating rather hastily, she signed for the check to be put on her tab, then left to take a quick stroll to the beach.

Cateline felt a bit more comfortable with others still out and about, and the walk was concise, as noted. Arriving at the beach, Cateline sat down and slipped off her shoes, feeling the coolness of the sand covering her feet. Even as a child, she had always loved the sand's texture as the sensation would sweep through her toes and encircle her feet with its chill that brought a calmness to her whole being. Moving her feet enticingly, she took in the sights from the seashore. It was a most peaceful night, as the moon cast vividly over the waters. Every sparkle of the stars shining atop the mediums brought forth a most mysterious essence to the waters of the sea as the illumination cascaded romantically downward. As she looked on, the vivaciousness of whitecaps that gushed passionately to the shores only added to the tranquility. The gusts of wind blew rapturously beyond with a radiantly northern resounding rumble as it echoed beneath the hills with bustling magical tones. Her hair being loosely down, caressed her shoulders, flowing with every breath of the sea as it carried the fresh breeze of the winter's chill. After about an hour of taking in the intense views that were utterly breathtaking, Cateline began to reflect upon her dreams and the journey which laid before her. As the chill of the night arose to generate a shiver within, she found herself in such a daze, for her thoughts were much engaged in the dreams. Finally, while the cold commenced to apprehend her soul, she decided it was probably time to head back and sleep to be rested and revived for tomorrow's journey.

Once Cateline arrived back at her room, she hastily phoned Mary to let her know of her safe arrival. They briefly discussed her flight and the specifics of the hotel. After their conversation had ended and her bags were unpacked, she soaked in the steamy hot waters of the jacuzzi tub before taking a sleeping pill and retiring to bed with a good book. It was not long before the drug effect could be felt, being quite drowsy, sleep soon followed.

CHAPTER
4

The morning was rather chilly, as Cateline was awakened by a lady of about middle-aged who had walked across the room and over to the window. Opening her eyes, she thought to herself, "I must be dreaming." Slowly sitting up in the bed, it became apparent this was not the hotel's room she had checked into the night prior. As the lady drew back the long, bulky draperies which revealed daylight, Cateline candidly remarked, "Excuse me, who are you?"

The lady who had begun to walk into the adjoining room turned to face Cateline with a most astonishing expression, exclaiming, "Miss Cateline, ma'am! I am so sorry that I disturbed you. I was only in hopes that a bit of sunshine might lighten up your spirits. Are you feeling better, ma'am?"

"Do I know you?"

"No, ma'am, you more than likely do not know me. I work for your uncle, ma'am."

As the lady spoke, Cateline could not help but notice her odd way of being attired, as she wore a most simplified long dress that would have been consistent with many years gone by. With the apron around her midsection, hanging down the length of the skirt and her hair drawn up with a bonnet, Cateline perceived her to be some sort of maid. Unsure of where she was or who her uncle was, Cateline spoke most abruptly once again to address the lady, "I'm sorry, but I have no idea where I am nor who my uncle is."

The lady, turning to face Cateline addressed her somewhat apologetically, "I am so sorry ma'am, the doctor was right—yes, he was! He said we should expect as much, said you might awaken and not remember much of anything."

"Doctor? —But where am I, and why was a doctor called?"

"You were hurt on your way to Ireland, ma'am—on the ship as you were headed to your uncle's."

"I was hurt; how was I hurt?"

"They said you slipped and fell—hit your head, you did. I believe there was some bad weather, and the ship was tossed about. The Mister and Mis'ess of the house, they brought you from the dock immediately. Sent for the doctor, and you have not hardly spoken

37

since that time. A moan and a few words here and there—we were able to get some substance in you, mainly broth."

"I—I'm not quite sure what you are talking about—I don't remember any of this. I was on a ship?"

"Yes, ma'am, from America."

"How long have I been here?"

"It was mid-week that they brought you here, ma'am."

"Well, what day is this?"

"This be Saturday, ma'am. I really am not at liberty to share with you any more details, ma'am. I must let your uncle and aunt know that you are awake; they will be much pleased to know," the lady said as she went over to a rather large fireplace against a wall that partially divided the second room. There she scooped up coal from a wooden bucket to rekindle the fire. "Let me just get this fire going good for you, ma'am, before I head to let the family know that you have awakened. It is a mite chilly in the mornings this time of year—you stay in bed, ma'am, until it warms the room. I will make sure breakfast is sent up to you. I am sure you must be most wanting," she finished while walking towards the door.

Cateline sat up, trying to take in all that the woman had said, which only added to her confusion. "How oddly the lady was dressed—look at this room, where am I?" Feeling a bit lightheaded, she sat there for a few moments, taking in her surroundings. Not entirely understanding what was happening, Cateline knew that she was still in Ireland according to what the lady had spoken but not in the castle hotel. She gently swung her legs over to the side of the bed with much effort. "I feel so weak," she murmured while trying to steady herself amid the excruciating pain. Lifting her hand, she rubbed her forehead lightly, which seemed to be the primary origin of the throbbing sensation of discomfort, which was pretty apparent as it radiated throughout her body. "Oh—my head, it aches so much." Gaining a bit of strength, sitting on the side of the bed, Cateline looked down at the delicate fabric of the bedspread, rubbing her hand across it gently. "Some type of a silky, refined material, quite soft," she noted, observing the frilly lace entwined along the edges, a deep beige in color—most elegant, indeed. Gazing around to gain a better view of the furnishings, the bed seemed to be constructed of an elaborate heavy wood—a four-poster canopy, deeply rich in golden color with gilded etchings of leaves and flowers engraved that were of a somewhat darker tone of gold. Extended overhead were thick wood crossings held up by the four vertical columns, which were considerably large and had a twisted look, as of rope, interlaced with fine light impressions. Over the wooden crossings, arrayed fabrics coincided with that of the bedcovering but sheerer in quality, with draping layers of lace bowing down slightly over the top extending from the edges on all sides. The canopy was of a light cream shade, with the lace being more vibrant in contours of deep beige. While gazing down, she noticed an upholstered hassock or footstool, which was almost the length of the oversized bed itself. The stool stood at a stature convenient for stepping down with its golden pegged legs, as it was doubtful one could simply climb in or out of a bed such as this, with its height far more significant than any bed Cateline had slept in before. The top of the stool was covered with thick, velvety gold fabric—very soft to the touch, she observed while stroking her feet softly over the surface. She stood on the stool while gathering her strength and then stepped down slowly onto the Victorian antique rug, which covered much of the first room, moderately ample in size. Cateline looked briefly around the immediate space and to the other adjoining region, both areas together, making a reasonably sizeable expanse that could easily have been a small apartment. With the ceilings of relatively a generous height, the two sections seemed most notable and quite spacious.

Cateline stood for a few moments as the dizziness subsided while she thoroughly studied the elaborate chamber. Being in deep thought of all the lady had spoken, she observed the long flannel nightgown she was wearing. "Where on earth did this come from? I have no idea where I am nor where my own clothes or belongings might be," her thoughts lingered as she stood observing all the vintage furniture in the first room. While admiring the furnishings and the rareness of quality, besides the enormously huge bed, there were two matching marble-top nightstands of an elegant design mixed with cream and beige colors in a half-moon shape, upheld by elaborate gold pedestals. On top of each nightstand were glorious lamps that held numerous candles, crafted of fine gold, adjoined by four legs extending from a large round base; all were admonished with delicate tracery as they enhanced the center of each table. The bases with extended branches were of a hand-crafted design that rose upwards, forming four pedestals, each holding a slight gold cup that encased the candles. As Cateline stood looking at all the candles, she gazed up to the ceiling once more before realizing there were no signs of any type of electrical lighting. Immediately she thought to herself, "Electricity, yes electricity," speaking those words aloud again and again, slowly she walked over towards the door, looking for any sign of light switches or plug-in receptacles. All she noticed was either candles or oil lamps on every table and, of course, the hearth for heat. In deep thought, Cateline remembered in her years of school that even once electricity had been discovered, it was years later before it was actually installed in homes. "Hmmm, everything from the clothing and furnishings seems to be consistent with the nineteenth century. I came to Ireland by plane, and I am evidently in Ireland based on what the lady said, but I came by ship— how strange!"

Cateline resumed walking through both segments of the adjoining rooms in a complete daze while observing every single aspect in hopes of finding some type of clue to where she was and what era this could possibly be. Feeling a bit unsure of herself, her thoughts renewed, "I suppose I should have asked the lady more specific questions. Why this is absurd, there is no such thing as being able to go back in time. Am I even awake, or perhaps, I really was in some type of accident, and I am dreaming while asleep—yes, maybe this is all a dream, and I will eventually awaken!"

Cateline observed the huge French doors which seemingly led to the exterior of the home. They were made of dense wood with the mid-portion encased with glass. Upon walking over to peer out, she perceived a somewhat sizeable balcony, and off in the distance across the lawn was another building that appeared to be some type of large barn with a stable attached. Not desiring to walk out on the balcony and be seen in her gown, she instead walked to the adjoining room, which had two substantial windows. Gazing out the windows, Cateline was able to view a partial fragment of the grounds, and from what she could see from the window, she was obviously on the second floor of a three-story home of sorts. It was pretty clear that it was an enormous house, perhaps even a mansion or a type of estate home. "This must be the back of the home," she curiously thought to herself. The grounds were immaculate with much shrubbery mixed with numerous kinds of flowers that sprouted forth along with a few delicately arranged gardens, which were also in bloom. "How breathtaking; I believe there is almost every color in view. It is much too far, but I believe I see some camellias," she thought to herself. Cateline had always loved camellias as they were a favorite of her mothers. Camellias had adorned their own home in Boston for many years. Her father would always remind her when she was just a child of how they were planted in various areas after purchasing their home.

As Cateline persistently observed the beautifully maintained lawn, she noticed walkways leading from the back of the house diverting to the lovely gardens on each side of the grounds and beyond. She knew that one of the walkways evidently went to her side where the barn stood, but she could not see the other side of the home from the back windows. The walkway then extended down to what looked like a lake off in the distance, but she could not see it well enough from her window. Large trees were scattered about in areas, and many were lined around the lake, much like those one would see at plantation homes, which reminded her of a time long ago. Reflecting back, Cateline recalled traveling to Louisiana with her family when she was relatively young. Yet, she did remember touring several of the plantation homes, which dated back prior to the Civil War days, many built along the rivers—Mississippi, Bayou Teche, and the Atchafalaya, among others. The homes, which were typically built beside one of the many rivers for trade in those days, were also enriched with the most stunning oak trees, well established in age. She had remembered thinking of how wonderful it would be if trees could talk. Many of the trees today, hundreds of years old, the stories they could tell of things they saw. As these thoughts lingered, Cateline cried out gravely, "Oh, —but where could I possibly be, and what could all this mean?"

Cateline stood observing the grounds and vaguely caught sight of a man and woman strolling along on one of the pathways, which led to a gorgeously landscaped garden. They stopped to engage in conversation with a man she perceived to be the gardener based on his dress and demeanor. "Hmm, strange their manner of dress," she thought, "from what I can tell, their clothing also looks consistent with the nineteenth century. Well, neither the man nor the woman's mode of fashion looks anything like what I have seen thus far in Ireland—oh, Ireland—yes, at least I suppose I am still in Ireland!"

While Cateline turned from the window, her concerns were more towards whose home she was residing in and why she could not remember anything since the castle hotel. She walked over to the hearth to stand as it brought warmth to her body. Turning to feel the heat on her backside, Cateline began looking over every inch of the Victorian room in hopes of gaining some type of clue as to what all this meant. Gazing at all the remnants of the past—paintings, décor, and taking into account the absence of electricity, heating, and cooling, among other items noted within her room alone, she was convinced this was impossible. With curiosity continually building up inside of her, she declared most ardently, "Unless I am either crazy or in some type of coma and only dreaming, I would have to say with everything I have seen thus far—their style of dress, the paintings which are replicas of years gone by, the décor and furnishings of the Victorian era—yes, this truly must be the nineteenth century. Perhaps, a few pieces look like that of the Georgian era, but primarily Victorian, I would have to say. I believe with the large rooms, and two rooms joined as such, in those days, they were called apartments, one for the sleeping area and the other was a boudoir—a kind of dressing room. I do presume the good thing is that possibly I was in some type of accident, which would explain my memory loss. Yes, the accident, I suppose, could be to my advantage since I have no recollection where I am nor whose home I am living." Cateline continued looking over the room as she warmed herself by the fire observing the Victorian wallpaper consistent with that time. In accord, the wallpaper was of diverse gold shades varied with darker browns and tiny designs of the French fleur-de-lis, assorted leaves, and other small flowers patterned throughout the expanse. Cateline being such a history buff, believed from everything she had thus far observed, there was no doubt that all was in conformity with the latter half of the nineteenth century. "I imagine I could have been a bit more explicit with my question to the lady when I asked what day it was— 'It is Saturday,' the lady said. Well, that's nice, but in what year? In the year 2000? No, of course not—in the nineteenth century, perhaps? Why—listen to yourself, Cateline— now, I am even talking to myself. Yes, I must have really been hit on the head, or else I have gone totally insane!"

Cateline, continuing to stand by the fire, noticed the antique washbasin in the adjoining room, which they used before running water and bathrooms. Walking over to the basin, she considered,

"Hmmm— it even has water in it." Picking up one of the flannel cloths to the side, she dipped it into the water. "Well, I suppose the lady that came in must have brought freshwater before I awoke as well. It is still warm." She squeezed out the cloth and sat down at the vanity to use the mirror to wash her face. Noticing the beautiful fresh-cut flower arrangement sitting to one side, Cateline leaned over to smell their fragrant aroma, which had spanned throughout that side of the enormous room. The display had long, straight coils sprouting out of the vase with star-shaped yellow blooms. The tiny star-shaped blossoms ran up and down each side of the twines, with sporadic pink clusters that hung down from cut twigs, embracing the chamber. The pink florets were adorned with small soft green leaves. Cateline closed her eyes and prolonged to capture the scent of the exquisite arrangement of the flowers while drifting away into a dream-like state. "Mmm," caught up in the moment, a most pleasant aroma filled her senses, as she proclaimed, "these smell so enchanting, such a light fragrance, spicy with a spring-like scent. This whole setting, Lord, if this is all real—I feel quite alive, more so than I can ever remember." Opening her eyes once more, Cateline looked into the vanity mirror and gasped, "Oh my, I look so pale, and my hair looks like it hasn't been brushed or cleaned for days. Well, the lady had said that I had been sleeping for what I imagine must be about two or three days." As Cateline washed her face, she gulped impulsively with a sudden shock of pain, "Oh, that hurts!" Pulling her hair away from her forehead revealed a significant bruise. "It is definitely evident that I was in some kind of an accident." Her hair could cover the area that was still swollen on her forehead, but it was also apparent that it extended into her hairline. The location was very sore to the touch, having to be most gentle while washing her face. "I feel as if I am literally starving," she thought to herself, "but then I must not have been eating much either. At least I am feeling better. I think I just need nourishment."

Upon standing, she observed her physique in one of the long mirrors on the side of a vast wardrobe. "Oh, I look so dreadful and in this cotton gown," impetuously, she gasped while exclaiming, "WARDROBE!!" Crying out rather loudly, she had failed to notice the massive wardrobe in her room. "Oh my, this is a wardrobe, which is what they used before closets," she asserted while looking around the two rooms for another door beside the ones that led to the outside of the bedroom and adjoining dressing room. There were no closets. Cateline opened the wardrobe and noticed that her backpack was at the bottom. Immediately, she picked it up very rapidly and looked inside even though it was apparent it seemed to be empty. Lying it back down, she looked once more, noticing her large duffle bag. Cateline lifted the bag, walked over to set it down on a small Victorian-designed loveseat adorning the second room in her apartment, which was reflective of the Victorian designs of golds and browns throughout both areas. Cateline began to sift through but found nothing of significance. "There are no clothes in here," she cried most fervidly, "were they removed?" She walked back to the wardrobe and noticed that many lovely dresses were hanging, which were of the Victorian period but nothing that belonged to her. Opening the other side of the wardrobe was just more of the same with a few hats and scarves, also from that period. Filtering through every single drawer, she observed some type of raiment that might have been consistent with undergarments, and then there were stockings and such, but there was nothing—nothing of her apparel. "Where could all my clothes be? What about my CD player and the book and various articles?" Hurriedly, Cateline walked back over and opened her bag once more, "Yes—yes, at least all of these things are in here—funny that they were in the bottom hidden underneath the insert of the bag. Hmm, but I do not see my cell phone. Oh well, at any rate, I still have my music," she declared, somewhat relieved as those items seemed to be the only things that connected her with the twenty-first century. This proved to her that she had come from America by plane but somehow had crossed over in time to the nineteenth century if indeed, that was even the case. Of course, Cateline had no idea what to make of anything at this point. All she knew was that before deciding to come to Ireland, she had felt that her answers to so many questions would come from her stepping out and leaving her life behind in her timeframe. "Could I have definitely been the Cateline from the book and articles? Yes—oh yes, the girl must have been me. Yet, I do not understand everything, but I do believe that God shall show me all that I am to see."

With her thoughts all over the place, she bravely decided to walk out on the balcony from her room in hopes she could glimpse something, anything that may help her to determine her circumstances. Opening the French doors, Cateline walked out to what was obviously a private balcony that overlooked the side of the house and then extended towards the posterior of the home vaguely. She noticed a young man at the stables who was evidently taking care of several horses. Not seeing anyone in the yard, she carefully walked around towards the back to get a better glimpse. On the balcony, she was able to gain an enhanced view of the grounds, which led to a most fabulous lake, while observing two moderately large buildings towards the back on the other side of the house, barely visible from where she stood. From those buildings, a number of servants were coming and going busily with their work. Not desiring that anyone should see her in the gown, she went back into the room.

Very buoyantly, she declared to herself, "Oh, what an awesome experience this shall be and such an awakening to my soul." Walking back over to the wardrobe, she took out one of the beautiful dresses, a most relaxed deep green, reflective of an emerald with a long sleeve bodice. The bodice was meticulously trimmed, the most exquisite mastery of lace she had beheld. The material felt so polished as it flourished with a glimmer of starlight against the radiance of the sunbeams streaming in vibrantly through the back windows. Cateline held the gown up against her frame, admiring the grace and feel as it beheld her beauty. As she observed its elegance, imagining being adorned in such, her smile became eccentric. Playfully Cateline remarked in a rather profuse voice, "Well, after all, tomorrow is another day, Rhett dear."[1]

CHAPTER
5

As Cateline was holding the most gorgeous dress she had seen of that period up against her body, she perpetually swayed back and forth, all the while admiring the ruffles which cascaded down the sides of the train as they extended to the back. Lost in her mirage, she remarked, "How glorious it must have been to have lived in those days and worn such handsome garments as these." Continuing in a trance state, she tried to envision days of eras gone by when the door recklessly flew open.

"Oh—my goodness! You are awake! We have all been so worried about you," the girl shouted as she came blustering into the room. Realizing how she must have startled Cateline, stepping back a few paces, she exclaimed softly, "Excuse me, I am so sorry, you are probably wondering who this person is barging through the door, scaring you quite to death." Extending her hand towards Cateline, she proclaimed warmly, "Hello and welcome. I am Anya, your cousin. You gave us all such a scare."

Cateline responding to the handshake, affirmed, "It is nice to meet you, Anya. I am so sorry, but I am not myself as yet. I fear that I do not know where I am nor how I got here, and I am beside myself, for I do not remember anyone." Anya was unmistakably adorable, probably in the same age range as Cateline. She was more of a medium build and somewhat taller but most attractive. Her hair was of a glimmering gold in a fashion of being crimped in waves and then pulled up and back, where it was perhaps twisted, secured with ribbons and a few flowers. "Definitely beautiful and graceful all the same," Cateline thought to herself as she persisted in observing the similarities in some of their features. "Yes, I suppose we could pass for sisters or cousins, for that matter," perceived Cateline silently while she prolonged in examining her cousin very thoroughly, from her style of dress to her demeanor. Wearing the Victorian attire of the nineteenth century, her stylish hair, which was worn in a fashion of the same, and her manner of dialect all contributed to more evidence in favor of Cateline, most certainly, somehow being in that period. As Anya maintained speaking, Cateline's thoughts were far off where she had begun fancying the possibility, if indeed, she had awakened to the era to be the exact timeframe as Oscar Wilde's. Her thoughts continued imagining just that, "What could this mean, and is this possible? Of course, it is possible if it is meant to be. For, this is why I came to Dublin—yes, to find out why I feel so connected to this man and those days from long ago, and why those photos I discovered have a lady in them that looks to be me. Although Mary said the girl must have been someone related in years past, I always felt like it had to be me!"

Finally, escaping from her contemplations, Cateline responded to Anya, who had not stopped talking. "I—I am extremely sorry, Anya—I believe my thoughts have run away with me as I have been so confused. Please, could you repeat what you were saying?"

"That is quite alright." Anya, having understood that Cateline was still recovering from her fall, paused before speaking once again, "I was merely apologizing to have startled you. Sarah had come to let us know that you were awake. We are all so relieved that you are going to recover. A minute ago, I also said that it is rather expected of you to have lost some of your memory. Our doctor assumed as much, and we will all be very patient and helpful in any way until you are feeling yourself. On the other hand, I also shared that you would probably not remember my parents or any of us, for that matter; we are family but have not seen you since you were very little. We were both children and played together during those days, but I only remember you because of stories communicated over the years. I have seen a few photos of you and your mother, but they were sent from America when you were somewhat older than our last encounter. Needless to say, we were both much too young at the time you and your mother left for America for either of us to really remember."

About that time, the lady who had awoken Cateline earlier entered the room once again, this time with breakfast that had been prepared for her. She walked over and sat the tray down on the table in the boudoir, which had a few Victorian-style chairs placed around. Looking up at Cateline, she exclaimed, "Miss Cateline, I do hope you are hungry. The cook prepared quite a breakfast since you have awakened and must be dreadfully famished."

"Thank you very much. I am extremely hungry, as a matter of fact," Cateline responded while hanging the dress back in the wardrobe before walking over to sit at the table to begin eating.

"Thank you, Sarah," Anya concluded, "I will let you know if Miss Cateline needs help with dressing and such."

47

"Yes, ma'am," the lady responded.

Once Sarah had left the room, Cateline spoke up, "I hope you don't mind if I eat while we talk. I feel dreadfully weak. I am sure I just need some nourishment."

"Yes, I would imagine you to be hungry, indeed. We have not been able to get much in you other than broth and water. Please eat. I can come back if you wish or stay, either way."

"No, please, I would love for you to stay. I do have questions and would like you to continue with what you were sharing with me. Please, sit down," Cateline said as she motioned to the other chair at the table.

"Very well," continued Anya while sitting across from her. "Where would you like me to begin?"

"You should probably start from the beginning, as I am at a loss for remembrance of anything."

"Alright," Anya responded while she resumed sharing the details of Cateline's arrival, "let's see, you were to arrive on Wednesday, which you did. My father and mother had gone to greet you at the docks and bring you home. Upon arriving, they quickly learned of your accident on the ship and your condition. We were not sure you would be alright, so we sent for our doctor, and he stayed overnight the first night to make sure you would recover. He did warn us to expect that you might awaken not remembering too much."

"I can recall nothing about the ship. You said that we are family?"

"Yes, I am your cousin, Anya. You were actually born and lived in Youghal, which is where your father's estate is located. I am not sure how much you know of those days since you were very young when your mother took you to America."

"No, I do not believe I remember anything of those days."

"As I have said, we were both very young when you moved away. Your mother left with family to cross to America when you were perhaps three or four, from what I was told. There were aunts, uncles, and some of our cousins who were heading off to America, and your mother left with them. Obviously, I do not remember many of those family members who also left during that phase, except for the few who have come back for visits. There were also those who moved back permanently but most never did. They all believed life to be much better in America, which I suppose it may have been since so many left prior. You know about the potato famine, I am sure." she inquired with an amiable smile.

"Without a doubt, I do. I have read about it in my studies. But, of course, that was back in the 1840s."

"Yes, but that is what led many to America from Ireland in the beginning. Since that time, families have maintained leaving for the *land of plenty*, as they say, and with so many Irish living there now, it makes it somewhat easier. The stories do come back to Ireland of how grand America is, and so, many Irish continue to leave for the new world even to this day."

"So, I believe that this is currently 1880 or 81?" Cateline pondered as she was inquisitive to know if, by chance, she could possibly be in that timeframe. To her, 1881 would have been the most probable year that she could have come based on the articles she found.

"Oh yes, it is 1881—see, you have not forgotten everything."

What a relief to know that what she had been feeling was right on target, even though it terrified and fascinated her at the same time of what lay ahead. She continued to eat breakfast, which was quite the meal for that period; never would she have thought the food to be so enjoyable, consisting of eggs and a variety of meat to include bacon and sausage, complemented with crumpets, so they were called. There was also a range of fruit, choices of bread, and even some type of oatmeal. The seasonings were not entirely to her liking, but all in all, it was a most favorable meal for that day and age. "The breakfast is very delightful," she politely remarked to Anya, continuing in conversation, "I am so thankful for all the hospitality and that I have been in such good care."

"You are most welcome, and I assure you, we are delighted to have you as our guest. Please, treat our home as your own. As for the breakfast, it is the English breakfast, but I would assume the Irish in America are relatively accustomed to eating much the same."

"Oh yes, we have nice breakfasts on occasions, but I have not heard the expression of an *English Breakfast*."

"Well, it is a full breakfast, to be sure. It is the routine in Ireland, a full breakfast on most days. Some, of course, refer to it as the Irish Breakfast."

"A good practice it is, and thank you so much, Anya, for all your kind words. So, I understand that I arrived by ship but was there a reason I was coming to Dublin? I am in Dublin, right?"

49

"You are, well, actually, you are in Clontarf, but that is a suburb of Dublin."

"Hmm," Cateline thought to herself, "Clontarf—the same location as the Clontarf Castle Hotel."

Anya maintained sharing with Cateline in hopes of stirring her memory, as she recalled, "In fact, we all used to live in Youghal, but my father came to Clontarf to be close to Dublin as that is where his office is located. We were fortunate to find this estate with land in such a location. It is quite pleasant here, as you will see. It was such a shame that we never were able to see you again nor your mother, before now, that is. I know much of the family thought about you and your mother often. It was after your father passed on—oh, I am so sorry, you did say you have no recollection of why you came."

"No, truthfully, I am afraid I do not have a clue. I suppose I need the full story so that I can understand, for I do not even remember my father," Cateline considered earnestly, knowing that Anya was speaking of her father in the nineteenth century, evidently.

"Well," remarked Anya with a most sincere expression as she resumed, "yes, your father, John McCarthy, passed away most recently, but you would not remember him anyway, as your mother never brought you back. None of us have seen you since you were a small child. Upon your father's passing, my father, your uncle, sent you a letter of his death. I believe that your father left you an inheritance. My father has all those details, as I am sure he will go over with you."

"So, your father sent me a letter to let me know that my father had passed on?"

"Yes, and we were so relieved when we received your correspondence to orchestrate your plans to travel to Dublin. In fact, it has been the most exciting news for some time of your traveling to Ireland, after all these years. We were expecting you as you were coming by ship on Wednesday. Needless to say, due to your injury, we have all been so worried. My father has been utterly beside himself," remarked Anya very strongly, adding— "I do believe he shall recover now that you have awakened," she concluded blissfully.

Cateline smiled gently as she inquired, "What was my father like?"

"Oh, Uncle John was so very kind. You would have loved him deeply."

"Why did my mother leave him to go to America, do you know?"

"I believe from what I have heard, they were already having difficulties in their marriage, and she had decided to leave with other family members. Uncle John did not want to leave Ireland, and your mother seemed to be set on going. Their disagreement on that matter only added to their troubles." After a moment of silence, Anya continued, "You do know that your mother and my father are brother and sister."

"No, I had no idea. I really have no recollection of my mother ever sharing much about her family in Ireland. Yes, Ireland was mentioned from time to time, but nothing of significance," Cateline elaborated as she tried to place herself in the life of that century, continuing, "Of course, I eventually grew up and never asked, as it was seldom spoken of. Does your father ever hear from my mother?"

"I am not quite sure. If he does, he doesn't talk about it. But honestly, I must say I do not remember much about your mother, Aunt Marion, for I, too, was very young since the last occasion of being graced by her company."

"Ah, yes—your aunt, I suppose that you would not remember her since we left so many years ago," Cateline affirmed while thinking about her name silently to herself, "*Marion,* why that is my middle name. From time to time, my parents would share a story of how they had chosen to name me after a relation in Ireland from many years back, someone they knew not but who had been spoken of by many. What was that story? Is it possible that I was truly the daughter of a *Marion* during this timeframe? Was it possible that I was actually related to the *McCarthy* family from this era?" A question she would always ponder with no parent living to confirm.

Cateline, realizing that Anya was still speaking, perked up to listen. "Uncle John, your father, he missed you terribly. He was very close to me as I reminded him of the little girl he lost to America," she paused with a smile before continuing. "Uncle John would speak of you often and never forgot you. I can remember conversations with my parents about his wish to cross to America to see you. Nonetheless, with it being such a very long journey, he could never leave his responsibilities, the laborious duties in maintaining a large estate such as his. Your mother, I suppose it was too long of a journey for her to ever come back, as well. I hear she remarried a man from America and was much involved in life there. Your

51

stepfather, is he a good man? I do hope that your memory of America hasn't faded as well."

"Some of this is coming back to me. Hopefully, I will regain my memory," assured Cateline, knowing she would have to be careful what she disclosed to not mix up her parents from this era and the next. Not even knowing who her stepfather was for this timeframe, she exclaimed, "My stepfather is a good man," keeping it most simple before continuing on the subject of John McCarthy. "But, seldom do I remember any mention of my father here in Ireland. You said that my father's estate is in Youghal?"

"Yes," Anya replied while adding a brief history of their past, "we go to Youghal from time to time, as both of my parents enjoyed living there. Such a small, quaint town—relatively peaceful, serene, and has the beauty of the River Blackwater, which flows out to the Celtic Sea. Of course, we also used to go to see Uncle John as often as was possible. In fact, we went to pay our respects at the funeral when he passed on recently. You are probably not aware that the Walsh and McCarthy families are also cousins. Not uncommon, you know, for cousins to marry."

"I am aware that was most probable back in the day, especially during occasions when there were few neighbors close. But I did not know that my father and mother were cousins."

"Oh, but it is still probable even today, especially among the very elite in society. And yes, they, to be precise, all the cousins grew up playing together as children. My father and Uncle John were not only cousins but the very best of friends. They were all pretty much a close-knit family in those days, and even today, we stay close with many of the McCarthy family."

While Cateline maintained eating, she was trying to take in everything Anya was sharing with her. "I am sorry, I suppose I am just not feeling myself quite yet, and so much I do not remember and even more which I never knew. However, I do remember Ireland briefly when I was very young. Nevertheless, that could also be because of my mother sharing those stories with me," she openly noted, thinking back about the time in the twentieth century where they had returned to visit family. Briefly looking down, rationalizing the knowledge she had thus far obtained, striving to separate her two lives, Cateline knew that she must listen closely to all that was told in order to understand how her life fit into that timeframe and if there was some explanation of why she lived in this century, as well as the twentieth and twenty-first centuries. Continuing with their discourse, she inquired, "Was my father not well?"

"I'm sorry to say that he was ill, very much so. In fact, he had been unwell for quite a phase, but none of us were expecting him to pass on. I believe with his remarrying his second wife and then her passing at such a young age, this certainly had taken its toll on his desire to live."

"So, he did remarry?"

"Oh yes, she was the most pleasant young woman. They had a son, James. He is, I believe, twenty. They were married for probably ten years when she became very ill and passed on. After that occurrence, it was merely Uncle John and James. I imagine that he lived as long as he did because of James, but once James became of age, many of us suppose that Uncle John had become lonely and saw no need in continuing life. After all, 'he had loved twice and unlikely to love a third time,' that was one of his famous quotes," she disclosed with a slight laugh.

Upon Cateline hearing those words, strangely, her father's words from the twentieth century rang out loudly through her mind, "Oh, my goodness! My own father, those were his exact words of my mother, except he had always said, 'he had loved once,' not twice. Could John McCarthy had actually been my true father in two different lives?" Perking up, Cateline continued to listen to Anya.

As she maintained her story, remembering Uncle John, Anya spoke, "Yes, he used to quote those words rather candidly when anyone tried to push him to marry again, and he did it so well—with a blunt smile and a quaint laugh! I can still envision his expression. Of course, we never really took him seriously, yet as the days and years lingered, it became evident that he had no desire to ever marry again."

"You said he had a son, James. He is my half-brother?"

"He most assuredly is at that! A most handsome young man who looks just like your father at that age. James is also most eager to meet you. He had no other siblings as Aunt Anne had never quite been well once James had been born. Oh yes, she lived up until James was about seven, but from his birth, she had remained sickly."

"I am so sorry for James; it must be hard at twenty to not have either parent."

"Yes, but as the only son and as is custom, he did inherit the estate in Youghal and has his hands much engaged in its upkeep. Not surprisingly, your father never forgot his daughter and made sure you would be well cared for, too. As is the practice, being the first daughter, you would have obtained a dowry once married. I believe your father wanted to make sure that you received what would have been yours. As I said, he talked of you often and never stopped loving you. Of the amount that he set aside, I have none of the particulars on that subject. My father will discuss that with you on a more personal level, I am sure," she laughed most gently before continuing. "I only know that your father made sure that the laws would not prevent you from receiving what would have been due to you upon marrying. As I said, he was a good man, and he genuinely loved you."

"I would so love to see his estate if it were not too far and visit James as well."

"Youghal is about a half day's journey from Dublin. It is actually a seaside town in County Cork and a most astonishing place to visit. As I have shared, both the Walsh and McCarthy family used to live there. The Walsh family moved many years ago closer to Dublin, but most of the McCarthy's stayed. Youghal was built on the edge of a steep riverbank with many beaches. The Clock Gate Tower, quite an antiquated sight to see, was built during the eighteenth century, which has a lot of history if you indeed love history."

"Oh yes, as a matter of fact, I do."

"Myself as well. You would truly love to visit Youghal with its history. The Tynte's Castle that is located there was built by the Walsh family dating back to the late fifteenth century. These, of course, were ancestors of great wealth and rank in those days, but they lost the castle during the Desmond Rebellion in the sixteenth century. It is still standing and was owned by the Tynte family, which is where it got its name. I know they sold it but not sure who the proprietors are now. Even so, today, it stands, as it is, on the main street of town. Not sure how much you know about castles, but it is considered a tower house with much history there as well. I am certain that you will meet James either by his coming to Dublin or perhaps, you can travel to Youghal. There is a train that runs to Cork, but as I said, it is about a half day's journey."

"Well, I have nothing but time and would so love to meet my half-brother and see my father's estate. I truly do not remember anything about my father and would naturally love to learn more about him and about our life when we lived in Youghal. Are you very acquainted with James?"

"Yes, we are cousins, even though at a distance, both families have traveled over the years to stay in contact. We were all very close to your father because he was still family, and so is James. I am a bit older than James, but there were many family gatherings over the years, where we enjoyed having fun together."

"Ah—a younger brother, how nice. I have no other siblings back in the states, and I would have traveled here sooner had I known, but I really didn't remember anyone from here. Since my mother never returned, I had never actually thought about coming to Ireland myself. I suppose your father's letter is what has brought me here, after all."

"Well, I do hope that you will be able to stay for a while and look forward to rekindling our relationship where we can be close friends as well. You also have another cousin to meet, my brother Cyrus. Cyrus is older than I am, and he is married with one son. They live in Clontarf as well, but along the coast, not too terribly far from here."

"Yes, I look forward to rekindling the relationship with all of you, and perhaps I can go visit your brother and his family before too long."

"Certainly, I actually haven't been to my brothers for several weeks, nor seen him here. We can definitely make a day of it soon."

"That sounds wonderful. I suppose I will need you to help me remember things since my accident, and I am not at all sure how to dress appropriately. In fact, I know none of the traditions or mannerisms of Ireland."

"Do not worry, I will instruct you on the customs, and as for the appropriate dress, we took the liberty of unpacking your belongings. Your dresses are all very lovely and meet the attire here in Ireland and England for that matter. We wear pretty much the same things. Perhaps, you should wear one of your dresses that is more practical for most days. I would save the exquisite ones, like the one you were holding when I walked in, for special occasions."

"Yes—absolutely, that makes sense," she responded while reflecting on all the excellent dresses in the wardrobe which actually belonged to her.

"Although we do entertain guests or go out on the town from time to time where a beautiful dress as such would be most admired. Oh, I almost forgot, my father was waiting for you to get better, but he is planning a special *welcoming party* here at the estate. There will

55

probably be many prominent gentlemen and ladies for you to meet while you are here, and I am sure that my brother will attend as well."

"That is so very kind of him to welcome me with a party. I will so look forward to meeting others. Will there be music and dancing?"

"Certainly, there is always dancing, music, singing, and eating. The Irish do know how to have a grand time. You will do fine. We do understand that you play the pianoforte and notice that you have a guitar. Do you play both?"

"Oh, I did not see my guitar."

"We took the liberty to place it in our more formal drawing-room where the pianoforte is located. I hope that is alright with you."

"Yes, of course, I had not even thought about it until you said something. And yes, I do play both, but I much prefer to hear someone else perform. Do you play an instrument as well, Anya?"

"Yes, I play the pianoforte and sing. Nevertheless—I am warning you now to be prepared; if I know my father and mother, they will expect to observe your accomplishments. The Irish love to entertain, and in doing so, if there is a particular guest with a talent, you can bet they will want to show off your attributes."

"Thank you for the warning," responded Cateline.

"Well, it looks like you were hungry."

"Oh, yes, I was, and everything was most delicious."

"I will send Sarah to take away your tray, and if you feel like getting dressed and joining the family downstairs, I know they are so very excited to get to know you."

"I would love to meet the family. I will get dressed and be down shortly."

"I would advise wearing one of your dresses with the long sleeve basque, as it is rather cool in February and March. March will tend to be a bit warmer during the days, but long sleeves are definitely appropriate, and perhaps, if you also have pantalettes, they seem to help with warmth."

"Pantalettes?" Cateline thought to herself. Yes, she had heard of the term but had never worn such a thing, nor had she ever the privilege of seeing the undergarments. Nevertheless, discovering that the clothes in the wardrobe actually belonged to her, she was so excited to wear some of those most beautiful gowns. Of course, she would also have to examine all the other articles to figure out how they were worn. "I believe I can do this," her thoughts evolved silently, "truthfully, how hard could it be?"

Anya speaking up, added spontaneously, "Oh yes, and before I leave, the maid who was in your room is Sarah. She is my lady's maid, mother's is Permilia. I am sure that you will see both of them quite often. They help with just about everything we need—hot water for cleaning, taking care of our hair and clothing. I was going to say if you need help dressing or doing your hair, either one can help you. If you would like, I can send Sarah to help you dress today and do your hair. She is very wonderful at making splendid creations."

"Oh, well, is it appropriate to have your hair down?"

"Well, yes and no. It is becoming more common, but as a rule, young ladies wearing their hair down means that they are eligible. If she is betrothed or married, it is frowned upon, I suppose you would say. Ordinarily, this is the most I wear my hair down, where it is really pulled up and back. I am engaged, though, and I am assuming that you are not?"

"No—no, I am not engaged nor married. You will have to tell me all about your customs and your engagement."

"Yes, I am sure as we spend time together, you will begin to learn our practices and for us to learn about each other, but please, feel free to ask me any questions, cousin dear."

"Thank you, Anya, and I will."

"As for your hair, you can wear it down if you like—especially at home, when there are no guests, it does not really matter. I do wear mine down when I am home and not expecting company at times myself. But, of course, when we are attending something more formal, we have our hair arranged properly. Even with my hair pulled back, I do not always wear it like this for a formal occasion, probably more up."

"Thank you, Anya; I will probably just do something simple for today and perhaps use Sarah for something more social. I believe the vanity table will work well with the mirror to manage my hair. I have a vanity as well at home."

Anya responded as she glanced over to the vanity table, "Oh, you mean the dressing table. Yes, we have those in all of the ladies' apartments. The mirror actually folds down if you prefer when not in use."

"Oh no, I love it like it is. Everything is so admirable, Anya. My room is quite lovely."

"I also took the liberty of having Sarah make sure that you had items on the dressing table to master your hair and face since we noticed nothing in your carpet bag. We were not sure if maybe it was misplaced due to your accident."

"Perhaps, some of my items are missing. I was actually looking through my bags before you came in and could not find some of my things."

"No need to worry; my father will make sure that you have what you need."

"You are most kind, thank you. I believe that I have everything I need to freshen myself and my hair without bothering Sarah today. Nonetheless, I would love for her to prepare my hair for special occasions, for I know by seeing yours that I am probably at a terrible disadvantage to dare try to create such a magnificent style."

"Then we will simply have Sarah create exquisite works of art for those particular days, which she is so good at doing. Now, I will leave you to yourself, and we will all be waiting for you downstairs to get acquainted. When you walk out of your room, there is a staircase to your right, these are the back stairs, and they lead down to the back of the estate. Once you get downstairs, go through the morning room on the right, not through the kitchen. There are two doors in the back of our estate, with one leading to the veranda and the other leads to the conservatory. We are routinely on the patio when the weather is pleasant, where we have our elevenses for the day. You will see us as soon as you go out the door."

"Thanks, Anya. What is elevenses?"

Laughing rather vaguely, Anya responded, "I am sorry. You may be Irish, but you have not been raised with the customs. Elevenses is referred to as the tea break, which follows a little while after breakfast, at eleven, to be exact. Which is why it is called *elevenses,* my dear. Bertha typically serves some light biscuits to accompany the tea."

"Interesting! Like I said, you will have to teach me because I will be at a loss without you," Cateline professed.

"I will teach you, and we are going to be great friends as well as cousins!"

With the door closed, Cateline walked back over to the wardrobe to pick out a casual dress that would be practical for everyday wear. Skimming through the various dresses on both sides of the wardrobe, she noticed a wool cape. "I suppose that is for when it is reasonably cold—perhaps, with a nice dress for a social event," she said to herself while continuing to look over each dress. Eventually, one particular garment seemed to capture her attention, quite perfect indeed, for a more casual appearance. The ensemble, deep wine in color, was trimmed in black velvet along the bottom to include the elaborate scarf-like extension draped over the shoulders of the slightly capped sleeves, which then extended to the back tied off with a dainty bow. The long sleeve basque, white in color, to be worn underneath the soft wool dress, would be much warmer for this time of year, not to mention the velvety texture provided for a most comfortable feel. Cateline thought to herself, "Yes, I will just relax today and enjoy conversation to learn more detail of my surroundings." Laying the dress on the bed, she went through the drawers of the wardrobe once again to locate the stockings of that period. Selecting a pair that would be warm and match the dress, she then found a few of the pantalettes, as well. In one of the drawers, she also noticed gloves, some short length and others were rather long to extend almost up to the shoulder, which could only be worn with a short sleeve dress. "That is definitely good to know," she said out loud, "but I dare say these are not needed for a day such as this." Next, Cateline looked for shoes, "Shoes, where are the shoes?" Upon opening every drawer again, there were no shoes. Rapidly, she took another look at where the dresses were and finally saw several pairs at the very bottom hidden in the back of the wardrobe underneath the robes. "Well, they did not make shoes in this period like they do in the twenty-first century. I dare say, I am not at all eager to wear any of these." Taking out a black pair of lace-up boots with a small heel appropriate for the dress, her thoughts persisted, "The good thing is that no one can see your shoes with the long dresses, but I suppose the bad news is they do look quite uncomfortable."

As Cateline began to dress, thoughts were continually racing through her mind, "I cannot believe that this is really happening to me. Oh, how I wish I could call Mary, and I wonder how long I will be here—and then will I simply wake up one day and be back in the twenty-first century? Am I merely dreaming? Why no, I could not be dreaming, for everything seems so real. It does not seem to be a dream, nor is it such at all. No, it is an adventure, and what an adventure it shall be. Perhaps, this journey will be one that I have no desire to even step back into the twenty-first century." Tears trickled

59

down her face as she sat at the dressing table, "Oh, why am I crying? This is so very real, as Anya even said. It is 1881, just like the pictures claim. How thankful I am, Lord, for you have brought me here for a reason. My being here has purpose, oh that I could see your purpose, but someday, perhaps, I will."

Looking in the mirror, she witnessed the paleness of her skin and started to apply some of the products unfamiliar to her that were spread out on the dressing table. There was some kind of cream that seemed to be a type of lotion. Applying it to her face felt quite pleasant to her skin and provided much moisture, which was needed. She then found something that almost seemed like wax, but it had a red color; using it on her lips, she proclaimed, "Yes, that works. This must be rouge, very common for this period. I will simply blot it a bit to make it a shade lighter, and that should be good, *voila*—red lips!" Cateline knew she needed minimal makeup since her skin was naturally smooth and soft. Adding a touch of the color to her cheeks, merely enough to give her face some clarity, she then brushed her waves of dark brown hair through to bring out the shine since it seemed to have lost its luster from the days spent in bed. As the sheen and beauty returned, Cateline gathered up the long locks and began to pull them up on the top of her head, leaving a few strands down on the sides and back. Once her hair was secured in a loose bun, she twisted the long ringlets where they curled meticulously, adding a certain charm to the overall beauty framing her facial features. As she maintained in arranging her hair just right, her thoughts continued, "So, they believe I am the Cateline from the past, and so I must be. It is apparent in both eras that I was born in Ireland. My parents must be those of the nineteenth century, as well as those of the twentieth. Hmmm—I wonder if they, too, were the same. Surely not, for my parents of the twentieth century loved each other deeply and would never have parted ways. Of that, I suppose I will never know. But, surely, with my parents of the twentieth century being of Irish descent and having the McCarthy name, they must have been of relations to these of the nineteenth century. Yes, I feel that in my bones. It must be, after all, even Anya has the same resemblance as myself. You can tell that we are family. How strange, but I suppose that my mother in this century is still alive and living in Boston, that is rather peculiar. It is indeed, yes, she had left for Boston. I must inquire more of her, but of course, I cannot inquire, as if I have not seen her for evidently, I left Boston to come here. I must then ask what she was like before leaving for America to compare her with my late mother. Yes, my uncle, her brother, should have great stories to be told. It is also quite obvious that this era of my family must have been from well-to-do families. My parents never talked of such that I remember, but they never really spoke of their ancestry at all except for those few whom they were very dear."

After dressing, finishing up her hair, and adding touches to her face, Cateline stood up and walked over to one of the large mirrors on the front of the wardrobe to make sure she was presentable. Admiring herself in the Victorian style dress with the long basque, she began to think about her real mother from the twentieth century. Cateline had been blessed with her mother's hair, dark-brown and thick. She had always chosen to keep it long as her mother had, as well. From time to time, Cateline would reminisce through old photos of her mother, pictures she cherished when her mom was very young, with the resemblance fairly noticeable between mother and daughter. Yes, if it were not for the photos being so old, it was hard to tell if it was her mom or her. Cateline could definitely see herself in her mother as she had grown into adulthood, remembering that her mother wore her hair up most days, but it was so beautiful when it was down. As she thought about those years of childhood, Cateline once again drifted off in her thoughts to where she was right now. "I know why I am here. Yes, I knew this was supposed to occur. I know I thought I was going crazy, but I wasn't. This is truly happening, and yes, there is a reason for me to be here; I am quite sure of it now. This is Oscar Wilde's timeframe, and my purpose for being here has to do with him. Yes, that has to be the reason."

She smiled, taking one more look in the mirror, and then gasped, "Oh my goodness, they are going to insist that I play the guitar. The piano is one thing; I know several of the classical composer's melodies that I enjoy performing—Beethoven, Wöelfl, Schubert—well, and a few others. I also love some of the tunes by many new composers, a few from my timeframe, yes—they would probably love them. The melody is clearly as superb as those of this era. Hmmm—Emily Barker is one of my favorites, but she is actually around my age. Oh, they would absolutely love her compositions, but that may not be a good idea. The problem is going to be my guitar. I can only play classical music on the piano and know no other genres from this period. My favorite songs are mainly from the 50s and 60s with a few more modern tunes, yet the newer music would positively not work for this age. Wow, I can't even imagine how they would respond to most of the sounds from the twentieth century! At least much of the music from the 50s and 60s are love songs, and they are relatively soft and slow—I will just have to make sure those that I choose are not too liberal for this era, and I must pay attention to the words." As Cateline thought about what their response might be to experience the more liberal type of music that plagued the 1960s, a quiet laugh escaped. At the same time, she contemplated, "No, they would definitely not approve of some of those tunes. I imagine I best be prepared ahead of time. Who knows, mixing a little of the 50s and 60s into the nineteenth century might actually be fun, and perhaps they may even come to love it!"

As Cateline walked out the bedroom door, she smiled roguishly and thought to herself, "This is certainly going to be hard. I am not sure they are ready for a woman from the twentieth or the twenty-first century for that matter, but that may actually make this whole experience more exciting."

CHAPTER
6

Cateline, walking into the wide hallway, noticed the stairs directly to her right, but turning to look down the extent of the corridor, she immediately stood motionless. In awe of what lay ahead, she gazed upon the front part of the home, which was filled with a number of Victorian-style chairs and tables. The walls were adorned with many of the era's glorious paintings, along with porcelain sconces holding tall candles in each cup. Doors were spaced out on both sides, which led to a range of rooms. Quite ecstatic, Cateline had enjoyed the decor and beauty of her own bedroom, where each and every space was embellished with luxurious treasures. But, gazing upon the relics which were dispersed before her, she had never seen such beauty in all her days, other than through pictures. However, even with the many photos she had come to cherish from this period, none did justice to the real world that extended beyond. The woodwork, especially all the trim throughout the extravagant passage, was of such flawless character to include the rich dark wood flooring with a Victorian rug stretched out the length of the entire hall, exposing the side sections of the floor. She began to quietly walk along, engaging in the prospect of various tables enhanced with antique oil lamps and many genuine articles, which included—a rose medallion vase and a few porcelain vases besides. Further down, an exquisite black basalt figurine accompanied one agate urn and one bronze, along with numerous silver candlesticks arranged nicely throughout. Lastly, there were several lovely enameled type bowls. "Oh," she thought to herself, "the value of all these delicate pieces of art, how elaborate." All the doors were shut soundly, and she dared not open any of them since she was a guest. Walking back towards her room, once again, she was in view of the most elaborate flight of stairs, one twirling downward and the opposite sprawling upward to what must be the third floor. "Hmmm—perhaps I have time to run up the stairs to see what is on the upper level," she thought to herself, persisting, "I am sure it wouldn't hurt, and I will just be quick about it."

Ascending the beautifully rich mahogany staircase, Cateline perceived the upper area to be considerably smaller than the lower levels. Still, there was once again a substantial hallway, much of the same décor with only four doorways visible leading to various rooms, all presumed to be apartments. With those doors fully opened, she slowly glided down the carpeted area to take a peek. They all seemed to be huge bedrooms entirely furnished with the likes similar to that of her apartment. Each room had its own décor in the particular style of furniture and furnishings, but they were all very exquisite in taste.

Hurriedly, running back down the stairs all the way to the first floor, descending to the last step, she ran into a gentleman to be middle-aged, one would say, but most charming, all the same, with dark hair, a slight mustache, rather tall, and to some degree, he maintained a muscular physique. "Excuse me," she exclaimed, somewhat embarrassed.

"Good day, Cateline," the older gentleman addressed her in a reasonably warm and gallant manner. With a sincere smile, he reached over to give her a big hug while continuing to speak softly, "Welcome to the Walsh estate. I am your uncle and Marion's brother, Samuel Walsh, my dear."

"Good morning, sir," Cateline responded.

With a straightforward chuckle, the man spoke in a most dignified voice, "Surely, my dear, it is not still morning, but we are delighted that you are awake and have come back to the living. You did give us quite a scare. And please, by all means, call me Uncle Walsh."

"Yes, Uncle Walsh," she responded as he took her arm in his.

"The family is out on the veranda, as it is such a marvelous day. Your aunt will also be much pleased to see you." At the base of the stairs, a trivial hallway seemed to lead to the kitchen in one direction, as several servants were busying themselves. Off from the stairs, straight ahead was another hallway of a vast expanse reminiscent of the second floor, which led to the front part of their home. Nonetheless, she did notice that the first-floor hallway did not have furniture lined along the walls. Instead, there were the most beautiful chandeliers hanging down with long candles to illuminate rooms adjacent to large openings, French doors visible on both sides. It was pretty evident those entryways led to huge rooms.

Mr. Walsh, directing her in the opposite direction towards the back of the home, escorted Cateline through what seemed to be a dining room, somewhat casual. It was a very sizeable oblong room but moderately narrow in width, with a long mahogany table and many Windsor-type chairs along both sides and armchairs on each end. As they entered, Uncle Walsh stated, "This is our breakfast parlor or morning room and where you will generally come for breakfast, unless you so choose to eat in your room. However, if you so desire, one of the lady's maids will be more than happy to bring up your breakfast."

"Oh no, I would not think of being a bother to anyone, Uncle Walsh. I shall very much like to join the family tomorrow for breakfast."

In his stately manner, while trying to curtail his laughter, her uncle responded, "Please know, my dear—many times we have breakfast in our rooms. That is also why you have a small table and chairs in your apartment. On Saturdays, especially, and sometimes other days, we tend to sleep later, and I am relatively certain you may not see your aunt nor myself, as we rather enjoy being served in our rooms."

"I see—America is fairly different. I must learn your routines," she responded while noticing the attractive mahogany buffet sideboard, which was to the back of the long table. It reminded her of the one in her childhood home, which had belonged to a great-grandmother. The bases were actually called *paw feet*.

"All in time, my dear. All in time," her uncle finished.

The French doors off from the breakfast parlor led directly to the veranda. As Cateline walked down the back steps, her eyes were filled with the most charming Victorian patio she had ever beheld. To her amazement, there were many gorgeous plants of every size and shape—quite a few were scaled along trellises while others sat in huge stone basins scattered about in various locations. Still, several others were delicately placed in most handsome jardinière pots located along the perimeters. Wrought iron tables were clustered throughout the area, with some assembled together for groups. Each table consisted of two to four chairs. They were small but maybe not entirely as small as the bistro tables that originated from Paris. At one of those tables sat her cousin Anya and a woman about the same age as her uncle, which she assumed to be her aunt.

The lady stood to greet Cateline while leaning over to give her a hug, speaking generously, "So delightful to finally meet you. I am your Aunt Martha, my dear."

"It is so nice to meet you as well, and I am so sorry if I have caused much distress with my accident."

"Nonsense. We have been so delighted from the first day we received your letter about your visit to Ireland. I cannot tell you how happy it has made your uncle. None of us have set eyes on you since you were such a tiny thing, and I dare say, we thought many times, we never would again. Of course, it is too sad that we have had to meet under the circumstances of your dear father's passing, but we are so genuinely elated to have you come and stay with us."

"I am so very pleased to be here, and I thank you both for your most gracious hospitality," responded Cateline with a pleasant and agreeable tone while making eye contact with both her uncle and aunt.

"You are so very welcome, my dear," Martha countered while commenting to her husband, "Samuel, it has been some time since our elevenses, and I have asked Bertha to begin preparing a light lunch for Clara to serve on the veranda a bit early. I do hope that is quite alright with you."

"Yes, that is perfectly fine, and besides, Cateline may still be hungry," he reflected with a congenial appearance while gazing slightly towards his niece.

"Well, I was served the most delicious breakfast and ate so much, but I will try to eat a little when it is served," she concluded while walking around, surveying all the various plants more closely.

"My dear," Aunt Martha pleaded, "please come and sit. I am sure that you are weak from this most dreadful ordeal you have encountered on that revolting ship. Let me pour you some tea." Aunt Martha picked up the teapot and poured a cup for Cateline.

"Thank you, Aunt Martha," Cateline stated while taking the cup and walking over to sit in one of the chairs closest to Anya.

"To enlighten you, my dear," Aunt Martha began, "we typically eat our English breakfast in the morning room between nine and ten. That usually depends on if your uncle is working from home or has to go to Dublin. We typically take our elevenses on the veranda on very pleasant days, as we have today, and some days our lunch. Are you familiar with elevenses, Cateline?"

"I wasn't, but Anya did share that with me. It is at eleven, and the tea is served with biscuits."

"Bertha does bring coffee as well if you prefer. I do hope that you had enough to eat for breakfast, I am afraid that our luncheon is a very light meal, but we do have our afternoon tea before dinner."

"Yes, ma'am, I had more than enough to eat. Everything sounds very agreeable. A light lunch is sufficient, I am quite sure. I am afraid that you must educate me on your practices. Our meals are most certainly not the same. The afternoon tea, is that just tea again?"

They all looked at each other, smiling as her aunt glanced back at Cateline to respond apologetically, "No, dear. I am sorry, of course, you are not familiar with the customs here, as in America. Our afternoon tea will consist of coffee or tea, whichever you prefer, and ordinarily sandwiches, scones, and baked sweet cakes, much later this afternoon, around four or so. However, it is only a light meal in which we sometimes have guests. It is served a few hours or so before dinner—our late evening meal, which is most substantial."

Cateline smiling back, answered, "Yes, ma'am, I am not familiar as of yet, but I assure you that I am excited to learn your customs."

As they conversed, a very young girl, small in stature, came with a tray of food items and began to spread it out on a long table. "I will be back with more tea, ma'am," the girl stated to Mrs. Walsh.

"Thank you, Clara," Martha responded.

Uncle Walsh rose first. Walking over to the serving table, he prepared himself a plate of sufficient items—tiny finger sandwiches and a cup of soup with bread on the side. "Please, Cateline, do not be shy. Help yourself to whatever you feel like eating. It looks like we have watercress egg salad sandwiches. What kind of soup is this, my dear?"

Martha responding to her husband's inquiry, replied, "Samuel, it is mulligatawny soup, can you not tell?"

"Yes—yes, I thought that was what it was."

Cateline rising along with the other ladies, prepared her plate while she acknowledged, "This all looks so good. I am afraid I will probably not be able to eat that much. I did eat all of my breakfast, as I was pretty hungry."

"Just eat whatever you like, dear cousin," Anya remarked.

Cateline, sitting back down, began to observe her surroundings. The veranda extended from the back of the house and was reasonably generous, with the floors made of some type of stone. Along the walls of the home adjoining the backside of the veranda stood tall plant-like trees, extending up a considerable

67

distance, evidently being the reason why the roof was protracted at such a significant height. The covering, held up with cross-sections for support, was lined with a steel-casing of some type to keep out the elements. Besides the large plants that lined the back walls, there were also lovely vines trailing along, making a rather nature-like appearance to the extent of the patio area. Throughout the vast space, numerous planters were extending down from the rafters, along with hefty pots in multiple locations scattered about, all overflowing with much greenery and flowers—the extent of the foliage to include various flourishing colors made for a serene garden type of retreat. Spaced out along the back wall were two sections between the vegetation, which housed two enormous stone fireplaces. Both hearths were well lit for added heat, with their tables being arranged fairly close, gaining some warmth from the chill of the day. The sides of the veranda were also lined with partial walls, and in varied locations, there were oil lamps for lighting at dusk, with the front being left open to the grandeur views of the grounds and lake. The whole area was most breathtaking with such beautiful scenery to enjoy while having meals outdoors or even merely sitting to enjoy a nice hot cup of tea.

Interrupting her train of thought, Aunt Martha inquired, "My dear, have you tried the soup?"

"Yes, ma'am, it is delicious, and the bread is very flavorsome, as well."

"Yes, the mulligatawny soup is always a fine touch to a light meal. I am glad to hear you are enjoying the Irish soda bread; it is most definitely a pleasant addition."

"Yes, ma'am, everything is perfect."

"Bertha is our cook; she has been with us for some time. She is quite excellent, wouldn't you say, dear?" sharing with Cateline, Martha looked over towards Samuel.

"Yes, dear, Bertha is an exceptional cook."

Cateline, observing her family while taking pleasure in the simple luncheon, discerned that her uncle had many of the same features as her father in the twentieth century. Her thoughts were consumed as Cateline silently continued to examine her relatives, "Hmm, my uncle is a tender-looking man just like my father with the same dark hair. A most distinguished gentleman, without a doubt—well-groomed and clean-shaven, a neatly trimmed black mustache with a touch of grey. Smartly dressed for the nineteenth century, if I do say so, with superbly tailored trousers as referred to in the Book of Exodus." With a relatively quiet laugh, to herself, that is, she thought of the actual Scripture, "You shall make them linen trousers to cover their nakedness from the loins even to the thighs. How silly to think of such." She continued in her reflections, "All the same, this seems to be what men wear with their distinguished overcoats to reflect their social class of this era." Cateline also took notice of her uncle's vivaciously agreeable smile, which revealed such a kind mannerism. "Yes," her thoughts lingered while observing her uncle, "he seems to be such a thoughtful man, as was my father." Her Aunt Martha was a blonde as that of her daughter, and it was apparent that much of Anya's good looks were a replica of her mother—moderately tall, slender, and still most attractive for her age.

As they were eating, the young girl, Clara, rather petite in stature, plain in appearance, and somewhat quiet in temperament, had come around to fill their teacups and to pick up empty plates and bowls. The tea was such a delightful addition, as it helped to warm the body. With it still being winter, she immediately contemplated in silence, "I may need to purchase some type of heavier coat than the wool cape in my room. I am certainly not used to the temperatures."

With their light meal finished, the conversations began once more with Mr. Walsh inquiring of America and questions of concern regarding her mother, his sister. Through various discussions in which she was able to follow along, it seemed that her uncle had seldom heard anything from his sister, a letter on occasions. It became pretty obvious, he was much closer to her father in Youghal, who had passed away. Of course, being his cousin, they did grow up together, which would account for their close friendship. Cateline used this opportunity of small talk to acquire the necessary information about this life in Ireland, which was so foreign to her. "Uncle Walsh, I meant to ask if there was a newspaper of any kind. I would love to keep up with the affairs of Ireland since I am at such a loss." Cateline already knew that the Irish newspaper had begun before the 1880s but wasn't sure if most people acquired them or not.

"Yes, my dear." At once, he called out to one of their servants, "Clara, please have Charles bring me the newspaper."

"Yes, Sir, Mr. Walsh."

As Clara walked away, Uncle Walsh resumed, "Cateline, I think that is a wonderful idea. I understand you have a love for reading, and I am sure that your stay would be much more enjoyable to explore our various museums and libraries on the history of Ireland."

"Yes, sir, I do love reading and history. I suppose I am happiest with a book in my hand," she declared with a quaint laugh.

"Anya, please be sure to take her to my library, as well. I am certain your cousin would be delighted with my moderate collection of reading material."

"Yes, father."

"Oh, I did not know that you had a library, Uncle Walsh. Thank you so much, for I know that I would so love to explore your books."

"You are most welcome. I also understand from your mother, you are quite accomplished on the pianoforte, and your voice is said to be almost like an angel. We look forward to hearing your achievements and your performance when we have guests, my dear. However, your mother never mentioned the guitar, but we do look forward to being entertained with all your accomplishments."

"Hmm, so I apparently did not play the guitar in this era," she thought to herself before responding to her uncle. "Yes, Uncle Walsh, I am certainly flattered; all the same, I am also very modest. I do love playing both but have never really performed for large gatherings other than those who are just friends. I can assure you that I would be most uncomfortable playing for anyone other than family and close acquaintances."

"Nonsense, we would love to hear you play. We shall be the judge and decide if we believe you are as gifted as we have come to understand. I know that Anya has told you of our plans to have a dinner party in your honor. At that time, we would be most appreciative for our guests to have the pleasure of experiencing your acquired gifts," Uncle Walsh determined.

Feeling embarrassed, to a certain degree but not desiring to offend her family, Cateline replied graciously, "As you wish. You may be the judge, and I would be honored if you think me to be proficient enough to entertain those in attendance."

As the discussions carried on in regard to the regal affair, her uncle noted, "Cateline, we are well acquainted with many of those who are affluent in Dublin where you will be able to meet gentlemen and ladies of good fortune. We were in hopes that your stay in Ireland would be to your delight and perhaps even a permanent stay if you come to love and know your heritage. I am sure America is rather pleasing, but you could come to also love Ireland, as it is your native country."

"Yes, sir, I am so looking forward to experiencing and understanding the culture as I have no plans to depart back to America anytime soon. I am also very interested in seeing London as well as Paris while I am here."

"Oh, there is quite a lot to see in Europe, my dear," her aunt replied, "but I do hope that you are with us for some time yet and are not in a hurry to travel far."

"Yes, ma'am, I definitely desire the time to come to know my family as well as learn about my father. Anya also tells me that I have a half-brother, James, who lives in Youghal, and I have a cousin, your son, Cyrus, who lives fairly close to here."

"Yes, dear," her aunt responded while she perpetually filled her niece in on more detail, "Youghal is where your father's estate is located, but it is certainly somewhat of a ride by train to get there."

"That is what I was told, but I would absolutely love to go see my father's estate at some point while I am here and meet James."

"I know there are still some of the McCarthy's in Youghal, so he does have family close as well. We do get to see him from time to time," smiling while she contemplated James's wonderful demeanor, Martha added, "yes, he is such a dear boy. I am sure you will love him,"

"We can definitely send a telegram to James. He may even be able to attend the dinner party. I think about mid-March or close to that timeframe would be good. What do you think, my dear?" Samuel inquired, looking over at his wife.

"Yes, mid-March sounds delightful," Aunt Martha replied agreeably.

Uncle Walsh continued, "We will certainly send out invitations rather quickly where those at a distance would have sufficient time to make plans to travel if they so desire to attend. Naturally, Cyrus and his family are not far and would undoubtedly join in the celebration. I hope this is agreeable with you, Cateline, my dear."

"Yes, everything sounds quite nice. I feel very honored," Cateline spoke amiably.

After a brief period, in a most firm manner, speaking up, Uncle Walsh addressed Cateline once more on a different topic, "Cateline, I also need to discuss your inheritance, which was specified in your father's will. As you may know, the custom is that the first-born son does inherit the father's estate; nevertheless, your father wanted to make sure that you received some sort of birthright which he entrusted with me. Growing up together, your father and I were the very best of friends, besides relations."

"Yes, sir, I am most thankful that you were so close."

"When your father became ill, I spent a good bit of time in Youghal. As he declined, one of his foremost concerns was making sure that you were aware of his intentions to leave you an inheritance. You see, my dear, he had never forgotten you. Therefore, he entrusted me with a reasonable sum to ensure that you received your portion. Your father never ceased talking about you all these years and longed for the day he would see you again, which never occurred. I just want you to know that he left me a letter written to you. His intentions were for you to know that he never stopped loving you. When we have time, I will give you the letter and go over all the legal documents. The funds will be moved into an account set up for you."

"Thank you so much, Uncle Walsh. I look forward to reading the letter and am very grateful that I received the invitation from you to come to Ireland. I feel terrible that I never knew how much he loved me and could never be reacquainted with him. He sounds as if he was a wonderful man, and I would love to hear more about him while I am visiting."

"But of course, there will be plenty of time for us to share your father's life here in Ireland so that you may know what kind of a man he was," Martha spoke up.

Charles returned with the newspaper, a tall man with a slender build, clean-shaven, and the most suitable type of apparel that Cateline would have pictured for that period. He was a most proper, mannerly gentleman's gentleman, as he handed the paper to Mr. Walsh. "Thank you, Charles," Mr. Walsh responded. Charles, bowing, walked away. Mr. Walsh had immediately handed the paper to Cateline. Without delay, her eyes went to the first page, as she was eager to know the exact date. Her thoughts were geared to herself at that point, "February—of 1881, yes, that I knew, and at the end of February with most of the year ahead." Cateline, folding the paper over, spoke kindly to her uncle, "Thank you, Uncle Walsh; I will take it to my room to read through later."

As the dialogue went back to the grand event to be held, Cateline inquired of her uncle if he was acquainted with Oscar Wilde. "It has been publicized in many of the newspapers in America of his coming next year to travel and lecture on the Aesthetic Movement. I am very much acquainted with studying this movement, as well as poetry, and I have written a few short stories, as well. It would be such an honor to meet him in person, as I understand he is from Dublin. I suppose one of my passions in life has been studying the various historical periods, such as the Renaissance and Elizabethan. Needless to say, I also love this current era, the Victorian. I am sure that Mr. Wilde is also extremely versed in these subjects."

Her uncle smiled cunningly as she spoke, and when finished, he replied, "I was actually a very close friend of his father, who passed away several years ago. William was a very talented man, respected in Dublin, appointed medical commissioner to the Irish census. In fact, Queen Victoria had knighted him for his services with the census. Sir William Wilde, yes, a very well-known surgeon and quite brilliant. Many have said that Oscar was as gifted as his father and had come to love the arts as Lady Jane, his mother. I have been in Oscar's company many times but have not seen him for some years, as he resides in London. I have heard that he seldom comes back to Dublin; nonetheless, I can send a telegram on Monday to ask the pleasure of his attendance for the occasion of welcoming my niece. Perhaps, if Oscar is available, he may travel and attend, and if so, the social gathering could be given in honor of my niece from America and Mr. Wilde for his achievements. I do understand that he was awarded the Newdigate Prize a few years back and continues to surprise all of us in Dublin."

"Yes, I have read that. It was for poetry at Oxford."

"It was, and I would find much delight in seeing the young man once again, myself. We could certainly send a wire to London and inquire."

"Thank you so much, Uncle Walsh. I cannot think of anything that would bring me more delight than meeting Mr. Wilde."

"You are most welcome, my dear," her uncle replied as he looked over at his wife to inquire, "Martha dear, I believe I will retire to my study and begin the planning of the dinner party. Would you care to join me?"

"Of course, as I will help by beginning a list of the attendees to invite. Cateline, please feel free to make yourself at home. And if you need anything, do not hesitate to ask one of our servants."

"Thank you, Aunt Martha," Cateline replied as her aunt and uncle rose from the table and began to walk into the estate when Anya spoke up.

"Oh, mother! Please, do not forget to invite plenty of gentlemen to dance with all the ladies that will be present. There is nothing worse than coming to a splendid ball and not having dancing partners."

"Yes, yes, I have planned a few balls in my day, Anya. I will be sure to invite a sufficient number of young gentlemen to satisfy all the ladies in attendance."

"Thank you, mother."

Cateline, having finished getting her fill of the delicious tray of food, Anya queried, "If you are finished eating, I would be delighted to take you on a tour of the grounds. If that would please you?"

"That would be most enjoyable, I am sure, Anya."

The two girls rose as Anya and Cateline went walking about the estate to view the beautiful gardens and the lake.

CHAPTER
7

The estate's grounds looking as lovely as ever, filled Cateline with such pleasure as she walked alongside Anya. "Oh, the stories to be told," thought Cateline— "if I could only share my life. Hmm, but what would Anya think? What would anyone think? Yes, the delight for one here to have such a glimpse into the twentieth or twenty-first centuries." With an ambiguous smile on her face, she continued listening here and there to Anya's reflection of the various aspects of the grounds. Yet, being lost in thought, a most sincere reverie of sorts filled her mind, "Oh, such enjoyment it would be, such pleasure that no one could be convinced otherwise. Ah, yes—the nineteenth century is to be consumed with such delight myself, as I am much fortunate to be able to touch it and feel it first-hand. Such splendor, and oh so serene as it consumes me with considerable gratification, I am lost in these moments—this time, forever flows through my inner-being. Yes, for I feel that this indulgence far exceeds all my expectations—what shall my life be, and shall I be here but a day? No, my waking hours will find me day after day, but for how long, my Lord, shall this life be mine, for can I not hold it forever that it never goes away? What is life if we live day to day and our expectations never satisfy, but what is life if we find ourselves where we have always dreamt? Would our time be any less, or would we find so much more? Can we hold on to it for as long as our days, or does it just all slip away? No, for it cannot slip away when it has taken but many years to find—how then, oh how then—can we hold on to time—this time—our time—my time? Oh, Plato, your wisdom does shine, for life must be lived as play."[1]

The flower gardens in the back of the grounds held their beauty with splendid colors of yellows, reds, pinks, purples, oranges in all different shapes and sizes. Hedges outlined the lawns in various shades of gallant greens mixed with brightly colored primroses. The slight wind that swept across the turf swayed the flowers back and forth gently but enough that their delicate scent danced along with every squall like tiny fairies twirling, skipping, and frolicking. Alive, yes, she was alive, and yes—she was in the nineteenth century satiating herself with every single aspect imaginable—conceiving, dreaming, visualizing her days ahead with such triumph. With the chill of the air hovering over, it fought for sovereignty against the sun, which cascaded down its warmth. How she could stay in that moment and bask in her thoughts, yet knowing there were reasons for her being there, her delight would be in fulfilling that which she knew to accomplish. "Yes," proclaiming earnestly to herself, "there shall be many days, not just one or a few—I shall savor every moment while here and take much pleasure in this journey."

As they strolled down the walkway, which led to a small lake not too far from the estate, both girls sat down on the quaint seating area, close to the waters. A bench for two to relax was nestled amongst such grand oak trees of substantial size, which hung vibrantly over to provide shade. Cateline noticed many unusual trees scattered about the lake gracefully with a distinct note of beauty in their resplendent grandeur state. Even though she had seen countless large trees in her days, these seemed quite different from any observed in America. Each branch which sprung out from their monstrous trunks grew thick and outwardly, radiating towards the ground as they summoned and lured those looking on with a welcome to explore. In profuse excitement, Cateline exclaimed, "These trees are magnificent! I am assuming they are an oak of some kind but never have I seen any of this dimension. I am tempted to sit on one of these branches which grow towards the ground, so intriguing if I were not in this dress."

"They are called the *King Oak*, noted Anya, "we also have a leaning oak tree," she remarked while pointing in that direction for Cateline to observe. "I always have loved the oak—all kinds really, they are clearly impressive, but this leaning one is rather unusual."

"Is that what it is called?"

"It is a holm oak tree, there are several over there, but that is the only one that leans. I used to love playing on both when I was younger, you can imagine. They provided for considerable entertainment and offered much to the imagination."

"Yes, I can see that. I believe I would have played in these trees as a child for hours. In fact, I am tempted to climb them as we speak," Cateline concluded, laughing most playfully while beginning to visualize doing just that in her dress. Looking over at Anya, who had joined in with the contagious merriment, both girls tried to compose their emotions.

At last, Anya gaining her poise, replied, "I am so sorry. When you said what you did, I remembered a few childhood moments with my governess. It is somewhat comical today, but I am sure it was not so for my governess. I would climb way up in the tree in my dress. She was adamant about getting me to come down where I would refuse. There was one particular day where I was most obstinate, and my governess tried to climb to where I could be reached, and she fell—oh, not to worry, she was not very far up and was not hurt, but her dress caught on a branch and, well, let's just say there was not much of the dress left. It was funny at the time, but not after my father found out."

Both girls continued in amusement until Cateline finally spoke warmly, "Your childhood must have been quite enjoyable."

"Yes, there are always wonderful things to remember of one's childhood."

Looking across the lake amongst a number of enormous oaks, there was a very unusual tree, substantially large in size, unlike any Cateline had ever seen. "Anya, that huge tree on the other side of the lake, the one that looks as if many trees all grew together, what kind is it? It is entirely unique, I do declare."

"That is the only one we have of its kind. It is called a horse chestnut tree. They can actually live for several hundred years and obviously, keep getting bigger. Wait until the fall, the leaves start turning on all of these, and with the lake, it is quite spectacular."

"I can only imagine. Why is the chestnut tree called horse?"

"The history is that these trees were brought over from Britain in the 1600s from the Balkans, and they received the name horse because the Turks would feed the seeds to their ailing horses," she resolved with a slight smile.

Cateline was amazed at all the variety of trees and how beautifully the lawns and gardens were landscaped in every direction. The lake's beauty blended with all the surroundings merely added to the tranquility as the girls sat on the bench to enjoy the scenery. They quickly began a conversation, eager to learn more about the other's life in the two diverse countries. Becoming more acquainted, their laughter persisted for some time, unbecoming to ladies of their age, yet—being most engaged and finding pleasure in time spent together, it was pretty evident the girls were both very similar in character. With that said, it did not take long to realize that they had much in common, even though they lived miles and miles apart, separated by centuries as well. Life was definitely different in America versus Ireland, not to mention two distinct periods. All the same, Cateline knew they would be close friends through this whole journey that lay ahead.

The day prolonged with much knowledge gained by both on various details about their lives. Cateline soon learned more of her cousin's engagement to a fine young man, "I'm sure you will be fond of Amos when you meet him. He is a junior barrister and works alongside his father, a senior barrister, and mine. We met at a very young age because our fathers have worked side-by-side for years in Dublin's High Court of Justice. After moving to Clontarf, that is. In fact, we grew up playing together as children. He is pretty remarkable, and I suppose we have been in love with each other forever. I always wanted to be married to someone like my father and am extremely fortunate that Amos is gifted with the same charm. I do believe that we will have a wonderful life together."

"I am so delighted for you, Anya. When will I be able to meet him, and has your special day been set?"

"He is ordinarily here on the weekends, but I seldom see him through the week, as he is very busy with work. You will probably get to meet him next weekend. We haven't really spoken on the exact date just yet, but we have both talked about a fall wedding, which would still give us time for planning."

"I do hope that he attends the dinner party; I cannot wait to meet him."

"He will definitely be here, and in fact, he will help my father where needed. He is such a delight to both of my parents, always willing to help with anything we have going on," Anya remarked with a most sincere smile.

After talking for some time, Anya acknowledged, "We could go back to the veranda to warm by the fire for a bit, and then I will take you to see the horses and the front of the estate if that is agreeable with you?"

"Certainly," responded Cateline, "I am enjoying the day immensely."

The girls walked back to the estate while Anya noted, "You will see off to your right," pointing in that direction, she resumed, "the covered area at the back of the home is our conservatory."

"Conservatory? A greenhouse?"

"It is where we grow many of our plants to protect them from the cold."

"I would love to see it sometime."

"Yes, we can actually enter it from the estate or from the outside."

"What are the buildings off to the right of the conservatory?"

"Oh, those are the garrets."

"Garrets?"

"Yes, our servant's quarters. We have one for women and one for men."

"Oh, I see."

The girls, entering the veranda, stood around the hearth to take the chill off while they continued talking and sharing details of their lives. After some time, they began walking towards the stables for Cateline to see the horses. Entering, there was a young boy who was brushing down a mare as they approached. "Hello, Daniel."

"Miss Walsh," replied the boy most pleasantly.

"This is Cateline, my cousin from America. She will be staying at the estate and may want to take a ride on one of the horses at some point; if so, please make sure that you assist her."

Daniel stopped what he was doing and replied, "Yes, ma'am."

Anya turning back to Cateline, curiously stated, "I was not sure if you like to ride horses or not."

"Oh yes, I love riding. There was a place in Boston—," realizing her words, Cateline changed her story abruptly, "well, I had a friend who I rode with many times in various places on the outskirts of Boston." Recovering from her first remark, she thought to herself, "Whew, I almost said a place to ride! What was I thinking, unquestionably, many own horses in this timeframe, to include America!"

"Well, you can see that we have several horses. Daniel can show you the ones that are best for riding. Some of them we use for our carriages."

"Of course, you have a number of coaches, I assume?"

"Yes, they are all in the carriage house; would you like a tour?"

"I would love a tour. Are they in the building connected?"

"They are, and you will meet our coachman if he is around."

79

Walking to the large building that Cateline thought to be a barn housed several horse-drawn gigs of various dimensions. "These are magnificent," Cateline declared.

"My father likes his carriages. They are rather impressive. I believe these are my father's leisure pursuits. It seems he has to keep up with the newest renderings."

As Cateline looked over all three of the different types, Anya inquired, "Those in Boston, are they similar to these?"

"Yes, they are. Yet, I do not believe they are identical, probably different renditions," replying, as she did, for Cateline was unsure how to phrase her response.

"Well, I see that Elbert is not here at the moment, but I know a little about each one of them. Obviously, besides my father, Elbert is the expert when it comes to carriages. He does all the upkeep and repairs. He is also our chauffeur when we use the brougham or the barouche. The small one over there is a calash. It is a two-passenger, pretty easy to maneuver where I have even taken it out by myself. It only takes one horse to pull."

Captivated with their variety, Cateline stated firmly, "Undeniably, these are very stylish, Anya."

Cateline follows her cousin closer towards the brougham to gain a better perspective, where she peeked inside. At the same time, Anya opened the door and elaborated on the design, "The brougham, with its enclosed carriage, takes two to four horses. This is my father's most recent purchase. Come, get a better glimpse of the interior—it is quite lovely and so plush."

"Yes, it is most lavish."

"This one is always used if the weather is questionable, and if the weather seems to be pleasant, we use the barouche." She clarified as Cateline walked over to take a quick look while Anya continued, "The barouche, as well as the brougham, will seat four inside, but another person could sit up on top with Elbert. There is a partial roof that collapses. Typically, my mother wants the roof up on her side to eliminate the wind and the sun to some degree."

"Miss Walsh," a young man of about mid-thirties walked up to Anya, "how do you do, ma'am?"

"Hello Elbert, this is my cousin, Cateline."

"Ma'am," Elbert bowed his head as he addressed Cateline, "pleasure meeting you."

A rather tall and thin man of robust stature, Cateline observed as she replied, "Thank you, Elbert, it is a pleasure to meet you."

"Is there anything I can do for you, ladies?"

"I was just giving Cateline a tour and sharing with her what I could about the carriages. I already told her that you and father were the experts," Anya remarked as she laughed vaguely. "I am sure that you could give her a bit of the history on them where I could not."

"Yes, ma'am, I would be delighted. The barouche here is a fancy type of coach. It has been a popular choice for many. I believe it dates back to the 1700s. It is well valued due to its roof, which may either go partially up or down, but the brougham is a newer model where the carriage is all enclosed. It was built in London in the 1830s—named after Lord Brougham, the man who designed it. Of course, depending on how many patrons would be riding determines the number of horses to pull each one—two or even four. This model has a window in the front, which was somewhat of a change from the previous and allows folks to see where they are going."

After the brief exchange, Anya replied, "Thank you, Elbert."

"You are welcome, Miss."

The girls walked out of the carriage house as Anya concluded, "Also, Elbert did not mention, the brougham is the favorite among the socialites today and is only affordable to those of class. You will not see the commoners in such, as they cannot afford it."

"Yes, it looks as though it would be one of the finer models."

As they walked towards the front of the grounds, Anya proclaimed, "We are much closer to the front entrance, and I am not sure if you have become familiar with our rooms."

"No, I have only walked from my room downstairs to the veranda—I can't say that I am familiar at all."

"On the ground floor, we have a small parlor, a drawing-room, and saloon. It is rather large and quite convenient when we have a dance. And, there is also the formal dining parlor.

Cateline, turning the corner from the stables, was able to view the beautifully landscaped front lawns, which were very precise with all the lovely shrubbery and the most handsome fountain. Upon the fountain stood an exquisite statue of an angel made of bronze with its wings spread out gallantly while maintaining a long narrow vase pointed downward as water surged from the spout into the rounded fountain below. "I love the fountain," Cateline proclaimed, "the angel is gorgeous, as is the whole front of the estate. I have thoroughly enjoyed spending time with you today, getting to know you better, and being able to see just how striking this time of the year is in Ireland."

"Thank you, dear cousin. I have had quite a wonderful time, myself. I am so pleased that you are here, as most days through the week can be somewhat tedious, where I am always looking forward to the weekend and Amos visiting. With you here, I am almost certain my days will be exceedingly noteworthy."

"I feel the same way. I am most obliged to your kindness in making me feel so welcome."

"It has been such a pleasure," Anya responded with an astonishingly jubilant smile as they walked towards the front entrance.

"What year was this estate built; do you know?"

"I believe it was the latter part of the eighteenth century—a Georgian architectural style."

"Revival of the Palladian architecture?"

"Yes, as a matter of fact—you are right," Anya said, "the Palladian was inspired over a thousand years ago by the ancient Greeks and Romans. I believe this particular style, the Palladian, was created sometime in the eighteenth century. I suppose you know your history."

"To a small degree, probably. Yet, I have always enjoyed studying the various cultures throughout Europe. Oh, and the estate is quite divine, Anya."

"Thank you," she responded and continued, "I am confident, with the sun descending, we are somewhat late for the afternoon tea. I am sure my parents are probably in the drawing-room waiting for dinner to be served. We should head in by all means." Walking into the front entrance, Cateline stood, surveying her surroundings in a most charming vestibule. Off from the latter was the wide hallway, previously observed when she had come down the stairway at the back of the estate. Having been most eager to see the adjacent rooms, Cateline was in awe of all the notable antique chandeliers hanging from the high ceiling outside of the adjoining areas, each adorned with many candles, brilliantly lit as the twilight hours were fast approaching. The chambers throughout had large openings where

French doors were stationed to the wall, leaving the grandeur chambers fully exposed for one to glance inside.

Following Anya, they walked past the first two rooms, where Cateline was then able to view the front staircase as it was nestled behind the room to the left. The elaborate stairs curved upwards towards the second floor with its pedestal lolled out in such magnificent contours inviting to any and all its elegance of such refined, rich wood. It was at the second set of chambers on the right where they joined her uncle and aunt, who sat in lush chairs opposite a sofa settee. An oval-shaped table sat beyond filled with the most delectable-looking food items, elaborately displayed on fine China along with teacups and saucers. The quaint grouping was complete as each piece of furniture lay on the outer edges of an elegant Victorian rug. A rather sizeable fireplace, most admirable, encompassed the wall off from the assembly, making for a more intimate design within such a significant room. "This is our more formal drawing-room, Cateline. It would be considered a saloon or some refer to it as a stateroom." Anya noted, "the family comes here before our evening meal to enjoy our afternoon tea. We spend a considerable amount of time in this area and entertain guests when they are present before dinner is served at the end of the day. The dining parlor is across the hall," motioning towards the room opposite from where they stood, being well lit with many candles as servants were busy preparing the room for their last meal of the day. "Perhaps, after dinner, we can enjoy entertainment on the pianoforte—and perchance the guitar," she finished with a slight laugh.

"It is about time that you girls arrived," her uncle noted. "Martha and I finished our afternoon tea some time ago; I assume you were unaware of the hour, even though it is quite late. I believe we do not have that much longer until dinner shall be served. Nonetheless, there is still plenty for you to enjoy if you care for a bite or two before our evening meal. I am sure you both must be famished. Cateline, please do help yourself."

"I apologize, but we were much engaged in conversation. I am so thankful that Cateline is here with us. For it does give me something to do through the week, father," Anya said as the girls sat down on the oversized Victorian sofa opposite Samuel and Martha before she concluded, "I suppose we did lose track of time. I had no idea it was so late."

"Very well, just save room for dinner."

"Yes, sir—we will."

Cateline noticed her guitar leaning against a large piano nestled into the corner off towards one end of the room. All of a sudden, she spoke up, "Oh, I see my guitar has been mysteriously placed by the piano for entertainment," Cateline playfully remarked with a trivial giggle.

"Yes, dear," Uncle Walsh countered most pleasantly, "we are truly delighted to hear you play and will not take *no* for an answer. If you girls had arrived sooner, we could have enjoyed listening to you perform before dinner. As it is, we can definitely recline back to the drawing-room after our evening meal."

While smiling at her uncle, she concurred agreeably, "I would never tell you no, sir."

The family engaged in conversation while the girls enjoyed the afternoon tea, which consisted of dainty crayfish sandwiches, pastries, and scones.

"What type of pastries are these? I am not quite sure that I have ever had any like them."

"Those are Irish apple tarts. They are delicious but be sure to try the scones with the marmalade and cream."

"Oh, yes, I most certainly will. Everything looks absolutely delicious," Cateline remarked while leaning over the coffee table to put a scone on her plate. "I had no idea they ate like this in the nineteenth century," she thought to herself, "not as many spices as what I am used to, but it is still excellent, and the desserts are simply splendid."

The family spent much time in discussion, catching up on life in America, as best as Cateline could reveal. All the same, she kept in mind the timeframe and only asked questions about life in Ireland, trying to keep the conversation steered in that direction, not so much on America. It was an enjoyable time for Cateline and her newly discovered family, where they talked, laughed, and shared much of their lives. How Cateline was so elated to this new life—a life she had dreamt for many years and was fortunate to have awoken in a period that was meant for her, even if it would not be forever.

While enjoying her time with the Walsh family, Cateline looked around the room often, taking in all the alluring relics, paintings, and furnishings of the Georgian and Victorian era. There were so many precious possessions and many that she had no knowledge of what they even were. The saloon was a much larger room than the first two they had walked past upon entering the estate. Surveying her surroundings, Cateline gazed towards the connecting room, which held two hefty French doors that seemed to be secured where they remained open, as well. The room was definitely lesser of the two but seemed to be somewhat of a replica; in spite of this, with the smaller room not being lit up with candles, it was hard to really determine much of the furnishings. The oversized saloon at present was designed in a way where it would provide for quite the enjoyment of many guests. Besides their quaint seating area, the remainder of the oversized room housed several other minor elaborate groupings, composed throughout the outer regions, each containing a slight table adjoined with two lush chairs all adorned with cabriole-type legs. These groupings lined about the walls left the vast majority of the chamber open, by preference, which provided for much space to host any elaborate festivity. It was a very tasteful room, primarily consistent with the Victorian era and a few Georgian furnishings scattered throughout. The furniture and all the furnishings themselves were of the highest quality for that period, as the pieces were not only comfortable but rather lovely, to be sure.

"The room adjoining, is it a drawing-room?" Cateline inquired.

"Yes, dear," Aunt Martha replied, "it is somewhat smaller and one that is not used often. When we have substantial gatherings, the first four rooms are all lit and open along with the hallway for dancing, and the veranda is accessible for those who desire to take a stroll outside."

"How superb, Aunt Martha," exclaimed Cateline, "then the other room opposite where we came in the vestibule, it is also a drawing-room?"

"No, my dear, it is our parlor and mainly used when we have a guest or two come to visit. However, we do open it for large gatherings. Otherwise, it is generally used only for myself when I have ladies visiting. Samuel, he has his rooms upstairs when gentlemen come to discuss business. Anya will have to show you her father's chambers," Aunt Martha smiled jauntily as she maintained, "he has his own study, the billiard room, smoking area, and his library. Anya, were you able to show Cateline your father's library, dear?"

"No, ma'am," turning to Cateline, she continued, "Cateline, I will take you on a tour after we retire for the evening if you would like."

"Yes—yes, I would like that very much." Changing the subject back to a point her aunt had made, Cateline inquired, "You said the hallway is used for dancing?"

"Oh yes, it is quite wide and makes a distinguished place for dancing."

"How nice it is, Aunt Martha," Cateline responded, "what kind of dancing is customary in Ireland?"

"Well, we do have Irish dances that are not as popular these days. You would probably see those dances more at weddings, wouldn't you say Samuel?"

"Yes—yes, of course, dear."

"At other social events, I believe even in most of Europe, it has just become the waltz and the two-step—am I right, dear?"

"Yes, Martha—I believe that is correct."

"Are you familiar with both of these in America, Cateline?"

"I am. I have danced to both of these. It has been a while, but I should most probably be able to pick it up again."

A few hours later, dinner was announced. The family all proceeded into the formal dining parlor, which was housed with very exquisite furnishings, in a similar fashion to that of the breakfast area. Although, the dining parlor was more grandeur and had an enormously impressive wooden encased fireplace with admirable carvings. There were cabinets of the same type of wood that held beautiful China, and a grand chandelier hung from the center of the room with tall candles. Several sconces adorned the walls, designed to add additional lighting to the room when in use. A large golden centerpiece sat in the middle of the dining table with elaborate etchings all around and golden leaves, holding six tall candles, enhanced by triple candelabras on each end. The table itself was certainly outstanding with its rich mahogany and armchairs stationed at each end, along with matching side chairs to seat a total of fourteen.

As a history buff, Cateline was truly enjoying every moment as many things she remembered from studying, but much more, she had no clue. To be able to actually be standing in the nineteenth century, she was absolutely beside herself on having the opportunity to not only experience this era but the culture as well. Being seated, once her uncle gave grace, various foods were passed around the table while talking commenced.

When Cateline reached for her glass to take a drink, she noticed it was wine. "Do you always have wine with your meals, sir?"

"Why yes, is that something that is not done in America?"

"No, sir, but I do believe I was knowledgeable that it was quite common in Ireland—well, in many of the countries in Europe, I suppose."

"Yes, we always have a good quality of wine with dinner. I believe you will like this one; it is imported from Italy, Chianti, a full-bodied white wine, fruity flavors, and underlying earth notes. I hope that you enjoy it, dear."

"Yes, sir, it is completely enjoyable."

While relishing the delightful evening meal—roasted leg of lamb with green mint sauce, creamed spinach, roasted parsnips, mashed potatoes, peas, and honey oat yeast bread, her uncle inquired of the styles of music Cateline knew on the pianoforte. She replied, "I really love a lot of classical music, but probably Chopin is one of my favorites, although there are only a few of his songs I have mastered to some degree."

"Very good; I look forward to retiring to the saloon to enjoy your accomplishments. The guitar, what type of music do you prefer to play? You will delight us with your endowments, I presume. You do sing, I am also told?"

"I do have a few songs from America that I can play well on the guitar, sir. Yes, I would be most honored to entertain my family, of course, but I fear that I am not as accomplished as many that you know—and, yes, I do sing as well, sir. I hope that you will find that I am not as comfortable playing for a large group, and once you have heard me, it is my desire that you would not have me entertain during the dinner party."

"Ah, my dear, if you play well, you will be well received. I will be the judge this evening on how excellently skilled you are."

Finished with the main course of their meal, a scrumptious Yorkshire pudding was passed around for the final touch. Having such a fabulous dinner, everyone seemed most quiet, walking back into the drawing-room to retire for the evening to be entertained with music. Cateline sat down at the pianoforte, feeling the fire's warmth circulating throughout the room, which was most relaxing. Beginning to play Frederic Francois Chopin's *Joie de Vivre*, everyone listened intently to the beautiful sound. Her uncle made notice of Cateline's fingers as they softly stroked the keys. She swayed to the tune fervently with every touch. So delicate was the rhythm—the solemn resonance, quality, and tone. Reminiscent of romance, virtuosic excellence, mysterious in want—the vibrations brought life. Alive in the moments, tingling and deep expressions were brought forth, dramatically enhanced, melodiously faint and touching—the pauses, the symmetry—lost in the dream, in the memory, memories now and forever, with every echo in harmony, alive to the last. Watching in amazement, Mr. Walsh very soon learned that she was, in fact, very talented, and it was especially obvious of her love for music. Yes, this was something that she could not hide; when Cateline played the piano or the guitar, she was always lost in the song, feeling every intimate caress to the very end. They all applauded and encouraged her to resume. Cateline continued with Joseph Johann Baptist Wöelfl's *Andante Sonata*, followed by a Beethoven. Once finished, she moved over closer to the fire and sat down while her uncle most anxiously spoke, "Cateline, my dear, you cannot be shy when it comes to your accomplishments. I have heard a few others master the pianoforte well, but you are very gifted, and our guests would be most honored to hear you perform."

"Thank you, uncle. If you wish, but there will also be other music where I do not have to be in the spotlight for long?

"Ah, your choice of words, my dear. And, no, Cateline, to be sure, my desire is not to bring you discomfort. To answer your question, we always have musicians present at any event held. Now, would you be so kind as to grace us with the pleasure of hearing one song on your guitar this evening?"

"Yes, sir." Cateline had already been contemplating what to play on her guitar when asked so that it would be suitable since she knew nothing that would be geared to this ear and appropriate, at that. Picking up the instrument, sitting down, and holding the guitar on her legs, she began to strum the chords to the song *Thousand Stars by Kathy Young and The Innocents*.[2] This was a song released in the early 1960s. It was a love song played many times on her guitar, and she was hopeful that they would approve since it was far into the future.

Once she had finished playing the song and singing the lyrics, her aunt responded first. "Oh, my dear, that was such an impressive love song. I don't think I have ever heard a tune such as that. What about you, Anya? Have you ever heard anything like it?"

"No, mother, but it was quite pleasing."

Being bewildered during her performance, her uncle responded pleasantly, "Yes, it was most agreeable. I would love for you to play at the very least one song on your guitar for our guests, as well. Although I am sure our guests will request the honor of your playing more. Of course, I will leave that up to you, but if so, be prepared for another song, my dear."

"Yes, sir, I will."

"You may spend your time dancing and socializing with our guests, and I will call you at the proper time to come and entertain."

"Thank you, sir."

The remainder of the evening, the family spent much time talking, as her uncle shared the days when her mother and father were just kids, and they all played together at the different estates. Cateline asked many questions to learn more about her father and mother's life of that timeframe, including all those days long ago when her mother and father had seemed to be happily married. It had been a good day filled with much laughter and enjoyment that reminded Cateline of the times she had spent with her parents in America before her mother's passing. As the sun had long gone down and the moon appeared, her uncle and aunt soon retired to their bedrooms, and Anya took Cateline to see her father's library.

Shuffling through the various books, such a fascinating sight, Cateline enjoyed herself immensely while skimming over countless volumes. Many she noticed were considered classics of her time, such as *Moll Flanders* by Daniel Defoe, Jane Austen's many novels, Percy Shelley, Charles Dickens, Shakespeare, and numerous other poetry selections. In awe of her surroundings, what amazed her more than anything was not the fact of her uncle's astonishing assortment of classics but the fact many were actually first editions. What she would have given to have had several of the books lined on his shelves in her home back in America. After spending a considerable amount of time looking over his enormous collection, she finally decided on a novel, *The Portrait of a Lady*, by Henry James, along with a book of poems by Lord Byron. "Would it be alright if I take both of these to my room, Anya?"

"Yes, anything you would like to read is quite alright."

"Thank you," she responded as both girls called it a night and went to their rooms.

Cateline, reading a fragment of the novel, realized just how drowsy she was—half-past eleven. Being most surprised dinner to be at such late hours, she supposed this was more in line with the social elite than those of the lower class, assuming the working class arose relatively early and more than likely retired in the evening once the sun had gone down. Moreover, with no electricity, it cost money to burn the many candles needed to provide light into the wee hours of the night. Whereas, those of the social class, when there were gatherings of parties and such, the hosts most assuredly could afford to light up all the candles and lamps. And so, they would spend much time until the early hours of the morning enjoying neighbors, family, and friends, before all returning to their own homes.

"This life," she thought to herself, "hmmm—this life is so full and yet still so modest compared to the life I know. They live, and they breathe—but oh, unknowing of the hustle and bustle of the modern-day world, the days of modern technology. Yes, indeed, which world by far genuinely has so much more worth? Which world lives day in and day out without the stresses and worry? Which period really knew how to live and how to love and how to appreciate life? I do find myself wondering, was technology so worth what it has cost our world? Have we not truly lost many things along the way? Does one honestly gain in living such a fast-paced life? Was there not some meaning of this period, a purpose for all life, something the modern world should have gained—something we should have experienced? I do believe there was something we should have acquired. I sincerely believe that life had meaning, and it did not take modern technology to produce such; in fact, modern technology has come at such a cost, so much is lost. Yes, those of wealth rose to such heights, yet they never seemed to worry about time in one's day—grand occasions—gatherings of family and friends. For, did they not know how to enjoy such leisure until the wee hours of the night—being morning rather. Yes, morning it would be—choosing not to end the night by mere time, for what was time? Time did not dominate them. No, for time was so dear. Yes, I could live this way by candlelight—by moonlight—by simple pleasures and so much more. This could be my life, and I would want none other. Lord, let it be for always that I stay—lead me back no more, for this is my way. Yes— oh yes, Lord—I pray thee to hear my voice as this life has so much more to offer to my soul than the life that seemed to be. Let this be my life, Lord, yes, let it be. I pray thee tonight that I never awaken from this life, my Lord, my Savior—for Lord, I was born too late—oh, yes, so late. Let my tomorrow remain forever here."

CHAPTER
8

The following day, once the family had breakfast and the elevenses, Samuel and Martha went to his study to finalize all the plans for the upcoming dinner party. At the same time, the girls spent the day out on the grounds enjoying the excellent weather.

Samuel first began to compose a letter to Oscar Wilde. He was rather intrigued over the dialogue which had ensued with their niece and shared such with his wife. "Did you not find it quite fascinating that Cateline's passions are those of Oscar Wilde's, my dear?"

"Why Samuel, you are the romantic. I suppose you have an ear for such, of course, I would never have noticed."

"I dare not impart with her what I am writing to Oscar; she is far too modest to see her talent and beauty. I believe if Oscar Wilde dared to attend and make her acquaintance, he would behold what I see."

"Yes, you are the romantic, but I love that about you, my dear. Now without further ado, I am ecstatic to hear the contents of the letter. Please go on—"

Samuel, finishing the last segment, held the letter up as he read over the thorough correspondence to his wife—

Dear Mr. Wilde:

It has been quite some time that I have had the pleasure of your acquaintance, and I have heard of your many attributes in London. As a friend of your late father's, I know that he would be most proud of his son.

I am writing this letter to you today, as my family will be holding a dinner party in two weeks—the date being 12 March. It would be such a delight for your presence at this affair. Our dinner party is in honor of our niece, Cateline, who has arrived from America. We would love your attendance, where the party would be in honor of your presence, as well as hers.

Cateline is such a beautiful and charming young lady, a few years younger than yourself. I am sure that you would be captivated by her beauty and many talents. She is most accomplished on both the pianoforte and guitar and has the most enchanting voice.

Furthermore, her passions are that of poetry and writing, where she has written a few short stories. I believe you would find Cateline much to your liking with your own achievements and would take pleasure in her company. I am delighted to say those in attendance will have the enjoyment of hearing her perform, as I am sure you will as well.

As our honored guest, your lodging would be provided at our estate; we have more than sufficient room. If there is a possibility of clearing your schedule to attend, please feel free to arrive the day prior so that you are well-rested for the affair.

In the past, you have attended various revelries at our estate on occasions, and I am confident that you will remember our location, which is just on the outskirts of Dublin in Clontarf. Please know I can also send my chauffeur the day you arrive at the docks if you send me your arrival time.

I look forward to your reply and your company at our residence.

With best regards,
Mr. Samuel Walsh

"How lovely, my dear. You always have had such a way with words. I do hope that Mr. Wilde will be available to attend our party."

"Yes, Martha, as do I. In the event I receive a telegram from Mr. Wilde of his acceptance, I do wish it to be kept a secret until the day of his arrival."

"As you wish, Samuel."

Placing Oscar's letter aside, he immediately began writing a second to James with the intention of giving him ample time to also make arrangements if he so wished to attend the party. With both correspondences completed, Samuel rose from his desk and placed them with his briefcase where he would not forget to convey them to the telegraph office to be wired the following day—one to London and the other to Youghal.

"My dear, would you like to join me in your sitting room?" Samuel inquired of his wife.

"I will join you as soon as I am finished with my lists in preparation for the party, dear. I must finish making a note of all invitees for Joseph, so he can take care in preparing the invitations and have them ready for you to take tomorrow."

93

"Yes—yes, that is good. That gives everyone who wishes to attend sufficient time to make plans. Please make sure that you do not forget any of our friends and acquaintances."

"I am using a prior list where I shall not leave anyone off, my dear. I do presume this to conceivably be a large ball, Samuel. My list so far exceeds one hundred."

"That is quite alright, my dear, but remember, many of those invited shall not attend."

"Oh, yes dear, I am aware of that, but I am also mentioning in the invitation of the French chef along with other details. I am confident, most will strive to make an appearance. After all, grand parties which we have held in the past were always well-attended. And I am requesting for our guests to *répondez s'il vous plaît.*"

"Do not be disappointed, dear, when they do not reply, as most seldom do. They just show up."

Mr. Walsh walked out of the study while Martha remained working away. In completion of the invitation list, she pondered many other details that need not be forgotten, such as placing the order for the necessary Port, Rheingau, sherry, burgundy, and claret of good quality to be sure. Additionally, she wrote down all the menu items to be served, knowing Bertha was more than capable of taking over from there. It was not as though this was Bertha's first affair, no, indeed. She would know exactly what would be needed to purchase for a most superb layout of delectable foods. Without a doubt, Bertha was well aware of how to organize and prepare all the courses.

Furthermore, Martha made a note knowing she would need to hire that excellent chef who had worked for them on other occasions such as this. Immediately, she added for Samuel to be sure to get in touch with him in ample time to secure his availability for that date. "One last list remaining," she sighed, "whew, there is always so much to do." Martha continued to carefully outline all the tasks which needed to be completed within the estate. Once finished, the list would be handed to Charlotte to delegate all the requisite duties—ensuring the entire mansion was spotless to include the third-floor bedrooms accommodated with clean linen for guests that would be traveling from afar. "Yes, that should just about do it," she thought. "Hmmm— oh yes, Samuel must take care to speak with the groundskeeper for all to be well-manicured and for Elbert to have everything in place for parking the carriages and horses that evening. Oh, my, and not to forget, we shall use two of the boudoirs on the second floor, one for the lady's toilet and the other for the men's hat room. Yes, I will need servants to be present in both of those rooms to assist our guests." Taking a deep breath, she sighed, "Well, I do believe that should do it!" With all complete, Martha handed each one over to the appropriate servants, making sure that Joseph knew to have all the invitations ready for Mr. Walsh the following morning. Relieved in having accomplished the planning, she was all set to retire to her sitting room to spend time with her husband.

The remainder of the day and evening was enjoyed immeasurably by the whole family, who soon retired to their apartments early, being that they were all pretty exhausted from the long weekend. Cateline, alone in her room, maintained reading the novel and finished off with a few poems by Lord Byron before retiring to sleep.

The following morning came bright and early. Sarah drew back the draperies to awaken Cateline for the English breakfast, and upon arising, she rapidly prepared herself for the day, heading downstairs to join her family.

Mr. Walsh, needing to stop off and wire the two telegrams before heading towards his chambers on Henrietta Street, hurriedly came out of his study with his briefcase in hand, along with the letters. Saying his goodbyes, Martha called out, "Do not forget the invitations, dear," as he turned towards her, she continued, "Joseph had these all finished for this morning; please drop them off at the general post office on your way."

"Yes, thank you for reminding me. I will make sure everything is taken care of." Mr. Walsh bent over and gave his wife a kiss on the cheek while he bid his adieus to everyone before leaving for the day.

Cateline quietly whispered to Anya, "You did say that your father was a barrister?"

"Yes, a senior barrister for the Irish Bar. His chamber is located right down in the middle of Dublin on the quay. It is somewhat crowded with so many people these days; we seldom go down there."

"It sounds fascinating. I am sure he does very well."

"Yes, he does at that. He practices in the higher courts of Ireland, which I believe I mentioned to you, and Amos is in the same general area, but he is only a junior. It takes time to work your way up."

Once they had all finished eating, Aunt Martha went over all the lists that had been tallied with the servants, while Anya and Cateline devoted much of their day on the grounds talking and sharing their deepest secrets, getting to know each other more and more. Cateline had begun to feel very relaxed with everyone and more at home among her Irish relatives, thoroughly enjoying the estate's peace and tranquil settings along with all the surroundings.

Most of the week had endured with pretty much the same routine: the girls spent an enormous amount of time talking, taking walks, and helping with organizing the party when needed. Although, they tried to stay out of the way of the servants as they were busy hustling about with so much preparation for the grand gala just shy of one week away.

Saturday morning had begun like any other, except there were still many things left that needed to be completed as the special day was drawing near. This particular morning started as a bright and merry day. Before the English breakfast was served, Amos had arrived to spend time with Anya. Cateline was very happy to meet him as he entered just in time for their morning meal, enjoying all the conversations while dining. Her uncle went over details of the upcoming ball and made a special announcement, noting that he had spoken with their son and felt it to be a great time to take a break. With all the hard work accomplished thus far, Uncle Walsh suggested the family ride out to Cyrus's to spend the day. A light lunch would be prepared, and the plan was for the family to remain for the afternoon tea later that day. It was a most agreeable thought, as Cyrus had communicated to his father, the desire to finally meet his long, lost cousin before her party. Both he and his wife, Isabel, were very much looking forward to making her acquaintance. Finishing up breakfast, everyone retreated to their rooms to dress for the outing. "Cateline," Anya spoke up, "be sure to dress rather casually. We will more than likely spend much time outdoors."

"Yes, I will wear something very simple. Thank you."

All parties meeting on the front lawn, proceeded to climb into the barouche to take advantage of the most splendid day in an open carriage. With Amos present, there was still plenty of room as Mr. Walsh rode on the seat next to Elbert. The ride was most pleasant as Cateline enjoyed the views of the vast countryside, the sea, and the overall beauty of Ireland. Cyrus and his family lived relatively close, with Clontarf's coastal community being a short distance from the Walsh estate. Turning off the main road, they ventured more towards the coast when they came upon a castle. "My dear," her uncle spoke hastily while looking back towards Cateline, "I told Elbert to drive by the Clontarf Castle where you may have a glimpse."

Cateline glared towards the massive structure which lay ahead and exclaimed, "Oh—my, I had no idea there was a castle here." Astonished, trying to capture her emotions, Cateline was unaware that the hotel where she had stayed was actually standing before her very eyes; of course, here it was one hundred years earlier.

"This castle was built around the 1830s," her uncle related, "and it sits on the site of the Battle of Clontarf."

Cateline observed the original castle stood before her eyes, without the modern wings that had been constructed years later. Considerable additions as they were, made for the refined luxury in which it had become. "Uncle, what is Clontarf most known for?"

"Well, it is most famous for the battle, which occurred in 1014."

"The battle of Clontarf, yes—I do remember studying that briefly."

"Brian Boru was the High King of Ireland during that time. He defeated the Vikings and their allies, the Irish of Leinster. It was that battle which marked the end to the Irish and Viking wars."

"It is utterly stunning—the castle, sir."

As they continued their journey, they soon entered the grounds of Cyrus's modest cottage, where Cateline could see Cyrus and his wife standing outside waiting for their guests. "Yes," Cateline thought, as they drew near— "Cyrus was definitely a younger version of her uncle, quite handsome, and his wife was a somewhat plain girl of a medium frame, with fair features and her light amber hair pulled up in a bun."

"Welcome, father," Cyrus spoke, shaking hands with his father and greeting all warmly one by one as they stepped out of the carriage. "This must be Cateline," Cyrus voiced, "she is as beautiful as you have described her. Well, well—at last, Uncle John's little girl has come back to her roots." He gave her a sincere hug as he smiled and continued, "Your father would have been much pleased to have

97

seen how his little girl has grown up to be a most charming young lady."

Cateline smiling, knowing from being Irish herself, they were not at all shy about the hugs and kisses. Appropriately returning his heartfelt hug and handshake while stating decisively, "Your kindness is most welcomed, for I have heard so much about all of you. It is such a pleasure to finally make your acquaintance." Looking around at the grounds and the house, she thought to herself, "After all this time—getting to see a cottage from the nineteenth century. And it is by no means an insignificant house as most would assume, but for this era, a cottage was quite comfortable in size for a sensible family, needless to say." Nevertheless, she already knew that one day, Cyrus would inherit her uncle's estate. Given a quick tour, Isabella took Cateline throughout the downstairs area, most pleasant in character, the rooms all of a sizeable dimension, Victorian décor for sure, with high ceilings and a most enchanting overall feel.

Unquestionably, the land was that of the countryside, with many trees covering large portions, but the majority was more of a wooded area backdrop. It was fascinating to see that Cyrus actually owned many farm animals to include his horses. As for servants, they only had one cook, a stable boy, and one maid. Naturally, it was unnecessary to have as many servants as her uncle, with the house being considerably smaller.

After all the greetings were concluded, and Cateline was introduced to their young son, Benjamin, of about nine years old, Cyrus took her to tour the property along with Anya and Amos. Walking over towards the stables, there was an attached field where all the horses were grazing. Cateline observing Cyrus's various assemblage of horses, inquired, "The miniature-looking horses, I noticed that your father has one that looks similar, and you have several. Is that a particular breed, Cyrus?"

"Why, yes, it is. Are you very knowledgeable about horses?"

"No, not so much. There are just some of the breeds that I find very fascinating, and I am fairly familiar with those. I do love to ride, but by no means have I acquired any considerable knowledge of these fine creatures to be an expert on their differences."

"Those horses, although they are small in stature, are much stronger and leaner than other horses you will see in Ireland. Their breed is the Irish Draught. Have you ever heard of them?"

"No, I cannot say that I have."

"Although they have been around for many years, these well-bred horses have the ability and strength to haul more weight than a larger horse and at a most efficient pace. For the farmer, they are a very valuable treasure indeed. They also can jump barriers far greater than other breeds, which for the hunter, they make superb companions, as they become much engaged. With my farm and love of the fox hunt, I dare say there is no better breed."

"I can understand why they would be so valuable. I presume they must make for a very fair saddlehorse."

"Yes, undeniably, they do."

"The white horse, that is also an Irish Draught?"

"No, that one is Benjamin's horse, or rather his pony. It is a Connemara pony."

"It looks just like a small horse."

"Yes, but it is a very popular pony in Ireland. They are very gentle, and Benjamin has become quite proficient in riding at his young age."

"Do all Connemara's have the long blond tail, as this one does?"

"No, the tail is naturally impressive, but that is not always the case, although it makes this particular horse most striking. Have you ridden any of my father's horses, Cateline?"

Cateline, looking at Anya, responded, "Not yet; I believe we plan to do so."

"Yes," Anya stated, "I told her we could, but we have been so preoccupied—although, today, we most assuredly can ride if you would like, Cyrus."

"Yes, we certainly can saddle them up and take a ride today—how about it, Amos?"

"A pleasant ride today sounds splendid," Amos assented.

"It is a most beautiful day, and there are many trails that lead down to the beach, but we are much too close to Bull Island. I dare say we should venture there for Cateline to have the pleasure of the views," Cyrus stated most assuredly.

"Oh—yes, how exciting," exclaimed Cateline, "that would be very nice. Bull Island, is there a way to cross?"

"You are familiar with Bull Island?"

"I am, I have not had the pleasure to see it, but I am familiar with the island."

99

"Fascinating, and to answer your question, we would ride down to Dollymount, which is not too far, to cross. There is a long wooden bridge—built over sixty years ago. Trams cross the bridge daily, taking people over, and it is entirely safe. We can ride the horses to the beach from here and then continue along the shoreline until we get to the bridge. It leads to the walls which were constructed years ago to prevent sand build-up in the mouth of the harbor."

They all agreed that it was a most excellent idea. "Then it is settled," Cyrus concluded while noticing his wife standing outside. "I do believe Isabella is looking for us. Lunch must be about ready; what say we head back to the house to eat and talk a bit, then a little later, we can take a ride. I will be sure and have my stable boy get four horses ready; how does that sound?"

"That sounds splendid," Cateline responded with everyone in agreement.

Walking back towards the cottage to enjoy a light lunch, they entered at just the right moment, with the family beginning to settle into their dining parlor. There was much discourse among all, laughter and sharing while enjoying their meal and getting to know Cateline. Finishing the last of the most flavorsome and delightful custard, they continued to converse around the table for a short time. The family all congregated to the drawing-room afterward, where Cateline enjoyed finally getting to know Isabella, being a most charming woman, very well-natured in all aspects. After a short period had elapsed, Anya and Cateline followed Isabella upstairs to be fitted with breeches for horse riding. "If I had known we were going to ride horses, I would have brought breeches from home. Isabella, hopefully, you have two pairs that we can wear."

"I never get rid of any of mine; you never know when they may be needed, such as today. I believe we should be able to find a pair to fit each of you."

Cateline inquired, "Breeches, that is a new word; what exactly are they?"

Anya and Isabella laughed at Cateline's remark while Anya finally educated her on the subject, "Breeches, my dear cousin, they are trousers for women. Truthfully, not to be seen out in public, but women wear them occasionally, especially for horseback riding, at least, women who love to ride and love to do so without a sidesaddle where you must sit aside rather than astride. I have several pairs at home. I will be sure to give you one; being a bit smaller than myself, I believe I still have a pair or two that I can no longer wear."

Cateline declared, "I am sure that it was a man who decided women must not be seen in pants, yes?"

"Well, you do mean trousers?"

"Oh, yes, of course."

"I suppose the answer could be yes and no—it all goes back to the Bible really, where women are to be adorned in modest apparel, but even in this day, women are not always adorned discreetly. There is a phrase as well, 'who wears the trousers in the family,'—or I suppose in America, the word used is pants, I am sure that you have heard this expression."

"Well, yes—I have heard that before."

"This phrase refers to the head of the household—which is the man, as it equates to the wearing of trousers with masculinity and power."

"Very intriguing," Cateline voiced.

Isabella went through all her breeches until she was able to find a pair for each of the girls. Dressing for the occasion, they went downstairs and out to the stables to begin their afternoon ride on the beach. With all the horses saddled and ready, Cateline rode on one of the Irish Draught, which made for a very smooth ride, her particular horse being most subdued. Cyrus rode up alongside Cateline to become better acquainted with his cousin. "How do you like the horse you are riding?"

"You were right, very gentle. She is delightful, quite agreeable."

They maintained talking and sharing until they came to the beach. "I will race all of you down to the bridge, off in the distance," Cyrus cried out to his companions. With that said, all parties geared their horses in a charge forward, with Cyrus shouting, "Go," in a rather loud voice, while hurling his horse towards the rocks clustered along the edges of the dunes, and with great strides, everyone fell into a gallop. While the others were all striving towards Cyrus, being as he was in the lead, there was much laughter and screaming, with Cateline's horse moving forward very fast, soon falling into second place. Cyrus finally having opposition, yet Cateline was unable to seize the quest.

101

As she laughed most energetically, Cateline cried out, "You know I would have prevailed against you if, indeed, I would have been prepared for the race?"

"Yes, perhaps you would have, as that is to your advantage being on the Irish Draught," Cyrus responded with a playful smile and a wink. They all climbed down from their horses to walk along the beach and view the beauty of the coastline before crossing the bridge.

"This is the Dublin Bay, is it not?" Cateline inquired.

"It is, to be sure," Cyrus responded.

Cateline enjoyed the crisp breeze that swept through the air over the sandy shores and the whitecaps of the water as it pooled into the bay. Thinking back to the hotel in Clontarf, she knew that this was the same beach except further towards Bull Island, being that Cyrus lived much closer to this area. Familiar with the island, having come across it in planning her trip, Cateline had actually intended to take a taxi one of her days in Dublin to spend on the island. Now here she was in the nineteenth century gazing upon the bridge to Bull Island.

Up and down the shoreline, as they continued walking with horses in tow, the beaches were moderately flat with picturesque sandy shores lined by dunes in the distance, capped with the whispery Pampas grass, and toppled with feather-like florets, which waved with each disruption of the blustery wind. In other places grew the European beachgrass with each blade bowing and coiling in rhythm followed by every gentle breeze of the moist air; their light green and greyish colors reflected the sunlight—beams came forth from each strand. As far as she could see inland, more and more of the flatland was filled with clumps of grass in some places very thickly and others in clusters. Off in the distance from the bay, one could see insignificant hills that toppled the midsection of the island, with more sandy beaches and verdant grassy dunes. The clouds drifted along the horizon as soft tufts of smoke puffing through the current, tumbling into the sphere, with the traces of heat from the sun bristling beyond like flashes of crystals fading off into the color schemes of blues, greys, and pinks. A most breathtaking sight, as she was filled with the subtle power of life—existence, tranquility, and vivid wonder. To herself, her thoughts were filled with that of a summer day, even though it was just barely March. The faint breeze and the majestic images were beheld in all its dignity, where she lived not for tomorrow but for each moment. Taking in everything as if it would not last, for in her thoughts, she knew her passions could hold onto all the memoirs to subdue her through a lifetime.

Getting back onto their horses, they rode across the wooden bridge onto Bull Island, a small platform of land built up gradually by sand formation out in the Dublin Bay. There were only a few trams along the way, with it being so early in March; nevertheless, many still came to spend the day on the island's sandy shores to absorb the beauty and relaxation. Once they arrived, many folks were scattered over the banks—some in groups, while others solitary and couples walking hand in hand—filling the busy beaches and basking in the sun of a cool March day. Children were out and about running and playing, others making castles in the sand. Off in the distant, few were observed, mainly couples taking brisk walks on the many trails, talking, laughing, and exploring throughout the expanse of dunes and grasses, while at the same time enjoying the brink of spring, which waited momentarily around the corner.

They had turned their horses from the gathering of folks to take a brisk run through thick acres of marram grass, which blustered in the wind. The silhouette of the Dublin mountains could be seen from the island, looking back towards the mainland. As they neared the shores on the far side in a more secluded area on Dollymount Strand, they veered their horses and hurled into a sprint. Simultaneously, they maintained following the beach along the way of the outer view of Dublin Bay—stretching its broad and mysterious waters forcefully out to sea. As they rode gauging the wind, the genial sight of Howth Head, a considerable distance away, came into view with its rugged cliffs and rocky shorelines. Cateline was enthralled with the island's beauty and the richness generated as they rode along on horseback. Bull Island was a nature lovers paradise, known for its refuge for wildlife. Besides the beaches and dunes, there was a wealth of mudflats, grassland, and marsh. Many geese, observed in such grace, populated its wetlands—mainly the Brent geese, which could be seen in great number. As they continued to ride, the current from the waters lashing in from the sea began to loosen the tightly secured strands of hair from both Anya and Cateline. Their long locks seemed to find freedom, lifting and

103

soaring—rushing, fluttering, flowing freely, falling all around in dazzling disarray.

Suddenly stopping, Cyrus had noticed seals a brief distance out from the shore. Gathering their horses around his, he pointed to the social group at a very close range in the bay. They watched in silence while the delightful mammals played and frolicked in the deep blue rumble of the sea. The day was much enjoyed as they rode along, relishing the feel of being so connected to nature. After spending such an enjoyable day in the briskness of wildlife, with dusk fast approaching, they steered the horses towards the cottage. The day had been quite long but so agreeable with no one desiring their fun-filled adventures to end. Yet, knowing that the afternoon tea had more than likely been served and finished, it was time to head back.

Once at the cottage, all dismounted their horses while Cyrus assisted the stable boy as his sister and the others waited. Together, they all walked back toward the country house and entered the drawing-room. Mr. Walsh was enjoying a splendid discussion with his grandson, Benjamin, while on the table before them sat the remaining items from the afternoon tea. The preparations were laid out on a fine tray, which seemed to have been enjoyed with an abundance. Being famished, as they were, they all sat down, taking delight in the dainty sandwiches of various meats and pastries, while Cyrus lifted the teapot to fill everyone's cup. "Thank you, Cyrus," Cateline responded.
"Where is mother?" Anya inquired.
"I believe she is helping Isabella in the other room. We have decided to stay for dinner since we were unsure when all of you would return," noted Mr. Walsh.
"I am sorry, father, for the time seemed to slip by. We did have a splendid afternoon. I believe Cateline enjoyed herself," Cyrus asserted.

The remaining moments were spent much engaged with conversation while having dinner in their parlor. The late evening flew by as Cateline had greatly enjoyed the hours employed with her extended family before they had to leave. Beginning to feel right at home with Cyrus and Isabella, she truly looked forward to occupying many more days in their company. How Cateline had loved spending the hours with all her new family and hated to think of the day she would no longer be with them. Before heading back to the estate, they all said their goodbyes, with Cyrus and his wife agreeing to be at the dinner party the following weekend.

Along the road towards home, Mrs. Walsh declared, "That must have been some ride. You girls are very quiet; it looks as though the wind was a torrent to you both—your hair is entirely undone."

"Yes, mother, we had a wonderful spell, but it was not fit for our hair, I'm afraid. But I do believe we will all sleep well tonight."

"We had such a good time, Aunt Martha," Cateline subdued softly.

"I am most delighted that all of you had such an occasion."

Mr. Walsh declared, "Amos, do feel free to stay the night if you so desire. We can all attend church together tomorrow."

"Yes, sir, I believe that may be a good idea. Thank you, sir."

"Much obliged."

Arriving back at the estate, her uncle called Cateline into his study. "Cateline, this will not take long; I know you are fatigued. I just wanted to briefly go over a few details regarding your father." Upon entering, Mr. Walsh first handed her an envelope in which he had already mentioned, "This, my dear, is the letter that I spoke to you about. I would assume that you would be more comfortable to read what he wrote in private." Her uncle then proceeded to go over her inheritance with her. "Your father has left you quite a substantial amount, but frankly, I believe that he was in hopes you would come back to your native country and fall in love with Ireland enough that you would remain. Nevertheless, the funds are yours to do with as you please. He left you five thousand pounds, which is enough for you to remain in Ireland if you so desire."

"Uncle Walsh, I am not sure I understand anything about the currency here in Ireland."

"Our currency is the pound sterling or rather just referred to as the pound. The funds are currently in the Bank of Ireland, which we will attend to opening you an account in your name and transferring it from mine."

"Are there legal documents required for such? Unfortunately, I do not have my birth record; being born here in Ireland, I am assuming it could be obtained."

105

"My dear, it is quite alright. Your father had several documents which he left in my care, one being your birth record."

In excitement, she exclaimed, "That's wonderful, Uncle Walsh. You have been so amiable to me already. I do not know how I will ever repay your family for all you have done."

"Cateline, you are family, and that is what family does. We are here to help you all that we can."

Cateline thought to herself, "Thank goodness there were funds left for me from my father, for my American money definitely would not work in this day and time."

"Shall we join the others, my dear? Or do you have any further questions?"

"No, sir, and thank you so much for all you have done."

Joining the family, the remainder of the evening was spent together in the drawing-room for a short time, as most were fully drained. Newton, the footman, brought the nightstand candle holders, as he did every night, with lit candles for each to take with them to their rooms. "Goodnight, girls and Amos," Mr. Walsh spoke gently as he escorted his wife to her bedchamber. Amos went to one of the apartments on the third floor, and the girls retired to their own rooms, depleted from their long day.

Nevertheless, as bushed as she was when Cateline came to her room, she sat down her candle on the nightstand and pulled out the envelope that her uncle had given her from her father. Opening it, she began to read as tears formed in her eyes and streamed down her cheeks. The letter had been most agreeable—rather pleasant, indeed. Even though Cateline had no recollection of her father from this period, the words had touched her soul, as if somewhere deep inside, she had known him, after all. With those sweet, spoken words arranged delicately on the paper in her hand, she uttered softly, "Father, it was evident that you so loved me, for my heart is full of sorrow—not having memories of you or this life, except for what I hold dear to me right now in my hand. With these words, I dare say that I have dreamt of this life and of family—perhaps it was even of you that I have imagined. For I have awakened many nights with tears, as I have foreseen these days, being of such times as these— time which has been spent. Yet, here I am, and here I will be, where I shall relinquish upon this life—this life, as if it were mine and were for me. Strength, I ask of thee, to hold me in arms—arms from years long ago, and be always my guide to unfold this mystery. Dare, I say—let my soul live to this life, to be such one, as you speak in these words—and to me that I behold all these days, as in such abundance, it shall be."

Sunday came and went, their morning passed in church, singing and quietly gaining perspective from the message. It was a peaceful day, with the family enjoying the Sunday Roast—a traditional lunch typically served after church with roasted meat. To their delight, the meal consisted of a pork roast with sweet apple sauce, Brussels sprouts, carrots, runner beans, potatoes—seasoned with salt, pepper, and lots of butter—a delicious flaxseed bread, and a most succulent dessert—apple charlotte cake in a mold with sliced up apples, filled with custard. It was a day of relaxation and rest for the whole family, as the coming week would be very demanding with the forthcoming event.

CHAPTER
9

Cateline awoke fairly early on Monday morning, having spent the day prior attending the small chapel where many neighbors had congregated, some of whom were to be in attendance at the upcoming dinner party. "Yes, it was an eventful time," she thought to herself, "I so enjoyed the fellowship yesterday." While lying in her bed, Cateline continued to reminisce on various conversations—interviews, as one would declare, in which she was engaged with several gentlemen, both young and old, along with the ladies who were present. The clergyman was a somewhat stout gentleman, middle-aged of sorts, and his message was rather reserved but well-spoken if truth be told—quite unlike those she had heard in America. Eventually, her mind drifted towards the magnificent celebration, as Cateline was utterly thrilled in anticipation of her very special event. Even though her uncle had not mentioned hearing back from Mr. Wilde, Cateline still believed that he was the reason for her being there in the first place, and in due time, she was confident they would surely meet. Finally getting out of bed, hurrying to get ready for the day, Cateline joined her family for the English breakfast, which was a most favorable meal, far better than what America considered breakfast—especially in the twenty-first century. By far, the breakfast was relatively superior to that of her day and surpassed most of the evening meals; on the other hand, she had overheard discussions about the preparations for the forthcoming stately ball, which would be quite a feast.

As the family was gathered around the breakfast table, her uncle remarked, "Anya, I thought perhaps tomorrow, you and Cateline could get up a bit earlier and dress for an outing to Dublin."

"To Dublin father, for what occasion?"

"Well, dear, I thought both of you could accompany me into the city, spend the day shopping for new dresses, and perhaps, we could all meet for lunch at one of the restaurants. There are a few extraordinary places to dine within the city."

"That would be wonderful, father, wouldn't it, Cateline?"

"Why yes, I have yet to see Dublin, and to be able to go shopping, that would surely be such a treat."

"Then it is settled. Martha, please be sure that Sarah knows to wake the girls early tomorrow morning."

"Yes, dear. I will certainly see to it."

"Oh—and Cateline, while we are in Dublin, we shall also attend to setting up your account to transfer the funds from your father."

"Of course, Uncle Walsh. Thank you so very much for everything you and Aunt Martha have done for me. I have entirely enjoyed my stay and am so fond of you all."

"Why that is very sweet, my dear," Aunt Martha concluded as Uncle Walsh rose from the table to leave for the day and gave Cateline a most sincere, warm smile, patting her on the back.

Leaning over, he affectionately hugged and kissed his wife before affirming, "Busy day today, Martha, but I will be home as soon as I possibly can," Mr. Walsh stated while walking towards the door.

The remainder of the day seemed to go by pretty swiftly, with Anya and Cateline spending a considerable amount of their time planning what they would wear and how they would have Sarah arrange their hair for their Tuesday outing to Dublin. They were so enthusiastic that it was all they could talk about throughout the day, as Anya eagerly shared insight with Cateline on the various shops, the quaint little cafes, to include the many historical sites.

The day hastily faded away with the excitement being carried over into the evening meal. Shortly after, all parties retired to bed very early in order to be up bright and cheery before sunrise the following morning.

It was barely daybreak, when Sarah hurried into both the girl's rooms to open draperies and awaken them for their fun-filled jaunt into the city. She then went to help Cateline with her dress since it was a more formal attire that included the bustle. The bustle, which helped support the skirt in the back of the dress, along with all the added ruffles and lace, was not that easy to manage without assistance. All the costumes for that period were so beautiful to Cateline. Still, she had never known how many layers of clothing had to be put on before the actual dress—her chemise and drawers, the stockings which were fastened with ribbons a little over the knee, the corset for support, and finally the bustle along with crinoline if the dress was to be full. And, not to mention, depending upon the dress, if one did not wear the bustle, it was multiple layers of petticoats underneath the crinoline. For ladies of this era, they had to have a maid purely to help with their attire for significant occasions. While Sarah was aiding Cateline, Aunt Martha had sent her maidservant, Permilia, to assist Anya. Once Cateline was dressed, Sarah began working on her long locks of hair, braiding several strands in an art fashion which Cateline had never seen in America. She then took the braids and created a masterpiece, which she lifted on top of her head with a few strands dangling downward, delicately curled. It was such a splendid detailed work in which it took more time than most Americans would dare spend each morning simply to go to town. Cateline soon learned that anything other than merely staying home required one's best apparel and the most magnificent hairstyles. Once Cateline had applied a bit of powder and blush with a slight color to her lips, being arranged quite stunningly, she first went to Anya's apartment before heading to the morning room to join the family for breakfast. Peering into her chamber, she stood admiring Anya's dress and hair, which were most charming. It was pretty obvious, Permilia was just as good as Sarah when it came to hair. With both girls being exquisitely prepared for Dublin, they walked downstairs to join the family for breakfast. Mr. Walsh noted, "My, my—girls, you both look absolutely superb. I will be flattered to be seen walking amongst you two today. Why men will wonder what I have that makes me so attractive to such elaborately adorned ladies."

"Oh, father, really. You get those looks every time you walk with mother," Anya responded.

Cateline giggled a little as she sat down beside Anya for breakfast.

Aunt Martha, as she discussed the various options with the girls for purchasing simply fabulous dresses in Dublin, submitted her recommendations, "Well, girls, I'm sure you will both have a wonderful day. I am assuming that you will make your rounds at the shops in the vicinities of Henry and Grafton Streets. I do believe there are several fine boutiques in that area, if I am not mistaken."

"Unquestionably, mother, but probably more so on Grafton. There are so many fashion shops, and many dresses come from either London or Paris," Anya stated confidently before addressing her father, "where will we meet you for lunch?"

"Well, first, my dear, we need to go to the bank and take care of Cateline's account. I suppose we can discuss our options on which café while we are headed into the city."

They all finished up breakfast as Mr. Walsh gave his wife a kiss goodbye, and the girls headed out the door babbling and chattering with such excitement and enthusiasm. Once they had all climbed into the brougham, Mr. Walsh inquired of the girls, "Seeing that you shall spend much of your time on Grafton Street, I believe we should meet up at Bewley's Café for lunch. How does that sound?"

"Yes, father, I remember where Bewley's is located. We will keep track of the time and meet around eleven or so?"

"Probably between 11:00 and 11:30 a.m. would be reasonable," Mr. Walsh made note while Elbert pulled up to the bank. "Cateline, if you would like to join me. Anya, it should not take very long."

"It is quite alright, father. I shall be fine."

Arriving alongside the enormous early nineteenth-century building with its curved façade and ionic columns, graced by sculptures representative of Wisdom, Justice, and Liberty, over the portico at the entrance, Cateline stepped out of the carriage. At the same time, her uncle took her hand to assist her down. They walked into the Bank of Ireland with Mr. Walsh approaching a clerk for assistance. Managing all the aspects, he handed over all the necessary documents where the account could be opened and secured with the funds removed from his account. Once all paperwork had been completed and the necessary signatures from both, copies were given to Cateline while the clerk prepared a small number of banknotes, which her uncle had requested. While waiting for the clerk to finalize all transactions, her uncle briefly explained how banknotes worked, where the bank would issue upon her demand whatever denomination needed. She was unsure of what the currency was or what items cost, for that matter, so her uncle instructed her on a minimal amount that should suffice. "Dear, you can come back to the bank to draw out funds whenever needed."

"Thank you, Uncle Walsh. I should hope that I will become better acquainted with the currency in Ireland."

"And you shall, my dear."

The gentleman at the bank handed Cateline the banknotes and a personal passbook. Mr. Walsh shook the man's hand as he thanked him for his time.

Getting back into the brougham, Mr. Walsh told Elbert to drive to Grafton Street. Arriving, Elbert helped both ladies out of the carriage while Mr. Walsh reminded them once again, "Have a good morning, girls, and I will see you for lunch." He then handed Anya banknotes to be able to purchase their dresses, mentioning to his niece, "Cateline, Anya has enough to buy both of you girls gorgeous gowns. There is no need for you to spend any of your money at this time. We planned to buy you this dress, my dear."

"Thank you, Uncle Walsh, but I do have my own money now."

"Nonsense," her uncle responded, "Anya, do not let her use her banknotes."

"I won't, father."

Anya and Cateline were most eager as they walked down the street, looking at all the numerous shops and businesses. There were so many people traveling about either walking or in various horse-drawn gigs and even trams. Cateline learned the trams were part of the Dublin Horse Tram. They were moderately spacious carriages, enclosed—double-decked to carry many passengers, and everywhere one looked, another could be seen. Gazing about, a number of trams could be spotted coming and going, whereas, Cateline had not expected so many people in the 1880s. Nevertheless, she soon learned that Dublin was heavily populated. Walking along, they went into one establishment after another. Both girls were looking for the perfect dress, and even though, Cateline knew she had her own money to pay for a dress from either Paris or London, there was no way Anya was going to allow her to do such. However, she thought to herself, "I will let Anya pay for the dress, but it will be my treat to purchase all our accessories for our new attires."

They entered one of the finer shops and explored with such delight. Within no time at all, they stumbled upon many very attractive originals. Browsing for quite some time, the girls observed some of Paris's latest fashions while admiring each and every one of them. With assistance from the clerk, Anya was fit in a Jacques Doucet ball gown, which was a light peach color having mid-length sleeves, assembled with dazzling gold lace, as it trailed around the low neckline of the bodice. Additionally, the lovely dress was gathered at the waist. It then flowed down extravagantly adorned with the beautifully sheered tulle and formed about two feet from the bottom, besides trailing upwards on the flowing part of the gown. It was encased with a somewhat long train extending in the back with more of the golden netting. Cateline was beside herself, admiring her cousin in the Jacques Doucet original, which was definitely the thing in Paris, being as they were so refined.

Another assistant helped Cateline in trying on several designer dresses herself. Finally coming across a Madeleine Laferriere evening gown, she knew this had to be the one. Adorned in a very faint pink color, the dress's bodice actually had large jewels at the top and along the gathered waistline. There was sheer light pink lace, which was encased around the top of the bodice and along the upper part of the sleeves. The dress was worn with long, pastel pink gloves extending above the elbows. The skirt was the same indistinct pink color yet mixed with gold adorned with gathered lace trailing along the lowest part of the border, formed in thick layers, extending all the way around to include the train in the back. The clerk at the store showed Cateline the gold and soft pink band with the same stone as on the bodice, which fastened around the neck to accentuate the dress, also included was a long gold feather carried in those days by women many times as a fan. Standing in front of the mirror in full dress, it was simply stunning. So, it was decided that both girls had made their selection—and what extravagant selections they were, the most marvelous dresses direct from Paris.

Anya still continued shopping for accessories to complement her dress, while the young clerk showed her the perfect accents to include a ruffled gold neckband that corresponded with matching gloves. They were so stirred with anticipation, eager to parade the exquisite elegance before their family later that evening. Anya paid for the dresses, but Cateline insisted on taking care of all the accessories. Once all sales transactions were settled, they walked towards the café to meet Mr. Walsh while spilling over with delight, as their conversations were enflamed the whole distance relating details of their very novel and spectacular dresses from *Paree*.

Before arriving at their destination, strolling in front of a quaint shop, Anya paused while reminding herself of a particular item she desired to purchase for her cousin. Escorting Cateline into

113

the shop, there were many odd articles, but the main thing that Anya was looking for was a diary. "Cateline, I noticed that you do not have a diary. Every girl must keep a diary, for it is her duty. Yes, here is just the item I was looking for," Anya remarked while picking up a rather drab-looking brown book. Quite plain in appearance with the word, *Diary* on the front.

"Anya, I can pay for the diary if I must have one."

"Oh no, cousin—this is my gift for you; let it be a token of sisterly love. You must be sure to use it, as I have mine for those most delightful memories and adventures my life has been fortunate to take." Anya walked to the clerk and paid for the modest brown book.

As the girls walked out of the store to continue towards the restaurant, Anya handed Cateline the diary, declaring, "Your diary is to keep mention of all your life's tiny secrets and your most precious memories. Do they not keep diaries in America?"

"Why yes, I believe some do, but I am not really sure how much of a necessity they are in America."

"Not a necessity—for goodness' sake, every girl of importance must hold her every memoir within those pages where none should ever see until she marries or unless it is her last breath. Oh, it is hard for me to believe in America, a diary is of little importance—girls do not hold their most vivid remembrances within their hands? —such reminiscence and achievements where they shall never ever be forgotten? You are so very young as it is, but your days will go by, and you will have regrets if the memories were but a trace to remain. Therefore, I beg of you, please be attentive to my request and keep your memoirs, for one day you will thank me for this, I am most assured. Every day, you should add to your diary, unless the day is full and demanding—nonetheless, the day after should have two entries. It is best to be kept by your bed, so when you retire, you can add the events of the day."

"I do thank you, Anya, and I promise that I will find it most pleasurable to keep track of my days and time—all of my adventures, as you say," Cateline responded with a heartfelt smile. Thinking to herself, "Yes, what a wonderful idea of keeping a record of all that ensued, for once I am no longer here, I may have my most valued memories to sustain my life."

As the girls resumed their walk, there was so much excitement between them with the day of the party at such a close range. Arriving at the café, they realized they were a bit early. As they were seated at a table, Anya told the young man—her father, a Mr. Walsh, would be joining them. While waiting for the server, they continued to spill over with joy about their spectacular dresses and the upcoming ball. When the waiter came to their table, Anya asked that tea be brought for the time being. Mr. Walsh finally arrived with quite a surprise, as Amos had accompanied him to have lunch with Anya. "Good afternoon, ladies," Mr. Walsh greeted the girls, "and I have brought my dear daughter a most gracious surprise."

Anya was so stirred to be able to see Amos, and with the feelings being mutual, Amos leaned over to kiss her lightly on the forehead, "Good afternoon. You look very lovely today, as every day," he professed most admirably.

"Thank you, Amos," Anya replied with their smiles toward each other, most apparent it was, to say the least, the profound love they both felt.

The girls, having already contemplated what they desired from the menu, the gentlemen quickly scanned over the choices themselves. Simultaneously, conversations continued to babble over as the excitement had escalated amongst the ladies; being as it was, they were in deep discussions on all the various shops they had come upon. Talks continued as they detailed the many pleasant items viewed. Needless to say, there was no need to mention their anticipation of the soon-to-be social festivity as it was without a doubt evident. Once Mr. Walsh and Amos had decided on their meal selections, Samuel inquired further into their day of shopping, "How has your day been, girls? I see from the number of boxes that you must have found gowns to your liking. And I might add, I presume you have also purchased the likes to go with them."

"Yes, father," Anya remarked with excitement in her voice. "We have had such an amazing time and found two of the most beautiful ball gowns that I have ever seen. Thank you very much for allowing us to spend this delightful day in Dublin."

"Yes, Uncle Walsh, thank you so very much and for the dress, which is quite charming," Cateline added with such enthusiasm. It was obvious that the girls were both glistening in their eagerness for the upcoming special day.

"I am delighted that you have both done well. I am sure I will have the satisfaction of seeing you girls try on those dresses this evening at home for the family."

"Oh, yes—yes, father, indeed. We can hardly wait to get home to try them on once again with all the accessories."

"I would expect as much, my dear. Have you both decided on your meal choice?"

"I believe we both would like to try the venison father. Is there a French chef at this restaurant?"

"Yes, dear, they do have quite a distinguished French chef. His food is most superb."

The server came back to the table with two more teacups, where he refilled both the lady's cups and provided for the gentlemen, while Mr. Walsh conveyed their choice of lunch selections.

As they cheerfully spoke of their day and the upcoming event, Mr. Walsh was pleased to see the excitement in both girls. The food was soon served, and they quietly ate to get their fill. While Mr. Walsh paid the bill, Amos helped the girls with their boxes, carrying them out where they hailed a hansom. "Do not worry about toting around all these boxes, your father and I will take them back to the office until the end of the day," Amos declared.

"Thank you, Amos," whispered Anya while leaning over to lightly kiss his cheek.

Mr. Walsh suggested, "Why don't you two spend some time at one of the museums or sightseeing until I leave work. I can cut my day short, so it will probably be a few hours more. Perhaps, you could show Cateline the museum or library; the Natural History Museum is on Merrion, a few blocks over, my dear."

"Yes, father, that sounds perfect, and I am sure Cateline will love the museum. Afterward, we shall walk towards your office."

"Splendid, I shall see you both a little later. Enjoy the rest of your day, Cateline."

"Yes, sir, Uncle Walsh," Cateline responded as the cab pulled away from the curb.

They walked along towards the museum, crossing an alley when Anya spotted St. Theresa's Church. "Oh my, come, you have to see this."

Cateline turned down the alley following her, heading towards a relatively large church, "This is amazing, the architecture of these old buildings—outstanding."

"We have to go inside," Anya remarked with excitement, "St. Theresa's is even more astonishing on the inside with statues and art that will amaze you."

Upon entering, Cateline was in admiration of the beauty alone, it being such a grand church. "When was this church built?"

"I believe the late part of the eighteenth century. Look, isn't the white marble statue of Jesus in the tomb simply breathtaking?"

"Utterly, gorgeous. The whole cathedral is so spectacular with such architecture. Why, what beauty it is, and the stained-glass windows, incredible. The paintings—every detail is so exquisite."

"Yes, I had forgotten about how beautiful this church was. I have come here before to merely sit in the back and feel the peace which it brings just being here surrounded by such magnificence."

"Yes, I can certainly feel that as well."

After a few more moments of enjoying their surroundings, they walked out to head towards the museum. Upon arriving, they spent at least an hour or so enjoying a small segment, becoming rather evident that they needed to begin heading towards Anya's father's office due to the time. Leaving, it was not long until they could see the Four Courts off in the immediate distance.

Once arrived, they walked to his chambers, where he was all ready to leave. Hurriedly, Anya rushed towards Amos's office to say goodbye before departing. On the ride back to the estate, the girls were so cheerful, knowing they would soon be able to adorn their dresses while presenting them to the family. Mrs. Walsh, greeting the girls, was very inquisitive on viewing their selections directly, yet, both girls hurriedly walked past her. At the same time, Anya admonished hastily, "No, mother, we are taking our dresses upstairs and will flaunt them with all the accessories where you and father may take delight."

"Alright, my dear daughter, we will be waiting with much anticipation in the drawing-room."

Both girls proceeded up the stairwell, with Sarah and Permilia facilitating, while the exquisite dresses and all the embellishments began to come to fruition. Once they were both fully donned in their gowns, they commenced their most elegant walk down the stairs to be presented for appearance before the family.

Entering the drawing-room, Mrs. Walsh addressed both girls, "Oh my, how absolutely gorgeous. Are the dresses from Paris?"

"Yes, mother. Mine is a Jacques Doucet dress, and Cateline's is a Madeleine Laferriere. How do you like them?"

"Like them, I am almost speechless. And, Cateline, the golden plume is always such a delightful addition, especially when one may find themselves impassioned. I must convey, you two will definitely be the prettiest girls at the ball."

Mr. Walsh's response in his fatherly manner, "Yes, I will have to keep a pretty stern watch over both of you. Why every gentleman at the festivity will be stricken with your beauty."

"Oh, father, you know that Amos is going to be with me. You will just have to make sure you keep your eyes on Cateline," Anya quipped with a slight wink at her cousin.

Cateline laughing sanguinely at her cousin, responded, "Thank you so much, uncle and aunt, for all you have done. I am so very enthused; I can barely wait for Saturday to come."

"Well, wait—you must, but it is only four more days. My dear," Samuel started while gazing over at his wife, inquiring, "I am assuming that everything is in order for Saturday, is it not?"

"Yes, dear, it is. Oh, Cateline, your brother James is coming in for your social event to meet you."

"He is? I am most excited to meet him, how nice that he will be able to attend. When will he be arriving, and how long can he stay?"

"He is arriving on Thursday and plans to stay through Sunday," Martha looking over at her husband, stated, "I have Lydia and Charlotte preparing the other bedrooms for those who will be staying, Samuel."

"Wonderful, my dear. I will only be going to the office tomorrow and have taken the remainder of the week off to assist with the preparations for Saturday, and with others coming in, I want to be sure and be here to be hospitable."

"How lovely, my dear. I am so happy you will be here for some days."

The girls went back upstairs to take off their dresses and put on more casual apparel for dinner. The remainder of the evening was much enjoyed around the dining table; afterward, they retired to the music room to hear Anya and Cateline play the pianoforte and persisted on Cateline playing one song on the guitar before withdrawing to bed for the night.

Once in her bedroom, Cateline retrieved her new diary and walked over to the davenport, where she sat down to begin going back as far as she could to make mention of all the days thus far and of everything that had taken place. Fully spent at this point, she blew out her candle and went fast to sleep.

CHAPTER
10

Wednesday flew by rather quickly, with everyone helping to exhaust all last-minute details since there would be family, James, that is to say, arriving the following day, and others on Friday. The excitement had spread throughout the house, and by the end of the day, when Mr. Walsh had come home that evening, all family members were pretty much expended. Both girls retired to bed promptly; Cateline, full of excitement to meet her stepbrother, wanted to awake as early as possible to be dressed before his arrival.

Cateline, waking the following morning, realized Sarah had not drawn the draperies, which meant it was more than likely too early. Lying back down, she began to daydream of the weekend close at hand, thoroughly beside herself with such anticipation, knowing there was no going back to sleep. A short time later, her door slowly opened while she watched Sarah go over to the windows. Giggling, Cateline called out, "I am already awake, Sarah—I couldn't have slept much anyway; this is all so thrilling."

"Yes, ma'am, I see you are wide-awake," she disclosed with a shrewd smile, continuing, "I will be back in to help you get dressed."

"Thank you," Cateline responded while sitting up in the bed, looking out at the beautiful day. "Yes, it is Thursday! I cannot wait to meet my brother and then just two more days!" She exclaimed with excitement while jumping out of bed. Sarah, having rekindled the fire, Cateline stood relishing the warmth, overcoming her body just enough to take off the chill. Once finished, she ran into Anya's room to bounce on the bed and wake her up. "Come on, sleepy-head, today is a great day. We have company coming; I can hardly wait to meet James."

"Oh, cousin dear, I am so sleepy, but I am getting up," Anya spoke drowsily, sitting up to stretch. "Sarah did come in and opened the drapes, but I guess I did not sleep well last night; I suppose that you did?" Anya inquired while her cousin seemed to be jabbering nonstop, so much so that Anya was having a hard time following. Looking over at Cateline's expression, Anya thought silently, "Where does that force come from? It is much too early, and my brain cannot keep up with her!" Stretching and yawning again, Anya decided to climb out of bed about the time Cateline happily darted back to her own room, all the while chattering a bunch of nonsense that Anya could not comprehend so early in the morning, as it was, she still felt half-asleep.

Back in her room, Cateline dressed as best she could when Sarah came in to assist. She wasn't too overly dressed for the day but was adamant that her attire looked presentable for her half-brother. Everyone met downstairs for the English breakfast to start off their day and relaxed out on the veranda, enjoying the elevenses with Mr. Walsh since he was not going back into the office for the remainder of the week. The afternoon finally rolled around, where Mrs. Walsh let everyone know that lunch was prepared while the servants arranged the meal eloquently out on the portico. It was a wonderful day in March, with a bit of chill in the air but not enough to be unbearable. As they sipped their tea and ate on the various sandwiches and savory cakes, dialogue regarding the upcoming weekend ensued. Shortly after lunch, Joseph approached to let Mr. Walsh know that Elbert had the brougham ready. "Thank you, Joseph; let him know that I will be right there."
"Dear, you are off to pick up James from the station?"
"Yes, Martha, he should be arriving in a little while."
"Father, can Cateline and I come with you?"
"No—you girls stay here and help your mother. I will be back with James soon enough."

Mr. Walsh left to head to the station while the girls helped with many of the final preparations for Saturday's grand ball. After some time had elapsed, hearing the clamoring noise of the carriage, the girls ran towards the front door with Martha following close behind. Enthused of James's arrival, they all stood at the front of the estate watching the brougham slowly draw near.
James immediately stepped out of the carriage and walked over to Cateline, "And, you must be Cateline, my older sister?"
"Yes, dear James, I have been so excited to meet you."
They gave each other a warm hug as James exclaimed, "You are quite beautiful; our papa had always said you would be."
"Thank you, James. That is very sweet of you, and you are a most handsome young man, taking after our father, I see."

121

Both, elated with smiles, they embraced again, "It is good to know that I have a sister, just unfortunate that we must meet due to his decease."

"Yes, I wish I could have known him, but you will share your stories with me."

"Yes, that would be such a delight; I would enjoy it immensely."

As everyone hugged and welcomed James, Newton brought his large bag into the house, handing it over to Charles, Mr. Walsh's valet. "James," Mr. Walsh remarked, "Charles will put your bag in one of the rooms on the third floor. If you need anything, be sure to let him know," turning to his valet, making sure his guest was fully serviced, he instructed, "Charles, be sure to take care of Mr. McCarthy while he is here."

"Yes, sir," his valet answered as he headed towards the stairs with James's bag.

Cateline addressing James, "That is rather nice to hear, Mr. McCarthy—someone else with my name," she finished with a smile to her brother.

Everyone retiring back to the veranda, Mrs. Walsh asked Clara to bring out more tea and the leftovers from the afternoon in case James was hungry. The day went very smoothly, as they talked to get acquainted, and the Walsh family asked enough questions to be caught up on James's current affairs. After a few hours, Cateline and James took a long walk on the grounds and talked about their dad. She had so many questions and loved hearing all the stories about him but especially all the times her father would impart to James, remembrances of his *little girl—Cateline.* It was evident that her father had loved her dearly, this she had come to understand. Even so, the distance had seemed to be such a hindrance, for neither one of her parents had wanted to travel the long journey by ship to the other country. Wondering to herself silently, she began to contemplate what her parents of this century were really like. Were they as kind and gentle as her other parents? What were their beliefs, their fears? Were there times of happiness and sadness? So many questions she would never know. Yet, Cateline seemed so connected to both of them. In fact, she was very attached to all those whom she had come to know thus far, loving each and every one of them deeply, with a love that seemed to have always been there—a love that would never die but last forever. With her thoughts, sadness continually came, for Cateline knew that these days would pass away, having nothing further but memories. Bringing her reflections back to the present, as James told of the treacherous journeys many had made to America, it would have hardly seemed likely that families would have traveled such a long distance. Yes, many families were probably separated by distance—by the expanse of the vast oceans and seas which laid before them. She, too, could remember all the discourses with her father of the twentieth century as he had shared many times of the journey, treacherous as it was, the voyage by ship. This had been their reason for having brought Cateline only that one time to Ireland when she was just a child

As the evening came to a close, the family had retired to the dining parlor for dinner, where afterward, discussions continued of the past, which brought much laughter. Cateline had enjoyed hearing the tales and had never laughed so much in her life. James could barely wait for Cyrus to arrive the following day, as they were both very close, even though Cyrus was somewhat older. They soon retired to the drawing-room for Anya and Cateline to play the pianoforte, and of course, James did insist on her playing the guitar at least once. Cateline was getting a bit more comfortable playing for her family since most of the songs had been pretty well received. After some time, they all went to their apartments, for they knew Friday would be such a big day, as well as the days following into the rest of the weekend.

Cateline had a hard time falling asleep, with her thoughts on all those she would soon meet. So many people from this century, the century that she had always been in love with and wished she had been born. Her dreams and wishes had come true, thankful that she was exactly where she was at that moment. From time to time, Cateline would think about Mary and what she must be contemplating—being worlds apart, neither could know nor would know what was transpiring in each of their lives, yet one day, her time here would end, and she would see Mary once again. The thoughts did cross her mind of Mary worrying, not being able to get in touch with her— despite this, Cateline had stressed to her friend of her need for time alone to think. "Surely," thinking to herself, "Mary will perceive that I separated myself deliberately and will contact her when the time is right." With those thoughts behind her, she pulled out her diary to make entries. After some time, Cateline stopped writing and lay down, swiftly drifting off to sleep.

Early the following morning, Cateline was awakened by Sarah pulling back the draperies. Arising from the bed, she felt as if she had just gone to sleep, yawning, Cateline thought to herself, "I feel drained. It is going to be a long day!"

Dressing for the day, she decided her attire would be somewhat simple with her hair down, no fuss—not putting much effort into her looks at that moment. Cateline was still so tired from the late night of talking and knew she could have slept a few more winks, at least. Heading down to breakfast, everyone was there waiting for her. "I am so sorry, I am late. I was clearly so invigorated last night that I had a hard time falling asleep."

"It's quite alright, my dear." Uncle Walsh said.

"Good morning, brother James—oh, Cyrus, you are here awfully early."

"Yes, I will be here all day to help where needed."

Mr. Walsh, glancing over at Cyrus, with a tedious laugh, responded, "You know your help was not needed." Turning away to address James, he concluded, "Cyrus could not wait to see you, James."

"Well, of course, father—it is good for a change to have another man that is closer to my age," he responded back to his father with a smile.

Once breakfast concluded, conversations subsided while everyone became relatively quiet. Suspecting she was not the only one that was still fatigued from this week, Cateline spoke up, "It seems that we could all use a bit of rest, for I know that we are not at a loss for words. Should we go to the veranda to relax?"

With an insignificant laugh, Uncle Walsh added, "I do say that I look forward to Sunday, where we can make up for lost sleep. Yes, let's go to the veranda. Joseph, please have Clara bring out tea."

"Yes, sir," Joseph responded and turned towards the kitchen.

It was a most refreshing and pleasant day. The bright sun shone down upon the grounds with a slight breeze filling the air, circulating the aroma from the gardens full in bloom with various arrays of flowers. The family was all seated in an area of somewhat small tables and chairs, which they turned towards the gardens to have a spectacular view while enjoying the beauty of the day. The elevenses soon arrived, and the discussions commenced once again, with everyone quite content on such a lovely and agreeable day as it was.

Cateline, looking over at Anya, it was most apparent that she, too, was wearied. "I see that you also decided to wear a very simple dress, more for comfort today, I presume."

"Yes, it was a matter of ease this morning, my sweet cousin."

"I suppose this is simply going to be a very relaxed day, Anya."

"Yes, I believe I am as drained as you. I did not feel like doing much to myself this morning, and besides, I think Amos will not be here until tomorrow to assist."

Being interrupted in their discourse, Cyrus commented, "Well girls, James and I decided that we are going to play a game of poona with brother and sister teamed to play against each other. We will see what team will be able to win."

Anya speaking up, "And, what makes you think that Cateline and I will join you?"

"Of course, you will join us, dear sister—James is company after all and needs to be entertained; you wouldn't say no to family—one which you have not seen in a while, would you?"

Anya, before responding, looked over at James, who was smiling about this time, "Well, alright, I suppose we can play."

"Cateline, have you ever played poona?" Cyrus inquired.

"I'm not even sure I know what poona is."

Laughing playfully, he responded, pointing in the direction of the lake, "We have the net set up on the lawns going towards the lake, do you see it?"

"Yes, it looks like a net for badminton."

"Well, you may call it that in America, but we are in Ireland, quite so! We refer to it as a game of poona."

"I see, and yes, I have played, and I'm not too bad at it either. So, it may clearly be that James and I will win!"

"Oh no, I can defeat James, I assure you," Cyrus noted.

"You just think you can, old man," he said with a most mischievous laugh, "ah—but I am younger and faster than you!"

"Well, I speculate the competition is on," Samuel spoke up with a laugh.

The two girls and boys went out on the grounds to where the net was placed while Cyrus brought the battledores and the shuttlecock. Tossing a battledore to all players, it did not take long for Cateline to understand the particulars of the odd, if truth be told, gadgets. As for the shuttlecock, it was somewhat of an unusual name and most peculiar in appearance. But if one were to hit the shuttlecock with the battledore, a point would definitely be scored— well, if it went over the net, that is. Laughing as gently as possible, hearing the silly names of the objects at hand, it did not take much time to figure it all out, but she certainly did not want to make fun of anyone; after all, this was a great history lesson.

They began playing with both her uncle and aunt sitting at the veranda watching the game. From time to time, when Cateline would look towards her uncle and aunt, she could see them having a marvelous moment of laughing at all the spirited maneuvers—and, yes, everyone was enjoying themselves most agreeably. The competitiveness between all the players was somewhat comical, yet it was also very entertaining. As the game continued, all participants were rather engaged and no longer had time to be observant of anyone watching, for they became terribly sincere about winning. The men kept score, and the match was on with whichever team won the most out of ten games, "Whew," Cateline thought, "unquestionably, we will all be exhausted if we aren't already."

It was only after a very short while, both girls called a break to change clothes. Walking back up to the veranda, Anya spoke in between, trying to catch her breath, "Father, this is much too hard for us girls, and it is unfair that we should have to play in these long dresses. Can we please go put on breeches just for the game? There is no one here but family."

Mr. Walsh thought for a moment and replied, "I quite agree! It is not fair; you girls dash upstairs and change."

Both girls took off running, while Samuel looked over at Martha, "Before you say anything, my dear—"

"No, no—I wasn't going to say anything."

"Frankly, I see nothing wrong with the breeches, and furthermore, I have never understood why women must wear what men deem to be proper. Even though it is the law, we are at home, so I approve merely for the game."

Upstairs, the girls went into Anya's room while she repeated a previous conversation, "Remember, I told you that I should have a few pairs that will fit you, which I have outgrown. Mine are custom-made and quite nice as they fit tightly to your frame. It is so much easier to play games and ride horses in the breeches."

"In America, women are not as confined to just wearing dresses for all occasions. We do wear a type of pants for riding horses, or at least some women do."

As Anya had supposed, there was a pair that she had outgrown, which fit Cateline perfectly. They hurriedly dressed and ran back down to the lawn.

Resuming the game, Cateline chided, "I suppose you boys will now be able to see that we girls can play as well as any of you."

"Boys! —you must be referring to your brother. This man and his sister are going to slam you and your boy."

"Ha-ha—you know what I mean, Cyrus. James is clearly as big as you, and remember, he is younger and faster!"

The game persisted while the family watched on, enjoying the entertainment with much laughter, all four running, tripping, and falling with such merriment, the girls giggled preposterously. Oh, the amusement and joviality, how Samuel loved seeing his family enjoy good days such as these. Breaking his thoughts, Joseph came out to the veranda and disclosed, "Mr. Walsh, there is a Mr. Wilde here to see you."

"Yes, thank you, Joseph, please show him out here and be sure to bring us a bottle of Port—that sounds mighty fine for this time of day."

"Yes, sir."

"Oh dear, Samuel, you did not tell me he would be here today."

"Well, I suppose that slipped my mind."

"But dear, the girls are in breeches."

"Martha, I am sure he has seen women in breeches—you do understand who his mother is, why she has been fighting for women's rights for many years. If it was left to her, they would all be wearing breeches."

"Yes, dear, I am sure you are right. Well, I am going to leave you, men, to yourself."

"You do not wish to stay?"

"No, I do still have a few items to tend to before tomorrow, dear. So, please, enjoy your visit with Mr. Wilde."

Oscar Wilde was led out to the veranda, with Mr. Walsh standing to shake his hand, "Mr. Wilde, it has been a long time. You are looking very well. I am so glad that you could join us. Was your journey long?"

"The journey was not too unpleasant. I did stay over in Liverpool with a friend for a few days, and then I sailed to Dublin in which I arrived yesterday. I stayed again with a friend here last night who has just brought me to your estate—and so, I would say that I am fairly well-rested."

"Well, wonderful! If I had known, you could have come yesterday."

"That is quite alright; I am seldom in Ireland a great deal—the visit with friends was utterly agreeable."

"That is most fitting to know."

Joseph returned with the Port, filling two glasses.

"A glass of Port, Mr. Wilde?"

"Yes, thank you, sir."

"Please, Samuel will do."

"Thank you, Samuel, and by all means, Oscar is quite sufficient, sir."

"One of my servants, I am assuming, took your bags up to one of our guest rooms?"

"Yes, sir, and thank you so much for your most generous offer to stay at your estate."

"I wouldn't have it any other way; your father was such a good friend of mine and was much admired. I hear you are doing very well in London?"

"Yes, sir—Samuel, things seem to be very well and most prosperous for me at this time."

"Glad to hear it. My niece, who I wrote to you about, is entirely engaged in a game of poona," he noted while motioning towards those frolicking about on the lawn. "She is such a lovely girl and so very accomplished. You will have to excuse my daughter and Cateline; I did give them permission to wear breeches just for the game. Never understood why women were so limited to what they can wear."

"I couldn't agree more; I am afraid that is so true. And I believe they seem to be having a most splendid time."

"Yes, that is my son and daughter on the one team; you remember both of them, I am sure."

"Yes, but it has been some time."

"The other boy is James McCarthy, who is Cateline's half-brother. I think you might have met him before. He is from Youghal."

"I believe I have. He is fairly young, or so it seems."

"Yes, I imagine he has turned one and twenty recently."

Samuel and Oscar maintained their conversation while keeping their eyes on the game. Oscar, extremely fascinated watching the girls, as they were giggling most hysterically, falling on occasions, but with every fall, they would get back up, laugh it off and continue. It was apparent that Cyrus and James were both pretty amused, carrying on and only agitating the girls more and more, as it seemed to provide for better amusement, which was entirely enjoyable for all spectators, as Samuel and Oscar definitely were. The entertainment resumed with screams and yells while Cyrus shouted out the number of games, keeping up with their scores. The merriment maintained, the shrieking, giggling, laughs, and many expressions on the girl's faces, which, by the way, seemed to be much more driven and fueled by the boys. "They are undeniably competitive. I cannot remember when I have seen such spirited girls compelled to fight so hard to win. I do believe I have not watched anything quite as pleasurable, Samuel."

Samuel, while laughing, replied, "Agreed, agreed, I believe I am having as much fun as they are—merely observing."

"Yes, I do concur," Oscar spoke with an invigorating laugh, as he continued, "in fact, I am rather glad I am on this side of the game; it does seem to be such tedious work. So much more enjoyable as a spectator, Samuel, sir."

"Yes, quite so, Oscar, quite so!"

The tumbles and falls endured throughout the game, along with laughs and giggles. There was a time when Cateline held onto the shuttlecock while taking a tumble, rolling over where she concealed the device underneath her body, refusing to get up. Yet, being tickled, she soon loosened her grip, and the fight renewed. Yes, it was a sight to see, and it was utterly humorous for both Samuel and Oscar as they watched nonstop while laughing boisterously. Oscar was captivated not only by Cateline's temperament but also her beauty as he thought to himself, "She could easily pass for nineteen or twenty, but I believe he had told me that she was four and twenty. If anything, his letter did not go in-depth enough to how beautiful she was and an American girl at that. Of course, of Irish descent but raised in America." Oscar was taken with her beauty considerably, and with the breeches on, it was evident she had a very slender frame and smooth silk-like skin of the most delicate features.

Once the game had ended, and Cateline and James won, jumping up and down ecstatically, she screamed with joy for triumphing over her cousin Cyrus. They had been having such a great time and were unaware of being watched by anyone other than Mr. Walsh. Walking towards the veranda, the two men stood to greet them. Cateline leaning over to speak quietly to Anya, "Who is that man with your father?"

"I'm not sure, Cateline. Is that not Oscar Wilde?"

"Oh no, please tell me it isn't."

As they drew near, Cateline soon realized the other gentleman was, in fact, Oscar Wilde. Feeling quite embarrassed by her appearance, simply mortified, she wondered while leaning over to whisper to Anya, "How long has he been watching us carrying on so childishly, Anya? Oh, I am so embarrassed. Did your father know all along he was coming and purposely did not tell me?"

"If he did, he did not tell me either."

Cateline, stepping onto the veranda, Oscar stood gazing at her with the most amazing eyes. Having the upper hand in this situation, one could tell that he was enjoying himself by the candid look on his face when her uncle spoke up, "Cateline, I seemed to have forgotten to mention that I did hear back from Mr. Wilde. And he most graciously accepted the invitation to your welcoming party. Of course, I told him to arrive early since it was such a long journey where he could be well rested for tomorrow's event. Oscar, this is my niece Cateline and Cateline, Oscar Wilde."

"It's very nice to meet you, but I see that my uncle seems to find all of this rather amusing, knowing that I would not have been out there tumbling around like a tomboy in breeches at that," she said, looking down at her clothes and also realizing how undone her hair must be. She continued, gazing towards Uncle Walsh, "If I had known we were expecting other company, uncle?"

Her uncle, laughing somewhat roguishly, looked from Cateline over to his daughter, son, and James, where he admonished, "Oscar came here to meet Cateline, let us all go in where we can have our luncheon and give them time to become acquainted. I will have food served on the veranda, Cateline, for you and Oscar."

Cyrus shook Oscar's hand before walking into the estate, "It's been a long time; we will definitely have to reconnect before you leave."

"Quite so; I will be here for a few days."

"Yes, and I will be here to help with the festivity. I look forward to hearing about your time at Oxford and London."

With the family leaving the veranda, Oscar formally extended his hand, taking Cateline's in his. While bending over to bestow a light kiss, he spoke candidly, "Cateline, it is my pleasure in meeting you. I have very much enjoyed watching the game. You are quite lovely. I also think you look simply delightful in breeches," teasingly he added, praising her with a cunning wink.

"Please, you are merely trying to be polite, but I feel very awkward. My uncle should have told me that we were expecting company, for I fear that I am not presentable to meet anyone looking as I do. Before I sit to enjoy your company, would you mind if I excuse myself so that I can freshen up? I promise that I will not be too awfully long."

"I find you absolutely divine as you are, but if you must go clean up, I will be here waiting."

"Thank you. I shall return shortly, and please, make yourself at home."

Cateline, walking into the estate, saw her uncle and gave him a look, which only contributed to more amusement and laughter as he regarded the whole scenario. Thinking to himself, Samuel perceived, "Very successful, I do believe—I could not have planned it to be any more prolific. He has been given the taste of seeing her in a natural state, most enjoyable at that."

Considering the trouble her uncle went to, Cateline decided to make an abrupt comment, "You might as well go and keep him company while I clean up since you failed to mention that he was even coming."

As her uncle continued to laugh, he headed back out to the veranda to have another glass of wine with Oscar and to learn of his exploits.

131

Once Cateline was upstairs cleaning up, she thought to herself, "I cannot believe that my uncle never even communicated to me that he had heard back from Oscar Wilde." Being a bit nervous, Cateline was also very happy as everything she had thought about while in America, all the dreams over the years, her hopes and desires, finally, they seemed to be coming true. With the excitement arising within, the uncertainty of what would happen from this point, Cateline knew deep inside that she was there for Oscar and could not help but feel emotions for this man—the one and only beautiful being she had ever truly loved in that way. Cateline picked out a dress for the rest of the afternoon and sat down to at least clean up a bit and brush out her long hair. There was no need to put it up so late in the day; adding a bit of powder and rouge, she headed back downstairs.

CHAPTER
11

Cateline, walking out to the veranda, observed her uncle seated across from Oscar with both men in profound discourse, not noticing her until she was almost upon them. They quickly stood to greet her, as was the routine in those days. Her uncle excused himself so that Oscar and Cateline could have time alone, remarking with a quaint smile upon exiting, "She does clean up very well, Oscar." At the same time, Cateline affectionately gave him a kiss on the cheek, where he would know she still loved him despite the unexpected visitor. "I will leave you two to become acquainted," Samuel proclaimed, walking back into the estate.

"Your uncle seems to be a perfectly splendid man, quite honorable, I am sure. As for you, my dear, exquisitely charming, Cateline, but I do assert that you were rather intoxicating even before refreshing yourself," Oscar noted admirably.

"Thank you for the compliment. I am assuming you are in town for the dinner party tomorrow?"

"Yes, I did receive an invitation, but in defense, I assure you that I sent a reply."

"Oh, I am sure you did, and I am almost certain my uncle purposely did not acknowledge this to me with his aim being that this would be a surprise."

"I find it even more fascinating that you were not expecting me, as I was able to see you out of your element, so to speak. I do hope that you are not offended by my arrival without your knowledge."

"On the contrary, I wanted him to invite you, for I do admire your work and the articles circulating in America about you and the aesthetic movement. I, too, am very much interested in the arts," she responded most politely with a slight smile, "I knew you would be in America next year, but I also knew you would be surrounded by so many that I would not have been able to meet you."

"Ah, but if I had noticed you in America, I would have approached cordially desiring an introduction."

"You say that, but when one is surrounded by so many, one does not have time to observe their surroundings."

133

"I assure you, Miss Cateline, I am always aware of my surroundings. Although, be as it may, fate has seemed to bring us together, has it not?"

"Part of that fate was the fact that my dear uncle knew your father very well. When I learned that truth, I thought there might be a chance that you would attend."

"Your uncle's letter intrigued me; I must have picked it up and read it many times."

"My dear sweet uncle, you know that he looks upon me as being quite more than I am."

"I would have to say, Cateline, my dear, I have yet to see that his words concerning you were exaggerated at all. Your beauty is rather captivating, as well as your mannerism. I have not heard you sing nor play the pianoforte and guitar, but I assure you that I am much interested in your accomplishments. You also write poetry, I am told?"

"I do love to write. I have written poetry and short stories, mainly, but I am sure that my uncle is biased, even though I do have some accomplishments. All the same, I am reasonably sure there are others far more talented than myself."

"Ah, tomorrow is your debut, my dear. If, in fact, you are as gifted as your uncle declares, you shall be well received not only for your performance but your beauty as well, and I should take delight to observe your skills this evening, if you would consent, before your unveiling at the gala."

"That is my uncle for you. He knows that I had no desire to be in the spotlight at the social event, but that is exactly where he plans to put me. As for this evening, I do say, my dear sweet uncle will more than likely insist that I perform on both the piano and guitar."

Clara, interrupting their discourse, walked out onto the veranda carrying a tray of light sandwiches along with other items since it was still a considerable amount of time before the afternoon tea would be served.

"Thank you very much, Clara," Cateline politely noted.

Their conversations continued where they discussed various subjects mainly to include different aspects of the arts and culture from Dublin to London. When Cateline suddenly inquired, "I don't suppose that my uncle also offered you a room here at the estate, or will you be staying with family while in Dublin?"

With a slight laugh, Oscar responded, "I am afraid that is another aspect your uncle failed to mention. He has invited me to be their guest while here if I so desired."

"Oh, he did, did he? My uncle is so full of surprises."

"You are disappointed?"

"No, of course not. I only wonder why my uncle went to so much trouble to get you here. Not that I am not pleased; on the contrary, I did so want to meet you because I feel as though we both have much in common. In America, there are not as many who love the arts as in Europe. I just find everything so fascinating that I read about in London and Paris, to include the diverse eras—Georgian—Victorian."

"You plan to visit both London and Paris, I presume?"

"Why yes, I very much want to experience both cities."

"You will discover—while in London one hides everything, in Paris one reveals everything." [1]

"How interesting; I will try to remember that."

Discussions continued with neither running out of things to say when Oscar reached out and took one of her hands, which made her somewhat nervous, while he inquired, "Do you mind?"

"Umm, no, not at all—," unsure of what to say.

"Your hands are very lovely; I could not resist. They are as elegant as can be and so very soft."

Blushing, she answered in a gentle voice, "Well, thank you. I've never really had anyone say that."

"That is hard for me to believe. Your beauty is quite rare. Perhaps men in America are not romantic?"

"I am sure there are men in America who are romantic but perhaps not as many as in Europe."

"Ah, I have been watching you from the first moment I arrived; I do not believe I have seen such beauty in all of Dublin nor London."

"You shouldn't say those things, Mr. Wilde. I'm sure there are much prettier ladies in London than myself."

"Yes, there are beautiful ladies, quite so—yet I find something rare about you, which brings about a strange feeling. Indeed, you certainly are different. I haven't a clue what that quality you possess may be despite everything, but I do know that I am quite taken with what I have seen thus far, and I do rather look forward to being in your company while here." Picking up the bottle of Port while speaking in his charming dialect, his words were most admirable, "Please, enjoy a glass of wine with me." While pouring two glasses, he maintained, "You know I have to agree with your uncle."

"Why, Mr. Wilde, I am not sure what you mean. In studying me, thus far, what have you determined?"

"Miss Cateline, there are many fascinating things in life. In observing you, I have found you to be just as enticing and attractive playing poona as I do right now, viewing you adorned in your splendid attire—freshened exquisitely," he spoke radiantly with a boyish smile. "You were most impressive playing with your cousins and brother, if I do say so—very competitive!"

Cateline responded, with a playful smile, "Competitive? — Why Mr. Wilde, I do believe you and my uncle have had quite a laugh, as you watched me in those breeches striving hard to win—even though we girls were at such a disadvantage to the gentlemen. I probably have a few battle scars that contributed to my playing so hard to win along with my younger brother at my side, of course. However, being the weaker sex, Anya and I did rather well today."

"Unquestionably, I would have to agree with you, Miss Cateline; I hope that you do not mind if I address you in that way, and please, Oscar will do."

"Please, call me Cateline."

"Cateline, a lovely name. I am afraid I must be quite sincere, when I received your uncle's letter, it intrigued me deeply in the way he described you. Initially, I thought nothing more about the letter until I read it once more, and then it seemed to capture my soul where I was drawn back to it again and again." Oscar's words lingered while his expressions were fashioned in such a way, with a bright smile and a most clever laugh. "I determined, after much thought, that I must travel to make your acquaintance where I could discover for myself if what your uncle spoke had any truth to it."

"And Oscar, what have you determined?"

"I do believe my countenance reveals my perceptions, Cateline. I am not at all sorry that I am here, on the contrary. Shall we walk the grounds and become acquainted? It is such a pleasant day."

"Yes, that would be enjoyable, I am sure," Cateline rose from the table while Oscar refilled both glasses with Port.

Reaching for his oversized fur coat, he handed it to Cateline, "Please, my coat is rather comfortable. You may wear it if you would like; it will certainly be beneficial with the slight chill lingering this afternoon."

Cateline took the coat graciously and slipped her arms into the warmth of fur while recognizing it to be the one in so many of his pictures, "Thank you, Oscar, I do believe this is the coziest and most wonderful coat I have yet to see since I have arrived."

"It is quite simple—for I do have the simplest tastes, and I am always satisfied with the best."[2] His face gleamed with each ingenious remark, and while Cateline met his dreamy eyes, she, too, was left with a smile at his clever wit. He then stood up and handed her one of the glasses while holding his own. Taking her arm in his, he led her down towards the lake. Noticing her splendid smile, Oscar inquired, "You are holding back laughter. Is it something I said?"

"I'm sorry, no—not at all; I was simply admiring your accent. Is that the English brogue?"

"Ah, no—it is the Oxbridge. At Oxford, my Irish accent was soon misplaced,"[3] smiling, he probed, "and, your accent, that would be Bostonian?"

"Not entirely, but yes, you could say so, I suppose."

Their discussions continued, with both having so much to say. It did not take long for them to realize they had a great deal in common. Oscar already knew he was completely taken with her beauty, as well as her grace and passions. At one point, Cateline, with a dazzling smile, spoke most sincerely, "I am delighted that you were able to leave London and attend."

"After reading your uncle's letter over and over, I knew I had to come and see for myself if such a distinguished creature could possibly exist, and here you are, a hidden gem. I was very intrigued, for you are as pleasant as described. And I do look forward to being entertained with your accomplishments this evening. I am sure that I shall not be disappointed, quite certain your attributes shall be as exquisite as your beauty. What a tragedy it would have been if I had never come and met you."

Cateline blushed while exclaiming, "My uncle is inclined to see me as much more than is perceived. I do not feel that I am as talented, and surely there are girls in Ireland and England that have more admirable looks than myself."

"Perhaps, but it is still somewhat rare for one to be as accomplished, as well. Yes, many may be as you say, but beauty as flawless as yourself, along with the accomplishments, are prone to be exceedingly scarce."

137

"Oscar, I am sure if you were around me long enough, you would also see my faults."

"Please, never mention faults. Behold the strengths and qualities in yourself; why should you look for that which does not benefit your improvements?"

Many things were discussed as they became acquainted, a few laughs here and there, but their interests seemed to captivate the desire to engage in much-longwinded discourse. Conversations ranged from the various periods and movements, the Renaissance to the Aesthetics, and others before and in between. Cateline, not as versed in the Aesthetics as Oscar, voiced areas of agreement and others of concern. The debate on the topics opened broad areas of discussion with both detailing their opinions, beliefs, and passions, above all, their love for the arts in all of its diverse forms.

"Like you, Oscar, I do love the arts in all aspects. Yet, I also believe that the Bible is the oldest form of art, magnificently created by God. If one believes in God, they must love art. After all, He made everything visible in all of its glory—and yes, brilliantly our world in all of its splendor, fashioned by Him. Everything in this world in its natural form is beautiful—the mountains and plateaus, the seas and the rivers, all of creation to include man. You look around at our world, and it is glorious. You search years back and read words written by poets and novelists. Then you look at the beauty of art on canvas from Michelangelo to Leonardo DaVinci, extraordinary—songs sung, plays created—all the wonders of our universe. Why yes, it is all art. And its beginning goes back to our Creator, but then you take yourself, Oscar Wilde—your life and your words impact many from your gifts and talents, all things which were bestowed upon you by God. I believe we all have gifts, and we all have a purpose, but it still goes back to that one book—the Bible, the oldest form of art in itself."

"Cateline, we all grow up being taught to believe what our parents believe, and then what the church believes. Do you ever question what you were taught as a child? Do you ever wonder if perhaps there are areas that you were taught which are not true?"

"Yes, absolutely, and you are no different than I am. Many simply go through life holding on to what they were taught, and then there are those, like you and I, we probe, and we live out our life with reservations, seeking and inquiring even more. That is the beauty of life, and it is what we are supposed to do. No one should grow up from their childhood and just live out their lives, believing everything they were taught. The Bible even tells us that we are to seek Him ourselves. It is not about seeking a church or anything else. It is about seeking one on one for those hidden truths. I can't say that I have all the answers—if I did, I would not be reading and contemplating other aspects out there, such as the distinct eras and their beliefs and the diverse movements and their purpose. We are all given a mind, and we all have the capacity to think, but most people go through life and merely hold onto what they have been taught without seeking anything further. I remember being told as I was growing up, *'Cateline, what you believe and trust in today that will change tomorrow, and then what you believe in when you are twenty will change when you are thirty.'* Yes, even what I believe today as truth, I can look back several years, and it was different. That is the good part, as we keep growing and learning, our beliefs keep changing, as well."

Oscar was quiet as he listened to everything she was saying. After a few minutes, Cateline resumed, "It is also such a shame because there are so many out there that have gifts and talents which were bestowed by God, and yet, they never seem to find them. Those gifts are deep within one's soul—from the heart. I read something years ago that helped me to understand—if I can remember it accurately, *'It's like the wind, you cannot see it, but you can feel it because it is all around you and you know it is there.'* Yes, it's the same thing with those who are gifted in many areas, it happens and is possible because it was always buried deep down inside, but once it is revealed, it comes alive in them and begins to pour out from their soul—just like the wind. They feel it in their inner being because it speaks to their soul—God speaks to their heart. If one could stand in front of a mirror and see not only their outward reflection but the reflection of the heart from within."

Oscar continued to listen intently as he persistently thought about what she was saying. At the same time, Cateline maintained, "There are moments when I do not even understand the words from within, which I then put down on paper, but I know they have meaning, and I know the meaning will come at some point. As I meditate on what I write, eventually, the words come alive, and I am able to see, to understand. It was always there, but I did not know it because I could not see it." There was a brief pause, and then she resumed, "When I write, it comes from deep within, and even I do not always know nor understand what I am writing—but it's there, and sometimes it's deep. I feel it, but I cannot see it, for it is like the wind. It is at this place where it comes alive in me. It is in this that one can express their self, who they truly are because it is inside of them—born from God's Spirit."

Oscar spoke cordially, "I love listening to your words—I cannot ever remember hearing a woman voice such things. You are indeed fascinating, and yes—I know what that feels like inside myself. And, I do believe it is a gift. However, I am not sure if you are familiar with William Wordsworth, but he felt the poet should learn from nature, not from books. In his poem *The Tables Turned,* Wordsworth believed those who were poets reflected back to nature as their teacher."

"Yes, I do agree that nature is the essence of the poet, where one must come back to their roots, back to that which was created by God naturally. Our world continually changes where man has become unfeeling to anything outside of civilization. I believe that Wordsworth made an accurate assertion in that man continues to become acclimated by inventions. More and more have lost sight of nature, by all means. When I write, I must be surrounded by creation. It is at those moments where my mind can wander, and the beauty of my surroundings come alive, then the words naturally flow."

"I do agree that one's mind must be silenced to the outside world where the imagination can be at work as the words do come from deep within one's soul. Wordsworth believed those who had that gift with words saw through what Plato referred to as the 'eye of the mind.'[4] I believe you would love his poem, *The Tables Turned.* I do know some of it—

> *Books! 'tis a dull and endless strife,*
> *Come, hear the woodland linnet,*
> *How sweet his music; on my life*
> *There's more of wisdom in it.*
>
> *One impulse from a vernal wood*
> *May teach you more of man;*
> *Of moral evil and of good,*
> *Than all the sages can.*[5]

There was silence for a moment while Cateline thought about the words in the poem, finally responding, "Oscar, that is so beautiful. Those words were from Wordsworth?"

"Yes. However, have you read much of his work?"

"Only briefly, I am afraid. It is spoken with such passion."

"His words are spoken with passion, deep conviction. However, if we take nature to mean natural simple instinct as opposed to self-conscious culture, the work produced under this influence is always old-fashioned, antiquated, and out of date. One touch of nature may make the whole world kin, but two touches of nature will destroy any work of art. If, on the other hand, we regard nature as the collection of phenomena external to man, people only discover in her what they bring to her. She has no suggestions of her own. Wordsworth went to the lakes, but he was never a lake poet. He found in stones the sermons he had already hidden there. He went moralizing about the district, but his good work was produced when he returned, not to nature but to poetry. Poetry gave him *Laodamia*, and the fine sonnets, and the great *Ode*, such as it is. Nature gave him *Martha Ray* and *Peter Bell*, and the address to Mr. Wilkinson's spade.[6] Yet, I see that you are most passionate in your artistic gifts— I, too, the great passion of my life is my writings, the love to which all other loves were as marsh-water to red wine."[7]

"I have to say, I do like your choice of words. I am rather passionate when it comes to fulfilling my gifts. Love of all the arts and the glimpse into history's past of many of the greats—why the Renaissance period, for instance, I believe it holds the wonders of some of the most glorious works of art by some of the most distinguished artists in history. Are you familiar with the German composer Mendelssohn?"

"I know what you are going to say," he responded, *"this is what I think art is and what I demand of it: that it pulls everyone in, that it shows one person another's most intimate thoughts and feelings, that it throws open the window of the soul."*[8]

"Yes," she agreed, "but, he also said, *'life and art are NOT two different things.'*[9] I cannot even fathom how anyone cannot be captivated by that period. No, it may not be 'Art for Art's Sake,' spoken by Shakespeare, was it not?"[9]

"Ah yes, Art for Art's Sake, the rendition of the French slogan, l'art pour l'art, which was coined by Victor Cousin,[9] the

French philosopher, and Shakespeare did use it, along with many others, Samuel Coleridge and Edgar Allan Poe—" [10]

"L'art pour l'art, hmm, yes, the phrase has become quite known," she added, continuing, "I believe without it—well, we would have lost a precious and valuable link to our past. The Aesthetic movement brought this to the light, yes?"

"Undeniably, many continue to strive to educate the world on the movement, myself included. Aestheticism is a search after the signs of the beautiful—to speak more exactly, the search after the secret of life.[12] Aesthetics are higher than ethics. They belong to a more spiritual sphere. To discern the beauty of a thing is the finest point to which one can arrive."[11]

As they continued their walk, there were moments they paused, observing the gardens while enjoying their conversations as both shared and laughed—regarding themselves so much alike in many ways. Soon they approached the bench which overlooked the lake; sitting down next to each other, they felt moderately relaxed. The discussions remained going from serious talks to personal beliefs, which brought giggles and laughter at times. After some moments, both had ceased sharing and began to just enjoy their surroundings, "It is a most pleasing day, is it not?" Cateline spoke quietly.

"Yes, a most striking scenery," he agreed, turning to face her before inquiring, "would you mind if I smoke?"

"No, of course not. I am sure that would be alright. My uncle does have a smoking area off from his study, where he smokes his cigars. I do know that my aunt is very adamant about not smoking in the estate itself, but you should be fine to do so out here," she remarked.

Lighting up his cigarette, he queried, "Does the smoke bother you?"

"No, I am not bothered by it, Oscar."

Cateline continued to speak on distinctive subjects while Oscar listened with a stunningly agreeable smile, enchanted by her beauty as well as her fervent energy and obviously her desires on various topics—topics that were also passionate to him.

Finally, watching his body language, she asked, "Why are you smiling at me like that?"

With a slight laugh, he answered very distinctly, "Youth smiles without any reason. It is one of its chiefest charms."[13]

"I am being very serious; why are you smiling at me?"

"Truly, I find you absolutely delightful. I am not sure I have ever met anyone quite like you—so passionate for life, extremely intoxicating, and refreshing, my dear. I dare leave Dublin without knowing there shall be other days and nights to spend by your side, as I find myself loving every moment shared with you, Cateline. I do believe you are the most enchanting person I have yet to meet. I would have to say that I have no regrets making this journey from London."

Cateline gazing up into his radiantly blue eyes, replied, "You are most gracious Oscar, and I, too, find myself desiring to have other days where we can become more acquainted. Do you have to leave soon to go back to London?"

"No, I can do what I do from anywhere, really. My life is far from idle wherever I may be. One can merely work hard as he rides in the row at ten o'clock in the morning, goes to the Opera three times a week, changes his clothes at least five times a day, and dines out every night of the season. You would not call that leading an idle life, would you?[14] For, I have always been of the opinion that hard work is simply the refuge of people who have nothing whatever to do.[15] In my opinion, when one has talent, it always takes hard work for the creative class. Why the mind never shuts down but continually is at work, wouldn't you say?"

"Quite so, I would have to agree, Oscar."

"Back to the subject, I have no immediate plans where I must return at a particular time to London. And yourself, will you be leaving to return to America anytime soon?"

"No, not at all. I planned to stay for quite some time. In fact, my plans include exploring Ireland to some extent and then heading into England and perhaps France. I also intend to go to Youghal, as that is where my brother James lives in my father's estate. I would like to see his estate before leaving Ireland."

"I would be most honored to be your escort in Dublin, for there are many sights, some being historical that I do believe would be most agreeable to you since we both seem to have the same passions. If you would do me the honor, I would very much love to spend my waking moments with you following the days after the dinner party. We could explore the city and perhaps the surrounding suburbs as well."

"Yes, I would love for you to be my guide to experience Dublin and the suburbs. Was there a timeframe that my uncle said you could stay?"

"Your uncle merely acknowledged that I was welcome to stay as long as I liked. If that is a problem, I do have other places I could stay."

"I wouldn't think it would be a problem. It is evident that he wanted us to meet."

"And I am so glad that he did," Oscar noted while he smiled aesthetically at Cateline.

Oscar and Cateline spent a considerable amount of their day together, talking and laughing immensely. Finally, being interrupted, Clara came out of the estate to let them know the afternoon tea had been set out a few hours prior, and Mr. Walsh had asked for dinner to be served earlier. With that cue, Cateline thought perhaps they should retire into the estate to spend time with the family. Taking her arm, Oscar escorted her back to the residence.

Within a short while, dinner was served in the formal dining parlor with all being seated; Mr. Walsh gave grace. During the course of the meal, the menfolk seemed to be much engaged in Oscar's life in London as the women listened on. There were intense discussions and enlightened ones, with many inquiries about his articles and columns published in London. With much enjoyment of his works, everyone was so engaged with questions, laughs, and comments. At one point, Mr. Walsh asked about his upcoming plans for America the following year, which brought more questions and much discourse. Oscar inquired of Cateline's opinion as to the various states and cities in America where he would be traveling. "I am not at all sure that I am your best guide to elaborate on the locations that you will generally be touring. However, there are many impressive universities from coast to coast, and from what I do know, your presence will be most welcomed, along with your knowledge of the aesthetic movement. The people are generally friendly, but I am sure that your presence will be of great importance and much welcomed regardless of what state. I, myself, have not traveled extensively to many locations in America. Primarily just the east coast area and one time to Louisiana. How long would you be in America?"

"I was told many months to complete the tour from the east coast to California and back."

"I am assuming they will be compensating you very well for all the speaking engagements," Mr. Walsh declared.

"Yes—the pay is to be most sufficient, sir."

Conversations continued as Oscar's life was truly fascinating, and everyone was so attentive to his tales thus far, even past dinner. Eventually, Mr. Walsh expressed, "Let us continue this discussion in the drawing-room, shall we?"

With everyone gathering into the room to relax, Mr. Walsh stated, "Cateline, my dear, I am sure that Oscar would love to hear you entertain us with song and music."

"Yes," Oscar agreed, "I believe that is one of the reasons I am here. Please do us the honor on the pianoforte."

"We have become quite accustomed to listening to her songs and have found them most enjoyable," her uncle remarked.

"Uncle Walsh, please, you make me out to be so gifted, but really many in America play as well as I do. Besides, I am certain Oscar has heard countless others with distinguished talent in London."

"That may be so, my dear, but we are most honored to have you and enjoy your playing. Please do us the honor, and besides, I know Oscar desires to hear you play and sing on the guitar, as well. Am I right?"

"Yes, Samuel, I did come far and would greatly take pleasure hearing all of Cateline's accomplishments. After all, I would dare to leave back for London and not have had the privilege and delight of her performing."

"I am sorry to interrupt, but I believe I am going to head out," Cyrus spoke apologetically, continuing, "tomorrow will be a big day, and I will be back in the morning, father."

"You are more than welcome to stay here if you would like, son."

"No, sir, I am too close to home, and Isabella is expecting me. Thank you anyway."

Upon his leaving, Cateline sat down at the piano and played Beethoven's *Moonlight Sonata*. Everyone listened intently as the sounds were beautiful. Playing one more on the pianoforte, she chose a most exquisite song by Franz Schubert, *Serenade*.

Afterward, Cateline stood up to address the family and guest cordially, "Thank you very much," looking at Anya, she resumed, "My dear cousin, it is your turn to grace us with your accomplishments."

Anya walked to the pianoforte and played a few songs while Cateline sat back down next to Oscar. "I do believe you are most accomplished on the pianoforte, Cateline. I look forward to your playing the guitar and to hear you sing as well—tonight?"

"Well, since you asked so sweetly, I suppose I cannot say no!"

After Anya rose from the pianoforte, Cateline picked up her guitar to play one song for Oscar. She chose *The End of the World,* a 1960s song by Brenda Lee.[16] The words were a love song, not meant for any particular reason—just a tune Cateline thought to be mellow. She sang the first chorus while playing the melody on her guitar. For the 60s, it was a gentle melody with lyrics that told of a broken love, but Cateline sang each verse as if from her heart. While she continued, everyone was very attentive to the very last chorus. Afterward, leaning her guitar against the piano, she went back to sit next to Oscar, who at that moment was most taken with her unique style and talent.

Aunt Martha declared, "I've never heard such a song. It seemed like a sorrowful love story to me."

"Well, yes, they do have songs as such in America," Cateline noted.

"I thought it was wonderful, Cateline," Oscar said as he leaned over and quietly inquired, "were the words meant for someone back in America?"

She responded cleverly, "Oh no, I am not brokenhearted over anyone in America. I merely think the song is very pretty."

"I am pleased to know this, and as I had assumed, your musical voice is heavenly—sweet mellow notes, all the assertive ecstasy that one desires to hear, the genius of nightingales resonating in wild passion. Your skills will bring forth much delight to all the guests tomorrow."

Mr. Walsh stood and announced, "Martha, I think it is time to retire. We have a big day tomorrow."

"I couldn't agree more, Samuel," she replied while rising from her chair.

"Oscar, my boy, you are all settled in your room on the third floor?"

"Yes, sir. Thank you very much."

"Cateline tells me that you do enjoy your cigarettes. So, by all means, feel free to smoke in your room. It is far enough away from the rest of the estate; Martha should not care."

"Thank you, sir; I will make sure that I open a window when I do smoke."

"Yes, that is most kind and, please do not hesitate to let one of our servants know if you need anything."

"Thank you, Samuel, sir."

"I think I am following their lead, Cateline," Anya remarked, finishing, "don't stay up too late; it is your big day tomorrow."

"No, I won't stay up too late, goodnight Anya."

"Goodnight, see you tomorrow, and goodnight Oscar."

James was already half-asleep on the sofa; as he rubbed his eyes, following the other family members upstairs, he addressed his sister and Oscar, "See you tomorrow, sis, goodnight Oscar."

"Goodnight, James, sleep well."

"Yes, goodnight James," Oscar replied.

It became rather tranquil as Oscar and Cateline sat side by side, listening to the occasional crackle of the fire on the hearth. Finally, Oscar turned to face Cateline, which seemed strange and made her a bit nervous, trying not to show her emotions, when he spoke, "I have enjoyed my evening immensely. You are quite accomplished on the pianoforte and guitar," before Cateline could respond to his compliment, he lifted one of her hands with his own and began to recite—

"Her ivory hands on the ivory keys
Strayed in a fitful fantasy,
Like the silver gleam when the poplar trees
Rustle their pale leaves listlessly,
Or the drifting foam of a restless sea
When the waves show their teeth in the flying breeze."[17]

"That was most beautiful, Oscar, but you surprise me."

"Surprise you? Why do you say that, Cateline?"

147

"I am sure that you are around many who are most talented. Unfortunately, I am merely an amateur."

"I believe you have yet to see just how gifted you are. Beethoven—I loved his *Moonlight Sonata*. Do you play much of his music?"

"No, I really love his music and wish I knew more, but I only know a few. He was such a fascinating composer, don't you agree?"

"Yes, quite so."

"I believe he said something one time about those who compose music, that it was inspired by God. I truly believe that—do you?"

"Beethoven had many well thought out quotes. I know he believed his music was endowed by God," Oscar concurred.

"Yes, it is the same thing as writing, I believe so. I know myself that the words come from somewhere deep inside when I write."

"Yes, they do come from within. One who writes and writes well is such a gift. Beethoven said, *'Music is the bond that unites the life of the spirit to the life of the senses—melody is the sensitive life of the poet.'*" [17]

"Ah—yes, I have read that one," Cateline agreed, continuing, "I also like this one, *'Music is capable of reproducing in its real form, the pain that tears the soul and the smile that it inebriates.'*" [18]

"It brings me such delight to see one who loves the arts, as you do," he replied, continuing, "I do believe that you are most talented, and you sing like an angel."

"You are too kind, but thank you, Oscar," Cateline said as she faced him, mesmerized by the beauty of his long flowing hair, the warmth of his eyes, and the appeal of his well-shaped full lips.

While gazing into each other's eyes, Oscar took his hand and ran it through the long loose curls which hung down along her face before he spoke again, "I know we have only met, but there is just something about you. I feel as though I have known you all my life. You are most beautiful, but I am sure that is revealed to you quite often."

With a slight laugh, Cateline spoke, "Well, no—actually, I am seldom told. What I mean, truthfully, I have not been involved with anyone in America. And—yes, I do know what you mean. I feel as though I have also known you my whole life."

"I hope you don't mind me running my fingers through your hair. Well, I am sure that sounded odd, but it is so stunning. It glistens from the light of the hearth, streams of gold and radiant reds illuminating from the sparkle of each flame protruding fiercely, through the rich luster of your dark-brown flowing tresses in locks of curls. Your face lit with the energy of the effervescent fire, and your eyes blazed in dazzling blues, your crimson lips lustered with taints of moisture shining radiantly in the darkness which surrounds the room." He paused, with a teasingly slight smile, before stating, "Your hair is so lovely. A temptation which I am afraid will be most difficult to restrain myself to be a gentleman. After all, the only way to get rid of a temptation is to yield to it. Resist it, and your soul grows sick with longings for the thing it has forbidden to itself, with desire for what its monstrous laws have made monstrous and unlawful.[19] Yet, when you look at me with your dreamy blue eyes, it just does something to me. I feel like I have lost all control. I know, that sounds like a cliché that I must use with all girls," he finished with a most enigmatic smile as he withdrew his hand.

"I suppose I could say the same thing, for I feel the same way as you. I love your hair—long as it is, and you have the most gorgeous eyes—blue, as well. And I do love your expressions. For a man, your appearance is most striking. I know that may not be a *manly* thing to say, but I love to look at your face."

Both mesmerized with the other, Oscar once more began to feel her hair as he ran his fingers through the soft thick locks that lay loosely over her shoulders and on down her back. As they persisted, looking into each other's eyes, it was a most tranquil romantic scene; the warmth from the hearth could be felt running up and down their bodies along with the tingling feeling deep inside. The sizzling of the fire brought the realization that they were both there together and both feeling what the other felt. There was no way to describe that moment, for Cateline had never fathomed a moment as such. Oscar, on the other hand, had believed himself to have been in love once before, but no sooner than the love was felt, it was also taken away, ending as she had found another. Despite this, here he was, side by side with this American beauty. In the balminess of the room, the smell of embers mingled with his cologne and the quaint fragrance of her perfume, a most tranquil night, alone in the dark with only the light of the fire and the sound of crackling, sizzling, an occasional snapping and tumbling as the logs burned, blazed, and smoldered. The sound of inhaling and exhaling, their breaths mingled, and their eyes spoke volumes of words without sound, for neither understood their meanings nor their hearts at that moment. If thoughts could be read, what would be discovered—for those moments of intimacy with a mere touch of hands—a depth of meaning in eyes that transcend upon hearts unknown. Her thoughts were silent but burned within, "This moment—oh, this moment, have I dreamt, but yet I dare not to have known. For, from the depths of my heart, it has been kept secret but is understood. Where is my love, are you my own—have I waited, for you alone. Let this moment forever be true, and never will we part—my love for you—our hearts be true, for they, too, have known, known you, my love." Her thoughts continued screaming within as she had only dreamed of a moment like this, but the dream had merely a glimpse of the truth.

The moment went on for what seemed forever. Even so, it was not near long enough when Oscar finally spoke in a very soft and discreet voice, "Forgive me, I am quite sure that this is the time we need to say *goodnight,* or I am afraid I shall have no control over our lips meeting intimately."

"Yes, that may be a bit awkward since we just met today. And, we probably need to get some sleep," she responded in a still serene voice.

"Yes, tomorrow is your big day."

"It is actually for both of us, remember?"

"Ah, yes—but I believe those attending will be more pleased with your appearance than mine."

Cateline smiled warmly. Oscar picked up the chamberstick, lit the candle, and then took her arm as they walked up the stairs. He led her to her room and made sure her fire was rekindled. "Goodnight Cateline, until we meet tomorrow, your passions shall appease me through the night."

"Goodnight, Oscar, sweet dreams."

With a most agreeable smile, he kissed her on her forehead and walked out of the room. Cateline walked over to the vanity table, sat down to wash her face, and reminisce about the whole day from the time Oscar had arrived. Feeling a bit mysterious as she thought of what had thus transpired, Cateline smiled with pleasure, rose to dress for bed in her long nightgown before she sat at the davenport to record in her diary all the events of the day. Once she had completed her entries, she climbed under the sheets to lie down while continuing to envision her day with Oscar once more as all their talks continued to float through her mind. Those things he had spoken, she knew in her heart that this felt right—he felt right! Yes, she had loved this man her whole life and would love him forever.

CHAPTER
12

The day had finally arrived for the grand ball to honor Cateline and Oscar, the latter well-known in Dublin. Having already risen very early to assist with last-minute preparations before the evening, Samuel and Martha knew it was soon to be such a memorable day. All staff was busily about finalizing the layout of the entirety of the first floor of the estate to include the veranda vicinity. Chairs were being moved from the dining parlor to be arrayed throughout the saloon as additional seating. The long-oversized table was moved towards the back area of the elongated grandeur hallway, to one side, conveniently displayed just outside of the kitchen area where much of the elaborate spread of various courses would be organized. The exquisite French chef, Monsieur LeBeouf, busily prepared his wonderfully planned cuisine, ordering about the kitchen staff with assigned tasks while adhering to extreme detail. Chef LeBeouf, having arrived the day prior, many preparations had already taken place, as well as discussions for adequate layout throughout the spacious hallway to include removal of the lengthy rug. After adhering to such, the setup of the musician's station was situated in close proximity to the entrance of the morning room, towards the back of the copious hall, opposite the kitchen. In addition, the piano was moved to the location where all the band's elaborate equipment, such as the violin, violoncello, and cornet, would be positioned after their arrival. Besides the site for the musicians, the extent of the remaining hallway was left bare for ample space to dance. At the same time, the adjoining drawing room to the saloon and the parlor were all opened, housing adequate seating areas to the sides with the principal space open for guests to mingle. Much of the furniture within the breakfast parlor was moved to the veranda with the exception of the long table, which was settled to one side. In contrast, the morning room would serve as the official refreshment area with additional elaborate cookery to be arranged throughout the table, along with tea, coffee, and lemonade. Of course, wine, liquor, and the likes would be served on trays by a few of their servants. Furthermore, the veranda would be set up beautifully for additional space for guests who wished to engage in fresh air, a smoke, or conversation.

Much time had already been spent cleaning and polishing all the select China and cutlery throughout the whole course of the week, along with tidying up the first floor, landscaping, and purchasing of all items needed for such an articulate occasion, as was the routine. The culinary arts of cooking, preparing, roasting, baking, steaming, braising, sautéing, all holding to a French flair, continued relentlessly with the kitchen crew, as many of the courses began to come to fruition. The fragrances and aromas had begun to fill the rooms with such pleasantness, making one's taste buds savor and relish the delight of such a well-fashioned festivity.

Charlotte, the housekeeper, along with the maid, Lydia, were busily at work with last-minute touchups of cleaning and organizing the estate. This untimely ordeal included the setup of the lady's cloakroom and the gentlemen's hat room. As they diligently worked on all the intricate duties, Newton prepared sufficient candles to be readily available for every room downstairs. Thus, the extent of the ground floor would be well lit for vibrancy, effervescence, and liveliness, bringing a sense of richness to the estate as a whole. Fireplaces were fully stocked with supplies of coal and logs along with an ample amount set aside, ready to be added as the evening would progress into the late hours and early morning. Joseph was assisting Samuel with the arrangement of the veranda, laying out fine linen tablecloths and décor, as well as stocking the bar with all last-minute touchups. Lyman, the gardener, worked tirelessly on final improvements to the grounds while cutting fresh flowers to beautify all rooms, as they would be added to the many elegant vases throughout the first floor, including being placed on tables arranged in the veranda. Elbert and Daniel were busy working out all parking details for the multitude of carriages to be ready in ample time for guests upon their arrival, including lying out the red carpet for their invitees to promenade towards the estate. Permilia and Sarah were assisting Mrs. Walsh where needed until the time to begin aiding the three ladies with dress, hair, and makeup.

"What a splendid affair this was going to be," Aunt Martha pondered to herself. Oh, how the Irish loved a majestic gathering, such as this, with many expected to be in attendance—family, friends, acquaintances—and perhaps a few unexpected, as was predictable. And, yes, there would also be many in attendance that had actually known Cateline's father and loved him dearly, paying their respects as well as cordially welcoming his daughter to Ireland. Aunt Martha thought about how Cateline would so enjoy meeting those who had known him quite well. And, not to forget, many others planned to attend, as they were colleagues of Oscars as well. Several young gentlemen were also expected who desired the acquaintance of Cateline, and no doubt, there would be young ladies who were eager for the company of Mr. Wilde. All in all, the whole affair would be one for many to speak of in the days following.

As the morning had ensued, Cyrus arrived early, but Samuel and Martha had decided to allow the girls to sleep in to be refreshed for the evening. With James and Oscar up and dressed, they all sat in the drawing-room, waiting for breakfast to be ready. While enjoying their discourse, Amos arrived, joining the family and being pleasantly welcomed by Mr. Walsh, "Good to see you, Amos, my boy. You are just in time for breakfast."

"Good morning, sir—Mrs. Walsh."

About that time, Oscar stood to shake his hand. "Amos, I had no idea you were betrothed to Anya until yesterday?"

"Oscar, so good to see you. And yes, we are soon to be married. It has been a long time since I have had the pleasure of your company, and I was unaware you would be here."

"It looks as though you boys know each other well," Mr. Walsh stated warmly.

"Yes," Amos commented, "Oscar and I were at Trinity together. Although, I have not seen him since he went off to London or rather Oxford."

"Yes, it has been quite some time, indeed," Oscar acknowledged.

They were soon called into the morning room, where they enjoyed a quick breakfast together, which extended into discussions of tasks still needing to be completed for the day. Mr. Walsh conversed to all the young men the range of duties each could manage while dividing it among the four gentlemen, in expectation all should be completed in a concise timeframe, as there were more than enough servants to continue with the duties. Most of the delegation involved mainly instructing the servants with details enough to finalize where all would come together in a sufficient time and be exact to specifications.

As they were in deep discussions on the various undertakings, Martha called for Bertha. "Yes, ma'am, Mrs. Walsh," Bertha inquired.

"Please make sure breakfast is prepared for the girls. I do believe they have had sufficient time to sleep in, and please have trays taken to their rooms."

"Yes, ma'am, I will make sure the trays are ready for Sarah to serve."

"Thank you, and can you send Clara to have Sarah and Permilia see me, please."

"Yes, ma'am."

Finishing up breakfast, all the men left to begin delegating their assigned tasks to the necessary servants while overseeing and assisting where needed. Once the bulk of everything had been laid out plainly for the servants to complete, the four young men decided to play a game of poona. In the meantime, the girls had already been awakened and were eating breakfast on the balcony outside of Anya's room when they heard the sounds of yelling and laughing out on the grounds. "That sounds like Amos," Anya stirred while rising to look towards the back of the estate.

"It sounds like all of them," Cateline joined in while they walked further towards the rear of her long balcony until they were able to have a clearer view of the gentlemen. Still dressed in their mid-length nightgowns, they stood while watching the boys playing poona together. It was Amos and Cyrus against Oscar and James. But, of course, with the girls not present, they were at their worst and most competitive nature.

Both girls laughed while Anya cried out, "What's the matter Amos, can't stand to lose?"

Suddenly all eyes turned towards the balcony at that very moment—Amos, in a loud voice, shouted back, "You must not have been there very long—or you would have seen my last play."

"Well, if your last play was suitable, you shouldn't be so competitive when the other team makes a point too!"

Amos amused as he gazed at Anya, "Why don't you girls come down and show us how to play if you think you know so much about poona."

"Well, Amos—I know as much as you do about poona."

"Then prove it!"

155

Oscar spoke up about that time, chiming in, "I've seen both of you play the game very well, indeed—I do believe it is time for some real competition, perhaps men against women."

Cateline smiling, turned to Anya, and in a low voice where the boys could not hear, "You think we can go play?"

"I don't see why not; let's hurry and get dressed. Just go and put your breeches on and throw your hair up. We will probably have to sneak out because mother may disapprove. All the same, she is so busy with the party, it would probably be to our advantage that she would not see us leave."

Cateline having put her breeches on, went back into Anya's room to see what she was going to wear as a shirt. Anya exclaimed, "I believe I am going to wear my silk bodice; what do you think?"

"That is really pretty; I love the deep blue color. I believe I have one that is similar, but it is emerald green, yet, it is French silk, is it not?"

"Why, yes—I love the French silk. Go and get your green bodice; we will both look rather stunning," Anya bantered with a roguish smile.

"Would your mother not approve?"

Cunningly, Anya replied, "She would definitely not approve of the breeches, but father believes there is nothing wrong with wearing them, especially for a game such as this. As for wearing the fine French silk, she would be livid, but it has its advantage. In our silk bodices, we will look most attractive, which will be a distraction to the boys providing for our gain, don't you see?"

"Why, yes—I do, quite cunning; I will be right back," leaving Anya's room, Cateline ran across the hall to find her bodice and brush out her hair.

Once they were both ready, they snuck down the back stairs into the kitchen and out of the conservatory to where the boys were playing. The game began with the two girls and Cyrus against Amos, Oscar, and James until the girls got upset because it wasn't fair. "I thought you said that you could play as well as us men," Amos reminded deviously.

"Amos, if you make one more remark, you can find someone else to dance with this evening."

Knowing when he had said enough, Amos responded in a low-keyed manner, "Why don't you and I play against Oscar and Cateline?"

With an uprising change in disposition, Anya proclaimed, "Yes, that sounds rather like an awesome plan, Amos."

Changing sides, they played while Cyrus and James sat it out watching. It was somewhat comical at times, with Amos and Oscar being very competitive and the girls getting in the way. After both girls being accidentally knocked down from the aggression of the boys, Cyrus finally spoke up, "Why not put the girls on your shoulders with the battledores where you have to run with them to be able to hit the shuttlecock."

"That sounds like a good idea; come on, Anya, get on my shoulders—Cyrus, help her up here," he stated while bending down to the ground while Cyrus assisted Anya on his shoulders as Amos held her legs tightly.

"You better not drop me," she warned.

"I'm not going to drop you," Amos responded irritably.

All the while, James assisted Cateline as Oscar bent down for her to climb up on his shoulders. "I'm not so sure about this," Cateline spoke cautiously.

"What are you not sure about," Amos responded to Cateline's comment.

"It just feels like I'm going to fall."

"You are not going to fall, Cateline," Oscar assured abruptly, "I promise I will not let you get hurt."

"But, what if either of you should trip? If you go down, so will I."

"We are not going to trip," both men agreed about the same time, beginning to be annoyed with their remarks.

"Come on, girls, either you want to play, or you don't," was Amos's final plea.

"Fine—Amos! I won't say anything further, but do not drop me!"

"You promise you won't drop me either?" Cateline inquired of Oscar.

Most quietly, he assured her, "Cateline, I am not going to drop you, I promise."

With the battledores in hand, the game commenced as Cyrus and James stood on the side, ready to assist in the event someone began to stumble. It became a very arduous game with much laughing, where it was more challenging than perceived for the boys

157

to maneuver in the direction of the shuttlecock in time for one of the girls to take aim. The game continued while the men strategized more closely on techniques. The girls giggled and laughed, quite apparent that it was not as easy as presumed—seldom were they able to make a shot. The sport became very intense, with all motivated to include James and Cyrus. It had definitely become very intriguing to watch and terribly competitive among both couples. Eventually, gaining a better perspective, each team had scored a few points here and there while carrying on with much laughter and giggling, especially among the girls. Being enthralled in the competition, they were oblivious to Mrs. Walsh. Having heard the ruckus, she hastily ran out of the estate onto the back of the grounds.

"Oh, my—girls—girls! Get in this house right now! Samuel—oh, Samuel—come and make these girls get in this house right now!"

Samuel walked out of the estate to observe the girls and boys, laughing while enjoying such pleasure in the sport. Amos responded, "Mrs. Walsh, we are only playing poona—come on, no one is going to get hurt. We are merely having some fun."

"Amos, do not make me come out there—Anya, you and Cateline get in this house immediately! You are supposed to be getting ready for this evening's festivity. Look at you, carrying on as such! Oh, my! And in your lavish silk bodices—Samuel, please say something!" she demanded.

"Martha, they are just having fun."

"Samuel—"

"Very well, Martha. Girls, come in the house so you can be ready for this evening."

"Yes, father," Anya replied while Cyrus and James helped them down. The boys accompanying the girls to the veranda, there was an occasional laugh and whisper among them.

"I had hoped that we would have been able to spend some time together today," Oscar spoke in a low voice to Cateline.

"We will once the ball begins."

With a trivial laugh, he responded, "No, Cateline, that is not going to happen. The festivity is in your honor—I am sure you will be quite popular this evening. I already know a few of my old friends will be in attendance, and I am sure they will all be desiring your attention. I am most certain that you will be dancing the whole evening."

She quipped in response, "This event is also in your honor. There will probably be many ladies who knew you before you left that will be longing for your devotion, too."

He responded with a slight grin, "Perhaps, but I am intrigued by you and believe that you feel the same."

"Yes, I do feel the same," Cateline spoke with a most charming smile. Briefly, in thought, she continued, "All the same, we must remember that our meeting only occurred because of this so-called celebration."

"Oh, I am pleased your family arranged this most pleasant gathering, for I rather enjoy a well-planned event. But my desire would be to have more time with you, that is all."

"Perhaps, you will not be in a hurry to leave for London."

As Oscar looked at her earnestly, he smiled once again, "I assure you that my thoughts have not been in the least about my traveling back to London."

"Well, then I suppose it is settled. If you're not in a hurry to leave, we should have more than enough time to get acquainted," she continued while turning to look up into Oscar's light blue eyes, "I will promise to save a dance for you."

"Perhaps, we can spend time together after the party if you are not too fatigued."

"Yes, that is also most probable."

"But we do have tomorrow. Once we are rested, perhaps we can set aside some time to spend together."

"What did you have in mind?"

"We don't have to leave the estate but can spend the whole day just the two of us out on the grounds, perhaps even a picnic down by the lake."

"Yes, that does sound rather nice—I still want the dance tonight; you know you merely have to ask."

"Oh, I will ask, and we will dance, but I would clearly like to spend time with you without others vying for your company. Yet, I am afraid that will be for another day, tomorrow, my dear."

"Yes—tomorrow, it is settled."

Martha, walking into the estate, escorted the girls upstairs to their rooms to make sure that Sarah and Permilia were in charge of getting their long beautiful locks of hair perfected in splendid creations, which would entail a tedious, time-consuming endeavor.

159

"Please make sure that their meals are brought to their rooms," she addressed Permilia and then turned to both girls, "do not let me see either of you downstairs. Once you are ready, please take some time to rest. Anya, you may come down at five o'clock, but Cateline, your uncle, will escort you down at the appropriate time. Until then, you remain upstairs."

Mrs. Walsh, heading back downstairs, joined Mr. Walsh and the other gentlemen on the veranda to wait for lunch, which arrived later than usual. Thus far, the day seemed to progress slowly, yet the remainder of the afternoon was spent leisurely, as the servants pretty much had everything running smoothly. Samuel and the boys retired to his study and billiard room for a few drinks and rounds of billiards before heading to their apartments to dress for the affair. In contrast, Martha also retired to her room, awaiting the arrival of Permilia to assist with her hair and dress before their guests would begin to arrive.

The afternoon quickly diminished with the men downstairs, assisting the musicians with the setup of all the many instruments for dancing and entertainment. Very soon, Isabella arrived to join Cyrus for the affair, and shortly afterward, the guests began to trickle in a few at a time. Everything seemed in perfect order, with the food preparations coming to an end, slowly being brought out by servants and arranged radiantly on the large table outside the kitchen area. At the same time, other dishes were laid out on the breakfast table, which adjoined the veranda. The bars were fully stocked with Port, and all the variety of liquors ordered with two servants placed in their station, ready to begin carrying trays of assorted drinks in tall glasses as the guests started to arrive.

Upstairs, the ladies all continued to be dressed and adorned with emeralds and diamonds for last-minute touches. Martha had finally joined her husband and son downstairs, welcoming their guests one by one, as those early began to arrive, until sometime later when others started to pour into the vestibule. Elbert and Daniel were busily parking the assembly of vehicles and steering guests to the front entrance as Joseph escorted them into the hallway, announcing the arrival of each with full title and name.

Anya, adorned in robe and her hair exquisitely detailed, walked to Cateline's room, where she was completely embellished in costume while Sarah was on the final touches of her beautiful locks of hair. Both girls had superb twists, braids, and flowing curls down from their delicate tresses, as well as jewels secured in various plaits and coils. Makeup was complete adding to their overall look of radiance, as reflected in one of admirable royalty. Standing side by side, they both looked flawless, especially with their Paris designer dresses, matching gloves, and accessories. "Well," Anya began, "I will go down first and let my father know you are ready for your entrance."

"My entrance? You make it sound like royalty."

"Yes, your grand entrance! Tonight, you are as royalty! For the ball is in your honor, and being a lady, you will be escorted in gallantly where father will announce you and share specifics in your introduction. I suppose one could consider you a débutante. This is somewhat like a coming-out party, being introduced into society. Although, that is French for a female beginner, and normally the girls are younger. All the same, father is still introducing you into society, so this is your night, my dear cousin. Nonetheless, be patient. I am sure he will not come and get you until most guests have arrived, so please, use that time to rest, and I will see you soon," Anya finished while leaning over to give her a big hug. "You look magnificent!"

"You do too, Anya. I am not sure I am ready for this. I am so nervous."

"It's perfectly alright to be nervous. Do not worry, father will have a hold of you so that you will not stumble or anything. You will do great, and you look absolutely gorgeous."

"Thank you, Anya, you look quite stunning as well. I suppose it runs in the family?"

"I will agree to that," she proclaimed with a radiant smile.

Anya headed downstairs a bit early as it was still shy of another hour or so before Mr. Walsh arrived at Cateline's room to escort her. "You look divine, my dear. I am so proud, and your father would be as well. Come now; the guests are all anxious to meet you."

"Thank you, Uncle Walsh, but I do not feel that I can do this."

"Nonsense, Cateline. You are a McCarthy. It is born in you, a natural—yes, you will astonish all of our guests, my dear."

As Uncle Walsh held her arm to escort her down the stairs, Joseph stood about mid-way, where he called out, "Introducing Miss Cateline McCarthy, born in Ireland and here from the Americas, escorted by her uncle, Mr. Samuel Walsh." They persisted, walking down the stairs, where Cateline could see myriads of folks filled within the rooms, people she did not know. All stared with the most pleasant countenances, as Cateline caught a word here and there of the small talk among the women on her exquisite appearance and beauty, as well as the men gazing with all eyes beholding her poise.

Descending almost to the final step, her uncle spoke up, "I would like to say, Cateline was my best friend's daughter, my brother by marriage, and my cousin—some of you may remember John McCarthy, a good man, gone too soon but never forgotten. We also have his son, James, with us this evening from Youghal. Cateline, John's daughter, is here with us from America, born in Ireland of Irish blood. We have only had her a short time but have come to love her dearly, and as you get to know her, you will also fall in love with her grace and charm. Lastly, I would like to welcome Oscar Wilde, who is also among us." Oscar bowed slightly as the guest acknowledged him, and her uncle continued, "Oscar, everyone knows, the son of Sir William Wilde and Lady Jane Wilde. He now resides in London and is making a name for himself. We are very honored to have him back in Dublin with many of his acquaintances present at our gala affair. Now, without further ado—please, eat, drink, dance, and have a wonderful time this evening!"

After her uncle's speech, she was flogged with introductions from one guest after another, conversations from acquaintances of her late father from the older men, remarks of her beauty by the elderly women and some of the rather gallant young men, and questions about the designer dress from a few of the younger ladies. The men bowed, kissed her hand while insisting on a promised dance, while the more voluble women adorned her with hugs, welcoming her to her native country. Cateline felt cheerfully acknowledged but seemed to have lost sight of Oscar since her uncle had announced his presence. She was sure that he was probably off in profound discussions, as well, since there were perhaps many attending very curious about his dealings in London. As the music started, she stayed much engaged on the dance floor with so many young men who were very eager for her attention. The party was so agreeable, with a multitude of guests, over a hundred, so she had been told. With all the rooms being set up to hold vast numbers, furniture moved around and even removed, carpet rolled away to allow for smooth dancing, all in all, it was a grand ball.

Cateline went from the dance floor to glasses of Port being handed to her from different gentlemen, as they were all engaged to conquer her consideration. She was very well received, having such a marvelous time talking and laughing while enjoying all the wonderfully prepared hors d'oeuvres and refined wines, which were relatively plentiful. The choice selections most favored were clairette blanche, a white variety full-bodied, and an Italian variation, Barolo—a most robust but elegant red wine with distinctive notes of dark fruit, tobacco, mocha, rose petals, tar, and truffles.

One man, in particular, caught her attention, as he was a most handsome young gentleman, tall with dark hair, of excellent stature, and extremely delightful nature. William was most intrigued by Cateline, and she found herself quite enchanted with all his tales and adventures, whereas the whereabouts of Oscar had seemed to diminish from her mind for the time being. William had swept Cateline off to the dance floor, where she temporarily found herself in a most dazed sensation in regards to this young man, stricken by his intellect and discourse. He, too, was a graduate of Magdalen College, Oxford but had come back to Dublin to carry on the estate of his late father's being the eldest son. They had shared many dances, waltzing, and time spent in the small parlor getting acquainted over drinks when not on the dance floor. Other young men had pretty much given up the bout for her attention, once William had seemed to conquer her distinct devotion.

Back on the dance floor with William, Cateline finally had a glimpse of Oscar, as he, too, was dancing with one of the attractive ladies in attendance. Cateline made sure that he never saw her observe such, but in reality, she already knew there would be many young ladies present who knew him from his years living in Dublin. After all, he had been very well-known among the higher class from his own father's achievements and then his popularity and accomplishments as well. Cateline also knew from his parent's level of fashionable society, Oscar had been most celebrated along with his presence requested at many a party during his years in Dublin.

163

As the dancing continued into the night, and more folks had arrived unannounced, it soon became apparent, the wonderfully planned ball, exceeding the intended number of guests, was labeled a crush! With that said, Cateline and Anya's trains on their dresses had become an issue where Sarah and Permilia facilitated a quick alteration. Both girls then continued in their merriment.

Back downstairs, in the midst of all the guests, Cateline was unable to locate Oscar as the attendance continued to grow. She became a bit concerned since they had not spoken from the time she had come downstairs and was announced by her uncle, nor had he asked for a dance, as was promised. What she didn't know was that Oscar had watched her for quite some time from a distance, whereas, in the beginning, there had been many young men desiring her attention, which had tapered off once Cateline's attachment had secured William's. From the back of the room, away from the crowds, Oscar observed her beauty, exquisitely dressed in her gown, a most stunning sight to behold. As beautiful as she was in merely a simple dress, the designer gown had made her look sovereign. Oscar could not explain precisely what he was feeling, which somewhat frightened him, knowing too well that she could have her pick of anyone in the room. It wasn't just Cateline's looks, even though they were of extreme beauty, but it was also her humor and intelligence which made her stand out far above any girl he had ever met. "The ideal companion," he thought to himself, "what a rare quality in such beauty as hers." Oscar also felt that he could love her forever if given the opportunity.

Cateline excused herself at one point and walked out to the veranda, away from the hordes, to get a breath of fresh air. With a few guests coming and going from the outdoor patio, she decided to walk out to one of the flower gardens where she could be alone to gather her thoughts. Enjoying the crispness of the night air, Cateline stood looking out at the lake while taking in the coolness of the gentle breeze, as the tantalizing effect felt much welcomed to her body after so many dances. Then, all of a sudden, a voice spoke out, "Needing fresh air, I see."

"Oscar, where have you been? I haven't seen you the whole night,"—which was not entirely true.

"I have been here, mingling and dancing, and I have noticed you from time to time. If I do say so, you are the most attractive girl here."

Cateline blushed while speaking rather nervously, "Thank you, but you have yet to dance with me."

"I do not want to fight the throngs of young gentlemen; besides, it is quite the crush if I do say so."

"That it is, indeed! I have never seen so many people crammed into one place. Why it is relatively annoying trying to go from room to room in this dress."

Oscar laughed, knowing this was her first experience with such, before he commented, "Yes, it is an experience one shall not soon forget. In London, you have not lived until you have been to a crush held in a townhouse, some being four stories, although, by no means, very spacious. As for dancing, we will have time later, and furthermore, I did not want to interrupt your time with William. It seemed as if you were enjoying yourself quite well."

"Oh, I wasn't aware that you knew him."

"Yes, we are acquainted. We were at university together, Trinity, as well as Magdalen College, Oxford."

"Oh, I see. William has never mentioned you."

"I do not suppose that he would when his attentions were solely focused on you."

Cateline responded tactfully, "Yes, well, he is the gentleman, if I do say so."

"It seems as though you are somewhat taken with him."

"What would give you that impression?"

"Your expressions and the looks that you give him when you two are together."

Before answering, she thought to herself, "I had no idea that he had been watching us," which made her realize that he must be a tad jealous at least. After the brief pause, Cateline responded, "Please, looks can be deceiving. Perhaps, I was merely trying to be sociable; after all, I am one of the guests of honor. It would be rather insolent on my part to not be cordial."

"Oh, but a lady does not dance multiple times with the same gentleman unless she is quite interested in him."

"Your customs, I perceive? But remember that I have lived all my life for the most part in America. That is not our belief, I'm afraid.

165

As I said, I was simply trying to be friendly, even though he is reasonably charming. Is that rule the same for men?"

"Perhaps, if a man dances multiple times with a lady, he does have an interest in her."

"And—you, have you been dancing with anyone in particular?"

There was a pause as Oscar thought about what to say, not sure if she had actually seen him dancing or not. He finally answered, "Yes, I have been dancing with an old friend from here, but we are merely friends." After a time of silence, Oscar spoke again, "I do believe that you owe me a dance. Would you give me the honor of this next dance, Cateline?"

"Yes, that would be wonderful," she responded while Oscar took her arm and escorted her back into the estate.

While they danced, there was silence between both of them. Oscar, being utterly taken with her beauty, eventually spoke, "I have looked upon your marvelous and incomparable beauty this evening. You are too captivating, my dear."

"You do have a way with words, Oscar. Thank you for the compliment. And yourself, you are most handsome. But, if I may inquire, I am quite curious as to why you haven't asked me to dance before now?"

"My dear, there are many young men here that came to meet you, and I am not one to fight for a turn to dance. I assumed as the night went on, I would have the pleasure of your company."

Entertained by his comment, she spoke discreetly, "Your lady friend, I am assuming, must be the lady off to the side. I see her gazing on occasions toward us. She seems to follow your every move."

"As I have stated, we are purely friends and nothing more. Does it bother you that her eyes follow me at times?"

"No, as a matter of fact, it does not; I delight that there are others who find you quite charming, as I do."

Oscar responded diplomatically, "I could also conclude that William has not turned his eyes away from you since we began dancing."

Again, Cateline said, "And, I am assuming that it does not bother you in the least."

In retort, whimsically, he settled, "I cannot say that it does nor does not bother me. I can only say that I know he will be leaving at the end of the night, and I will still be here with you. My advantage to his, I presume, would be of much greater conflict on his part than mine."

They continued dancing to the end of the song when Oscar inquired, "Refreshment, my dear? Perhaps, a glass of Port?"

"Yes, a brilliant suggestion, Oscar," Cateline responded.

"I will meet you on the veranda with the wine—fresh air, yes?"

"Of course," she replied as her countenance lit up beautifully, "a most dazzling idea, Oscar. I shall be waiting for you on the veranda."

As she walked towards the veranda, Cateline was unaware William had been watching. No sooner than Oscar had turned away, he joined her.

"I thought I saw you come out here. Would you care to dance to the next song?"

"Well—"

Before the words could come out, Oscar had arrived and handed her a glass of wine.

"Hello, William, it has been some time since I have seen you. I hear you are doing quite well in Dublin?"

"Yes, I have taken over my father's estate and business, and you?"

"In London, naturally, writing and publishing various lyrics and poems in magazines. My book of poems, which I have long been working on, shall be published this year, and needless to say, I do continue to work on plays. Having finished one, I am in hopes of it being produced next year. Besides my personal work, I am also helping to lead the aesthetic movement and planning the trip to America next year, which should be rather extensive."

"Yes, I would say so. I was surprised to see you here in Dublin."

"I was invited; my father was friends with Samuel—Mr. Walsh."

"Yes, I did hear him announce you, as well. Where are you staying while here?"

"Oh, I am staying here as a guest, of course. You should stop by one day and spend time with us, Cateline and myself, to be precise."

"Oh—so, how long will you be here?"

"No plans at this point. Cateline's uncle has invited me to stay as long as I would like. I plan to take Cateline around Ireland to show her many historical sites. I could be here for some time, my boy. As I stated, I have no plans at the moment. Being a writer, I can work freely from anywhere—simply impeccable, wouldn't you say?"

"Yes, I suppose it is, without a doubt. Well, I will probably not be here much longer. I will leave you two and head back into the estate to start saying my adieus."

"It was quite pleasant to see you, William, remember, drop by anytime. Cateline and I would love to have you as our guest."

"Yes, I will keep that in mind."

Once William had gone back into the estate, Cateline turned to Oscar smiling, as she said, "That was awful; you made it sound like we are a couple. I believe you hurt his pride."

"I am not sure I understand. Does that bother you?"

"Well—yes, I mean—well, I mean, you did not have to make it sound like—well like I belong to you and that he is wasting his time."

"Is he not wasting his time? Or were you wanting to explore your options?"

"I really don't know what I mean. No, I do not want to explore my options—what does that mean, anyway?"

"You wanted to get to know me, did you not?"

"Yes, of course!"

"Then, there is no need to explore options. I came all this way to meet you and have enjoyed it immensely. I have no desire to explore any other possibilities."

"You were jealous."

"No—jealousy is the green-eyed monster ¹—for, I was only eliminating the options, or I should say distractions. The time I stay here at your uncle's is meant to get to know you, my dear."

"Hmmm, a Shakespearean! But what about the girl?"

"The girl? What girl are you speaking of? You mean the girl I danced with?"

"Yes, precisely."

"There is nothing between us," he reassured, with a flirtatious smile.

As the music could be heard from the veranda, Oscar, being quite taken with Cateline's beauty, extended his hand most insistently, "Let us dance right here, just you and I on the veranda."

"You wouldn't rather go in and dance among the others?"

"Why should we—do you need to be surrounded by others to dance? Not to mention, it is so very crowded inside."

"No, I do not need to be among the crowds, Oscar," Cateline acknowledged. Taking his hand as he put his arms on her waist, they danced slowly, gazing into each other's eyes, mesmerized by time. Neither spoke but held each other, swaying to the music—with their body language speaking volumes.

With the song ending, Oscar advised in a sensible manner, "You should probably be sociable, wouldn't you agree? We can spend time together after the revelry."

Cateline gently smiled and strode back in while Oscar was spellbound by her every step, clearly pleased at how attractive she was. After a few moments, her uncle announced, "Attention everyone, as some of you know, my niece from America is exceptionally gifted, and it is with the greatest pleasure that she will indulge us with her outstanding music and voice. First, Cateline will play a few songs on the pianoforte in the drawing-room while the musicians take a break, and afterward, she will also delight us with her guitar and lovely voice. Cateline—"

"Thank you, Uncle Walsh, and I would love to thank everyone for attending. This has been quite an evening, and I feel I have made so many new friends. Thank you for joining us this evening." Cateline sat down at the piano playing two songs, one which was by Chopin and one by Domenico Alberti-Presto. After completion of the classics, she picked up her guitar and sat down on a chair to play *I Love How You Love Me* by The Paris Sisters.[2]

With every word beautifully sung throughout her performance, young men gathered around to listen to her stunning voice while gazing at her exquisite loveliness. From a distance, Oscar had his eyes fashioned upon her demeanor and was lost in her voice, as well as the words harmonized. He felt something for her that he had never felt for anyone else. Captivated by the sound of her voice throughout the song, her eyes gazed into his from a distance, but he knew she noticed him standing at the back of the room. Oscar dared not to look away, for he was lost within her every breath and her every word that proceeded from her lips. Cateline, absorbed in her song, also felt something for this man that she had never felt for anyone in her life.

With her voice immersed in the last chorus, Cateline put down the guitar while everyone clapped fervently. All eyes followed her as she mingled among the guests. At the same time, many young gentlemen approached to compliment her proficiency with the piano and guitar, to include her brilliant voice. Feeling like a princess, even if it was for a spell, Cateline knew she had an advantage over the other women; after all, she did have talent, but the songs were not her own songs—but songs from her era. She also had beauty, but other women during that timeframe were also quite remarkable, even though her being from America did seem to make it much more fascinating for that period. Still, there was another advantage Cateline had over other women, and that was her education. Yes, there were women in the higher ranks who were educated, but coming from the twenty-first century, none could have the knowledge as she. Cateline knew that her advantages were not just her accomplishments and beauty but the wits of an American woman from the twentieth and twenty-first centuries. Women had changed over the years, and there wouldn't have been a young man in that era that would not have been fascinated with her. In fact, her demeanor was nothing like girls of her own age, even in her period, for her dreams captured the thoughts and expressions of the novels and poetry that consumed her days. In her time, there had not been a man who was able to seize her attention nor her gaze. Was Cateline different from other girls? Yes, in her own timeframe but far superior to those from Oscar's time. This advantage had its rewards, but it also came with uncertainties. For Cateline wondered if she had actually been born in the nineteenth century, would she have been as attracted to Oscar as she currently was. She also had to wonder if he would have been taken with her. Yes, Cateline was an educated twenty-first-century woman from America that could even speak some French, although that had not been disclosed. She was smart and even street smart—living in Boston and Chicago. She was beautiful but also wise, knowing what men liked in a woman and what they did not like. She could carry on a conversation with anyone and fit right in, whether it was a woman or a man and even a highly cultured man at that.

By the end of the night, Cateline was exhausted, as most of the guests had left, while some remained into the wee hours out on the veranda. The older gentlemen were mostly discussing business matters; nevertheless, she noticed Oscar among them and decided it was probably best to retire and get a good night's sleep. Ascending the back stairs to the second floor, she heard steps coming up behind her. "I was under the impression that we were going to spend some time together after the party?"

"Oh, well—I saw you out with the other gentlemen deep in discussion. So, I thought that maybe you were having a good time, and we would see each other tomorrow."

"Yes, we will see each other tomorrow, but I would also delight in your company before we retire—that is if you are not too weary."

With a pleasant smile, she disclosed, "Yes, I am rather tired, but we can go back down and talk for a while if you would like."

"Yes, perhaps we can go to one of the rooms where it is quiet. I do believe most guests have left except for the few on the veranda."

"Yes, I believe so," she responded while he reached up and took her hand to lead her back downstairs.

They settled into the front parlor, where it was pretty cozy, sitting down on the sofa facing the fireplace. Oscar rekindled the fire where the warmth could be felt before he sat down beside her. They were both relatively quiet for several minutes when he turned to face her. Looking into her deep blue eyes, he spoke most elegantly, "When I look at you like this, it drives me insane."

"Whatever do you mean?"

"You have such a curious influence over me. When I look into your eyes, filled with pools of passion, they seem to hypnotize me where I have no control. Your rose-colored lips tantalize my own. I do understand that we have only known each other for such a short time, but I desire you—desire to kiss you, Cateline. I want to kiss you—I desire to hold and kiss you."

"How many times have you used that line with girls, Oscar?"

"Yes, it does sound like a cliché, but I assure you, it is not as you would imagine. My life is quite complex. With college here in Dublin, Oxford, and now in London, I have been set on a course and have seldom allowed obstacles to cloud my vision or produce havoc in my life that would change that path. My life is destined to be one in the spotlight one day, to be great and remembered as making my mark in this generation. Yes, there have been distractions, my dear—but, by far, you have disturbed my thoughts from the moment that I met you."

Cateline knew his life more than he realized since she had devoted much time studying this era and him in general over the last couple of years. Obviously, that was to her advantage, but still the same, she knew that she also loved him. Cateline knew where all this was leading because of her many dreams. As she looked into his dreamy eyes, her words of agreement spoke softly, "Yes, you are right—we have not known each other but for a few days. I, too, Oscar, have not really had time in my life to focus on the simple pleasures, but I do hope that you will decide to stay for a while where maybe we can become better acquainted."

"Yes, I do plan to stay longer. But, of course, that will also depend upon your uncle. I dare say that he has asserted I could remain, as long as I desired. I am not quite sure why he has spoken in that way to me, even though he was a friend of my fathers."

"More than likely, I would have to speculate that my uncle desires that my attentions are drawn to you where I will remain and not go back to America. I do know that is his wish."

Satisfied, Oscar exclaimed, "I do believe that is to my advantage. Please, tell me, was there someone in America that has captivated your heart?"

Pleasingly amused, she gave her response, "No, Oscar—I lived alone and spent most of my time with my closest friend, Mary. As far as my attention towards any young man, I am afraid I have found none that could hold an intelligent conversation. My *loves* in this life have been somewhat the same as yours—the pursuit of the arts. That is my downfall, I am sure, but nothing pleases me more than having discourse with those who possess the same passions as I."

Oscar, speaking with a delightful countenance, proclaimed earnestly, "Ordinary people waited till life disclosed to them its secrets, but to the few, to the elect, the mysteries of life were revealed before the veil was drawn away. Sometimes this was the effect of art, and chiefly of the art of literature, which dealt immediately with the passions and the intellect."[3]

They continued talking about many of their joint interests, despite the fact, Cateline and Oscar were both extremely exhausted—yet, neither had wanted the time together to end. Gradually, their conversations paused at intervals, with both feeling rather weary but neither desiring to bring a halt to their time together. Eventually, they drifted off to sleep while comfortably sitting next to each other on the sofa. Oscar, awakening in the deep darkness of the night, noticed the fire was barely producing any such light and no warmth at that. Gazing over at Cateline, her body had fallen slightly towards him, with her head resting on his chest. He sat for a short time, adjusting his eyes to the darkness while he admired her beauty and the feel of her warmth next to him. Turning, with his arms around her, he noticed her beautiful locks of hair that had begun to loosen and fall gently onto her face. He ran his hand through the curls, gently sweeping strands over to the side where he could see the beauty of her appearance and feel the softness of her skin. Kissing her ever so gently on her forehead, he spoke softly, "Cateline, wake up."

As her eyes opened, she looked up at him, forgetting where she was, sitting up slowly while speaking tenderly, "Where am I?"

In a jovial manner, he remarked, "We fell asleep in the drawing-room."

"It is so dark."

"Yes, everyone must have gone to bed, and no one noticed that we were in here. All the candles are out, and it is quite dark."

"Oh—well, we must get upstairs to bed."

"Yes, we must be very quiet. Hold my hand, and I will try to lead you upstairs in the dark. I have no idea where there is a candle."

"I have one by my bed, but that doesn't help us down here."

Arising, Oscar held her hand while leading her slowly to the back of the house where the staircase was located. They gradually ascended the stairs, cut off from any moonlight coming through the windows, making for quite a climb in the abrupt darkness. Taking one step at a time to not trip and fall, they gradually made it to the second floor. Cateline's room, the first one on the left, once ascended, they were able to slowly locate the door while she giggled at the situation, as there was not a stream of light to be seen. Stepping inside her room, it was obvious that Sarah must have closed all draperies, leaving them faced again with sheer darkness. "I can find my candle by the bed, Oscar," Cateline assured him, walking steadily until she felt the bedstead and then the table. Lighting the candle, they finally were able to see.

"Here, let me have the candle, and I will make sure your fire is well lit for the night before I leave you."

"Thank you," she responded to his kindness while sitting on the side of her bed, watching him at the hearth. Her thoughts were so interwoven with the image of a life with him. Watching his tenderness while he rekindled the fire for her warmth alone and his kindness as he had been such a gentleman. Did he love her, could one tell? Yes,

173

her life and these moments were for him. But what then—what awaited her? After all, this time was his time—her purpose for him— her life as it was right then and right there, it was all for this man— this gentle soul, yes, a soul that felt pain—felt hurt, and would one day know tribulation, experience rejection, loss, and failure. But one day, he would also remember these times. He would think on his purpose, the plan—and he would triumph in the end. Yes, his end by all fleshly perspectives, but that would only be his revision, his gain—truth, as it would hold him through those trials and bereavement, the passing, the loss, and ultimately the death— nonetheless, the beginning of life.

While Oscar revived her hearth, his thoughts drifted to desires that she awakened in him. Yet, he knew it was best to patiently await the right moment and the suitable time. Once Oscar had the fire blazing, he sauntered languidly back over to Cateline, leaned over to kiss her lightly on her forehead, followed by a sincere closing note, "Goodnight, sleep well, Cateline."

"Thank you for getting the fire going for me, Oscar. Please, carry the candle holder with you so that you may find your way in the dark," Cateline spoke while she lit the lamp beside her bed and handed him her candlestick.

With a warm smile, he winked while sharing most precociously, "I see your uncle owns courting candles."

"What do you mean?"

"This candle holder, it is a courting candle," observing the holder, she did not understand, he continued, "you do not know the history?"

"No, I suppose that I do not."

"You see how the wrought iron coils up to hold the candle?"

"Yes."

"When a gentleman comes to court a young lady, the father lights the candle and places it in the room. Once the candle burns down to the first coil, the courting is over for that evening," he paused with a somewhat dubious laugh. "Of course, these are not used in this timeframe. At least I assume that your uncle does not plan to use these."

Curiously, Cateline smiled while responding, "I have never heard this, but it is quite fascinating. Not all of their candle holders are like this one, but I had no idea its meaning," she giggled.

"Goodnight, Cateline—tomorrow, we will be able to spend more time becoming acquainted."

"Yes, I am so looking forward to it," Cateline spoke cheerfully while gazing in his direction as he left her room.

Once alone, Cateline dressed for bed and went to the davenport, picked up the quill pen, and wrote down all her thoughts and all the affairs of the whole day in her diary where she would have every moment of this most wonderful day recorded forever.

CHAPTER
13

The following morning came way too soon—everyone, including the servants, was exhausted and in dire need of rest. Breakfast was served a bit later, as most had slept in. One by one decided to join in for the Sunday morning breakfast, which was served exceedingly late. Not to mention, once all were gathered around the table, the silence was quite obvious.

Mr. Walsh was the first to break the quietness following grace, "I believe the grand ball to be a huge success, Martha, what do you think?"

"Yes, dear, I believe it was. Cateline, did you have a good time?"

"Yes, ma'am, I did."

In excitement, Anya exclaimed, "Last night was such a crush, for it shall be talked about for some time! I never thought one such as this would be held at our estate! But, by no means was it a grand ball, father! The Walshes have entertained their first crush!"

"Yes, undeniably, they have." Mr. Walsh agreed. "How on earth did this happen, Martha?"

"I am not sure I know, dear. I do believe it must have been by word of mouth. Most of those late-comers, I did not know. Did you?"

"No, I did not recognize many of them. Yes, it was some party, yes, indeed!"

There was silence once again as everyone ate and had their fill of coffee and tea. Spending a short time in small talk with James since he would be leaving at daybreak the following morning, the family inquired on various topics of the happenings in Youghal.

Afterward, Mr. Walsh spoke wearily, "I believe I will retire back to bed, Martha dear. Would you like to join me? The servants will be able to handle putting everything in order and cleaning the estate."

"Splendid idea Samuel. I am right behind you." The family had all agreed it would be a day spent somewhat lazily, deciding to retire to their own apartments. It being Sunday, they had opted out of attending church since the party had gone on into the wee hours of the night or rather early morning.

With Amos leaving after breakfast, Anya concluded, "Sounds great to me too. I believe I will retire to my apartment; see you later, Cateline." Anya stood as she headed upstairs.

It was just James, Oscar, and Cateline remaining at the table before James finally spoke up, "I suppose I will leave you two to yourselves and head into the study to read a bit myself. I plan to lay down later this afternoon to get a bit of sleep before I head out for home early tomorrow. Cateline, I will see you later this evening."

"Yes, brother, we can spend some time together a little later."

Cateline and Oscar, having made plans for a rendezvous, intended to spend the entire day together. Once they had all cleared out, she looked over to him while acknowledging, "I am assuming you are probably as fatigued as I."

"Yes, I am at that. Why don't we take a blanket down by the lake? It would be quite enjoyable to relax on such a beautiful day—if that sounds pleasing to you, of course."

"Sure, I am still exhausted, but that does sound wonderful."

Cateline went to grab a few blankets and met Oscar out on the veranda. Handing her his oversized fur coat, he took the blankets from her, "I thought you may enjoy the warmth of my coat."

"Thank you, I do need to buy myself a warm coat while I am here, but I do appreciate using yours."

"You may wear it any time."

As they strolled down to the lake, Oscar spread out one of the blankets for them to sit upon. Lying down on his back, he looked up at the radiantly blue sky while Cateline lay on her side, gazing towards him. "I can tell you are really exhausted, Oscar. It is quite alright if you would like to go back to the estate and sleep awhile."

"No, I would rather be by your side. I may fall asleep, but at least I will still be here with you."

"I hope you had a good time last night."

"I did—a most perfect time at that, how about you?"

"Yes, but it was a bit too much. I seldom had a break from dancing."

"Yes, I observed such, but I did expect as much. Several of my friends—besides William, made remarks regarding you, which did not surprise me."

"What kind of remarks?"

"Desiring to know more about you, naturally."

Cateline laughed while she spoke, "I don't suppose it bothered you, the amount of attention I received."

"Why no, I assumed you would be flogged by gentlemen," smiling reticently at her, he resumed the discourse, "of course, I also knew that I had you for today all to myself, and so, it was the least I could do to let all the other chaps believe they had a chance."

Cateline smiled as she replied inquisitively, "And, I suppose that you are pretty confident that fate is on your side?"

"I do believe we shall see," Oscar responded with a grin.

They were both quiet as Cateline retrieved the other blanket to spread out to take the chill off and share with Oscar before rolling over on her back to look at the late morning sky. The silence was marked, with both not having much rest. Oscar soon drifted off to sleep while Cateline covered him before falling asleep herself.

After a few hours, Oscar woke and rolled over to see Cateline sleeping soundly. Moving closer to her, he pulled the blanket up securely around her for warmth while he lay on his side, looking into her face as she slept peacefully. He then ran his fingers through her long hair until she was awakened. "I'm sorry, I must have fallen asleep."

"Yes, but I have enjoyed watching you."

"You should have awakened me."

"I believe that I did, for I have suffered from temptation; my hands seem to have a mind of their own when it comes to your hair. Truly, I try to abstain, but the desire is far too great."

With a quaint giggle, Cateline sat up to stretch and began to twist her long locks, arranging them in a most attractive way secured with a hair slide, revealing her face to the fullest.

"You do not have to remove the temptation, my dear."

"I think it distracts you, so probably better that I put it up."

It was still a chilly day but not too bitter with the sun cascading down upon them radiantly. Everything seemed quite mysterious, it being the first time they had actually ever been alone without anyone close by. For a while, Oscar lay there looking up at Cateline as she continued to twist and work her hair ornately into a fashionable detailed design. Stricken by her beauty, he sat up and brought her hands down while he loosened the clip to allow her hair liberty as it fell once again across her shoulders onto her back and covering her breasts. "Please, leave your hair down. It is rather lovely and natural," he spoke, most sincerely.

With a radiant smile, she did not have to speak, for her countenance spoke volumes. They talked and laughed, enjoying each other's company. There were so many things he did not know about her and so many questions to ask. Oscar had been so taken with Cateline and intrigued by every word she spoke. It was apparent they were both so compatible and loved being in the presence of each other. Oscar felt it so very relaxing to be with a girl that he was actually comfortable with sharing any and everything. To him, it was pretty rare in relationships for men and women in those days to have so much in common and to share the same passions for life. He knew there was just something special about her that was so unlike other girls he had met, and he thoroughly loved being in her company. Yes, Cateline made him feel so good, so full of life—alive, an inner feeling he could not explain.

At one point, Oscar inquired about the songs she had sung on the guitar. It was music, which was so different yet undeniably pleasing. In sharing about the music, Cateline had to let him know that it was music from America, but she was not the artist. Even so, her music was part of her life—a part of her life that he could never understand. Although she was able to impart to him her love for music, her overall love, but not just for music, it was all art in general—paintings, songs, poems, novels, plays—everything! When Cateline talked about any one subject, he could see the passion inside of her like he had never witnessed in a girl before. While he was secretly trying to analyze her, she continued pouring out her most precious thoughts filled with emotions, which melted his heart. Cateline was the most perfect girl he had ever known, beauty, brains, passion, culture—yes, she had it all. Nevertheless, here he was, in deep thought that she was taken with him for some reason he did not understand. While in his most critical contemplation, she asked, rather impulsively, "Do you sing at all?"

"No, not at all, poetry, yes, but I do not have that gift as you. Your music is quite unusual but very enjoyable. I believe that I could listen to your voice without ceasing, such a sweet harmonious resonance, one of the angels, to my ears."

"Thank you, that's very sweet of you to say. I love to sing but prefer to sing when there's not a lot of people around."

The afternoon continued to drift along as they sat on the blanket looking out at the lake when Oscar asked, "Are most girls in America like you?"

"How do you mean?

"I mean it in a good way, of course. I find you so different from girls in Ireland or London, for that matter. Ordinary women, there is no mystery about them; they are what they seem. I find you quite the opposite. You do remind me of one girl—someone I met some time ago. She is from Jersey," he spoke earnestly with a quaint smile before continuing, "she is very unique and most beautiful. She has a rare personality, reasonably intelligent, like you. When I first met you, I thought you had some of her ways—unquestionably her looks, except she has long golden hair. Her name is Lillie, she is a very close friend of mine. Perhaps, one day, you shall meet her. Yes, she turns heads, which I see you do as well."

"It sounds like someone that you admire very much."

"Yes, she is much to be admired, but I believe once you have been introduced to London society, it will be the same for you. It did not take her long to be accepted into the right social circles with her beauty. Yet, I have told her that society is wonderfully delightful, but to be in it, is merely a bore—and, to be out of it is simply a tragedy.[1] I have tried to convince her that she needs to become an actress— she would take London by storm, if so. For she seems to have that air about her that attracts others. And, therefore, those of substantial opulence seems to capture her attention."

"I would have to say that is one area that I am unlike your friend. No matter how much wealth someone has acquired, it would take more than that to capture my attention."

Oscar looked seductively into her eyes while he spoke, "You have captured my attention, Cateline. I am rather captivated by everything about you. You seem to be most confident about yourself and life—debonair as if you could conquer the world. As I have said, you are quite distinctive from girls in Europe. Most seem to be waiting for that certain gentleman to come into their lives where they can become a wife. They seem to believe life begins once married, and then they set up home and commence to have babies. It is the rare woman who appears to have a mind of her own and not necessarily in search of marriage to find her place in life."

Thinking about what he said, Cateline replied, "I would have to say that most girls are not like me. I've always been different. But, I, too, like most women, desire to be married and have that special man in my life. Yet, it would not ever be at the expense of where I become what he desires that I be. It must be where he loves me for who I am, my desires, and my ambitions in life. I suppose that I'm a dreamer, and I live by the inspirations that flow through my inner being. Sometimes they come through a song or music, but other times through writing. I love all forms of art and history. I can't imagine a life without the things in this world that bring beauty and happiness. There is too much sadness in the world if one desired to think about those things, but it is much easier thinking of the things that bring joy."

"Paradox though it may seem—and paradoxes are always dangerous things—it is none the less true that life imitates art far more than art imitates life,"[2] he replied to her address.

"I like that. Is it something you wrote?"

"Yes, I do declare that my life is full of expressing myself in words, as they also flow through as inspirations—it is a passion of the greatest kind."

"I know exactly how you feel," she responded while continuing with that train of thought, "it makes me sad sometimes because I realize that most people do not possess this kind of passion. My life would be nonexistent without the thoughts that come to mind that I can actually articulate on paper."

"It seems that we are much alike, indeed. What was your family life like growing up as a child?"

"I was raised in a most pleasant home, even though I did not really know my father from here. I was an only child, though, and was taught many valuable lessons in life—Biblical lessons. The Bible was actually an inspiration to my life, as it has been my guide many times in my walk and has brought me through much heartache as well."

"Yes, I have had my own battles in this life with good and evil. I, too, have turned to the church many times or the Scriptures, but I am not as sure as you about God guiding me in this life."

"I believe that everyone at some point in their life cries out for a God they may not know. I also believe that many of the trials in this life occur for a reason; it's His way of getting our attention. However, I know I am thankful that I was fortunate enough to have the

Bible at hand anytime in my life when I felt that I needed Him. So, tell me, what are your passions that you love to write about?"

"I would have to say that I am very passionate about the Aesthetic movement, Art for Art's sake. I am passionate about many things, really. In Europe, women have not had the same rights as men, and I believe that to be unfair. I sometimes feel I am an advocate for people who cannot speak for themselves, and in my writings or articles in columns, I can express thought, where others can reason what makes sense. I also have a deep passion to one day be a great playwright. As you have pointed out previously, it is as if the words I write clearly flow from within. I do understand your thoughts and the many things you have shared. I suppose someone who writes understands this while others may not."

"Yes, and I am sure you would agree, those who write also love to read. Even so, it is not about what one reads but about how one reads. People can read anything, but if they are only reading to read, they will gain nothing. It is reading to listen and to hear the words that bring life from within."

He stated while gazing into her eyes, "Yes, I understand that as well. I believe all true writers and artists truly feel what you are describing."

"To me, it's God's voice which I feel deep inside," she said, placing her hand over her heart while continuing, "it's not your physical heart but deep inside, you hear, and you know that He is speaking, the words just come alive to you. When I write short stories or poems, I feel them inside, and they are life to my soul—they are passionate, and they guide me through this life. In fact, the artist sees and feels what others never will."

"I believe it was Mozart who said, 'When I am... completely myself, entirely alone... or during the night when I cannot sleep, it is on such occasions that my ideas flow best and most abundantly. Whence and how these ideas come I know not nor can I force them.'"[3]

"Ah, yes, but Brahms declared, 'Straight-away the ideas flow in upon me, directly from God, and not only do I see distinct themes in my mind's eye, but they are clothed in the right forms, harmonies, and orchestration.'"[4]

"Yes, I have read that as well," Oscar remarked, "but Brahms also said, 'In my study, I can lay my hand on the Bible in the pitch dark. All truly inspired ideas come from God. The powers from which all really great composers like Mozart, Schubert, Bach, and

Beethoven drew their inspirations is the same power that enabled Jesus to do his miracles.'"[5]

Both laughing, Cateline professed, "I believe we both love the arts, Oscar. You honestly amaze me."

Responding with a most charming smile, he declared, "Always remember, the meaning of any beautiful created thing is, at least, as much in the soul of him who looks at it, as it was in his soul who wrought it.[6] Vice and virtue are to the artist materials for an art."[7] He paused for a moment before continuing, "Yet, it is not only about what we consider beautiful, Cateline, for the young artist who paints nothing but beautiful things... misses one half of the world.[8] An artist must be true to himself, true art lies within the beholder, and the artist must stay focused. The moment that an artist takes notice of what other people want and tries to supply the demand, he ceases to be an artist and becomes a dull or an amusing craftsman, an honest or a dishonest tradesman."[9]

There was silence for a while as they looked out over the lake at the lovely scenery, and Cateline pulled his coat tighter around her to break the chill in the air. Finally, Oscar inquired, "Are you too cold? Should we go in?"

"No, I like it out here. I will be fine; your coat is quite warm. Oscar, how long do you plan to stay, or do you have to be back in London anytime soon?"

"Well, yes—at some point, I do have to go back to London but not tomorrow at least. Of course, if you are tired of me, I can leave tomorrow."

With a most intense smile, she laughed before speaking, "Why no, I am not tired of you. I just didn't want this to end. I enjoy talking with you and learning from you."

"Learning from me? I find myself acquiring so much from you."

"That's very kind of you to say. But truthfully, I do hope that your stay will be most sufficient. I would enjoy getting to know more about you."

"Unless you are ready for me to depart, I have no desire to leave at all until I have conquered this feeling that you seem to bring about," he avowed with a most enigmatic smile while gazing into her captivating eyes.

"Feeling—and what might this feeling be?"

Oscar leaning over, ran his fingers through her hair as he gazed into her strikingly illuminating eyes before speaking, "I am not quite sure, but I do know that you do something to me." He paused briefly before continuing, "I really love your hair, leave it down for me, please, and—I do believe that you also are feeling what I feel, Cateline," he spoke in a most elusive voice while lifting her hand to his mouth where he placed a light kiss.

At that moment, Cateline felt tingling all over her body and was speechless for the first time in her life. Trying to change the subject, she established, "You have heard me play the pianoforte, as well as my guitar. I think it only right that I experience your accomplishments, Oscar."

"Are you trying to change the subject?"

"No, you just left me speechless. But, in all reality, I would like to experience your talents as you have mine."

"What did you have in mind, Cateline?"

"You have said that your desire is to be a great playwright, yes?"

"Yes, over the years, I have written not only poems but short stories and, of course, the one play. Thus far, many of my poems have been published, and I have won awards at both Trinity and Magdalen, but I do desire to be an eminent playwriter one day. I have written a play called *Vera* and have begun a few others, which I consider well written. I do plan to solicit *Vera* when I go to America. I believe I need the right actress for the part, and it would be a sensation. It is one of my passions, and without passion, nothing will come to fruition. So yes, I think I have a good chance of being celebrated one day as a playwriter. Have you ever acted?"

"Why no, not at all, but it definitely sounds so exciting. I have seen many plays, and they are very intriguing; however, I cannot imagine being an actress. I assume that would be the correct word."

"I would think you would rather do quite well."

Cateline lightheartedly responded, "I think not. I have no such knowledge in acting unless one could include her childhood escapades."

"Ah—we experienced some childhood acting, yes?"

"I wouldn't exactly call it that, but yes," she responded with a most fascinating smile while remembering all her exploits growing up with Mary by her side. Continuing, "My closest friend Mary, we were so inseparable. It was the best of times. We would actually write a play to perform for our neighbors each summer. I remember how serious I would take this quest. I would even go around in the neighborhood and talk several of the other children into participating when other parts were needing to be filled, minor roles, that is," she concluded. With a slight laugh, Cateline continued, "Naturally, Mary and I played the major roles; after all, it was our play. So, you see, I have never really acted; it was merely child's play."

"I don't know; it sounds to me like there was something within that gave you such a desire to act and maybe even write."

"Oh, but I do love to write, Oscar. I have written many articles that have been published. Of course, I write on specific topics that I spend time researching."

"I would love to see your work sometime."

"Yes, as I would yours as well. I was thinking, perhaps since you have heard me perform on the piano and guitar, and you have heard me sing, I, too, would love to see you act out a scene from a play of some sort which you have written."

"Hmmm—," Oscar thought. "Well, on one condition."

"And what might that be?"

"Sing me a song right now, any song but something quite magnificent."

Cateline laughed as she replied, "Surely not right here. Besides, you have already heard me sing."

"Yes, but I would like to hear you sing just to me right here and now. You sing me a song, and I will act out a scene from a play."

"I don't even have my guitar."

"I want to hear you, your voice—not the guitar."

"Let me think about what I can sing for you," Cateline responded as she thought about what song would be really pleasing. Finally, she replied, "Well, let's see, um—there's this song called, *Can't Take My Eyes Off of You*. It's such a beautiful song that was sung by a lady named Brenda Lee."[10]

Oscar smiled playfully and replied, "Sounds wonderful; please sing it for me."

Cateline stands up and walks a few steps closer to the lake before she begins to sing while looking out over the water with her back towards him—

The words drifted lightly about as Cateline turned with her eyes fashioned on Oscar, beholding this man whom she admired deeply, singing harmoniously with a soft touch. Romantically, she was moved, feeling the pleasantry of the melody as each lyric coasted through the air with such force. As she walked closer and closer towards him, singing the final chorus, Cateline briefly captured his eyes, finding herself lost in his world, mesmerized by his expression. Closing her eyes as she felt the sensations invigorating her essence for a second in time, memorizing the moment, Cateline felt caught up in this life—this instant—this world, one which she desired to embrace forever.

With the last words articulated, Cateline knelt down on her knees, sitting beside Oscar as he was elated by not only her beauty but also her talent. He gazed upon her quite pleasurably, with an astonishing reaction, "I believe you took my breath away, Cateline. If truth be told, you have an exceptional gift, and the song was utterly amazing. I must say something about your voice moves me in a way that I am not sure how to explain. When you sing, it is as a breath of passion."

"Thank you, Oscar, now it is your turn to act out a scene," she prompted with a most infectious smile while covering back up with the blanket.

Smiling obscurely at her, he responds, "I find it hard to tell you no on anything. I truly cannot think of a setting that could easily be performed right here, but I do suppose I could perhaps come up with a few lines to a short play of some sort. You know I do not act either, yet—that does not mean I could not; even so, I cannot pretend to act without another actor to play a part with me or rather an actress, which means you will need to perform alongside me."

Cateline laughs slightly, replying, "I definitely cannot act either. It was so many years ago, and it was not really acting."

"Never say you cannot do something. It seems that you have at least played a part, even if it was in your childhood. Remember, acting is the same as writing; you live and breathe it on the inside of you, Cateline. You take on the life of the person you are portraying where you can literally see and feel what they see and what they feel. Come, stand; we shall see what you are capable of doing. Besides, this will all be done purely for fun. We shall see how well you will do. I am sure it will all be quite entertaining. Perhaps, even a few laughs," he finished with a quaint smile.

Standing, Oscar shares, "The story is simply this, let's assume we are betrothed to marry, and the day before the wedding, you discover that I had an affair with your best friend. We are desperately in love, but you are distraught by what has been revealed and broken-hearted, even though you are still very much in love. Remember, you must feel the part as if it is factual, understand?"

"Yes, I think I do."

"We can use our own names to make it easier. You are at your home outside like we are right now. The day before the wedding, I arrive to see you, knowing nothing about what you have discovered. I am walking towards you as I notice you have been crying. I will begin with a line, and you merely feel the part and perform."

"We are just going to come up with our own lines as we go?"

"Yes, that makes it easier and more interesting," he replied with a wink.

"Alright, I think I can do this," she concludes with a most eager and luminous smile.

They both walk away and then turn around to face each other as they begin the scene. Cateline looks up to see him approaching, wiping away a tear while simultaneously, she turns around, not desiring to look directly into his eyes, all the while trying to hide the fact that she was crying. Oscar approaches her and puts his hand on her shoulder while she is standing facing the opposite way. "My dear, you are crying. Is there something wrong?"

She wiped away another tear before speaking softly, "Yes, there is. In fact, everything is wrong." Turning to face him, she continues, "Please, leave me alone, for I do not want to see you right now."

"You must tell me what have I done?"

"You should not ask me, but you should ask Alana as she came to see me early this morning. Please, do not pretend you do not know—and of any girl you could have chosen to disgrace my name, it had to be my best friend!" Feeling the part, Cateline's expressions intensify exceedingly. At the same time, she continues most earnestly with an exceptionally harsh voice, "YOU DARE say that you love me, for I will not listen anymore to your lies! PLEASE, sir, I ask that you leave me at ONCE, for I cannot bear to look into your eyes, those same eyes that have filled me with false hope, of a love which could never satisfy. For, it is true love that does not leave one with a broken heart—"

As Cateline continued to speak, Oscar started rolling over with severe laughter. While she looked up at him, articulating rather curtly in a charming dialect, "Are you laughing at me?"

187

"No, no—I am absolutely not laughing at you."

"But you are laughing."

"Not because you are not good at the role-play but because you are so sincere. It merely made me smile, and then I could not help but laugh; although, it was not at what you were saying, only at how serious you are taking this."

She responded while joining in with his laughter, "Well, Oscar, I do take everything quite seriously. You wanted me to play a role, and that is what I am trying to do. Shall we continue, or is this enough?"

"I dare say we finish where we left off. This has been extremely entertaining, and I do look forward to what you will say next," rather amused, he resumed, "so, where were we—ah yes, you had just finished telling me how you could not bear to look into my eyes and for me to leave."

Stepping back into her role, in a determined voice, Cateline spoke intensely, "YES, so as I was saying, my dear, I cannot bear to look into your eyes, those eyes that have looked into my own and revealed to me they loved me but have also deceived me, as you have broken my heart! Please, sir, if you would be so kind as to leave me, for I cannot endure seeing you! For how can you say that you love me and want to marry me, but yet you desire the company of another as well?" At this point, Cateline had real tears flowing down her cheeks as she turned from him to walk away.

"I'm not sure what to say, my dear. I will not deny what Alana has spoken, but upon my word, you must know that what you have been told is not entirely true. Yes, I admit that I was weak, but it was only one time—precisely one vulnerable moment in time. You must know that it is genuinely you whom I love. I have never loved anyone in the world but you. Good heavens, I could never love another," he spoke while following her steps.

As she spun around, tears streamed down her cheeks, and her words began to be expressed from somewhere deep inside—pain felt from within, her voice trembled, and tears broke out uncontrollably, "Why do you not start by telling me the truth. Why were you with her? If you say you could never love another, was I not enough?" Putting her hand up to stop him from moving any closer, she continued, "No, do not even answer that! There is nothing further to say. Please leave; I beg you." No longer able to look into his eyes, she turned back towards the lake.

"Yes, Cateline, you are enough, and I love only you," he cried out tenderly, "please turn around so that I can look you in the eyes and tell you how much I love you," with those words, he placed his hand on her shoulder while trying to turn her to face him.

With tears streaming down, she responded, "No, I do not and cannot look you in the eyes any longer! You have broken my heart," Cateline states while Oscar turns her around to face him. Looking down, she dared not make eye contact at that moment.

Oscar placed his hand under her chin, lifting her head to look into her eyes. He wiped her tears while speaking gently, "Look at me, Cateline—I love you more than life itself. Yes, I was wrong, and I am sorry. Please do not throw away our love, as there will never be another that I shall dare feel affection for but you, my dear."

Cateline stood looking up at his face, admiring his profile, tall and robust. His hands were of such strength yet so gentle as he wiped away her tears, she continued to gaze directly into his eyes. Captivated by every movement, she was suddenly silent, truly feeling something deep inside of her stirring. Oscar then proceeded to lean towards her as his lips touched hers, and his hands pulled her towards his body. With Cateline standing on her toes, they held each other as she welcomed the most passionate kiss she had ever experienced. With the kiss lingering, she found herself putting her arms around his neck. Entwined together, the kiss seemed to last forever. Once their embrace ended, they both stood there with their arms intertwined, and their eyes immersed one to the other for what seemed like an eternity. Neither spoke a word. All the same, their lips seemed to find each other once again, the second kiss lingering briefly. In those fleeting moments, Cateline gently pulled away from his arms and went back towards the blanket. She sat down and tried to act as though what had occurred was merely acting and nothing more. Feeling a bit embarrassed and unsure of what just happened, Cateline pulled her composure together before speaking, "Well, so how was my acting?"

Oscar, not really understanding what had befallen him, thought silently, "Was she simply acting, or was there something more there?" Hesitant on what to say, nervously, he smiled softly as he sat down beside her, "Your acting was impeccable if I do say so. You were magnificent. The tears, how did you manage such, my dear? Were they fake?"

189

"Perhaps they were not fake tears. Perhaps a woman can think of something sad that brings about the tears when she needs them for a reason. That's just something I have always been able to do."

"Is that the secret?"

"Perhaps it is."

"And what was the thought that produced the tears?"

"Well—that, I cannot say, at least not now—I do not know you well enough."

Leaving it at that, Oscar did not persist, but instead, he replied after several minutes, "Well, I must say your acting was very well indeed, please never say you are not talented in that area. Perhaps, I may want you in one of my plays someday, after all."

As they sat on the blanket, smiling at each other, Cateline finally broke the silence, "In real life, that is not at all the way I would have handled the situation."

Oscar laughing while inquiring, "I think I am afraid to ask, how would you have handled the situation?"

"I think I would have probably slapped you across your face, and then perchance, I would have pushed you into the lake, as I stated my case harshly and walked away," she responded abruptly with a mischievous smile on her face.

They both laughed while he concurred, "I think it would do me good to remember that; nevertheless, I do not perceive you to be harsh. On the contrary, your spirit is too gentle, Cateline!"

"Yes, you are probably right, but the thoughts of acting rashly would more than likely be present," she finished with a trivial smile.

Some time had passed while they sat silently on the blanket, looking out over the lake. Both seemed to be in deep thought, Cateline wondering if the kiss was Oscar's way of acting or if he felt something more. Thinking back on his conversation, she remembered he had said this was purely for fun. With that thought in mind, Cateline determined the kiss must have been merely acting. However, it was quite evident, the kiss had stirred her unexpectedly. Yes, it felt so natural—completely different from other experiences during the times she had briefly dated. In fact, one of her reasons for seldom dating was because she had never experienced that spark—the feeling one should feel when it was real, meaningful. Yes, she was truly a romantic inside and had enjoyed hearing her father share the moment when he knew her mother was the one, so to speak—and then there were the novels and movies. Love was not to be something one just accepted as so; it was to be felt, a feeling deep inside where one knew it was genuine! This time, the tender kiss between them had ignited that spark, the feeling she had dreamt but never experienced. Yes, she knew there was definitely something that stirred her deep within, leaving her without words.

Oscar, too, had continued to sit next to Cateline, quiet and absorbed in his own thoughts—drifting back to the kiss, wondering, and questioning what he was feeling. Caught off guard by her quick response to pull away from his kiss, he thought to himself, "Was she merely acting. Yes, that must be so, for she did pull away swiftly to inquire of her performance. The kiss must not have meant anything, and now, with her not speaking, she must be upset that I pursued her inappropriately, only knowing her for such a short time at that."

Neither of them knew what the other was thinking, which made it somewhat uncomfortable with the silence stifling the air. Unbearable as it was, feeling a bit awkward, Cateline eventually spoke first, "Perhaps, we should go back to the house where it is warmer."

"If that is what you want to do. I assume you are cold."

"Well, no, I am wearing your coat. Are you not cold?"

"No, not at all, but we can go back if you so desire."

Looking at each other face to face, Oscar finally remarked, "Cateline, the kiss—well, what I mean is that I never meant to kiss you like that, and I am sorry if I offended you."

"No, you did not offend me. I simply did not know if you were just acting, or it was something more."

"Truthfully, it was not acting. I would have never kissed you in that way. I suppose it clearly happened—because—well, because I had wanted to kiss you from the first day that I saw you when you were playing poona. I am truly sorry if it was not the right timing."

With a slight giggle, she looked up at Oscar most disputably to declare, "I don't think I looked attractive at all that day."

"Ah, but Shakespeare said, 'Love looks not with the eyes, but with the mind; and therefore, is winged Cupid painted blind.'"[11]

"Oh—so, you agree that I did look horrible that first day?"

"Why do girls always add words to what a man says?"

"But you said—"

"No, my dear—I did not say you looked horrible that first day. I merely spoke one of Shakespeare's quotes based on what you said. And so, to answer your question, no, you did not look horrible, not at all. On the contrary, I thought you to be most charming, but my dear, you must understand that it was not your looks that first caught my attention—no, it was observing your interactions with others. To me, you were the most fascinating creature I had ever laid eyes on, and I knew I had to have you," clearing his throat, he corrected, "I had to kiss you."

"From the first moment I met you, I, too, wanted to kiss you, to know you. I am not at all offended, really," she spoke most genuinely while Oscar leaned in towards her; being caught off guard, she suddenly began to laugh most abruptly. Pushing him backward, Cateline jumped up and ran while enticing him to chase her. "If you want to kiss me again—you will have to catch me."

Lit up with smiles, he stood and pursued the quest laughing along while Cateline became quite hysterical—screaming, running, and giggling. They playfully ran along the edges of the lake with Oscar in pursuit while she steadily dodged his every move. Cateline was able to hold her own while twirling around, running towards the tall row of trees, dodging and giggling like a young schoolgirl. How she felt so alive, experiencing the joys of love—a love she had already known. Oscar, too, was enjoying the adventure just as much as Cateline—and of course, it was not long until he was able to take her in his arms, as she had backed up to a tree. Still and silent, they stood gazing into each other's eyes, examining the contours; both were deeply engaged in knowing every single facial feature with such clarity. Oscar gently traced his fingers along her face, outlining the curves, learning each facial expression, from her smile and lips to her brows and the symmetry of her eyes. Hypnotized, they stood without a sound being spoken, yet their eyes captivated every thought and desire. In due course, Oscar leaned towards her as she inclined to him while he planted tiny kisses on every fragment of her face. Ultimately, kissing her lips intimately, holding each other, wrapped in an embrace, his lips persisted in seizing control over her senses where she was lost in the moment.

Once their lips had parted, he continued to gently stroke her face before taking her hand to lead her back towards the blanket. Hand in hand, there was silence, but it was no longer awkward, for both knew what the other felt. Lying on the throw, Oscar held Cateline in his arms. At the same time, they enjoyed the serenity of their surroundings—the tranquil water with an occasional duck splashing about, birds hovering overhead, and a rather busy-body male robin perched on a somewhat high branch peering down upon them. He was a most beautiful species wearing his bright red-orange vest over his grey-white belly. Gaining their attention with his shrill call, they gazed upwards, fascinated by his demeanor as it was apparent the robin desired their allegiance. Holding their gaze, he looked down at them and began his most melodious twittering. Enthralled, his gleaming presentation brought much laughter as they maintained observing the maestro of the tree. With life feeling complete, they were both captivated by time while the wind lingered, gently bristling over their flesh with the sensation of refined plumes. A day most perfect, lying side by side, feeling the love that neither had experienced before, captured by a devotion which was not understood, yet lost in what felt complete. Having only just met three days prior, it was as though they had known each other forever. While cuddling to keep warm, conversations evolved with an occasional kiss from Oscar on her forehead and, from time to time, her lips. It felt so right for both of them. To Cateline, it was as if she was living in a fairytale. Nonetheless, she knew her time there would be limited, but Cateline felt so much in love with this man whom she had spent much of her life living within the dreams that once was. They stayed out by the lake for most of the remainder of the day, enjoying each other's company with no desire for their time together to ever end.

CHAPTER
14

Having said all his farewells to the family the night before, James awakened Cateline early the following morning, before daybreak, as she had insisted on saying one last goodbye. He gave her a great big brotherly hug and encouraged her to visit Youghal. She was much inclined to accept his invitation as soon as a trip could be arranged. Upon Elbert entering the estate, ready with the brougham, Charles assisted James with his bag, and he was off to the station. Cateline, walking back into the home, climbed into bed for a few more winks before the draperies would be drawn.

The family woke to a bright and cheery Monday morning; having retired to bed early the evening prior, they were ready to begin a fresh week. A late breakfast was served that morning, while the house had seemed to be back to normal from the long weekend. Discussions progressed, here and there, through the course of the meal, as Mr. Walsh noticed quite a difference in the way Oscar and Cateline looked at each other with their continual dialogue, smiles, and an occasional giggle from Cateline. The talks continued around the table about the exceptional weekend, along with much discourse regarding Anya and Amos setting a date for their wedding. Once everyone had finished breakfast, Mr. Walsh still had a short time to spare before leaving for the office, having planned to arrive late. Looking over at Oscar, Samuel spoke candidly, "My good boy, why not come into my study before I have to leave so that we can talk."

"Yes, sir, Mr. Walsh—Samuel."

The men left the table while the ladies headed out towards the veranda to enjoy a cup of tea and fresh air for the day. Aunt Martha started the discussion, "Cateline, it is quite obvious that you and Oscar have become rather comfortable with each other."

"Yes, ma'am, we have much in common. I dare say we could probably never run out of things to talk about when we are together."

"I know you have only been here for a short time, but have you thought about plans for your future? You know that your uncle and I do so wish you would not leave for America. Perhaps, there could be plans for you and this young man?"

"Well, we haven't actually spoken of anything long term, Aunt Martha. I do believe that Oscar is not in a hurry to leave for London. We have talked about spending some time in Ireland together, as he would like to show me much of the history and give us more time to become acquainted."

"That sounds like a marvelous idea. You know that your uncle is currently speaking to him on his intentions with you, my dear, that they are most honorable, of course."

"Yes, ma'am, I understand. I do believe that his intentions are very honorable towards me, Aunt Martha. He has been such a gentleman and very kind. I do love being in his company."

"That all sounds well, dear. We just do not want to see you hurt in any way. And well, your uncle does plan to let Oscar know that as long as his intentions are honorable, in that his address to you, my dear, would be the object of his admiration, he would be more than welcome to stay and court you if he so desires."

"Yes, ma'am. Thank you again. I have had such a wonderful time, and I would have never dreamed there would have been such a connection between us. I am very grateful for everything you and Uncle Walsh have done for me."

About that time, Mr. Walsh and Oscar joined the ladies on the veranda as Samuel leaned over to kiss Martha before heading out to the office for the remainder of the day. Conversations continued among the ladies and Oscar until they had finished enjoying their time of tea. Mrs. Walsh had Anya join her inside, leaving Cateline and Oscar to themselves. Cateline assumed that it was intentional to give them time alone. Reaching out to take Cateline's hand, he inquired, "My dear, it would be simply gratifying to spend the day together in Dublin, as your uncle has been most gracious to allow us the use of the calash. I do hope this suits you."

"Why, yes, Oscar. I would love to spend the day with you, anywhere you desire."

"Entirely divine, we should visit some of the historical sites, and perhaps, go to the museum. And, we could have a delightful lunch in a quaint little café. I do hope that is agreeable."

"It sounds very pleasant, but you must give me time to prepare myself. I should dress appropriately for the city."

"I would expect as much. I will just stroll the grounds while waiting for you, my dear."

195

Cateline walked into the estate, heading upstairs to begin getting herself arranged nicely for a splendid day with Oscar. Sarah came in to help position her hair in a marvelous updo with twists, braids, and curls. She decided to wear her cream-colored, lacey dress, which was very soft and sheer, sheathed with many gathers of tulle extending throughout the bodice, around the hem, and covering in multiple layers on the bustled dress flowing down the back. An array of various earth-toned shades of satiny material were formed in a fashion to resemble roses and petals which paraded over one shoulder and down the side swirling around above the hemline. To complete her appearance, she powdered her face and lightly applied a bit of rouge. With Cateline's features quite impressive, it did not take much makeup to outline her beauty. Once dressed and heading downstairs, Cateline observed Oscar in the drawing-room waiting for her. Rising when she walked into the room, he approached her; bending down, he gently took her hand and instilled a gentle kiss. "You are the visible personification of absolute perfection, Cateline. I am beside myself to be seen in the city walking with you, my dear. I dare say all eyes will be fixated on you before they glance towards me, where they will then wonder why on earth you are with me," his words were spoken with a slight chuckle.

"Oscar, really? Everyone already knows who you are, and they will simply think that you have me because of your great talents. Why there is probably not a woman out there that would not want to be at your side."

"To whom do you allude? I dare not remember women lined up at my door desiring my attention. Needless to say, it is only by your side that I desire to be, my dear Cateline. Would you like me to bring my coat?"

"Perhaps, I've come to enjoy its warmth."

They walked out of the estate and got into her uncle's calash to head towards the city. As they rode along, Oscar looked over at Cateline; with concern, declaring, "Please, wrap yourself in my coat, dear. And there is a blanket under the seat if you prefer."

"Oh—thank you, that is most thoughtful. You know I will always prefer your comfy coat," Cateline said while draping the furry warmth over her shoulders.

Towards Dublin, they ventured along while Cateline enjoyed the views. Oscar, sharing much of the history of the city and surrounding areas, noted, "I am not sure if you knew, but Dublin is the largest city on the island of Ireland."

"The Emerald Isle—"

"Yes, *When Erin first rose*—"

"What was his name—William—"

"William Drennan, excellent. He was also a physician in Ireland besides a poet."

"Now, that I did not know. Do you remember how it goes?"

"Yes, I believe I do. Well, I remember a segment—

When Erin first rose from the dark, swelling flood,
God bless'd the green island and saw it was good;
The em'rald of Europe, it sparkled and shone,
In the ring of the world the most precious stone."[1]

"So pretty—but then, Ireland is most remarkable. Were the Vikings the first inhabitants of Dublin?"

"The Vikings founded Dublin, which was spelled D-u-b-h L-i-n-n—meaning *black pool* around 800 AD. But, in the twelfth century, the Normans took over the city where Henry II declared his son, John—Lord of Ireland. He inherited the kingship, and Ireland was then tied to the English throne. You may already be familiar with much of this; if so, please just tell me if I am boring you?"

"No, not at all. I love history. This is most entertaining to me; please go on."

"There are young ladies, I am sure that may love history, but that is typically not the case. Nonetheless, most ladies have not been given the opportunity of education, unless, of course, their families were wealthy enough to have their own governess."

"Yes, I suppose you are correct. However, I believe things are changing in America, where some cities allow girls to attend and be educated. I have been most fortunate and have even attended college."

"Yes, I thought as much. Your knowledge on various matters far out way most ladies from here."

"Please, share more of the history with me," Cateline entreated while Oscar steered the calash along the road by the bay.

197

"You are familiar with the Dublin Bay, which runs into the Irish Sea?"

"Yes, I am. Cyrus has a cottage very close to the bay. We rode horses out to Bull Island the other day."

"I see; it is simply delightful that he lives so very close. There are many beautiful beaches and scenery in Ireland. I have a few places I would like to take you as we are exploring. Perhaps, we may also be able to ride horses to some of the locations very soon."

"I would like that very much."

Cateline looked at the beauty of the bay as they rode along, with many buildings in the vicinity. "It seems as if the city never ends. I suppose the population of Dublin is quite substantial along with all the surrounding suburbs."

"Yes, I would say with all the adjacent towns, it is probably close to two hundred thousand. I believe it has the third largest port in the UK."

They continued to ride along while enjoying being deeply engaged in the discourse, which was most distinct in their body language; the attraction was felt not just outwardly but a profound connection of their individual passions and desires from within.

Traveling on, Cateline was able to see many ships and boats at the various ports along the way. "When I came to town with my uncle and Anya, we must have gone another route; we did not ride along the bay."

"There are other roads which lead into Dublin, probably faster, but I chose the more scenic route for you."

"I am glad you did. It is quite picturesque and full of so much history."

Continuing their course, they crossed over a small canal. "This is the Royal Canal. You would have crossed this any route taken from Clontarf."

"Yes, I do remember this."

As they came into the city of Dublin, traveling the road along the quay, the buildings were prominent on both sides. Oscar expounded, "We are on the north side of the river right now, and the other side is considered the south."

"What river is this, Oscar? I don't remember being close to this location when I came into the city before."

"You had to have crossed the river; you were probably not paying attention. This is the River Liffey."

"Yes, I am sure you are right. When I came with Anya to purchase our dresses, we were much too engaged in a discussion regarding the upcoming revelry. Yes, I do remember the river upon leaving the city but not when entering," laughing slightly while thinking back on their enchanting day filled with the excitement of shopping in the exquisite locales.

"If you look to your right, we are coming up to the Custom House."

"The Parliament buildings, I suppose. They are most beautiful, and the Four Courts on Inns Quay where my uncle works."

"You were fortunate to have been in the Four Courts building?"

"Yes, after Anya and I finished our shopping, we walked to my uncle's office."

"You are also familiar with the various courts?"

"Oh no, I never asked, and it wasn't offered."

"It houses the Supreme Court, the Court of Appeal, the High Court, and the Circuit Court. We could try to stop in and visit your uncle, but he may be rather busy and not expecting us—"

"Oh no, that is quite alright. I am sure that my uncle is very busy, but the buildings are so wonderfully designed."

Cateline noticed while riding along the quay numerous structures, such a large city with the riverside so full of every kind of boat imaginable. The architecture was most impressive—Georgian urban buildings, Palladian, Gothic and neo-Gothic, to include Norman. Cateline could only perceive it to be comparable with some of the old buildings in Boston and, of course, in many of the first states, Delaware, Pennsylvania, and such. She also knew much of the European architecture had heavily influenced America, even though she had not ventured across the country to many locations.

After viewing the diverse sites along the north side of the river, Oscar turned the cart around to go back towards the direction they had come. Continuing along the quay for a short time, Cateline looked across the river at all the glorious architectural buildings lined about. How she loved history and wondered what changes had been made to many of those buildings by the twenty-first century.

Pulling the calash over close to a long bridge that crossed the river, Oscar jumped out of the buggy and tied the horse to a post. The bridge was absolutely stunning, and it seemed as if it was clearly for walking across, not any kind of transportation. "What is this bridge, Oscar? I'm assuming it is just for pedestrians?"

"It is," he acknowledged while walking over to take Cateline's hand and help her down. "This is the Ha'penny Bridge, or in Irish it would be, Droichead na Life. It received its name because a toll was set to pay for the bridge and the cost a half-penny or ha'penny to cross. It is only for pedestrians, but it is most notable, and I believe if in Dublin, my dear, it is something you simply must do. Please, come, and we shall walk out on the bridge where you can gauge a different view of the river."

They first walked over to look at the river, with Cateline commenting, "It is so gorgeous with such a rush of current."

"The Liffey begins in the Wicklow mountains, a superior location. I shall take you there one day very soon. The mountains are striking with a charming waterfall that is quite popular—the Powerscourt. The river then flows through Wicklow, Kildare, and Dublin, where it emerges into the Irish Sea."

"And Clontarf, where my uncle's estate is, it is also close to the Liffey River?"

"The Liffey flows to the Irish Sea, south of Clontarf. There is a much smaller river, the Tolka, which flows beside Clontarf and then into the sea."

Oscar paid the toll; taking Cateline's arm, he led her towards the center of the bridge where many other couples were standing here and there. The expanse of the city of Dublin could be seen across the way, filled with many a pedestrian, carts, and wagons of every size. "The bridge was built the early part of the 1800s and is made of cast iron," Oscar disclosed.

Coming to the center, they both stopped to look out at the stunning views, beholding the river and city that lay beyond the banks on both sides. It was breathtaking. Oscar had stood behind Cateline as he wrapped his arms around her and held her close while they viewed the beauty. A few times, he leaned down to kiss her on her neck. Everything seemed so perfect and so right, Cateline kept pushing the thoughts out of her mind that her time would one day end, and she could not in any way stay forever. She struggled to live for the moment, knowing that was all they had, and her feelings for him remained, growing deeper and deeper with each minute they shared. Even though they were not completely alone on the bridge, it felt like there was no one around. They both were only attentive to each other, and neither allowed distractions to enter their moment together. As she turned to face him, looking up into his enticing eyes, he leaned down to kiss her tenderly. They embraced while distancing themselves from any disruptions. To them, they were all alone and cared not what anyone thought. With such a deep attraction and a yearning to be in each other's arms indefinitely, they both continued to embrace as their eyes were held spellbound—beholding, gazing, mesmerized. Oscar, enticed by her beauty, occasionally leaned forward to kiss her tenderly. In a very soft voice, Cateline commented, "I could remain right here in this moment forever, Oscar."

"As could I, Cateline. Plato stated, 'Human behavior flows from three main sources: desire, emotion, and knowledge,'[2] or rather Plato quoting Socrates. For when I am near you, I feel that I want to hold on and never let you go." Laughing, he sustained, "For I have a hard time controlling my appetite as the majority of the population, I am sure. My passions seem to be out of control, whereas my reasoning is no longer my own."

Cateline asserted, teasingly, "I suppose I have cast my spell upon you, my most humble cavalier."

They walked back over to where Oscar had left the buggy, holding hands along the way. "My uncle, I know he called you into his study to speak of me."

"Yes, he did, and I had assumed as much. Does that distress you?"

"No, my aunt had informed me of the matter he discussed with you."

"Oh—so, you know that your uncle and aunt saw us at the lake yesterday when I was chasing you?"

Cateline, stunned, stopped to look up at Oscar, "Why no, she never mentioned that. She only told me that my uncle was speaking to you on your intentions."

Smiling, he continued, "Yes, I suppose he did want to know what my intentions were since we have yet to know each other less than a week, and they witnessed my kissing you."

"Oh—my, I had no idea. What did you say?"

201

"Well, of course, I assured your uncle—as, I will also assure you, my intentions towards you are most honorable."

"I never thought otherwise; you have been a complete gentleman towards me."

"You are quite special to me, and I look forward to sharing many days by your side. In fact, I look forward to knowing everything about you, if that be possible," Oscar finished, with a slight chuckle as he was charmed by her presence and mystified as he gazed into her eyes.

"My uncle, was he upset?"

"No, not at all; I believe he was merely concerned that we have not known each other very long for me to have kissed you," he responded with a most playful smile.

"And what was your reply?"

"Well, I was not prepared, by any means—after all, I was unaware anyone saw us. The only thing I could say was that it was wrong of me to do so in such a short time—even so, the times I had spent with you, I just felt like we had known each other for much longer."

"I suppose that appeased him?"

"Yes, I do suppose, and with that, I agreed to remain for a time to get to know you properly and to court you, that is if it pleases you."

With his last statement, Cateline felt so relieved and happy inside but did not want to show her feelings so soon. She cautiously countered, "So, you do not have to return to London and will be able to stay longer than you had planned?"

"I intend to stay as long as it takes."

"Meaning—"

Oscar stops and stands to face her, "Cateline, I believe that you have feelings for me as I have for you. I dare say that I shall not leave without knowing if what we are feeling is real—and if so, I will not leave without knowing one way or the other." He then leaned down and kissed her affectionately as she reacted and melted into his arms. They continued to walk towards the calash in silence, knowing what the other was feeling.

Oscar held Cateline's hand, helping her into the buggy before climbing in himself. He then took the reins to steer the horse along the quay towards the Grattan bridge, where they had to backtrack a small distance. The Grattan bridge could be crossed by carriages or trams, as it was much broader than the Ha'penny. Crossing the bridge, they headed towards Dublin's south side while Oscar suddenly stated, "I would like to take you to see Trinity College. It is where I graduated before attending Magdalen. Normally, when I am in Ireland, I stop by to visit some of the faculty. They do appreciate my coming when I am in Dublin, which is very seldom these days."

"Yes, I would love to see Trinity."

"It is also next to St. Stephen's Green, a very enchanting park opened to the public. There are restaurants close by, and I thought we might order a take-out meal to eat in the park if that sounds pleasing to you. There is a most delightful lake with a quaint bridge that crosses."

"That sounds wonderful. I am so enjoying seeing all these sights and being with you, Oscar."

As they approached the college, Oscar steered towards an area where he could secure the horse to a post and, once again, came to help Cateline down from the buggy. Taking off his coat, she declared, "This is amazing. I so love all the architecture in the city."

"Yes, the architect is quite old, with the college being founded in 1592."

"Really, it is that old?"

"Yes," Oscar replied while walking beside her towards the tower.

"Is that the bell tower?"

"It is, mademoiselle," he responded while revealing a bit of his French, "built about thirty years ago."

"It is quite beautiful," Cateline expressed while she gazed profusely over the many interests throughout the college grounds while nearing the statues.

"This is Oliver Goldsmith, and the other one across the way is Edmund Burke, both graduates of Trinity."

"Oliver Goldsmith was a novelist from the eighteenth century?"

"Yes, born in Ireland and moved to London, also a poet and playwright."

"I'm not sure I know who Edmund Burke was."

"Eighteenth-century, as well. He was a statesman and philosopher, and a member of parliament in the House of Commons in London with the Whig Party—*There is a boundary to men's*

203

passions when they act from feelings, but none when they are under the influence of imagination.'"[5]

"I like that. Who wrote it?"

"Burke, he was also known for his many quotes. That is one of my favorites."

"Hmmm, there is a boundary to our passions when we act by feelings—but none when, what was that?"

"None when we are under the influence of imagination."

"Ah yes, I can see that. Feelings can sometimes mislead us, but our imagination is free to use as we please without limitations—restrictions."

With a most clever remark, smiling, he probed, "Which is your victory and which your ruin?"

Before answering, she pondered his question, "Truthfully, I would have to say that my feelings as well as my imagination share in my conquest and my defeat. I am unsure that I know which would be more dominant, and you?"

"I live in my imagination, as I am sure you understand. It is part of my writing and creating—we are all actors in this life; being oneself is a form of playacting, with the most important act of creativity is the creation of one's own image.[4] Still, I do love my senses in which there are moments where they overrule me."

She thought about this as they walked about the grounds seeing many a gentleman along the way, with stares and discourse among those walking in groups and pairs. Holding her hand, he leaned over to whisper, "Do not be surprised if all eyes are upon you, as there are no girls that attend."

"Should I not be here with you?"

He responded with a copious laugh, "Yes, of course, you can come with me. It is just not every day these chaps who attend get to see such an attractive lady on the premises." Once they had covered the campus's outer areas, he led her back to the front entrance.

Entering the building, they approached the main office, where several faculty members were present. The gentlemen all looked up, surprised to see Oscar while they stood from their desks, walking over to shake his hand. Introducing Cateline, they were delightful in welcoming her and Oscar both. Communication erupted on his whereabouts, life in London, and the stories they had kept tabs on concerning his career. One of the gentlemen immediately had left to walk into another office while he exclaimed, "I must let Professor

Mahaffy know you are here. He would be so disappointed to not have had the pleasure of seeing you. Please do not leave, Oscar." Conversations continued on his dealings in London and the American tour, which had spread throughout Dublin while waiting for the professor.

In a short while, a very jovial man walked into the room, "Oscar, my dear boy, so pleasant to see you," the man exclaimed as he stepped forward to greet him. Introducing Cateline, the professor extended his hand to receive her as well. "Please, please," Professor Mahaffy addressed one of the other men in the office, "we must take pictures. It is not every day that we see Oscar." One of the gentlemen walked into another room and came back with some sort of old-type camera. "Take one of Oscar with Miss Cateline but take two of them so I can forward one to Oscar. Then I would like you to take a photo of me with both of them, of course, two once again." He first took two pictures of Oscar and Cateline together, with Oscar having his arm around her waist, and then the man took two with Professor Mahaffy in the picture with them. Cateline had immediately recognized the professor when he walked in the room, as being in one of the images from the old articles found at the library, and acknowledging the background, she was certain this was one of the photos along with a second one of just her and Oscar together. This made her heart sink, knowing the pictures had begun and would continue to the last one— realizing, once all photos were captured, there would be no reason for her to remain. They stayed for a while, Oscar catching up with the professor on his dealings before saying their 'goodbyes.'

"My dear boy, once we have the pictures developed, I will forward your copies to you in London, unless you will be in Dublin for some time."

"Yes, sir—I do plan to be in Dublin for a while. If you could simply forward them to Cateline's uncle, Samuel Walsh. He is a senior barrister at Four Courts."

"Ah yes, I will do that, and you should have them very soon. It is so good to see you."

"Thank you, Professor Mahaffy. It has been good to see you as well. I would like to show Cateline the *Book of Kells* before we leave, sir."

"Yes—yes, by all means, please take your time; you know where it is located. If you need anything, please let us know."

"Thank you, sir," Oscar said as he led Cateline down the hallway into the old library to view the book.

In the library, Cateline inquired, "Has the book been here for an extensive length of time, Oscar?"

"It has; I want to say it was brought to Trinity in the seventeenth century but was only placed on display about thirty years ago or so."

"It is so old, hard to believe that it has survived as long as it has. What century does it date back to?"

"I want to say 800 AD and written in Latin."

"Oh, do you speak Latin?"

"No, no Latin."

Cateline subtly inquired while they walked outside, "Trinity is a liberal arts college, right?"

"Yes, but they have expanded over the years, where it is not just liberal arts."

"The colleges in Ireland, none of them accept girls, is that correct?"

"There are some that take women in Cork and Galway, I know for sure. There may be a few more places, and this only began a few years back, but it is merely for those families who can afford tuition."

Walking back to the cart, Oscar shared different stories of his years spent at Trinity—many first-rate memories. He smiled and laughed with her as she delighted hearing of all his escapades during those early years. Upon leaving Trinity, they had to pass by the park where Oscar noticed all the construction. "Well, it looks like St. Stephen's Green is shut down for renovations—ah, *Faiche Stiabhna*, I hope eating inside the restaurant will be fine?"

"Yes, you are the chauffeur, anywhere you desire. Too bad about the park; it does look very inviting."

"Perhaps, next time we are in Dublin."

Puzzled, she questioned, "Next time, WE are in Dublin?"

"Yes, I am assuming that you are not staying indefinitely, am I right?"

"Well, yes, you are correct."

Oscar, changing the subject, mentioned, "We could still order food and find a grassy place along the river to spread out the blanket and eat—stunning views."

"Yes, that sounds even better."

Finding a quaint little café, they went in and were seated as they looked over the menu. Oscar, placing their order, advised the server, they would like to take it with them. Waiting for their cuisine, Cateline curiously inquired, "What was your life like growing up, Oscar?"

"What would you like to know?"

"I want to know everything about your father and mother, other family members, your likes and dislikes, those things that made you happy and sad."

"Yes," he spoke with a slight laugh before continuing, "I understand you would like to know everything and in due time. I, too, would like to know more about your life, as well—needless to say, it cannot all be said in one day, am I right?"

"Of course, but we can start."

"Yes, we can. I will begin by sharing one thing, and then you tell me something about your life. I believe that would be quite reasonable, yes?"

"I believe so."

"My father was Sir William Wilde, and my mother was Lady Jane Wilde. My father was an eye and ear surgeon. He was also an author, but essentially, he wrote on medicine. However, he also composed numerous articles on the culture and traditions of Ireland. His father, my grandfather, was also a prominent medical practitioner. My father earned his medical degree from the Royal College of Surgeons in Ireland. He loved to impart tales about his life after he had received his degree, of course. This was before he met and married my mother; I used to love hearing his stories. He had embarked on a cruise to the Holy Land with a patient, visiting various cities, but porpoises were caught and flung onto the ship at which he would dissect them and took notes on their habitat. He eventually wrote a book on the nursing habits of the porpoise. My father won many awards and was ultimately awarded knighthood at the Dublin Castle, which by the way, is in this same vicinity. I would love you to see the castle, it is most impressive. And to make a long story short, after his knighthood by the Queen, he became Sir William Wilde, which made my mother, Lady Jane Wilde."

With a genial smile, she responded, "My uncle had shared some of this, but most of it I did not know. You sound like you gained much of your love for writing and your cleverness from your father."

207

"My father did influence my life, but it would have been my mother that played a greater part of my love for art."

"Ah, yes, of course. I had heard that your father passed on?"

"Yes, my father died about five years ago."

"Your mother, she is still living?"

"She is, and she is in her late fifties—also a writer, but women have always been discouraged from writing unless under another name, so her pseudonym is *Speranza*. She wrote for the *Young Ireland* movement in the 1840s and published poems. My mother has always been a strong activist for women's rights and education, as well, and continues to this day. She actually left Dublin two years ago to move to London, closer to myself and my brother—currently living with my brother, Willie, who also writes."

"I suppose you are close to your mother even now?"

"Yes, there were many things that occurred before my father's death, and upon his passing, my mother decided to finally come to London. I love my mother dearly, and it was probably her compelling influence in my life that led me to be where I am today. She is very talented in her writings and poetry and has spent much of her life fighting and advocating for women's rights, doing so fearlessly. My father was a good man, but he came with certain faults, yet my mother kept our home together and loved him, defects and all. She was the light in our home and brought happiness as we grew up. I also had a sister, Isola, who died a few months before she turned ten—I was twelve at the time."

"I am so sorry, Oscar. How did she die?"

"Isola had been sick for a time, with a fever. They believed she was getting better when she suddenly died. We were told that it was a sudden effusion on the brain."

Their lunch had been prepared and packaged for take-out. Being brought to their table, Oscar paid for their order, gathered everything up where they left to find a quaint setting along the river to enjoy their meal.

Continuing the dialogue where they had left off, Cateline concluded solemnly, "I'm truly sorry to hear that you lost your little sister. That must have been very hard on your family. Does time seem to heal the pain?"

"Time heals it to a degree, but I do not believe one ever gets over the death of one to whom they are very close. It was a most dreadful ordeal for my whole family. It has been so long ago. And yet, I have never forgotten her. I believe that her death, to some degree, has shaped my life. No, you never really seem to get over losing someone very dear to your heart."

"Yes, you were only two, three years apart. So, you must have been quite close."

"Indeed, we were, and being older, a brother is always protective of any sisters. I still tend to go to her grave from time to time. In those days, I would go several times a week. I also wrote a poem for her when I was nineteen, and I have finally decided to publish it this year."

"I would love to read it."

"I have it with my papers; remind me when we are back at the estate. I would love you to read it."

"Thank you, that means a lot to me."

They continued along the quay in search of the ideal spot, where on another note and being somewhat concerned, Cateline exclaimed, "Oscar, you smoke too many cigarettes; you do know that is not good for you?"

"Nothing is good in moderation; you cannot know the good in anything till you have torn the heart out of it by excess."[5]

Cateline, unable to keep a straight face, smiled oddly, for she knew many of his favorite quotes.

"Ah-ha, you smile?"

"Well, yes—you do have a way with words, but that is quite foolish, and you know it. I only say what I do because I care about you and know that tobacco is not good for you."

"Ah, but women love us for our defects. If we have enough of them, they will forgive us everything, even our intellects."[6]

"You think so, do you?"

Oscar replied proficiently, "Please, do not worry, just enjoy spending time with me. Let's never spoil a moment in disagreement when there are far too many points we can agree."

Cateline knew he was right with his last account, and besides, she knew her coming had nothing to do with changing who he was inside nor outwardly. Any changes would be his choice and his choice only.

Riding along the river and on the outskirts of the city, they eventually found the perfect location for lunch—a spectacular grassy area with several trees for shade. Oscar steered over to the side of the road and secured the horse to one of the trees. Spreading out the blanket, Cateline assisted Oscar with all items from the buggy, where they sat down to enjoy the flavorsome lunch together as they talked endlessly. "Oscar, this is so lovely. I so love the river and hearing it as it rushes forth with such intensity."

"This may actually be better than the park."

"A most quaint setting and rather soothing, if I do say so. If I didn't know any better, I would have to say that you are a bit of a romantic."

While articulating his words, Oscar stated, "I assure you, whatever my life may have been, ethically, it has always been romantic.[7] I do assume that you find that character of mine quite charming?"

"Most certainly, I do. But I also believe that this has been the best day of my life, so far," Cateline mentioned as the closeness she felt towards this man continued to evolve. Relaxing while looking over the beautiful scenery, feeling the crisp breeze from the rush of the rustling waters of the River Liffey, they enjoyed the delicious cuisine. Engaged in shared stories of countless past memories, much laughter and times of seriousness were exchanged, making their day most memorable.

Once they had finished eating and relaxing by the river, they rode back into the city, with Oscar showing Cateline several historical places and sharing stories with her of his years growing up. The journey proved prosperous as he drove past multiple locations, which sparked additional memories and supplied yet another account. They both were so settled, with Cateline enjoying the various narratives of years past, which provided exceptional humor, many laughs, and far more questions. As time passed, Oscar pulled the calash over to a quaint area in the vicinity of a few small cafes and pubs. "Would you like to have some refreshment—tea?"

Looking up to observe their surroundings, Cateline inquired, "The famous pubs in Ireland that America always hears about, is that one of them?"

"Mulligan's, I suppose it would be. It has been here for quite some time."

"Are ladies not allowed to go in?"

"There's not a law to keep women out, but most who are respectable will not be seen in a pub. Unfortunately, there are also those owners who will refuse to serve women. Are you interested in Irish pubs?"

"Oh, I simply wanted to see what it was like at an Irish pub since there are a few in Boston. I just wondered if they were the same, that is all."

"In America, it is acceptable for women to socialize in pubs?"

"I believe in America, there are not as many rules for women and, even though it may not be appropriate, it is allowed."

"I see, very well—come, I shall get you in. You can sit at a table in the back, and I will go to the bar and order us a couple of Guinness's. If you are going to do this, you might as well do it right. People come to Ireland to go to a pub to have a Guinness."

Pleased with his comment, Cateline agreed, "Yes, as long as I am with you, I can do this. So, let's go in."

They walked into the pub, and as expected, it was filled with many older gentlemen and a few younger whose eyes were fixed upon Cateline. Oscar knew anywhere he took her, men would all stare at her phenomenal beauty, "Get used to the stares; you are out of place in here, I assure you."

"I've got this. Just point me in the direction where we are going to sit."

"Any of the tables in the back of the room should be most sufficient. I will get the beer and join you."

As Cateline walked back to the table, all eyes continued to be on her every move. Of course, it did not bother her because she was with Oscar. As she sat down, three young men approached the table. Evidently, they knew Oscar, for she heard one remark, "Boys, we must be doing something wrong, look what Oscar has brought in." While ordering the Guinness, Oscar watched the young men approach the table where Cateline sat; recognizing who they were, he was utterly amused walking back to the table. They all seemed to be conversing with her, and Cateline was doing a pretty good job holding her own.

Oscar speaking up, "I beg your pardon, gentlemen, I believe the lady belongs to me."

211

Squeezing through the men who had gathered around her, one remarked, "Ah, do not be so certain Oscar, ole chap, until there is a ring on her finger, you can never be so sure that she is all yours!"

"Oh, I am quite sure indeed, for I have already charmed her with my good looks and my wit. Perhaps the ring is not too far off. All the same, you chaps are welcome to join us. This is Cateline, an American; I suppose I should say she is Irish but was raised in America. Cateline, these are some old friends of mine during my days at Trinity."

They all pulled up chairs, catching up on Oscar's happenings in London and talking with Cateline to learn more about America. It was fairly obvious the young men were fascinated with her beauty and charm. The gentleman who sat closest to her at one point addressed Oscar, "Parle-t-elle francais?" Once spoken, they all looked towards Cateline to see if she understood French.

Cateline, deciding to play along with their game, responded, "You speak in French so that I will not know what you say?"

The gentlemen all seemed to laugh playfully, as they assumed, she did not speak French. Oscar then spoke up, "Non, elle ne parle pas francais." **All laughing**—Cateline smiled, knowing that this would be entirely entertaining.

"Sa beauté est rare, n'est-ce pas? Talent de beauté intelligent, non?"

Oscar replied, "Oui, tout un tresor."

As they all smiled, Cateline decided to end the charade, "Oui, messieurs. Je suis tout à fait le trésor et je fais bien de rendre mon homme heureux. Droit mon cheri?"

Everyone laughed to include Cateline, while Oscar responded, "You never mentioned that you spoke French."

"You never asked. Truthfully, I am much better at understanding what one is saying than speaking it fluently. Still, I am reasonably knowledgeable in French.

Soon, Oscar announced, "Sorry, boys, but we only stopped in so Cateline could see what an Irish pub was all about. I am afraid we need to be heading back to the estate. It has been a pleasure to see all of you."

Upon leaving, Oscar held Cateline's hand as they walked to the calash. He then helped her into the seat while inquiring, "So, what do you think about a pub now, my dear?"

"It was interesting—so, a ring perhaps soon to come? You do seem to be pretty sure of yourself that I belong to you, even though we have only just met?"

"Yes, if I do say so, we were meant to be together," with a playful laugh, he continued, "I am sure you feel the same. Please tell me if I am wrong, for I cannot imagine my life without you. Of course, I do know that I must make you love me, and I am working on that." With his last spoken words, Oscar winked as he gazed into her alluring eyes.

Responding with a smile, "Hmm, and how do you propose to make me fall in love with you, Oscar Wilde?"

"It is quite obvious, my dear—kiss me!"

"Kiss you?"

"Kiss me unless it frightens you."

"Why should I be frightened? You have already kissed me."

"Yes, but you kiss me this time."

As Cateline smiled, she leaned over to kiss Oscar, a kiss that lingered as every part of her tingled. Once their lips parted, Oscar spoke, "You see, it is the kiss. We were destined to be together, and the kiss awakens the inner self; you have felt that as I have, my dear. Tell me if I am wrong."

Cateline, looking into his eyes, lit up with a smile, knew she could not deny what he spoke. "Yes, Oscar, you are right. I do feel the same way as you, and I wish that every day could be as today, and it never had to end."

"It does not have to end, my dear. Oh, and by all means, I did forget to mention your language skills, rather impressive, if I do say so, it was quite amusing. I am only thankful we said nothing that would have been inappropriate."

"Well, I did enjoy the conversation. You speak other languages as well?"

"Yes, besides English, I am fluent in German and French and have some knowledge of Italian and Greek—enough to understand perhaps."[8]

"Ah, how remarkable—Irish—Gaeilge?"

"No, not at all," he said with a quiet laugh.

213

CHAPTER
15

The following day, Oscar planned to take Cateline into the city, once again, to continue exploring various locations—the Dublin Castle, a few museums, and a quaint dinner before heading to Dan Lowrey's Star of Erin Music Hall. Beginning their day, they first enjoyed the English breakfast and elevenses with the family before loading up in the calash to leave for Dublin.

"I thought we could first drive by the castle and the home where I grew up since there was not sufficient time yesterday, my dear. They are both a short distance from one another," Oscar elaborated.

"Yes, I would love to see your home, also the castle."

On their ride into Dublin, Oscar reached down to pick up his briefcase. Pulling out his journal, he handed it to Cateline, "I have not forgotten the poem I wrote for my sister—please, I have the page marked, if you would like to read it."

"Yes, I would love to," she said while filming through the booklet—

"Requiescat
Tread lightly; she is near
Under the snow
Speak gently; she can hear
The daisies grow.
All her bright golden hair
Tarnished with rust
She that was young and fair
Fallen to dust.
Lily-like, white as snow
She hardly knew
She was a woman, so
Sweetly she grew.
Coffin-board, heavy stone
Lie on her breast
I vex my heart alone
She is at rest.
Peace, peace; she cannot hear

Lyre or sonnet
All my life's buried here
Heap earth upon it.
Avignon.[1]

After reading the poem, she noticed he had crossed out several lines. Before inquiring, she browsed over those words, "The additional verses, did you decide not to include them?"

"Only the ones not crossed through shall be published. I have been working on it and made a few changes."

Cateline reread the verses which were marked through once silently to herself—

"Had we not loved so well
Not loved at all
None would have tolled the bell
None borne the pall.
O bitter fate
When some long-strangled memory of sin
Strikes with its poisoned knife into a heart
While she has slept at peace.[2]

Having finished the complete poem, Cateline became quiet, thinking to herself, "What did those other verses mean—was there something far greater hidden that he lived with his whole life—something that perhaps, he took to his grave with him." Finally, looking at Oscar, she proclaimed, "Oscar, I am so sorry for your pain. The poem is beautiful. I will always wish I could have met her. She must have been very special to you."

As he remained silent to her remark, Cateline could tell it was a topic extremely difficult for him to express, even after so many years.

They continued to ride along while Cateline was in deep thought on the pain he obviously felt within. At the same time, she enjoyed the lush views of Ireland until they had eventually arrived within the city.

"We shall be passing the home where I grew up first; it is just around the corner." Approaching, he slowed the horse while steering over to the side of the road.

215

"Is this it?" Cateline inquired while observing a Georgian architectural style home.

"Yes, I wish you could see the inside. There is a staircase when you first walk in, which is truly quite impressive. My father actually had his practice here, as well."

"It is so wonderful, Oscar, and the architecture is most inspiring. Your childhood must have been very fulfilling."

"Ah, indeed it was! I cannot complain, really—except, for the loss of my sister, my childhood was most pleasing."

As they sat looking at the home, Cateline addressed him, "Your father, you have special memories of him, I am sure."

"Undeniably, he was a good man, most intelligent. He had his faults, like many, of course, but my mother stood by his side through everything. She is quite a remarkable woman—possesses beauty, intelligence, kindness. I suppose I have always admired how she loved my father despite his flaws—all women are not like that," he spoke with a solemn look on his face—a countenance of silence, but words were not needed for what was said in his discreetness.

"Your mother sounds very amazing. I can see that you love her deeply," Cateline responded to his silence, knowing in her heart his idea of the perfect wife was one who would stand beside her husband clearly as his mother had always done with his father. Cateline also knew that one day, she would not be there. But yet, never would she desert him. Even though her presence would no longer remain, she would never be gone in thought or feeling, always loving this man despite those things he would one day be accountable for, incidents he may question and perhaps even regret. "Oscar," she began to speak, placing her hand upon his, "I do believe that one day, you will find someone who will love you unconditionally." With those words coming forth from her lips, Cateline already knew that she did love this man as such. As she continued, her words were spoken softly, "I believe that your mother is a most remarkable person, and I so admire her for the woman she was with your family and with you."

"Yes, she is rather incredible. One day, you will meet her."

After a brief moment, Oscar steered the calash back onto the road, during which they were both occupied observing the various points of interest in the general area before Cateline spoke again. "Oscar, thank you for sharing the poem written for your sister with me; that really means a lot. I do desire to know more about your life."

"I am quite enjoying this time with you, myself."

"I believe you have spoken of short stories and even plays—Vera, for one, yet have you any other work which is close to being published?"

"I have written man poems over the years during my days at university, and I am currently working on publishing a book of poetry this year, which I do believe I had mentioned to you. Other than that, I have only finished the play *Vera* and have had others read it. I would love for you to read it, as well, if you would like."

"*Vera*, is it a romance?"

"It is based on the life of Vera Zasulich, from Russia. Are you familiar with her story?"

"No, I'm afraid I am not."

"She is a most phenomenal woman, born into an impoverished minor noble family. Her father died when she was relatively young. Her mother sent her to live with relatives—wealthy relatives. It was soon determined she was quite brilliant, becoming involved in radical politics, where she became a respected leader in the movement."

"I would love to read your play; she does sound fascinating."

Oscar steered the horse in the direction of the castle, "We are near the castle, just a few streets over." Approaching the Dublin castle, Oscar pulled the buggy over as they got out to walk closer for Cateline to gain a better perspective of the structure. To her, it was like watching a movie.

"It is such a massive fortress, Oscar. You said it was not open for the public?"

"Sometimes, they have balls, and if you are one of the aristocrats, then you are invited. I have been there with my father and a few times since. I am sure that your uncle and aunt have been invited before. Yes, it is most substantial and quite prominent in appearance. I believe it was built back in maybe the thirteenth century; however, it was damaged severely in the seventeenth century by fire, but the damages were renovated."

After a few moments, they returned to the calash. "Yesterday, I believe I disclosed a great part of my life with you," Oscar alleged, "I suppose it would be your turn to reveal something to me about your life."

217

"Well, let me see. You already know I was born here and went to America. I had a pretty awesome childhood."

"It was just your mom who raised you?"

Cateline thought before answering to not mix up the two eras, "No, my mother remarried a respectable man. He died a few years ago," she added while thinking of her real dad in America. "But he raised me, and I loved him very much. I was fortunate to get a good education, as I have shared with you. There are a few colleges in America who allow girls," continuing while relating to how her life would have been in America in the 1800s.

"I suppose in college, you do gain much knowledge, as education is an admirable thing, but it is well to remember from time to time that nothing that is worth knowing can be taught." [3]

Thinking of his statement and knowing it was one of his quotes, she established, "Yes, I agree. Someone can spend many years attending college, and once they go back into the real world, they may have learned nothing about life."

He countered, cleverly, "The secret of life is in art.[4] The gift deep within one's soul."

"I do believe we see things quite alike."

"Please continue; tell me about your parents."

"Well, my parents had an Irish Pub," she noted, making the decision that could possibly be the case in the nineteenth century.

"Ah, so that was why you desired to see what our pubs were like in Ireland."

"Yes, I suppose it was. I wanted to see inside a real Irish pub," she concluded while continuing, "and I spent much time growing up helping to run the business. I also played the piano and guitar for different occasions or when the pub allowed those with talent to perform."

"Why did you not tell me all of this before?"

"I wasn't sure if it would have been a suitable occupation. However, my stepfather and mother did very well with the business."

"What did I say which made you think that?"

"You told me that most respectable women would not be seen in a pub, and well, I grew up in one."

Oscar laughed jovially, "You do not know me as well as you think. I am quite a rebel, as you may know, and so is my mother. What the Irish look at as unacceptable, I do not agree."

After a few moments of silence, Oscar inquired, "Did you have any siblings growing up?"

"No, I was an only child; of course, I have James that I did not know about," she smiled most affably. "Life was pretty good in America, but I always felt like something was missing, and that is why I had to come to Ireland."

"Well, I am glad that you did, or we would have never met."

"Maybe it was meant to be."

"Yes, perhaps you are right, and did you find what seemed to be missing in your life?" Oscar asked while leaning over to kiss her gently.

She responded to his kiss and then replied, "Perhaps, I have found what seemed to be missing."

While gazing into each other's eyes, Oscar finally spoke, "Are you ready to see some other sights?"

"Sure," Cateline replied while Oscar steered the calash back into the street.

They crossed the river into the livelier section of Dublin, where there were many people out and about in all the countless shops, pubs, restaurants, businesses, and areas that were over-populated. "We can take in some sights which you are probably not familiar with before we have a light lunch, afterward, visit a museum or two—maybe explore a library before we have dinner this evening at one of the restaurants."

"As long as I am with you, I am delighted with any of your plans, Oscar."

The day seemed to be filled with much exploring, sharing, and laughter. They rode for a few hours, looking at various historical sites, enjoying a light lunch at a small café, exploring a few museums and one of the libraries. Time had evolved swiftly as they began to contemplate a place to dine for the evening. Oscar suggested a favorite of his, which was incredibly delightful to Cateline. The restaurant was very secluded, quiet, and romantic as they enjoyed their meal.

After their delightful meal, they headed for the theatre, where they immensely enjoyed the entertainment with much laughter and merriment. Leaving the theatre, Oscar eagerly continued in dialogue on the somewhat dramatic yet comical play. Cateline could tell Oscar truly came alive when engrossed with theatrical performances. It seemed to occupy his mind and aroused a part of him in a way she was privileged to observe. While beaming at him in his enthusiasm, caught up in his persona, Oscar tenderly responded to her demeanor, "What? Is something wrong?"

"No, nothing is wrong. It's just that everything is so right. I really love being with you—you know that, don't you?"

Oscar leaned over and gave her a kiss as they rode back to the estate.

The time flew by, with Oscar and Cateline spending every waking moment together, exploring Dublin while enjoying each other's company and falling in love. During the week, Oscar spent many hours in her uncle's library writing and composing, and by Friday, finishing up, he sent his work to London. Being in touch with his roommate, who was aware that, more than likely, Oscar would not return in March, and any business needing attention, Frank would handle for him. Despite this, with the upcoming trip to America planned for the following year, there were also many engagements Oscar had to take care of beforehand to build up his image in Europe. Naturally, this had weighed on him to a considerable degree, knowing he had to leave at some point and head back to London to take care of the pressing obligations. Yet, Oscar had also known that Cateline had been a breath of fresh air for him, which had resulted in different perspectives in his writings. As they continued to roam Dublin and the surrounding areas, there was never a dull moment and so many thoughts and occurrences that gave him dialogue for creating poems and short stories. All the while, ideas for plays seemed to accumulate deep within his mind, jotting down each one on paper. At this conclusion, Oscar had felt that this past week had been all but prosperous, which temporarily soothed his thoughts from making any drastic decisions hastily. Yes, he had determined another week or even two spent with Cateline might be more beneficial to his disposition than returning abruptly to London.

Monday rolled around, a bright and sunny day in mid-March; the family had all gathered around to have their English breakfast. Cateline's uncle had finally left for the office while the family sat out on the veranda, enjoying their usual tea. Martha was in deep dialogue with Anya regarding her wedding date, as they were still unsure what month would be best. Anya, stating to her mother, "Amos and I continue to discuss the dates for a wedding but just have not decided."

"That is quite alright, my dear, but we do need to begin preparations at some point and would love to see you married while your cousin is here."

"Well, I would hope that Cateline would come even if she is not in Dublin, Cateline?"

"Of course, Anya. I would not miss your wedding for anything. I have no plans to go back to America anytime soon, so I am sure I would be able to attend."

Oscar leaned over to Cateline while Martha and Anya continued to talk on the subject of the wedding, "Cateline, I thought it would be most pleasing to you if we do something special today."

"Yes, absolutely. What did you have in mind?"

"We have talked about going horseback riding. I believe that would certainly be enjoyable since you love to ride, and I have yet to see your riding skills," he finished with a questionable smile.

"I suppose we could have Daniel get two of my uncle's horses ready if you would like."

"No, there is a place I would like to take you. One of the chaps you met at the pub last week, he has excellent riding horses. We spoke of it briefly, and he told me to bring you anytime. His home is pretty close to the shores, in Portrane, which I believe is farther down from Cyrus's. There are several beaches; one is the Tower Bay Beach with fabulous cliffs."

"I've never heard of Portrane. Is it a minor suburb?"

"It is a small seaside village, known for the Round Tower. Portrane is a most quaint town and a beautiful location to ride horses on the cliffs and seashore."

"Round Tower?"

"Yes, I thought you might like to see the tower. It is very tall, and initially, it has been said, round towers were built to protect against the invasion of the Vikings. However, this particular tower was rebuilt, as the original is no longer standing. The one there now was constructed about forty years ago and is an imitation of the original. It is called the *Tower of Love*," Oscar said as he smiled tenderly at Cateline, knowing that she would want the whole story.

"The Tower of Love, and—?"

"And the imitation was built in memory of George Evans," Oscar elaborated with a spirited smile, as he maintained, "Evans was

221

the local MP for Dublin, and also his family was the last ones to live in the original tower. His wife had it built in his memory, and at one time, there was a bust of him on the property where it was noted that it was erected because of her deep love for her husband. The bust is now at the Magdalen College, Oxford."

"That is very interesting. Yes, I would love to see it and on horseback. How soon could we leave?"

"As soon as you are ready."

Cateline stood up, "I only need to change. I will meet you back downstairs."

"My goodness, you two are going to run off once again today?"

"I'm sorry, Aunt Martha, but I am so enjoying Oscar showing me so much of Dublin and the beauty of Ireland."

"It's quite alright, my dear. I just hope that you two have a wonderful time."

"Thank you. Oscar, just give me a few minutes. I will be quick about it, if you want to have Elbert get the calash ready."

"I will do that," he concurred while rising from the table with farewells to Mrs. Walsh and Anya.

Within minutes, Cateline was ready and dressed in her breeches, a long skirt covering, besides, and her hair thrown up in a simple twist, secured to be out of the way for riding horses. She walked to the front lawn, where Oscar was waiting with the calash.

"Here, my dear, let me help you," he spoke tenderly while taking her hand and assisting her into the cart. They rode to Portrane, where Oscar's friend lived who owned the horses. "I also brought a few blankets in case we want to eat on the beach or the cliffs, whichever you prefer; we will have something to sit on. Oh, and a lunch basket full of food, compliments of Bertha, and I believe I brought enough drinking water for the day. Of course, not to forget a bottle of wine, so we are all set for a delightful engagement."

"I am so excited. I love to ride horses."

"That is what I hear, and also, I hear you are pretty good at riding."

"Yes, I have ridden horses since I was a child."

As they rode along, Oscar pointed out different spots on the way with a story to each one. How she loved hearing his narratives about his life growing up in this most exciting culture. She thought to herself, "Why could I not have been born and lived my life out during this timeframe. It was always this era in which I was so entranced."

Pulling up to the home of Oscar's friend, he steered the buggy to the side of the house where the horse stalls and barn were located. Helping Cateline down, he affirmed, "I will let Henry know we are going to saddle up two horses to ride out to the cliffs and beach. You can go into the stalls to get a glimpse of his horses if you would like. I should not be too long."

Cateline smiled agreeably at Oscar and then proceeded towards the barn. Within a short while, Oscar and his friend accompanied her, with Henry speaking up, "Good day again— Cateline."

"Hello Henry, it is so nice of you to let us ride a few of your horses."

"I am only glad that it delights you, Cateline. I do hear you love to ride."

"Yes, I have been riding since I was a little girl. I love horses."

"Well, just pick out which ones you two would like to ride," Henry addressed while he leaned over quietly to Oscar and whispered, "although, the dark brown horse, I call him Ardan, is very high-spirited, the others are fairly temperate."

Not hearing what Henry had shared with Oscar, Cateline had already fallen in love with a beautiful white horse. "Henry, I think I adore this one. She seems to be so gentle; what is her name?"

"Fionna, which means fair white one. She is a most gentle horse. I think you would enjoy riding her."

"Thank you, Henry. Oscar, are you going to saddle them?"

"Yes," he answered while thanking his friend for his hospitality before gathering the saddles, harness, and reins. While Oscar saddled both horses, Henry took care to unbridle the horse from the calash to be cared for in one of his stalls.

"Oh, and do not put a ladies saddle on my horse," Cateline exclaimed, "I do not ride side-saddle. I was taught to ride astride."

"Well, my dear, I do not think you dressed for the occasion. There is no way you can ride in a man's saddle with that dress on."

Cateline unfastened the skirt to her dress to reveal her breeches. "I came prepared."

Oscar laughed overtly as he declared, "Please, do not forget your skirt because it is frowned on in this country by many. I know

223

women have been fighting this, my mother for one, but until Parliament makes that decision, there will still be those who oppose and instances where women will be arrested in public."

"You wouldn't let them take me to jail, would you?"

"No, I would think not, but it would be rather dramatic."

"Yes, I suppose that it would," she answered with a laugh.

"You always know if one's government is good or bad—life under a good government is rarely dramatic, whereas life under a bad government is always so."[5]

"If that be true, I am quite sure America has its share of drama like Europe."

"I would think that most governments who enforce rigid rules fill their lives with unnecessary drama. For to be entirely free, and at the same time entirely dominated by law, is the eternal paradox of human life that we realize at every moment."[6]

"Yes, so true. In fact, women are governed by so many more laws than men—and, I am sure, it has been a man that decides those laws of what we—women, may wear and not wear. It is somewhat silly, but I do suppose that women will continue to fight for their freedoms and their rights as citizens in any country."

"Truthfully, there is hardly any form of torture that has not been inflicted on girls and endured by women, in obedience to the dictates of an unreasonable and monstrous fashion.[7] Being raised watching my mother, she has always been at the forefront of fighting for women. I know that you would love her very much."

"Yes, I do believe that I would. I just hope that I do not go to jail today for what I am wearing," she responded with a laugh.

"We may not even see anyone, but do have your skirt in case we are in an area where there are others." Oscar saddled and bridled both horses, where he then brought Cateline *Fionna*. As he started to assist her into the saddle, she put her foot in the stirrup and jumped right up. "I see that you do this quite well, my dear."

"Yes, quite well, indeed!"

As they were both on their horses, they rode along slowly, deep in conversations through much of what was a forest of trees immersed with all varieties and color. There were trails, it seemed, which had been trodden down by many rides and perhaps even those taking walks through the thicket of woods. Filling her senses with the smell of wildflowers, her sight cast upon all the vibrant colors as there were flowering shrubs of forsythia and luscious trees filled with various shades of greens. The scents through the air of spring in season drifted about while birds sang their songs, in flight from branch to branch, along with scampering sounds throughout the dense expanse of woods. After some time, they had finally come to the end of Henry's property line, and beyond that point, there was a vast field of great beauty. "These are the cliffs. There are fields as far as you can see straight ahead, and to your right is the cliff's edge with paths which lead down to the sea."

"How beautiful. The field seems to go on forever. I see a large tree way out in the middle; can you see it?"

"Yes, I see it."

Cateline, using her heels to nudge her horse to take off in a gallop, loudly exclaimed, "I will race you to the tree." Having already started in full gallop, catching Oscar off guard, he immediately engaged his horse unconcerned, for he knew Ardan was the faster of the two. As he caught up with Cateline, she screamed out in excitement, "My brave knight in shining armor, you must win the love of your princess by taming her. If you cannot tame me, you shall never win my hand!"

While she spoke those words flirtatiously to Oscar, he retaliated, "I fear not that I cannot tame thee, my fair maiden. I will win this challenge and tame you all the same time."

"I dare say, Sir Knight, you speak with such confidence, but I, sir, cannot be tamed," Cateline continued with her game.

Oscar retaliated, "Ah, but hope I adhere to, for I shall not be demoralized. I am quite convinced that you shall be conquered." All the while, both were much engaged in laughing while Oscar gained ground. As they neared the lone tree with Oscar right beside her, Cateline screamed, "NO—NO, you cannot win!"

Finally, arriving at the tree, Oscar was victorious by just a few feet. At the same time, Cateline proceeded to abruptly station her horse, jump off, and commence running towards the tree while proclaiming loudly, "Ha, you have to touch the tree, and you did not! Therefore, I have won Sir Knight, and it is you that shall be tamed!"

Oscar jumped off his horse while both were engaged intensely in laughter. Gaining his composure at one point, he added, "I should have known you were so competitive after watching you play poona, but I never imagined you would go to the extent of changing the rules to fit your device. Ah, so much energy and spark in you, my dear!"

"I assure you, there are probably many things you do not know about me, my dear charming knight," Cateline commented while Oscar approached her as she stood with her back to the tree. Leaning in towards her, he kissed her before she whispered lightly, "I am the princess of this land, Sir Knight. I ask you kindly to remove your hands from me, for I do not know you."

"Oh, my fair maiden, your claim is wrong—for you do know me—for you have been put under a spell by the dark knight, and I am here to save you."

"Save me, you dare say. How do you intend to save me?"

Oscar leaned in closer to her and lifted her face to his while he proclaimed, "My lovely lady, princess of this land, it is only by one kiss that the spell will be broken, and you will know that I am your knight in shining armor and have come for no other reason but to rescue you."

As he pulled Cateline into his arms and passionately kissed her, she responded to his advance while whispering in his ear, "You are my valiant knight who has loved me and fought to save me."

"Yes, I have and do love you—my fair lady." Releasing her, he proclaimed, "And yes, you have won. You may do with me as you please, for I am at your disposal." They continued to lean against the tree in a deep passionate kiss. After some time, Oscar spoke assuredly, "I never knew you could ride so well. I do not believe I have ever seen a lady ride as such. You must have spent much time in the saddle while you were growing up."

"I did and always loved horses. What about you?"

"There have always been horses, and I have ridden them since I was very young. And, by the way, you never really had a chance in winning if I had not allowed it, for the horse I am riding is Henry's most spirited."

"Is that what he whispered to you?"

"I am afraid so. Henry felt that you needed to be on a horse that was gentle being a lady, but I believe you could have handled my horse for that matter."

"Unquestionably, I have ridden many high-spirited horses in my days."

"I also suppose when you were a little girl, you must have acted out creative scenes, such as I just witnessed?"

She responded with a most appealing smile, "Yes, I always loved to play knights, chivalry, and such. I read a lot about various knights and kings, such as the tales of King Arthur."

"Ah, King Arthur, the history of Britain and the mythical Brutus of Troy."

"The poet Wace, right?"

"Yes, Robert Wace, he was a Norman poet, and I suppose you also have read Romeo and Juliet?"

"Oh, yes, without a doubt. I do love all of Shakespeare's works."

"Indeed, as I do myself."

Standing by the tree, Oscar took out his pocketknife as he began to carve his name and Cateline's on the bark. "Ah, carving up the Chestnut tree?"

"Yes, a chestnut tree it is. Do you have them in America?"

"I am not sure. My aunt and uncle have them on their estate; that is why I knew what it was called. So, you are carving our names?"

"Yes," he answered, stopping to look over at her, resuming, "please, turn around where I can surprise you once I am finished."

Doing so, she inquired, "How sweet. Is this something you normally do when you meet a girl?"

Oscar laughing, "No, I have never done this. I simply thought it would be a good memory. Me beating you to the tree and all."

"No, I beat you to the actual tree," Cateline insisted impertinently.

Oscar smiled affectionately while he finished carving— 'Cateline loves Oscar'.

When she turned to see what he wrote, she exclaimed emphatically, "No, Oscar loves Cateline."

"Does that mean you do not love me?"

"Well, yes—I do love you, but you could have put it the other way since you wrote it."

"I am just working on taming you," he declared shrewdly with a smile.

At that, Cateline leaped back on her horse and announced, "Well, you better keep up if you want to tame me."

Jumping back on his horse, they rode off slowly towards the edge of the cliffs while they continued to share memories of their lives. Getting close to the edge, both jumped down to stand and gaze out in the distance of the beach and out to the sea. It was so beautiful and serene; Cateline had never experienced a seashore with such beauty. Oscar inquired, "Do you like it here?"

"I love it here. Can we go down to the beach with the horses?"

"We can; there are trails to get down. Come, follow me," he answered as he mounted his horse.

They rode a short distance until they came to a slight trail that led down to the coastline. Once on the shore, Cateline inquired, "Where is the tower located?"

"It is a bit further down from where we were. We can go once we leave the beach if you would like."

"No, this is so incredible. I love the sound of the waves and the feel of the breeze. I could stay right here forever. We have all day and can ride to the tower later, yes?"

"Certainly. I have blankets and the lunch basket; are you hungry? We can spread everything out right here."

"Yes, this is quite perfect, so secluded—no one to be seen."

"Like I said, it is just a small village, and we are really not close to any homes. I am going to gather up some branches and build us a cozy fire to take the chill off," Oscar imparted while he handed her the blankets. "Here, my dear—if you would like to spread out one of the blankets and our food while I am gone, the lunch basket is secured to the side of my horse."

"Yes, of course. I will get everything ready for us."

Cateline, unfolding one of the blankets, spread out the various food items Bertha had packed for them while Oscar went back and forth for more wood. He finally started the fire relatively close to where the blanket was lying. Once it was blazing satisfactorily, he sat down next to her. Warming by the fire, they enjoyed their lunch together while Cateline perpetually talked about the beauty of the sea. Oh, how she was becoming so used to living in Ireland and enjoying her heritage. Once they had finished eating, Oscar mentioned, "I may have said this before, but just to emphasize—I do love the way you look in those breeches."

"You are not to say that. It is probably not proper."

"The way I see it, our country says it is not proper for you to wear them. But, since you choose to wear them, I cannot help observing how good they make you look. Of course, I could have been dishonest, but as your brave knight in shining armor, I knew my integrity and honor must be superb."

Cateline, entertained by his remark, replied, "Thank you, my brave knight, for being so honest with me and also to know you approve of my breeches."

"Yes, absolutely. You can wear the breeches in front of me anytime," he emphasized while smiling playfully.

As they finished their lunch, Cateline secured the other blanket for added warmth while the chill of the breeze flowed over them. The fire felt quite inviting in between the phases of the brisk wind as grey clouds off in the far distance could be seen drifting along out over the deep blue sea. Lying down on the blanket, she enjoyed the feeling of warmth upon her body while she watched the waves continue to crash upon the shoreline. Oscar laid behind her on his side, cuddling up close with his arm stretched out over hers, holding her next to him. Sharing her blanket, she reached over to make sure he was also wrapped in its warmness. They laid there for a long time in serious discussions about their distant lives and desires for the future, either agreeing on topics or debating, but all in all, they were much pleased with their time spent together. This was one thing that enchanted Oscar, having never before met a girl such as Cateline, who was filled with so many opinions and such intelligence. After some time, being quite relaxed, the talking had subsided while they continued to enjoy the view and the closeness of their bodies lying next to each other. Everything became so serene and peaceful, a perfect setting; nothing seemed better than the moments they shared. The quietness brought a feeling of peace and relaxation much needed and much enjoyed, a moment of complete ecstasy where they eventually fell fast asleep in each other's arms to the sound of the waves and the crackle of the fire.

With evening on the horizon, Oscar was awakened by droplets of water. Realizing a storm seemed to be approaching fast towards the bay from out at sea, he hurriedly woke Cateline, "Cateline, wake up—wake up! We must have fallen asleep. Rain is on its way; we must find shelter."

Cateline jumping up rather startled began to assist Oscar in securing their belongings on the horses. Darkness would soon be covering them while the cold was rapidly settling in. Saddling their horses, Oscar led them back to the trail where they could ascend the cliff. "What shall we do, Oscar? The rains are so very close, and it is getting quite late. Will we ever be able to get home tonight?"

"That I am unsure, at present, we need a place where we can stay dry and warm. Even if the rains were to stop, I am doubtful it would be safe to guide the horses into the thicket of woods to find Henry's home. If we are lucky enough to find his place, we still may not make it through the darkness as far as Clontarf. I think we must find shelter where we can build a fire to make it through the night until the wee hours of the morning. We must hurry, the storm is imminent, and the winds are becoming more forceful."

"Where are we heading?"

"The tower, it is not too far," Oscar responded as the late wintry gales had become more persuasive. The winds thrashed to the shores, roaring waters immerged powerfully, sending sprays of dampness into the air, which could be felt while they rode along—the rains lingered and drizzled lightly upon them. Once they had come to the trail, which led the way to the top of the cliff, Oscar yelled through the sounds of the approaching storm, "WE WILL HAVE TO WALK OUR HORSES UP THE CLIFF!" Dismounting their horses, they journeyed up the trail to the top of the cliff, where they mounted once again to gallop at a fast pace through the fields and on into a wooded area before coming to an opening where the tower stood in such grandeur, tall as it was with various outlets, windows of sorts.

They arrived about the time the rain began to pour compellingly. Jumping down from their saddles, Oscar secured the horses to a tree and hurriedly assisted Cateline in carrying all their belongings inside. It felt damp and was very dark once they entered the interior of the structure. Oscar looked over at Cateline while speaking most sincerely, "I know it is dark, and you are cold, but please remain inside while I find dry limbs in the wooded area to build a fire. I will return shortly."

Cateline, sitting down in the dark hollow of the cold room, listened to the howl of the winds while the storm continued to bring torrential rains along with strong gales. It was a dreary sound with darkness filling all of her surroundings. Feeling so helpless, all she could think about was Oscar's safety and occasionally looking around her towards the diverse sounds, unsure what could possibly be lurking inside. As she tried to quiet her mind, thoughts continued to surface of creatures creeping about until she finally heard Oscar approaching. Bursting into the tower with many limbs, Cateline exclaimed, "You are soaked, Oscar. You must be dreadfully cold."

In between shivers from his damp state, he replied, "Yes, I am cold." He fumbled around in the darkness with only faint lights from time to time coming through the openings as he tried to find a safe place to build a fire. Securing the door where wildlife could not access, he worked on getting the fire going. Even with the openings of the window areas, due to the storm and the darkness that prevailed upon them, there was barely enough light for him to see to ignite a flame. After several attempts, a fire raged successfully. Oscar then removed his outer attire to lay near the heat to dry. Turning to Cateline, he spoke, "Your clothes are soaked too—it is very cold, Cateline. The fire will not provide enough warmth for the night with the exposure to the window openings. You should take off the outer layers to dry as I have. You will still be clothed, and you have your skirt that you did not wear while riding. Is it not dry?"

"Yes, it is dry. It would have been wonderful to have your fur coat about now."

"Well, I assure you that I will be a gentleman. Besides, there is not sufficient light, and our blankets are still very much dry. You can cover with those."

"Thank you, Oscar. Now, please turn around while I undress." Once she had taken off her outer garments, she put her skirt back on and wrapped herself in one of the blankets. Oscar hung her clothing about the fire to dry while she laid out the other blanket for them to sit and enjoy the remaining food that Bertha had sent. Luckily, Oscar had packed plenty of fresh water for them to drink.

The storm had sustained, howling and roaring as a tempest in the night, yet they seemed to be secure in the tower, with the fire raging. Having had their fill of food, Oscar resolved, "We have the bottle of wine. Would you care for a glass?"

"Yes, please. I believe it may help provide warmth to our bodies."

They sat down on the blanket side by side, enjoying the crackle of the fire while spending their time sipping wine and enjoying the conversation. Once they had polished off the wine, Oscar stated, "Please lie down on the blanket and get some sleep; it does not seem that the storm will pass anytime soon. Besides, with the amount of rain, it would be hard for the horses to trot through the muddy terrain."

231

"No, Oscar, you use this other blanket to wrap yourself," she responded as his chest was completely bare, and his only attire remaining on had been his pants.

"Cateline, you are shivering—please, you can use both blankets; I will sit by the fire tonight."

"No, you are also cold, Oscar. I am wrapped in one of the blankets—I do not, nor will I take the other one," she assured him stubbornly while lying down with her blanket secured for heat.

Oscar sat for a while close to the fire with the other blanket wrapped about him—cold, very cold, noticing how she, too, was shivering from the elements where he finally moved over closer and laid next to her for added warmth. "You are very cold, my dear. I cannot let you freeze tonight," he spoke solemnly while he held her in his arms.

Cateline responded by scooting closer to him, replying, "Oscar, you are freezing too. I will not let you freeze either. Our body heat is needed to keep each other from the elements." Both lying next to each other, wrapped together to provide the warmth needed as the night continued. With the storm in its fierceness, the intense sound of the gusting wind was heard as it violently whooshed through the openings that could not be secured. In complete darkness with the slight glow from the fire, an occasional flash of lightning would give a brief glimpse of light to their dismal surroundings. To Cateline, it was a bit eerie, but she felt safe in his arms.

Before they had drifted off to sleep, Oscar commented, "Donner and Blitzen."

Cateline, realizing what he spoke, inquired, "Did you say, Donner and Blitzen?" as she thought about the reindeer song, which was not heard of in the 19th century.

"Why, yes, I did. Do you know any German?"

"No, I can't say that I do. What does it mean?"

"Thunder and lightning, my dear."

As the storm persisted, Oscar made one last comment, "Perhaps, there is a reason for this storm."

"Why do you say that?"

"Thunderstorms are quite rare in Ireland. We do have rain but seldom the thunder and lightning."

"I did not know that; perhaps you are right—there is a meaning to this storm."

After several moments, he spoke once again with a smile on his face, "I suppose we could get up and play one of your knight and chivalry games if you would like."

"Yes, this would definitely be the perfect place."

"And do not forget that this is the *Tower of Love.*"

"Ah, yes, how could I forget? So, Sir Knight, it is in this very tower that you shall claim my love forever and I yours."

"If it is your wish, my dear lady, but I already claimed your love before venturing to this tower. Perhaps, this will be the place that we make vows to love each other to the end of time."

When Oscar said those words, it saddened Cateline because she knew she would love him until the end of time, but they would not be together but for a short period. In the darkness, Oscar was unable to see her tears flow down her face, and as she gained her composure to think only of one day at a time, her words were spoken softly, "Yes, Oscar, at this place I do vow to love you until the end of time."

"And I also vow to love you until the end of time," he concluded while rolling her closer towards him, where he kissed her tenderly. They lay for a time in the quietness of the tower until they both became sleepy. It was definitely warmer than it was on the beach, which was to their delight. Oscar got up once more, placing additional wood on the fire where it blazed fiercely; lying back down, he fell asleep with his princess by his side.

CHAPTER
16

Early the following morning, the sun was clearly beginning to rise as Oscar eagerly awakened Cateline while exclaiming, "Cateline, wake up. We probably need to get Henry's horses back and hurry to your uncle's estate. I am certain they will all be awake when we get there, and not sure how they are going to feel about us not coming home."

"I do believe they will probably just be worried, Oscar. My uncle would not have wanted us to have traveled in that storm, I assure you."

"Even with the storm, I am unsure your uncle will be so understanding. Perhaps, he will assume we should have anticipated the storm approaching and have begun our journey back to the estate."

"Oscar, it is not as if I am not a grown woman, and besides, everything was innocent. Stop acting so guilty."

"I feel guilty since I did not get you home at a decent hour. I promised your uncle that my intentions were most honorable."

"It is going to be fine; you have not overstepped your boundaries and have behaved as quite the gentleman through this whole ordeal. But yes, we do need to begin heading back."

Having dressed in their clothing which had dried in the night, Oscar made sure the fire was out and then saddled and bridled both horses. He loaded the blankets onto his horse and went to assist Cateline. "What are you doing? You know I can get on my horse without your assistance."

"I forget that you are not like most girls," he added with a smile.

"How many girls have you taken horseback riding, anyway?"

Oscar, thinking to himself, responded, "I don't think I have taken any before, but I have been where there were several of us riding, and most girls ride with side saddles."

"Just remember, I am not *most girls*."

As they rode along next to each other, Oscar leaned over to give her a kiss while declaring, "I never even said, good morning." They both smiled and rode off to Henry's house. Upon arriving, Oscar made sure the horses were secured in the stalls, including the saddles and such, where all items were put back in place before they left. "There is no need to wake Henry since it is so early. He will see the horses are back when he comes to check." Securing their horse to the calash, he then helped Cateline up into the cart, and they journeyed towards the Walsh estate.

As they entered the vestibule, the family could be heard in the morning room. Walking in to join them, Cateline proclaimed sincerely, "I am so sorry, Uncle Walsh, about not getting back yesterday. We went to the most glorious place to ride horses, which was quite a journey from Oscar's friend's home, where we borrowed the horses. Before we knew it, a most fierce storm had approached, and it was not long until we were in utter darkness. Due to the weather, we were unable to get home safely."

Oscar looked over at her uncle to add, "I take full responsibility, sir, and assure you that it will not happen again. I did make certain that Cateline was safe for the night."

Mr. Walsh laughed a bit with a somewhat grave smile before he answered, "You both sound guilty, as I had yet to inquire about where you were last night."

Cateline, in a cheerful manner, started to speak when Oscar interrupted, "The truth is that we did have a wonderful ride in the fields by the cliffs at Portrane, sir, and then we took a trail down to the beach where we sat to enjoy the food Bertha had packed. I gathered wood to get a fire going since it was cold, and we each had a blanket to wrap up and keep warm from the chill. We laid about for some time talking, and I suppose we were both feeling quite weary from the long day and journey on horseback—and well, we fell asleep. I woke first when drops of rain began to sprinkle upon us. I did not think it would be safe to try and find our way back in the wooded area to my friend's home in the storm, which very soon approached. With the coldness setting in, we were able to find our way to the tower house where I built a fire for the night, and we went back to sleep until daylight. I assure you that I have the utmost respect for Cateline, sir, and I would never dishonor her or your family in any way."

Mr. Walsh smiled at Oscar before he concluded, "I respect your honesty Oscar and appreciate the comment. Now, breakfast is getting cold; you two best be seated and start eating. I am sure you are probably hungry."

Smiling, they both sat down, and Cateline stated most thoroughly, "Thank you, uncle, and yes, we are famished."

Their days prolonged, with Cateline and Oscar spending almost every waking moment together since the Friday he had arrived. For the remainder of the week, they continued to explore Dublin, where they visited the Dublin Zoo, which was built around 1830, to include many other amazing sights. One of their week's unique highlights was the evening of enjoyment at Dan Lowrey's Star of Erin Music Hall. Being entertained first by Bessie Bellwood with style somewhat unrefined and other times comical, she was very well received by the number of patrons who had attended. Following her performance, an impressionist came on stage to mimic several well-known folks, and before each impersonation, the man announced the subject of his aim. It was pretty amusing, but amid the various acts, Oscar mockingly remarked, "And, I do think it, so kind of him to tell us who he is imitating. It avoids discussion, doesn't it?" [1]

Cateline resolving in a cheerful fashion, "Yes, I suppose it does?"

The remainder of their week was spent taking countless walks throughout the streets of Dublin, viewing much of the history and points of interest to include the statues of William Smith O'Brien, leader of the unsuccessful rebellion of 1848, and Sir John Gray, an Irish physician. Gray had served the people and society in many ways in Dublin. Their excursions also entailed walks or views of numerous bridges that crossed over the Liffey River. To name a few, the O'Connell Street Bridge was constructed in the eighteenth century, the Grattan Bridge was reconstructed in the 1870s, and last, the O'Donovan Rossa was rebuilt in the early part of the 1800s. Their days were mixed with much enjoyment, pleasure, and adventure.

The following week, towards the end of March, Oscar surprised Cateline with a planned journey by train from Dublin to the Cliffs of Moher, located in County Clare on the southwestern edge of the Burren region of Ireland. He had planned a long weekend since the train would only take them so far, and they would travel further by carriage, where arriving in Lisdoonvarna Friday of that week, their plan was to secure a cab to take them to the Queen's Hotel, where Oscar had reserved two rooms side by side.

Leaving as planned, their travels went smoothly, where they eventually arrived at the hotel, which stood tall and impressive for its time. The hotel sat at the top of a hill with a wide stepped colonnade leading up to its grand entrance. It was an immense building of three stories, bricked in white with lined windows down each side of the cubed structure on all floors. Entering the lobby, it was quaint in appearance, nothing outlandish, but rather that of a country-club feel. Once they had checked in, they went to dine in the restaurant and then spent the remainder of their first day enjoying the quaint town and learning of its spa wells. Back at the hotel for the evening, Oscar came to Cateline's room to enjoy a more intimate setting together. "You know you would not be in my room if we were at my uncle's."

"Of course, I wouldn't, not with your uncle there. But I mind my manners, do I not?"

"Yes, you do," Cateline replied, honestly. "I can hardly wait to see the cliffs with everything you have shared. We will be spending the day there, yes?"

"We shall. I have already taken care of arranging food to take with us, and we certainly must stay for the sun to set. It is the most splendid sight." Kissing her one more time, he stood to go to his room. "Get some sleep, my princess. I will awaken you in the morning."

She answered with a gentle smile, "I do hope that I can sleep."

"It does not matter if you can't; we more than likely shall fall asleep tomorrow as we lay amongst the beauty of nature."

Oscar leaving her room, Cateline opened up her diary to catch up on her writings, with it being a few days since she had written at all. She finished up her last sentence, changed into her gown, and climbed into the bed.

The following morning, Oscar used the key to her room to enter. Quietly, gazing at her beauty while she slept, he sat down and gently swept her long hair away from her face. He then leaned over, kissed her on the cheek, and softly professed, "Good morning, beautiful."

Cateline, opening her eyes, affirmed, "You always love to surprise me when I am not looking my best."

237

"You are amazing when you are most natural, without your hair arranged in any particular fashion or having applied to your face," he concluded with a most amiable smile.

"It seems so early, or maybe I merely did not get enough sleep."

"Remember, you may sleep at the cliffs, my dear. Arise and commence to ready yourself, and I shall acquire coffee to awaken my princess."

"Yes, coffee, please. That sounds quite enjoyable," she spoke softly while sitting up in the bed. Oscar left the room, and Cateline began to arrange herself, selecting something more casual to wear to the cliffs since their day would be spent enjoying the views and laying around on blankets to eat and relax. This would be a most pleasant day, just the two of them amid nothing but nature. Cateline could barely wait, knowing she needed this time with him alone.

Returning with coffee and a light breakfast of crumpets for Cateline to enjoy at that moment, Oscar had taken care to pack plenty of food for their time away, not expecting to be back at the hotel until much later that evening. Cateline was basically ready. After adding light touches to her face, she had decided to simply brush out her long hair and allow it to flow freely in the breeze of the cliffs. Seeing him standing there with her cup of coffee in which she desperately needed, advancing swiftly, Cateline took the cup from him. Immediately taking a sip, she exclaimed, "Ah! Refreshing, how sweet coffee tastes! Lovelier than a thousand kisses, sweeter far than muscatel wine!"[2]

Smiling, Oscar noted, "I knew not of your desire for coffee as such—*Bach-style*, I must have pleased you!"

"Oh, you always please me, and the coffee was much needed! Thank you!"

As they left the hotel, Cateline ate her breakfast and finished her coffee while Oscar led the horse and carriage they had acquired towards the Cliffs of Moher. Lisdoonvarna was about seven miles to the cliffs, which would take them a little over an hour. The ride was most pleasurable as the scenery was breathtaking, making their journey seem much shorter, and before they knew it, the cliffs were in direct view.

Oscar, drawing nearer, found a place where he could secure the horse. Unhitching the lone steed, he fastened him to a tree, close to a most verdant green grassy setting where the horse could relish. Cateline, gazing out over the richness of what lay ahead, looked forward to a relaxing day while appreciating the lush and vivid scenery surrounding them. Hand in hand, they walked out on the grassy plateau, while at one point, Cateline bent down to take off her shoes, proclaiming with an exuberant smile, "I must feel the lavishness of the meadow. It is so silky feeling, Oscar."

While laughing at her, he responded, "Perhaps, I shall join you." Removing his shoes and tossing them to the side, they continued their walk.

"See, doesn't it feel astonishing to your feet?"

"Quite pleasant, to be sure," he replied.

A feeling of peace swept over both of them, for their surroundings were filled with awe as they walked further out onto the cliffs; it was like standing at the top of the world. The view amazed Cateline while she stood in awe of the jagged rocky cliffs extending out into the ocean. Positioned towards its edge, the sound of the roaring waters below continually crashed onto the rocky serrated walls of limestone with a thin layer of shale visible between the stone, whitecaps mounting with such intensity, as Cateline persisted envisioning the cliffs in all their splendor.

She had worn her hair down to freely swirl through the wind, but also because she knew Oscar loved her long flowing locks. So here she was, at that moment, feeling as if she were stationed on the edge of the world, where the fierce gales could be felt while they whisked every strand twirling about her face, down on her shoulders, and towards her back. Suddenly, Cateline noticed a mass of seabirds with their white wings outstretched as they soared from below, coming out of what seemed like secret underground caverns from deep within the vertical black stone walls. The tall formations stood above the Atlantic Ocean, reaching forthright, standing proud with such a magnificent force—a force that formed the cliffs, with a height above seven hundred feet. It was a height of splendor, row after row shooting forth as a stout battalion of forces standing in allegiance, on top of the world—proud, strong, forceful, vigorous, magnificent, in all its glory and splendor. A new awareness was brought forth from within where Cateline felt so alive, standing at the rocky promontory that jutted out into the waters below—viewing—feeling all the energy of nature or the strengths of God, feeling His presence in the bristling wind—the roar of the seas—the splendor of the rock—shining black rock, limestone, shale. Every sense was stimulated in those moments, in that place. It was God, and it was her and the man she had come to love, the man she would soon impart something far more significant than anything else that mattered—something from God—something for him to hold onto one day, something to give him hope and love beyond any other meaning that life had. These moments they shared together, amid creation, were moments that would one day dissolve but would also be forever.

  Oscar watched Cateline while she sauntered out on the expanse of the lush plateau of deep green grass, bending over plucking tall stems of sea pink wildflowers, twirling them through her fingers while in deep thought of her surroundings. As she stood close to one edge of the cliff, enjoying the vigor of the winds, Oscar sat down on the lushness of the meadow to enjoy his view—the view of her. He watched and enjoyed every second of her reflection, in tune with her inner-self as she relished some of the best sights that Ireland had to offer. Closing her eyes and spreading her arms like an eagle, Cateline felt the force of nature envelope through her whole being. Her hair brushed away from her face flying with the breeze and sprawling upwards with such energy. Oscar gazing at her image with a satisfying smile, he was able to see just how much her devotion was for nature and beauty. How much he enjoyed every single moment with this magnificent woman who had seemed to capture his soul.

  Was it real, or was it a dream? The dreams they had come, and they had gone. They returned again and again, never-ending, remaining over and over—days—weeks—months—years—over a decade, her affection had grown, and his feelings had begun. Where was this destiny, was it to continue, was it sincere or merely a dream? Could life be so good, could love feel so authentic? Yes, oh yes, life had so much to offer, life was real, love could also be so real. We sense it, we know it, we seek it, and we embrace it. These moments, these hours, these days—they are ours to take, ours to hold on to, ours to never let go. If love departs, where would we be? Without love, how do we survive? Oh, how she had come to know the answer, for Cateline had lived without the love for so many years—and knew that one day, she would live without it once more, but for now, Cateline would hold onto it every single moment, every moment where she had that love with her right then and right there.

Cateline, turning from the view of the ocean and the waves as they continued to crash to the shores, walked over and sat next to Oscar. "I love you so much. This is the most beautiful, the most romantic place I have, up till now, experienced, and it is even far greater to be right here this very moment with you."

"There are many places near these cliffs that are also quite remarkable, Cateline. I can remember some years back seeing Lough Corrib, a most splendid and romantic lake not too far from Galway. I felt the same as you. There could not be a more romantic place on earth; nonetheless, the cliffs are just as breathtaking."

"All I know is that everything seems as if it were a dream, Oscar—please, never awaken me for if it is, I wish to remain right here forever."

Oscar, taking her arm, pulled her back, where she laid beside him on the plushness of the grassy meadow where he held her close and reflected, "If it is a dream, then I am a dreamer. For a dreamer is one who can only find his way by moonlight, yet his punishment is that he sees the dawn before the rest of the world."[3]

Before speaking, Cateline knew his quote very well. It was one that she kept in her quiet place where she would sit and dream, a rather brilliant passage written by him. "I do love those words, Oscar. Did those words come from within?"

"Certainly, those are lyrics, composed from my heart. For I astound myself as I am most clever, am I not?"

As he spoke those words, his laugh came forth while Cateline joined in with him before responding, "Yes, you are quite ingenious."

"To be truthful, from the first day those words came to me, I never felt their full meaning until lying here next to you in this very moment in time." Smiling gently, he leaned over and kissed her passionately. Facing each other, lost in the complexities of their eyes intently drawing into their very souls, Oscar's words were spoken somewhat romantically. "Your eyes speak to the depths of my soul; there is no need for words. I feel your thoughts mingled in my whole being clearly by your gaze into my own eyes. Your mouth does not move, yet it speaks to me—those red-roseleaf lips of yours should be made no less for the madness of music and song than for the madness of kissing[4]—kissing me." As he leaned towards her, their lips met in an utterly surrendered embrace, which spoke volumes to both. Turning to face the ocean, they maintained lying next to each other with Oscar's arms entwined about her while they gazed out at

241

the remarkable sights. There were no words spoken, but they both knew each other's thoughts, designs, feelings—every second was enjoyed. With a spectacular scene of such repose amid the natural energies of creation, it was the perfect setting for two beings to fall deeply in love. Oscar knew he had chosen the ideal place and the most precise moment to spend with this woman whom he had come to love dearly in such a short time.

Viewing their surroundings endlessly, they looked on at the outstretch of the Aran Islands, which were off in Galway Bay. Seen as a backdrop in the distance beyond, they formed a silhouette against the waters below, elevated discreetly from the ocean. The smokey views of the Twelve Pins Mountain range off to the north stood tall and proud, lifting high, protruding into the clouds, and opposite lay the Maumturk Mountains, meaning—*the pass of the boar,* with its reach being long and broadly straight. Finally, off in the far distance at the southern tip, Loop Head—barely seen from an expanse past the mountains. The day continued on with such pleasure in their resplendent surroundings, engaged in time shared, along with their many relished discussions.

As their day progressed, Oscar spread out the blanket while he lined the edges with their belongings and the food items to secure it from the gusts of wind, after which they sat to enjoy lunch together. Pointing off in the distance to a rather large structure, Oscar began to impart the history of O'Brien's Tower, which rose in height, not too terribly far from where they sat. Located at the highest point on the cliff, it had been built in the earlier part of the nineteenth century. Cateline, desiring to explore the tower, having had their fill of lunch, ventured hand in hand with Oscar towards the magnificent structure. The views were superb, as they stood at the top overlooking the ocean below, observing the various boats and ships in the great distance of the oceanic waters. They wandered through the rustic flat, irregular-shaped stone in which the tower was constructed, a medieval allure reflecting a kind of magic to that of a small castle. Alone in this vast historic part of Ireland, Cateline pressed Oscar into performing feats of chivalry, being her knight in shining armor once more—she, his lady in waiting. With laughs and merriment, they ran around the tower heartlessly—playfully—mischievously, ending with him surrendering to her every whim—if she merely promised her love forever. This was a simple request, having already loved him for most of her life, knowing that she always would. Cateline, standing at the highest point, threw her arms around his neck as he held her tight while looking into her midnight blue eyes, which captivated his whole being. Oscar leaned down to meet her lips with a most passionate kiss that lingered on and on.

With their lips parting, in his most passionate voice, Oscar spoke these words—

> *"And her sweet red lips on these lips of mine*
> *Burned like the ruby fire set*
> *In the swinging lamp of a crimson shrine,*
> *Or the bleeding wounds of the pomegranate,*
> *Or the heart of the lotus drenched and wet*
> *With the spilt-out blood of the rose-red wine."*[5]

Looking into each other's eyes, there was silence for some time while they stood atop the tower as the gusts of wind flowed through their hair. With the moment being as it was, Oscar decided to approach the subject of his returning to London. "Cateline, there is something we need to discuss," he spoke sullenly and continued, "I am sure you know that I cannot remain at your uncle's estate forever. I have been working here and there, sending articles and such back to London, but I need to leave for home very soon. In a matter of days, I will have been here almost a month."

"Yes, I knew that you could not remain forever," she answered with a sullen smile, "you have someone that has been taking care of your place in London?"

"Frank, we are close friends. It is his house where I reside. I have written to him several times since I have been away."

"How soon must you depart?"

"Perhaps, I can remain another week or two. But, Cateline, it is not that I want to leave. I simply have obligations that I need to see to, and well, I cannot continue to live at your uncle's forever. As much as I would love staying right here with you indefinitely, I am afraid I must go back to London."

Cateline, looking up in his persuading eyes, decided to say nothing at that moment—waiting for his next words. Although, when he spoke nothing further, she resolved, "I understand Oscar and am so happy for the time that we did get to spend together." Even though she spoke those words, her thoughts were much different, for

243

Cateline knew that it could not end like this. According to all the dreams and the pictures, she knew that their life together could not be over—not yet. For three weeks, they had been inseparable, even though she knew in her heart that he could not remain in Dublin forever because his work was in London.

Oscar finally spoke most gently, "I do not want to leave you, Cateline. You mentioned when I first came that you did plan to visit London and Paris. If so—perhaps, you could leave with me."

"Yes, I do plan to do so. Nonetheless, I would like to see my father's estate in Youghal before leaving Ireland; I told James that I would come. You are welcome to go with me if you so desire. After I pay him a visit, I can leave for London, but I would have to find a place I could let for a while."

"Cateline, Frank's house is quite large enough. There is plenty of room for you to stay."

There was a pause, as Cateline was not prepared for that comment and unsure how to respond. Turning from his arms, standing towards the warm views of the ocean, she looked out at the majestic landscapes, reminiscing on the wonderful day they had shared together before she replied. "Oscar, I cannot leave with you just like that, and I could not live with you at your place; it would not look right." He started to speak when she interrupted. "Please, let me finish. Yes, I plan to come to London, but I also promised my brother that I would visit him in Youghal to see our father's estate. After that time, I will be coming to London and into Paris, but I would also like to stop in a few of the cities in England before my arrival to London."

Oscar thought about what she was saying, as he, too, had stood facing the ocean, gazing down at the beauty and charge of the waves rushing forth with such energy. He then spoke softly, once again, "I never meant to imply that I wanted you to live with me, not like that. We have an extra bedroom; it would be yours. It is no different from us being at your uncle's."

"No, Oscar, that is not like at my uncle's. People will assume the worst of me if I live at your place with no supervision. They will talk, and my reputation would be damaged."

Silence once again had filled the air, except with the echoes of the current, the resounding of the waves—colliding, hurling, thundering, and collapsing against the pillars of rock—towers of strength. At the same time, neither spoke, as their minds were filled with the unpleasantness of their dispute. In the solitude, standing side by side, looking out at the waters, thinking of something to say, something to make the pain end—the discomfort of what they both knew was inevitable. Their unending passion and feelings had grown over this short period with neither desiring to let their love diminish nor did they want their times together to end—longing to hold on to the last remnant, the last hope to be together. In their seclusion, both thought about a recourse—a design to yield, a solution to make it work—isolation enveloped them, their beliefs—judgments—feelings—opinions. It was quiet for some time before Oscar spoke first. "Cateline, I love you dearly and would never do anything to hurt you. I leave for America next year, a very long trip. I do not want to commit to something that I cannot honor right now," he paused while turning towards her, looking deep into her eyes before continuing, "once my trip to America is over, I will come back to you. I know you are the one that I want to be with forever. Therefore, I believe it would be most unreasonable for us to be married right now, and then I leave you."

Cateline said nothing for several minutes while she pondered his comments. "Oscar, I do understand—really, I do. And well—your reasons make it much clearer that I do not need to commit myself to live with you in London since you will be leaving. When I do come to London, I would love to see you, but I will find a place to stay before I arrive. I do hope that you understand."

Silence fell around them as their most beautiful day had all of a sudden darkened. After some minutes had passed, Oscar finally turned towards her, as he earnestly asserted, "Please, I do not want this day to end like this. I still love you dearly." He reached out to pull her close to embrace her as he gently kissed her.

Ending their day, they laid on the blanket, looking out at the ocean side by side, watching the magnificent view of the sunset at dusk. A glorious sight, the light of the sun descending into the low-lying clouds with its reflection upon the waters of bright streams of yellows and oranges—then most gently, the hues disappeared on the horizon as if swallowed by the seas. With the moon overhead, they cuddled while Oscar kissed her lightly, "We should leave and get some sleep. We have a train ride back to Dublin in the morning."

"Yes, this has been a most memorable day, Oscar. I wish to never wake from times like these."

They kissed deeply and then rose to begin packing up to head back to the hotel in Lisdoonvarna.

Sunday morning came all too soon, where they arose and began their journey back to Dublin.

CHAPTER
17

Mid-week, on a Wednesday morning in late March, directly after breakfast, Oscar followed Mr. Walsh into his study prior to him leaving for the day. "Samuel—sir, I would like you to know I have profoundly enjoyed your hospitality for my extended stay, but I have been here for almost four weeks. I will need to be leaving soon to take care of business in London."

"Ah, yes, I had supposed you would not be able to remain forever. Have you spoken of your plans to Cateline?"

"I have, sir, and I wanted you to be informed as well. I do extend my deepest appreciation for your kindness while here."

"My dearest boy, I do understand, and I knew you would need to return home at some point. Have you a day in mind when you would be departing?"

"No, sir, I have yet to decide, but in all probability, it shall be one day next week."

"Yes, I do believe you have deeply enjoyed your stay and time spent with my niece. However, if possible, I would be most gratified if you would accompany me on a fox hunting trip with a few of my acquaintances. We would be leaving this Friday, very early that morning, and would not return until late Saturday night. I am sure you would have a most enjoyable time."

"That sounds excellent, Samuel. I am rather honored you would think of including me in this venture with your acquaintances. I can't say that I have ever been on a fox hunt, but I am sure it would be a most remarkable experience."

"You have used a gun?"

"Yes, I have, but it will be my first fox hunt."

"Well, I am sure you are in for quite an adventure. It is then settled, and you would not leave to go back to London until perhaps the following week if I heard you correctly?"

"Yes, sir. I will make plans to depart the first part of next week."

"I will let the family know of our plans at dinner this evening. Good day, Oscar."

"Good day, Samuel."

While Mr. Walsh was at the office, Oscar had asked Daniel to get the calash ready. Cateline began to dress for the occasion to explore other points of the city—the Natural History Museum, to be exact. Leaving the estate, they soon arrived at their destination.

"I understand that you visited the museum with Anya."

"Yes, I did, Oscar. Although, we were very pressed for time and were only able to explore a small portion. I am naturally delighted to be able to experience it fully with you."

Oscar, pleased to be able to share the experience with her, noted, "I am not sure if Anya mentioned, but this museum has been here since 1857, Cateline. I simply love coming here myself and have been here many times over the years." They walked through, looking at all the various histories of Ireland, with Cateline asking many questions.

"What would you say Ireland is most famous for, Oscar?"

"There are probably many things it is famous for. Music would be one; there is a variety of music—either traditional, Irish, or Celtic."

"Did Celtic music originate in Ireland?"

"It originated from Ireland but also from Wales and Scotland. It is music that is sung as a ballad. Instruments can range from the bagpipe, violin, harp, the lute, and others."

"Oscar, is there a difference in Irish and Celtic music?"

"Not much difference; other than, Irish music just originated from Ireland."

"You said it is famous for many things; what else would you say?"

"In addition, Ireland is also well-known for its food—bread, several varieties—the Irish stew. Oh, and of course, Saint Patrick."

"Saint Patrick—yes, tell me the Irish story."

"The celebration of Saint Patrick's Day—he, Saint Patrick was the advocate who transformed Ireland to Christianity, where many walked away from Pagan Gods—chased away the snakes," he said with a laugh.

"What does that mean?"

"The serpent was a metaphor for the early Pagan faiths of Ireland."

"Oh—so, in a sense, he is credited for driving out paganism, which was the serpent or snakes."

"More or less."

After a brief pause, Oscar exclaimed, "And, my dear, we mustn't forget our Guinness—the Irish pubs—Mulligans!"

Cateline smiled cheerfully, remembering their time at the famous pub.

"And I suppose other things Ireland would be known for—horse racing and rugby," he finished.

"Well, that is quite a list. You should have also noted the most gorgeous views. Ireland has truly been breathtaking. I am not sure any country could match its beauty—the Emerald Isle it is."

They continued walking through the museum, enjoying the many displays in the fields of geology and zoology. They viewed various specimens, Irish animals and such, to name a few, there was the skeleton of a giant Irish deer from the Marquess of Bath; a basking shark; a polar bear shot by Admiral Sir Francis Leopold McClintock; numerous mounted birds, fish, other mammals; and the botanical collections.

Ending their day in Dublin, they walked back to the calash, where Oscar steered the horse towards the estate. With every moment occupied together, Oscar knew it was going to be hard to say goodbye. He had wanted more than anything to take her with him. Yet, he knew they had only known each other for such a short time, even though they had spent almost every waking moment together. With his decision to leave the following week to head back to London, Oscar was having a hard time imagining life without her. In the back of his thoughts, he still somehow believed that perhaps, there was a way to convince her to leave and go with him to London. Although, he had no idea what he could do or say to sway her decision. Knowing she was pretty headstrong on her convictions, it seemed like a hopeless cause.

At dinner that evening, Mr. Walsh announced to the family that Oscar would be accompanying him on a hunting trip where they would leave early on Friday and return late Saturday. Following his notice, Oscar then announced he would be leaving for London the Monday after. Cateline, hearing the news, felt heartsick as most of Oscar's remaining days would be spent with her uncle. She knew their time together would shortly come to an end. The anguish was evident to all as her features changed, and she merely picked at her food.

"Cateline dear, are you not feeling well. I see you are not eating," her aunt observed.

"I'm sorry, Aunt Martha, I am quite well—I just do not have much of an appetite. Could I please be excused?"

"Why yes, my dear," the response came with the whole family, including Oscar knowing the cause of her distress.

Cateline, leaving the table, walked out back to the veranda and decided to venture to the lake in the dusk of the evening to be alone. Oscar very soon excused himself to follow her, knowing what she felt because he was also experiencing those same feelings deep within. Walking down to the lake, observing the illumination of the gas lights which gently shadowed over the waters, he was able to witness her sitting on the bench, staring out in the distance, absorbed in thought as she wept gently. Looking up, seeing him approach, she immediately wiped the tears from her cheeks while trying to turn her face where he would not notice.

As he sat down next to Cateline, she turned towards him while his fingers lightly touched her face to gently wipe a tear off her cheek. "I feel we are reenacting our play from those first days, yet I believe these are real tears this time. Please, do not be sad. I, too, feel what you do, my dear. But I must return, Cateline. I do hope that this is not—goodbye."

"It's simply that you are leaving with my uncle, and then when you return, we only have one more day together. Oscar, it's not that I am not happy with your spending time with him; I am most pleased with this occasion. But I cannot help my being sad of your going away entirely." Naturally, Cateline knew if this man was to be a considerable part of her life, it was reasonably imperative for him to also spend time with her uncle. If truth be told, it was a most comforting thought for him to be loved and welcomed by Uncle Walsh and completely agreeable for him to be in her uncle's life, as well.

With his arm around her, they continued to look out at the lake in solitude—words were not spoken but both having many thoughts, thoughts which crossed their minds in silence. In their seclusion, away from the estate and away from family, they were feeling the loss of what they had come to know—the loss of intimacy, unity, and togetherness. All they had gained over the many days spent together, the feelings of deep devotion towards each other— love, adoration, all seemed to be drawing to a close, drifting away, out of their reach. After all the meetings, dialogues, discussions, debates, the deep feelings which were produced equally on both sides, the nights of wanting and longing for the intimacy desired, looking forward to the days of embracing and caressing, the closeness, tenderness—memories gone, but would they be gone? If they both felt this burning for each other, to spend every moment together, never tiring of the other, why should it end? Why would it end? Was life cruel that it should separate those who were meant to be together, those drawn to each other, those who lived for the moments, however short or long—but just to be beside each other, welcomed with yearnings, happiness, fulfillment—does this life take away that which was meant to be? Would this life now, forever dispel their love, their affection? The world in which we live, our very existence, our lives, the lives we live to advance our own gain, our self-wills, desires—do we trade those things which are meant to be, for far less? Do we live for love or, do we live life to make our mark in this world, a world that can be cruel, a world that lives for self, a world that minuses out an existence—our existence and reality of truth, of love—that love which is God-given, for He is love—love without Him, is it truly ever love?

Cateline was heartbroken to know he would not be with her, distressed to imagine he would be leaving all too soon, but happy to recognize that God had a bigger plan, even if she did not understand His purpose at that moment. She had learned to trust—and, in that trust, she had peace. After some time, Cateline spoke, "We should probably go into the drawing-room to spend time with the family, Oscar—"

Waiting to hear his response, and it came hesitantly, "Yes, you are probably right." They held hands while walking back to the estate. In the drawing-room, Anya was on the pianoforte playing a lovely tune, while at the same time, the family sat around enjoying the warmth of the fire along with the beauty of the music as the sounds drifted delicately through the air with such splendor and harmony. Cateline took her turn playing the piano and time on the guitar as the evening continued. Everyone retired to bed early except for Oscar and Cateline, who routinely had sat downstairs night after night, spending those quaint hours together before retiring. Oscar, putting his arm around Cateline while she leaned in closer to him, held her hand and spoke most passionately, "We just have one more day together before I leave with your uncle. I thought perhaps we could make tomorrow really special."

"What did you have in mind, Oscar?" Cateline spoke with no felt emotion at this point.

"A short trip to the Wicklow mountains."

Cateline, perking up at his response, excitedly inquired, "Oh, do you mean where the Powerscourt Waterfall is located?"

"Yes, but Bray is also in Wicklow. I very much want to take you to Bray besides Enniskerry, where the waterfall is actually located. There are many amazing sights to see. It is only a short distance by train where we would arrive in Bray. Bray has many distinct memories for me, which I would love to share with you."

"You have spent much time in Wicklow?"

"Yes, my father and mother built our seaside resort—Elsinore," he allocated as his countenance lit up, "it was our holiday home. There were many good times, exceptional childhood memories, and quite beautiful, overlooking the Irish Sea on Esplanade Terrace. Most exquisite views with the sea, Bray Head, and the Sugar Loaf Mountains off in the distance."

"Your father sold the home?"

"No, I sold the property several years back along with other properties my father owned. One day, I am sure I will have my regrets—but, nonetheless, I would love you to see it, for it is a part of me. I perceive that once we arrive in Bray, we could acquire a carriage to view many of the sights, spend the day and be back by late evening."

"That sounds so delightful, Oscar. I would love to go and would love to see part of your childhood," placing her hand upon his knee, she smiled most passionately at this man who had long ago captured every part of her being.

The following morning while everyone gathered around for breakfast, Oscar shared his plans for the day and evening with Cateline.

"Yes, dear boy, the countryside is very spectacular. I am sure Cateline will thoroughly enjoy the views," Mr. Walsh spoke, "just be sure and remember, we will be leaving bright and early tomorrow morning. Please try to be back to the estate to get enough rest for our trip."

"We shall not stay too late, sir. You have my word."

Once breakfast had ended, Oscar and Cateline prepared themselves for Elbert to take them to the train station. Getting in the barouche, they headed out when Oscar noted, "You look quite lovely, my dear."

"Thank you. You look very impressive yourself. I am so very excited to spend the day in Wicklow with you."

"Myself, as well, Cateline."

On their journey by train, discussions remained while Oscar entertained Cateline with his stories of Ireland and its history on diverse places they passed along the way. In view of the Wicklow Mountains, which extended from Dublin to Wicklow, were known in Dublin as the Dublin Mountains, Oscar had explained to her. The steam train arriving in Bray, Oscar acquired a small buggy for the day, and they soon headed out towards the falls, which were on the outskirts of Enniskerry.

It was a most tranquil late morning; riding along, they were encircled by nature at its finest. Oscar pointed out the various mountains off in the distance, and Cateline reflected on the well-known *Great Sugar Loaf*, isolated with its tapering shape and sharp vertical inclines. Immediately past, the Djouce Mountain, notorious for its pleasures with many walking trails. The views were reflective of a relatively smooth, bare surface—a most garrisoned height with a curved shape, splotches of brown earth, dark blue-grey slate, and bedrock. Along the route, scenic plateaus of grassland were scattered about, with many a wildflower—green twigs with yellow sprays flowing and bowing—shoots erupting among evergreen shrubs, in full bloom. As they continued along, off in the distance sat a splendid pool of water, Lough Tay, or rather, Guinness Lake, nuzzled in the soul of the glorious mountain range where it was hidden in splendor, loveliness—smoothly curved, formed and filled with the darkness of the filtered peaty waters. Streams fed its expanse, colors of brown in depths of blackness. Atop the summit drifted visions of clouds, floating nearby, tints of grey mixed with white into the blues of the sky, along with twilights of pinks and yellows, as the sun ascended the peaks—touching and caressing earth to the heavens. Coming to life in all its form, birds soared through the air—their songs being sung, a merlin or peregrine falcon to be seen on occasion. Then off in the far distance, the falls spewed

253

from the hills, into the expanse of the valley below, settled among the backdrop of the apparition of the Wicklow Mountains range.

Traveling as far as they could, Oscar secured the horse to a tree while they continued their journey on foot to the base of the waterfall. Along the way, they enjoyed the peace and quiet of their surroundings. With the birds of the air and an occasional rustling of leaves, small creatures could be seen in the grassland peering and wandering in the early light of the morning. The tender breeze was felt as it gently massaged life—a pure life, one of splendor. Nature, as far as could be seen, that which is natural, God made and breathed—life and revelation—light upon the dawn—darkness diminishing and all energy awakening. With trees scattered about, one could appreciate the oak, pine, beech, and the larch—coniferous and deciduous woodlands deep. Shrubs met and were viewed—plush, greens and yellows—flowers in bloom among the lushness of grass—the hills inviting, alive and breathing—streams of water with rocks near, abounding and fulfilling—memories created, lived, and aspired.

After a distance of hiking, in the quietness, they arrived towards the base of the magnificent waterfalls, where Oscar, sitting down in a verdant stretch, drew Cateline to sit closely in his arms, holding her ever so near as one together. Overlooking the magnitude of the atrocious falls, lying amongst the river Dargle, Cateline and Oscar were both in admiration of their surroundings. The falls in their impressive grandeur, soaring in heights, 397 feet, was considered the second-highest on the Emerald Isle. Towering, as it stood, flowing in vibrancy, joie de vivre—cascading waters, streams of rivers lost in nature—rushing, rippling, demanding in all its glory and beauty. Shrouds of deep blues and twilights of white, glittering and enticing, the waters sprung onward, pooling in such suddenness with splashes of life as it gushed forth anew—spilling, circling with sudden sprays of droplets shattering about. The beauty and loveliness were indescribable, mixed with the sounds of delight and quietened peacefulness. The views, alive to the artist, the contrast of colors—the poet of words, spoken sounds in accord—standing in pursuit, harmony awaiting—the suddenness and moment to capture all genres, seasons, splendor—transformed by thought and feeling. The smell of the moist dampness, crispness, the energy, delight of flavor—freshness remembered for always—time and the moment of lovers which meet in the brusqueness of serenity.

Moments of solitude having elapsed, Oscar pulled Cateline up to walk with him closer to the falls. "We will probably get a bit wet, but we cannot come this far without you experiencing the strong force at a much closer distance."

"I cannot even imagine attaining more than I feel and see right now—getting wet, that has never affected me, and I can only perceive the showers from the falls to establish this moment for eternity. Please, let us proceed further, I want more, and I want to experience it beside you."

They walked on further, feeling the first tender sprays of the falls—the audible vibrations, the depths of the waters crashing fiercely to the base with a lurid charge. The waters exploding in the valley below. The sounds of a stampede, loud and rushing, sending currents and heaps of waters in all its strengths into massive streams—about the rock, gushing, flowing, and running nearby—forming, gliding into the valleys—lowlands with waters continually approaching, filling—an endless supply. While alongside, wildlife could be seen in the forested terrains taking a drink on occasion or a peep through the wooded surroundings—a red squirrel about its day scampering a tree or running through the brush—a family of deer, the native Sika, passing along in contentment of the serenity—the peace. Drawing ever so closely, the considerable sprays were felt, as clouded views prolonged with a white mist—covering, dampening, delighting. Cateline screamed with glee, raising her arms in the air as she felt the force of the wet spray streaming and covering both of them.

Enchanted by this woman who captured his soul, Oscar joined her with love and joy, holding hands as children. They were alive—at play, youthful in nature, loudly shouting, shrieking, frolicking about, chasing and being chased, tumbling and delighting in creation—a vivid awareness that nothing seemed to matter, their time at that moment centered around a love that was so pure and so natural. If only moments could be bottled and kept forever. If only time could be stopped on those days remembered. If only youth could be secured where neither grew old, savored where one could taste the sensation for eternity and if only, love could always remain from whence it began.

Leaving the rushing waters of the fall, soaking wet from play and laughter, they walked towards the meadow, where they laid out on the softness of the grassland. The sun shining at its peak gradually began to dry Oscar and Cateline's apparel while they talked, laughed, and shared intimate secrets. Then, suddenly, Oscar watched a fawn in the distant wooded area, "Look, my dear, her mother must be close by."

"Oh, how beautiful; she sees us."

"Yes, be very still," he spoke most gently, continuing, the words of a poem came to mind—

"Out of the mid-wood's twilight
Into the meadow's dawn,
Ivory-limbed and brown-eyed
Flashes, my Fawn!" [1]

The fawn walked back into the wooded area as Oscar and Cateline continued to lie side by side. With their fingers entwined, she observed the large ring he wore, "Is this ring special?"

"Yes, my mother gave it to me. It is an Egyptian scarab ring." [2]

"It's very impressive—a lovely green stone, quite unusual."

"It is a very ancient ring," he replied, taking it off to let her look at it more closely.

Placing it back on his finger, she smiled, "You should treasure it always, especially it being a gift from your mother."

Once they had enjoyed a prepared lunch from Bertha, they left the falls while Oscar steered the horse to the locale of the Powerscourt Estate, where Cateline could get a glimpse of the gardens and view of the castle. The gardens were a genuinely glorious sight, with much beauty and loveliness. The château, established among all the scenic views they had thus far experienced, was one of bewilderment with its lavish verdant grounds surrounding the structure of Palladian architecture. Continuing on, they ventured towards the quaint village of Enniskerry.

Along their short journey, the view remained relatively scenic, and upon seeing the picturesque village nestled in the distant valley, it was as a world gone by. Enniskerry was a quiet and charming town whose landscape was drawn into the mind—one of artistic thought, captivated by the low-lying trees that bristled gently from a slight breeze. The vista spread throughout gracefully as it was colored with obscure taint pinks toppled from the hilly regions in the vast terrains along with shaded hues of light and dark greens. In the midst, a much-settled sky had formed in faded colors of yellows with hints of pinks and greys. The sun shone in its brilliance, looking over the frail yet subtle village. It gave forth its vibrancy where life stirred under the warmth, as the antiquated settlement was a place known to every man, a center among few. To the unknown the community was a sought-after locale, proclaimed in thought, seen in dreams, and experienced by those in search of that serene place. It was a place that would all too soon be gone—remembered only in view, as in an epitome. Yes, a scenic image, standing in the midst, sharing the life of long-ago—life, so far gone, life dreamt but never known. Reality— yes, it was a reality that life existed in the quaint—the insignificant, solitude of towns, years past.

Leaving Enniskerry, they headed back to Bray to spend the remainder of their day walking the beach along the Irish Sea, where Cateline was able to view the surroundings, which included the Elsinore as she listened to the many stories of his childhood, on into adolescence. Some of Oscar's best memories had occurred on this quaint stretch of beach. The Wilde seaside retreat was quite extravagant. A most exquisite three-story terraced home built up a level on a hefty concrete foundation with a large entrance opening up to wrought-iron railings and widespread stairs. It was fairly substantial for a dwelling with the outer façade reminiscent of a fairy-tale castle on a somewhat smaller scale, but nonetheless, it was by all means elaborate.

"I cannot even imagine how wonderful your childhood must have been, Oscar—the home, the views—I can't begin to even conceive how you could have ever parted with memories of such. You said you would someday probably regret doing so?"

"Yes, of course, I think about it. I still come here on occasions, not often, for I do have to lease a place to stay. I love it here, but living in London, I could not have kept this nor have been able to care for it as my father had."

Cateline feeling the regrets in his voice, somehow understood what he suffered. After all, she, too, had a hard time letting go of her parent's home—their dream and business, once she decided to settle in Chicago. "Oscar, I can only imagine how this makes you sad. At some point in our lives, I believe we all have to make decisions based on where we are in life. For you, your life and your dreams were to go to Oxford and now London, you are an artist, and you desire to write plays and poetry—you are absolutely right, you could not have taken care of this, being as far away as London. But you will always have those memories. Be thankful for all the remembrances that your father and mother gave you," she concluded, reaching over to take his hand in hers.

After a long day exploring so much of Wicklow, Oscar and Cateline headed to the railway station to begin their journey back to Dublin. "This has been a most delightful day spent with you. You know how much I love you; I do not believe there have been many days that I have not spoken those words since we first met," Oscar revealed.

Cateline smiled and looked into his most enticing eyes while responding tenderly, "I know that you love me, and I also love you. I have very much enjoyed this brilliantly romantic day, Oscar. I do hope that even though we may be separated in body, we shall always be together in spirit."

He then leaned in to kiss her intimately when the whistle sounded for boarding the train. Both being overly fatigued, they gazed out in the distance along their journey, enjoying the quiet solitude of the evening—observing the vibrancy of the sky. At the same time, the sun slowly descended towards the horizon. Cateline leaned in closer to Oscar, putting her arm on his shoulder, nuzzling her lips into the cress of his neck while kissing him ever so gently. She whispered, "I am so in love with you, my knight in shining armor." It was a gesture that assured Oscar, she really loved him, and he wanted nothing more than to be with her forever. Knowing he had never felt this way before, he also knew time was running out since he would need to get back to London very soon.

Arriving in Dublin, Elbert awaited them at the station. On their way back to the estate, Oscar held her in his arms, meeting her lips as they passionately kissed. Once arrived, he leaned against Cateline as she stood with the barouche behind, looking deeply into each other's eyes. They embraced under the faint moon, with it hazily ascending the sky, unaware of their surroundings—holding, loving, lost in each other's presence, they continued to kiss until both were startled by Daniel. "Oh—hello, Daniel."

"Miss Cateline, ma'am. I am sorry to startle you. I was just coming to get the horse and carriage."

Within the estate, they were greeted by the family, who had retired to the drawing-room following dinner. "Please, help yourself to the spread of food in the dining room. Bertha left everything on the table for you two. We are on our way to retire since we will be up before dawn, Oscar. I will see you bright and early in the morning. I do hope that you both had a most marvelous day; you will have to share details tomorrow."

"Yes, sir," Oscar assured Samuel and then followed Cateline into the dining parlor.

Finishing their evening meal, she leaned up to give Oscar a quick kiss, "Goodnight, my love, you do need sleep for tomorrow. If I do not see you in the morning before you leave, I pray you will have a most enjoyable trip with my uncle."

"Merci, my love, but I will be exceedingly wretched without you."

With a most playful smile, Cateline laughed softly before responding, "I am glad that you will be miserable, but please do not be too despondent. Goodnight, my dear, pleasant dreams."

He resolved with an elusive smile, "I will try to enjoy myself. You have delightful dreams, as well."

"Oh, my dreams are of you always, my love."

The following morning, Oscar and Samuel rose very early to ready themselves for the hunting trip. Bertha had packed the men plenty of food for two days. As they were getting ready to leave, Mr. Walsh told Oscar he would meet him outside while he hastily went over everything with Charles to make sure all had been packed into the brougham. Oscar, having a few moments, hurriedly ascended the stairs and entered Cateline's room. He leaned over next to her and looked on quietly while watching her sleep, then lightly kissed her lips while whispering, "I love you, my sweet darling."

Awakening, she concurred, "Oscar, I love you too. Are you leaving?"

"Yes, but I had to tell you goodbye and kiss you once more. I cannot imagine a day where our lips never meet," he stated while leaning closer to embrace her ardently.

259

"Please be careful, and I suppose we will all be asleep before you get back on Saturday night, according to what my uncle has said."

"Yes, but I will still come and kiss you goodnight if that is alright with you."

Amused, Cateline responded, "Certainly. I love you."

Getting up from her bed, he smiled, confirming once again, "I love you."

The men left the estate to meet up with Mr. Walsh's acquaintances. It was moderately early, but it gave both men the chance to talk where Oscar shared his thoughts with Samuel, as he knew that they desired nothing more than for Oscar and Cateline to be together.

In the meantime, the few days Oscar was away seemed like a lifetime to Cateline as she moped about the estate in her own quiet, little world. When her aunt or cousin would speak to her, it was as if she heard nothing. "Cateline, my dear," Aunt Martha declared, "Anya has been speaking to you, but you seem to be in such deep thought, do you not hear your cousin?"

"Oh, I am so sorry, Aunt Martha. My mind was merely elsewhere. Cousin, were you addressing me?"

"Yes, but it is quite alright. It wasn't anything important. I have clearly seen how quiet you have been since Oscar has been gone; it must surely be love," Anya said with a quaint smile.

Cateline, smiling back at her cousin, responded, "I suppose it is somewhat obvious. Yes, I believe that I have been drifting away in thought. It's simply that I know he will be leaving Monday for London. I have solely become so used to his being in my company, that is all."

Aunt Martha spoke up rather solemnly, "My dear, we have all been able to tell that you are most in love with this young man, but I assure you that it is not one-sided. We can all tell he is pretty smitten with you just the same."

"Do you really believe so, Aunt Martha?"

"Yes, my dear. If he does have to go to London, he will certainly be back. I am sure of it. Well—girls, I believe it is time that we should be off to bed. After all, Samuel and Oscar will be fairly late coming home, and we will see them first thing in the morning."

"Yes, perhaps that is best. The sooner I go to bed and fall asleep, time shall pass swiftly where I will be with him once more, even if it is but for a very short time."

"Yes, my dear. Goodnight, Cateline, and goodnight, my lovely daughter," Martha spoke affectionately as she smiled at the girls while walking up the stairs to her chamber.

Cateline and Anya both arose and ascended the stairs, engaged in deep discussion until they both said their *goodnights*. Cateline laid in her bed, thinking of Oscar until she finally fell fast asleep.

At some point in the night, Samuel and Oscar had arrived back at the estate. Quietly, they came into the home and went to Samuel's study, having been engaged in the most marvelous dialogue. To celebrate, Samuel noted while addressing Oscar, "This calls for a bottle of wine, dear boy. Do you prefer white or red?"
"Do you have a German wine, Samuel?"
"Yes, I do believe that I do."
"Then, a hock and seltzer will do quite well, sir."
"It is a riesling?"
"Yes, that will be most pleasant, Samuel, sir."
They sat in the study and continued on with much discourse about the particulars while enjoying some of Samuel's choice wine varieties. After a while, Samuel decided to retire for the night and bid Oscar goodnight, at the same time, suggesting, "You may want to take a bottle of champagne in to celebrate with Cateline."
"At this hour, sir?"
"I believe at any hour; she would be quite pleased to know of our conversation."
"Thank you, Samuel, sir. I believe I would not have been able to sleep at all." Oscar rose from his chair in the study and gathered a bottle of champagne and a few glasses to take to her room, being that he would have had a hard time waiting until morning, and with her uncle's blessings, that made it even more, the reason to awaken her.

Oscar walked up the stairs and stood by Cateline's door, where he laid down the champagne and glasses on a table in the hallway before entering. Realizing there was enough illumination from the fire to see his way to her bed, he decided to leave the candle outside on the table while picking up the champagne and glasses instead before walking quietly over to where she lay. Oscar sat the bottle and glasses on her nightstand and then lounged beside her, where he leaned forward, gently sweeping Cateline's hair away while lightly kissing her cheek. She turned over and opened her eyes to see Oscar reclining next to her. First, her thoughts were those of happiness as she had missed him so much, but her second thoughts were of him being in her room at such a late hour and lying next to her in the bed while her uncle might still be awake. "Oscar, I am so delighted to see you, but do you think it is wise to lay here as such? Why my uncle may be awake. If he were to find you in this room stretched out beside me, well, I am not sure what he would say or do for that matter."

"My dear, I am in a very pleasant state. Your uncle and I just arrived home and have been in his study talking of a thousand things."

"I'm quite sure—talking and drinking, I suppose," acquiring a bit of the odor from liquor mixed with stale cigarettes, she resumed, "I can smell it on your breath, Oscar. What would my uncle think of you coming in here like this?"

"I think he would be pleased, as it was his idea that I awaken you. Your uncle is also most aware that my intentions of being in here are most honorable."

"What on earth are you talking about? I cannot imagine that my uncle wanted you to come to my bedroom at this hour. Whatever do you mean?"

Oscar, sitting up on the side of the bed, opened the bottle of champagne, pouring two glasses, one for each of them while he spoke, "Perhaps, you will hardly believe it, but your uncle and I have been celebrating, at which I hope to also celebrate with you."

"For what occasion at this hour?"

"My dear, I have missed you so—your lips touching mine, the feel of your hand as it brushes through my hair, and the warmth of your body when I hold you close. For I am most incomplete without you beside me. I could not wait to see you at this very moment; morning would not come soon enough. We are to celebrate good news in which your uncle is most thrilled, and I dare not wait until tomorrow to share with you, as I would never be able to slumber."

"What is it that you desire to tell me, Oscar? I cannot imagine such news as would allow my uncle to give you access into my room at such an hour."

"First, your glass of champagne," handing her a glass, he maintained, "I desire for you to know how much I have come to love you."

"Are we to drink at this hour? Oh, excuse me, for you have already been drinking; should I drink at this hour? And, for what reason? It seems as if you have already had enough to drink for both of us by your countenance."

"Ah—say what you wish, my dear, but it is not what you think. Besides, your uncle is to blame for entertaining me with drink, not I." Oscar then taps his glass to hers while he continues, "This is to us."

Cataline, not quite sure what was going on, drinks her champagne down, and then Oscar takes her glass and kneels beside the bed. Cateline's heart began to flutter when he gazed into her eyes to speak. "Cateline, my dear, in spending time with your uncle, I spoke with him about my feelings for you and the desire that I did not want to depart for London without you. I assure you that I have been in such a bad state, knowing I would be leaving you behind, and I have come to my senses to realize that I cannot depart without you. Your uncle has made me see the light, so to speak, and because of such, he has given me permission for your hand in marriage. I know I said I did not want to commit since I would be traveling to America next year. But my dear, I cannot imagine my life without you. Yes, we have known each other for only a short while, but we have also spent almost every waking moment together since we first met. Besides, spontaneity is a meticulously prepared art,"[3] he finished with his poetic smile she had come to appreciate.

"As you have stated, we have not known each other for that long. Do you feel that this decision is being made in haste?"

"I assure you that I feel as though we have known each other a lifetime already, and I cannot see myself living this life without you by my side. I do hope you feel the same, my dear."

"Yes, oh, yes—I do feel the same."

"Then, would you give me the honor of becoming my wife and making me the happiest man in this world?"

As tears trickled down her cheeks, she declared most excitedly, "Yes—why yes, Oscar, I love you, a thousand times I love you."

Oscar rose to sit on the side of her bed while holding her in his arms and kissing her fervently. Handing her another glass of champagne where they could officially make a toast, he stated, "Let this toast celebrate our lives together. This, my dear, is to the rest of my life with you by my side." Leaning back on the headboard, they sat side by side while finishing off the bottle of champagne, all the while sharing their deep feelings of love, which had overtaken them.

Finally, Cateline inquired, "Does my uncle really know that you are in here?"

"Yes, you know he loves me and desired that we would marry."

"Well, it has been easy to see from day one that my uncle wished this day would come. I suppose I am just surprised that he allowed you to come into my bedroom."

Oscar kicked off his shoes to get more comfortable before settling next to her once again. He leaned back and placed his arm around her while he shared the stories of his hunting trip. Cateline asked many questions while laughing several times at his tales before she declared, "You sound like you had such a marvelous time."

"It was quite a rewarding experience. Yes, a most wonderful time spent watching the gentlemen galloping after a fox—the unspeakable in full pursuit of the uneatable![4] How droll, I do detest the fox hunt, my dear!"

Cateline laughed, "Yes, I can see what you mean—besides, a fox is such a beautiful creature, why would any man desire to hunt them?"

"I can say that I did miss you something horribly."

"I'm glad that you missed me and hope that you will always miss me when I am not with you."

"I will always miss you, but you may actually become tired of my being around so much."

"I long for days to be together, and when we are not, I will forever think of you."

Cateline leaning her head over on Oscar's shoulder, very soon, she fell asleep. Oscar arose and laid Cateline down upon the pillow, afterward planting tiny kisses on her face while enveloping her with the coverlet. She mumbled a bit, being half asleep while he softly whispered, "Goodnight, my adorable princess."

CHAPTER
18

Sunday morning, the family sat around the dining table enjoying breakfast before readying themselves for church. Spending the few hours amongst the community, the service was reasonably enjoyable, but Cateline also loved seeing many of the families she had become acquainted with since her arrival. Having Oscar present to observe the Sabbath made the time even more delightful.

Back at the estate, the family sat around the dining table enjoying the traditional Irish Sunday Roast—roast beef with hot white horseradish sauce and stuffing, cauliflower cheese, roasted butternut squash, colcannon, and Yorkshire pudding. During the meal, Oscar announced to the family that he had petitioned Mr. Walsh for Cateline's hand in marriage, and upon his consent, she had accepted. The news was delivered most suddenly, as it was further noted, they wished to be married without delay, seeing as Oscar needed to return to London. With the family being relatively astonished, Martha declared, "Oh dear, this is entirely unexpected, indeed. Forgive me. It is not as though I am not pleased, but this is purely surprising. The other day, I was simply saying how it was so obvious the two of you were so much in love. I am utterly thrilled; honestly, I am. But we must plan a wedding, and that takes time. As you see, Anya and Amos are to also be married, but we have yet to even set a date for that occasion."

Cateline spoke up, "Aunt Martha, please do not fret yourself over this. I haven't shared this with Oscar," she continued while gazing towards him, "but I do not want any sort of substantial wedding. My idea would be something moderately simple, just with family. Besides, Oscar needs to be back in London very soon, and I would only ask if he could possibly wait one more week?"

Oscar, replying rather earnestly, acknowledged, "One more week would be fine, my dear. If you only want something simple, that is quite alright as well."

"My thoughts are that I would love to be married at my father's estate, Oscar. Perhaps we could send a wire to my brother tomorrow, and if he agrees, we could leave immediately to be

265

married. We could merely stay one night and then begin traveling towards London if that would be agreeable with you?"

"Yes, dear. That sounds perfect, but I think we would need to stay for more than one night. I would hate to marry, celebrate into the night with family, and then leave the following morning by train."

Uncle Walsh spoke in agreement, "Yes, I would dare say Oscar is quite right. And my dear, if you wish to marry at your father's estate, I believe that is acceptable to us, right Martha?"

"Yes, dear. I suppose so, but I do hope that you should not regret the large wedding. Oscar, do you have family that would also want to attend?"

"No, ma'am. My mother and brother are in London, and I am sure they could not make the trip. They will be able to meet Cateline after our wedding."

"Perhaps, you could arrange the ceremony for Friday of this coming week, that way, we could leave on Thursday by train, which will give us more than enough time to take care of particulars since it would be a simple affair," Aunt Martha noted.

"Yes, I suppose that would work, but perhaps Oscar and I could leave a bit earlier, as soon as we hear back from James, that is. Will that be alright with you, Oscar?"

"Yes, dear. I do not have to be in London for that Monday, but as long as I am there before too long, it should be fine."

"I assume we are having a wedding then," Mr. Walsh declared. "I believe this definitely calls for a bottle of champagne. Joseph, please bring champagne and glasses. I knew the first day I saw you two together that it was meant to be. I am very pleased, Oscar, and I am especially delighted for you to be part of our family."

"Thank you, sir, you have been awfully kind and hospitable during my stay here. I have thoroughly enjoyed spending time with the whole family."

Joseph brought the champagne, and they ended the Sunday Roast with toasts made to the young couple. Once all the commotion ceased, Cateline and Oscar went into Samuel's study to compose a wire to James in which her uncle could send by telegram the following day. As Cateline wrote out the note, she made it clear to James that this would only be close family, having no need for any publications in the newspaper; her desire was for a somewhat personal affair. Oscar, sitting beside her, observing while she composed the letter, Cateline quickly voiced her opinion, "I hope you understand; I prefer this to be intimate with just those whom we invite. I love you so much, but it is of no one's concern for our affairs. It is a private occasion, to some degree, wouldn't you say?"

Cheerfully, he concluded, "If that is what makes you happy. I find you to be incredibly rare—most girls, I dare say, would want a grand ball with everyone invited to celebrate their day of marriage. I am quite alright with it being intimate—as you say, after all, I am marrying you, and that is all that matters."

"If you would like your mom and brother to attend, Oscar—," before she finished, he interrupted.

"No, I seriously doubt either would be able to come so far in such a short time, and my mother would more than likely insist we wait some time and even that we marry in London, which is out of the question. You will meet them in due time; as for now, let us plan out our week."

Cateline, smiling at Oscar, added, "I suppose we should hear back from James by Tuesday if Uncle Walsh sends the wire tomorrow. We need only pack and be ready to leave on Wednesday if you are in agreement."

"Indeed, that sounds splendid. But, all the same, we do need to buy you a ring."

"Agreed, and I need to buy you one too. You will wear one, will you not?"

"Certainly, my dear. I would wear anything you desired me to wear," Oscar smiled as he continued, "but we should go tomorrow to pick out the rings where they can be sized if need be."

"Yes, I think tomorrow will be such a hectic day, as I will also need to purchase a fabulous dress for the occasion, but I would not want you to see the dress until the day of our wedding. Perhaps, we can go buy the rings tomorrow, and I can have Anya go with me to shop for a dress on Tuesday."

"And, in the meantime," he added, "we need to plan our time in Youghal and the wedding."

"Very simple, of course. I am sure that James can find a minister to marry us at the estate. I assume it will take most of the day on Wednesday to even arrive, where we will probably be too tired to do anything other than spend time with my brother. The only other thing that I can think of is having someone there to take pictures. I will be sure to inquire in my letter to James, as well."

267

"Perhaps add in the letter that all we need him to do is find a clergyman and a photographer. I would also let him know that it would merely be your family in Dublin attending, so there would be no need in preparations for a huge feast. You need to give James a particular time for the clergyman and photographer to know when to arrive."

"The time, I could just let him know any time in the afternoon; would that be sufficient, Oscar?"

"I think that should be fine; that way, the time can be worked around the clergyman and photographer since it is such short notice."

"Yes, that's right. Well, let me finish the letter. Is there anything else that you can think of?"

"The only thing I can think of is how much I want to hold you right now and never let go," he smiled passionately while Cateline looked up into his most tantalizing eyes.

Cateline, smiling herself, spoke rather calmly, "Be serious, Oscar. We need to make sure that we do not forget anything."

"I am serious," he replied with a slight smile before continuing, "but we do need to stop by the station to inquire about the tickets and times of departure."

"Yes, that is a good idea."

Oscar, standing, reached down to take her hand, "We have finished the letter; I would love to accompany you to the lake where we can spend time together this afternoon, alone—if you so desire."

"Yes, of course. I feel that I am in a dream, but I never want to wake up."

Cateline, leaving the study, let her uncle know she had the letter ready to be sent to James and had left it on his desk. Oscar went and gathered up a few blankets as they walked down to the lake to relax for the day. The afternoon went by fast, and night approached, where they all retired to bed knowing that the following day would begin the week with much to do and little time for anything leisurely.

Monday morning, Mr. Walsh left reasonably early to wire the letter to James. Oscar and Cateline, finishing breakfast, hurriedly dressed appropriately to spend the day in Dublin, where they would shop for rings. Cateline had already asked if Anya could accompany her on Tuesday to pick out her wedding dress. Quite excited, Anya was more than anxious to go with her, especially since her wedding would follow not too far ahead. Anya thought to herself, "Yes, a marvelous notion it was. While assisting my dear cousin, I can also browse the shops, searching for my own perfect gown."

Shopping for rings, Oscar shared with her about the Claddagh ring given to the woman by the man as a gift. "First, the ring would be worn on the right hand and turned facing outward—once in a relationship, it would be turned inwards, and then once betrothed to be married, it would be worn on the left hand pointing outward and then married, the ring would be turned inward."

Cateline was so overcome with the custom and the beauty of the traditional type of ring, she declared, "Oh Oscar, I love it. That is unquestionably what I want."

"You are sure?"

"Yes, completely sure."

"Once it is sized to fit, you would wear it now on the left turned outward, and when we are married, I will take it off and turn it inward."

"That sounds most enchanting; I so love this. What about for men, do they, too, wear the Claddagh ring?"

"Yes, they have them for men as well; the band is just wider."

"Oh then, I would so love to buy the same for you."

"That is fine, my dear, but I can buy both of them. You do not have to use your money."

"No, absolutely not. I am giving you the ring, so I will pay for it."

Oscar, speaking casually, with a whimsical smile, remarked, "I can certainly see that this marriage will never be tedious."

"Whatever do you mean. I am simply giving you a ring, so I shall be the one who pays for it."

"As you wish, my dear. Let us pick out two and hope they can be sized by tomorrow."

"And I would hope you were never to expect this marriage to be dull."

"No, surely not; you are quite different from any other. With you, I find every day to be exceptionally joyful, as I never know what you will do or say."

"And I, my dear, plan to keep it that way."

The rings were even more beautiful than Cateline had imagined. They were solid gold bands with the top having two hands holding a heart with the heart wearing a tiny crown—several choices in their decision—design and expense. Of course, those adorned with diamonds in the heart and/or on the bands were exceedingly posh in their appearance.

"Oscar, I do want the finest ones for both of us, with the diamonds. They are so exquisite." Being in agreement, they selected the two desired, as Oscar explained the need for the rings to be sized by the following evening to the shop proprietor before their leaving town in two days. The man assured him that he could do a rush order and have them ready by Tuesday evening.

Leaving the shop, they enjoyed lunch at a quaint café and then rode to the train station to inquire about the tickets for Wednesday, along with the departure and arrival times to Youghal. Oscar, leaving Cateline in the carriage, had decided to purchase the tickets prior to hearing back from James. Whereas in the event their plans were altered, he would simply make the necessary changes at the station. Returning to the calash, he noted, "It looks as though we will be leaving very early on Wednesday, seven o'clock to be exact. So, I decided to take care of acquiring the tickets now."

"Oh, I suppose that will have to do, quite early it is—and I am sure that Elbert can drop us off early that morning. We will need to have our belongings packed up the night before and promptly be awakened—perhaps around five or so, wouldn't you say?"

"Yes, but we can sleep on the train. It is a bit uncomfortable, but when you are tired, you will sleep."

Upon leaving the station, they arrived home to rest for the day since Tuesday would also be full of preparations, and then their long journey to Youghal would follow. Everything had gone according to plan with the letter wired to James and the family discussing all the particulars during dinner, once Mr. Walsh had arrived home late from a most tiresome day. As it was a busy week with much packing for the whole family, everyone retired to bed early once again.

Tuesday morning, Oscar carried Cateline and Anya in the barouche to shop for her dress, dropping them off in the midst of Dublin's business district, where afterward, they had all decided on a time to meet for lunch. While the two girls shopped, Oscar ventured about, visiting a few acquaintances he had not seen for some time.

While browsing through many shops looking for that perfect dress, Anya shared with Cateline the history of the long-established wedding gown—as customarily, it was a light blue symbolic of virginity and purity.

"So, they don't wear white?"

"Oh yes, many today do wear white—but it was Queen Victoria who chose to wear a white wedding dress in 1840. Her choice started a new trend of wearing white versus the traditional blue. However, there are still those who aspire to wear the conventional color. There is a saying on the color of the dress, if I can remember it—*marry in white everything's right, marry in blue lover be true, marry in pink, hmm,*" Anya contemplated in thought before she continued. "*Ah, yes, it goes, marry in pink spirits will sink, marry in grey live far away, marry in brown live out of town, marry in green ashamed to be seen, marry in yellow ashamed of your fellow,*" pausing to laugh, she exclaimed, "*well, I believe I am almost there. Marry in black wish you were back, marry in red wish you were dead, marry in tan he'll be a loved man, and last, marry in pearl you'll live in a whirl.*" Anya, giggling, stated, "I can't believe I remembered all of those. And I do believe white or blue either one will simply do, right?"

Cateline, laughing along with her, "Ah, so you rhymed!"

"As a matter of fact, I did!"

Deciding perhaps she would choose the light blue, Cateline remarked, "I really believe I would love to stay with the traditional blue. That is most unusual, and I love hearing about all the customs here, which we do not have in America. What do you think, should I go with blue?"

"That is up to you, but I know when I get married, I do want to stay with the old-style wedding myself."

"Yes, I couldn't agree with you more. I think blue, it is. Please help me find something that is ingenuously gorgeous."

"As you are looking, keep in mind that the more lace, the better. That is also another tradition, and you will either want a veil or a headdress of some sort. Just remember, on the day of your wedding, whichever you choose, you must not put it on yourself. I will do that for you."

"Why is that?"

"Bad luck, cousin dear," Anya said with a sincere smile.

"Well, I think I would rather have the veil."

271

"They make beautiful veils in the blue, as well, with added lace where they are very exquisite."

The girls began to look at all the blue gowns, with Cateline heading to the boudoir to try several on.

"Remember, if it needs minor alterations, Sarah and Permilia do very well at making the necessary adjustments and can work on it today."

"That is quite nice to know," Cateline replied while walking out of the dressing room with an incredibly elegant, designer-quality blue dress. She courted around a small area for Anya to critique one way or the other. "What do you think?"

"Breathtaking is the most proficient word I can utter. This is the dress, why you look like royalty. Oscar is going to have a hard time keeping his hands to himself, cousin," Anya declared while both girls laughed. With Cateline in her dress, Anya began making a few gestures of areas to alter. She remarked, "Sarah can simply take a minor tuck in here and there, perhaps a slight alteration here, and I believe you are going to be the best-looking bride of the year."

"Well, Oscar better keep his hands to himself at least until we are married."

"Yes, that he will have to do with all the family around."

The attendant at the dress shop carried Cateline's dress and the accessories she had chosen to accentuate to the front of the shop. Looking at a few other items in the store, Cateline noticed a small section of men's articles. Stopping to browse, she perceived an exceptionally handsome necktie of sky-blue, which would correspond with her own dress, "Anya, look at this necktie for Oscar. This would be a most astounding touch to heighten our apparel at the wedding, would you not agree?"

"Oh my, it is quite lovely, and yes, I believe it would be an amazingly welcome addition to your whole ensemble. You both will be the envy of every young lady and gentleman present."

"Miss," Cateline spoke to the clerk, "could you please add this to my selections?"

"Yes, ma'am," the lady agreed while taking the necktie to package it up with her other purchases.

As the girls left the dress shop, Cateline had made sure that her elegant gown was tucked away in a box, safely concealed from Oscar's view, as they headed towards the café to meet him for lunch.

Upon arriving, they were surprised to see Mr. Walsh and Amos sitting with Oscar. "I decided to go and visit your uncle after a few friends, and then we determined to surprise both of you for lunch."

Both girls smiled and looked at each other as Cateline declared, "Well, it is sure a surprise, but we are both excited that you are all here."

Uncle Walsh, looking over at Cateline, inquired, "My dear, were you able to find the perfect dress?"

"Yes, sir, it is absolutely gorgeous."

"Yes, and I think I found the one I want when we get married," Anya added while gazing over at Amos.

The men all smiled, observing the vibrancy of the girl's faces, lit up with joy and happiness, when Mr. Walsh declared, "Gentlemen if you could wed your bride every day, she would remain in such ecstasy. Why look at their glowing faces." Studying Oscar and Amos, Samuel continued, "Remember boys, your wife is always your bride—keep her happy, and you will always be happy!"

"Wisdom at its finest, Uncle Walsh," Cateline added with a smile, "my, you do surprise me, but I see how wonderfully in love you remain with my aunt."

"If only our young men understood the wisdom passed down through the ages, they would not make as many mistakes. Oh, I almost forgot to let you know a wire has come from James. He is pleased that you want to be married at his estate and said for you not to worry about anything; he would have a clergyman, as well as a photographer. James also mentioned that he has friends who would attend to have Irish music for dancing afterward," Mr. Walsh proclaimed.

Anya exclaimed with excitement, "Yes—you must learn how to do the ceili, Cateline."

"I am not sure what that is, Anya."

"Ceili means dance—it is Irish dancing in Gaelic, often referred to as an Irish dance party."

"I have never heard of such; please explain."

"It is a traditional Irish dance which is often seen at weddings. There are unique Irish tunes for this dance, but first, you must learn the dance. If his friends are going to play Irish music, you can bet there will be ceili tunes."

Cateline trying to pronounce the name, "Kei-lee—," before she was interrupted—

"It is spelled c-e-i-l-i, but pronounced, **kei-lee**," Anya declared.

"Kei-lee—you can teach me the dance?"

"Well, yes, but it involves more than one couple. Oscar, you do know the dance, right?"

"Of course, we should all get together and teach it to Cateline. Amos, you can come this evening after work?"

"I don't see why not."

"We probably need at least one more couple. Father, you and mother, would join us for this?"

"I'm sure your mother and I could join all of you this evening. It might make for some good entertainment, yet we have no one to play the tunes," Mr. Walsh added.

"No, father, we can just hum a tune if we need to. As long as Cateline has the steps down, she should do fine."

"Yes, once Cateline gets the steps down," Oscar shared, continuing, "I can also work with her at James's on Wednesday evening and Thursday so that she is more confident."

"Then it is settled; after dinner, we will all teach Cateline the ceili," Anya finished.

"I suppose we will need to retire to bed as soon as I learn this dance step as well since we will need to be up very early to dress. Uncle Walsh, would Elbert be able to drop us off at the station? The train leaves by seven; we would probably need to leave the estate by six to check-in before departure."

Uncle Walsh noted, "I will also arrange to get you two there at the station, but by all means, once we have secured the dance steps to a degree, both of you should retire thereafter. I will make sure you are awakened in the morning, very early. As for the rest of the family, we will be leaving on Thursday afternoon to arrive late that evening, which was the best I could do to clear my schedule at the office. Amos, are you able to get away for a few days?"

"Yes, sir, I made plans to travel with Anya."

"Good—yes, very good. We will arrive on Thursday, and they are to be wed on Friday; we should be rested by then for a joyous time. We will also be bringing Sarah and Permilia with us on the trip to help with all the lady's hair and dress for the occasion."

"Thank you. By far, you are the greatest uncle ever."

The five of them had a great meal and excellent conversation. Upon leaving the restaurant, Mr. Walsh and Amos headed back to work. At the same time, Oscar mentioned to the ladies, "We should go to the Gaiety Theatre to see what is playing. It is still quite a while before our rings shall be ready. There is no point in heading back home and then turning around to come and get the rings."

"Yes, that sounds delightful. How about it, Anya?"

"Absolutely. Anything but going home. Thank you, Oscar."

Oscar steered the barouche to the theatre, where they watched *Bluebeard*, a French folktale. Once the play had ended, the three of them walked to the carriage. Hand in hand, Oscar looked at Cateline, "I could tell by your demeanor in the theatre, you were not that thrilled with the performance."

"Oh, no—you are terribly wrong. I do say that I have never seen *Bluebeard*—and it was not what I expected, that is for sure. The performance was very well, I found the plot reasonably interesting, and the ending was most pleasant. The play being in pantomime did make for an extremely dramatic production, quite brilliant indeed. I really did enjoy it immensely, Oscar," Cateline responded while thinking to herself, silently, "I cannot believe I have never heard of this play. I did find it somewhat fascinating, not surprising that there are so many horror films during this timeframe." Continuing on the subject, she concluded in contrast to the production, "Although, Oscar, I am not a huge fan of watching someone murder all their wives."

"Of course, the tragic effects could have introduced comedy,"[1] Oscar declared.

"I think it was anything but comic."

Grinning, he maintained, "A laugh in an audience does not destroy terror, but—by relieving it, aids it. A playwright should never be afraid that by raising a laugh, you destroy the tragedy. On the contrary, you intensify it."[1]

"I do believe you will make a fine playwright one day, Oscar," turning to Anya, "and my dear cousin, how did you like the play?"

"It was very interesting. Although it may keep me awake tonight, it was rather frightful, don't you think?"

Oscar laughing, "Women—it was just a play, not reality."

"Women! Please, Oscar, I said that I found it quite interesting. I shall have no trouble sleeping tonight," Cateline snapped.

Oscar, looking over at her, affirmed, "I suppose the times that you jumped and screamed, you were not afraid?"

"No, I was not afraid," she declared firmly. Continuing with a smile, "It was the strong dynamics to the music at times that made me jump. Did it not you, Anya?"

"Yes, it most certainly did."

"And, I dare say, Oscar, I never screamed, as you say."

"Indeed, if you say so," he stated, truthfully understanding there were times it was best to not try and prove a point.

They rode along in conversation or, more accurately, debates regarding the performance until they had arrived at the jewelry shop. Oscar jumped out and proceeded to run into the store, where he obtained the rings while the girls waited in the carriage. Once he was back in the barouche, Cateline could not wait to show Anya the ring Oscar bought for her. "Oh, it is so incredible, Cateline. It makes me want to hurry and get married."

"It is quite lovely at that, and here is the one I purchased for him. It is also a Claddagh ring."

"So, remarkable. I do love the history on the Claddagh rings," Anya stated.

"When Oscar shared it with me, I knew that was what I wanted. Oscar, what does the crown represent?" Cateline inquired.

Oscar asked, "Anya, you know the story of the ring, yes?"

"Yes, I do."

"I did not reveal the entire story; I merely conveyed what the rings mean to wear them. The story originated, I believe, in the seventeenth century, in the little village of Claddagh in County Galway. They used to put the initials R.J. on the rings. It is said that Richard Joyce was taken captive by pirates at a time when he was in love and to be married. He was sold into slavery in Africa, where he worked in a goldsmith shop. Joyce kept pieces of gold until there was enough to fashion into a ring, a Claddagh ring. He never stopped loving the girl he was to marry and was gone for many years before his release. Finally, Joyce returned to find his love, still waiting for him. The heart, of course, represents love; the crown is a symbol of royalty, which symbolizes loyalty; and the hands come together to hold the heart and crown representing friendship."

"That is truly beautiful, Oscar. I am so glad that is what we bought."

"Ah—but, you know—with the crown representative of friendship, between men and women, there is no friendship possible. There is passion, enmity, worship, love, but no friendship."[2]

"I disagree; I believe that a man and a woman must, by all means, be friends if they are to be lovers. There are no arbitrary rules that one must take a wife and then denounce her friendship, for what chance would there be to happiness if they were not as loyal as true friends?"

"I believe that falling in love with a woman, one can no longer treat her as a friend. The relationship would not work."

"Oscar Wilde, I can tell you right now when we are married, you will not only be my lover, but you will also be my one true friend because you will care for me like no other could. Please tell me if you disagree. I would hope that you know there will be no other that will ever care more for you than I."

He concurred with a smile, "I will not argue with that point."

Cateline leaning over, kissed him lightly on his cheek, "I will love you as my husband but also as my friend."

Arriving back at the estate, Cateline called Sarah to assist her with the dress, explaining the slight alterations needed. Ascending up the stairs into her room, she tried on the dress where Sarah could pin those areas needing minor adjustments, making tucks here and there for the dress to fit precisely. Once they were done, Cateline took the dress back off while addressing her, "Will you be able to have it ready by this evening, Sarah?"

"Yes, ma'am, it should not take me too awfully long."

"Thank you," Cateline smiled most earnestly before heading back downstairs, where Oscar met her in the hallway and motioned for her to walk with him to the veranda.

Outside, in somewhat passionate dialogue, Oscar reflected, "I wanted this to be a little more intimate where I had you alone."

"Whatever do you mean?"

Oscar, taking the rings out of his pocket, prompted, "Remember, we wear the rings now, and once married, we turn them around."

"Oh, I had almost forgotten."

Oscar took her left hand and slid the ring on facing outward, showing they were betrothed while assuring, "I love you with all my heart, Cateline." He then handed her his ring, and likewise, she slid the ring on his finger with the heart also facing outward.

"I, too, love you, Oscar, and cherish this very moment with you." Leaning down towards her lips, he kissed her intimately while Cateline wrapped her arms around his neck. How she would never forget that moment—the moment of closeness, sharing their love with rings of such meaning, the embrace they held, awaiting the day they would become one.

Upon walking back into the estate, looking at her ring, Cateline thought to herself, "Why is outward with the heart pointing towards me? To me, that would be inward." Not quite understanding, she inquired openly, "Oscar, why is it considered outward when the heart points towards me?"

"Simple, my darling. It shows others that you are promised to someone else. Once we are married and I turn the heart around, it points towards me, which shows that you belong to someone which, of course, is me—since that is the direction it points."

"Hmm, I suppose that is simple, and on the right hand it means differently as facing towards me would mean that it was a gift from someone but turned facing the other way, it would mean that I am not betrothed just promised to the person in which it points, yes?

"You are correct," Oscar responded, "and I thought you may wish to show the family the rings at dinner."

"I would. This is very exciting, and I do love my ring. I will cherish it forever as well as cherish you, my love."

Walking back into the estate to join the family for their evening meal, Cateline was all lit up and beaming, where she immediately showed everyone her ring as well as Oscar's. "Oh, how beautiful," Aunt Martha said, "I have always loved the tradition of the Claddagh ring, my dear. They are very stunning." After everyone made such a fuss over the rings, the subsequent discussion drifted towards the dress, as Anya could not wait to emphasize Cateline's gorgeous wedding gown.

"I wish you could have seen her with the dress on, mother," Anya said, "oh, I cannot describe it to you because Oscar must have no clue until their special day, but I informed Cateline she looked just like royalty."

"Oh my, it must be very lovely, my dear," Aunt Martha spoke.

"Oh yes," Anya concurred, "why I even told her that Oscar was going to have a hard time keeping his hands to himself once he sees her in that dress," Anya spoke hastily with a playful smile while looking over towards the imminent groom.

Cateline feeling a bit embarrassed, blushed while Oscar smiled cleverly, resolving, "It must be quite a dress."

With everyone now bursting with laughter, her uncle added, "Well—we will have none of you two sneaking off after the wedding. You must first celebrate with your family before the night ends."

"Yes, sir," Oscar established, "I would not want to disappoint the family and will make sure that Cateline's beauty does not overtake me." With his last statement, he glanced over to smile generously at her.

"So, my dear," her aunt commenced to inquire, "Sarah is making a few minor alterations?"

"Yes, ma'am, I believe she is at work on those now where I can try it back on after dinner."

"Very good, why don't you allow us to bring your dress when we come on Thursday. It will make it much easier on your journey tomorrow."

"Yes, ma'am, I will have Sarah bring the box down in the morning."

Conversations endured throughout the meal with much talk of the wedding and inquiries unto Anya and Amos's special day to come. With dining having concluded, Oscar and Cateline went to their rooms to pack their bags swiftly for the extensive journey the following day. Upon finishing, they hurried back downstairs, as agreed, for the family gathering to commence teaching Cateline the Irish dance steps. Oscar stopped by Cateline's room to gather up her belongings for the journey, carrying everything downstairs in advance. They then joined the family in the drawing-room to begin the ceili.

"Is everyone ready? There is more room out in the hallway," Anya declared with the party following her. Stepping forward to begin teaching the dance steps, Anya remarked to the group or, to be more precise, explained in detail to Cateline, "We will make two lines facing our partners. Each line, goes boy, girl, boy, and depending on how many are dancing will depend on how many are in each line. It can be very long lines in large ballrooms, Cateline." Everyone stood in their place facing their partners while Anya

279

resumed, "When the music begins, but we can simply hum, the first step will be for you to promenade in and out two times. Amos and I will run through the first step, pay close attention, so you will understand."

Amos and Anya took their steps towards each other two times showing Cateline how it was done. "Now, we will all do that first step together—ready, promenade in and out one time and then again two times. The next step couples exchange positions, if you are stepping to your right, you pass at the rear, just follow our lead and do as we do in slow motion first." The three couples then exchanged positions, moving to the right, passing at the rear. Anya continued, "Wonderful, now let's do that again a few times until you are sure you understand." Once again, the couples all exchanged places, then Anya stated, "Now, let's start from the beginning and get those first two steps down"—doing so numerous times until Cateline understood. "Now, once all couples have exchanged places, you are no longer in front of your partner but someone else. Then set in place, like this," Anya began to show her; once that was done, she admonished, "the next step pertains to the middle couples. In our case, there is merely one couple, but when you are doing this in a ballroom setting, it will be several couples. So, all the middle couples for eight counts do the right-hand star, then the left-hand star, like this," Anya started showing Cateline with her partner. "While the middle couple is doing eight counts of the right and left-hand star, the couples at the end are doing the swing buzz." Anya maintained while Cateline watched to see how that was done. Cateline practiced this move a number of times as the middle couple doing the eight counts of the right and left-hand star and the outer couple doing the swing buzz. "Once again, you set in place, like this, and then everyone heads home to their partner like so, and once home, you set in place again. After that, it is in and out two times with the top lady at the line making an arch for pass-through to progress, like so," they all do this to show her while Oscar holds her hand to bring her through. "Once that is done, it begins all over again."

Cateline laughing, "I do believe this is going to take some time."

"You will get it," Oscar declared with a tender smile. They continued and continued while everyone was immersed in laughter, including Cateline. With many mistakes and start-overs, Oscar held onto her through the entirety until she caught on. A few times, Oscar stopped to laugh hysterically, and Cateline being a good sport, would giggle with him.

"This is really fun. I have never danced anything like this before," Cateline deliberated. They spent about an hour dancing and drinking wine, which her uncle had Joseph bring out for everyone to have a splendid time together. Finally, Cateline spoke up and declared, "I think that Oscar will just have to work with me further on the steps for the next two days. It is much later than we had planned to retire, and we must be up relatively early." Cateline walked over to her aunt and uncle and gave them each a light kiss on the cheek, "I love you both, and thank you for everything you have done for me."

Oscar shook hands with the men and told everyone how he had enjoyed himself immensely during his stay, with Uncle Walsh concluding, "Good night to you both, and I wish you a safe journey. We shall not be far from arriving ourselves and look forward to being a part of your incredibly blessed day."

Cateline and Oscar bade their adieus to the family and then ascended the stairs. Once standing at Cateline's door, he reached over to kiss her goodnight and then followed her into the room. Kissing her once more, he lightly whispered, "Goodnight, my dear. I will see you in the morning."

"Oh, I almost forgot, my darling," she spoke softly while walking over to her dressing room. Opening her box from the dress shop, which her aunt and uncle would be bringing with them, Cateline pulled out an article and turned once again to Oscar, "I bought you this most handsome necktie of sky-blue for you to wear at our wedding. I do hope that you like it; it is the same color as my dress, and I felt that your necktie would add such a welcoming emphasis on blending us together as one. Do you not agree?"

Oscar holding the tie, "It is absolutely delightful. I could not agree more, together we will be as one, my dear."

In her enchantment, Cateline reached up and wrapped her arms around his neck as she kissed him, "Goodnight, darling."

Wednesday morning soon arrived, quite early at precisely 5:15 a.m., as Sarah came bustling into Cateline's room to awaken her. "Sarah, I know it is so early. Please go back to bed; I will just go and make sure that someone woke up Oscar, and then I will get ready."

"Thank you, ma'am. And were you able to try on the dress before you retired last night?" Sarah inquired.

"Oh, yes I did, thank you very much. The dress fits superb, but I am so glad you mentioned this, for I almost forgot. Will you make sure that my dress is brought downstairs for my aunt and uncle to bring with them when they come?"

"Yes, ma'am, I will see to it."

"Thank you, Sarah."

Cateline arose from the bed and walked up the stairs to Oscar's room; opening the door, she ran and jumped on his bed quite impetuously while laughing, "Wake up, wake up, my love! I am so excited and ready to be your wife."

Oscar rolled over, rather pleased, as he took her in his arms, pulling her close to him under the covers, all the while kissing her intimately. "Good morning, my love."

Glowing, as she laid next to him while responding, "Good morning to you. I love you so much."

Oscar leaned up vaguely while casually lying upon her frame in a subtle mode. His lips tenderly stroked hers faintly, lingering as he drew her towards him, teasing her with every compassionate kiss. Minutes passed while he held her intimately, compelling her nearer; his touch intensified with every caress. Cateline finally reacted, "We have to stop, or we will be late. Just think, in three more days, we will be able to sleep next to each other every single night forever." With those words coming forth, in the back of her mind, she knew the word *forever* would not really be forever.

Provocatively, Oscar responded, "If you amuse me for half an hour more, you may do as you please."

Cateline smiled most firmly but playfully, with her response coming forth somewhat brusque, "You sir, will release me, or we will miss our train, and there will be no wedding, nor will I be your bride to do as **you** please."

"Well, if you put it that way, I must refrain from keeping you hostage." Oscar, releasing her, rose from the bed to begin getting ready for the trip. Oh, how she loved the way he looked in his nightshirt, but as he began to undress, Cateline knew it was time to leave the room.

Rising up from the bed, she hurried out of the room while he smiled bravely, unashamed of disrobing himself in her presence. She spoke up while he laughed, "Men, they are such unruly creatures, unashamed of walking about naked in front of ladies."

Both finishing up dressing casually for the long journey, Oscar stopped in Cateline's room to gather any additional items she would be taking with her. Packing very light as they had, knowing they would be staying one last night at her uncle's estate on their return, and from there, they would leave for their final travels towards London with all their belongings.

CHAPTER
19

Elbert loaded the couple's trunk and carpetbag in the carriage while Oscar and Cateline finished gathering a few other items needed for the long journey. Bertha, arriving at the door and presented them with a basket of food items to enjoy along the way. "Thank you so much for preparing this for us, Bertha," Cateline spoke softly, adorned with a most loving smile while continuing, "you are so very thoughtful."

Oscar helped Cateline into the brougham and then settled down next to her when Anya came running out of the estate to say her goodbyes. "Cateline, my dear cousin, I know I will see you in a few days, but I just wanted to wish you a safe journey."

She responded cheerfully, "Thank you, Anya; I cannot wait until you are with me in Youghal."

"Yes, I am so looking forward to this trip. And, please do keep up with your diary and never mind what Oscar thinks; it is a woman's treasure and to only be shared once he has said his vows to you, my sweet cousin," Anya finished glancing over towards Oscar with a mockingly playful smile.

Amused at both ladies, he quipped, "Yes, ma'am, I will not take a peek at it—not once, I assure you, until I have said my vows to Cateline."

Elbert steered the horses towards the train station while Oscar resumed the debate with Cateline, "Ah—but, you do know that I, too, keep a diary, and I never travel without, my dear. One should always have something sensational to read on the train."[1]

"I had no idea. Do most men have diaries?"

"I do not know about most men, but I do know that many writers and artists, in general, do keep a diary, or some refer to it as a journal. I keep a diary to enter the wonderful secrets of my life. If I didn't write them down, I should probably forget all about them."[2]

"I have yet to see you writing in any type of journal."

"Memory, my dear Cateline, is the diary that we all carry about with us,"[2] he concluded with a sly smile.

Discussions continued regarding their travel when Oscar began sharing details, "It is around 140 miles from Dublin to

Youghal—we should arrive within three hours." Cateline was aware that the trains did not travel as fast in the nineteenth century, but she was confident they should still reach their destination before noon with their early departure.

At the train station, Elbert unloaded their belongings, and they promptly boarded the cars. Settling into their seats, Oscar shared, "You will probably be more comfortable if I sit next to the window where you can lean against me if you are planning to try and sleep."

"Yes, I thought we probably both would sleep some; that is why I brought the pillow. If you are going to be by the window, please, you take it," Cateline said, handing him over the comfy pillow, continuing, "Oscar, lay it against the wall. It will be more relaxing, and we can both cover up with the blanket to stay warm."

"That is fine; the trains are not so cozy, are they? Have you ever ridden far by train in America?"

Cateline, thinking about his question, remembered once traveling in her era, of course, where it was reasonably comfortable. "Yes, but only for a short distance," she alluded to the fact.

"Well, you will get used to long-distance traveling by train as we will have quite a journey to London."

"You crossed from England to Ireland on the Irish Sea, right?"

"I did; the best place to cross is from Liverpool to Dublin. Liverpool has one of the largest dock systems in the world. The river where ships come in is relatively deep in Liverpool to accommodate substantial vessels, where most ports are not. It is supposed to be one of the most significant trading centers due to the ease by which ships can maneuver. Nevertheless, the ship from the Dublin port to Liverpool takes around seven or eight hours. However, this does include stopovers at various ports to deliver mail. But it is a much smoother ride than by train. The first segment of our journey to England will be on a small steamship, and then the remainder will be by train."

"Oh, I had no idea it took such a long time by ship to get to Liverpool. I suppose we should leave early that day as well?'

"No need to leave that early, of course, depending on what time the ship departs. I assume the first day we arrive will be late that evening, where we can grab a bite to eat and then get some sleep. We

285

can sleep late our first morning and then go about the town once we awaken, perhaps even take in some sights before leaving by train to Bath. You did say that you would like to see Bath?"

"Yes, if it is not out of the way."

"It is traveling the same direction but a bit out of the way. It is perfectly alright; Bath is a very fashionable sight—I am sure you would like it, and if it makes you happy, I am happy."

"You make me very happy, Oscar."

"Well, then there is no need to leave early for Bath either, as we do not have to be rushed. I know I said that I would like to be back before the end of this week, but it will be our honeymoon, and I also want to enjoy this time with you, more so than rushing to be back in London."

"Yes, but I would also like to spend a little time in Liverpool. Is Bath very far from there?"

"From Liverpool to Bath is about three hours. If you want to spend more time in Liverpool, perhaps we could stay for a few nights. Once in Bath, to London is only another two hours."

"That was an awfully long trip that you took to get to Dublin."

"More so when one must wait at each location until the mode of travel has arrived, delayed once more as they prepare for new passengers. Not to mention, ships are not always available at any hour, which pushes your departure to the following day. However, I have traveled many times to Dublin over the years. You just sleep along the way, bring food, unless you prefer to purchase from their selections."

"Such a very lengthy journey unless you were staying for a while, which you did. I am assuming that makes it much easier."

"Yes, it is quite pleasant when you do not have to hurry back. So, my staying as I have, has made for rather a pleasurable excursion—naturally, it was unexpected. I had no plans to prolong my stay. That would be your fault, my dear."

She responded playfully, "My fault? I can hardly take the blame for you falling in love with me."

"I certainly cannot blame your uncle—no, I doubt that would be the right thing to do. I dare say that it is entirely your fault," he finished with an unrepentant smile.

"And so, do you regret meeting me?"

Oscar, looking down into her eyes with a genuine smile, replied, "I think you know that I dare not regret meeting you. I just never expected this to occur, and so hastily—what were your expectations, Cateline?"

"Oh—well, I thought after the first day we met, you were going to fall in love with me," she spoke bravely, followed with a slight laugh.

He stated adamantly while procuring an appealing smile, "Yes, go ahead and blame it all on me but remember, I do know that you also fell in love."

"Yes, I am very much in love with you, Oscar," Cateline replied, leaning over to kiss him.

After a brief silence, Cateline expressed once again, "Perhaps, we could stay a few nights in Liverpool and then a few nights in Bath before we head to London unless, of course, you need to be back sooner."

"I really am not looking forward to living on a train for such an extended period. This will be our honeymoon, Cateline—I would much prefer to enjoy the week, or rather, next week. If we need to stay longer at each location, we will. As long as I am at least heading towards London, everything will be fine."

"You do know how to say the right words, my love. I, too, would love to enjoy our time together for our first week of marriage. Perhaps, we should at least leave early from Dublin to head towards Liverpool, so we can enjoy our stay there."

"Indeed, but to go to Bath, it may be more feasible to take a later train where we merely sleep and arrive before daybreak the following morning."

"Yes, I believe that is a good idea."

"Now, stop worrying yourself over such a tedious subject. Let's relax and enjoy the journey, my dear."

Getting settled for the trip to Youghal, Cateline snuggled up against Oscar as the steam train geared up to leave the station, with billows of steam and gas escaping as it gained speed. Covering themselves with a blanket for warmth, she strived to get comfortable while cuddling up closer. It was not a very comfortable ride, that was for sure, but at some point, having slept inadequately the night before, they were both sound asleep within no time.

About mid-morning, Oscar awoke and began to stir, which woke up Cateline. "Are we almost there?" she inquired.

287

"No, I believe we have only traveled a little over an hour or so. I was simply getting a bit hungry; how about you?"

"Yes, did you look to see what Bertha packed for us?"

"Just started looking, but I believe there are many breakfast items to choose from, and it seems lunch items, as well. We will definitely need to thank her again—Bertha is such a prize to them, I am sure." They each pulled out various fruits, cheeses, and pastries to begin with. "It looks like there are a few sandwiches if you would like one now."

"No, thank you. I believe what I have is sufficient," Cateline remarked, as they enjoyed their breakfast while looking out the windows to such resplendent views of the Emerald Isle with all the opulent terrains. The train mostly traveled along the coastal region, which showcased ornately scenic views of the most stunning emerald green countryside. Cateline soon understood why this great land, the land of her ancestors, was referred to as the Emerald Isle. One could only be in awe when standing gazing upon its lush coverings of immeasurable dark greens, mixed with tones of yellows forming numerous shades streaming throughout the luscious sacred ash trees. These gallant trees, scattered about along their journey, trunks stood tall—to allegiance, and their full bodies rounded with throngs of leaves hiding every twig—prized for their strength and healing properties. Likewise, the native wych elms could be spotted along the route—mountain elms, positioned along the rocky cliffs, oval fuzzy green leaves with splashes of purple flowery buds. The broadleaf Irish oaks were seen occasionally among the panoramic settings— the ancient Sessile, native to the country, the symbol of strength, the king of trees throughout the immensity of flatlands perched high above the precipices that ran along the clear blue waters. Vistas of beauty could all too well be perceived as mixed foliage formed in clusters of shrubs while overlaying the jagged ridges of bluffs. The brightest hues of blues in the vastness of the seas as the waters stood tranquil in silence, small ripples pooling in much of the expanse with a bit of white foaming waters that fizzled along a few of the shores. Bridges adorned the landscape, iconic stone, rustic red iron with trusses perched over waterways and rivers. Time stood still, history waiting, stories to be heard and told—a different time, a diverse place. Ancient and picturesque, as Cateline took in every moment and every scene to savor the views, the scents, the sounds, the taste, and the feel. All her senses were alive; she was alive savoring every moment, every detail, and each day as if it were her last. Yes, Cateline knew time would stop once again; time would end for her, time would end for her with him. These moments and memories would last her a lifetime; it was all she would have and all she could hold on to. Oh, how she thought about life—life being so short, time running out, and yet, life was far too often lived for tomorrow, never absorbing every moment of today as if it were one's last. Life was too brief, yes—time was fleeting and, life was seldom lived to savor, to truly spend one's days meaningfully. She would one day know that these moments with Oscar were the best days of her life, the days that really mattered, days that would not last for all time. Cateline suddenly felt very empty inside. This train was taking her to her destiny; nevertheless, she knew it would all be short-lived. Life was passing along too rapidly. Her life with him would be much too short.

The sun continued to rise as the morning commenced to quietly drift away, and the whiteness of the puffy clouds shone with smears of oranges and various hues of yellows, floating cleverly in the sky underneath a most delicate pale blue background. Cateline looked over at Oscar, admiring his appearance as he, too, was staring out the windows at the scenery, a most handsome young man. This was the epitome of the man she had long dreamed of—strong, tall, with his long hair so carefree. He was in his youth, vibrant, alive—his mind always free, brilliant thoughts escaping, talents, artistic, poetic—works of art in every verse, prose, sonnet—a master of creation, one to be remembered, always and forever. He would never know the pathway of his life after his death. He would never know the lives he touched, the spectacular creations that worked through him and were apparent in his life throughout his adolescence and into his twenties, thirties, forties. His was a mind awakened, one that questioned, studied, looked into the future, born before his time. Yet, it was in an era that failed him. Although, it was a time of reflection where he found life and meaning, not for this life but for the next.

After the calm of her train of thoughts, Cateline inquired, "Have you traveled to this part of Ireland, Oscar?"

"Yes, I have pretty much traveled most of Ireland in my days with family and even as I became older. I went to many places with friends as well."

"Ireland is so picturesque. It has a bit of everything with its mountains, rivers, the sea. I believe it is more beautiful than the east coast of America, which is also very striking."

They enjoyed the closeness felt, talking and sharing while Cateline asked many questions about Ireland and Oscar sharing its history. Before too long, they were getting close to Youghal, as it was almost eleven.

As they drew near the station, Cateline started to pack everything back in the basket and folded the blanket. Stepping down from the train, she spotted James entering the depot. Cateline ran to him, sharing her excitement with a great big hug, bubbling over with anticipation to see the estate. The two young men shook hands as James congratulated Oscar and Cateline on their upcoming wedding. "I am very pleased to have both of you here and to have you married in my estate. Father would be so thrilled to know you came back, Cateline, and that you also decided this was where you wanted to marry. I think you will both be content, as I have had my servants prepare the grounds and the core rooms downstairs for your pleasure and have taken care of all the necessities with the clergyman and photographer. There is plenty of room for all the family to stay as well, and I have arranged the large room with a balcony for the suite once you two are married."

"Thank you so much, brother. I do hope that you did not go to too much trouble."

"No more than father would have done if he had lived to see this day."

"Please, let us know the cost for the photographer and minister, and we shall take care of it."

"No need for that, my dear sister. I have already taken care of all the particulars. Let this be my wedding gift to the happy couple," he concluded with a smile.

"James, you are such a prize and the best brother that any sister could have." Cateline smiled affectionately at her brother, and the men loaded their belongings into his carriage.

Oscar and James talked considerably on the ride to the estate discussing many things that the menfolk seemed to enjoy. Before too long, James spoke up, "Cateline, we are approaching the clock gate tower."

Off in the immediate distance, she could see the enormous arched tower that sat astride their main street, topped by an immense clock encased with a most ancient appearance. "The tower was built over one hundred years ago, and it was a jail up until about 1840," James shared while the carriage proceeded through the arch.

"It looks somewhat medieval," Cateline replied, "have you seen inside?"

"Why yes, I have been inside. It's not a place one would want to sleep, or at least I would not."

As they entered the estate, it was such a grand home, much more so than Cateline had ever imagined. She was so delighted that her wedding would be held at her father's estate and believed that Oscar was also quite pleased. The coachman acquired all their belongings while Oscar helped Cateline down. "Oh please, I must take a look a bit longer at the front of the estate, the fountain and all the shrubbery; there is such beauty in everything. Let me just linger here for a moment or two before we go inside, dear brother."

"Yes, but of course. I grew up here at this estate and the only place I have ever lived."

"You surely plan to marry and have children; I do hope that you will, brother," Cateline pleaded.

James laughed, "Well, yes, I hope to marry, and I do have someone that I am courting at the moment. Perhaps, it will occur soon enough."

Cateline smiling, "I am very happy to hear this, and shall we meet her?"

"Yes, definitely, you will meet Sophia at your wedding."

Getting settled in rooms, Cateline went about the second and third floor, looking at all the assorted furnishings as they outlined each room splendidly. One of the rooms, assuming it to be her father's, had a picture of her on the bedside table when she was relatively tiny, along with a picture of a man and a young boy— Cateline assumed it to be her father when he was a young man with James. Continuing on her venture through the range of rooms, undoubtedly, she found the room for her and Oscar once they were married, a most elegant chamber with fine furnishings. The apartment had evidently been adorned with gorgeous, fragrant flowers and a bottle of champagne accompanying two glasses for the bride and

291

groom, unquestionably. It seemed to be the biggest of bedchambers and the most astounding at that, with French doors opening to the balcony, which overlooked a most alluring flower garden. The terrace was truly delightful with its extravagant width curving prominently on both sides to a somewhat rounded shape, many substantial ormolu columns, which stood with such distinction to appear as a chateau. Yes, quite spacious and impressive, the very estate where Cateline must have been born, in reality, that is, if she did live two lives.

As she walked out onto the sufficient grandeur balcony, many lavish chaises were scattered about with a wealth of greenery and a surplus of flowers—a few smaller sculptures in various locales, all overlooking the expanse of the grounds, which went fashionably off in the distance. The land was moderately extensive to that of her uncle's estate, yet all in all, her father's was perhaps a bit larger but not by much. Cateline sat on one of the plush chairs to unwind from the long journey as she continued to reflect on the breathtaking scenery of the grounds. Off in the distance at a much greater expanse than her uncle's, Cateline was able to get a glimpse of the stables where the horses were apparently kept, having already known that James loved horses and owned several for riding. Taking in the scenery a bit longer, she wondered what the estate looked like in her timeframe.

Cateline, leaving the upper floors to join the men downstairs, began to examine the vestibule along with the choice drawing rooms that were all opened to elaborate the overflow for guests and the central area embellished for where they would soon take their vows. In the main drawing-room, a rather grand pianoforte sat in a corner. Off to the side, an arch was constructed where many flowers in vibrant blooms were gathered around the edges, embellishing a slight pathway covered with a beautiful light blue carpet leading to the bow. It was at this site where Oscar and Cateline would stand, amongst romantically colored flowers, showcasing such warmth, feelings of love, transforming their aroma and softness to the touch. The ardor—passion with every breath could be felt, the presence of nature, of a higher power. God in His wisdom and mercy, bringing together two souls, lost in love—lost in the moment, together as one, one with the Lord in all His magnificent benevolence and clemency.

"James, this is so thoughtful of you. It is most romantic. I don't know how to even begin to thank you. There are so many flowers and plants which make everything look so enchanting," she exclaimed while walking over to the various arrangements which adorned the room meticulously. "Please tell me, dear brother, what kind of plant is this?" Cateline inquired, reaching forth her hand to a green plant where the leaves were as shells mixed in with tiny fragrant white flowers.

"Those are called Bells of Ireland which symbolize luck," James replied while he walked over to another plant, continuing, "and these are Myrtle plants," touching a green plant with many fragrant flowers, some of white and others were a light fragrant blue. "The Myrtle was a plant used centuries past and were sacred to Venus, the Roman goddess of love. They have been used as a symbol of marriage for centuries."

"I am familiar with the Myrtle, but I have never heard of its history. How did you know my dress is blue?"

"I received a telegram from Aunt Martha," James answered with a most heartfelt smile.

"I should have known; I do say that I am not in the least surprised," Cateline responded with a slight laugh. At the same time, while walking around the room, viewing the magnificent features and beauty, she observed where they would stand on Friday under the arch taking their vows to be joined together as one. Tears coursed down her cheeks as she wiped them away and apologized. "I am so sorry, this setting that you have made so special has overcome me with emotions, for I never expected such beauty or thought from you, dear brother. I am only sorry that we never met until this year, but I am so thankful that you are now in my life."

James walked over to Cateline, circling her with his arms as he gave her a brotherly hug, "I, too, my sister, am so pleased that we have finally met and vow that we shall strive to grow close for years to come."

"Yes, I would so like that and hope you would visit us in London."

"I would be most honored, and perhaps that may happen sooner than later, especially if I marry. However, you have made my day by just coming and giving me the honor of having you married under our father's roof. I am so happy that you like it. Oh, and I almost forgot, Sophia plays the pianoforte very well, so I thought she could play while Uncle Walsh walks you down the carpet to Oscar."

293

"You thought of everything. I never even considered the music for the actual wedding nor who would give me away."

James, lit up with smiles, proclaims, "Even us men can surprise our women, as we do think of many things to please. And I assumed our uncle would want to give you away."

Cateline, overcome with joy, instantaneously, walked over to clasp her arm around Oscar's before inquiring to James, "Are there any other surprises that I do not know about?"

James reciprocated, "Well, yes, I did take the liberty of hiring an additional cook to assist Margaret, partly so that your cake will be most magnificent in accord with Irish customs," with a slight laugh, he looked towards Oscar. "The tradition with the layers of cake stacked as high as possible." James continued in his merriment, where at this point Oscar joined in, for they knew that Cateline had no idea what that meant.

"Well, I see that you two are being most discrete. Please spare me the ridicule in front of our guests. What is so funny about the wedding cake being stacked high?"

"It's quite alright, my dear. You will love it, I am sure," Oscar replied.

James maintained sharing with Cateline other items that he had yet to disclose, which would take place on their special day, "And, my dear sister, I have a few friends as well that were delighted, when I inquired of them, to join us for entertainment. They have many instruments to include the fiddle, flute, harp, and the Uillean piper."

"That is a bagpipe, brother?"

"Yes, have you heard one played in America?"

"I wish I could say yes, but I am afraid I have not." Cateline smiled warmly, continuing, "I am rather excited to be part of this culture—and, am so glad to meet some of your friends and also be entertained with the traditional Irish music. I can hardly wait."

"Well, they are just a small group, but they play very well, and I believe they will also be bringing their wives or girlfriends, as some are not married—if you have not seen Irish dancing, you will also have that privilege."

"As a matter of fact, I have not seen much Irish dancing, but Anya did arrange for several of us at their estate to dance to the Irish tunes, where I could learn. What was that dance called Oscar?"

"She's speaking of the ceili dance."

"Good—good, because they will be playing tunes specifically for the ceili, which is very prevalent for weddings, so you will surely have a splendid time."

"All of these customs of the Irish have amazed me, and I am so excited to be finally able to experience them, especially at my own wedding."

Oscar laughing, "Oh yes, you will definitely get to experience a traditional Irish wedding in all its aspects. I believe that the Irish conventions far outweigh other cultures, wouldn't you say, James?"

"Yes, I believe you are probably right. This will be a day for Cateline to remember for sure. And, perhaps, she may be able to acquire a few other Irish dances as well."

Cateline spoke up very quickly as she smiled profusely, "Oh no, I learned one of your traditional dances but would much rather watch any other. I do not want to bring embarrassment to you or even myself for that matter."

"Believe me, my dear, the amount of drinking that takes place at an Irish wedding, no one would even know if you made a mistake or at least they won't remember it by the following day. I promise you after the many drinks of mead, you will be out on the dance floor," Oscar spoke as he laughed along with James.

"What is mead?"

"Why the traditional Irish wedding drink," James declared.

"I suppose it must be strong," Cateline probed.

Oscar speaking up, "It is just yellow wine with honey and herbs."[3]

"Yellow wine, I do not believe I have heard of such," she declared.

"I suppose you call it white wine, but you should have questioned based on the color. Red wine is called red because of the color, is it not? White wine is not white; it is yellow; therefore, I call it yellow wine."

James and Cateline were both amused, where she responded to Oscar's remark, "Yes, I suppose you are right, and I shall try to remember that in the future. But please continue; you have failed to answer my question. If mead is merely wine and honey, why will I be inebriated to the point of making a fool of myself on the dance floor?"

Oscar added, "After this wedding feast, you will come to know that the Irish do throw quite a celebration. The toasts with mead will be many, and with each toast, we will be drinking—besides the mead, there will also be other sophisticated wines and champagne for sure, perhaps harder liquor, as well."

Entertained with the discourse, Cateline commented, "I can see that we shall all be feeling pretty well. I clearly hope I remember my wedding day on Saturday."

"Oh, and I also failed to mention that I did inform my friends of how well you play the guitar, and they are most anxious to hear you perform and sing," James added.

"Oh no, please, I feel so uncomfortable playing, and besides, I did not bring my guitar."

"Not to worry, one of them has a guitar. Oscar, wouldn't you love her to play and sing a song personally to her husband after you two are married?"

"I think that is a great idea, and besides, it is also the tradition."

"Oscar, you are making that up."

"No, he's not," James noted, "it is really a custom if the bride can carry a tune; she is to also be part of the entertainment."

"So, you see, it was not I trying to manipulate you to perform, my dear," smiling at his soon-to-be bride, Oscar continued, "we only require one song for you to sing to me, that is if you love me."

Somewhat amused, she answered, "I can hardly say no when you say it like that."

"Well, it is settled; just be prepared with a song."

Looking up at Oscar, smiling, she addressed her brother, "James, I almost forgot the most important element. What time worked for the clergyman and photographer?"

"Ah, yes, they will be here around two in the afternoon—naturally, I know both of them well, so we do not have to be in a hurry. I thought we could begin the ceremony around three or four on Friday; that should be sufficient."

"Well, yes—of course, I assume that means I should spend Friday morning preparing. Perhaps we could take our vows by three, Oscar. Would that be fine with you?"

"Yes, whatever you think."

"Three it is then, and thank you, James, for everything."

After getting settled in, they went out to the back of the house, where James had a similar veranda as the Walsh's, which was also decorated with many elaborate flowers and greenery. James brought a bottle of Barolo red wine with robust flavors, distinctive notes of rose petals, dark fruit, tobacco, mocha, tar, and truffles. The imported wine from Italy was enjoyed along with the various cheeses and biscuits spread out on a table. "I thought it appropriate to celebrate and would like to make a toast to the happy couple soon-to-be-wed," James concluded rather romantically while pouring three glasses, "may your love flourish throughout time and your days be filled with abundance." In agreement, they all tapped their glasses together before taking a drink.

"Oh, James, I am not sure this has been mentioned, but we plan to stay until Sunday if that is quite alright with you. We had thought about leaving the Saturday after the wedding; however, Oscar reminded me of how the wedding party would possibly go into the wee hours of Saturday morning, and we would probably not be fit to travel on Saturday."

"My dear sister, you may stay as long as you wish."

"Thank you, James," Oscar stated graciously, "Cateline and I really appreciate you doing all you have for us at the last minute, to say the least."

"Think nothing of it, Oscar. It pleases me that Cateline would marry in our father's estate. I do know you must get back home, but I do look forward to spending as many days as possible with both of you."

"Thank you, brother. I think that Sunday will be sufficient since Oscar needs to be back in London."

"Yes, I understand. On another note, there is a place, quite a surprise, where I would like to take both of you while you are here. If perhaps, we may do so on Saturday—obviously, that afternoon."

"What surprise are we to encounter, brother dear?"

"I have a friend who has a boat. He agreed to take us out to see Bull Rock Island or Teach Duinn, as it was referred to as far back as the second century by the Greek writer Plutarch. Oscar, you are very familiar with Irish Mythology, yes?"

"Yes, of course, why my mother has written on the Irish myths and legends for many years. I am highly familiar with *Donn, the Dark Lord—Lord of the Dead,*" Oscar spoke most mysteriously in an obscure-mystic voice, continuing, *"the legend has it that Teach Duinn is where all the deceased go and the three red-haired men, sons of Donn ride their horses, crying out, 'we ride the horses of Donn, although we are alive, we—are—dead!'"*

297

Cateline, along with both men, seemed to be caught up with such intense laughter before James finally responded, "Oscar, you did that quite well!"

Still laughing, he responded, "Needless to say, my mother did read me every Irish legend as a boy many times over. I am reasonably sure I know most of them by heart."

Cateline, cheerfully, inquired, "I am so impressed. I assume that you are very familiar with the island?"

"Yes and no, I have read of it but have not been there. James, it would be such an experience to be able to witness Bull Rock—*and the entrance to the gateway of the underworld*," ending the last part of his sentence seductively in his extremely grim-shadowy voice.

Cateline, smiling, inquired, "Gateway to the underworld, so mysterious, Oscar, and just what may that be?"

"It is merely an opening, an arch between the rock."

James added, "Ah yes, a truly glorious sight, Cateline. It is settled then. I will let my friend know, and it is not a long ride, but we should probably leave after a late breakfast on Saturday."

Cateline responded, "It sounds terribly fascinating. You have both given me such thought of this island. I am unsure if I am more excited about my wedding or going to this enchanted, mystical place you have described so thoroughly."

Oscar playfully acknowledged, "Ah, too easy, my dear, to lose your attention. You have crushed my heart!"

Lovingly, she responded by leaning over to kiss him lightly, "I hope that assures you of my love."

They spent the remainder of the day being entertained by James and into the evening. Once dinner was over, everyone decided to retire early since they were exhausted from the journey and needed to be rested for Friday. Before withdrawing, Cateline inquired of James, "Brother, we would like to go to the beach after breakfast in the morning, if you don't mind. I want so much to be able to simply relax and unwind before our big day and would love to see the ocean, or is it the sea?"

"It's referred to as the Celtic Sea, but it joins with the Atlantic."

"Yes, that is what I wasn't sure of. It would be so enjoyable to walk along the shore and take in all the views. I am sure they are quite breathtaking. And I thought that perhaps, later tomorrow, we could all ride your horses together?"

"Better yet, why don't the two of you ride horses to the coastline? I have early plans tomorrow, and I may be gone for most of the day, but the estate is only a short distance from the most beautiful secluded beach."

"Yes, that would be great. Oscar, will that be fine with you?"

"Certainly, just steer me in the right direction, James."

"Oh, it is quite easy; I even have a trail that leads right to the seashore. You will see it from the stalls."

With that said, they all retired for the evening to their bedchambers as Oscar first pulled Cateline close to kiss her very intimately. Once their lips had parted, he concluded, "Only two more nights without you next to me. I love you, my sweet darling, truly, I do."

"And I, my dear, love you as well."

Once Cateline was dressed for bed, she picked up her diary to account for the few days when there had not been time to recall the moments spent with Oscar and family.

CHAPTER
20

Thursday morning came bright and early, with Cateline bubbling over in excitement, knowing it was only one more day until she would be Mrs. Oscar Wilde. Oh, how she loved him and wanted this to be forever but knew it would not last. Never desiring to even think about what was to come, but instead, aspiring to simply live for the moment. Arising from her bed, Cateline dressed and secured her hair for the day, along with having her breeches on under her dress for riding horses. She adored her father's estate and the enjoyment of being there—such grandeur, and oh, how immaculate, so much like her uncle's, for she found herself very elated, looking forward to the morning escapade on horseback to the beach. What magnificence, being close to the sea, to be able to venture to the shores, the two of them—alone. Her mind drifting back, in her own era, Cateline had always loved riding when her parents would take her to the stables and later on just her father, who had loved journeying to the countryside, riding through the fields and streams on horseback. One summer, they had even decided to take a long excursion with a group of families, loading up horses to trail ride across fields and streams, sleeping along the trek, and cooking by the fire at the campsite. It had always been so exciting, and for the first time, Cateline felt that loss once again of her father back in Boston. Shaking off those feelings, knowing her focus had to be on this era and her purpose for Oscar, but still, Cateline was saddened by the fact that she was torn between two periods. Feeling the love for all those known for such a short time since her arrival in Dublin and mixed emotions of the timeframe she had left behind seemed to haunt her. In spite of everything, Cateline knew that the twenty-first century seemed a lonely period in her life to venture back at that moment—a time of loss, losing the one man whom she had loved so deeply, her dad. Still, in Oscar's timeframe, Cateline had grown to love so many, nevertheless, knowing it would only be for a season—a brief moment of time, she thought to herself, "How strange life can be. You think you have everything until you lose it, and then somehow, you have to find a way to keep living."

Cateline went downstairs to join Oscar and James, as they were already up and standing by the hearth talking while waiting for

Cateline to dine with them for breakfast. "Good morning," James said, "I hope you slept well."

"I slept very well, thank you. I suppose I was tired from the journey, and the train is definitely not comfortable. Oscar, did you sleep well?"

"Yes, my dear, it certainly beats sleeping in a train," Oscar replied as he walked over to kiss her lightly on the cheek and take her arm to escort her to the breakfast parlor. James had several servants busy with the upcoming wedding, and the cook had already begun to prepare quite a feast with the company present.

"I normally do not have all this prepared just for me, but with guest, I have had Margaret cook for today as well as the weekend. I am assuming that all the family plans to be here through Sunday, as well."

"I believe so, James. Oscar, did uncle tell you when they would be returning?"

"Yes, they will be taking the same train on Sunday morning, leaving the same time."

"London is such a distance, Oscar. Will you and Cateline be traveling nonstop?"

"No, we were discussing that on our journey here. We will stop off a night in Dublin at the Walsh's estate, where our other belongings are, and then we shall be taking a ship to Liverpool. Cateline would like to see Liverpool; we may stay there a few days before departing to Bath and remain there a day or two before our final destination, London. Yes, it is quite an extensive trip, but stopping along the way, should make for a delightful honeymoon."

Finishing breakfast with much small talk, they all rose from the table as James bid them goodbye and shared with Oscar the particulars regarding the horses, whereas his stable boy would fully take care of all the preparations. At the stalls, Oscar relayed to the young boy which horses they desired to ride while they waited for a short time as the lad readied two of James's finest breeds. Of course, Cateline reminded Oscar to make sure her horse would also be saddled correctly. "You did not have to remind me. I had already assumed as much and instructed the stable boy accordingly. I do suppose you have your breeches on under your dress," Oscar acknowledged with a most clever grin. Cateline smiling candidly, undid her skirt to take it off, which revealed her breeches, while Oscar

301

laughed, knowing she was one of a kind—yet he also felt most fortunate to have found her.

"Oh, and I know that you love the way I look in my breeches, but my dear Sir Knight, you can look, but you cannot touch!"

"Yes, and I will definitely look and will certainly touch in one more day, my dear," he replied playfully.

Riding out of the stalls, seeing the trail off to the right, Oscar led the way as they rode along. The path was narrow, where they could not ride side by side, but it was only a short distance before the beach was in sight. A somewhat alluring and secluded beach, as far as they could see, very stunning and isolated. Oscar jumped off his horse and went to assist Cateline; with a rather enticing comment, he declared, "My dear, it amazes me that you want no assistance getting into your saddle but require my aid to get down."

With a most playful gleam, she replied, "Ah, but yes, it is not that I need help getting down; it is that I enjoy your arms around me while I gaze into your eyes, my charming knight."

Oscar, grinning rapturously, responded, "I do believe that you seduce me with your smile, my dear."

"Oh, no, I assure you that I would never do such a thing. It would be most dishonorable," Cateline concluded while gazing into his eyes, her ravishing smile melting his heart.

Tying the horses to a tree at the edge of the shrubbery, where they had plenty of grass to feed on, they walked down to the beach hand in hand. Both were delighted in such an awe-inspiring day with the sun splashing down bright rays at an angular view, reflections coming forth from the waters of the sea splendidly casting a most serene picture. Reaching the shoreline, they sat down, enjoying the warmth brought about by the refreshing breeze which skimmed across their faces. As the wind blew strands of Cateline's hair about, it danced freely, whispering loosely in the air; the gusts from the waters rushed to shore, bringing a sense of energy to their bodies. The temperature was climbing into the fifties, in Fahrenheit, that is, making it a relatively pleasant day. It was such a delightful and welcome sensation that swept over both of them while Oscar continued to hold Cateline's hand. Sitting so very close together in silence, time seemed to elapse while enjoying the peace and tranquility. Finally, Oscar being in deep thought, spoke rather quietly, "If you could live anywhere in Europe, where would it be?"

"I'm not sure I could answer that, as I have yet to see much of Europe, other than Ireland, but I have read a lot about England and France. You know I really love the charm of the city, but I also like the seclusion of the countryside."

"Hmm—interesting. What about in America? Where would you choose to live?"

"I lived in Boston most of my life and loved the charm and history, and then I moved to Chicago, only for a brief time. Chicago is also charming, considered one of the most beautiful cities. It is also known for its art and culture. But I think that someday if I were to return to America, I would love to live someplace on the east coast where I could write while surrounded by the beauty of the ocean. Of course, it would have to be in a location by the shores, but I do enjoy the mountains as well. Our world is surrounded by so much peace and quiet in its natural habitat, don't you agree?"

"Yes, I, too, love to be surrounded by nature, but I do love the charm of the city as well—the charm and history, like you said."

"I just know, as one who loves to write, you must have your quiet place, I'm sure you understand," Cateline uttered with a pause, "there was a place we used to go often when I was a child. As I grew older, I would also go with friends and sometimes just by myself, especially during the fall months. It was in Maine on the east coast, not that far from Boston—Wells, Maine, to be exact. I used to love going there. In fact, the last time I went was probably a few years before coming here. It is a quaint town of sorts; I can remember mornings sitting on the beach at dawn, as it was normally always secluded during off-seasons. It's somewhat peculiar, I suppose, for I would spend my time dreaming about coming to Ireland." Silence ensued around them as Cateline was in deep thought. After a brief period, she shared once again, "I remember sitting on the beach in the mornings, drinking coffee—or hot tea—funny, I haven't thought about Wells lately. I recall meeting a ship captain once and asking him the coordinates from Wells to Ireland's coast. I had actually researched for a location fairly close to this side of Ireland, straight across the Atlantic. I would dream about a place, somewhere like this—somewhere quaint, a seaside town of sorts, like Wells." Cateline related with a gloomy smile and a most sincere expression as she stared deep into Oscar's eyes before continuing, "It was strange, really. I would imagine what it was like in Ireland, what it was like along the coastal regions in this part—and, if there was perhaps

303

someone sitting on the beach like I was, at that same moment, dreaming of America." With a slight laugh, she resumed, "I presume with the time difference, there would not have been anyone at the same hour as I, but I still would somehow daydream that possibly it was so." They both sat silent, gazing out at sea, with the breeze from the waters surging through their hair, sauntering down their skin— the warmth of the sun shining radiantly upon them, bringing a sensation to their senses—moving, stirring, producing an awareness of familiarity, perception, and numbness. Feeling as if time had stopped, their existence comprising of two—Oscar and Cateline— nothing else mattered for those moments. Their thoughts were lost in the depths of the sea, revolving with every wave, flowing through every sentiment—the seconds refreshed with the prickle of air, tinges of rawness, the fervor of flames, gravities of love—time arranged in silence, stillness, calmness—yet, vibrant and alive. Their time alone in those moments in deep meditation and remembrances, forever and ever.

As a brisk force of nature barreled to shore with wisps of water splashing forth in time, the depths of their reflections once lost were stirred. Being flaunted with the dampness unexpectedly, they jumped up laughing, surprised by the sudden crest of a wave, propelled with such force, splashing down, rolling towards the shores.

Oscar looking over at Cateline, "Well, it doesn't look like you are very wet."

"No, but it was cold," she cried with a most vivid smile.

Walking down the beach farther while holding hands, Oscar spoke after a few moments of silence, "Please, finish what you were sharing about the coordinates."

"Well, it was just that I love the beach and the ocean, I suppose. I would often dream of Ireland. I imagine because it is my roots. I always remembered the distance in miles; it was somewhat over twenty-nine hundred, in nautical miles, of course. So, I presume if I were to pick one place in America where I would desire to live, I would buy a home on the beach in Wells. It's a wonderful location that is somewhat secluded and tranquil."

Silence ensued while Oscar thought about her response, contemplating all she had clearly shared, realizing the tranquility of the sea, along with being by her side, had to be the most remarkable feeling he had ever experienced. He could very well understand why writers need those quaint places of peace, but being with Cateline—well, there was something quite unique, a sense of being alive, a feeling that he could not explain. Yes, lost in his love for her, a feeling like nothing he had ever felt, knowing he had loved before, but this was different; she was different. After some time, Cateline turned to Oscar while looking up into his enticing eyes before kissing him passionately. Softly she whispered, "Oscar, promise that you will love me forever."

"Cateline, you know I will always love you—forever! I do promise!"

"I mean, even if I am no longer here, you will never forget me and always love me."

"Of course, you will be here. Where would you go?"

"I'm just saying, if something happened to me, you would never forget me, would you?"

"Nothing is going to happen to you, but no, I would never ever forget you and would love you forever."

"You know, looking out into the deep blue waters, it was the same thing I did many times in America. Along the coast of Boston, there were many quaint places to go, where one could merely get away from the noise of the city. I would always sit on the beach gazing in a dreamy state out into the Atlantic. I would oftentimes think about Ireland and how it was the country of my ancestors. Sometimes while I sat there, I would think about how the Atlantic Ocean was the only thing that separated me from here, right here on this very beach, the same body of water."

After a brief pause, Cateline continued, "I never knew I could love someone like I love you, and all this time, it was from this point right here to a point on another beach in America that was separating me from the one person I could love forever. It was you. I came to Ireland to meet my family, but also because I had never been able to connect with any of the men I had known. I needed to find out who I really was. I had spent many years thinking something was wrong with me because I never fell in love like all my friends had. This was part of my reasoning for coming to Ireland. I knew I had to come back to my heritage to at least find out more about me, in hopes of finding that person deep inside, and then I met you. It was always you that I was supposed to meet and fall in love with." Cateline looked up at Oscar with tears in her eyes.

"Why are you crying, my dear? You have found me, and we are together, forever," with a brief pause, wiping away her tears, he continued, "Cateline, do you ever think that you will want to go back to America?"

"I don't think I want to go back to America, for if I ever did, I would once again sit on the beach looking out at the ocean dreaming of you, wanting you."

Oscar smiled most affectionately, "You never have to go back, my dear. When I cross to America next year, I will bring you with me. You can be at my side, and we will then come back to London together."

"Yes, of course," she responded, knowing that would not be the case.

"So, it was in Wells, Maine; that was your favorite beach?"

"Yes, I suppose it is for America. Wells is a most charming place. In fact, I had always thought that if I did not stay and returned, I would not go back to Chicago but buy a house on the beach in Wells. Oscar, promise me, if you are ever in America without me, you must go and visit Wells and walk along the beach."

"I can't imagine that I would be in America without you, my dear. But perhaps, while we are there together next year, we can go to Wells. I would very much love to see this place that has filled your heart with such memories."

"Yes, perhaps."

After some time, Oscar and Cateline rode back to the estate. Cateline waited while Oscar helped the stable boy get the horses back in their stalls. Hand in hand, they walked towards the manor, enjoying the cool breeze which could be felt lightly from the sea. The lawn was so beautiful and handsomely landscaped. With the light of the day, it made one want to enjoy the seclusion, not to mention the delightful views, as they savored every moment. "Can we spend time outside today, Oscar? It is so peaceful, and the breeze is most pleasant."

"If you would like," he responded, "but we should probably check to see if lunch is being served, and maybe we could bring a few plates out on the grounds."

"Yes, perhaps."

"Oh, but wait, my dear—we have not practiced the ceili since we arrived."

"Truly, I was hoping that you would not remember. I feel as though I will be such an embarrassment to you at our wedding."

"Nonsense," he related while taking her hands to begin the steps as best they could, with none present to determine the appropriate moves for those centered and those at the ends. Both laughing, they frolicked about on the grounds for a short while to establish she had at least not forgotten what had briefly been taught at her uncle's. Then, with much pleasure at the moment, they were overcome with hunger and thus maintained their walk towards the veranda.

Before entering the estate, Oscar pulled her towards him and held her tight as they kissed each other. "We should retire directly after dinner this evening, my dear. We need to be well-rested for tomorrow," Oscar proclaimed as he regarded the beauty of her eyes.

"Yes, tomorrow is our big day, and I cannot wait until we begin our lives together," Cateline replied before resuming, "Oscar, there was something I completely failed to mention."

"What is it, my dear?"

"Even though my father is no longer alive, he did leave me a dowry in hopes that I would not go back to America. I have five thousand pounds in the Bank of Ireland in Dublin. We will need to transfer it to London, yes?"

"We can take care of that in London. Your uncle did mention that your father had left you a dowry, but I have never alluded to the fact. The dowry never seemed to matter. I would have married you penniless, my dear."

"Well, I just wanted you to know that it is yours, and we can also use those funds to enjoy our honeymoon on our travels to London."

Oscar, smiling at her, "We will have a wonderful time. It will not end in London; you did want to travel to Paris, yes?"

"Oh, yes, very much so."

"Excellent, our leisurely spell while in Europe will be much relished before leaving for America. Ah, and I will be paid very well for my time in your country."

They walked in and saw that James had come home earlier than planned. "I hope you had a pleasant ride to the beach. No trouble finding it, I'm sure."

"None whatever, we merely followed the trail. It was a very excellent ride, and your horses are some of the finest I have ridden," Oscar responded.

"Father always bought top-quality horses; there was only one in which I selected," James added with a slight laugh.

"Thank you, brother dear, for allowing us the use of them," Cateline commented while she walked up the stairs to freshen herself before lunch.

"I see you are fitted in breeches, Cateline. I do hope that Anya has not influenced you severely." James countered.

"No, James, Anya has not persuaded me. And, in America, girls seldom ride in side-saddles."

"You best be glad your father never saw you dressed as such. He was very old-fashioned and believed a woman never to wear anything but a dress."

"That is rather interesting, for Uncle Walsh was quite alright with us wearing them as long as it was not in public. How do you feel, James?"

"I am not as old-fashioned as our father was," he deliberated with a cunning smile while Cateline continued upstairs to attire herself appropriately for the day.

Shortly emerging back downstairs, Cateline walked out to the veranda to join the men for an enjoyable lunch. Partaking in the pleasantries with the gentlemen while finishing up the spread of exquisite sandwiches and such, James inquired, "Well, sister dear, would you enjoy a walk on the grounds. I am sure you would love to hear some of the stories about our father in which you have missed."

"Oh yes, I will not be but a moment to retrieve my shawl; I would so love to hear the tales," she replied, thinking to herself, "I suppose laying out on the grounds with Oscar will not happen as we had hoped. Oh well, I do want to spend time with James to hear all the narratives of our dear father."

Once Cateline had come back downstairs, Oscar was in James's study writing an article to send to London and declined the walk, as he felt that the two siblings needed time together to reflect on the stories growing up since they had not had that fortune.

Therefore, Cateline walked with James while he shared so many accounts and answered the countless questions Cateline petitioned as she strived to learn of the father she had never met. Through the many stories and tales, Cateline soon learned his personality fit precisely to her real father in her timeframe. She often wondered, could she have really lived this life, and could it be possible that her real parents were also the same. All of this sounded quite bizarre, knowing she needed to keep her perspective, for her reason of being there in the first place was for Oscar, and it was God who had sent her for that purpose only. Even though Cateline did not understand everything, none of that mattered. The reason she was there was significant enough.

During dinner, James noted that he would be leaving to pick up the Walsh family at the station since they had taken a late train. "I know both of you want to retire early, which is a good idea, and if you do not withdraw before I return with the family, you will probably not be able to go to bed until late. As it is, I will let Uncle Walsh and the family know that both of you have already retreated for the evening, with such a big day forthcoming, they shall understand."

"Thank you, brother. Yes, it is probably best that we get some sleep before tomorrow."

James soon left to go to the station while Oscar and Cateline made their way up the stairs to their apartments to undress for the evening and retire to bed. Once Oscar had changed into his nightshirt, he went to tell her goodnight. Walking into her bedchamber, Cateline was already lying in her bed, where she exclaimed upon him entering, "Oh my, you are getting most comfortable at just walking in on me when I am not properly dressed, my dear."

Oscar smiled while responding to her comment, "I only have one more night to be able to do so, whereas tomorrow it will be legal. Besides, I am having a hard time waiting, for I want you something desperately right now."

Cateline responded with a laugh, "Yes, but you know that is not happening."

He walked over to the bed as he proclaimed defensively, "Yes, I know, but I can at least kiss you, right?"

Looking up into his most appealing eyes, she responded, "I think I would be sad if you did not, since you have come thus far."

Oscar sat on the side of the bed, where he leaned over to kiss her goodnight but eventually laid down next to her while he held her close to himself. They continued to kiss passionately as he whispered in her ear, "You are most beautiful, and I want you so much, Cateline."

"I want you clearly as much as you want me, but it is just one more day."

"I shall not touch you if you simply let me lie next to you all night, I promise."

"If I let you stay, it would take away part of the excitement for tomorrow."

"It is not as if we have not laid beside each other all night before if you will remember at the tower of love."

"Yes, but we were both somewhat clothed, more so than now. I love you, but you must leave so we can both get some sleep."

"I will leave, but first, I must tell you that you are the *Ideal Woman* according to Irish tradition."

"And what is the ideal woman?" Cateline inquired with curiosity.

"My dear, it is one with a pleasant speaking and sweet singing voice, also one who is quite clever and pure."

Smiling at him, she responded, "You are most gracious, and I do love you so much for it."

Oscar rose from the bed and sighed as he wanted so much to stay with her all night, but he knew it was solely one more night. Leaving, he concluded softly, "I love you, Cateline, goodnight."

"Goodnight, Oscar. I love you too."

After some time, James returned with the Walsh family to include Amos coming with Anya and Mr. Walsh's valet, Charles. Two of their lady's maids were also in tow, as they were needed to assist the women with their wardrobes and hair the following day. Once home, James showed everyone to their rooms as his servants carried their belongings up the stairs. The women decided to retire early, but James, Amos, and Mr. Walsh sat down in the parlor having a drink before bed to conversate on the various happenings in Dublin and Youghal, all retiring somewhat later.

CHAPTER
21

Friday morning, Cateline lay awake dreaming of her wedding on this most special day. It was not long until Anya came running into her room with such excitement to see her cousin and share in this most delightful time. "Good morning, my sweet cousin. I can hardly wait for the day to begin. You must be so excited, and I gather you scarcely slept a wink last night."

Cateline, shining with exuberance, sat up in her bed, replying, "Anya, oh yes, I am so excited and most pleased you are here. Yes, I did have such a time trying to sleep last night until my mind could no longer wander, and my body finally so drained from thought—slumber, at last, came upon me. I am happy to see you indeed! The family, they are all here?"

"Oh yes, everyone is here, to include Amos. I believe he is actually excited to share in this most remarkable occasion, knowing we shall soon be much engaged in our own wedding. As you know, I think this will be such a delight to be part of your special day while planning ours—not too far off at that. I can barely wait to see you in your magnificent gown. Oh, and James filled all of us in on his plans for this memorable day, last night. I believe your dear brother is as excited as we all are for having such a role in this glorious affair."

"Yes, he disclosed to me briefly his arrangements when we arrived on Wednesday. It was quite surprising for me to listen to such expertise, especially those things which I overlooked that he most graciously deliberated himself."

"Oh, I almost forgot to mention. I thought about this after you left us and not sure if you knew—the day of the week you chose is so very portentous according to Irish traditions."

"No, I have not heard of any customs regarding the day. What does it mean to be married on a Friday?"

"Let me see if I can remember all of them. Monday is for health, Tuesday for wealth, Wednesday—the best day of all, Thursday is for losses, thank goodness you did not choose that day! Let me see, ah yes, Friday is for crosses, and Saturday is no day at all," Anya finished with a laugh.

"Friday for crosses, hmm—I suppose that could be a spiritual reason, so yes, I am rather delighted that it is Friday. You did not mention Sunday."

"No, I did not. There is nothing for Sunday—that is a day most do not marry; it is considered a mark of disrespect to the church."

"Well, I am quite pleased that it is Friday and also completely excited." Thinking to herself after considering the meaning of crosses, "Hmm, bearing my cross. Yes, indeed, this was my course in this life, my purpose, after all!"

After a time, fascinated with ingrained notions, Cateline spoke, "The month being April, is there any tradition about what month to marry?"

"Ah, yes, I thought I had already shared the months, did I not?"

"Perhaps, but, if you did, I am afraid I do not remember."

"I am unsure if I have all these down. However, in choosing my own month, I have definitely taken into consideration most of these customs. I do remember March was not a good month; thankfully, you are in April. They say, *marry in April when you can, joy for maiden and for man.*"

With the girls laughing, Cateline remarked, "That is pretty cute. And—you have chosen the month you shall marry?"

"Yes, it will be in June."

"Not too far away, and what is the saying about marrying in June?"

"It goes, *marry when June roses blow, over land and sea you'll go.* I discussed this with Amos, and it was decided once we are married, we could cross the sea to come to visit you and Oscar in London," Anya finished with a sincere smile.

"Yes, you must promise!"

"Of course. And before I forget," taking a folded piece of paper out of her pocket, Anya handed it over to Cateline, "another tradition in Ireland once you have been wed. Secretly, you give Oscar a drink and utter these words which I have written, but remember, it is done in secret where no one hears you."

Cateline reading the words, silently smiled, "Quite nice; I think I am really going to enjoy all these traditions. It does make this such a memorable day."

"Well, I must go down for breakfast, but I will send Sarah up with a good selection of cuisine, my sweet cousin. And, just so you know, we did bring Sarah and Permilia both to assist with the dressing, hair, and all the makeup—you will be the most stunning bride in all of Ireland, I assure you."

Cateline smiled joyfully, stating in a most genial tone, "You speak of me as being such a goddess of which I am not, but I thank you still the same. And you, too, will be a most beautiful bride soon enough."

"Yes, and I do hope you will be able to return from London and attend, my dear cousin."

"I would certainly hope that I will. Oh, and no need to have Sarah bring my breakfast; I can join all of you downstairs."

"Oh no, no, no—the groom must not see the bride at all today—until you come down the stairs ready for the ceremony."

"Well, that is something I did not know. It is not as if one gets married every day. I will definitely wait on Sarah. Thank you, Anya."

Anya left the room while Cateline dressed very simply, where she then lay back down on the bed, waiting for Sarah. It was not long until she entered the room with Cateline's breakfast. While she ate, Sarah laid everything out needed to have Cateline dressed, hair creation in a masterful updo, and her makeup applied superbly. Anya, very soon, came back into the room with Permilia. "I thought we could at least be in the same room while they work on our hair and makeup. I am much too anxious about your special day that I wanted to be in the same room so that we can talk."

"I am so glad you are here. I can hardly even eat and literally have to make myself take bites. I am so nervous; I fear I am going to faint."

"Oh, we will have none of that, Cateline," Anya replied about the time Aunt Martha entered the room to check on the bride.

"My dear, how are you this morning?"

"I am quite nervous, Aunt Martha."

"That is to be expected. Your uncle and I have been speaking with James, and I believe we all feel that it would be such a tribute for your brother to give you away in place of your uncle. James would be most honored to take the place of your father. Of course, that is your decision, and your uncle would be flattered, but with your father

313

no longer being with us and James is hosting your wedding, we believe it would mean so much to him."

"Oh, Aunt Martha, that is such an excellent idea, and James has been most gracious. He has far surpassed expectations on making everything so precise. Yes, by all means, I would love for James to give me away."

"Then, it is settled. I will let the men know of our talk, and we will proceed as such," Aunt Martha finished before leaving the room.

Sarah and Permilia both worked enthusiastically on both girls' hair, which took a considerable amount of time. Each long lock was either curled or twisted for perfection, creating the most extravagant styles to complement the girls' Irish complexions and features to be observed on this most honorable day, as it was. Cateline was beside herself as the creation of a beautiful up-do started to be unveiled. The sheik design was slightly lifted with curls streaming gracefully downward, meticulously for the sky-blue, sheer veil to gently flow over her shoulders, back and to lightly cover her face. The veil was enhanced with a lacey band affording enough width where tiny flowers were epitomized and spaced along in shades of blues mixed with creams to complement her colors. To be the final element added, the band would be elegantly fortified over the masterpiece of locks to secure the flow of tresses as a covering.

During the grueling process and time involved, the girls continued with talks and laughter for what seemed like several hours. There were so many things they loved to share, as their lives were both focused on plans, although diverse as they were. Following Cateline's wedding, she would soon begin her new life with Oscar, and Anya's time would by far be filled with the planning of her own unique wedding day. With conversations continuing, Cateline finally inquired of Anya, "There are so many Irish customs which are quite different from America. Is there anything I need to know before I go downstairs? Or can you just tell me what to expect from the vicar?"

"Well, let's see. First, the clergyman will recite some vows, and I heard there would also be the *tying the knot*, not to worry, the clergyman will explain the tradition, but once he has done so, at one point, you and Oscar will be given a chance to say your own vows—following will be the changing of the rings."

"Yes, I heard the phrase, *tying the knot*, but I am not sure what that entails. Last night, James and Oscar were laughing about this *tying of the knot* thing, yet, when I asked, they would not reveal to me what it meant."

Anya smiled as she stated, "Oh, I love this. You have never heard of it?"

"Why, no!"

"I'm sorry, but I cannot tell you either. It is evident they desire this to be a surprise, but not to worry, you will do fine. It is an amazing custom and very romantic."

"Is there anything I need to know about it?"

"No, the minister will take care of the whole thing," Anya assured her with such a warm smile before continuing, "in fact, the clergyman will lead everything. There is nothing to worry about. The only thing I would do is to be thinking about a vow that you would want to make to Oscar since there will be a time for you to recite your own. I am not sure about the traditions in America, but Irish cultures are exceptionally beautiful. Oh—and remember to stand under the horseshoe!"

"The horseshoe?"

"Yes, but James will lead you there. It is another Irish practice for good luck or rather luck of your house. It also symbolizes fertility." Anya paused with a smile as Permilia had finished up her hair and started to master Anya's makeup, which did not take too much time. Makeup for the nineteenth century was not anything like that of the twentieth; therefore, Permilia had Anya just about all set except for her dress. Standing, ready to head towards her own room, Anya turned to Cateline and concluded, "I will see you downstairs shortly; I am sure I will be ready before you are. But remember, do not leave—James will come up and get you before three. Oh, I will also send someone up with your lunch momentarily. Please make sure you eat; Irish weddings have many toasts, which means much alcohol. So, you will need food in you."

"Thanks, Anya," Cateline said nervously.

"Relax, it will be over before long," Anya reassured while walking out the door.

Soon afterward, Sarah had finished the completion of Cateline's hair and stood back to observe her work. "How do you like it, ma'am?"

Looking into the mirror, she acknowledged, "It is simply divine, Sarah, thank you so very much."

315

A light knock was heard on the door with Cateline speaking, "Yes, please come in."

One of James's servants brought Cateline lunch, which included small sandwiches, pastries, and scones. While, at the same time, Sarah briskly began doing Cateline's makeup and her nails. The time continued to pass, where it was presently two-thirty in the afternoon. How Cateline was getting so very nervous, but at least, Sarah had finished all the necessary touches where she was finally helping her into her lace corset and petticoat, busily working on all the ties, buttons, and clips to her gown. Anya, having finished dressing and being ready to go downstairs, swiftly glanced into Cateline's room. "Oh, you are almost ready, and you look astonishing, but I almost forgot," she noted, approaching Cateline. Handing her a bracelet with tiny little silver bells all around, Anya explained, "You must wear this on your wrist. The belief is that the bells bring good luck, but they are also a gift from me to you." Pausing briefly to fasten the bracelet onto her wrist, she gave her a kiss on the cheek and a great big hug, "You look gorgeous, and I will soon see you descending the stairs."

Cateline smiled as she looked down at the elegant bracelet before commenting, "Thank you, Anya, it is most attractive." The bracelet was so very delicate, yet the bells made faint jingling sounds as she moved her wrist about.

"Oh, and one more thing—your veil. I wanted to be the one to put it on you, and that is the last touch—Sarah, can you please hand it to me?"

"Yes, ma'am," Sarah responded, gathering up the sheer covering and handing it over to Anya as she placed the veil in the precise place, with it flowing gracefully down the back and along the sides, a most exquisite sheerness, and rich lace quality. Anya, drawing the front over to cover her face, declared, "Flawless, yes, quite lovely—you are absolutely magnificent dear cousin." Anya gave her one last smile before leaving the room to head downstairs.

The final moments flew by, where Sarah had finished all the last-minute touches. Cateline, standing up in front of the mirror to view herself before time to leave the apartment, exclaimed, "Sarah, you have quite outdone yourself. I cannot thank you enough. My hair, the dress, everything truly exceeds perfection."

"Thank you, ma'am. You look very pretty, and I wish you a wonderful and happy marriage."

Cateline smiled at Sarah, giving her a hug about the time James knocked on the door. "Come in," Cateline spoke up with James entering the chamber. Sarah, standing off to the side, James walked over to gaze at his adorable sister, a most elaborate view. Here she was, a fabulously adorned bride, her brother speechless for the moment, observing, before he remarked, "You look amazing!" Brotherly affection spilled over, feelings he had not known, proud of this day to finally know his sister and be absorbed in her most memorable day. Words could not be spoken; all he could do was gaze at her beauty, being able to see some likeness of their father's but the feeling of stepping into that place—the place which had been meant for their dad, gone too soon, James was overcome with emotions. Cateline gazed at her brother while he looked on admiringly, as his sister was most impeccably arrayed in her long flowing sky-blue designer gown intertwined with ivory, magnificently elated with filigree throughout. Her dress was draped gracefully in layers, two-toned, with lacey embellished edges along each tier. The full skirt, formed by trifling hoops from the waist down, provided for a most stylish touch of pure elegance. Underneath, she wore her silky petticoat, which provided for a rather smooth feel, with the corset fitted warmly to the contour of her frame and slender waistline under the satiny bodice modestly low cut. The intricately detailed long sleeves were richly crafted of refined lace, which cascaded softly down her delicate arms, extending midway, exquisitely flowing outward trimmed about with elegant cream-colored lace. The elaborate veil was made of sheer sky-blue tulle infringed with exquisite tracery, and her feet were adorned in blue French brocade one-inch heels embraced with ivory lacelike trim. James continued taking in her beauty before he spoke forth in awe, "Our father would have been so proud, and he would have loved to have been here for this most blessed day. I cannot tell you how happy I am to be part of your special day and to have the honor of giving you away," James concluded while he walked over to his sister and kissed her cheek very lightly.

She leaned over to give her brother a great big hug, smiling, "Brother dear, I love you more than you will ever know and will remember this day forever."

He took her arm in his, as he stated, "The photographer is also here and will be taking random pictures. I will be sure you receive those in London."

"Thank you, James."

"Well, are you ready for this?"

"Oh yes," speaking hastily with her whole demeanor radiating from excitement, she leaned over to acquire her handkerchief, which her aunt had given her for this glorious day, embroidered with the initials, *C.W.* Cateline declared, "I am ready to go—more than ready." James stepped out of the room first to motion for Sophia to begin playing the pianoforte. "Oh!" In excitement, Cateline observed, "that must be Sophia on the pianoforte, am I right?"

"Yes, you will meet her soon."

Cateline, hearing the music flowing gently with the most awe-inspiring romantic tunes, proclaimed, "If Sophia is as pretty as she plays the piano, she must be quite lovely indeed."

"She is," James answered with a most pleasant smile.

"Playing the wedding march, yes?"

"It is the one written by Felix Mendelssohn but was the Bridal Chorus from Richard Wagner's opera."

"Ah—it is excellent."

James glancing at Cateline, "Shall we begin?"

"I am quite nervous, but yes—let's begin."

James led Cateline out of the room into the hallway. At the top of the stairs, the arch was not in view until they had descended about halfway down. Once there, Cateline was able to capture a glimpse of her most suave and soon-to-be husband standing underneath the bow, knowing in a short while he would be her husband. Oscar was most handsome—charmingly dressed in his light grey Victorian frock coat. Underneath, he wore a white pleated Victorian turn-down collar shirt obscured by his double-breasted waistcoat with coordinating button trousers and grey spats covering the tops of his dark Loake loafers. His attire was accentuated by the brightly colored sky-blue ascot necktie, which was knotted loosely in a cravat fashion, emphasizing the midsection of his high collar with only the uppermost portion being perceived. Keeping her eyes glued on Oscar, he seemed to be clearly as nervous as she was herself. As they smiled at each other, James continued to lead her towards where he stood when she finally noticed the horseshoe, which hung overhead where they would take their vows.

Now, facing the man she loved, the vicar spoke while James took her arm and gave it to Oscar. Turning to face the clergyman, Cateline was in such a daze that she could hardly contemplate the words being spoken. The clergyman, a middle-aged man of sorts, maintained addressing their guests, sharing the particulars of a traditional Irish wedding. While all the specifics were being disclosed, Cateline glanced over at the man she loved, standing so tall, most fetching, adorned with the lavish necktie she had given him to match her wedding gown. Not just any tie, but the tie he would one day wear in America to be observed by all. Oscar smiled most lovingly at her and silently whispered as he drew nigh, "You are ravishing, my dear." Cateline smiled while looking deep into his arousing eyes with such love, gazing back at her with a most dreamy look, which sent a tingle throughout her body. Yes, Cateline had waited for this day for so many years, a day she never thought could have come true, and here she was, 1881, standing next to the man she had loved most of her life, momentarily to be her husband. Even if it were only for a short time, he would very soon hold her in the night and be by her side each day. They would at least have known love, love that many never find—the passion, the devotion, the tenderness, the caring and sharing everything about each other. Yes, Cateline knew his faults, but she also knew his strengths, and she very well knew that one day, he would make things right—one day, they might even be together once again.

After the vicar had finished speaking to those in attendance, his gaze fell upon the young couple, "We will honor the handfasting ceremony which is known as *tying the knot*," he professed. I was told Cateline has no clue to this custom, but we will not be too hard on her," a brief laugh echoed through the room from all who were present with those words shared. The clergyman resumed, "Oscar and Cateline, standing here facing each other, please join your right hands and left hands together; your hands will be crossed. James, in giving away the bride, will have the honor of tying the knots of the cords while the vows are recited one by one."

Cateline, unsure precisely what any of this meant, stood facing Oscar, looking into his eyes, feeling so secure and loved. James approached with gold and silver cords waiting for the clergyman to begin. While the vicar explained the custom, James started tying the cords around their hands where they were bound together. "This is an old Irish tradition which James had asked that we do," the minister acknowledged, "tying the knot symbolizes the bond of marriage. As these cords are intertwined together, cords that

319

cannot be broken, Oscar and Cateline's lives are also bound together and the union of their hopes, dreams, and desires. They become one today, joined together not to be separated but always together as one through our Lord and Savior. At this time, I invite you, Oscar, being bound to Cateline by the cords which symbolize your free will to enter into this marriage, to speak forth your vows to Cateline."

It was at that moment, looking deep into her eyes, Oscar spoke tenderly, "I take you, Cateline, this day bound together by marriage. You are blood of my blood and bone of my bone. I give you my body that we might be one. I give you my spirit, 'til our life shall be done."

The clergyman maintained while he looked to Cateline, "Cateline, as you are joined by the cords to Oscar which symbolize your free will to enter into this marriage, I also invite you to speak forth your vows."

Cateline looking back into Oscar's eyes, feeling as if there was no one in the world but the two of them, spoke tenderly, "Oscar, I take you this day bound together by marriage to honor and to love you. I will be by your side through all the good times and those times of sorrow and pain. I will stand by you through trials and will uphold your name with honor, all the days of my life."

The minister continued as he spoke blessings over their union—

"Blessed be this union with the gifts of the East.
Communication of the heart, mind, and body
Fresh beginnings with the rising of each sun.
The knowledge of the growth found in the sharing of
silences.
Blessed be this union with the gifts of the South.
Warmth of hearth and home
The heat of the heart's passion
The light created by both to illuminate the darkest of times.
Blessed be this union with the gifts of the West.
The deep commitments of the lake, the swift excitement of the
river
The refreshing cleansing of the rain
The all-encompassing passion of the sea.
Blessed be this union with the gifts of the North
Firm foundation on which to build
Fertility of the fields to enrich your lives

The clergyman continued, "Lord, bless Oscar and Cateline this day and consecrate their marriage. Oscar and Cateline, according to their free will and love for each other, have vowed to love and cherish each other as husband and wife. With the husband cherishing and loving his wife as Christ loves the church and the wife honoring and obeying her husband to complete him." Motioning for James to begin taking off the cords, the minister resumed, "While James is removing the cords, at this time, Oscar, I ask you—do you take Cateline to be your wedded wife, to have and to hold from this day forward, for better or worse, for richer or poorer, for fairer or fouler, in sickness, and in health, to love and cherish, till death us depart, according to God's holy ordinance?"

"Yes, I do."

"And do you, Cateline, take Oscar to be your husband, to have and to hold from this day forward, for better or worse, for richer or poorer, for fairer or fouler, in sickness, and in health, to love and cherish, till death us depart, according to God's holy ordinance?"

"Yes, I do."

"At this time, Oscar and Cateline have chosen the Claddagh rings, which are also an Irish tradition. Oscar, move Cateline's ring to face her husband," the vicar spoke while Oscar took the ring and turned it to place back on her finger, at the same time, the bride was addressed, "Cateline, move Oscar's ring to face his wife." Cateline removed his ring and turned it around to place it back on his finger, as well.

"The rings are symbolic of your love for each other—the Claddagh rings also symbolize that Oscar belongs to Cateline with the heart of his ring facing towards her, and Cateline belongs to Oscar with the heart of her ring facing towards him. May these rings they have exchanged be a symbol of their faith in each other and a reminder of their love. Bound together in holy matrimony, I now pronounce you husband and wife. You may now kiss the bride."

At that moment, Oscar raised the veil to reveal Cateline's face while he quietly whispered, "Our souls have become one, my own dear wife, you have become everything to me in life." and he intimately kissed her. They continued to kiss, unaware or unconcerned of others watching; it seemed that no one mattered but the two of them.

Finally, as the family crowded around, they turned and faced their guests with the clergyman announcing, "I now present to you—Mr. and Mrs. Oscar Wilde."

The congratulations commenced with the family and acquaintances shaking their hands and many hugs. It amazed Cateline how the men were so open about kissing the bride and did so right on the lips.

Oscar, seeing the look in her eyes, leaned over and whispered, "Irish weddings, it is customary for the men to kiss the bride on the lips. I know it is somewhat tedious. Yet, your loveliness and fashionable manner are irresistible, my dear," he concluded while smiling at his exquisite bride.

James escorted his girlfriend, Sophia, to meet Cateline—Sophia gave her a big hug and congratulated her and Oscar. Once everyone had given their congratulations to the happy couple, Cateline walked over and selected a glass of wine from one of the servants to take to Oscar secretly, as Anya had shared. Cateline had time to memorize the words on the slip of paper that her cousin had given her while getting ready upstairs before the wedding. She then walked back over to Oscar, who was in conversation with one of James's friends. Interrupting apologetically, Cateline led him over to the side away from their guests. Handing him the wine, she quietly spoke these words in his ear—

"This is the charm I set for love, a woman's charm of love and desire:
You for me and I for thee and for none else;
your face to mine, and your hand turned away from all others."

Once she had spoken the words, Oscar finished the drink and leaned over to kiss her gently, responding, "I will always be for thee, and none other shall there ever be."

Cateline was quite taken with all the traditions and excitement, having never experienced a wedding as such. She watched her uncle approach the front of the room to get everyone's attention. "Please, friends and family, at this time, we will begin the toasts. The servants are handing out the mead, be sure to get your cup ready for toasting the bride and groom," Mr. Walsh spoke while he motioned for Oscar and Cateline to come and stand next to him. "I will begin with the first toast, and the servants will be coming around to continue filling your cups."

Cateline thought to herself, "At least the cups were not that big," but then James walked up to hand the bride and groom matching goblets for the toasts. "Oh my, surely we are not to drink with these filled for every toast."

Oscar smiling, "Invariably, they shall not be filled completely, darling. Yet, I fancy with each drink that our night shall become more and more marvelous."

Once everyone had their cup of mead, her uncle commenced—

"First-let me say, Sláinte chuig na fir, agus go mairfidh na mná go deo!"

"Cateline, in English, it means *health to the men, and may the women live forever!"* Her uncle gave one more toast to the happy couple—

"May your mornings bring joy, and your evenings bring peace.
May your troubles grow few as your blessings increase.
May the saddest day of your future be no worse than the happiest day of your past.
May your hands be forever clasped in friendship, and your hearts joined forever in love.
Your lives are very special; God has touched you in many ways.
May His blessings rest upon you and fill all your coming days."

All held up their cup to the bride and groom and then downed the first round. James gave the next toast once all the cups were refilled—

"Friends and relatives, so fond and dear, 'tis our greatest pleasure to have you here.
When many years this day has passed, fondest memories will always last.

So, we drink a cup of Irish mead and ask God's blessing in your hour of need."

Once again, everyone raised their cups to toast the couple and downed the mead. Amos came forward to make a toast once all the cups had been filled again, as he proclaimed—

"May the road rise to meet you,
May the wind be always at your back,
May the sun shine warm upon your face,
And the rainfall soft upon your fields,
And until we meet again, my friend,
May God hold you in the palm of his hand."

The toasts came, and the drinks were consumed. With that third drink, Cateline hoped there would not be very many more, even though she had thoroughly enjoyed the tradition. Still, one of James's friends also came forward to give another toast, waiting once again until all the cups had been refilled.

"On this special day,
Our wish to you,
The goodness of the old,
The best of the new.
God bless you both who drink this mead,
May it always fill your every need."

Once again, the cups were lifted and then consumed. Thankfully, that had been the last of the toasts, and James came over to Cateline to escort her into the drawing-room to sing a song to Oscar on her guitar. "Oh, James, I am a bit tipsy. I do hope I can do this."

"I am so sorry, sister, I should have had you play before the toasts, but I am sure you will do fine." Oscar took her arm and finished escorting her to the front of the room, where all the instruments and band members were. A chair had been pulled out where she could sit, and one of the guys in the band handed her a guitar. Oscar sat down in another chair, secured fairly close to Cateline, and turned slightly to face her.

"Family and friends, some of you have heard my sister play the guitar and sing, and some of you have not. She has a most amazing voice and was asked to sing a song to her beloved husband at this time. I am sure everyone will be pleased to hear her talent," James announced.

After his statement, Cateline began playing, *Pledging My Love*,'' a song from the 1950s by Johnny Ace. She looked over at Oscar, singing while gazing into his eyes, taken by his look, captured by his regard, deeply engaged in the romantic words sung for her beloved husband.

After finishing the song, everyone was clapping and talking about how her voice was most astounding and the music so enchanting. Oscar took her hand in his and led her into the center of the floor as the bride and groom took center stage for the first dance of the evening. Sophia played a splendid song on the pianoforte as the band members joined in while Oscar held Cateline in his arms, dancing as they all observed. Yet, to them, they felt as if they were all alone because they both only had eyes for each other. Oscar whispered in her ears, "You are all the great heroines of the world in one, my dear. You are more than an individual, and I love you and must make you always love me. I want to make Romeo jealous, and the dead lovers of the world hear our laughter and grow sad. I want a breath of our passion to stir dust into consciousness, to wake their ashes into pain. Cateline, I am so taken with your beauty, for I worship and desire you, my own one."

"Oh, Oscar, I love you so much and am happier than I have ever been in my life." Once they had finished the official bride and groom dance, the band began with tunes chosen for the ceili dance.

Oscar taking her hand, "I am afraid, my love, that I now hunger for your presence on the dance floor. I do believe you are ready for some Irish dancing."

"Yes, I am ever so excited to do the dance with quite a line of people. I do hope that I don't make a mistake."

"Never speak of mistakes. Why what nonsense you talk. For you, my dear, have genius! With your harmony of soul and body, your simple and beautiful nature shall be seen. Come, let us celebrate this night with all the candor of youth."

The ceili dance commenced with the *Seige of Ennis*. Dancing the steps in which she had learned at her uncle's, the happy couple gallantly twirled about with every song, in tune to the music with each pace, thoroughly enjoying themselves. Cateline, thus far, had been doing quite well at remembering all the strides and having a grand time at that. Once the first tune ended, the band played, *The Walls of Limerick.* After a few dances, Oscar took Cateline's hand breathlessly, saying, "Let us break a moment. I believe a drink would be excellent." Together, they walked over for a glass of champagne, laughing and carrying on like two children in love, young lovers with the world at their feet—enchanted—separated from those around them, only in deep thought of each other, satisfied and wanting to please. If love could only be bottled and kept, a reminisce of love that is lost too often—moments as these to hold on to, never to let go, never to cease from being bound together by vows—to love and to cherish, to be joined until death—love that comes and sometimes leaves. Yet, Oscar and Cateline thought not about tomorrow or the days to come, for they were caught up in the moment—those moments that one can never return once they have been spent. After a break, they went back to join in with the ceili dance.

After several dances, Oscar led Cateline to the dining parlor to get a bite to eat. "I do believe we should break for refreshment, my love, for you have not eaten anything since you came downstairs. I shall not have my bride become wearied from lack of nutrition. James prepared quite the feast, and everyone besides yourself has been eating for some time before you made your grand entrance," Oscar declared as he escorted Cateline into James's dining parlor. The room was set up superbly, adorned with the most handsome fine floral China holding various dishes of roast mutton, duck pheasant, cucumber sandwiches, piles of fresh berries, plum pudding, mince pies, tiny petit fours, and lemon tarts. Each dish was elegantly placed on lace doilies and garnished with little rose petals and orange blossoms.

"What kind of cake is this, Oscar?"

"I presume that to be a fruitcake."

"It has icing on it?"

"Yes, fruitcake is normally served as a wedding cake in Europe, which typically has icing."

Cateline, taking a small bite, concurred, "Mmm—this taste delicious," continuing with a second and third bite, she enjoyed the sweet fruity flavors, zesty tangs of citrus, and the quaint nutty taste all savored into one, complemented with the richness of the homemade white icing.

"Cateline, I insist that you need something more filling than just the cake, my dear."

In agreement, she declared, "I am going to eat some of the other dishes, as well—do not worry."

After they had both tasted several of the delightful hors d'oeuvres, they went back to the dance floor.

Time had elapsed when James stopped the music to direct everyone into the dining parlor for the bride and groom to partake in the tradition of the wedding cake, which had been brought out and set on a separate table. Cateline, unaware of what the Irish custom demanded, was not prepared for what she observed. With a somewhat piercing gasp, spotting the cake upon walking into the room, it was undeniably stacked exuberantly high. Cateline laughed while she declared, "You were not kidding when you said a cake stacked high."

Everyone laughed, which had Cateline wondering if there was something she was missing. Looking over at Oscar, who stood by her side, she inquired quietly, "Is there something I am not aware of with this tradition?"

Amused, trying to compose himself, he responded, "Listen, my dear, James is about to share the details."

"The cake is rather astonishing," James spoke while laughing. "I am truly sorry, but I have not communicated this with my dear sister. She may disown me after this one. I apologize, Cateline, but living in America, you have just missed some really great practices. I thought it only right that you would be able to experience some of them." Everyone was laughing, with the last laugh on her, of course. "Sister, I need you to stand on this side of the cake—and Oscar will stand on the other across from you," James continued, "the tradition is that you two have to lean across and kiss each other, over the top of the cake. A successful kiss, where you do not fall into the cake, means you are guaranteed a prosperous life together."

Cateline was beside herself, smiling with everyone else before speaking, "That is so unfair. Oscar is so much taller than I. Can I have a stool to stand on?"

With everyone laughing, not surprisingly, the answer was—No! Cateline took off her shoes, leaning up as high as she could, standing on her toes, but naturally, Oscar was so tall that it was easy for him. They leaned over and finally were able to kiss at the top when

327

Cateline lost her balance and partially went into the side of the cake, crying out, "Ah—but the kiss was done successfully; I only fell afterward." With everyone laughing, Oscar came around and kissed her most passionately. "This has really been an awesome wedding," she acknowledged to her charming husband. Speaking to everyone in the room, Cateline shared, "Now, we must do cake, America's traditional way." She took the knife and cut off a piece of the cake, laying it on a small plate before cutting that slice into two relatively large portions. "The American way," she began, "the bride and groom each pick up a piece of the cake, and they feed that portion to the other one."

Oscar, in a cheerful demeanor, "Is that all? It sounds rather easy," he replied while picking up one of the slices as Cateline picked up the other. As they both went to feed their pieces to each other, upon Oscar beginning to part his lips, Cateline hastily smashed the cake all over his mouth and face. She laughed so hard while trying to get away from him as he rapidly seized her arm. While struggling and screaming, Cateline put her head down, turning to keep him from smearing cake all over her face. Trying to get loose from his grip, he persisted in striving to reach her face with his other hand, which still held his piece of cake. Shrieking uncontrollably, Cateline frantically tried to get out of his grasp when they both slipped down to the floor, laughing hysterically. She was trapped beneath his grip, lying on the floor while he smeared the cake onto her face. Yes, it was quite a sight and most amusing at that.

At this point, all in attendance were hooting and hollering intensively. While, at the same time, Oscar maintained holding Cateline down, planting kisses all over her face, smearing the icing that much further. Unable to stop the unrelenting laughter, she started screaming in the midst, "Oscar, STOP—STOP, it is covering my whole face, and you are getting it in my hair."

He backed away from her slightly but proceeded to hold her arms while looking in her face, laughing as he declared, "You are truly in disarray, darling."

Cateline, in a giggling state, responded, "I don't think you look any the less, my dear."

Oscar turned to their family and friends as he helped his new bride to her feet while announcing, "Presenting, Mr. and Mrs. Oscar Wilde at their finest."

Everyone joined in with laughter while the newly married couple announced their departure for a brief period, "Please excuse us; my wife and I are perfectly hideous at the moment. We shall clean up and resume our fête with friends and family momentarily," Oscar declared, excusing them from their guests.

As they walked from the room, James acknowledged loudly, "I think I like the American way better, Oscar—and you will be pleased to know that the photographer has captured many of these poses. I dare say this has been a most memorable wedding."

"Yes, I must agree, James, quite memorable at that," Oscar replied.

They walked up the stairs to the bridal suite, where Oscar took hold of Cateline's arm as he spoke, "Wait, my dear one, I must carry you over the threshold." Before she could say anything, he had swept her up in his arms, and Cateline smiled, being most satisfied with her wonderful husband, as she was so much in love.

In the bridal suite, all their belongings had been thoroughly arranged neatly in the wardrobe, as well as items on the vanity and such by the maidservants. They both went to find something appropriate and comfortable to go back downstairs with their guests, as the evening was not quite over. Oscar looked at his lovely wife and walked to where she stood as she had begun to slip out of her dress, standing only adorned in her soft satiny corset, sleek petticoat, and silk stockings. Oscar continued to take notice of her body, enticing as it was with such splendor. Observing her delicate features, the allure of her frame, he finally spoke, "I would much rather remain here with you, my dear, and make love to you this very moment."

Cateline turning to look into his eyes, remarked in a most sensual voice, "As would I, but we do have company to entertain, and the evening will end soon enough."

At that moment, he took her in his arms, and they fell back on the bed, entwined in passionate kisses and intimate embraces. "It is legal now that I can at least touch you before we go back downstairs with our guests." Lying beside each other, absorbed in passion, they remained kissing with Cateline knowing that there had never been a man in her life whom she had desired as she had Oscar. With restraint, at last, he spoke, "Perhaps, we should not be rude and show ourselves to our guests for a time. I am afraid, if we continue this, they shall not see us for the remainder of the night. We at least know what pleasure awaits us for later."

Arising, they both got dressed and cleaned all the cake off as best they could. "Do I look alright, Oscar?"

"You look ravishing, my dear," he responded while walking over to give her a kiss. "Come, my bride, our guests do await our return."

Once again, joining their guests, they continued into the night with joyous moments of dancing, wine, champagne, good friends, and family. At one point, James noted that the bride and groom had yet to open their gifts from family and friends. Oscar and Cateline sat down as each present, one by one, was handed to them to unwrap. They received Irish linen, a tradition as the linen represented commitment; there was pottery—Belleek pottery and Waterford crystal. They also received, in addition, tall toasting glasses of excellent quality and many other delightful items. They were both very thankful for all the generosity of those who attended, along with the hospitality from James and the use of his estate. Once they had finished with the gifts, the celebration lingered into the night. It had been a most exuberant occasion which secured many memories that would remain with both Cateline and Oscar for a lifetime.

As much of the guest outside of the family had left, few family members endured with drink and address, which would probably continue far into the wee hours of the morning. Oscar looked at Cateline and remarked, "My dear, while the family seems to be engaged in conversation, let us quietly slip out of the room. I dare say they probably will not even notice our absence for some time." He took her hand as he led her to the bridal suite, and once again, he wished to carry her over the threshold. Inside the room, Oscar shut the door and walked over to Cateline to disrobe her. As he did, he kissed her intently and laid her upon the bed, and then began to undress. Climbing in next to her, they embraced and kissed intimately, making love for the first time. Lying next to each other, Oscar persistently held Cateline in his arms while talking between kissing and cuddling. Oscar sharing with Cateline, spoke quietly, "Our most fiery moments of ecstasy are merely shadows of what somewhere else we have felt, or of what we long someday to feel,"[3] after a brief pause, he resumed, "I must reveal something with you, my love."

Caitlin raising her head and looking down at him, spoke quietly, "You sound so serious."

"I am quite serious."

"Well, my wonderful husband, with the words you have just spoken, I am most anxious to know what they mean. Please, do tell?"

"You must know that I had dreamed about you before I ever met you. The first time I saw you, it disturbed me, I assure you, but instantly, I was captivated by your beauty."

Cateline smiled as tears streamed down her cheeks, responding, "My dear, I, too, have dreamt of you most of my life."

"But it was you, Cateline. It was your face that I dreamed of, and I had never laid eyes on you until that first day at your uncle's."

"I do understand because I, too, dreamed of your face, as well." She leaned over and kissed him passionately.

"Whatever do you suppose this means, my love?"

Cateline, of course, understood more than Oscar did, but it wasn't time to share at this point. She thought a moment and then responded, "I'm not quite sure what it means—except, God must have brought us together for a reason, Oscar, but I have loved you for most of my life."

Looking deep into her eyes, there was silence for several minutes—Oscar then reached up to pull her towards him, holding her so very tight, he responded, "I love you dearly, Cateline—I will love you forever."

They kissed and held each other until sleep finally had overtaken them.

CHAPTER
22

Saturday morning soon came, as Oscar and Cateline were awakened by a slight knock. Hurriedly, Oscar threw on his trousers while Cateline rolled over to watch him open the door. His exquisite physique sent chills over her as she loved this most gorgeous man in all his enchantment. In the hallway stood one of James's servants with a breakfast tray for the newlyweds. Thanking the young girl, he returned and lay the tray on the table to the side, disrobing himself once again before he climbed back into the bed next to Cateline. Leaning over, Oscar gave her a kiss, mumbling softly, "How are you this morning, my beautiful wife?"

"Oh, how can you say such a thing," she muttered sleepily, "I am sure my hair is most repulsive, and I am not quite awake. I believe I could sleep for hours on end."

"As could I, my dear one, for I do have no desire to socialize at the moment, for I would much rather remain next to you all day. Although, we must show ourselves in society from time to time, just to remind the public that we are not savages.' One must have the reputation of being civilized, after all. But, as it is, I dare to share you or your repulsive hair at the moment; that simply would never do," Oscar spoke facetiously with a seductive grin.

"You do not have to agree with me, my love, but I, too, would much prefer to lay beside you throughout the day if it were possible. Yet, I do suppose we should arise and go downstairs to be sociable."

Oscar, running his fingers through her lengthy hair, countered, "Invariably, I would agree if, indeed, this were not our honeymoon. Must we be so gregarious, my darling?"

"I am afraid we must. I am surprised at you, Oscar." she quipped.

"Oh, please do not be surprised, for I assure you, it is your wonderful soul in that delicate little body that holds me captive."

"I am surprised that you would enjoy running your fingers through my repulsive hair?"

He smiled at her wit while whispering rather romantically in between light kisses placed along her face, "My lovely one, I assure you, repulsive hair as yours, is by far what I prefer."

While responding to his gentle advances, the food seemed to stimulate her senses, "Mmm, our breakfast does smell awfully good, but I do believe I would take you over food even though I am quite ravenous. But truthfully, my dear, we must arise and get dressed for the day."

Sitting up in the bed, Oscar declared, "Whatever for?"

With a slight laugh, she reminded him, "Do you forget our obligation?"

"I—I suppose I must have. Please, do enlighten me, my dear."

"Bull Rock?" Cateline jogged his memory with a smile.

"Ah—yes, it is true, I had forgotten. How horrid of you to smile. I do suppose we should eat and prepare ourselves. But first, my darling, turn around and kiss me," Oscar spoke while pulling Cateline back into his arms to cuddle and embrace once again. "You are not going to run away so soon. Certainly, we have time if we hurry," he pleaded.

"Yes, if we hurry."

A short while later, they both climbed out of bed to get cleaned up and dressed. Cateline was having difficulty trying to manage her hair because Oscar would not keep his hands to himself. Finally, with a most playful smile, she acknowledged, "Oscar, if you are ready to go downstairs, you may go without me. I cannot get ready with you all over me."

With a slight laugh, he agreed, "You are a distraction, my dear, so lovely to look at. Am I to go?"

"Yes—yes, please, Oscar, you must go so I can get ready," she acknowledged, kissing him lightly on the cheek.

Once presentable, Cateline joined the men where the three of them left to meet James's friend at the docks. Arriving, they climbed aboard a nice-sized schooner. Cateline recalled memories of a time she had spent with several friends on the Bagheera, a nice-sized schooner at Cape Ann, north of Boston. Meditating on that timeframe brought a smile to her face, the sailboat had been so much fun, and now, here she was in a different era, once again anticipating their day in this delightful vessel.

Once all the sails were lifted and secured, the ride became most pleasant. As the winds carried them along, over waves whooshing here and there, the brisk ride brought a thrill to all. Oscar and Cateline sat quietly, relishing the breathtaking views of the sea and the feel of the sun cascading down their bodies, which provided a refreshing sensation. The freshness of the breeze and the occasional spray of waters brought forth a mist which lightly infused over them while James carried on in deep conversation with Maurice, a long-time friend who had also attended the wedding. Occasionally, Oscar engaged in their tales. Still, for the most part, they were too absorbed with the comforts of the scenery and tranquility to gather up the energy or stamina for too much discourse, as it was. A delightful ride of an hour or so had ensued before off in the distance, the enormous rock could be seen. With such excitement, the energy seemed to come alive within Oscar and Cateline while they stood on the rather nice-sized sailboat owned by Maurice. "Oscar, how utterly fascinating; can you see the tunnel underneath? It is most enchanting, is it not?"

"It is indeed! Unspotted from the creation, an antique world. It seems to be in every way what I had imagined. Most incredible," he concurred.

Drawing nearer and nearer, Bull Rock resembled something of medieval times with its jagged rocks and plush verdant green grasses growing sporadically in alcoves and niches along the sides. Plateaus sprawled at a variety of elevations, covered in velvety softness joined with mounds of rock formation molded astringently as sharp diabolical blades, followed by smooth casings. Diverse shapes formed upwards, rising into the sky, penetrating structures, unique characteristics—distinctive, rare, as an ancient turret. It was a sight to view, one of awe. The waters which surrounded, a most tranquil blue, were so inviting—exuberantly invigorating, splashing upon the sides of the boat, buoyantly.

Oscar, reaching down to hold Cateline's hand, as he reacted, "Simply wonderful."

"Yes, quite so. I would love to swim in these waters, wouldn't you?"

Oscar looked towards her as he inquired, "Ah—the secret of one's own soul. Should this be what fate has in store for you?"

"Well, yes, it's only once in a lifetime opportunity. We shall probably never be here again."

"Whatever would your motive be, my dear, to immerse yourself in such cold water?"

"It would be such a sensational moment, Oscar. Purely breathtaking, an extraordinary experience. Surely you can sense this, can you not?"

"A curious sensation, I perceive."

Cheerfully, she responded, "Yes, perhaps so. But I don't care if the water is cold, Oscar Wilde, let's just do it. I believe it will be a memory that we will cherish forever."

"What would you wear, Cateline? You cannot swim in your dress."

"I can simply take my dress off. I do have on pantalettes and a short chemise underneath. I will merely tell James and his friend that they cannot watch."

"You seem to be quite serious."

"Is it alright with you if I am serious?"

Oscar, envisioning them swimming to the rock, filled him with awe of this remarkable woman who was tremendously different from any woman he had ever met. Lit up with a big smile, he responded, "You truly absorb my whole nature. This is, of course, perfectly hideous that you would influence me in such a way, and at the same time, I am sincerely fascinated by the rare creature whom I am bound to by marriage."

She responded with a somewhat significant laugh, "Yes, I am by far a rare find, Oscar Wilde. So, that means you will do this with me?"

"It is not my conscience that leads me to do so, my dear, for if that was what was leading me, I would remain warm and dry."

Cateline threw her arms around Oscar's neck and kissed him intimately. With both caught up in merriment, she went to tell James and his friend, who thought it was a bizarre idea but agreed, as long as they did not remain in the water for a considerable length of time, with it being cold as it was.

"Cateline," James spoke with concern, "do you swim well enough?"

"Yes, James, I am from America; girls often swim in America."

The two of them readied themselves and then dove into the water, swimming over to Bull Rock, just shy of the gateway to the underworld, all the while laughing and acting like two children in the waters. As they entered into the arch, they tread over towards an area that protruded where they were able to climb up to a slightly flat portion of rock, with Oscar assisting Cateline. Briefly, out of sight from the boat, he leaned over to give her a most romantic kiss, "I shall love you forever, my lovely bride, may this kiss remain in your memories where our love shall never part."

It was a most romantic encounter and one Cateline would treasure for a lifetime.

Swimming back to the boat, they raced, but Cateline was no match for his muscular frame even though she remained reasonably close. As they climbed back into the boat, with assistance, being quite chilled but so very thankful as there were blankets to wrap around for added warmth and to assist with drying off. James's friend turned the boat back to shore, everyone in agreement that the trip had been an incredible journey, with the men thoroughly enjoying the discovery of Cateline's hidden personality—a side never before had they witnessed in any girls they knew. "James, please promise that you will not tell the family that I swam."

"I promise, sister, but you should hurry and get dressed before we arrive."

It was later in the day before they had returned. As they arrived at the estate, Oscar and Cateline had decided to take their dinner in their room, where they could spend time together and get to bed early to be ready for their train ride back to Dublin the following morning. Placing the tray of food between them in bed, they first drank the mead which had been sent up in their goblets and then enjoyed the tasty meal, all the while laughing about their day and trying to feed each other food while making such a mess. Finally, Cateline was able to get the best of Oscar as she instigated a food fight with a bowl of shepherd pie where it fell delightfully into his lap. Cateline was laughing so hard while Oscar grabbed hold of her arm, and as she leaned backward to resist, she completely fell off the bed, screaming rather loudly! Oscar then leaned over to see if she was hurt, and when he did, she pulled him off as well. They were both lying on the floor laughing so hard, entirely covered with various foods. Nevertheless, Oscar started to kiss her while she screamed, "Oscar, stop—stop—let me get up. We are both covered with food," but he remained steadfast in his persuasion until she yielded.

After a space, climbing back into bed, they laid in each other's arms, reminiscing about their most memorable day, which of course, included their time at Bull Rock. "How pleasant it was swimming alongside you today, Cateline. You do fill me with awe, my dear. I believe we have had an unusual and adventurous wedding weekend; would you not agree?"

"Yes, Oscar, most incredible memories. I will always cherish these days and yearn for many, many more."

"I assure you, there shall be loads of memoirs, my dear."

"And, my love, I would also like to remind you of something you said a while back," Cateline stated suddenly!

"And what might that be?"

"First, you do agree that we had a lot of fun together today, do you not?"

"Why, yes, certainly. It was quite the venture, yet I detect that I am plummeting into a snare, my dear."

Cateline giggled at his remark before she acknowledged, "You told me not too long ago that a woman and a man could never be friends."

With a grin on his face, he concurred, "Ah, but I knew where this was going, such a tedious subject if I do say so. I suppose one would have to talk seriously about it."

"Well, let me just add to this conversation. You vowed to be my constant friend, did you not?"

"I am at your mercy, my dear. I do agree; my days have been filled with endless adventure since I made your acquaintance. Even so, in defense, most women do not have your temperament nor charm. Nonetheless, I agree that we are lovers and friends."

No longer sleepy, they continued to reminisce of their most delightful week spent at James's, chatting of their days ahead. Both shared the same passions and were so excited about what lay before them. With conversations continuing, Oscar made a comment, "One looks for pleasure in life, yet pleasure is found in those places that one desires to be. Next to you, Cateline, that is what brings me much pleasure, perpetual perfection when I am with you. The days which follow, I am no longer concerned with hurrying to London, for my desire is to learn of the beautiful creature whom I have married, for that will simply do."

"I thought you needed to be there sometime this next week."

"Ah, London means nothing to me compared with you. When I am beside you, Cateline, you represent something to me that I have never known. I should be wretched if I rushed back to London and failed to find pleasure in my wife. After all, it would not be right to not make this next week a memorable honeymoon, my dear."

337

Cateline, beaming at him, responded, "Mmm, that all sounds quite wonderful. I am glad you feel that way."

"Well, it did originate with the Irish, and who better than the Irish to create a honeymoon which is impressive?"

"The honeymoon's roots come from the Irish?"

"Unequivocally, once married, the couple spends intimate moments together during the course of their honeymoon, but the words—honey and moon are a tradition with the wedding. As we drank mead, it is the sacred drink in an Irish wedding, and it is made from fermented honey, which is where the word honey comes from in honeymoon. We were given the goblets as a gift, which is another practice. The custom is that the newlywed couple uses the goblets daily to drink or toast the mead for one full moon after their wedding. That is where the word moon comes from, thus making it honeymoon. Of course, the belief is that in doing so, there would be fertility for a great marriage."

"Oh, that is why they sent us mead in our goblets this evening."

"Yes, you are correct, my dear."

"But where will we get mead once we leave James's?"

Oscar smiling, proclaimed, "James made sure there was enough made for the bride and groom to take with them. It is a tradition where the family takes care of such, as they do want our marriage to have fertility."

"I do believe I am going to love all these practices. Even though I am Irish, I feel that I missed out on so much history while living in America. I really love hearing all these stories and the traditions at the wedding. I believe the wedding was so notable with all the different customs we partook in."

With it being their last night and fully awake, they decided to get back up to spend an hour or two with the family. The family, having retired to the drawing-room, Oscar and Cateline, joined them with all three girls taking turns on the pianoforte. The tunes made for a most splendid evening with her family, including her brother James and his girlfriend, Sophia. Cateline relished in time spent with her brother, knowing it would probably be their last. Everyone remained up late, in which Oscar and Cateline decided to take pleasure in the evening and on into the night, where they could have these memories with family before retiring to bed.

Sunday morning rolled around quite early, with everyone packing their belongings before breakfast. Afterward, the whole family retreated to the veranda until time for James to drive them to the train station, close to noon. Being that the entire family was gathered together, they decided to toast the mead with Oscar and Cateline and then enjoy an early lunch before leaving for the station. The newlywed couple took pleasure in their time at her father's estate, where Cateline felt it quite hard to say her final goodbyes to James. "Brother, please tell Sophia that I said goodbye, and I give my sole approval for you to marry that girl. We would love to have you visit us in London along with Sophia."

Giving her a final hug, James said his goodbyes, and they parted.

Her uncle, having taken the liberty to pay for their tickets back to Dublin, first-class tickets at that, they all boarded into a most elegant Victorian-style décor car. It was significantly different from the other classes—tasteful and luxurious from its carpeted aisles to its curtained windows. The family all reclined in posh upholstered seats, which were obviously comfy. The girls sat close to each other to spend time together, whereas Oscar and Amos were within close proximity as well. Cateline leaned over to whisper to Oscar, "We should have purchased first-class seats on all our escapades thus far by train."

"I am so sorry, Cateline. Truthfully, I never take first-class, traveling alone. At any rate, I never even considered first-class. But, of course, now that I am married, I will make certain that we travel in comfort."

"Oh, please, pay no attention to my words. Honestly, I do not care how we travel as long as we are together. All the same, this is unmistakably lavish, Oscar. And very comfortable. I merely thought all train rides were uncomfortable."

"No, you are quite right. In England, we shall travel in comfort."

She concluded with a smile, "Whatever you desire, my love. But just know, I really do not care how we travel."

As they settled in, Mr. Walsh mentioned, "We should arrive in Dublin around four or five o'clock depending on how many stops are made. I had told Elbert to be sure and pick us up around that time. Oscar, have you purchased tickets yet for Liverpool?"

"No, sir, we will take the Rob Roy, the same ship in which I traveled from Liverpool. If I remember correctly, I do believe they leave fairly early; I want to say around half-past eight or nine. We would need to arrive at the docks early on Monday."

"No point in leaving earlier than is needed. When we arrive in Dublin, I will simply have Elbert drive by the shipyard to purchase your tickets this evening. That way, you will know exactly what time the Rob Roy leaves tomorrow."

"Thank you, Sir."

"How far a distance is it to Liverpool?"

"It takes about seven hours. Of course, there are ports where mail is delivered."

"I will be sure and let Bertha knows to prepare an early breakfast, and I will have Elbert ready to take both of you to the shipyard," he concluded while looking over at his niece, "I do hope you keep in touch, my dear."

"Of course, uncle. I will write often and will miss all of you something terrible."

A short time after departure, a waiter approached to bring complimentary drinks and hors d'oeuvres. Enjoying the wine and mixed drinks, conversations continued with Cateline and Anya talking endlessly about many personal things. At the same time, Oscar was so involved in communication with Mr. Walsh and Amos, he was unconcerned with hearing their girl-talk. Occasionally, Cateline would glance over towards him, just to be sure that he was not listening, while confiding many intimate details to Anya on how romantic and quite gentle a man he was. She was so much in love and expressed to her cousin the delight of being married to someone who shared that love. Aunt Martha had fallen asleep within less than an hour of their departure, which had been excellent, giving both girls ample time to discuss many things that they wouldn't dare if she had been awake. Having company on the journey back made for such an improvement, as there was so much time to be filled catching up on each of their romances, which young lovers so enjoy sharing with their most reliable confidants.

Anya had undoubtedly become like a sister since the time Cateline had arrived. With all the moments they had spent together, she knew there would never be another in all of Europe who could fill the role of such an intimate friend as her cousin. How Cateline knew that the days ahead would leave such a void in her life, as Anya would be incredibly missed after seeing her so often, as it had been. Cateline could not even imagine how dreadful it would be once her time had ended, where she would return to her own era. It was no longer just about the unbearable thought of never seeing Oscar again but of the sister she had found through Anya and how much pain there would also be in her own absence. However, Cateline knew she must trust God. Oh yes, she must depend upon Him solely because this had never ever been about her but about Oscar in the first place. Her thoughts were many, which filled her deep within. As a writer, Cateline knew it wasn't entirely about being here; it was so much more. This life was real inside, and that was something which would never leave her—no, not ever. No matter how long her days would be once Cateline returned to her time, these days and these feelings which filled her right now would never end. They would never ever go away. It saddened her, but Cateline was also filled with much joy at merely knowing she had been able to love Oscar, even if it was so short-lived.

As time continued to pass, Anya seemed to have become somber. Perhaps she, too, was thinking of tomorrow and how Cateline would no longer be with her daily. The men folk's discussions at one point seemed to have ceased, as well. Oscar leaned over to Cateline in adoration; taking her hand, he squeezed it in his, saying so earnestly, "I love you passionately, my dear."

That was all she needed to hear at that moment, looking into his eyes, knowing he also loved her clearly as much as she loved him. Cateline thought deeply to herself, "Time may separate us, but it can never take away the love we had—no, not ever."

Uncle Walsh seemed to have fallen into a deep sleep along with Aunt Martha, while Anya and Amos talked quietly together. On occasion, Anya would giggle, and Amos would smile. Yes, the love they shared was quite obvious, as well. Cateline sure hoped that she would be able to attend their wedding, as she had no idea what lay ahead once they left for London. She only knew that most of those pictures discovered from the library were taken in England, with perhaps a few in Paris. Of course, it was not precisely clear the location. Cateline so looked forward to their journey together but

341

feared it as well, for she also knew the farther along in their passage, the closer it came to her departure. A few tears rolled down her cheeks, looking away from Oscar to hide her sorrow, for she had no way to explain what she was feeling, at least not now.

Oscar, relaxing in the plush recline of his chair, persistently held Cateline's hand while she nuzzled up next to him. They cuddled close together until overtaken by slumber. Within a few hours, the family commenced to stir, and all decided to go to the dining car for an early dinner. It was explicitly impressive, delightful tables with luxurious chairs about with large windows encased for exuberant views of the countryside. After ordering, the waiter, before long, brought out scrumptious smoked poultry, savory spinach, potatoes with gravy, and the most delicious apple charlotte cake. This was definitely remarkable for the nineteenth-century railway and much better than second class. They all enjoyed their meal with much conversation and laughter for a pleasurable late afternoon shared with family.

Much time had passed when the loud whistle of the horn shrieked boisterously while the train hissed loudly with the screeching of the brakes as it slowed down and finally came to a complete stop. The noise had quite stirred all when the announcement came of their arrival in Dublin. The porters soon arrived to gather all their belongings while they were ushered off the train into the station. Uncle Walsh quickly saw his coachman, "There's Elbert." Everyone headed in his direction while Elbert, along with Charles, walked towards them to assist with the many trunks and baggage. With the addition of family and servants, it had been necessary for the brougham and barouche to accommodate all parties and luggage. As soon as everyone was loaded into the two carriages, Uncle Walsh let Elbert know to head over to the Dublin shipyard before going to the estate. At the same time, Charles carried the remaining family home.

"Yes, sir," Elbert responded as they headed towards the shipyard.

Cateline leaned over to Oscar to inquire, "What is the Rob Roy? Is it the name of the ship?"

"It is, my dear, they provide service for patrons to cross the Irish Sea from Dublin to Liverpool. They are mainly a small steamship service that carries mail and cargo to include passengers daily. You will enjoy the ship; it is relatively comfortable, more so than our train ride to your brothers."

"I would think anything would be more comfortable than our travel to James's. I probably could ask you a thousand questions, but I am much too tired right now to even think," she responded while laying her head on his shoulder as Oscar put his arm back around her to draw her close.

It was not a far distance to get to the docks, and once arrived, Oscar swiftly jumped out and went in to secure two tickets for their travels for the following morning. Getting back into the barouche, he remarked to Mr. Walsh, "The ship will be leaving around nine, sir, and we should arrive in Liverpool about four o'clock. We would need to arrive by eight-thirty in the morning in order to be loaded before that time."

"Yes, yes, of course. I will see to it that all arrangements are made to have you both up early and at the shipyard on time," Mr. Walsh concluded. Elbert continued steering the horses towards the estate while there was much silence amongst everyone. It was clear the long journey had taken its toll, even though some had slept during their excursion.

Arriving at the estate, Elbert swiftly unloaded all their belongings while Charles and Newton took all remaining trunks and baggage into the estate to the appropriate rooms. Oscar let Charles know to leave all his and Cateline's belongings downstairs since they would be leaving the following morning. At the same time, Charles informed Oscar that all of his articles from his apartment on the third floor had been moved to Cateline's room.

As it was fast approaching half-past seven, once everyone had settled, Bertha had made a small spread of food in the event anyone was hungry. Uncle Walsh suggested everyone make a plate to bring into the drawing-room, where there could be last-minute dialogue before retiring for the night. He had also insisted that Amos stay the night in one of the third-floor bedchambers, where they could leave for work together the following day.

It was a most pleasant evening, as the family enjoyed their last time together with Cateline and, of course, Oscar, to whom they had become so attached during all the weeks he had stayed. They all

343

talked about the particulars for Oscar and Cateline's future, as well as plans for his writings of poetry, short stories, plays, and other clever talents, to be sure, as his dream was to be a great playwright. Cateline soaked in the moments of that night where she knew the memories would last her a lifetime, even once she was back in America. Yes, it was nights like this where Cateline would sometimes lay awake to write down every moment, most memorable as they were. If she must leave this timeframe and go back to another, at least she had her diary, quite customary for the nineteenth century. And as such, Cateline had secured every memory to date thus far and hoped for many more in the future.

After some time, everyone was ready to retire, as the journey had been rather extensive and tedious. Whereas in modern times, the twenty-first century, to be precise, a trip as such, would have taken half the time, and other places of considerable distance could be traveled by air.

Saying goodnight to all of the family, Oscar and Cateline retired to her old room. Cateline, having laid out a chemise to sleep in and removed her dress when Oscar pulled her towards him, "No need to bother with such. I spent many a night in your room when you would turn down my advances since we had not made our vows. Tonight, my bride and I shall share this room." He smiled seductively, helping her undress before removing his own attire. Oscar went over to put a few more logs on the fire to relieve the chill in the air, kindling it to bring an abundance of flames. Cateline, watching him at the hearth, climbed into her bed while admiring the beauty of his frame. Walking back from the fireplace, he poured each of them their goblet of mead. After toasting their marriage, Oscar took the goblets to the table in the other room while observing Cateline watching his every move with her most gorgeous smile. He stood beside the bed and leaned over to kiss her, "Your eyes have remained fixated upon me, are you charmed by what you see, my dear?"

"Come to bed, and I will show you just how much I am charmed by what I see," she responded as he climbed in next to her. They cuddled together all the while kissing, and in between kisses, Cateline exclaimed, "You are most romantic, Oscar; I would have never thought as much."

Kissing and caressing her, he added, "You should have known me to be romantic, my dear, for I am a poet as well as you.

Romance comes naturally to those who live it with every breath because it is within their soul."

"Mmm, but who can know the depths within one's soul?" Cateline inquired as she succumbed to his every breath and touch.

"To recognize that the soul of a man is unknowable is the ultimate achievement of wisdom, my dear. The final mystery is oneself," he spoke in a whisper as he leaned in to kiss her lips before continuing. "When one has weighed the sun in a balance, measured the steps of the moon, and mapped out the seven heavens star by star, there still remains oneself," kissing her once more, he finished, "who, my dear, can calculate the orbit of his own soul?"[2]

CHAPTER
23

Monday morning came around quickly; the house was still quiet when Cateline awoke, sat up in the bed, and leaned over to see what time it was on Oscar's pocket watch. "Just six in the morning, but we really should be getting ready to leave," Cateline's thoughts stirred while rolling over towards her prince charming, kissing him until he began to rouse. "Good morning, my love," she said.

Turning over on his back, he looked up into her eyes and responded, "Upon my word, morning surely has not arrived; I do feel quite sure of that."

"I am afraid so, Oscar. It is so very early."

"What o'clock is it, my dear?" should I make note this is how he said it?

"What o'clock is it? Oscar, you amuse me so. It is barely past six, but we must arise; the ship shall not wait for us."

"Ah, I forgot all about it. It shall be most delightful once in London, for those of fashionable society are rarely seen about the town before late afternoon, at any rate. We must seriously consider remaining in bed while in Liverpool and Bath, where we become acclimated to the lifestyle of London's upper echelons. It would be atrocious to be mistaken for one of the working class, my dear."

"As long as I am by your side, we do not have to stir until a time which pleases you, my dear." She kissed him again until he responded to her gestures. "Honestly, we should get up; it is a little after six. I am sure my uncle is probably getting ready for work, along with Amos. We probably need to say goodbye before they leave."

"I certainly agree. Your uncle has become very dear to me. If it were not for him, I would have never met you."

They began to get dressed, with Oscar finishing first; he then packed all his belongings. "I will meet you downstairs and will let your uncle know that you wish to say goodbye to him," he said, continuing, "and I will also send Charles to bring the trunk and other baggage down to be loaded in the barouche. Once you are dressed, please make sure you have packed all your things, my dear one."

"Yes, I will, and I shall not be too long," she replied with a loving smile while Oscar walked towards her and kissed her once more before leaving the room. "Yes, you are definitely romantic, and I am much pleased," she concluded.

Oscar smiling, related, "You, my dear, are the greatest romance of my life."

As she beamed from his comment, her reply was spoken softly, "You are my first romance, Oscar. I shall love you forever. Please, let my uncle know that I shall be down shortly."

Cateline swiftly secured her hair in a rather loose updo and added just a touch of makeup before promptly going through the room, checking to make sure she had not left anything behind. Opening up the wardrobe, securing her original bag along with belongings that must accompany her to London, fully packed at this point, she took one last glance in the mirror to make sure that her form was quite pleasing. Standing in radiance, while observing her choice of dress with its soft flowing contours enveloping her most subtle curves and trim waistline, she felt that her appearance would be very presenting as Oscar's new bride.

Cateline, walking out of the bedroom, observed Anya on her way up to assist where needed. "Is there anything I can do to help you, dear cousin?"

"You are up quite early, Anya."

"Yes, I wanted to be sure and see you off."

"Thank you, that is so sweet of you. And, no, I do believe everything is packed and ready to go. I simply need Charles to bring all the additional belongings down and load them into the carriage, and we should then be ready to leave a little after breakfast. Oh, do not let me forget my guitar, cousin."

"I will make sure it gets in the barouche."

"Thank you. Is my favorite uncle still here?"

"Yes, of course, he is. He would not leave until you have come down. That was another reason I was checking on you. I believe they are about ready to head to the office."

"Well, then let's not slow them down," Cateline replied as she walked over to take Anya's arm, and they headed downstairs.

As they descended the last step, still in deep discussion, Anya continued, "Have you had time to keep up with entries in your diary, dear cousin?"

"Oh, but yes, I did write for some time while on the train, you know. I will have to write more on our trip to Liverpool," Cateline

347

responded while looking over to make sure that Oscar was not within earshot before she continued, "I just have to make sure that Oscar is not trying to see what I write. After all, it is my diary, and I do know that a husband has the right to see it. But I do declare that he may find what I write to be much on the side of romance, and I would not take it very kindly if he were to make fun of me. It is with that sort of logic I do conclude a woman's diary is the business of a lady and not for a man."

"I thought you shared with me how romantic Oscar was."

"Ah, yes, that he is. But all the same, it would be somewhat embarrassing if he were to find my writings quite silly."

"Agreed! But eventually, you will have to reveal one's thoughts, for he is your husband, my sweet cousin."

Her uncle was standing in the vestibule off from the stairs, waiting to greet and hug his dear niece goodbye. Cateline ran over and jumped into his arms, knowing she would miss him dearly. Uncle Walsh hugged her back, with Cateline sincerely allocating, "I love you dearly, uncle. You have been such a father to me in the absence of my own, and I have most assuredly cherished our times together. I thank you for everything that you have done for me and will miss you dreadfully."

With a big fatherly hug, Samuel replied, "You are as my daughter, and I have so enjoyed our times spent. Martha and I must surely visit you and Oscar in London, and you both shall come to Anya and Amos's wedding." Samuel kissed her on the forehead before turning to shake Oscar's hand while acknowledging, "Oscar, my boy, you and Cateline have a most wonderful trip, and please send us a wire from time to time. Take care of my girl here," he ended with a most amiable smile. Turning to the family, Samuel said his goodbyes for the day and proceeded out the door. Cateline watching him leave in his brougham saddened her immensely, knowing that as much as she loved all of them, her time was very limited, for she was uncertain if she might ever see any of them again.

Oscar accompanied Cateline to the breakfast parlor, where he sat down beside her while Aunt Martha and Anya, already having breakfast with Mr. Walsh, had waited to be joined by them both for last-minute discourse. As they would be leaving within the hour, their final moments with family were enjoyed around the table, where they soon wandered out on the veranda for tea. It was such a beautiful morning, and they all sat and talked for a brief period, with Joseph advising them it was almost time to depart.

"Thank you, Joseph," Mrs. Walsh stated, "please come let us know once the barouche has pulled up to the front. Continuing in their conversations, she reminded Cateline, "When you receive your wedding pictures from James, we truly would love to have one, my dear."

"Yes, ma'am, I will be sure and send one for your remembrance. I am really going to miss this estate and miss all of you so very much. Anya, you and Amos should take a trip to see us in London very soon. Perhaps before your wedding date."

"I am sure we will be much occupied with planning the wedding to even think about such a long trip. Why June is not too terribly far away, I am sure that we are both set on London for our honeymoon. Please, I pray that you do look forward to our meeting again for that occasion. I assure you that we are both most excited to spend some time with the two of you. In the meantime, we will both write to each other, agreed?"

"Yes, of course, you know I will. You have become like a sister to me, one I never had. I will miss you so dearly," Cateline said with tears in her eyes.

"Oh, cousin, please do not cry. We will still be able to see each other, and we can write often," Anya spoke sympathetically as she hugged her cousin.

After a short while, Joseph returned to the veranda to let them know all their baggage was secured, and the barouche was pulled to the front of the estate. Everyone stood, hugged, and bade their adieus with Aunt Martha wishing them a safe journey on their travels as they walked out on the front lawn where the carriage awaited.

Oscar helped Cateline into the barouche; they waved as Elbert steered the horses down the long road from the estate while Cateline looked back at the family she had grown so close to. Waving one last time, with tears beginning to flow down her cheeks, Oscar feeling her pain, drew her close as he enveloped her in his arms. "Cateline, I do understand that you will miss them, but we shall come to visit, and besides, they spoke of traveling to spend time with us in London. Whatever it may be worth, I have never been so happy. You are the one thing I have been looking for all my life, and this is the beginning of our life together. There is so much for you to see once we arrive in England, and I feel that you will love London, as I do. Furthermore, when we cross to Paris, you will be overcome with adoration, I am sure of it."

"I know you are right, and I am very excited about what lies ahead for us. You know that I love you so dearly and cannot wait to experience all the pleasures of England and France with you by my side."

Arriving at the docks, Oscar helped Elbert carry their trunks and bags to where the Rob Roy was located while a few crew members loaded them onto the steamship.

"Well, I am most assured that it was simply inevitable that I was to acquire two trunks plus an additional carpetbag since the time I came to Ireland," Oscar spoke sarcastically while laughing.

"Yes, but you also acquired one more person to travel with. I am sure you are not displeased."

"Displeased? I would dare to be displeased, my dear—even if there were ten more pieces to carry."

Cateline smiled lovingly while putting her hand on his arm to walk along beside him, thinking to herself, "A good thing indeed that he only brought one bag. I am not at all sure how this was managed, to be quite the dresser as he is, why I believe Oscar loves clothes as much as myself. Besides, I have become so accustomed to the mode of dress from this era, I shall simply have a hard time trying to keep my wardrobe under control."

After saying their goodbyes to Elbert, they boarded the small steamship where an older gentleman welcomed them aboard. Oscar and Cateline, standing on the deck, looked out over the backdrop of Dublin Bay with Bull Island set in the slight distance overshadowing the rather grey contrast of the sun as it whispered through the many clouds that slowly swam across the sky. The radiance of light trailed down upon the meadow of the island, where pampas grass could be seen swaying with the cool of the morning. Geese were in flight while in their natural habitat, bringing the dawn to life with each swoop conquering the terrain. The boundless sea was aroused to the morn, with all its life, as a group of seals clamored close to the shores, frolicking amongst each other, and an occasional clapping or barking in their own intercourse could be heard. The ship progressed through the Dublin Bay past the island, heading out to sea. Looking towards their destination, it was a most stunning morning. The sun gently climbed the stark blue sky as it plummeted through the many shadowy puffs and stripes of clouds mixed with tints of grey, shading the dark still waters with fleeting mists of golden yellows which shone beyond as it strived to breakthrough. Water and more water could be seen to the breadth of the horizon. In the extreme distance, a mirage was foreseen so slight, one-two, perhaps three vessels a drift—ships out at sea with wandering souls in quest of lands, some far and others familiar—souls all in search of a destiny whether known or unknown. Cateline's calling would be a land unfamiliar to her but one that would be shared with her husband—her fate had been one mysterious for many years but had become a reality. How she was beside herself with anticipation of her life to come. Her life desired and dreamt of would shortly belong to her and far too soon be taken away.

In her serenity, gazing at the various landmarks, dreaming of a new life, distracted by the beauty bestowed and sounds heeded, Cateline beheld the Baily Lighthouse. Erected high on the hill of Howth Head, it stood proud, a tower unyielding, imagining its welcome to the rugged and worn from the sea into the harbor of Dublin. Bright shining lights amidst the fog, through the dark hours, dusk, and on into the deliverance of dawn—most welcoming to those returning and those arriving anew. Its siren to be heard, resounding across the waters as it roared and blared with warnings to sailors afar on their merchant ships. Standing proud, a welcome to travelers coming and a farewell gesture for the lonely souls. Revealed in white, a solid beacon to guide—a securing watchtower, a sudden reminder to those lost to the sea—crashed by the rocks, swallowed by the torrent waves. A phare, in her beauty adorning her post—a memory, a valediction to the Emerald Isle, forever may be gone, but to live on in one's heart eternally.

Eventually, the ship was surrounded by the dark, still waters excepting the ruffles of whitecaps made from the vessel, as her course remained steadfast. She was phantomlike through the deepness setting off ripple effects upon the surface of the waters—the sound of surges and breakers—movements of swaying, threshing, and flails—the abruptness of air plunging over their bodies along with the warmth of the sun in its glare.

351

During their progression, time had begun to pass by lazily, with Oscar and Cateline beginning to feel the twinges of hunger. Pulling out the basket, which Bertha had sent packed with all sorts of nourishment for them to enjoy while on their voyage, they sat down next to each other, relishing the cool breeze from the sea and the beauty that flourished before them. Cateline feeling a bit nostalgic, with a few tears tumbling down her cheeks, remarked, "Bertha really outdid herself. She must have spent a lot of time preparing all these delightful treats. Why, she made many of my favorites—cucumber sandwiches, fresh berries with cream, her plum pudding, and the dainty little trifles. Mmm—this is wonderful, Oscar."

"You shall miss them dreadfully?"

"Yes, of course, I will miss all of them."

"Do you regret—," before Oscar could finish his words, Cateline interrupted him.

"No, please do not even think such a thing. I will never regret my decision to marry you nor to follow you wherever you choose to go. Besides, marriage is permanent."

"It is an irrevocable vow, one that I chose to take, Cateline."

Filling themselves with the most pleasing fare, they decided to walk around the ship's deck, enjoying the fabulous seas in all its splendor. With the vessel mounting and subsiding through the plummeting waves, they continued to stroll hand in hand, quietly savoring the moments shared—an unspoken feeling of two souls joined together by a force that could be felt but not seen. The swift drafts that befell them tenderly moved Cateline's hair about her face, which brought feelings of life—sensual passions, so beautifully diverse and flowing vehemently through both, a connection not understood but known. Oscar looked over towards her as his heart melted at the beauty that she owned in her looks and also her demeanor. Cateline could see in his eyes the love which held him so bound to her as she exclaimed, "I love you too, my dear. You have made me so very happy."

"I was merely admiring you and your beauty. I feel as if I am dreaming, and I pray that I should never awaken."

"My love for you, Oscar, will never die. For it will live on to the end of time, I promise," Cateline spoke fervently with a most vivacious smile while she leaned over to kiss him lightly on his cheek.

Many hours had gone by when land could finally be seen. Oscar pointing out Holyhead, proclaimed, "Land, at last—Holyhead, located on Holy Island, which is part of Wales. That is the South Stack Lighthouse on the summit, Cateline," he concluded. The lighthouse, marking its coastlines, standing on the far tip, a warning to ships of the impending dangers with the rocky cliffs protruding into the seas, a gallant fortress—stronghold, illuminating the shores stretching out down the coastal region, as far as the eye could see.

"We must be close to Liverpool?" Cateline inquired.

"Once around this peninsula, we shall be very close to the River Mersey. You may be able to see the Isle of Man off to the left very soon. It is still quite a distance but sometimes can be seen if weather conditions are favorable."

Within a short timeframe, Cateline could see the apparition of land far off in the distance, "Is that the Isle of Man, Oscar?"

"Yes, that is it. Had you ever heard of the island?

"Actually, I have. There was someone I knew—well, someone I knew of that was from there." After speaking those words, Cateline started to reminisce about the band from the 1960s, the Bee Gees, who were from the Isle of Man. She had always loved their music and sang one song, particularly, many times which stirred memories deep within, memories of Oscar, the man she had often dreamt of and carried with her secretly all these years. As she looked out at sea with the island in the far background, the memory of the tune drifted through her thoughts, clouded her mind, when she softly sang the chorus to this favorite of hers, *To Love Somebody,*[1] by the Gibb brothers—

There was silence as they both stood side by side entranced with the beauty of the sea but also with the splendor felt of their life together, joined as one, with a bond that could never be broken when Oscar quoted—

"There be none of beauty's daughters
With a magic like thee;
And like music on the waters
Is thy sweet voice to me:

Cateline spoke as she continued the poem—

353

When, as if its sound were causing
The charmed ocean's pausing,
The waves lie still and gleaming,
And the lulled winds seem dreaming:

Oscar finishing—

And the midnight moon is weaving
Her bright chain o'er the deep;
Whose breast is gently heaving,
As an infant's asleep:
So, the spirit bows before thee,
To listen and adore thee;
With a full but soft emotion,
Like the swell of summer's ocean. [2]

Both smiling at each other, Oscar commented, "Lord Byron, he is one of my favorite poets—yours?"

In response, Cateline declared, "Yes, I enjoyed reading his poems at my uncles. At night before bed, I would read various books. I believe that poem was one of my favorites."

"Like Keats and Shelley, England never appreciates a poet until he is dead." [3]

As they closed in on Liverpool, the ship emerged towards the River Mersey, with land being seen on both sides. "The New York of Europe!" exclaimed Oscar.

"Liverpool?"

"That is what they say."

"I had no idea."

"Liverpool grew very rapidly due to their dock system and the many Irish immigrants who came during the potato famine. Today, it is bustling with much trade from all parts of the world."

Approaching the channel into the harbor, Liverpool slowly appeared into full view while they stood on the deck. Cateline was ecstatically overjoyed to finally be at one of the places of her dreams, and as they drew near to the famous dock system laid out on the River Mersey, her heart fluttered with eagerness. Now her eyes thoroughly captivated at the fascinating sights, far superior and grandeur, more so than she had ever imagined. The city on the hill stood in its majestic splendor, so many steamships—ships with the sounds of their masts flapping in the wind, the full-rigged vessels carrying large cargos. Multiple crafts lined the pier: a British Barque or rather a Baltimore clipper, with its square masts unloading its freight; a Barquentine, which was uncommonly seen around these regions; a Brig spotted, known for its speed during naval battles; and many schooners bringing in their catch for the day. Droves of people were all scurrying about, busily going to and fro in such haste, conducting business, commerce—selling, buying, and trading.

The various docks beginning to fully emerge were laid out one after another. Cateline never imagined so many people in such a vibrant port in Liverpool's central waterfront. Beyond the enormous quay, the sun shone down from the stone-carved buildings that lingered out as far as one could see, a massive industry of ships, sailors, merchants, and everyday folks. A painted view evolved to be captured by the artist, as it stood most radiantly picturesque for all to behold—buoyantly placid it was. Enchanted in its nineteenth-century landscape of a time long ago, it was a time beyond thoughts, perceptions, reflections—the many stone-carved buildings seated along the wharf beyond afforded a panorama of great worth. Off from the harbor, a wide road lined with many a carriage, horses coming and going, and men loading and unloading from the multitude of ports, along with people covering the street, buildings lined up one after another. In the background, such a broad perception of a city with such vitality, emerging into the main thoroughfare—the center of business lined up on the central waterfront. Building after building was visibly stretched out as far as could be seen, with the sun casting an illumination upon the still dark waters of the River Mersey as it descended lower into the sky, making way for a late afternoon of four or so.

Cateline's eyes were shining bright as she took in the architecture of some of the more prominent buildings in view. "Oh, Oscar, Liverpool is so much more than I imagined. This is such a magnificent view from the waters. I cannot wait to explore."

Oscar smiled at her enthusiasm, as he was so very happy with every moment spent beside this woman whom he loved.

The ship pulled up to secure at George's Dock, one of the older docks built in the 1700s, possessing a certain amount of character, as they all did, each was lined up consecutively along the extended stretch of commerce. After such a prolonged journey, here they were, finally, able to step onto England's soil at one of the finest cities outside of London. Standing on the dock at the edge of the harbor, they waited along with many other weary passengers as the ship's hands worked tirelessly, unloading their wares along with the many crates and bags. Oscar lifted the smaller bag while several ship hands assisted passengers with their heavier trunks and baggage. While managing, with assistance, to carry their belongings towards the main boulevard area, known as Strand Street, Oscar was able to secure a clarence, a much larger sort of carriage and more common for transportation with trunks and such. Strand Street diverted in both directions, running along the channel as far as the eye could see. With late evening fast approaching, Cateline's senses were stirred by the sight of much commerce and the sounds of Liverpool's mode of transportation with trams and carriages busily passing along amongst the many patrons, mustering up quite the noise, rattling and clattering throughout the avenues. The chauffeur of the clarence assisted Oscar in loading the trunks, who, in turn, was instructed to take them to the North Western Hotel on Lime Street. Fully loaded, the journey began towards their hotel as the young man steered the team of horses onward into the business district.

Cateline, full of admiration, looked upon the many variations of architecture, but the Renaissance captured her attention at length. They had first traveled down Hanover Street, which must have been one of the main thoroughfares with much history lining both sides. She could not stop inquiring what each grand building was and the history of such. Turning left, Cateline saw that they had reached Lime Street, where the hotel was located. The road was not very long, perhaps two blocks in her estimation, but the hotel was the prominent force that stood out among any building she had yet seen. It was a glorious French Renaissance empire as she would have described it from its beauty and its breadth that spread out at least the length of a block and perhaps more. It denoted a baroque style of European architecture from the seventeenth century, such as that of the Palace of Versailles. Conceivably there was some detail of the Neo-Renaissance oriel style windows that either protruded or were that of Neo-Gothic. The upward towers rose towards the sky on each side of the entrance and once again at each end of the massive structure—standing tall and proud, as any building would have of this magnitude due to the artistic creation of its creator. As Cateline stood looking over the beauty and art of such a fine period, she was in total awe of her surroundings and could have walked around the building for hours observing every intricate detail. The construction was made of stone, which resembled a French château, and the entrance was that of a round arch lined by fluted Doric classical columns, which elaborated the beauty in such a way of ancient Greece and Rome. Cateline spoke in excitement, "This must be very expensive, Oscar."

"I suppose you could say so. All the same, it is our honeymoon, and we can afford it."

Cateline smiled and stepped out of the carriage with Oscar holding her hand to help her down. He then assisted the young man with their trunks and bags and paid him for his services when several hotel porters came out to gather all their belongings. Oscar took Cateline's arm to escort her into the lobby of the grand resort. Completely in reverence, Cateline walked around observing all the intricate details while Oscar took care of checking them into a room. As she had been so intrigued by the building's outer perimeters, she had not been prepared for the artistic detail inside. Cateline began to think about how modern architectural design had lost something from the periods prior, as she had never seen such delight in all her life. She was so thankful for having chosen diverse courses on the historical periods in college because the past had always been something that had intrigued her aspirations. Just as she had always desired living in the nineteenth century, Cateline was also an admirer of the various architectural styles dating back as far as medieval times. It was in these studies that she had learned so much about the different varieties and designs, which had only brought her to a place of desiring more and more to be a part of those eras. Even though she had seen many pictures of the architect, no depiction could describe standing amid the vestibule with all its surroundings while she waited on Oscar to secure their lodgings.

The staircase alone took her breath away, as its layout was such a magnificent force with a great expanse and antique carpeting of superb quality. The intro, grandeur as it was with finely polished wood railings on both sides. The stairs climbed and coiled gracefully as if piano keys were swept away, one by one, in a gentle breeze, being laid daintily step by step, ascending to the heavens, curving as they lifted higher and higher. The rhythm felt as the elevated steps joined harmoniously with the room, then flowing generously from left

357

to right, dividing into two sections at the uppermost portion, winding gallantly to one balcony on each side of the enormous reception area. The terraces surrounded the outer layer of the grand expanse with railing all the way around. There were stately columns spaced along the entirety of the gallery, which protruded to the ceiling, being as it was several stories high. From the entryway, looking up was nothing short of awe-inspiring. The whole lobby was filled with resplendent treasures, as there were paintings by known artists, gold candelabras, and sconces along every wall, along with chandeliers suspending throughout the immense ceiling. With lit candles illuminating vibrantly against the golds and silvers, wealth and splendor were showcased, bringing forth life—glorious energy to each jewel. Illumination brought forth, casting off shadows, reflective through long suave mirrors, trimmed in gold, together with stunningly lit elegant vases. Flashes of silvers were mixed among the tantalizing florals, filled with flowers and greenery which added fragrances—fresh aromas dancing about. To complement the elegance, the finishing touch was the overstuffed sofas and chairs of exquisite taste and quality, which sat in attractive groupings for guests to recline. Being caught in a daze, she finally realized that Oscar had been speaking to her. "I'm sorry, what did you say, dear?"

"I was merely letting you know they have carried our belongings to the room. Shall we go to their dining parlor to eat a bite before retiring for the evening? It is probably much too late to take in any views, and I am sure we both need a good night's sleep. I would think a light meal in their dining parlor should be sufficient, wouldn't you say?"

"Yes, that's fine. I suppose their restaurant should be most pleasant."

"I am aware they do have more than one. But there is a small one around the corner which should suit our taste."

With a most pleasing demeanor, she took his arm as he led her to the dining area. Once again, they stepped into a room that was a replica of the grand entrance. Being seated, Cateline was so busy looking at all the details, lost in thought, where she was not really paying attention to Oscar.

"Cateline, I see you are very distracted, my love," he smiled, enjoying seeing her delight in all the surroundings.

"Yes, it is clearly the most beautiful hotel I have ever seen."

"America, do they not have hotels as such?"

"Yes, there are some glorious hotels, I suppose. I think it is just being in Europe and seeing much of the old historical buildings of such grandeur. I do suppose America will never have the history or roots found in the ancient world. I believe America has what they call a Renaissance Revival architecture, but I do not think it comes close to what is seen in Europe."

"Perhaps, you may be correct, but the North Western Hotel is fairly new, Renaissance architecture, but it was only built about ten years ago."

"Oh, I had no idea, but it is quite lovely."

"All the same, my dear, you have yet to see London or Paris. They are far more impressive than what you perceive here."

"Oh, I am sure. Especially, Paris, no?"

Oscar replied, "Oui, *Paree*—you will fall in love. Liverpool has the stateliest architecture, somewhat similar to London, but London is much larger and more to see."

Before the server came to take their order, Oscar spoke up, "My dear, would you rather we order to be delivered to our room where we can relax?"

"Yes, that sounds fine, my dear. I believe the long journey of seven hours has made for such an exhausting day, and I am quite fatigued, even though the boat ride was much more comfortable than I had anticipated."

Once Oscar had placed an order to be delivered to their room, they ascended the glorious staircase to their elegant accommodations. Upon entering the stylish upscale room, Cateline walked around to examine the beauty of their surroundings, which entailed a small quaint drawing-room equipped with a most radiant fireplace. An s-shaped love seat or rather a tête-à-tête sofa, with matching chairs and a sofa table to complement the grouping adorned the center of the apartment, whereas off to the side sat a charming dining table exquisitely placed near the windows for viewing the landscaped grounds on the backside of the building. Completing the room, a secretaire sat in one corner and opposite a chaise lounge of a delicate nature. To accompany the décor, elaborate paintings of intensely landscaped views embellished the walls, all fashioned for a most stylish and cozy apartment. Off from the dining parlor, the bedchamber was adorned with a most graceful sleigh bed, plush pillows and spreads, a lovely vanity and wardrobe

359

with a long-standing mirror opposite the bed, and a tallboy in one corner, to include a slight dressing area with a water-closet off from that locale.

Cateline, taking off her shoes, laid on the bed, relatively comfortable as it was. For the most part, she was fatigued from the extensive journey, and the bed was quite inviting. Walking over next to where she lay, Oscar sat down beside her. "I fear, if we both lie down, we shall fall asleep."

"I suppose the concierge would awaken us with his knock, would he not?"

"You are probably correct," he replied, as he stood up to disrobe down to merely his shirt and his underpants, or rather drawers as they were called.

"Oh, Oscar, I am much too weary to even think about removing my clothes."

Oscar, lying next to Cateline, gently positioned his arm around her, where he pulled her closer to him. Snuggling up to him, Cateline gently swept his hair away from his face while looking intimately into his eyes. He spoke gently, "I knew this was going to be a long venture. I do believe I could lay here and not move the rest of the night, myself."

"Mmm—yes, just hold me close. I could so fall asleep lying next to you like this. We do need sleep, after all, my dear."

In the quietude of the evening, with nothing further said, they both drifted off to sleep until Oscar was awakened by a knock on the door. As he sat up and looked at his surroundings, he finally remembered they were at the hotel about the time another knock came. He arose and put on his robe while walking over to open the door. The concierge, having arrived with their dinner, was ushered into the room. Following Oscar, the young man walked into the dining area and sat the food on the table; turning to leave, Oscar handed him some coins for a tip.

As dusk had filled the sky, Oscar rekindling the fire in the hearth for warmth, lit a few more lamps to brighten the rooms, and then walked into the bedroom to awaken Cateline. Sitting down next to her, he noticed she had not flinched since lying down. Knowing she must really be exhausted from the prolonged journey, Oscar decided to set out all the various courses before awakening her—roast duck with cranberry, candied yams, fresh corn, rhubarb pie, and pumpkin fritters. All was complemented with a glass of Bordeaux red wine imported from France for his bride and champagne for himself. Once everything was ready, Oscar leaned over and planted kisses on her neck ever so gently again and again until she began to stir. Cateline, turning around, gazed into his eyes, "I'm sorry, I assume that I have been sleeping since we arrived. Were you able to sleep?"

"I was asleep with you until they brought up our dinner. I have everything spread out on the table. The food looks delicious. Come, we shall eat and have some wine, then we can go back to bed and sleep late tomorrow."

"Yes, that sounds wonderful. Will we have time to see Liverpool tomorrow?"

"I promise we will not leave Liverpool until we have rested and enjoyed our stay."

"You are so sweet. I must be the luckiest girl in the world to have met you."

Pleased, he pulled her up and stated, "My beautiful princess, let us get some food in you."

They sat enjoying the meal together and the bottle of wine and champagne, which had been provided by the concierge. "Oscar, I know you like champagne more so than wine, but I also like champagne. Please, you do not need to order both. I am more than happy to have champagne with you."

Oscar smiled as he spoke, "I like wine, but I love 1874 Perrier Jouët Champagne, that is iced-Perrier Jouët, a most favorite drink of mine—pink, made to order, please taste to see if you like."

Cateline, taking a sip, inquired, "Yes, it does have a pleasant taste, rather refreshing and sweet, a bit fruity, I believe. What did you have added?"

"Strawberries, it makes the color and adds to the flavor, a small amount of sugar and cognac, poured over ice—presto—a Wildean cocktail."

She laughed, "You are too funny. But, yes, I seem to love everything, Wildean."

Their meal soon came to an end and being somewhat wearied, they retreated to the quaint parlor to relax, as they were in dire need of rest. Oscar prepared two glasses of champagne, Wildean-style, before pulling out the bottle of mead for them to finish off. "You do realize that there is a full moon tonight?"

"Ah, yes, I see there is, which means that we do not have to continue drinking the mead, yes?"

"That is correct. We can finish it off tonight or take it with us, but we do not have to remember any further."

Cheerfully, she concurred, "I must admit, I am relieved that we no longer have to continue that ritual. I would hate to have had a night where we forgot."

"Agreed, my dear," Oscar replied, with a slight grin, "not to say that there is any truth to these traditions or should I say superstitions."

"You are quite right, but they did make for a most outstanding wedding."

"Yes, indeed, they did."

After finishing their champagne, they drank the remainder of the mead while watching from their windows the various people walking about on the marvelously lighted landscaped grounds.

CHAPTER
24

Oscar and Cateline, having retired fairly early, were both unable to sleep late. "Where have you been, my darling, since last night? I have missed you something dreadfully while in slumber."

"Mmm—and I have missed you too, Oscar."

"As it now is much too early, it would be ludicrous to leave the confines of such a warm bed. I should object very strongly if we were not to remain lying next to each other until noon; it is quite alright if we do."

Cateline responded with an agreeable smile, "It looks to be such a beautiful day, Oscar. And yes, I would love to spend the entirety of it in bed with you. But—"

Oscar interrupting her, "No, my dear—please, do not use that horrific word—but!"

Bluntly, she replied, "Oscar, I was going to say that I do believe I could sacrifice staying the whole day in bed with you to visit the shops instead and take a wonderful stroll on the beach. We can always sleep late another day—please, can we get ready?"

With a deep sigh, he spoke candidly, "It makes me shudder to share you with the world, my dear. Needless to say, I am awfully obliged to do so if it satisfies the delicate filaments of your nature." Following his verbiage, he leaned over to kiss her intimately once more before he finished with one last query, "Are you most certain you would not rather remain in bed?"

"Mmm, you have almost persuaded me, but—no!"

They both arose and dressed for the day. Cateline had decided to wear something relatively modest since they would be promenading on the beach. Yet, now that she was married, her hair would need to be fixed up properly. Oscar, finishing first, went to the lobby to acquire a newspaper. Returning to the room, he inquired, "You are almost ready, my dear?"

"Yes, I believe I am. Do you think I am dressed well enough, Oscar? I know we will be going down to the beach; I thought this would do?"

"You have never seemed more exquisite to me than right now, Cateline," he replied with a thoughtful smile. Continuing his discourse, "For you are divine beyond all living things, my dear."

"Oscar, please—be serious!"

"I should be miserable if I thought I should ever be more serious than I am at the present moment, my dear. Let us go!"[1]

In a cheery manner, she picked up her bag and joined him at the door as he asked, "Shall we feast in the hotel dining parlor? I do hear they have a most delightful English breakfast."

"Yes, that is fine with me, Oscar."

Oscar and Cateline enjoyed breakfast in the hotel while the concierge arranged for a hansom cabriolet to convey them to Crosby Beach. Upon leaving the hotel, they enjoyed the short ride in the cab, where they were soon walking down to the sandy shores. By far, Crosby was not as attractive as some of the coastlines in Ireland or even America, but it was secluded and somewhat peaceful. As with all beaches, there was the charm of the waves hovering over the sand, the feel of the gentle breeze, the delight of the sun with its fervor that floods one's soul, and the sense of a connection to earth—or rather, the correlation to God. For one could feel the strength of nature, the force of waters, and the abruptness of the wind that envelopes one when standing in the vastness of all the miraculous wonders visible with the senses.

Strolling along the sandy shores, they soon decided to sit and enjoy the views, the perception of the moment, the humid air from the sun, and the sounds of the waves rolling and roaring onto the beach. Closely sitting next to one another, the breeze from the sea flourished over them while the sun shone down, warming their bodies. In complete solitude, Cateline took off her shoes to feel the sand on her feet and between her toes, a most pleasant sensation. Leaning back to enjoy the view, Oscar was in his own zone while quietly looking out at sea. Cateline, also in her own world, began to reminisce about the Beatles who had arrived in America from Liverpool. She thought about how famous they had become in the 1960s—tragedy much too early for John. Cateline had grown up listening to their music in her father's Boston pub, with many artists coming to play their instruments, bands—all unknown, striving to be discovered. The pub had several memorable nights to honor the music born out of the 50s and 60s. Yes, there were many of those occasions, she pondered silently, "How very strange to be on this beach, the same beach they must have spent time walking, the same seaside town, where they originated in their time. As it was the nineteenth century, they had yet to be born," she continued in her thoughts. "Hmm—those four men would eventually be born in her time and then evolve to be so very well-known. Yes, so famous they were," Cateline remained in deep thought. A particular song spoke to her heart and rose within her soul as she stood and wandered towards the waves with her back to Oscar. Overcome with the moment of what it felt like to be standing on the beach at Liverpool and how it had played such a significant part of history, Cateline bent over and picked up a handful of sand. Once again, standing looking out at sea, she softly sang, *The Long and Winding Road,*[2] an old song sung by the Beatles from her era. Yes, Liverpool had brought such memories. There were many songs played by the Beatles in her father's pub over the years. So very reminiscent of being in Liverpool, the place where the Beatles were from. Even so, no one knew that one day, this group of young men would rise up to be one of the greatest well-known bands of Cateline's era. Her notion was that perhaps, she was standing on the very beach where Paul, John, George, and Ringo would one day stand. Opening her hand, Cateline watched every grain of sand fall softly and slowly to the shore, each tiny granule disappearing amongst all the other small fragments of the same, as her voice remained singing those words by the Beatles from long ago.

Cateline continued with the melody, singing along. She turned and sauntered back towards Oscar, looking in his eyes as he quietly attended to every word sung and watched her every move. She reached down and took his hand, looking deep into his eyes, feeling in that moment—love that she had never experienced in her life. As Cateline sustained with the lyrics, tears filled her eyes while she let go of Oscar's hand to turn towards the sea. Walking a few steps forward, she stopped to lift her hands, facing unto the heavens to worship her God. Cateline knew that it was through Him only that her life had evolved and would prolong to advance regardless of what road lay ahead. She turned once again, with tears in her eyes as her voice became softer with each chorus. Cateline stood with the waters behind and the city in her gaze. Slowly, she looked down upon Oscar, deep into the eyes of this man whom she so loved, finishing the song very quietly as there were times her eyes were shut, feeling the words deep within her heart—her soul, that could not be expressed. Concluding, Cateline walked again down to the shores. Oscar rising, joined to where she stood as he took her hand and brought it to his lips, "That was touching, Cateline. It has filled you with sorrow, for a mist of tears has formed in your eyes, my dear."

She responded with a smile, "Yes, the song has such deep meaning to me. I only had tears because of how much I love you, Oscar."

"It seems strange, yet, when I look upon you, it is as if I see you not with the eyes of the body but with the eyes of the soul. Having been consumed with your outward beauty, suddenly I find myself drawn to your beauty from within your soul, the essence of your being. Beauty is a form of genius; it is higher than genius, as it needs no explanation.[3] For it has its divine right of sovereignty, my dear. You are perfectly wonderful. I shall love you through all time, Cateline. Please say that you shall never leave me."

"I know you love me, and you know I love you just as deeply. You will always be with me, always," she replied.

Oscar took her into his arms and gently kissed her before he replied with an affable chuckle, "Always! I used to express that was such a dreadful word. It made me shudder to hear it,[4] needless to say, that was before I met you, my dear."

They stood holding each other, enjoying the beauty of the sea, when Oscar changed the subject, "Cateline, there is a matter we must address."

"You sound rather serious, Oscar."

"It is something I have thought of many times since we met, my dear. I dare say with your talent in singing and your good looks, you are simply a born artist, far too gifted not to be noticed. It would be utterly monstrous not to consider the theatre?"

She laughed faintly, stating honestly, "Oscar, really—I have no desire to become an actress. My life is by your side. Please, do not even mention such a thing. Besides, truthfully, you would not desire that I become involved in such; there would be little time for you."

"On the contrary, I insist, for I would not want you to pass up an opportunity. I know women are wonderfully practical, such as they are, yet, you have all the delicate grace and personality to flourish, my dear. Furthermore, one day, I may have a part in one of my plays that would suit you."

With a slight smirk, Cateline replied, "If—I am just saying, if there is a part that you write for me, I may consider it the one time. Otherwise, Oscar, I truly am not interested in fame and fortune. Please, it means a lot to me that we are in agreement on this matter."

After taking into account her thoughts, he finally replied, "Agreed! Nonetheless, if you were to change your mind, I do have many acquaintances in London and Paris, a good many lady friends who are actresses where I could arrange an interview. I am sure that you have heard of most of them, even in America—Sarah Bernhardt, Ellen Terry, and Helena Modjeska."

"Yes, I have. But I do not believe acting is something I care to pursue, Oscar."

"Very well."

As they walked down the beach holding hands, Cateline knew there was something she desperately needed to discuss with him. Being so very close to London, she knew it was only a matter of time until she met friends of his. Loving Oscar as she did, there was no way that Cateline wanted this marriage to hinder publicity that could work against him in America, which would undoubtedly change the course of time. She also knew that one of the pictures in the book from the library supposedly was taken in Liverpool or perhaps even Bath. If that were correct, it might be sooner rather than later before they would come face to face with acquaintances of his that would know her as his wife. "This would not be a good idea," Cateline thought silently while anticipating the possible outcome of others becoming aware that Oscar was married. "Yes," she pondered again, "this needs to be discussed now before it is too late." With deep concern in her voice, Cateline spoke openly, "Oscar, there is something else that I believe we should discuss."

"Now, it is you who sounds so very serious."

"I believe this to be very serious."

"Proceed, what is distressing you so?"

"I have been thinking about this even before our wedding. And now, well, I believe it is of utmost importance."

"Please, carry on—"

"It concerns your image before leaving for America. I love you more than anything—but, when I told James that I did not want our announcement in the papers, there was more to it than that."

"I am not sure I quite understand."

367

"Please, hear me out, and we can then discuss this. Your tour to America, the publicity leading up to this is crucial, as I have heard you state—this was the reason that you needed to hurry back to London. Is that not, correct?"

"Your assumption would be most accurate. Appearances, interviews, and such are an important element in gaining adequate exposure—hype up the articles, as one would say, whether good or bad. There is only one thing in the world worse than being talked about, and that is not being talked about."[5]

"Yes, I am most aware of how it works. And well, I feel being married will hurt your popularity; it will taint your image, so to speak, especially among the young ladies. I do know that this tour is vital to your success and would not want anything to damage your character."

Oscar, laughing profusely, responded, "I entreat you; what do you want me to say? This has quite strangely stirred me, Cateline. Would you desire that our marriage be dissolved?"

"Of course not, don't be ridiculous."

"I dare say that your points are a bit overdue, wouldn't you agree?"

"I have another plan that should suffice until after your tour."

"Proceed—"

"I feel that we should keep our marriage a secret for now."

"You would care for such an arrangement, my dear? For over a year?"

"Well, if need be, yes."

"Are you serious? And, we just live together?"

"Well, truthfully, we wouldn't be living together. We both know we are married."

"My dear, your reputation would be spoken of most unpleasantly; would that not be offensive to you? I dare say, others can be cruelly unkind."

"Oscar, I love you, and it is really no one else's concern what we do behind closed doors. We both know that we are truly married."

"I believe we had this very conversation before we were married, you coming to London with me. At that time, you refused because of your reputation being damaged, and now, it no longer bothers you?"

"Yes, I suppose it does bother me to a degree; yet—"

Before Cateline could finish her sentence, Oscar interrupted her abruptly, "I must speak, my dear! This is simply foolish, and I object to this absurd silliness. We are married, and we must always remain so!"

"Oscar, I have been in deep thought about it since our wedding. You mean more to me than what others choose to believe, and besides, eventually, the whole truth will come out, and then my reputation will be cleared."

"I wonder, is that really so? It would pain me something fierce to hear of unjust gossip behind your back."

"I assumed you would say as much, but there is still another way. When we get to London, we will both claim to only be friends. We met in Ireland; being an American, I planned to head to London and Paris, and you offered to be my guide. We became very close, and you suggested that I stay with you and Frank. No one will even know the difference except, perhaps, Frank. He will know that we sleep in the same bedroom, but you did say that you were very close to Frank, yes?"

"Frank and I are close, and he would not say anything, even if we told him the truth. This is beside the point, Cateline. I am torn between approving this madness or disapproving."

"Oscar, it is possible to get away with this, at least until you have gone to America and have gained the publicity needed."

"I plan to take you with me to America, Cateline. How on earth would that be explained?"

"That is easy; I purchase my own ticket to be on the same ship with you. When we arrive in America, I can remain with friends and family while you tour. In the event you truly miss me, I will take a train to where you are—no one will ever know," Cateline concluded. "Ah, yes, he is going to address the rings," she thought to herself, noticing him looking down at his band. With her thoughts continuing, "Thankfully, I have already contemplated what to do and have the perfect solution to alleviate any concerns."

"We merely stop wearing our rings? Or, had you not considered this small detail?"

"As a matter of fact, I knew you were about to ask, and of course, I have thought about how to handle this minor detail, as you say. We could purchase you a chain to go around your neck. If you want to wear your ring, you can wear it on the chain hidden under your shirt. Myself, I can simply put my ring on my right hand turned the other way—that just means a gift from a friend, correct?"

369

"Yes! I have to say, this is still an absurd stance to take towards our marriage. It is entirely foolish, and I must be insane to oblige you. I am much concerned with how this would affect your reputation. I will agree on one condition—if at any point there is any conflict or hardship on your character or reproach, I shall declare that you are my wife and have been all along."

There was a brief pause while Cateline was considering his words before she spoke, "Yes, I agree."

The walk continued down the beach with Oscar and Cateline, both being very quiet. The conversation had been strained and not wholeheartedly agreed upon, but the subject was left alone where it stood on the terms set down.

Time passed rather swiftly, with Oscar securing a hansom cab to be chauffeured back to the shopping district where they could saunter through the quaintness of the seaside town. They walked along admiring many items, purchasing a few 'must-haves,' which included a chain for Oscar's ring. They browsed in and out of shops, admiring many relics, apparel, and trinkets, a day quite enjoyable to Cateline. At one point, Oscar encouraged her to purchase a new dress in which she declined in order to wait on doing so in Bath. During their stroll, Cateline observed that Liverpool was a most fascinating town with much industry. It was filled with busy streets and many patrons coming and going, stores bursting with luxurious indulgences, charming cafes scattered about the somewhat sociable town, and enticing pubs catering to the many tourists along with locals. They stopped in at one of the restaurants and decided to enjoy lunch while observing the activity of the seaside settlement.

Finishing up at the quaint cafe, they persisted in wandering along, delighting in each other's company, while Oscar shared the history of Liverpool. With evening finally approaching, they walked back to their hotel to dress for dinner and a night out on the town. "I have to say, Oscar, I am so very excited to be going to the Grove House; you have been there many times?"

"There were a few occasions I came with acquaintances from my Oxford days. The Grove House has been a haunt for many of the lads. I must say, you shall have the fortuity to perform on stage."

"Perform—as in sing? Oh no, Oscar, why would I do that?"

"My dear, we both know how very endowed you are. I have agreed, for the time being, you have no desire for the theatre. But please, you must recognize, all delightful things are to be adored. The Grove House allows those who are brilliant to perform. It would be horribly unjust of you to completely conceal your gifts when the opportunity stands before you. Besides, you would sing to please me just this one night. You don't really mind, do you?"

"Well, yes, I will. If that is what you desire."

Pleased, Oscar maintained, "Your dress, my dear, is stunning. Do you plan to wear your hair up?"

"Since we did acquire the chain for your ring, I thought I could wear my hair down. You do like it that way, don't you?"

"I adore your long beautiful locks, but I find this to be an excuse for you to wear your hair down, as you say. Married women would never do such in public. Of course, who would object, seeing that you seem to be single, Cateline? I would much prefer you not give the impression that you are available."

Cateline, walking over to him, put her arms around his neck, beaming while looking up into his eyes, "Oscar, you are not jealous? You do know that I only have eyes for you?"

Responding to her advances, Oscar kissed her intimately before he paused to speak, "I should be jealous," he determined. As he brushed his lips lightly over hers, he resolved, "Kissing you has narrowed my life to one perfect point of rose-colored joy.[6] I passionately adore you, Mrs. Wilde. If you desire to wear your hair down, I should like that awfully much. You know that I am a supporter of women's rights, and part of those rights are the rules that govern women on their manner of dress and hair, of which I find yours thoroughly fascinating. I shall relish seeing other men desiring that which is mine."

Upon leaving their room, they decided to experience a dinner in one of the hotel's fine dining rooms. After enjoying a bottle of Perrier Jouët with their meal, Oscar had the hotel acquire a hansom cab to chauffeur them to Penny Lane while he hurriedly ran back to their room, leaving her in the lobby. Heading back down with her guitar in hand, Cateline questioned, "You went back to get my guitar?"

"Why do you ask? You have already agreed, have you not?"

"Oh Oscar," smiling, she did not know what to say, "I suppose it must happen."

"Yes, it must."

371

The cab was waiting when they walked outside. "Good evening, please carry us to the Grove House on Penny Lane."

"Yes, sir."

Arriving at the famous pub, Cateline had known that the Grove House, later called The Dovey, was where the Beatles had performed before they became famous. As they walked inside, Cateline glanced around to where the stage was located while thinking to herself, "The Beatles actually sang on this very stage." Walking towards a table, Oscar ran into a few of his friends from Oxford, who invited them to join their party. Cateline immediately had recognized all three, but then she had suspected that the photo from Liverpool was taken at this pub. One of the young men spoke, "Oscar, let me introduce you to my friend Benjamin," looking over at Benjamin, the man continued, "Ben, you've heard us speak of Hosky—the demy who hailed from Trinity in Dublin before Oxford and received medals and things. Hosky is a most interesting chap; you will enjoy hearing his discourse." All of the men joined in with laughter and greetings, shaking hands before Oscar turned to Cateline, "Gentlemen, I am honored to introduce Cateline, a friend of mine from America. I should say, a very virtuoso friend. Cateline has a dazzling voice, and she is most proficient on the piano and guitar."

"I see you have come prepared," the young man acknowledged as he nodded towards the guitar.

"Indeed!" Oscar acknowledged, continuing, "However, it may take a few drinks for her to acquire the courage to stand before the many gentlemen here this evening. Cateline, these are two very good chums of mine from Oxford—Reginald and William. Benjamin, did you attend Magdalen?"

"I am currently at Magdalen, Oscar; I was just beginning, I believe, when you were a senior. I knew who you were but had not been introduced."

As they ordered a round of drinks—absinthe, the attention soon fell to Cateline with each of the young men desiring to know more about her. The server returned with their drinks while Cateline took a sip, exclaiming, "Oscar, what is this? It is quite potent."

"Powerful, Cateline! You are indulging in the drink of London and Paree—there have been many late hours where we have all spent the night with absinthe—la fée verte," his friends began to laugh.

"Yes, Hosky, I remember many nights trying to get you home," Reginald laughed, looking over towards Oscar.

"Ah, *Kitten—the green fairy,*" Oscar speaking in his mysterious voice, with a slight laugh, continued, "but my love for absinthe was to be more improved, do you not concur?"

"I am in accord that your love affair with absinthe went far too long into the night, *Hosky*—right, *Bouncer?*" Reginald inquired of his friend.

"Right you are! Remember the night where you were carrying on a conversation with her," looking over at Cateline, William corrected, "her—referring to absinthe, *Hosky?*"

"Yes, I do. After the first glass of absinthe, you see things as you wish they were. After the second, you see them as they are not. After many, you see things as they really are, and that is the most horrible thing in the world. Like the time the waiter came in to water the sawdust when the most wonderful flowers—tulips, lilies, and roses, sprang up and made a garden in the café. I inquired, *'Don't you see them?'* to the man, but he responded, *'Mais non, monsieur, il n'y a rien.'*⁵ Nonetheless, I will have you know, all the greats were inspired by absinthe, and they still are to this day—why she brings out a part hidden deep that dances into the night and into the early mornings," Oscar finished, as he was laughing along with all his friends.

"Yes, Guy de Maupassant—Van Gogh—" William agreed with a jubilant smile.

"Oh, do not stop," Oscar declared, "Lord Byron, Edgar Allan Poe—."

"Do not forget Paul Verlaine—," Reginald added.

"Arthur Rimbaud," William noted.

They all laughed with each new addition; Benjamin inquired, "What was his name; he was a poet from Paris, Charles—with the decadent movement—."

"Charles Pierre Baudelaire, mon ami," Oscar added.

"And—Edouard Manet," Benjamin shared laughing very hard, "remember, he is the French painter who created his masterpiece entitled, *The Absinthe Drinker.*"

"Ah, such recollections! That is most memorable, the rag-picker, another notable painting by the impressionist who frequented the Louvre," Oscar added with laughter and his friends joining hysterically. Continuing, he recounted, "You musn't forget the man whose poem immortalized his fondness of absinthe."

373

"Yes, the poem, *Lendemain*, Charles Cros," William stated emphatically.

Cateline, listening to all their dialect in regards to not only this era but those long gone, also remembered the stories of Picasso and his adventures in the midst of absinthe. However, Picasso was actually born in 1881 and was not known at this time. Lost in her thoughts of the history for this period, hearing her name repeated, she once again listened to their prolific accounts. "Cateline, if you drink enough of absinthe—well, you will understand why it is so loved by the creative class. It is rather amazing. Please, you must have at least one."

"I am actually not sure that I want to partake in what you have described, and these names," gazing into Oscar's eyes, "Hosky?" Cateline responded.

The boys all laughing, Oscar replied, "Our Oxford days, Cateline," glancing over at his pals, he inquired, "Have either of you seen *Dunsky* lately?"

"It has been a while. I do believe I heard he was married," William commented.

"Married! Oscar, I remember your philosophy on marriage," Reginald noted as he continued, "what was that you used to say? Oh, I believe I remember, marriage was a vulgar recourse in striving to find simple pleasures only to awaken the following day to realize your life was quite finished."

While all the men were in an uproar, Reginald noticed that Cateline did not seem to find the remark so amusing, where he elaborated, "Cateline, please do not take this personal. When men get together and drink, our conversations are not always acceptable to a lady."

"Oh," Cateline replied, "I have been around men before to hear how they carry on in regards to women. So, I am not at all offended. But I am quite curious to hear from Oscar more about his concepts on marriage. I do find all this most enjoyable."

All parties looked to Oscar, awaiting his reply. Then, knowing that he must turn the conversation around, he proceeded to find a way to make amends for what had thus far been said. "In my defense, I must come clean. What I felt during my Oxford days, I have matured since that time. Of course, I am not married, but I do look forward to one day being married. Even so, with that said, I will not settle for just any woman. She must have the personality that fascinates me where the world would mean nothing compared to her."

With those words spoken, Reginald replied, "I never thought I would hear you say that, Oscar. And I suppose with those words, you shall never marry. There are no women who can fascinate a man to that extent."

Discussions continued with stories told of many adventures during their Magdalen College, Oxford days—much laughing and carrying on. Cateline was thoroughly enjoying hearing all the tales. On occasions, she would smile earnestly at Oscar, seeing that he was so much in his element with his friends, conversing of their big senior days as the big men on campus.

After a few drinks, Cateline proclaimed quietly, "Oscar, I better slow down; this is very strong."

He leaned over and whispered, "You know that I will take care of you."

"Well, I hope you would, but I'm not so sure that I want to be in that position."

Three drinks later—drinks of absinthe, the dialogue went back to Cateline singing on stage with Oscar sharing with his friends her distinguished talent. Cateline, by this time, was feeling the effect of the alcohol along with Oscar and his friends, where the stories gained much more clarity along with lots of laughing and giggling on her part. Having such a grand time, they all encouraged her to get up on the stage—to which she finally agreed. Oscar and his friends all accompanied her to the platform, remaining to have a good view. Excited to be on the same stage where the Beatles would one day perform, Cateline resolved to sing one of their songs. In the spirit of absinthe, totally relaxed, being confident in her performing in front of a room of almost entirely men, Cateline selected the song she would sing. Although, instead of playing her guitar, she chose to play the piano. Walking over to the side of the stage, Cateline sat down and commenced to play while singing—*Imagine*⁹—

With her voice softly singing the words, the love affair with absinthe exposed her skills on the piano and that of her impressive vocals, less reserved due to the alcohol. Her style and essence flourished through the melody, lost in oblivion, heedless of those present—those that gazed on. Cateline was lost in this world, a world desired but unknown, a world of the gifted, the creative class of those days, the elite—superb artists, playwrights, and poets. Countless had walked these paths, paths where feet trod on the same dirt, sand, slate, rock—crossed the waters of the seas and rivers, lived and visited in these seashore towns, cities. They were the painters of masterpieces, the playwrights of eminent plays, poets of poems, sonnets, a verse in prose—the actors and actresses that began on stage—the singer and songwriter—novelists of the classics. The greats of their days were surrounded in this timeframe, this period—experiencing and contributing to these men and women who walked these lands—fighting for freedoms, fighting for rights, and creating beauty in life while living, loving, and dying.

Performing from her inner being, feeling the music while playing the piano, the pub became most quiet while all listened to the sound of her voice—the style of her song. While Cateline played from her heart within, mirroring her own era—the era in which she came, she was quite different they knew, but they knew not why. Talent never before had they seen, a gift that did not belong to them, yet moved them. The place was filled with many a young man and those of age, as well. They began to stir, coming towards the stage, all standing in awe, watching this young woman, eyes fixated on her presence. Oscar, alongside his friends, was mesmerized by her charm and her beauty. Cateline dazzled in her own world with her eyes closed, felt so very much alive. Those words in the Beatles' song, she could feel more than ever their meaning at that moment—touched by the significance of her being at that place in that timeframe. Oscar looking around could see there wasn't an eye in the place that had not stopped and stood paralyzed by her brilliance. He knew now more than at any time, just how genuinely accomplished she was. Cateline captivated her audience, all standing in allegiance, tuned into her every word and every move. They were absorbed by her essence, lost in her thoughts, entranced in the sound of her voice—one of angels and gracefulness, one of self-possession, appeal, charisma, magnetism, attractiveness. She was one who conquered desires, hunger, yearnings, longings, hypnotized by all that was within her. She mastered what most artists in those days could not.

In the midst of her song, a couple of young men walked up on stage—one with his guitar, the other walking towards Cateline, who sat down at the piano beside her. Picking up the key in which she played, they performed in tune with the melody. Singing the last reprise, Cateline turned and smiled at the two young men who had joined, and upon standing to walk towards the edge of the stage, all those in the audience applauded, many whistled, and then the shouts erupted, "ENCORE—ENCORE!" Cateline smiled and looked over to Oscar while he shouted, "Yes—Cateline, yes—sing again!" Oscar dazed at how all seemed to love her—it was Cateline's moment, she knew, and oh, how Oscar loved watching her.

Cateline walked back over to the other young men, giving them the key to play, along with a few strums on her guitar, sharing the tune enough where they were all in sync. Strolling over to the center of the stage, Cateline looked back at the other musicians to nod that she was ready and started to strum her guitar while singing *Rhiannon,*[10] by artist *Fleetwood Mac*—

Cateline knew this song of the 1970s was considered rock for those days and quite different from anything they had heard. Yet, in her reasoning of choice for this song, she was without a doubt swayed by the influence of absinthe—the drug of choice for that period. Absinth, being the drug romanced among the social class and the elite, was consumed by the poet, playwright, and other artists in all aspects. This infatuation had continued from the Romanticism on into the Aestheticism movements for those who desired to be the Shakespeares of their day, the Raphaels, the Picassos, the Jacques-Louis Davids, the Johann Sebastian Bachs, the Frédéric Chopins, the Christopher Marlowes, the Johann Wolfgang von Goethes, the Charles-Valentin Alkans, and the Alexander Pushkins. In her romance with absinthe, it was Cateline's moment—her moment to be part of history, part of that age—to enlighten those of great talent, to give way to those emotions that she had carried most of her life. This was her—who she was inside, one who longed for this time, longed to make a memory and to give her dream to those who dared to go forth believing—always believing there are moments in time that are meant to be, moments shared for reasons unknown, moments to reflect on one's life and to fly into the bliss, if only for that season. There would be no regrets, none.

Yes, Cateline was alive in the absinthe. Yet, she would not regret the memory of the night in a world, another world—one of absinthe, one of romance, the aesthetics, in a world only known to her by books until now. This was a brief encounter through time— into an epoch. By far, this was the most celebrated era of the artists. It was a time dreamed of but never before experienced, a time where she felt alive—her time, the time she was born to encounter, indulge,

377

and exploit every sense, every feeling, every part of who she was on the inside, the creativeness. Awakened, yes, she was aroused to the period she was meant to be, even for that brief moment. Indeed, Cateline was stimulated, inspired by absinthe, and stirred by her emotions, ingenuity, and artistic awareness that she had only once dreamt but now encountered. As she sang the song, all eyes were fixated on her every move while they all listened to the words—words that painted a different story of women from what they knew for their era. At one point, after she could tell they had the rhythm and tune perfected on the other instruments, Cateline lay her guitar down to focus just on singing while the two young men finished harmonizing the melody.

At the end of the song, she spoke briefly of the woman that they may have never encountered—the woman from her time, such as the song proclaimed, one free, not ruled by life, carefree, alive—alive in this one life given. Finally, Cateline closed by saying, "Perhaps, this speaks of the American woman, or so they may say." Excusing herself, she agreed to sing a few more songs before the end of the night.

Cateline sat back down with Oscar and his friends as they had another round of drinks, "Oscar, this must be my last one; I am already having a hard time walking straight," she urged with a laugh.

"As you wish," he whispered softly, "we are supposed to merely be friends, remember?"

"Well—as a friend, I am asking you to not let me have any more."

With a sarcastic smile, he responded, "Agreed!"

Other musicians provided a steady flow of entertainment, and one by one, Oscar's friends escorted Cateline to the dance floor. The night had continued with every one of his friends arguing over whose turn it was to dance with her, along with many other admirers not of their circle trying to step in, as well. Oscar, becoming frustrated with all the attention his friends were giving Cateline, spoke in a ridiculous manner, "I wish you chaps would not squabble over whose turn it is to dance with Cateline."

Even feeling the effects of absinthe, Cateline knew Oscar was somewhat jealous. Of course, he did have reason to be since every man in the Grove House believed her to be available. Not to mention, it was evident she was the life of the whole place. Cateline was so free and laidback, after more than a few drinks, she possessed a certain charm that was very rare in young ladies, especially those in England. Perhaps this was because she was raised in America, an American girl, but more so due to her living in an advanced era. All Oscar knew was that she possessed something entirely different, even though he was unsure what that element was. How he loved watching her come alive—seeing her dance, laugh, giggle, and smile—one could only get lost in those moments; no wonder every eye was captivated by her every move and the sound of her most sensual voice. Yes, she loved the attention, and Oscar observed that her most unique personality clearly knew how to flirt enough to capture the devotion. Eventually, it never seemed to fail as Cateline often glanced his way with a most alluring smile. A silent expression but one which told Oscar she loved only him. It would have been very easy for jealousy to seep in, as there was not one man there who wouldn't have given just about anything to have Cateline's consideration. Yet, Oscar knew that this most charming and beautiful lady loved him deeply. Knowing this, he found himself continually gazing upon his wife, watching her with admiration as she danced brilliantly. She was full of life, full of such joy and happiness in her every move, entertaining, talking, carrying on with all his friends who adored her at this point. Nonetheless, Cateline did not realize that they all thought it a possibility to gain her affection, unknowing that she was married, married to him. Without a doubt, she was married to Oscar—it was this which bothered him. Yes, she did belong to him, yet no one had a clue.

As the night carried on, the moment finally happened—a moment that she had known when they had first sat down at their table, but she had soon forgotten. Here they were—Oscar, Cateline, and his three friends gathered together at this table when a man came to take a picture of their group. Cateline had noticed the background where they sat and knew this was the place of that picture in the book she had found. From the time she met his three friends, she knew they were the ones in that photo—the first picture she had come across in the library that day.

Before long, Cateline was persuaded into singing one more song. In between her laughs from the experience of absinthe, she stated, "I don't know—I am not sure that I can stand up to sing."

"We will carry you up there and carry you back down," William responded.

All laughing, Cateline spoke again, "No, I am not going to be carried. But, yes, someone will need to help me get up there and just promise to catch me if I fall."

They all walked back to the stage, as those playing cleared off and the two musicians that had performed with her prior approached once again. She walked over to show them briefly the key and tune of the song. Cateline then turned and walked to the center of the stage to sing, *We Belong Together,*[11] by artists *Ritchie Valens*—

Cateline sang while holding those listening, captive to her voice and choice of song, where all who entered the pub that night became part of her, part of her era. Unknowingly, they entered into her world. Many who may have stopped in for a quick drink would never forget this night. Those who perhaps came to hear a few performers, they would live on in her music—the music of her timeframe, connected through time, even if for a short while. They desired more—more of her talent, more of what she possessed—in song, tunes which had never been played nor heard, melodies which had never been experienced nor felt. As the song came to an end, the shouts came once again— "Sing again, Encore!"

Enjoying the responses, Cateline spoke briefly, deciding to sing one more song. Oscar looked on, realizing that she was in the spotlight. Quite different from any girl he had ever known, Cateline was such a natural with her audience at her feet and clearly attentive to her every word and move. Cateline was a most accomplished performer, one that he would have to encourage to share the gifts she possessed, gifts that need not be wasted. Once the other musicians had the key and tune suitable for her last song, feeling the absinthe flooding through her whole being, it was as if her body no longer belonged to herself; it belonged to them—to those who desired to hear more, more, and more. "Just one more song!" Cateline thought to herself. "Yes, absinthe—get me through one more song!" Beginning to sing, *At Last,*[12] by artist *Etta James,* a song of the 1960s—a sultry, bluesy type—

In the moment of the song, Cateline strutted across the stage, performing with her movements and proclaiming every word. Her eyes were closed, as she was lost in herself with her love, absinthe, beside her. Cateline entertained with all her emotions and passions, pouring forth words that seemed to bring her audience of admirers to full attention with her sense of style, gestures, and sultry movements. With her explosive personality, candor, and sincerity,

Cateline dazzled those watching as she felt the meaning with every word as if it spoke to her own heart. Young men and old alike were mesmerized by her beauty and sensuality, yet her thoughts were on her life right at that moment. She swayed with her eyes closed, feeling the words deep within—words alive to her life with Oscar. She sang most enticingly, walking down from the stage towards where Oscar stood. Singing the last part of the song, Cateline put her arms around Oscar's neck to dance close to him, slowly resting her forehead upon his shoulder with her eyes shut, softly Cateline spoke, "I love you so much, Oscar. I really love you."

The musicians continued playing the tune while Oscar held her close, dancing slowly with her every movement, speaking tenderly, "I love you too, Cateline." With a soft, quiet laugh, he continued, "I do believe that you blew it; all the fellows must now know that we are more than just friends."

A vague laugh came forth as Cateline whispered, "I don't care right now. You will clearly have to promise that you will not let me have a love affair with absinthe ever again. I will do this better in London, I promise."

"What have I to do with this? I take no credit myself. This was your silly idea of us pretending to simply be friends."

Gazing into his eyes, she kissed his lips intimately, "Well, we might as well make it look good. Perhaps, you can tell them I merely had too much to drink."

With a faint laugh, "It is quite finished. I congratulate you on the final touch, the kiss that is. Probably was not such a worthy notion, especially in public."

Cateline giggled as she spoke, "I know, but I do not care right now. Oscar, I think I have had too much to drink."

"That, my dear, is rather obvious. I am sure that all eyes are upon us right now, but from where I stand, I am absolutely enthralled for you to be in my arms, knowing every man here would give anything for what I have."

Quietly, Cateline replied, "Oscar, I don't think I can walk out of here; can you please take me back to the hotel?"

About that time, Cateline felt as if she was floating, her legs no longer holding her. As she commenced to fall, Oscar quickly seized control. Holding her in his arms, he proclaimed, "I think it is time that I take her back to where we are staying. William, Reginald— I need to get a cab to carry us to our hotel."

Reginald spoke up, "Oscar, I have a carriage outside. I will get her guitar and meet you at the door."

"Thank you." Oscar carried Cateline to the front of the pub, with Reginald following close behind.

CHAPTER

25

The following morning, Cateline awakened as a headache had begun to rapidly consume her senses. Oscar lay beside her, still asleep, when she realized she had no clothes on. Suddenly, rolling over, she began to awaken him.

"I feel like I have died, Oscar."

"Well, my dear, you were fairly inebriated last night, I'm afraid."

"And I see you wasted no time in taking advantage of my circumstances."

"Ah, I am afraid that **you** were the one who took advantage of me—you were entirely scammered," smiling, he continued, "I will say it was quite enjoyable or rather fascinating. I had no idea that American women could be so aggressive. I do say that your advances were utterly splendid; a night I am sure I will never forget," he concluded while laughing.

Cateline, feeling a bit mortified, responded, "I am not quite sure what happened last night, but I am so overjoyed you have found such pleasure in this situation."

"Oh, I do believe that you found as much pleasure as I, my dear—I assure you."

"Oscar, you embarrass me with your words. I dare say that I remember nothing of what you speak. I feel terribly ashamed, well, not as a lady should. Please forgive me, for it must have been that repugnant drink that beheld me."

"Ah, yes—absinthe! Yet, your passion you cannot deny, nor will I. Your free spirit was alive and not hindered, and I cannot refute that your craving stirred within me a desire for my wife in a way I had not known."

"Well, I am most delighted if it pleased you. I do hope that my manner has not made you think of me as less of a lady, for I assure you I would never carry myself in a way if it were not for the absinthe."

"Indeed, absinthe, by far, will lead one to be absorbed in a caprice, but I assure you that your aggression enthused me most delightfully. My thoughts will often remember your fervor, for I shall never be able to escape the memory. I should forever be drawn to you, my dear, never away," Oscar concluded, rolling over to kiss her most gently. "You look rather pallid, my love. I do believe it is time for your *mal aux cheveux*. I will go to the restaurant and have them make you a prairie oyster."

"*Mal aux cheveux*, Oscar?"

"Ah, you are not familiar with these words?"

"Well, yes—*sore hair*, but what do you mean by that?"

"Are you not feeling well from the absinthe?"

"No, I do not feel well at all."

"You have not heard the expression—*even my hair hurts*?"

"No, that one is new to me. We simply call it a *hangover*. What were you going to get me for my mal aux cheveux?"

"A prairie oyster—you have never heard of this concoction?"

"No—perhaps, I don't want to know what it is."

"Good assumption, you probably should not ask," he concluded while dressing.

After a brief time, Oscar returned to the room with the most awful-looking cocktail. Handing it over to Cateline, she sat up in the bed while observing the utmost gruesome blend, quite disgusting, a somewhat dark bloody substance in appearance. She declared, "This looks repulsive, and it smells sordid."

"It may appear to be hideous, my dear, but it will cure your soul as your senses begin to thrive once again. I strongly advise you musn't look at the horrid brew—just drink it, and you must drink it all."

"How do I know it will not kill me?"

With a most prominent laugh, Oscar responded, "After being seized by such a capricious lover, how could you possibly even consider that I would dare take your life?"

"Very funny," lifting the drink up to her lips, taking a sip before continuing her discourse, "oh Oscar, I do not think I can get this down—if I try, surely it will come back up."

"Cateline, stop being so silly and drink it!"

While gathering up her courage, she decided to down the mixture as fast as possible. Her mouth felt on fire as she declared loudly, "Now—what was in that?"

Oscar could not help but laugh while he noted, "A cocktail mixture which one musn't ever talk about, I assure you, a monotonous blend of tomato juice, a raw egg, Worcestershire sauce, hot sauce, vinegar, salt, and black pepper."

"That was so vile; I do hope that it works."

"Oh, I assure you it will work."

"If it does not kill me first."

"Would you have rather been buried in the sand? Of course, that would have been quite wearisome, for I would have had to carry you to the shore."

"Are you serious? Do people really do that for a hangover?"

"Your Irish ancestry, you have not heard of that cure?"

"I have not; surely, you are joking."

Somewhat amused, he responded, "Not at all. It actually helps a *mal aux cheveux* or should I say *Katzenjammer,* from the Germans for *screeching cats.*"

Cateline, overcome with amusement, declared, "Please stop—it hurts me to laugh; this is all too funny. However, you must tell me the remainder of the Irish cure."

While he smiled back at her, Oscar continued, "You merely go down to the river or the seashore where there is moist and damp sand, dig a place to bury yourself up to your neck. The coolness feels quite pleasant and helps your blood to stir, having a most cleansing effect."

"It actually works?"

"They say that it does; I never used that method when I had a Katzenjammer. But growing up, my brother and I did bury each other in the sand, and it was quite cool and refreshing."

Changing the subject, Cateline began to think about the time, knowing they were to be traveling to Bath, "Oscar, we are supposed to leave today for Bath?"

"I knew that would not happen after a night spent with absinthe. Not to worry, I secured another night at the hotel. I thought we could do absolutely nothing today unless, of course, you would like to enjoy the simple pleasures, or should I say, a reprise of last night's performance."

"You are too funny, Oscar. I cannot even remember last night, much less reenact it."

"I am sure it would all come back to you. After all, it was a performance of your deepest passions, part of whom you are secretly hidden within. And, my dear, if you are feeling well enough later, we could go to one of the hotel's restaurants to eat, or I can just have food delivered to our room."

"The choices I have, how delightful they are. In truth, Oscar, I do not believe I want to leave this bed. Can I sleep for a while?"

"Yes, by all means. Sleep as long as you would like. I shall read for a while and may join you later," Oscar countered while he leaned over and kissed her lightly on the cheek.

The day soon turned into night, while Cateline only moved when Oscar would bring her water to drink. By late evening, she was finally hungry and sat up to eat dinner in the room with him. They retired early to bed and were well-rested when they were awakened by the front desk for check out the following morning, deciding to get a head start towards Bath early rather than arriving late.

After they were dressed and all packed, Oscar helped a young gentleman who worked at the hotel to load their trunks and bags in a clarence where they were transported down Lime Street to the Liverpool Station, which was in very close proximity. Once arrived, the gentleman saw that their belongings were safely loaded onto the train while Oscar secured first-class tickets to Bath.

Cateline boarded the train with one carry-on bag; all the other baggage was secured by the porter. Once inside their elegant first-class car, they settled in plush chairs, side by side, while Cateline cuddled up next to Oscar. Taking a blanket, Oscar draped it over her, inquiring, "Are you cold, my dear?"

"Just a little, but you would have been all I needed for warmth," she noted, "although it is considerably pleasant that they have blankets in first-class."

Jauntily, he responded, "I am much obliged to assist you in keeping warm," as he drew her near, engulfing her in his arms. "Oh, by the way, I underestimated you," he declared in a most portentous voice.

"Underestimated me? Whatever do you mean?"

"I have learned that you are most fond of doing dangerous things. But it is quite alright, for it is one of the qualities in women that I admire most."

Cateline, looking over at him, inquired, "I am not entirely sure what you are talking about."

"I watched you extensively the night at the Grove House; you seemed to enjoy all the attention of the gentlemen. A woman will flirt with anybody in the world, as long as other people are looking on."[2]

She smiled most profusely while exclaiming, "Oscar, I do believe you are jealous."

"Hardly am I jealous, for I rather relished witnessing your reaction to all the gentlemen that had no idea you would be leaving with your husband. Yet, it was certainly uncouth on your part, I do declare. Myself, I was the lucky fellow to benefit from your mad passion, but how sad it was for all those lads who fell in love with your extraordinary beauty which, by the way, I am sure they will never forget!"

No longer able to hold it in, she giggled, knowing that he was indubitably jealous. In a teasing manner, she affirmed, "Why Oscar, you may continue to believe that you were not jealous!" She leaned towards him and kissed him lightly on his cheek— "You are my knight in shining armor, my love. It is only you that I love deeply and only you that I desire."

Completely drained from the lingering journey back from James's estate and not really having enough time in between places to just relax before heading to another destination, they settled in for the trip ahead. The train blowing its whistle finally began to rumble along the tracks, gradually gaining speed after being delayed for some time. As it was, Oscar and Cateline were very quiet, as their desires were more for slumber than anything else. If they were only able to fall asleep, the journey to Bath would not seem to be so tedious. After a brief period, cuddled closely together, they finally were comfortable enough to where they soon dozed off.

Time elapsed when Cateline had awakened first, where she reached over to look at Oscar's pocket watch. Evidently, they had slept for about two hours, even though part of that period was during the layover at the station. "Oscar," Cateline whispered close to his face, "it is almost noon. You should be hungry, dear. Should we go eat in the dining car?"

Opening his eyes, "Yes, indeed! I am ravenous! That sounds wonderful—the dining car, it is."

They walked to the diner and sat at an elegant table while viewing picturesque landscapes soar by. Ordering lunch with the waiter, the cuisine shortly arrived. The presentation was superb, as they savored boiled ham with champagne sauce, baked sweet potatoes, roasted parsnips, and English plum pudding, along with a bottle of champagne with strawberries. Unfortunately, the train did not have all the ingredients to make champagne Wildean-style, but the added strawberries and sugar came close. "I believe we only have a little over two hours left to Bath," Cateline shared.

"You would be correct. Are you rested and feeling better from yesterday, my dear?"

"Quite so, I felt as though I had not eaten in days. Lunch was so agreeable, along with the champagne. I do believe I am beginning to feel like myself once again."

"We should arrive a short while after two, and then we should probably check into our quarters before doing a bit of shopping. You did say that you wanted a dress from Bath?"

"Oh yes, I would love to look for a dress, and I know that you love clothes as much as I. You do plan to buy a new outfit as well?"

"Yes, of course! A splendid idea; new outfits for us both."

They finished up the last of their champagne and rose to head back to their seats in first-class. Cateline soon removed her diary from her bag and jotted down all the details since her last account.

"Writing in your diary, I see—," Oscar stated with a pause as he waited for her reply.

"Yes, many fascinating experiences to add, wouldn't you say?"

"Oh—yes, indeed. Do not forget to include our late-night encounter after your love affair with absinthe, my dear," he retorted in laughter.

"Perhaps that was not very memorable to me. I do recall telling you that I had no recollection of what you tried to declare happened," Cateline replied with a slight smile.

"Oh, then, by all means, let me fill in that day for you," he countered as he swiftly grabbed the book out of her hands.

"Oscar, give that back to me, right now! Don't you dare try to read any of it," she yelled loudly, looking around to see other passengers beginning to look on.

Amused at her demeanor, he had already begun to read some of her writings as he acknowledged, "Ah, you did not forget that night, my dear. It is most definitely noted." As Oscar continued to read her notations in regards to the whole night, he began to laugh.

"Oscar, give that back to me; you are making fun of me."

"No, I am not making fun of you. Although, I do find your mode of expression rather fascinating. And, my dear, absinthe did not make you sleepy where you could not remember anything; it made you inebriated, to say the least. Yet, it seems you had no problem remembering the minutiae to our late night of passion."

"Well, it is only noted based on your knowledge," she quipped.

Shutting the diary, he handed it back to her, giving her a delicate kiss on the cheek while softly speaking, "I love everything about you, even your silly diary. You are divine, my love, beyond all living things."

She responded with a most angelic smile, "I know you love me, and I love you too!"

For the remainder of the journey to Bath, Cateline enjoyed the splendid scenery as she pulled back the curtains where they sat and continued to take delight in the extensive discourse with her beloved knight in shining armor. "Oscar, I promise I will do better than the other night; I will not start kissing you in public. I know I can do this right while in London, where we simply seem to be friends, for your sake. I do not want to be the cause of you not getting the publicity needed for the American Tour. I will do this as agreed. Frank will be the only one who knows the truth for the time being."

"Needless to say, I am not in accord with your crazy notion, it being quite ridiculous. But it does not matter to me in the least. I will find amusement in the repercussions which this shall bring, I am sure, not to mention the delight at the close of each gathering in which we shall attend. Seeing as you will not be able to emit your passions in the midst of acquaintances, once we are alone, I am sure that your cravings towards your husband, thus being contained throughout those evenings in which we shall be engaged, will be ravenously released."

"I am so glad that you find all of this amusing, Oscar. However, it is merely your story. As I said, I do not remember a thing. Furthermore, since you seemed to enjoy my night on absinthe immensely, you should also be glad I came up with this crazy idea, as you call it. For without this plan, that night may never have materialized."

"None of this really matters, my dear. For, I feel that I am irresistible to you. I am not sure you will be able to keep your hands to yourself for months," he quipped with laughter.

"That is not funny, Oscar. And I do not have to keep my hands to myself, only when we are in front of other people. As long as I never drink absinthe again, I should be good."

"Oh, but you were good on absinthe."

"Very funny, you do know what I mean."

"Oh, but do I? Let me see—," he replied while fumbling through his briefcase for a book, "ah, here it is, and I marked the page—."

"What is that?"

"Poems—John Keats, I marked one to read to you and almost forgot, but you have kindly reminded me by remembering your night on absinthe, my dear. This one reminds me of you—

Where be ye going, you Devon maid?
And what have ye there I' the basket?
Ye tight little fairy, just fresh from the dairy,
Will ye give me some cream if I ask it? [3]—

Before Oscar could finish, Cateline interrupted him abruptly, "Oscar, I am very familiar with Keats' poem, but please, you do not have to quote his words any further. I do get the point, and I am quite sure you will never let me forget that night."

"Forget that night; why would you want to? I will never forget that night."

As the discussions continued, Oscar decided it was time to bring up the topic once again about her talent. "Cateline, I know you have said you were not interested in performing on stage publicly or rather professionally, but I fear that you do not clearly understand how genuinely gifted you are."

"Oscar, I agreed if you were to write a part in a play for me, I would consider. Otherwise, I have no desire to be on stage nor famous for that matter."

"I wish you could have been standing where I was the other night at the pub. There was not a soul in the place who had not walked up to hear you sing and play your guitar. Their eyes were fixated on you, well—groveling at your feet, if I dare tell the truth."

"Oscar, I do not want men groveling at my feet," she commented with a playful smile while she maintained, "I am content to just have you."

"You do understand they earn a very handsome salary. The actresses that I know have fame and fortune handed to them easily, and they love what they do. You dare say that you do not love to sing and play your guitar."

"Of course, I love to sing and play my guitar, but I am not interested in the money. Money seems to change people. Is it not alright if my being with you is quite enough for me?"

"I am flattered. Truly, I am, but I believe that you are making a mistake by not taking advantage of your opportunity while it is to be had. The proprietor of the pub in Liverpool gave me his card before we left and wanted to be sure that you knew they would welcome you back to Liverpool at any time to perform at their establishment. He did not say the amount of money they would pay, but he did say that they would make it worth your while. I merely want you to be aware if one establishment such as the Grove House feels you are worth their effort to bring you back, I cannot even fathom what an establishment in London would pay for your talent."

Cateline smiled and looked into Oscar's eyes while speaking softly, "I am gratified that you believe me to be so accomplished, Oscar. I really am, and I will not tell you no, but I do ask that this not happen right away. I want my time with you right now, and I want the focus to be on you and your journey to America. That is all I ask; surely this can wait. Can it not?"

"Of course, it can wait. As long as you are not saying no, that is a start. I do love you, you know that, right? Even if you do not take advantage of your opportunity, I would still love you. I cannot say I will understand, but then women are meant to be loved, not to be understood."[4]

"Yes, I know you love me, and perhaps, one day, you will also understand," she spoke seriously while kissing him gently. A few moments passed where she thought to herself, "I know he believes these songs I have been singing were written by me, even though I have told him they were not. But, nonetheless, this is not my time. This time is for him. My time here is for him, not for me."

391

Time swiftly flew by, and before too awfully long, they had arrived in Bath, Somerset. Bath, known for its Roman-built baths, located in the valley of the River Avon.

Oscar acquired a carriage to take them to the Royal Crescent, where they would obtain a terraced house for a few days. Riding through the town, the Georgian architecture could be seen at its finest, with Cateline gazing at every building in awe. There was so very much to take in that she was lost for the moment in the astonishing views of such history, as she had yet to perceive. She listened to Oscar's every breath as he named the various structures in which she so longed to experience. As they passed alongside several buildings, Oscar noted two places they would be enjoying the following morning, the Grand Pump Room and the Roman Baths. The pump room was named for the hot springs, which continually drew water into the room where many visitors traveled to drink from the fountain believed to have medicinal properties. The latter, adjacent to the pump room, housed the hot water springs. Both landmarks drew many to Bath for their marvelous cleansing and relaxing properties. The baths were an experience in themselves; on the other hand, besides the baths, the Roman Temple was most captivating, to be sure, with its Sacred Spring and a museum of artifacts dating back to the eighteenth century.

Off to their right, an enormous bridge made of the Bath stone could be seen. "Oscar, what bridge is that?"

"That is the Pulteney Bridge; it crosses the River Avon."

"I do not believe I have ever seen a bridge of such character."

"A Palladian design, my dear. It is quite grand. We will see it much closer while here and will cross it if you would like."

"Yes, I would like that very much. What are all the buildings that connect with it? It seems like some sort of fortress."

"Those are shops on each side."

Continuing on, they drove fairly close to the Circus, where Oscar had contemplated their staying the few days while in Bath before deciding on the Royal Crescent. One could see the glory of the outer perimeter with its curved shape divided into three sections, its name being that of Latin—meaning a ring, oval, or circle which depicted its form. The outer façade with its graceful curves was adorned in three classical orders—Greek Doric, Roman/Composite, and Corinthian. The Doric depicted insignias of serpents and nautical symbols along with other representations of the arts. A classical Palladian landscape, the Circus was considered John Wood's masterpiece, an English architect who never saw his project's completion. Wood had died shortly after the project had begun with his son completing the grand chef-d'oeuvre to his father's blueprint. Oscar depicted the inner court, which could be accessed by carriage as it encircled the gardens—a most attractive landscape for their tenants to enjoy, with its completion in the latter part of the eighteenth century.

They continued to travel towards the Royal Crescent, passing by the Assembly Rooms, another *must-see* while visiting Bath. As they drove past this 'U-shaped' building of Georgian-style crafted with the creamy gold bath stone obtained from limestone, Oscar portrayed the many socials in their grand ballrooms having taken place over the last century. He further noted that the Assembly Rooms consisted of not only the grand ballroom but also the tea room for gathering about, not to mention the octagon room where people would meet before the ball. To conclude, there was the card room where many a gentleman and lady had played their hand at a game of luck or skill for that matter.

Finally, arriving at the Royal Crescent, it was consistent with the architecture of many of the buildings, thus viewed—curved façade, narrow columns, with the overall structure depicting scenes of the parkland which were paradigms of *rus in urbe*. Laid out in a wide-ranging crescent sat a row of terraced houses. While the porter attended to their trunks and bags, Cateline's eyes wandered, taking in the glorious landscape while waiting for Oscar to secure the keys to their accommodations. On opening the door to their spacious lodgings, Cateline was overcome with the lavish décor and furnishings of the Georgian era. An abundantly elegant drawing-room of grandeur dimensions lay before them endowed with an elaborate seating area and pianoforte, not to mention a most distinguished dining area where an opulent table sat adorned with intricate candle holders spaced accordingly. Every wall seemed to be garnished with fine paintings of regal taste, and a most radiantly designed fireplace stood prominently positioned to one side. Lastly, an ornate candelabra was suspended from the center of the room with a uniquely vivid intensity, along with substantially generous windows covering one wall, allowing for more brilliance to saturate throughout the room. It was such perfection and splendor, standing amid this nineteenth-century accommodation, a manner of glory seemed to overwhelm Cateline to a world that she may one day leave but carry with her buried deep in heart forever.

They entered into their bedchamber, which was just as extravagant as the drawing-room. Relatively large in size, situated within were elaborate furnishings dividing the apartment with an intricate sleeping area to one side and a parlor to the other. Upon entering, fixated in the bedchamber, sat a mahogany four-poster bed with a complementary bureau to one corner and a cheval mirror opposite. To one side of the elaborate room, the parlor, a most spacious seating area, was also furnished in mahogany to include an empire sofa settee positioned favorably along with two matching chairs. The ensemble centered around an oval sofa table, and off to one side sat a most attractive cabriole chair with a mahogany console— "Quite charming and delightful of rare quality, if truth be told," Cateline thought to herself.

Briefly unpacking their trunks and a few other items, they refreshed themselves before heading out for the remainder of the day to take advantage of shopping and sightseeing before dusk. Venturing into the streets while viewing the area firsthand and taking in the shops, Cateline fell in love with a most exquisite Charles Frederick Worth ball gown. Cut with a slender frame to fit sleek throughout her curves, a smooth flair flowed from her hips to the floor, trailing down the back with a modest train. Sleekly designed in a most fashioned pastel orange-colored satin with detailed designs of golds embroidered throughout, adding an elaborate artwork of ornamentation. The bodice, adhered with a v-neckline, low cut, fit precisely to Cateline's shape. As she was in awe of the design, additionally, the slight sleeves briefly capped over her shoulder, intricately with an earthy silk tone of golds. Cateline tried on the dress and stepped out of the boudoir for Oscar to view, "What do you think?"

"Superb, it is quite lovely on you, my dear. You must purchase it." Oscar selected a suave brown velvet suit, consisting of a padded doublet, brown knee-breeches with silk stockings of the same, and a most extraordinary pastel orange cravat fashioned necktie to be in sync with Cateline. He would also adorn his cloak, which he so loved, and a corresponding broad-brimmed hat. Once

Oscar had taken care of the payment on their items, he had them delivered to the Royal Crescent.

With the time slipping by, they stopped in at a quaint little café to place an order of simple finger-type food for takeout in which they could eat along the way while they maintained exploring the city.

As they left the café, Oscar noted, "Before we go any further, we must climb the tower," pointing in the distance to where it stood. "That is the Beckford Tower built in the earlier part of the nineteenth century, and from the top, the panoramic views are truly a sight," he finished.

"It seems that most everything is within walking distance, is it not?"

"Yes, quite so," he replied while they continued on their trek toward the turret. Once they were close, they veered off on a dirt pathway fully landscaped along the way with flowers, shrubbery, and many trees. The tower could be seen standing proud in all its grandeur style, a neo-classical form that sat on Lansdown Hill. "The turret was built for William Beckford, who collected art and was an art critic, as well as a novelist," Oscar noted.

"Oh, an art critic. How does one such as yourself feel about the art critics?"

Oscar, grinning at her, commented, "If it were not for the artist, there would be no need for the critic. The critic has to educate the public; the artist has to educate the critic."[5]

As Oscar walked up toward the steps, he declared in enthusiasm, "I will race you to the belvedere."

"Wait, what is the belvedere?"

"Do you see the dome structure at the top?"

"Yes, I see it."

"That is called the belvedere," he noted while he began to run up the stairs.

"You cheated," Cateline screamed, "you started before I did."

Slowing down, he turned— "Come, I will wait for you, and we will begin again." When she arrived on his step, he spoke, "Ready?"

"No, let me gather my dress up some, where I will not trip. Yes, I believe I am ready," she declared as they both commenced running. Cateline could not stop laughing while observing his competitive nature. "You will just have to win," she yelled loudly.

"Are you giving up?"

"How can I compete with your long legs and stamina? I am afraid that I cannot come close to beating you." Exhausted by the time she had arrived at the belvedere, Cateline announced, "You win! I dare say that I do not have the energy in which you have, my love."

Oscar leaned over and gave her a gentle kiss before he commented with a sly smirk, "But, you win, my dear. I am your prize."

Standing at the top, they gazed around, taking in the panoramic views of the countryside, as far as the eye could see. Luscious meadows of green on the hillside waiting to be explored while clusters of shrubs and trees outlined the fields and valleys embellished in shades of emeralds and dazzling yellows. Clouds laid low over the tops of the horizon from afar, providing a canopy for the historical cemetery with graves from long ago. Standing together as one, joined by love, by vows, the memory of this day, their laughing, talking, sharing, and loving, forever would be embedded deep within her every breath. Oscar pulled her close to him and looked into her eyes of blue, lost inside of her for those moments. He swept her hair to the side, kissed her tenderly and then more ardently, seizing every part of her which belonged to him—his love, his wife, the woman who had touched his senses in a way that had never before been known. She was alive to him forever, she was his, and he belonged to her. Cateline whispered in his ear, "Oscar, I feel more alive these last few days spent next to you, more so than I have ever felt in my whole life."

He responded, "To live is the rarest thing in the world. Most people exist, that is all."[6]

While smiling, she replied, "I never wish to just exist but to live within your arms for all time."

With Oscar's arm engulfed around Cateline's shoulder and her arm around his waist, they walked back down the lengthy staircase from the tower. Words did not have to be uttered, for their demeanor spoke it all. Young lovers enjoying every day together as if it were their first—the seclusion and tranquility, their devotion, gentleness, and tenderness towards each other, no one could ever measure its worth. Nothing could be compared to their feelings, which were felt from deep within, the love they held dear, as one. Before they had fully descended, rain began to fall. At first, it was light, but then it came down heavier. Oscar, hastening along, spoke while taking Cateline's hand, "Perhaps, we can get on a horsecar if we hurry. You can't come to Bath without experiencing rain."

As they ran side by side, Cateline declared, "I love rain, Oscar. It does not phase me in the least."

Looking over at her, soaking wet, "You are just as pretty wet as you are dry, my dear."

They both laughed as they persisted, rushing towards a horsecar in hopes of acquiring a ride back to the Crescent.

Settled in the vehicle, heading back to the Crescent Royal, Oscar spoke, "The evening is getting quite late; we should merely have a quiet romantic dinner and then get some rest, my dear. For tomorrow, we will go to the Roman baths once we awaken to be revitalized. Later in the day, we should take in a performance at the Theatre Royal before we head to the Assembly Room ball."

"Yes, I am looking forward to tomorrow; it sounds most pleasant," Cateline responded.

CHAPTER

26

The following morning, having slept late, they decided to dress comfortably to head out for a proper breakfast before relaxing at the Roman Baths. Taking one of the horsecars, they were dropped off in the thick of town where most activities were going on. Walking along the streets, there was already much hustle and bustle, with many flocking into the bathhouse and pump room. The roads were somewhat narrow, adorned closely by the golden-colored stone buildings of two and three-story height on each side. Much charm was visible with rather quaint shops lined about, eating establishments, and the typical businesses one would find in a boisterous township. The rich architecture was quite prominent to that of the Georgian era with its Palladian revival. Cateline enjoyed all the views and the culture of the nineteenth century, being most pleasingly preoccupied with the surroundings of that timeframe and the exuberance among those visiting Bath, where she failed to hear Oscar. "Cateline, we should go have Bath buns for breakfast," he spoke once again in a higher tone, "one cannot come to Bath without savoring their sweetness. They are served deliciously hot, enticing one's senses. Ah, they are simply mouthwatering."

"By all means, they sound remarkable. What exactly are Bath buns?"

"They are made with sweet dough covered scrumptiously in sugar nibs and currants, and a whole sugar cube is baked into the bottom, most heavenly."

"Why, yes, I would love to try them. You do make them sound so tasty."

"Sally Lunn's is across the street, they make the buns, and I am sure they have crumpets if you prefer," Oscar noted as they crossed the lane.

"No, no—I would much rather try the Bath buns."

The front façade of the café, a generous show window, had many items on display in the picturesque restaurant. They stepped inside and were seated at a table, which was moderately cozy. Oscar had immediately asked that they be brought hot tea and would be ordering Bath buns, in which the server had cordially responded to his request.

"I love the atmosphere, Oscar. It has a very cozy feel."

"Quite so, my dear. It is most pleasant, indeed."

The server soon returned with their order, laid out divinely in Churchill China cups and saucers, creamer, and teapot—the Blue Willow pattern. The design depicted an exquisitely hand-painted scene: a slight bridge shadowed by a large willow tree where three men stood, two birds in flight, a type of pagoda surrounded by many trees and foliage, a lake with a boat, and a small house which sat in the middle of a distant island. Cateline, observing the willow pattern, thought to herself, "The Blue Willow, hmm—quite a collector's item in my era." Being distracted, as the server delivered a fabulous dish filled with the buns, Cateline could not help but notice how scrumptious they looked. As she took a bite, the warm, sweet, and soft bread filled her senses with the most succulent experience. "Mmm—," she professed, "these are amazing, simply ravishing, to say the least."

"Who wouldn't like them?"

"Like them—I love them!" she exclaimed.

As they continued to enjoy the buns, Cateline decided to inquire into the China, "Oscar, this is the Blue Willow pattern, is it not?"

"It is. You are familiar with Churchill China in America?"

"Yes, of course, I do love this particular pattern."

"It is the English pattern, but it was inspired by the Chinese. Do you also know the legend behind the scenes?"

"I'm afraid not. Can you share it with me? I would so love to hear the tale?"

"The legend has it that there were two lovers who were separated and denied the right to marry due to the difference in their social status. Yet, they were able to meet each other once a year when the stars aligned. Eventually, the young lovers eloped, running over the bridge where they escaped in the boat which took them to the little island. On the island, they lived for many years in the house shown, but in due course, they were discovered, captured, and brought back, where they were put to death. In spite of everything, the gods transformed them into a pair of doves where they were together once again."

"What an amazing tale. I love the story, and it all fits together with the various scenes," she declared, thinking to herself how wonderful it would be if they, too, were given a chance to also meet once a year.

Upon finishing breakfast, they relaxed and enjoyed their hot cup of tea while appreciating the outside views of the comings and goings, many folks enthralled in the quaint city. "Yes," Cateline contemplated silently, "what a delightful breakfast this was, fabulous buns, simply scrumptious, to include the diversion of the romantic fable of the young lovers."

After leaving the café, they proceeded to walk to the bathhouses, which were in close proximity to their current location. Having already seen the outer buildings of the Roman Baths and the Grand Pump Room, Cateline was very anxious to experience the inside of both. From the standpoint of a tourist wandering into the baths, the views were seen as outstanding. The opulent architecture was sustained with its elaborate neoclassical style, as well as Victorian, with much of the Roman structures and expansions being established and preserved in the eighteenth century from the ruins of years gone by. Like most of the construction in Bath, the same cream-colored stone was superbly made from limestone and used throughout to include the Sacred Spring, the Roman Temple, the fascinating Roman Bath House itself, and a museum of sorts. The gallery itself held many excavated artifacts of the main core temple courtyard, such as the stone sculptures, Denari silver coins dating back to the third century, and many other fine relics.

Oscar first wanted to take her to the upper floor, where they could view the entire length of the large bath in all its splendor. Overwhelmed, Cateline was amazed at the beauty. Yet, seeing so many pictures of the buildings in her timeframe, no photo could do justice to what one felt standing in the midst during the nineteenth century. Gazing down, the magnificent creation of exquisite splendor from centuries prior could be sensed and imagined. Countless hours were expended soaking and relaxing by all who had lived before. Kings and queens, dukes and duchesses, lords and ladies, all the aristocracy had frequented this sublime element of Bath, England. They had spent numerous hours indulging in these waters, soaking, relaxing, refreshing in the waters of hot springs that continually surged into the vast stone-encased pool. The many conversations among those rejuvenating could only be imagined. Those meeting for the first time, lovers were found and engagements formed, marriages came to be, and ladies were brought out into fashionable society. The magic was felt as Cateline stood peering out upon the history, the luxurious waters, knowing that she would soon experience all of it with the man whom she had loved and dreamed of for years. Never had she thought there would be this moment in time where she was right then and there in the midst of this unique locale in history. How she wanted to savor these days, hold on to each moment forever—never to let them pass, never to let them go.

Cateline, walking around the terrace, enjoyed the immense view of the pools of water below, the infusing of bubbles from the hot mineral streams spewing forth, producing a fog of steam from the algae green-tinted wells. As they were observing the outer assembly of the sizeable basin below where large colonnades were structured about the edges, uplifting to the second floor, Oscar spoke calmly, "It is fabulously scenic viewing it from here."

"Yes, it is remarkable—breathtaking!"

"Shall we proceed to the pools for a day of leisure?"

"Oh—yes, oh, yes! I do believe that I am so ready and so happy that we came here. Above all, I am most happy that I am here with you."

Oscar smiled as he led her back downstairs, where they could get ready to go into the water. Separated into different dressing areas, they both changed into outer garments that covered their bodies and met once they were in the huge bath. To Cateline, the experience was quite unusual walking along with Oscar while many others were about them. The waters felt enticing to their bodies, exceptionally warm and refreshing. It was said to be therapeutic, which brought many annually to Bath. The history alone made for a most serene feeling, overwhelming, to say the least. A day which could never be repeated in her timeframe, the beauty of the ancient, standing where many before her had stood—history as far back as one could imagine, or could one even begin to imagine the experience as far back as the times of Emperor Claudius?

After considerable time spent enjoying the spa, they dressed and left the Roman Baths to walk to the adjacent building, the Grand Pump Room. Upon entering, the sound of music could be heard as a pianist sat to one side, skillfully orchestrating his works of art in a delightfully romantic setting. Many fashionable folks were strewn about the room, standing in parties conversing on who's who repertoire. Corinthian columns in grandeur style were set in the chamber, along with a marble statue of King Nash that rose nobly in its brilliance to one side. The main attraction, the marble vase, was positioned to the center of the relatively large room. The vase stood elegant, with water flowing forth elaborately through several spouts where attendants provided guests the fresh spring to sip. Oscar and Cateline stood in line to experience the therapeutic spring water, where they were given their cup to drink of its freshness. At the same time, Cateline looked around as she observed the surroundings.

As she gazed about the area, fireplaces were positioned towards each end, and remarkable paintings adorned every wall. Cateline walked around the perimeter regarding the masterpieces which embellished the room. Many were portraits by William Beach, a British portraitist of the eighteenth century. Of his works, there was a brilliant painting named *Miss Davis as a Bride*. Such history, a bride who had been married in Bath Abbey during the eighteenth century, of a most prominent family. Miss Jenny Davis, another member of the Davis family, adorned one section, having thick and long black hair of fair complexion, a most attractive young lady. There were many other works of art, to name a few—Sir Robert Walpole, an Earl of Orford from the eighteenth century, painted by a French portrait painter, Jean-Baptiste van Loo. Walpole, seated in the masterpiece, wore a lengthy robe of red, gold, and white, adorned with his rather long wig; in addition, there were works by William Hoare, known as *Hoare of Bath*, the first English artist to visit Rome where he studied art. Hoare had come to Bath to paint portraits and stayed the remainder of his life; his creation of Richard Beau Nash, known as the *King of Bath* due to his role as the Master of Ceremonies in the city, portrayed one wall in elegance. Nash was adorned with his white hat in the portrait, which had become his trademark. To conclude, one should not fail to mention, besides the statue of Nash, there was the bust or rather sculpture of Richard Nash, which was attributed to Prince Hoare. However, it is said that it was Joseph Plura, not Hoare, that should have been credited for the bust of Beau Nash. Prince Hoare was the brother to Hoare.

"William Hoare, his paintings are quite remarkable, Oscar. I cannot believe I have not heard of him, such perfection."

"Ah, but man is not perfect, nor is his work, my dear. 'To banish imperfection is to destroy expression,[1] for if we are to have great men working at all, or less men doing their best, the work will be imperfect, however beautiful. Of human work, none but what is bad can be perfect, in its own way,"[2] as Ruskin taught."

"John Ruskin, your professor at Oxford?"

"Indeed, he was. John is a very bright man, an enormous influence in my life."

After a most relaxing and enjoyable day, they walked back to their terrace house to begin dressing for the evening.

Cateline walking by him in her pantalettes to achieve her new dress stopped to give him a kiss. Beginning to walk away, he held onto her wrist, "It would be terribly grave for you to dress, my dear, when one might fancy making love to his wife. For, I do believe we have a little time to spare."

With her wrestling out of his grasp, she replied, "No—no, no! We always have later, Oscar. My hair has already been perfected." Cateline, feeling his disappointment, kissed him passionately while adding, "Most definitely later, my love!"

"You should not tempt me as you do."

"You shouldn't be looking," she quipped.

"I cannot help but look when you flaunt yourself in front of me so blatantly, or should I say nude."

Amused at his remark, while continuing to dress, she stated, "First of all, I am not nude, as you say. Secondly, it is my duty to entice you where you do not grow unfavorable of me."

"Grow unfavorable? I should think not."

"One day, you may."

"How could I?"

Cateline smiled at him and concluded, "Just think, you have something to look forward to later tonight."

Ready for their evening out, they decided to ride in one of the horsecars since they were dressed so exquisitely in their evening wear. As they arrived at the Theatre Royal to take in the play, *She Stoops to Conquer,* the streets were lined with carriages where many anxiously walked towards the entrance, as much conversation and laughs could be heard. Cateline observed the British royal coat of arms above the main entrance, the emblem—an insignia portrayed in the center with a substantial crown on top. Atop the generous crown stood a small golden lion wearing a crown. To one side of the crest, standing tall, was a large crowned lion, and on the opposite side

403

stood a silver unicorn, chained—for legend notes, a free unicorn to be considered a dangerous beast. Of the insignia, the first and fourth quarters were symbolic of England's guardant lions, the second quarter the rampant lion depicted Scotland, and the third quarter a harp for Ireland. The bottom of the crest, *Dieu et Mon Droit*—God and my right! To conclude, the exterior of the three-story building was of a Georgian architectural design with three arched entrances framed with columns and the second and third floors lined with significant windows across the front.

Upon entering, the interior had been rebuilt to the design of architect C. J. Phipps, after the fire in 1862. Inside was a single-storied auditorium, a wide spacious area with many seats and additional stalls towards the back with the curved stage protracting into the open space. Along the walled regions were three tiers that provided for further seating, with those closest being level with the platform—the dress circle situated above the orchestra. A number of large chandeliers hung throughout the theatre, which brought much light along with the many windows on the upper levels. Billows of ruffled draperies hung down on both sides and front, covering all but the anterior part of the stage. The proscenium arch separated into sections with allegoric figures representing comedy, tragedy, farce, melodrama and spectacle, pantomime, opera, ballet, and medallions of Shakespeare.

They made their way to the box seats Oscar had secured on the second level, reasonably close to the stage area. While waiting for the play to begin, Oscar poured them a glass of champagne, which was complimentary at the box seats, when a man suddenly introduced himself as he was taking pictures of all those seated in the loge sections. "Will they send us the pictures, Oscar?"

"I should think they would. After all, they do have our information," Oscar replied.

Cateline, in deep thought, remembered seeing a photo taken of her along with many others at what seemed to be a theatre, but it was not this particular one nor the background. This somewhat disturbed her, but she assumed there would be many other occasions where they would be present at theatres, with it being quite the entertainment in those days. Oh, how she would have loved to have had a copy of this evening, of that picture. Perhaps, there were pictures in other articles that she had not discovered.

Within a short time, the curtain was drawn upwards and the stage illuminated with several chandeliers at different dimensions overhanging. The performance commenced, a comedy by Oliver Goldsmith, with its light humor and romance all bottled up in one. Quite an enjoyable film that provided much merriment throughout the theatre, with laughing continuing during the entirety of the performance.

After the show, they soon left and walked towards the Assembly Room while Oscar inquired, "Were you entertained by the play, my dear?"

"Very much so; it was rather amusing. I suppose that young love does make couples act in the most peculiar ways. It would be easier when there is love between two, to not hide what they feel nor shy away from a commitment due to others' disagreement, wouldn't you say?"

"I would have to agree with you. Although, the days in which we live, women nor men have always been free to marry whom they love. A great many of these marriages, I fear, have been arranged, of which the result of these so-called engagements, far too often, one finds themselves spending their days with someone not of their choosing and being terribly miserable."

"Yes, such a tragedy," Cateline agreed, continuing, "yet, I do believe that a drama of this sort opens those doors to see that it is possible, even today, for those who truly love, to be free to marry regardless of the consequences they may face."

"Such as our marriage? It was not for fortune nor for class."

"I would think not. Of course, you were given a dowry, but I believe that you loved me even before you knew of such."

"And, you being an American girl, primarily, that is also frowned upon amongst the English many times. But I was madly in love when I first laid eyes upon you; could you not see that?"

She concurred with a vague laugh, "I could, and I still do."

They entered the vestibule of the Assembly Room and walked towards the ballroom to their left, noticing there were many people gathered in groups engaged in conversations and much laughter. As they walked into the Grand Ball Room, Cateline observed a most transcendent Georgian rectangular room of much elegance. Lined throughout the center of the room hanging from the significantly high

405

ceiling were five Whitefriars crystal chandeliers, the finest of the eighteenth century. They were attached to moldings of intricate design, which were fashioned to the upper extremity. Each held forty candles, which provided for a well-lit room. Columns were lined respectively alongside the elegant windows, which were detailed elaborately. Four extravagant fireplaces were positioned, two on each side of the elongated walls, unlit, even though nights could still be chilly. Nonetheless, with dancing, the added warmth was not needed. The vast open floor space of grandeur size allowed large crowds to enjoy their evenings in dance while the fashionable orchestrated musicians carried out their tunes.

Adorned, in her designer dress, purchased her first day in Bath, all eyes seemed to be focused on Cateline's most beautiful frame and appearance. "It seems as though men and women are fixated on your beauty, my dear. You are splendidly dressed—a ravishing angel in appearance with your dazzling hair partially flowing over your shoulders and your alluring contour," Oscar spoke very quietly while smiling.

"Please, sir, if you remember, we are merely friends while here," Cateline responded playfully.

"Oh, I do remember, but you fail to see that there is not a man in here that would not love to take you in their arms—,"

"Oscar, please, you are making me blush. I do not like the stares. Can we at least dance?"

"A blush is very becoming on you, my love, and might I add, there is a good deal to be said for blushing if one can do it at the proper moment. To answer your question, my dear, I would be most honored to be seen in your company on the dance floor," he related with a laugh.

As they danced, Cateline asked, "Why are they all still staring?"

"I would suppose that the women stare because they are jealous and the men stare—well, I already told you why they are gawking at you."

"Yes, perhaps, while here in Bath, we should be together where the men will leave me alone."

"Possibly, for they do come to Bath exclusively to secure a partner. Women, more so than men, desire to find their husbands. Men get snagged when they either find one with too large of a fortune to say no or one to whom they become enchanted."

Cateline, slightly laughing, added, "I suppose you were enchanted with me, or was it my fortune?"

"Your fortune, I dare say, could have conceivably persuaded me if I had not already been taken by your charm. I do say that I was enchanted; you performed a type of spell on me where I lost all reasoning of who I was."

"And you do not regret marrying me?"

"Regret, how could I regret? We were meant to be."

"Yes, my life was meant to find you."

Oscar and Cateline spent much time on the dance floor and made their rounds to the tearoom for a bit of refreshment in between. The tearoom was most gorgeously designed and of a reasonable size, yet, not as significant as the ballroom. Its ceilings rose to an extensive height passing its second-floor balconies, which overlooked the expanse of the chamber equipped with tables and chairs to relax and have refreshment to include a somewhat quiet place to conversate when not on the dance floor. The room was also equipped with Whitefriars chandeliers, three strewn down the center length from one end to the other, hanging from the arched ceiling, which rose at a substantial height from the second floor, all the way down to the upper part of the first. Several arched doorways lined one end, and elaborate fireplaces stood to the center area of each of the two lateral walls, which unified the extent. Lastly, there were massive pillars that held up the balcony spaced throughout with black iron railings.

To some degree, it was toasty in the room, without dancing, for the hearths were blazing. While there, Cateline was able to see the Octagon Room, obviously shaped with eight sides, a much cozier chamber with four fireplaces throughout. Many were seated playing cards, as this was the room's sole purpose; while they strolled about observing, Cateline pondered silently, "This is quite the space, very large indeed for a card room."

The night remained as they immensely enjoyed their time together, spending a considerable amount on the dance floor. Stares ensued with a few young and older gentlemen approaching to request a dance from time to time. Politely, Cateline had refrained from dancing with anyone other than Oscar. "If you would like to dance with someone else, you may," he stated.

"I really have no desire to dance with anyone else, Oscar."

As they stood over towards one of the hearths, discussions had transpired among several couples within close proximity. They enjoyed the discourse for a change, soon being engaged in laughter along with a group that had become attached to them. To Cateline, mingling with others meant so much more than anyone would ever know. Living a different life at a different timeframe, it seemed harder to fit in with the conversations of that era. However, Cateline merely stepping out to make that effort, she was able to see that time may separate—but people were still people who shared in the same emotions and feelings, knowing at times, days can be filled with diverse emotions. For there are times of sadness yet times of happiness, times of joy and laughter, success and failures, times of war and times of peace, and there are times of deep heartfelt love! It was during their intense discussions and talks, much laughter and happiness, that a gentleman approached, desiring to take a picture of their group. No sooner than he asked, Cateline remembered, this group—these complete strangers, she carried the picture in her bag as one she had found in an article. Only later, they must have realized that it was Oscar Wilde in this group where this photo became of value.

They began to head back to the Crescent as the night rapidly came to an end, with the dawn beginning to spring forth. Both being exhausted after enjoying such a memorable evening, which had surpassed into the wee hours of the morning. Yet, they still looked forward to the much-needed time alone. Oscar, anticipating a more romantic escapade once they had entered their quarters, went to the sideboard to roll out the cellaret, where he pulled out a bottle of Italian prosecco and two glasses to take to the bedchamber.

Saturday morning soon followed, where they arose fairly late for breakfast and then decided to take a horsecar to view the Pulteney Bridge, walking about while enjoying the shops. With London only being a short journey, they had decided not to take an early train. Arriving at the bridge, the view was breathtaking. Built of limestones, in the Palladian style, the façade had the form of a shrine. Walking out on the bridge, they stopped midway to enjoy the genial view of the river. On a much smaller scale, the calm dark waters surrounding the massive stone structure portrayed a view similar to that of Venice. The tranquility felt so serene standing alongside Oscar, being in the old world, in another time. Nothing could depict the profundity of the stillness, the depth of the loveliness. For some time, they shopped at the various stores and markets, after which, they happened into a charming little café for lunch before heading back to the Crescent to gather up their belongings.

Later that day, arriving at the Great Western Railway, they boarded to take the short train ride to London, where they would reach their destination by late evening. With it being such a short trip, they declined for traveling in first-class but instead chose to travel in second.

Not having quite enough rest from the night prior, both Oscar and Cateline fell fast asleep before long and did not awaken until the sound of the whistle could be heard blowing vigorously, signaling their arrival in London. Cateline sitting up straight, stretched from the tiring effect of riding on the train, as she thought to herself, "At least this was not as long of a trip. I do believe that I could never get used to the comfort level compared with modern days, other than in first-class. Yet, I would not trade these days for anything ever in my whole life."

Upon exiting the train, Oscar looked around until he spotted Frank, "Ah, there he is, the rather tall chap." As they walked towards him, Cateline observed that Frank was quite tall with an athletic build, a young man, dark-haired, neatly trimmed mustache, a nice-looking gentleman with a most pleasant demeanor. The two men smiling, Frank reached out to shake Oscar's hand with a warm and slight embrace. Cateline remembered much about Frank during her in-depth studies in America since his life had been so entwined with Oscar's. Frank was artist-in-chief for *Life Magazine* and also, he contributed to *The Garden*, a weekly journal in London. As an artist, he painted many portraits of known ladies of society to include Lillie Langtry. However, Cateline knew most in her era were probably unaware that Frank wound up being a suspect in the highly proclaimed case of *Jack the Ripper* murders. Although, eyewitnesses who had apparently seen the real Jack the Ripper peering through darkness during times of his assault described the man to be about five foot five to five foot seven and stout, which Frank was not.

Oscar, looking towards Cateline, introduced Frank, who, in turn, gave Cateline a friendly hug while his eyes trailed towards Oscar, unsure exactly what sort of relationship he might be involved with this young lady. It was evident, she was the young woman Oscar had described in his telegram and just as lovely as he had portrayed. Frank, stepping back, smiled as he gave Cateline a thorough approving stare, proclaiming to Oscar, "Well, I certainly can see why you could not leave Ireland without her; your description is most accurate."

Cateline, gazing over at Oscar, "Whatever does Frank mean?"

Frank finally came clean, with a quick smile towards Oscar. He then addressed Cateline, "I received a letter from Liverpool of your accompanying him to London; what were your exact words, Oscar?"

"Words! Mere words, Frank. There is really very little to tell, and I am sure my words were nothing that I have not said to you before, Cateline. You are quite perfect—wonderful eyes, beautiful long coils of hair, most agreeable in every way."

"Among other items not mentioned," Frank quipped with a smile while they gathered up all their baggage with the assistance of a few porters.

Conversations continued while walking among the masses at the station, "And, what other details did you seem to mention to Frank?" Cateline inquired.

"I am afraid I do not remember everything that I wrote," Oscar replied slyly, assisting Cateline into the clarence while their trunks and bags were being secured. Tipping the porters, their driver was soon maneuvering through the heavily traveled London Paddington station in the slightly dense fog of the twilight hours. There was much discourse amongst the noise of the *growler* as its wheels hobbled along on the cobblestone streets. The two men carried on in conversations about the happenings in London during Oscar's absence, to include very general topics and those of delicate nature shared by Oscar on his adventures while away. With Cateline quietly listening to his words, they very quickly were in close proximity to Frank's house. Once arrived at No. One Tite Street in Chelsea, Frank's place was situated between other dwellings of the same character. As dusk had begun to settle, the front façade of the brick home with a mansard style roof behind the brick parapet and a most admirable Flemish-type gabled roof flowed skillfully along the frontage. Immense windows were arranged in a way to illuminate vivid light from inside, viz., the grand expanse of windows stretched for two levels beginning on the second floor and rising to the third—lining the majority of the façade. Upon a closer view, a bottom floor was revealed, the basement, which provided for additional living space, storage, and not to mention a great location to preserve and age wine.

Oscar tipped the chauffeur, after which the man assisted them with unloading their belongings to the front entrance stairs. Oscar and Frank, lifting one trunk at a time, ascended the stairs, which trailed upwards with handrailing of iron bars and extended down the front of the home, securing the premises. As they entered through the front door, Frank began to laugh slightly regarding the weight. After carrying all the various baggage up the stairs into the foyer, they still needed to be brought to the upper-level floor.

"I know you did not take all these trunks and bags when you left," Frank noted while looking over at Cateline— "either these belong to Cateline, or she took you shopping."

"I did acquire a trunk while there, and the other one is Cateline's, Frank! And we did shop on occasions; truthfully, we probably spent many instances among the retail class. Although, I dare say, you do know how I feel. The costume of the nineteenth century is rather detestable. It is so somber, so depressing.[4] Myself, I must suffer to ravage through shops to find one item which I cannot seem to live without. I feel that is not the same with women and their obsessions with fashion."

Cateline entered the premises and observed large rooms on each side, with stairs situated to the right just past the extensive vestibule. She quickly glanced into one of the great rooms located on the other side of the entrance. As she gained perspective, it was splendidly decorated for that era with overstuffed sofas and chaises of complementary fabrics, a small console table to form a grouping, and pianoforte at one end, for vibrancy. And one must not fail to mention the sizeable chandelier centered in the room, well-lit with many candles, and a most enduring fireplace closely arranged to provide added warmth.

Interrupted in her thoughts, the conversation had continued among the two men, with Frank asking, "Are we carrying part of these into one of the spare bedrooms?"

"No, Frank! Everything is going into my room. Cateline will be sleeping with me."

Frank, now looking over at Cateline, who was having a hard time keeping from laughing when Oscar finally spoke up— "The surprise in which I wrote in my letter, besides Cateline coming to London, was that we were married."

"Married? Why did you not mention this in your telegram?"

"That is something we need to discuss once we have carried everything upstairs," Oscar noted. They continued hauling all the baggage into Oscar's room which was only one more flight of stairs, due to Frank's studio being brilliantly open to a two-floor height. The substantial area beheld glorious views overlooking London through windows that stretched the length and height on one side of the sizeable home. However, the stairs climbed to one more level, a third floor that housed a lesser room opening up to the roof. And, to the right of the studio, the home entailed additional bedrooms, with one being Oscars. Leaning over to kiss Cateline, he proclaimed, "Do you mind giving me some time to talk with Frank alone? It should not take too awfully long."

Cateline smiling at him, responded, "Just take as long as you need. I will freshen up and be down a bit later."

The gentlemen headed back downstairs, with Frank opening a bottle of champagne. "I suppose we should celebrate with a toast, a shot of whiskey with your champagne?"

"Eau de vie! Indeed! That sounds delightful," Oscar responded.

Frank handed him a glass, asserting, "To your marriage, your happiness, and hopefully to your mother's understanding why you did not share in your special day with friends and family."

Oscar replied to his comment, "It is a little more complicated than that, Frank. Once you get to know Cateline, you will love her. I truly played with the idea of marriage, and at first, I believed it would be a mistake, especially since we had not known each other but a matter of weeks. I certainly struggled with the decision. Then, I realized, the only things one never regrets are one's mistakes.[5] If it were to be a mistake, then I shall never regret it. Besides, I could not have left without her. I can't explain it, but I fell in love with her almost the minute I saw her. And, then, it was her charm, her compassion. And, of course, her beauty, just look at her."

"I have, and I can see the attraction. Even though she seems entirely perfect, you have not known her long."

"Yes, how strange it all was. I considered that for some time, and I do know it is all so sudden. But, Frank, we are both desperately in love. And, it's not merely her looks; we are so much alike, we complement each other," he paused with an appealing laugh before continuing, "she reads the same books that I do, loves poetry, she's witty and funny, and she loves all the same poets as I. She is even familiar with Whistler's paintings. Furthermore, Cateline believes that I am the most clever and accomplished man she has ever known. What more do you want me to say? When one finds such a woman, one should not let her get away."

"Quite so, quite so!"

"Frank, her beauty may turn every head in the room when she presents herself, but her talent, you have yet to hear her perform. Her voice is music that fills the air. You will understand when you hear her sing. It is extremely lovely. Why the birds cease to exist when her voice floats through the air in song, so angelic, such beauty."

"I hope to hear her sing very soon. She is from America, yes?"

"Cateline was born in Ireland, but her family moved to America when she was very young. I suppose you could say that she is an American but still has Irish roots. Not to mention, it has become rather fashionable these days to marry Americans."

Frank concluded, "Yet, I do hear a long engagement seems to exhaust the American woman, not to mention, the English do frown upon marrying them."

"Yes, Frank, that may be true. But I suppose this will give them something to talk about, which by the way, is far better than not being talked about at all."

"I noticed you brought back a guitar; does it belong to Cateline?"

"Yes, she is most accomplished on the guitar and piano. While in Liverpool, we went to the Grove House, and she sang while playing her guitar. You should have seen her, Frank. Why, every man in the place was swooned by her beauty, charm, and talent. I clearly could not see myself coming back and never seeing her again."

"I understand your infatuation, Oscar, but such a brief engagement, how could you possibly know anything about this woman, knowing her for such a short time?"

413

"I know, I thought the same thing, Frank. But we devoted every waking moment together, which was probably more time than I would have spent with any woman if I were to court one for a full year. Why I have never felt this way about anyone. When I am beside her, I want to place her on a pedestal of gold, show the world she is mine. Cateline's trust makes me faithful, and her belief in me makes me good.[6] Frank, I know your views on marriage are somewhat stern, but I do love her dreadfully. I want you to give me one good reason why I should not have married her?"

"Besides it being a rather rash decision, you should have at the least informed your mother. You could have also waited and married in London?"

"It would not have worked. Cateline wanted a simple wedding, and she wanted to be married at her father's estate in Youghal. I needed to get back to London to begin the publicity for next year's American tour. Well, it was simply easier to be married with a few family members and friends present where we could begin our trip back to London. As far as saying anything to my mother, we are not telling anyone that we are married just yet."

"How horrid you are! Why on earth would you not, at the very least, let your mother know?"

"It was Cateline's idea but a most delightful theory, at that. She felt that my being married would hurt the publicity for next year's tour. Thinking about it, I seem to agree."

"How are you going to pull that off?" asked Frank, while simultaneously handing him a package that had been delivered the day prior, "I almost forgot, this came for you yesterday."

"Thanks," Oscar replied, while he proceeded to open the parcel, and at the same time, responding to Frank's question, "We—Frank, we are going to pull it off. You are the only person that will know our secret in London. I have my wedding ring on this chain," Oscar shared as he pulled the chain out from under his shirt, "and Cateline is wearing her band on her right hand as a friendship ring. You will also be the only person who knows we sleep in the same room. Everyone coming over here or wherever we go, for that matter, we will inform them we met in Ireland, she was heading here for a visit, we became friends, and I invited her to stay while in London." He paused for a moment before resuming, "Ah, yes, our wedding pictures, here they are. Proof that we are married," Oscar said as he handed the photos to Frank.

"I never doubted that you were married. So, that is your plan?"

"Certainly, what do you think?"

"It is irrational, unwise, and downright bizarre. That is what I think. You, Mr. Wilde, are passionately wild. But, if that is what you want to do, I will adhere to your confidence. You do know that our friends will be ruthlessly determined to seduce her; she is absolutely gorgeous. These photos of her are—I don't know what to say, very seductive. But I suppose I should rephrase that to very charming," he said, smiling, "ah, and," he continued with a laugh, "I really like these of you two lying in the floor frolicking about while all your guests watch on."

Oscar laughing, "Ah yes, remind me to tell you about the American way to have cake at a wedding. It was rather exciting."

"Without a doubt, Cateline looks to be quite invigorating. I can see the enchantment, very attractive! You will let me paint her, will you not?"

"Beautiful, she is beautiful, Frank. Let you paint her? I should say not."

"What, you think I would try to seduce your wife?"

"I should hope not, but I know you too well, Frank. I am not so sure I am that confident in your loyalty."

"I do not think I am the person whom you should be concerned. We do share many friends that would not hesitate to try to get Cateline in bed, even if they knew you were married to her. But, not knowing you are married, they will not even falter to seduce her in front of you."

"I am not that worried. Cateline is an American girl by most standards. She can handle herself. I just don't want anyone to suspect that we are sleeping together. I dare say that I would not want her reputation damaged. And, as for painting her, you may ask. I shall leave that decision up to her."

Frank rationalizing their discourse, paused before he added, "Cateline is probably right, it pains me to say. It more than likely would damage your popularity in America if they knew you were married. But what happens when it is time for you to leave? Will she remain here with me?"

Oscar laughed and then replied, "No, I would not leave her with any of my friends. Cateline will travel with me or not with me, but she will be on the ship traveling to America at the same time. While I am touring, she will be visiting friends and family."

"Perhaps, it may work unless she becomes with child."

"Yes, I have thought of that, and we will cross that bridge if it happens."

As their discussions continued, Cateline finally came down the stairs, and Frank brought her a glass of champagne, "Congratulations are in order, Cateline. Your secret has been revealed. Let me pour you a glass of champagne." While each held their glass, Frank continued with the toast, "To the newly married couple, may your days be filled with love and happiness, and welcome, Cateline, to our happy bachelor's establishment."

They all drank down the champagne when Cateline addressed Frank, "It is such a relief for you to know. I was already starting to feel that I was not going to be on your good side."

Frank laughed, "Well, this may be for the best right now, I hate to confess, but your motives for this charade more than likely will benefit the advancement of Oscar's fame. As for your own eminence, I was just asking Oscar if he would allow me to paint you. I am sure with your beauty, you would have other offers, and I would like to be the first in line to capture your loveliness on canvas."

"Oh, and did he say that you could?" she inquired while glancing over to gaze into Oscar's eyes.

"Why, no. He has not said one way or the other. That would be your decision. In London, you would surely become a P.B."

"A—P.B.?"

"Professional Beauty, my dear. You do have the looks. You would draw a lot of attention."

Entertained, Cateline assured Frank, "I have no intention of doing anything that would draw consideration to myself, Mr. Miles."

"Before you say—no, your portrait would be reproduced and sold throughout London. Couturiers and milliners provide their latest fashions to the Professional Beauties simply for wearing them in public; it boosts their business and fills your wardrobe—"

"Please, no need to say anything further; Oscar knows that I have no desire to bring any interest to myself."

"Yes, I do understand, but if you change your mind—"

"I promise you that I will not, but if I did, I would allow you to be the only one to paint my portrait, Mr. Miles."

Frank concurred with a smile, "That is settled, but please call me Frank. Oh, by the way, your wedding photos arrived."

Oscar handed the envelope to Cateline, as she exclaimed, "Oh my gosh, Oscar, they are beautiful, have you seen them?"

"We were scrutinizing over them right before you came down, my dear," he replied while walking over to stand next to her.

"So, Frank, you had already seen the pictures and knew about the wedding?"

While laughing, Frank replied, "No, I had not seen them. They only arrived yesterday. Oscar just opened them."

With everything settled, Frank became an accomplice to their scheme. And so, they spent the remainder of the evening enjoying many conversations and sharing stories on their courtship in Ireland with all their escapades.

CHAPTER
27

During the past week or so, Cateline had joined the gentlemen in their exploits throughout London. Oscar and Frank's lifestyles were admired by many, as they were pretty involved with those of consequence. Cateline soon met many actresses, poets, and various artists, where she was quickly in the good graces of Lady Jane Wilde. Entertained as they were, surrounded by those relatively distinguished throughout the late afternoons—evenings, and until the wee hours of the morning. Many invitations were received to spectacular afternoon teas, superb suppers, London dinner parties, soirees, galas, and invites to attend all the latest theatrical spectaculars. Then, on occasions, there were those sporadic late nights spent at one of Oscar's favorite pubs, the Golden Lion, as was most often the case.

On her first Saturday in London, Cateline met Lady Jane as she was accompanied by Oscar to his mother's famous salon that evening. During her soirée, Jane fell in love with Cateline's charm and very hastily made sure she knew of her very fashionable literary Wednesdays. With all the mingling among those privileged, it was very gratifying to observe Frank and Oscar's proficiencies on entertaining weekly, as well. Their expertise with any type of affair, not taking anything informally, on the contrary, was viewed with the best of taste. For their exclusive list was always precise with those of the upper classes. Their invitations employed on those carefully selected were labeled, *Tea and Beauties* to everyone's delight, with many making their appearance—not desiring to miss the occasion of two great hosts, or rather, one might perceive them to be arbiters. Yes, it was somewhat apparent with Oscar's demeanor and temperament that he was most adept in influencing those of high society to his tastes, which were often mentioned throughout a most engaging evening. Oscar, with his decorating skills and his very colorful furnishings of Sevres fine porcelain platters, pots, and vases with the romantic blooms of white lilies adorning the drawing-room—his elaborate mode of beautification also included select French porcelain, Greek Tanagra figurines, and not to forget, peacock flowers to complement the décor arrangements graciously positioned throughout the room. All provided for a most aesthetic mood, while Frank's pastel portraits of his latest beauties on canvas were displayed about their home, where he was always most eager to make the commission with a sale or two. Besides the hors d'oeuvres of simply delightful cuisine, the bar was reasonably set with Venetian glasses to delight the desires of their extinguished guests to a hock and soda, gin, whiskey, or a refreshing glass of champagne—Perrier Jouët, of course. The soiree would not have been complete had it not been for the music box which adorned their drawing-room and filled the air with instrumental tunes. Not to mention, choice tobacco was freely available to all guests if they so desired to venture out on the veranda to enjoy the luxurious and vibrant garden while having a smoke. Oscar was known to steal the show, so to speak, with his witty sayings and his suave voice spoken with a certain, *cri de coeur.* He remained delicately smooth in his charm, even though he always overflowed with a somewhat poignancy in his quips, which were very ingenious. Cateline, knowing him intimately, understood those things he spoke, and she believed them to be embedded deep within his soul. Remembering Oscar's remark one evening on his belief to break into society, his words drifted through Cateline's mind, "There were only three ways this could be done, to feed them, amuse them, or to shock them."[1] Yes, it was quite the life, one in which he lived by adhering to those three tactics faithfully, which were to his advantage.

Those in attendance at the *Tea and Beauties,* Cateline soon learned, were many of the elite of London worthy of being mentioned: Lillie Langtry, *The Jersey Lily,* who one day would be classified as a British-American actress; Helena Modjeska, an American actress of Polish descent, who spent several years in London; Ellen Terry, English actress; Sir Edward Burne-Jones, a British artist known for his paintings; James Whistler, a most accomplished artist who was also known for his portraits and landscapes, not to mention his witty quotes—born in America, arriving in London where he remained; and last but definitely not least, Prince Albert Edward VII, the Prince of Wales, who was captivated by the lovely Lillie Langtry. Many other artists and actresses of London frequented their *Tea and Beauties* from time to time, which brought a superb following of the influential, who were also accustomed to purchasing Frank's paintings.

Arriving late, Walter Sickert, who was another British painter. Chills went through Cateline as she remembered in her timeframe, the article which had circulated, after so many years, it was believed that Sickert was Jack the Ripper. A bit frightening, as it was, Cateline decided to make sure her time in London would always be spent beside Oscar if possible.

All the socializing in London had placed Oscar and Cateline in the midst of many of his acquaintances. It had been more challenging for Cateline to pretend they were only friends than for Oscar. Yet, thus far, they had been successful in carrying on their ruse, with none being of suspect. Of course, with not one having a clue that they were actually married, except for Frank, this left the door wide open for many of his confrères to surround Cateline while trying to captivate her with their charm. On occasions, Oscar would catch a glimpse of her being in the spotlight amongst the available gentlemen. Still, he carried on with his wit and cleverness without further ado in the matter, while he held the majority enthralled. Cateline, too, was very much in tune with his rapport and enjoyed hearing bits and pieces of his quotes and tales. There were times when she would find herself standing by his side, far enough from any others to hear, and on one particular occasion, she whispered, "So, Mr. Wilde, what mask are you wearing this evening?"

Whereas he smiled most prominently and replied, "What a bore it is putting on one's attire. I can't see that it shall ever altar, my dear. You truly had better lose no time in telling me what mask you find me wearing, Cateline."

"Oh, I am not entirely sure. I believe I would have to study you further and your manner of dress, but my only desire is for you to know that you needn't ever feel you must wear any mask when in my presence."

"I do grow willful, my dear. For the praise of folly from the world is not always clear and vivid. How terribly cruel they can be at times. Nothing is ever quite true, indeed! To the world, I seem, by intention on my part, a dilettante and dandy merely. It is not wise to show one's heart to the world, and as the seriousness of manner is the disguise of the fool, folly in its exquisite modes of triviality and indifference and lack of care is the robe of the wise man. In so vulgar an age as this, we all need masks."[2]

"Yes, I, too, have worn many masks, and I do understand their purpose. Yet, surely, I am not just the world to you; I am the woman whom you love. I do assure you it is wise that I must see your heart."

Oscar grinned and replied, "No one talks so wonderfully as you, my dear. I am most fortunate enough to possess the key to your heart, indeed! And, I shall only be charmed by one such as yourself. It is in your presence that I have no desire to wear a mask of any kind, ma chérie."

At many of these events, Cateline found herself immensely enjoying meeting several of those she had studied and esteemed in her timeframe, with one being James Whistler. She had singled him out during tea regarding one of his famous paintings, "Mr. Whistler," Cateline spoke—
"Your name was?"
"Cateline, sir—"
"Please, call me James. You are visiting from America?"
"Yes, James, I am. You are also from America, I understand."
"Yes, I arrived in Paris when I was one and twenty, and I never returned."
Cheerfully, she announced, "I have greatly revered your paintings, but my favorite is *Symphony in White.*"

Conversations continued with Oscar, observing them from a slight distance while they seemed to be deeply engaged in much laughter and delight. Approaching, he spoke wisely, "Whistler—my most admired painter, I see that you have met my friend, Cateline, American as yourself. And I feel that her love for Europe has captivated her. Like you, I do not see her returning."
Cateline, laughing, "Yes, I do believe that I may have no desire to return. Oscar, I see why you admire James, as you do. Not only is his work of the highest standards, but his charm is absolutely captivating, as well."
"His work," Oscar laughed, "ah—yes, I will have to say, Jimmy being American, it is quite fortunate he lacked in the qualities of the American man, where art has no marvel and beauty no meaning and the past no message. He thinks that civilization began with the introduction of steam and looks with contempt upon all centuries that had no hot-water apparatuses in their houses[3]—but not Jimmy. For some of his work is rather done quite well."
"Please, Cateline—pay no attention to Oscar, for what has he in common with Art? Only that he dines at our tables and picks from

421

our platters the plums for the pudding, he peddles in the provinces," Whistler finished with a laugh.[4]

"My dear James, don't flatter yourself. I am afraid I have nothing to declare except my genius.[5] In fact, would you like to know the great drama of my life? It's that I have put my genius into my life; all I've put into my works is my talent."[6]

"Of course, Oscar—and where would we be without your cleverness?"

Oscar smiled and concluded while looking over at Cateline, "Jimmy, my dear Cateline, is indeed one of the very greatest masters of painting, in my opinion, that is. And, I may add that in this opinion, Mr. Whistler himself entirely concurs."[7]

Both gentlemen laughed, with Cateline realizing that Oscar and James were unmistakably pretty cordial with one another. "I suppose that you both like mocking each other?"

"We do see each other often, wouldn't you agree?"

"I am afraid that is true," Oscar concurred.

"Besides, I must make Oscar use his talents at times; otherwise, I am afraid it would all go to waste, Cateline."

"Ah—but when you and I are together, my friend, we are both quite brilliant, for we never talk about anything except ourselves."[8]

"No, no, Oscar, you forget—when you and I are together, we never talk about anything except me."[9]

"Yes, it is true, Jimmy—while we are talking about you, I am thinking of myself."[10]

The two gentlemen maintained their dialogue regarding themselves while laughing at their comments, with Cateline extremely amused at their friendship. At one point, they realized that Cateline was still standing there, listening to their banter, when Oscar, speaking in his Italian lingua, quietly whispered to James or rather Jimmy, as he was known by his friends, "Trovi la Cateline più affascinante?"

Whistler replied, "Lo voglio— Lei è parlato per?"

"Credo che lei sia."

Cateline smiling, interrupted, "I do believe it is not proper for two gentlemen to carry on a conversation in front of a lady trying to conceal their words."

Both laughing, Oscar agreed, "You are absolutely right. It is not every day that we are with others who speak Italian, but we will speak nothing further in front of you."

The three of them engaged in perpetual discussions and laughter for some time until Oscar's attention was requested elsewhere, while others continued to be drawn to Cateline.

With the midnight hours passing swiftly into the wee early morning, one by one, the guests had dwindled where Oscar and Cateline found themselves entirely alone. As they lounged around, she inquired of the Pre-Raphaelites, knowing they were established in the late 1840s and lived in London being relatively well-known. "Oscar, you do like the works of the Pre-Raphaelite Brotherhood?"

"Why, yes. Why do you ask?"

"I think much of their paintings are very enlightening. Jimmy had brought up the subject tonight which, was most informative as I have enjoyed their work over the years. In fact, I simply adore Rossetti's painting, *Proserpine.*"

"Dante—I grew up admiring him greatly. Rossetti was entranced in his youth by my mother's translated version of *Sidonia;* in fact, he quoted from her translation many times."

"How fascinating. I am sure, as a young boy, they played much in influencing your life, besides the influence of your mother, of course."

"Yes, they were also associated with John Ruskin, one of my professors at Oxford, if you will recall. It was Ruskin and Walter Pater, another professor, who were huge influences in my life. The Brotherhoods' works were highly influenced by Romanticism. *Proserpine,* Jane Morris was his model. She married William Morris, one of the other brothers. Holman Hunt, he painted, *The Eve of Saint Agnes,* are you familiar with that painting?"

"No, I do not believe so."

"The painting is based on Keats's poem. I know Hunt's daughter, Violet, a lovely woman, lives here in London."

"You know her well?"

"I suppose I do. I have spent considerable time at her home, but it was quite some time ago," amused, he continued, "do I detect a bit of jealousy?"

"No, I don't have a reason, do I?"

Oscar, leaning towards her, kissed her most romantically, whispering, "I think not."

423

Slightly annoyed, Cateline thought to herself, "The jealousy must have shown, for I do know who she was, and there was a time when he courted her. I am almost sure of it."

The following Saturday had arrived, 23 April, which had been the topic of every conversation over the past few weeks since Gilbert and Sullivan's premiere of *Patience* was to open at the Opera Comique theatre that evening. This two-act operetta had been heavily advertised in every newspaper and magazine, while its motive was to satirize the aesthetic movement in England through humor. In the operetta, two poets were typecast: Grosvenor to that of Swinburne and Bunthorne of Wilde, with Whistler's trademarked white truss of hair. Both characters, Grosvenor and Bunthorne, ardently contrast each other in personalities and styles, becoming rivals throughout the performance while ladies affectionately adored them. It was imperative that Oscar attend the premiere, which would be heavily publicized to promote his popularity and publicity before his American tour.

The evening of the premiere, dressing the part, Oscar wore his black velvet jacket, knee-breeches, with a most vibrant red waistcoat and complemented with black clocked silk stockings. Underneath, a white shirt barely visible was accompanied by a superb black tie in cravat fashion. Stepping into his patent leather pumps, he achieved a lily to carry and was ready to leave for the theatre. Cateline, dressed impressively for their evening, knowing how important this night was to Oscar, had purchased a new evening gown in the most vivid blue color made of gendarme silk. Her beautifully ornate skirt flowed amongst narrow pleats, topped by puffs of white silk, delicately lined with ruffles and a square-neck bodice, trimmed with embroidered tousles of elegant white taffeta to accent. The sleeves, cascading midway, were ornamented with dainty white petals of soft tulle. Completing her ensemble, she carried her new evening fan, purchased to complement her dress in the color of blue elaborated with tiny flowers, as well.

Oscar, purchasing box seats for his friends, accompanied Cateline and his other guests, Frank and Whistler, to name a few, as they followed the porter to their section. Very soon, complimentary champagne was brought for their delight, which Oscar had previously arranged, along with whiskey for those who desired to add a shot to their glass. It had been decided before their leaving that

Cateline would sit next to Frank to not bring any attention to Oscar looking as though they were a couple.

"Ah, I see you are most bizarrely dressed, Oscar. Quite decorative, may I add—but oh, so debonair," Jimmy spoke with an air of certainty.

"Jimmy, oh, Jimmy! You should know me quite well, indeed. For if I were all alone, marooned on some desert island, and had my things with me, I should dress for dinner every evening."[11]

It was undoubtedly, Oscar at his best, and what a night this would be. Once in their box, he passed around white lilies for all his friends to hold before leaving his seat to walk down into the theatre. As he joined in conversation with various folks, he continued to hand out more lilies while cameras were continually all about him. Most knowing Oscar from his attire and with the performance staged in a way that was meant to mock the aesthetic movement, he was definitely one of the champions for their cause. As the theatre became very crowded, everyone who was anyone was in attendance, all stalls seemed to be filled at full occupancy, balconies overflowing—box seats at capacity, and the dress circles were well taken with many of the elite. Back in his chair, Cateline leaned over to whisper to him, "It is pretty apparent that you and Whistler are very popular with this movement. Yet, many, I am afraid, find all of this amusing. I truly admire you for standing up for your beliefs and daring to be unlike others, Oscar. I have always said that it is perfectly alright to be different."

"You are quite right to think that, my dear! One's real life is so often the life that one does not lead."[12]

With all seated in their sections, eagerly awaiting the performance, Frank inquired of Oscar, "Is there a reason we are all holding the white lilies?"[13]

"I wanted a good number of men to hold them. It will annoy the public."[13]

Frank asked, "But why annoy the public?"[13]

"Well, it likes to be annoyed. I made sure a young man on stage would also be holding a lily; people will stare at it and wonder. Then they will look round the house and see, here and there, more and more specks of the white lily. 'This must be some secret symbol,' they will say; 'what on earth can it mean?'"[13]

Cateline probed, "And what does it mean?"[13]

"Nothing whatever, but that is just what nobody will guess."[13]

425

It was during the intermission, between acts, many wandered into the bar close to the theatre to enjoy drinks while conversing thus far on the splendid performances and much laughter on the comparisons of those portrayed. Cateline, off to the side, enjoyed watching Oscar amongst his many friends relishing in the moments, able to share the experiences of his life.

Back in their box seats, awaiting the second act, anticipations were exhilarated throughout the remainder of the play. Such a magnificent experience, seeing the entertainment of the nineteenth century, the ending soon at hand, a most massive applause to the performance being received, echoing throughout. Everyone stood and began to congregate, with much conversation and excitement being heard. Cateline managed to stand next to Oscar for a few moments, yet long enough to exclaim, "Ah, poor Oscar, 'Nobody is Bunthorne's bride!'"

He smiled at her and quietly replied, "There is no other bride for me. You are quite delightful, my dear."

Oscar walked down into the crowds with all his guests as many eyes were fixated on him, amazed by his appearance, adorning a lily. More photos were taken, which captured a few that included Cateline in the background since she was among those in his circle. Oscar and Whistler were then escorted backstage to meet the cast.

A number of days had passed, where Cateline many times found herself left in the company of Frank. At the same time, Oscar took to his commitments on publicity stratagems for the benefit of building his reputation before leaving for America. Oscar and Cateline's time alone had become sparse with his lifestyle and multitude of friends always being in their company. Cateline, on the other hand, had seemed to fit right in with his contemporaries, yet she deeply missed their times alone and longed for those days of past, where they only had each other. With the days trailing on, it was easy for Cateline to observe Oscar's popularity among all, owning a certain magnetism where people seemed to be drawn to him regardless of their social status. He seemed to charm the crowd relatively small or large with the ladies, as well as the men. Cateline became most admired among the gentlemen, with several making obvious advances towards her, almost immediately bringing about

Oscar's awareness. All the same, Cateline was very adamant in handling any of the young men in a ladylike fashion. It was always late nights, which surrendered them once again to their home, where they could, at last, be alone and together as husband and wife. At these times, Oscar's tenderness could be felt and assured of his devoted love towards her. Although, Cateline could foresee that he, too, needed the assurance of her love and devotion after observing all the gentlemen of consequence steadily taking an interest in getting to know her. On one particularly late night or, to be more precise, the early hours of the morning, as was their usual time to finally be alone, Oscar inquired, "Do you regret marrying me?"

"Why would you ask that question, Oscar?"

"Most of our days are spent in the company of others, in which we are merely friends. It has been a great privilege to observe you in polite society but rather horrid to hear the whispers, most audible, I assure you. I have felt somewhat vexed. Perhaps, there has been a bit of jealousy possess my soul."

Cateline smiled as she leaned over to kiss him gently, "I married you because I love you deeply, and no one will ever change the way that I feel for you, my love. These whispers, have they been vicious rumors?"

"No, I would not have stood for unwarranted gossip, Cateline. If someone were to taint your reputation, I would be furious. It was purely some of the fellows talking of your beauty and with that, their desires pertaining to you, of course, not in a bad way, I assure you. But it was enough to have put me in a sulky mood. I dare to imagine other men desiring you, that is all."

"Oscar, I love being married to you, and I shall never regret my decision."

Most nights had been filled with exhaustion where they had fallen asleep promptly, but that night was one filled once again with the love they had for each other—a night of tenderness, caress, and adoration.

The following morning, Oscar awakened and cuddled closer to Cateline, having no desire to arise but to remain next to her for the day. Awakening, she spoke softly, "Good morning, my love."

"Good morning," he responded, kissing her intimately. "Why don't we simply spend the day together in bed—I am pained at spending each and every day acting as though we are not in love. I desire to be with *ma femme* and not share you today."

Cateline laughed while replying, "I love to hear you say that—but—,"

"No—do not add a *but* please!"

"I think you should know that it is Wednesday, and we promised your mother we would attend her salon, *mon mari.*"

"Yes, but that is this evening."

"Right you are, except she asked if we would accompany her for elevenses with perhaps a light lunch today at the Savoy."

Oscar looking at his watch, "We still have some time. We do not have to begin getting ready just yet—," he countered as he pulled Cateline closer to him and kissed her fervently.

Later that morning, Oscar and Cateline hurriedly prepared themselves to be presentable for Lady Wilde. Riding in one of the omnibus's, they arrived at the Savoy Restaurant, located beside the Savoy Theatre, both owned by the Carte's family. Cateline, finally able to view the Thames River by daylight, observed selected tables, quite charmingly lined along the riverfront adorned with fine linen. Several couples were enjoying their tea alongside the most exquisite view of the many gondolas drifting about. While they waited to be seated in the Thames Foyer for lunch, momentarily, Lady Jane joined them as they took pleasure in much small talk. Shortly, they were led into the notable dining area, where numerous tables were scattered about with white tablecloths draped over. Off to one end, Cateline observed the pianist playing intensely in smooth tunes while the room was much engaged. Rather busy, as it was, folks were seated throughout as they enjoyed their fare and company. Oscar took charge of the ordering, with the server soon delivering their tea in a most lavish British Burleigh crockery, a teapot with three accompanying teacups in a pink Asiatic Pheasant design. Having requested Assam tea, the server filled their cups with the brightly colored brew. Cateline added cream and sugar to her tea before taking a sip of the malty and robust flavor, "Mmm—this is most delightful, Oscar."

"Yes, Oscar does choose a good cup of tea, Cateline," Mrs. Wilde concluded.

Promptly following, the server returned with their choice of food items, which were skillfully spread out on a three-tier serving stand and placed in the center of their table. Cateline looked on at the most splendid selections, where she found herself lost in the variety of delectable foods. There were fabulous egg and mayonnaise finger snacks, charming cucumber sandwiches, delicious scones served with clotted cream and preserves, thin slices of orange cake, adorable bite-size square cakes, and fresh raspberries. Oscar, motioning for the waiter to return, expressed, "Please, we would like some fine champagne."

"Champagne? Whatever is the occasion?" Cateline inquired.

"We are here with my lovely mother. What could be a better occasion? Besides, one never needs a reason for fine champagne, my dear."

Everyone was quite engaged as they enjoyed the scrumptious food items when the waiter soon returned and filled three glasses with a most select variety of champagne. The discourse continued among their small party, lingering for a brief time until Lady Jane unexpectedly left Cateline astounded when she remarked, "Come now—neither of you has succeeded in deceiving me of your intentions."

"Whatever do you mean?" Oscar inquired.

"You know very well what I mean, Oscar. Remember, I am your mother, dear! Besides, Professor Mahaffey did not know where to send these pictures, so they were sent to me," Jane concluded, pulling out the two photos and handing them over to Oscar. "You may have been able to fool others; however, you cannot fool me. I can see, not only in the pictures, of you two standing side by side but also in observing your interactions together, as I assure you that I have been able to discern without a doubt. Your eyes give it away entirely. It is clear, your relationship goes beyond friendship."

Cateline spoke up and inquired, "Oscar, I thought Professor Mahaffey was supposed to send the photographs to my uncle?"

"I believe that is true, but perhaps he forgot," Oscar replied. At the same time, he glanced up to Cateline, trying to contemplate what he would say next to his mother when Lady Wilde relentlessly spoke again—

"Oscar, it is quite alright with me whatever you do with your life—but let me remind you of the importance of not falling into some scandal."

"Mother, that is very nice and very wrong of you! Even though nice is a nasty word! I assure you it is not what you think.

429

Yes—," he sustained, glancing over at Cateline, "there is more than just friendship—but I assure you that Cateline and I have done nothing to be worthy of a scandal."

"You are then admitting that there is more than friendship?"

"Yes, you are correct in your assumptions."

"Will you also try to declare to me that you two are not living together?" There was a brief pause while no one spoke when Lady Jane rephrased her words, "Come now, Oscar, I am not blind to what I see. Once again, the question stands, you are living together, are you not?"

Pausing before he spoke, Oscar stated, "You might as well know the whole truth, and I assure you that it was in our best interest to not share this with anyone. I married Cateline while in Ireland—."

"You did what?" his mother exclaimed rather loudly!

"We are married—legally, and before you say anything else, let me finish. I leave for America next year, and it was really Cateline who was more concerned with my popularity not being what it should if Americans were to know that I was married. Therefore, we decided to merely portray our lives as friends for right now, until after all the publicity and my tour to the Americas."

Jane was speechless for some moments before she responded, "Well, yes, I can see your concern and naturally so, but couldn't both of you have postponed your engagement and marriage until after your return from America?"

"I suppose we could have, but I, or rather we are both extremely taken with each other—desperately in love, mother. I could not leave Ireland without her, and Cateline would not have followed me to England not being married, which you should understand that if she had, her reputation would have been damaged."

"It's not that I am disappointed, dear," Jane continued while casting her gaze towards Cateline, who had remained quiet, "and, Cateline, I have nothing against you. In fact, I enjoyed your company immensely the other day. I do find you quite charming, and naturally, you are Irish, which means a great deal to me. You make a lovely daughter-in-law. I only wish that I could have been a part of your wedding and have known your intentions before now," she finished while casting her eyes back towards Oscar.

"I will take the blame for that, mother. But if we had indeed told you our intentions, would you not have tried to persuade us not to marry yet? Please, be truthful with your answer."

Lady Jane, thinking about his question, finally replied truthfully, "Yes, I suppose you know your mother very well. I do say I would more than likely have tried to persuade against the marriage until after your tour. It just saddens me that I could not be a part of your special day. Were there photos taken?"

"Yes, mother, there were—many photos, in fact. I also assure you if the wedding means that much to you, once I return from America, we can have a ceremony where everyone can be present."

"I suppose that would be a good start," Jane added and then placed her hand upon Cateline's as she spoke to her daughter-in-law, "Cateline dear, I do hope that we will have sufficient time to spend together. I would like us to be very close."

"Yes, ma'am, I would like that very much as well."

"Mother, there is one other thing, now that you know. You musn't share this with anyone, not even Willie. The reasoning behind this absurd farce was to keep this from going public. The more that discover this truth, the sooner it would leak to the wrong source."

"Very well, I will keep your secret for the time being," she resolved while continuing on the same matter, "but tell me, have you had time to prepare yourself for speaking on the aesthetics while on your tour, Oscar?"

"Ah, prepare or not prepare—my one concern, perhaps, I do not have a talent for public speaking, mother. Yet, I would want a natural style, with a touch of affection,[14] and my hopes are to acquire such."

"My dear boy, you are your mother's child. I would think it should come naturally to you."

"Oh, would that I could live up to my blue China."[15]

Lady Jane and Cateline laughed at his remark, and conversations continued with all enjoying their afternoon.

They finished their lunch and left the restaurant promising Jane that they would be at her salon later that day.

The week went smoothly, staying engaged in all the usual affairs when Friday finally arrived. Oscar, giving instructions, Frank and Cateline were to adorn themselves most stylishly, for he had made special arrangements, a surprise of sorts. Cateline being most anxious to have an evening out with Oscar, even though it included Frank—she was still enthusiastic, as she loved surprises. Dressing the part most elegantly, momentarily, Cateline joined the gentlemen

431

downstairs for their adventure. It was evident that Frank had already been informed of Oscar's plans, though none would disclose any details as to where they were heading.

They very soon arrived at a rather upscale hotel, The Langham, which had a quaint pub tucked away inside, one of Oscar's hangouts with his acquaintances. The three of them walked into the pub, where they were met by many of Oscar and Frank's friends. Yet, little did Cateline realize at the time, Oscar had planned a private gathering where Cateline would entertain with her guitar and voice. "Oscar, how could you do this without asking me?"

"Cateline, you know how much I love to hear you sing," he concluded quietly, walking her to a room in the back where they would not be seen, their relationship being as it was. He then put his arms around her and looked deep into her eyes before finishing his plea, "I know how annoying this is to you, Cateline. I ask that you do this for me, please!"

"I am really disappointed. You know that I do not have a desire to be in the spotlight."

"I am sure I do not know what to say to make this right. It is true; I do know you have no desire to perform. But, please, if you love me," he spoke quietly into her ear while kissing her lightly on her neck, "you will do this for me, I beg you. I think you are wonderful and just want my friends to hear you."

She smiled and responded, "Well, only because I love you—Oscar."

Cateline headed back into the front of the pub, where a stool had already been placed on the small stage for her to be seated. Thinking about what song to sing, she decided to start with a sassy number by The Ronettes from 1963, *Baby, I Love You*[16]—

Upon ending the song, there was much applause and encores among Oscar's friends. Cateline performed more than a few songs that night, taking breaks in between. Many a gentleman engaged in dialogue with her and one particular who continued to try and persuade her to leave with him. Throughout the evening, a photographer took several pictures; Cateline assumed this was due to the many actresses and upper echelons present—including many taken of her when she was standing amongst some of the elite. Nevertheless, she realized she had not recognized the background as being among any of the photos in her possession nor the many acquaintances of his who were at the pub. It became quite apparent to her there may have been additional photos taken that had never materialized or pictures she had yet to find.

As the night lingered, there were many laughs among Oscar's friends as his clever words and wit seemed to keep their whole group amused. It was pretty obvious that a party simply was not a party without Oscar's presence, which somewhat explained just who this *Oscar Wilde* person truly was. Conversations emerged from among passing friends who had not known him at length, where one would realize why his presence was always required when the social elite gathered. During one such discourse, discussions had geared off towards a psychiatrist who had become fairly well-known among the privileged, while many felt Max Nordau was nothing more than a quack, and others seemed to delight in seeing him. Oscar, in his brilliance, summed it up most cleverly when he responded to the topic of conversation, "I certainly agree with Dr. Nordau's assertion that all men of genius are insane, but Dr. Nordau forgets that all sane people are idiots."[17] Laughter and applause could be heard, for any night in Oscar's presence, one could be assured of the utmost premier entertainment.

Later through the night, Cateline soon learned that one of the gentlemen with their group happened to be Squire Bancroft, an actor but also the manager at the Haymarket Theatre. Once they had left, she also discovered that Mr. Bancroft was very interested in getting Cateline into the theatre. Of this, a late-night discussion occurred between her and Oscar once they had arrived home. Undressing for bed, Cateline elaborated, "Oscar, I know that you arranged for my entertaining tonight in hopes that I would be persuaded by the offer of Mr. Bancroft to get into acting." While starting this conversation, she walked over closer to where he stood and looked into his eyes before saying what needed to be said, "I know you love me and believe that I am most talented, but I assure you that I am right where I want to be for the moment. I love you; I am not in love with the idea of being a famous actress." It was at this moment, Cateline put her arms around him, leaning forward, she kissed him softly on his lips.

Oscar responded to her advances as he held her close, kissing her most intimately. "I love you too, my dear. They all loved you; you know that, don't you?"

"Yes—so, it seems, but some of them could hardly keep their hands to themselves. I do not think that I want that kind of attention. On another note, I would like for us to spend a whole day together with you showing me some of the sights in London. We have been here for some time now, and I have spent it solely in the presence of your friends, and I have only seen your main hangouts, which I love, by the way. But I want to experience London with you and not with all your friends."

Oscar smiled as he tenderly asserted, "For you, I would throw over all my friends. An engagement it is. I will promise to spend all my time with just you, my own one, for my desire is to explore London at your side. We sleep late, and then we go into the city until the wee hours, if you so wish."

CHAPTER

28

The morning started as a bright and energetic day, with Cateline awakening around ten as she cuddled up to Oscar. She kissed his neck lightly until he stirred. Excited for their day of ventures planned in London, Cateline whispered, "Good morning, my love—wake up, we have a big day today."

"No—expound to me, my love, what is so good about it? It is far too early to be good; besides, wickedness is far more enjoyable, wouldn't you agree? May I ask if you intend to arise at such a time?"

"I believe it to be a cheery morning, my love."

"Oh, but please indulge me, my dear, let's just sleep for a while. It is much too early," he responded lazily.

"I am hungry, Oscar."

"You, my dear, are dreadfully roguish and extremely dangerous."

"Why would you speak in such a way, Oscar? You do know I love you, so much so; how could you think me dangerous?"

"Cateline, my own one, you influence me in such a bad way."

"You think me to be a bad influence?"

"To influence one in any way would be a bad influence, my love, for there is no such thing as a good influence. All influence is immoral—immoral from the scientific point of view.[i] You must remember, I have strived to adhere to the standards of the elite, those of London's fashionable society. One would never be seen among the working class so early in the morning. Do let me sleep, my dear; it is one's duty."

"I'm terribly sorry, Oscar. Do you feel that I am bad for you?"

"Very bad, indeed, my love." With his eyes barely opened, Oscar looked up at her charming and fairly captivating expression as he inquired, "Are you really hungry, or is this a trap to awaken me?"

"Is it working?"

He smiled and replied, "No! It is not working."

She responded with a slight giggle, "Yes—it is working; I can see it in your sarcastic smile. You love me and would never deny me food."

435

"Ah, I am afraid you can see my heart. For, I am too much in love to tell you no. And, you are correct in your assumption, I would not let you go hungry, but you do not look like you are starving by any means," he remarked mischievously.

"WHAT? Are you saying that I am fat?"

In a jovial manner, he responded, "No, I was just trying to get even with you for waking me, but this is going to cost you dearly," he remarked while reaching over to pull her next to him while kissing her passionately.

Responding to his advances, their morning took somewhat longer than planned before they commenced to get ready for the day.

They had a delightfully late breakfast, as it was, with Frank, before leaving to begin their day shopping at Liberty, one of Oscar's favorite places. Liberty's department store was quite substantial and had many items for sale. They were known for their elaborate fabrics, having all the latest and most exclusive for any taste—silks from India such as the Nagpore, Corah, and Tussore. There were soft ivory-white silks, art cretonnes, chintzes, cashmere, woven muslin, and various cloths—kamil, valley, and cotton for spring and summer. They also carried a generous variety of millinery for ladies and many specialty items of perfumes, jewelry, art, and articles of clothing. "My dear," Oscar mentioned as he watched Cateline looking over all the fine silks, "I have purchased an abundance of their fabrics, most favorably priced, I assure you, and the quality I have simply worshipped."

Overwhelmed by the many choices and the elaborate colors, she responded, "Yes, they are exquisite. Oscar, please do help me decide which ones I should buy."

Oscar walked over closer to where she stood and reached down to examine the quality before making his decision on a few of superior worth in the most alluring colors, "I believe this one, the rich amethyst, will bring out the beauty of your eyes and hair, my dear. Ah, and the scarlet, it is purely astounding."

"Yes, they are quite lovely, thank you." Gathering up those selected, Cateline stopped to gaze at all the elegant ladies' hats. Deciding among the various options, she joined her husband as he wandered over to look at the home furnishing items and art.

As they made their final purchases, Oscar desired to stop by James J. Fox cigar merchants, "This is where I normally purchase my cigarettes; they carry such a large medley of smokes, gold-tipped, indubitably."

Cateline smiled and noted, "Yes, if you so desire, but I wish you would stop smoking, Oscar. It is a most dreadful habit that is not good for you."

"Ah—but a cigarette is the perfect type of a perfect pleasure. It is exquisite, and it leaves one unsatisfied. What more could one want?"[2]

"I believe I could bring forth a good argument on that point."

"Please, if you must, but do remember, my dear, one who is civilized often takes things too seriously. I would much rather be unrefined than to be overly serious." Cateline stopped walking while Oscar turned towards her as he spoke once again, "How tedious, you had better lose no time with your argument, my dear. But must we stop?"

"Yes," she declared while putting her arms around his neck. Cateline leaned forward and kissed him passionately. As she released him to continue her argument, she proclaimed most earnestly, "Oscar, this conversation is not boring. Your perfect pleasures, are they not times like these when we are intimate, mon chéri?"

"I beg your pardon, my dear. There is nothing about you I find boring. On the contrary, I am quite charmed, yet emotions can be advantageous, many times, where one is led astray.[3] To conclude this conversation, you are my perfect pleasure, I must confess. All the same, before I met you, my cigarette held that realm in my life."

She gazed into his eyes while elaborating, "Hmm, I do believe I am satisfied with your final comment, my dear. It is much improved, and, I might add, I believe it is far better to be satisfied instead of not being satisfied."

"Ah—but that you misunderstood. When we are satisfied, there is no need to seek anything further. Enjoying one's pleasures should never completely satisfy in that you continue to desire that pleasure more and more."

"Yes, I can see where that makes sense. I hope that you are never entirely satisfied with what we have so that you desire *us* more and more daily."

He stopped and leaned over to kiss her intimately, once again, "Oui, ma chérie, I desire more and more of you."

437

Continuing their walk towards the cigar merchant store, they soon arrived where Oscar could purchase his standard Turkish brand tobacco. While they waited for his brand to be packaged, he commented, "I am afraid nowadays people know the price of everything and the value of nothing.⁴ Ah, the highly aromatic delight when one smokes, the mild flavor, gratifying, my dear."

Afterward, they enjoyed a delicious lunch at Café Royal, one of the places Oscar frequented and where the regulars knew him rather well. It was a most enjoyable time as Cateline loved watching Oscar interact with many of the patrons, of course, introducing her as his friend from America.

As they left, Oscar took Cateline to Hatchards' bookstore, which dated back to 1797. Once again, he was a regular where she was introduced. Cateline, loving to read as much as he did, spent a substantial amount of time enjoying sorting through the many volumes of books before being drawn to two, *Nana* by Émile Zola and *The Way We Live Now*, an Anthony Trollope narrative. *Nana* was relatively a new release, and Trollope's novel was released several years back, but she was pretty familiar with both in her time. To her surprise, *Nana* was the third edition even though it had been released not quite a year since. Still very excited, Cateline exclaimed, "Oscar, have you read either of these?"

"I am familiar with both. *Nana* was published not long ago. Although, Zola is determined to show that if he has not got genius, he can at least be dull.⁵ As for Trollope, there has been considerable talk of his becoming a play. I am certainly familiar with him; he does reside in London. Trollope has written many books, but he is not as well-liked as he once was—yet I believe this is one of his best works. I am sure it would be a good read."

"I have read *The Warden* by Trollope and enjoyed it immensely. I do believe I would like both of them. I am surprised to see *Nana* is the third edition if he is dull, as you say."

Oscar smiled and noted, "*Nana*, upon its release last year, sold fifty-five thousand copies in one day. Personally, I am not fond of him, nor his works, but you may very well enjoy the book."

Being shocked to know the number of sales, as she had no idea, Cateline responded, "Fifty-five thousand? That is astounding; you did not purchase one?"

"No, but if you are set on having the first edition, I am sure we could find you one."

"No, that is alright. I will just take this one."

Oscar, having also picked up a few new books, paid for their selections. Opening the door for Cateline, they resumed their exploits, seeing many sights of London.

"I hope this day has not bored you thus far."

"Not at all; why would you think such a thing?"

"I suppose it has not been very romantic," he concluded.

She slipped her arm around his and answered, "Just being with you and not having any of your friends with us has made me very happy."

As he smiled from her last remark, Oscar stated, "I would like to take you to Kettner's for dinner. Their restaurant, excellent if I may say, is located within the hotel. It is French cuisine at its finest, of course, prepared superbly by chef August Kettner. And it is quite the compliment to *l'art de la cuisine*, I do declare."

"August Kettner, the proprietor?"

"Yes, indeed! It is rather remarkable, but I feel we should go home and dress for the occasion; after all, it is fine dining."

"Yes, I would find much delight in getting myself all dolled up for the evening—to be beautiful for you, needless to say."

"You are already beautiful, we should merely dress the part, and afterward, we can go have drinks at the Golden Lion's pub."

Hailing a cab to head back to Frank's home, Cateline was somewhat dazed, dreaming of their most romantic dinner and evening out on the town. After tipping the chauffeur, they were soon busily about donning themselves for their splendidly arranged date. Cateline arrayed herself in a very soft satiny dress of deep burgundy with a squared neckline—mid-length sleeves trimmed with cream-colored lace to complement the deep cherry shade. The fitted bodice curved over her form, flowing gracefully down as it gathered with sufficient ruffles where delicate roses laced with ribbons of cream were stationed at intervals. Cream-colored lace fashionably enhanced the bodice and adorned the extremity of the hem gracefully. To complete her look, Cateline wore her new hat of the same elusive hue fashioned atop her luscious hair, which was formed in a slight updo. Strands of her curled ringlets dangled sparingly on

439

each side and along her back. She looked over at Oscar and inquired, "What do you think?"

"I think it will be my pleasure escorting you this evening, my love. You are an extraordinarily stunning creature, Cateline." With those words spoken, Oscar went over to pick up a small bag lying on a table before he turned back towards her. "I do believe this should be added to your attire for the evening, a bit of decoration to enhance your charm, my dear." As he stood in front of her, Oscar pulled out a Victorian locket, floral repousse with a shamrock slide hanging delicately from a very dainty chain.

"Oh my—Oscar, it is so lovely. When did you buy this?"

"While we were shopping and you were preoccupied—that is not all, earrings to complement the necklace," he disclosed while fumbling in the bag to pull out the remaining items.

"Oscar, I don't know what to say. Why the necklace even has a 'C' engraved—I love them."

With an appealing smile, he fastened the necklace around Cateline's neck and then assisted her with the earrings. "I wanted my wife to stand out amongst the London crowd tonight—and, to know how much I love her."

With tears in her eyes, Cateline leaned over to kiss him deeply, "You do know how much I love you, don't you?"

"Yes, I do—please, no tears. I will not have you looking sad; we will have a most memorable night."

"Thank you, Oscar. I do say that your taste surpasses most men. I find myself quite intoxicated with your choices. This is a locket; I will have to put a photo of us inside," she concluded.

"That would be a fascinating addition, perhaps one of our wedding photos."

Leaving for their romantic evening, Cateline felt so in the moment, knowing that she would never love again—never could love again, how could she? Oscar was everything to her and everything she could ever want.

They arrived at Kettner's and entered a most prodigious building, and were immediately ushered through a plush dining room. Fine linens draped over stylish tables were lined throughout a spectacularly decorated room adorned with select paintings. Their lavish surroundings of the most splendid taste brought Cateline such delight. As they were seated, Oscar took charge of ordering their drinks and the cuisine. Cateline felt like a princess being charmed by her prince. It was a most intriguing evening, as they enjoyed excellent hors d'oeuvres before their main course of superb French cuisine. Champagne supplied the night with a most romantic flare, and flattery resumed with Oscar exposing himself unashamed of his admiration and love for her. But, of course, the best part of the night was the fact none of his friends were present, where he could be her husband and not her friend.

The evening continued as Cateline felt highly cherished and desired by the man she would never forget. All the times she had faithfully written in her diary would be kept beside her to the end of her days, as she would sincerely treasure every moment. All in all, they had a most romantic evening that soon turned into night, where they headed to the Golden Lion's pub to end the day over a few drinks. They enjoyed their time shared where, luckily, none of his acquaintances were to be seen the entirety of their rendezvous.

As the night endured, Cateline remarked, "Oscar, I do miss these times together. It reminds me of all the moments we were able to share in Ireland. Unfortunately, it has not been the same in London, with all your friends. It is not that I do not like them; I have enjoyed getting acquainted with all of them very much, yet, it does pain me to pretend that we are merely friends instead of lovers. I miss the intimacy throughout the day—whereas, we only have those times once we are in bed—which again, comes very late due to the time spent surrounded by others."

"Don't you think I, too, have missed those times we used to spend alone at your uncle's? I had no clue you felt this way." Oscar, sighing, stated, "Ah, women represent the triumph of matter over mind, just as men represent the triumph of mind over morals."[6]

Cateline, feeling perplexed, declared, "I do hope you are not referring to me as the normal woman, Oscar. I assure you, circumstances around me do not sway my decisions. My mind is quite clear to be able to reason the importance of spending quality time with my husband, and by no means do I look upon things based on my surroundings. And, even though my feelings may come into play from time to time, I do tend to settle with seeing that which is above and not below. My emotions may get in the way, but once again, I will quickly choose to look on the bright side of things."

441

"Hmmm—interesting! You always seem to amaze me, dear. But I must say, this was your idea that none know we are married, Cateline. If you desire that everyone knows, we will announce our marriage."

"No, I do not want to jeopardize your popularity for America. I was merely stating how I miss those times together—just the two of us. Once we leave for Paris, I am assuming there will be more days where we can enjoy each other as husband and wife. That is if we will not be surrounded by your friends while in France, as well."

"I do have a few friends in Paris, but of course, I do not live there—I have no residence for others to stop by. While there, I usually reside at the Hotel Voltaire close to the River Seine."

"I do hope that we can leave for Paris before long."

"Yes, I have been thinking about it to some extent. If you care to, we could leave one day next week. Would that suit you?"

"Yes, I would love that. Thank you, mon chéri." A few moments had passed when Cateline revived the conversation, once again, "Oh, and Oscar, I do have another question," she stated with a most seductive smile.

"Hmmm—I'm not sure I like that look."

"Do not think I was not listening to what you said earlier. Your comment about men representing the triumph of mind over morals, is that the method most use where they feel no remorse for living sinful lives?"

"Ah, my dear, is it not better for women simply to love us, defaults and all?" Oscar ended the conversation, leaning towards Cateline while kissing her intimately.

Soon afterward, they decided to leave for home. Oscar, paying for the cab, took Cateline's hand and expressed, "No, let's not go inside just yet."

"What did you have in mind?"

"A walk down to the river. I believe your only view was when we dined at the Savoy, and it is not more than a few blocks from here."

"Yes, I knew it was close; that sounds somewhat enticing."

They took the short walk towards the River Thames, holding hands, taking in the glorious views of London at night, with the vibrant flare of the gas lamps lining the streets and their yellow mist rising up eerily along the quay. Off in the distance, the quaint pubs were illuminated nebulously, with an occasional patron seen going in and out, while the brief twilight coursed along the brick mortar pathways. The distant dark green waters glistened from the streaks of moonlight, where a tiny image was briefly visible—a ship heading towards the channel filled with commerce and a large barge close by. They enjoyed the night air with a slight chill and the feel of a gentle breeze as it whisked over their bodies, tousling strands of hair that were hanging down around Cateline's face. After some moments, Cateline spoke, "Oscar—"

"Yes?" He responded, taking her hand in his.

"I was merely thinking, London is known for its fog."

"Fog—or rather Dickens *London ivy*?"

She laughed, "Well, yes, I do know it is not really fog."

"London is too full of fogs—and serious people, whether the fogs produce the serious people or whether the serious people produce the fogs, I don't know."[7]

"I like that. Your words always amaze me. But I hadn't noticed anything significant other than when we first arrived by train."

"Ah, and you may not see it hardly as much. The fog is more noticeable during cold weather. However, if you will notice, closer to the river, it is a bit more visible."

"Yes, I can see it vaguely, but I thought the fog was much more prominent."

"It is more blatant dependent on the time of year," he concluded, adding, "the great advantage of the fog—an artist's delight, my dear, a most romanticized touch if you have had the pleasure to see the works created."

"I have, and yes, they are magnificently depicted."

They had briefly walked along the river when Oscar sat down on a grassy area that provided for a genial view and pulled Cateline down to sit in front of him as he wrapped his arms around her. She leaned back into his chest, feeling the rhythm of his heart while they both looked out over the dark waters, with the light of the moon shining down—a glow streaming sleepily over the banks. The occasionally quaint sound of the waters could be heard eerily from a distance, with the echo of a boat's steam whistle sounding quite sporadically. Nonetheless, London seemed to be asleep, at least on the end where Oscar lived. Only a faint mumble could be heard from time to time, and an indistinct silhouette of a man or woman from a distance could be seen. It was a most lovely night, sitting out under the dark sky with the solitary glow of the moon in all its grandeur, the vast horizon dotted with thousands of stars, some twinkling while others seemed to stand vibrant yet desolate with a sense of seclusion. They were both quiet as they listened to the stillness around them, the sound of their hearts beating in unison. Oscar's hand gently ran through Cateline's hair, loosening the slide that had held it up gracefully, watching as it fell in loose curls upon her shoulder cascading onto her breasts. His breath could be felt on her neck with each soft kiss planted as she responded to his gentleness along with every soothing touch. She turned her head, and their lips seemed to gently find each other as they became intimate, then more forcefully desiring each embrace, caress, and every kiss. Lying on the soft grass, they became lost in each other's touch, with the desire for more and more being felt within. When suddenly, Oscar began to look around at the darkness about them, finally he spoke, "Ah, I want you something fierce, but I am afraid we must go."

"Is there something wrong?"

"Not at all. We should probably go home to finish what we started, that is all."

Having no desire to leave, reluctantly, she agreed, "I suppose it may not be so safe out here at night."

"Mmm—yes, you would be correct in your assumption, but do not lose that look you are wearing."

"What look might that be, Oscar?"

As he leaned over one more time to tenderly kiss her, between light strokes, he whispered, "The look, Cateline, that says you want me."

Oscar stood and pulled Cateline to her feet, once again, holding her close while kissing her lightly on her face and neck. As he held her hand, they started walking back when Oscar quipped, "I will race you—."

"Ah, my knight in shining armor once more," Cateline responded while removing her shoes and twisting her dress where she could hold it out of the way to be able to run, "Yes, let the competition begin, but I should get a head start—that is only fair."

"You may have a head start," Oscar agreed, continuing, "but I will still win."

Cateline smiled and declared, "Do not say so until it has been proven," she finished, taking off with a quick lead before he had time to say anything.

She laughed with every stride, even as Oscar passed her. As they arrived at the house, she could not stop giggling for several minutes until she finally caught her breath, proclaiming, "Your prize, my knight, for winning—I will let you go to sleep without having your way with me!"

"No—no, I am the winner and get to choose the prize, my dear."

Despite everything, in a state of laughter, she responded, "I never agreed on such. Your prize is that you get to go to sleep without!"

Pulling her close to him, he commenced to kiss her as they both were filled with laughter. Oscar declared rather abruptly, "I believe I can change your mind." And, if truth be told, her mind was changed as they spent the remainder of their night together, enjoying the pleasure of each other, with giggles and laughter being entirely discernable. Yet neither seemed to be concerned that particular night, while Oscar exclaimed, at one point, "I am sure Frank has heard our laughter, my dear."

"Yes, that is if he is even home."

Neither seemed to care, as they were much engaged in spending those long-awaited moments together, like old times. With Cateline, she had desired that night for quite a while, knowing that time was of the essence for their very existence and all they had left would quickly end.

The following day, sleeping late, they eventually arose to join Frank in the parlor. To their surprise, a few of Oscar and Frank's friends had stayed over that night. Yes, it was revealed those acquaintances of theirs were well aware who shared a bed with Oscar. Of course, with this knowledge, they were also taken into their confidence on telling no one of their marriage.

The days seemed to fly by, with Oscar busily working on finalizing his works of poetry that he deemed to submit to David Bogue Publishers before their leaving for Paris. As he was busy with more pressing matters, Cateline spent time packing for their soon-to-be journey across the channel to Paris and spare moments catching up her diary with journal entries here and there. On one particular day, Oscar was so absorbed in his work that Cateline had barely realized he was even home. As she walked into Frank's studio and

445

observed Oscar busily working away on his writings, Cateline strode over to where he sat and inquired, "How is it coming, Oscar?"

"After working on the proof all morning, I took out a comma."[8]

"And this afternoon?"

He replied, "Well—I put it back again."[8]

"Seriously, Oscar, I see you working away; you have done more than merely taking a comma out and putting it back."

He smiled and stopped, looking into her eyes, while replying, "I am almost finished."

Later that evening, they enjoyed entertaining one last time at their home with Frank and a few acquaintances, along with his mother. Lady Jane had become very close and loving towards Cateline.

On their last day in the city of fog, Oscar and Cateline arose fairly early to have a romantic breakfast in bed before hailing a cab to take them sightseeing through London's richness of history laid about the banks of the Thames along with many sights in between. Oscar had planned an itinerary to surprise her, which started with a ride close to Buckingham Palace, where he had the chauffeur pull the carriage over for Cateline to get a better view of the French neo-classical design enclosed by wrought-iron gates. "Have you ever been inside the palace, Oscar?"

"I have, indeed. I have been invited by Prince Albert on a few occasions—he is most taken with Ms. Langtry, as you know."

"Yes, that is quite obvious. The palace is outstanding, I am sure."

"Of course, the prince has entertained many of his friends in the music room when he would have splendid performances on the pianoforte. I have also been in several rooms nearby, mainly those close to the blue and white drawing rooms, one on each side, and the green drawing-room across. I have also seen the throne room, which is next to the green room."

"It all sounds so wonderful, or I should say colorful," she finished with a laugh.

"Ah—I do believe you have been in my presence much too long, my dear."

Leaving Buckingham Palace, they ventured towards the river, passing Westminster Abbey, built in the Gothic style of architecture with two towers standing erect on the front façade. "The church was first built in the year 960," Oscar noted.

"But—it was rebuilt?"

"Yes, in the thirteenth century in the style of Anglo-French Gothic. The towers were added in the eighteenth century, a more Gothic Revival design."

"It is beautiful, Oscar."

The driver turning the corner from the Abbey, they were facing the Westminster Bridge, riding up beside the House of Parliament with the adjoining Clock Tower, when he noted, "Here we are at the "Big Ben."

"Big Ben?" inquired Cateline.

"The clock tower is referred to as such. It is rather a moniker—having the great bell among four lessor bells."

"I assume it chimes loudly?"

"Have you not heard it?"

"I believe I have, but honestly, I have not paid much attention. Was it the loud bell sound while we were at Buckingham Palace?"

"Yes, it is quite loud. Westminster Palace was destroyed by fire in 1834 but rebuilt several years ago. The clock tower was the only part which survived—perpendicular Gothic Revival."

"So, magnificent; I am really enjoying all the history. You have pleased me immensely, my gallant knight," she concluded with a playful smile.

"Ah, I always love it when you proclaim me as such. It pleases me, as well, my princess."

Oscar had the cab driver stop, and he paid the fare as they would carry on exploring by foot. Proceeding, they walked out upon the Westminster Bridge, predominantly a green shade, made of cast-iron, with seven arches of Gothic detail. Walking along with many others going in all different directions, they stopped to look back over the scenery of the city after a short distance. Cateline was able to get a more suitable glimpse of the famously known Westminster Palace, along with the adjoining clock tower, which provided a most enjoyable view along the quay. The expanse of all the Gothic architecture lined along the river provided for a most pleasant landscape. Oscar continued to narrate much of the history of those areas of importance, knowing how much Cateline loved hearing of centuries past. Once again, the clock struck noon as it chimed beautifully, arousing a sense of vibrancy and energy to its core, awakening the masses to its antiquity—stirring and reviving, a city which seldom slept at all. How lovely a view it was and with many artists having painted London's historical sights, a most notable city, overflowing with much character, one of such magnificent charm, holding the key to times gone by.

"Oh, how I wish I could have a picture of us together, standing on this bridge with the city in the background, Oscar."

"That would be splendid. London is quite the city, with such grandeur," looking down while holding her hand, he maintained, "a city which draws the artist, the painter, poet, writer, actor, and actress. My dear, many from America have come, art being their passion, they seldom leave."

"Yes, I can understand that thoroughly, for if Paris only gets better, I may never leave."

"Ah yes, *Paree*—the city which beholds one's inner thoughts, it captures a man's soul where there is no escape."

Cheerfully, she concluded, "I am sure once I have experienced *Paree*, I may never be the same again. Perhaps, I will never have the desire to return to America."

Oscar gazed into her eyes, inquiring, "You have thought of leaving, Cateline?"

"No, Oscar. I am far from being homesick at present, and I don't know if I ever will," she finished with a loving smile.

They enjoyed the sights from the bridge, standing for some time, taking in the beauty of their surroundings before they walked back to hail an omnibus. Riding along the quay, Cateline enjoyed the views of the river. London's populace was utterly impressive at such an astronomical size, seeing the streets filled with thousands, along with massive carriages and trams going about in all directions. It was hardly feasible to go any length of distance without taking much time to enjoy the picturesque scenes. With the lunch hour at hand, they both were feeling a bit wanting for a decent meal. "We will get off the bus once we are close to the London Bridge and have lunch before walking out on the bridge if you would like," Oscar affirmed.

"Yes, I am feeling quite hungry."

Many other bridges were passed until they finally arrived close to the famous London Bridge. Oscar paid their fee, and they stepped down from the bus, proceeding to locate a café, where shortly one was discovered situated in a charming locale along the quay. Yes, it was filled with a certain charisma—a French appeal and a *Paree* flare. Being seated at a small bistro-style table for two, Cateline remarked, "Please, I would much prefer that you order for me since you are more familiar with the cuisine than I."

"Certainly, I will order a few items for us to indulge."

Cateline smiled, replying, "Yes, that sounds splendid."

Their food soon arrived, as Oscar and Cateline enjoyed the view of the river while relishing their meal. Once they had finished, they walked towards the bridge and joined much of the populace walking across. Cateline tremendously adored being able to walk out on the London Bridge, knowing that it had been dismantled in 1967 and shipped to America. Its new home became that of Lake Havasu City in Arizona. In current times, there was a new bridge over the River Thames, which resumed the name London Bridge. Witnessing the old bridge, which connected the city of London with Southwark, was impressive in itself. The admirable feat of the architecture stood in such grandeur at almost one thousand feet in length and fifty-four feet in width with notable granite arches of immense breadth and stature for boats to pass through. Tasteful lamp posts, cast of the metal from French Cannons seized in the Peninsula War, were dispersed about the walkways on each side of the bridge. There was much activity with persons on foot walking along the perimeters. Oscar and Cateline stopped almost mid-way and observed all the many gondolas along with many other pleasure boats. At the same time, the traffic lingered extensively down through the center of the bridge, being as it was, filled with many a carriage of all sizes and horse trams. Standing in amazement at the waters beneath, they enjoyed the feel of the beautiful day and the loveliness of the views. "Oscar, it looks so enchanting out on the water. Have you been on any of the pleasure boats?"

"There have been times, yes. Would you like to experience a ride on one of the gondolas?"

"Oh, could we? Yes, I would love that so very much."

"It is settled, let us walk down to the shore and secure a boat for pleasure, besides my cigarettes and you, my dear—I do believe drifting about on the water, we shall also find much delight."

"You are too funny, my love—but, yes, I do believe it will be most agreeable."

Before heading to the gondolas, Oscar ran into a restaurant, where he came back out with a bottle of Perrier Jouët. "We cannot spend any amount of time afloat without enjoying a glass of champagne," he concurred with his most charming smile.

"You do think of everything," she replied, taking his arm.

They secured a gondola with a guide, enjoying their time floating about on the river while appreciating the views along the quay. With the breezy feel of the afternoon, drifting on the smooth waters amidst the many Londoners, it became a most romantic adventure. The city's panoramic vistas from the river were most astounding, yet to Cateline, the enjoyment was felt even greater sitting beside the man she loved as they both experienced the admirable landscapes as one. Spending a considerable amount of time, lazily laid-back next to Oscar, he opened the bottle of champagne to share with Cateline as she exclaimed, "I suppose we have no glasses."

"I don't think that could have been managed," he replied as he turned the bottle up to take a drink and then handed it over to her.

She laughed before taking a sip as they resumed relishing in their time spent together. While they glided about on the waters, Oscar had taken out his small journal, which he often carried with him to write down any thoughts. Cateline watched as he took in the scenes and continued to jot down his reflections on paper. "I see that you are in your element of being creative, my dear."

With a slight smile, Oscar countered, "I am always creative; even when I do not write it down, it is stored in my memory. Yet, I have finished this masterpiece. Shall I recite it to you?"

"Please do," she answered.

An omnibus across the bride
Crawls like a yellow butterfly,
And, here and there, a passer-by
Shows like a little restless midge.

Big barges full of yellow hay
Are moored against the shadowy wharf,
And, like a yellow silken scarf,
The thick fog hangs along the quay.

The yellow leaves begin to fade

And flutter from the Temple elms,
And at my feet the pale green Thames
Lies like a rod of rippled jade.[9]

After a few hours, they walked to claim a cab to begin their journey back towards Tite Street. "We can end the day by going to Hyde Park. It is in the direction of Frank's," Oscar exclaimed as he continued, "the park is lovely and is home to the marble arch which used to be at Buckingham Palace. It was relocated to the park, I believe, in the 1850s, quite clever of them, if I do say so. It adds a rather noble touch." In agreement, Oscar let the chauffeur know where to drop them off.

Arriving at the location, Oscar assisted Cateline down from her seat. Paying the man, they then walked hand in hand towards the arch, which stood on one corner of Hyde Park. Of such a remarkable architectural design, the arch was based on the Arch of Constantine in Rome and the Arc de Triomphe du Carrousel in Paris, constructed of Carrara marble from Italy. Built in the early part of the nineteenth century, it stood upright, supported by eight massive Corinthian columns. Sculptured panels were fashioned in the upper corners, and to the left were three females, symbolic of England, wearing Britannia's helmet—Ireland, with her harp, Scotland with the shield of St. Andrew, and to the right was Peace with the Trophies of War. They walked past the arch and wandered about the park until coming close to the Serpentine, a recreational lake, where they sat down in a most luxuriant verdant grassy area, enjoying the remainder of their day. Families were out and about, ladies and gentlemen, all dressed pleasantly—an artist could be seen from time to time, painting landscape scenes.

"This is a very agreeable park, Oscar. I can see why it would appeal to the artist. Does everyone always dress so kindly to come here?"

"It is a very voguish park, my dear. But never mind that, verily, it is used by the fashionably elite, which is quite droll. Nothing ever colorful amongst those of class, and if there was, it would seldom be worth mentioning."

Cateline relaxed as she leaned back into Oscar's arms, feeling secure with his touch and his light kisses upon her neck. "Cateline, I

451

know our time in London has mainly been spent entertaining my friends. I promise when we return from Paris, I will take you to see much more of London, and we can also spend time viewing the historical sites which you have only had the pleasure of a glimpse. I have yet to show you Oxford and am afraid we do not have time for that venture either, but we will have plenty of occasions once we return. I know how much you love castles and there are so many close to London—Windsor, Highclere Castle, and others you would enjoy. While we are in Paris, I will spend time indulging you with all the history, and there are castles we can see while in France, as well."

Cateline smiled and acknowledged, "Oscar, I love being with you. I also enjoyed getting to know many of your friends and watching how brilliant and clever you truly are amongst your acquaintances. As I have observed you in your milieu, I have come to realize just how much more I love you and every aspect of who you are on the inside."

"Ah—indeed, you are really very comforting, but it is only I. Please, do not perceive to speculate that I am far more, my inner-self, than one can see outwardly. Yes, I may be clever, but sometimes I don't understand a single word of what I am saying."[10]

With a slight giggle from his ingenious words, she leaned over and kissed him lightly on the cheek as they headed back to the main thoroughfare where they could acquire a cab home. Along their journey towards Tite Street, Oscar gave the driver directions to go past the palace slowly, while he acknowledged to Cateline, "Kensington Palace is on the other side of the park. I thought we could at least drive by for you to view on the way back to Frank's. Nonetheless, we must be going."

Arriving, the chauffeur slowed the carriage where Cateline was able to get a better glimpse of the palace, inquiring to Oscar, "Which royal family lives on the premises?"

"I believe there have been several—offhand, I can only say there are many apartments which have been occupied by various dukes and duchesses, and it was home to Princess Victoria prior to becoming queen. Although, the palace at one time was known as Nottingham House. It was chosen to be a country retreat among the monarchs until it was transformed into a palace for young Britain royals."

They continued their journey, reminiscing on all the amazing times they had enjoyed together and conversed about their upcoming jaunt to Paris. "Oscar, I know that we have to take a train to the English Channel where we will board a ferry to cross over into France. Could we stay in Dover for one night?"

"All right, I believe you would enjoy being able to see more of Dover. Are you familiar with the white cliffs?"

"I have heard of them and their beauty. I believe it would be a very romantic place to stay."

"It would indeed, and while there, you will accompany me to see the Dover Castle."

"Yes, everything sounds so enthralling. Please, do go on. I love hearing about our upcoming travel, Oscar. Will the journey to Dover take long?"

"From London to Dover will only take us a little over an hour to arrive. We could leave early and have the remainder of the day to explore if that pleases you."

"Yes, it all sounds so wonderful."

"Our travel across the English Channel and then by train to Paris will be quite a journey, I am afraid. We may want to stay a night in Calais as well, my dear. In fact, I shall insist upon it."

"How far is it to Paris?"

"To cross the Channel will take close to two hours, and the train to Paris is over seven, once we leave. We will definitely want to go first-class."

"That is a rather long trip. Yes, perhaps we should stay one night."

Before they arrived at Frank's, Oscar turned to Cateline and leaned over to kiss her passionately. Then, in a most crucial tone, he professed, "I just want you to know, I believe with all my heart that this marriage—you, are the one person that will always love me."

She smiled and responded, "I will always love you unconditionally, my darling."

Finally, as the chauffeur pulled up to their resident, Oscar paid the gentlemen for his services, including tipping him most generously. They quickly hurried to freshen themselves for the London social. Yes, a dreadfully remarkable dinner party in which they were invited to attend along with many of Oscar's friends who were to be present at the luxurious estate of the well-known Richard D'Oyly Carte. Cateline, finishing up the last details of her attire, was dressed exquisitely in an alluring French satin gown of a most

453

radiant deep blue with refined lace. Oscar, alongside, was adorned in his piped velvet brown doublet over his waistcoat, corresponding trousers, and pumps, all complemented by a silky necktie, in accord with Cateline's dress. However, with Cateline viewing his overall appearance, she hastily addressed Oscar regarding his tie, "My darling, you are most superbly dressed, but you cannot wear that tie?"

"You do not like my choice?"

"Of course, I love your choice, but you must not correspond with my attire. After all, we are merely friends."

"Ah—yes, forgive me. What was I thinking?" he chided while leaving the room to go and swap for a necktie in a different color. With the final touches, Oscar chose his cloak and wide-brimmed hat, in accordance with his style, and then he stood gazing at Cateline, "I am quite ready, my dear, and you look as lovely as ever. I am afraid we are due at the party and mustn't be late, my dear. Although punctuality is the thief of time, and one must never have regrets. Myself, I gave them up long ago."

With everyone dressed and eager, Frank had made arrangements for a hansom which was waiting, where they very soon were secured and set to head out for the estate. On their way, Frank and Oscar had become heavily engaged in an in-depth discussion on an article in the journal, with Oscar made a sound statement, "I assure you, Frank, murder is always a mistake. One should never do anything that one cannot talk about after dinner."[11]

Frank laughed, "Yes, I would say the chap was not very smart when in fact, he could not keep his mouth shut—it was certain that he would be found out almost immediately."

They arrived and were greeted at the door, as they were escorted to a most elaborate drawing-room, where many guests were gathered in discussions and cocktails while awaiting the elaborate meal. Cateline had no sooner walked through the door than she was approached by a very handsomely dressed gentlemen whose resident they had the privilege of being invited. Mr. Carte was not only a talent agent but also a theatrical impresario, owner of two London theatres, and a hotel empire. Quite impressive, he had also established an opera company, and as of recent, he was the mastermind behind the American tour in which Oscar would engage. Needless to say, this was not only to bring awareness to the aesthetic movement but also to popularize the play *Patience* for the American touring production.

There were many in attendance, with Mr. Carte introducing Oscar, along with Frank and Cateline to several of his prominent guests of whom Oscar had no knowledge. Feeling a bit out of place, as this was the most elegant of dinners in which she had attended, Cateline was still able to hold her own in keeping with the conversations. She commented here and there, being received very well, with much delight to those whom she was engaged. As time went on, it became pretty clear there had been a gentleman of the estate who had his eyes on Cateline from the time they had arrived and who had eventually swept her off her feet to be her escort throughout the evening—not leaving her side, that is. From time to time, Oscar would look around to see where his wife had been taken, but with no one having a clue besides Frank of their being married, both seemed to be stuck in playing the charade for the whole evening—which carried on throughout the meal and besides.

Cateline was placed next to the gentleman after the butler had announced the meal at about the hour of eight that evening. All were escorted to the rather grandeur drawing-room to partake in the simply scrumptious dinner, with the first course being exceptionally arranged. It became obvious to Cateline that the gentlemen of substantial rank made sure her name was inscribed on the card next to his. As it was, *Service à la Russe*, the first course was soup accompanied by sherry and followed by fish for the second sequence with a most pleasant wine, clairette blanche. Enduring his company, Cateline was somewhat listening with an occasional nod of seeming to be engaged in topics of discussion, which became tedious at times.

Not surprisingly, as time went on, it became quite evident why everyone who was anyone desired Oscar Wilde's company at their exclusive and alluring dinner parties. He, in fact, was without a doubt the entertainment. Oscar was able to keep conversations going with much laughter, for he always had exquisite remarks for any and everything. Trying to use the times of his comments to draw the attention of this man who seemed to have his eyes glued exclusively on her, Cateline found herself always turning from him to Oscar when he would speak. In that, she was able to laugh and listen to other's parlances from what he said so cleverly.

"I adore a London dinner party. The clever people never listen, and the stupid people never talk," Oscar elated.[12]

Laughter following with many speaking forth, one such reply on occasion, "Ah, I believe our group all talk or at least, most of us do. I presume that all your friends are simply clever, Oscar."

"Man is least himself when he talks in his own person. Give him a mask, and he will tell you the truth."[13]

"Yes, Oscar is the man of many masks. What was that you said one time about wearing a mask?"

"A mask tells us more than a face."[14]

"I suppose one can pretend to be anyone or anything while wearing the mask, but—one can actually be himself wearing the mask, and no one would know," a gentleman disclosed.

With the discourse set on masks, Oscar made one final comment concerning this witty topic, "I do perceive, there may come a day which I surely will never see, where all men shall wear their masks. None shall see nor hear, for the blind will be leading those deaf. If one from this time were to step into that sphere, they would perceive all to have suffered from some rare disease."

The eruption of laughter could be heard as the conversation continued, all taking much satisfaction in Oscar's discourse. It was apparent that he held the attention, as everyone waited for his next remark, when he candidly proclaimed, "A man who can dominate a London dinner-table can dominate the world."[15]

"And—Oscar, one day will dominate the world. I do hope that I live to see this," another man responded.

The third course arriving, the entrée, sweetbread served with claret, the sequence following, the relevé, a meat pie graciously presented with burgundy and accompanied by various vegetables. "As if this was not enough food," Cateline thought to herself, "I dare say the dinner parties held by the elite are quite substantial pertaining to these days." The roast course followed, a roasted pheasant served with game chips, or rather disc-shaped potato chips, very thinly sliced. And, not to forget, with every indulgence, more alcohol was consumed. A most delightful red wine, sangiovese, was served with this course, which was of a savory flavored range, grown in Tuscany, fruity rustic qualities with notes of cherries, dark stone fruit, spices, tobacco, and dry herbs to accompany the pheasant.

After a reasonable amount of time had passed, they were finally on the last course. It was hard to imagine one could eat so much and at such a late hour, as was society's custom in those days. This sequence was the entremets, as it was a series of dishes divided into three—dressed vegetables, savarin of peaches, and devilled sardines.

The many servants busy about the table started to clear off all the exquisite dinnerware and cutlery while serving all the guests more wine at about the time, dessert platters arrived, topped with ice-plates of which were finger bowls and dessert cutlery. Fruit and nuts were served while conversations still evolved with a number of the guests so relaxed by this time, while many were no longer engaged at all. One by one, guests left the table and retired back into the other drawing-room to settle. At this point, Cateline, not used to the late hours and extensive food consumed, was not very talkative. Nonetheless, the young man still remained by her side. Standing in close proximity to a group centered around Oscar, men lit their cigarettes while one older gentleman stood off to the side smoking a cheroot. Conversations could be heard, primarily as Oscar was much engaged in his parlance. The laughter continued to roar through the room, with men and women alike, encouraging him to continue. "Indeed, it is the secret to the charm of the American women, I do declare. They all behave as if they are beautiful."[16]

It was a long and tiresome late evening, which turned into the early hours of the morning before Oscar was ready to leave, where they arrived back home to be able to get a few winks of sleep before they would have to arise and head to the station to catch a train.

Wednesday morning came far too quickly. With Frank half asleep, he assisted Oscar with their trunk and bags. "I am glad to see you are only taking the one trunk," Frank noted.

With a slight laugh, he replied, "Yes, I am surprised that Cateline did not try to bring another one."

"Do not let her hear you, for it may have been a mistake. If it was, she would not realize it quite yet."

Both men were laughing when Cateline appeared. "What is so funny, gentlemen?"

"Nothing, my dear—nothing that concerns you," Oscar responded while approaching her to lean over and give her a slight kiss on the cheek.

"Are you going by train to the ferry in Dover?" Frank inquired.

"Yes, I believe it is by far the quickest route," Oscar professed as Cateline thought about the Orient-Express and boat trains which were still a few more years out before this mode of travel would come into play.

All loaded in the clarence which had previously been arranged, saying their goodbyes to Frank, they were soon off to the South Eastern Railway to board the train to Dover. Oscar, paying and tipping their chauffeur as he had also helped in loading their luggage with the appropriate porter, momentarily, they boarded and were settled into their seats. Upon the train pulling out from the station, Oscar took off the chain he had worn for weeks around his neck, which held his wedding band. Then, looking over at Cateline, he noted, "We are wearing our rings from here. I want others to know that you are my wife," he finished as he slid his gold band back onto his finger. Cateline, pleased with his remark, removed her ring from her right hand and put it in the place where it belonged.

"What if we meet up with any of your friends in Paris?"

"I really do not care what anyone thinks, Cateline. I would rather not watch my acquaintances trying to seduce you or to secure your attention, for that matter."

She smiled and replied, "Oscar, you are the only one that secures my attention. Do I sense a bit of jealousy?"

"Perhaps, I may be. Yet, the gentleman last night kept you much to himself, did he not?"

"Yes, as a matter of fact, he did, and if it is any consolation, I grew quite tired of his efforts."

CHAPTER
29

Time flew by quickly while on the train, and within an hour or so, they had arrived. As they had little baggage for this leg of their journey, a hansom was acquired, and the chauffeur took them to a hotel located within their central business district. They rode along, turning onto Castle Street, where the main part of the quaint town seemed to be composed. On this long stretch of road, there were various businesses, restaurants, and hotels. Off to the far distance at the end of the thoroughfare, the Dover Castle sat high upon a cliff offering a most historical view. The young man pulled over to one of the hotels and assisted Oscar with their belongings. Oscar and Cateline secured a room for the night and unpacked a few items before freshening up from their travels. Cateline, having decided to keep it simple, adorned herself in a French neoclassical style, soft-silky dress with a high waistline and sleek silhouette—modest elegance, no-frill, nor ruffles. Oscar dressed fashionably in his attire, consisting of a brilliantly patterned shirt made of liberty silk, festooned in his black velveteen jacket. Completing the assembly, his necktie knotted in cravat fashion. Dazzling as he was, Oscar remarked, "Ah—sentiment is all very well for the buttonhole, but the essential thing for a necktie is style. A well-tied tie is the first serious step in life."[1]

Cateline looking over at her husband in his most stunning apparel with the complement of his tie, inquired, "Oscar, should I dress more elegant?"

"Pray don't, my love."

"It's just that I thought since we are going to the cliffs and beach after we get a bite to eat, I should dress comfortably."

"My sweet darling, you of all people should know that I believe in beautiful apparel, but it should also be practical. You are without question marvelously robed, and the dress is simply divine. Besides, I can remove my jacket at the beach, and then I shall be most appropriate."

Cateline smiled as she responded, "Thank you. You always know the right thing to say."

"Ah—yes, fashion is such an essential part of the *mundus muliebris* of our day, that it seems to me absolutely necessary that its growth, development, and phases should be duly chronicled."[2]

Cateline looked over towards Oscar as he spoke those words, where she concluded, "I am not quite sure what you meant, nor what *mundus muliebris* means, but I will conclude that we shall go eat and then to the beach."

With a slight laugh, he noted, "*Mundus muliebris,* it is Latin, simply meaning ornaments, my love."

Cateline knowing that they were going to the cliffs to spend time, picked up her small bag where her CD player was stored and all the pictures she had brought from America, feeling it to be the perfect place to impart her story—the true story of who she really was. Oscar started out the door, taking a blanket from the hotel for their comfort.

"The blanket—a good idea for the beach."

"My dear, when one loves someone as I do you, they do plan ahead to initiate those pleasurable moments. Like old times, I too reminisce of those instances shared at your uncles," he elaborated with a smile.

"Oh, how I miss those moments," she responded.

"I, as well. I would sooner lie with you on a deserted beach than spend hours on end at a superb dinner, my dear," he spoke affectionately, adding, "the views are very romantic at the cliffs, no reason not to take advantage of the scenery and use it to our leisure."

She smiled back at him as they left their room and headed out to have lunch.

Wandering down the road, they came to the White Horse Inn, a quaint pub that served food either to enjoy in their dining area or outdoors in the back garden. They were seated outdoors in a most charming area with much greenery and various flower gardens spread throughout. The outdoor locale, sitting behind the three-level building in which the façade was mainly of stone, portrayed the feel of an ancient castle background. Ordering two meals from their menu, Oscar then asked for champagne with ice to be served prior. A bottle of champagne soon arrived, and Oscar poured them both a glass over ice. "Here is a toast to our life Cateline—our life and the love which we have been so fortunate to have known."

"Please, you will make me cry."

"Impossible! I could never say anything to make you cry, at least not intentionally. I only want our time together to be moments we can cherish forever."

"Yes, you are absolutely right, my love. Here is to us," she spoke, tapping his glass before taking a sip.

They enjoyed the champagne and discourse while awaiting their food when in a short time, the server brought their selections. It was a delight to share the salmon fillet and chicken curry, while afterward, they continued to enjoy sipping champagne. Cateline eventually became very solemn with Oscar discerning there seemed to be something amiss, and so, he inquired, "You are awfully quiet, is there anything wrong?"

"No—no, not at all," she spoke gravely, "I suppose I am a bit weary."

"We can go back to the room and rest if you prefer, Cateline. We do not have to be in a hurry and can stay another night in Dover if you would like."

"No, I will be fine, Oscar," she assured him, leaning over to gently kiss his cheek.

Once they had finished their meal, he secured a cab from the hotel to drop them off at a most secluded location at the cliffs with arrangements made for the chauffeur to return at dusk and convey them back to their lodgings.

With the remainder of the day before them, they were surrounded by the natural beauty of the White Cliffs of Dover, the grassy green plateau which laid above, and the brisk winds blowing in from the English Channel. It was the most romantic scenery that enveloped them from every angle. Oscar spread out the blanket while Cateline dropped her bag and proceeded to walk out closer to the edge for a most splendid view of the Strait of Dover. Oscar, following her, stood behind as she was captured by the beauty of the waters. Folding his arms tightly around her waist, he held her close. They both stood looking out over the beauty, watching in the far distance many ships and ferries coming and going in solitude. With the wisp of the gentle breeze and the smell of the waters, a pure cleanness— The Channel—La Manche in the strait, plummeted and towered as the waters flowed out to the Atlantic in one direction and eastwardly to

461

the North Sea, lost in those moments together—moments which would be remembered forever.

"It is a most agreeable day, yet somewhat cloudy," Oscar affirmed.

"Yes, it is, but I believe the clouds plainly make it a bit more romantic."

"My being next to you makes everything romantic, ma femme. Gazing into your most enchanting, *forget-me-not eyes*, you do have a curious influence over me, Cateline."

How Cateline loved the times when he spoke such words to her—words which seemed to move her inside. She closed her eyes and leaned back against him while he continued to hold her in his arms, whispering lightly in her ear, "When the days are clear, you can actually see the coast of France, my love."

Opening her eyes, Cateline spoke quietly, "I believe it is just as beautiful with the clouds." Oscar kissed her neck softly as she turned to face him, speaking forth romantically, "I love you. I love you, Oscar Fingal O'Flahertie Wills Wilde."

"And I love you, Cateline Marion McCarthy Wilde," finishing, he lifted her up in his arms and took her over to the blanket where he laid her down. While lying beside her, Oscar continued to kiss her gently, proclaiming, "It looks like we are very secluded out here."

"Yes, it does," she responded.

"Does this remind you of the Cliffs of Moher?"

"Not only the cliffs in County Clare, but it also reminds me of all the times we spent at the lake while at my uncles lying on the blanket. It reminds me of so many of our intimate times we shared," she spoke with tears streaming down her cheeks.

"Why are you crying, Cateline?"

As she tried to wipe the tears, Cateline replied, "I'm sorry, I did not mean to cry."

Cuddled up close, he looked down into her eyes as she lay on her back. Oscar raised himself slightly while inquiring, "Is there a reason you are crying?"

"Yes—yes, Oscar, there is a reason for my tears."

Oscar rose into a sitting position and assisted Cateline as she sat up as well while he inquired, "Please, tell me what is wrong. Have I done anything to upset you? Do you regret marrying me, Cateline?"

While sitting next to him and looking in his eyes, she responded fervently, "Oh, no—never, I would never regret marrying you, my love."

"What is it then? Why—you are quivering!"

She sighed and spoke softly, "I never wanted this day to come, but it has and, well—I want you to know that I never wanted to hurt you. I wish that I could stay here with you forever and—well, just love you forever."

Oscar looking intently at her, trying to understand what those words could mean, finally spoke again, "You are leaving, Cateline? Why are you leaving me? You said that you never wanted to hurt me. What are you saying—that you are leaving me?"

Cateline cried as she stood, slowly running back towards the edge of the cliffs, where her words echoed through the breeze, "I don't know how to say this—I never wanted to say this—."

Oscar, standing, ran after her, stopping behind as he turned her to face him, "Then do not say it—do not say that you are leaving me, not if you say that you love me."

Cateline looked intently into his eyes, with the tears beginning to flow immensely before she spoke, "If it were up to me, I would never leave you—I would never, ever leave you! But it is not up to me, Oscar."

"I do not understand. Who is making you leave me, and where are you going—back to America?"

"Please," Cateline cried out as she walked back to the blanket, "come, I have something that I need to show you, so you will understand."

Oscar followed as they both sat back down on the blanket while she rummaged through her bag before pulling out the book. With the page marked, she handed it over to him, proclaiming, "Look at the picture."

He opened the book to the marked page and glanced at the picture taken at the pub in Liverpool. It contained the two of them along with his three friends, "Where did you get this from? How is this picture in a book—what is this book?" he inquired while closing the cover to read what was printed. "I do not understand, Cateline. What is this?"

"There's more, Oscar," she spoke quietly, pulling out the copies of all the articles which had been brought with her.

Oscar shuffling through the various papers and looking at the photos—confused, he spoke with alarm in his voice, "These pictures, how did you get them? Is not this the one taken in Bath with all those we met while standing at the hearth?"

463

"Yes, Oscar."

"And, the picture at the premiere of *Patience*, I have not even seen these," he stated bluntly while looking up at her, "here's a photo when you sang at The Langham, Cateline, where did you get these pictures? How did this one get printed in this book? I do not understand. Where did these come from?"

She sighed and voiced, "You will not believe me when I tell you, but there is something else that I need to show you that may help." Once again, Cateline opened up her bag, and this time, she pulled out her portable CD player. Clicking on the button, one of the songs she had played on her guitar could be heard coming through the quite unusual object, to Oscar, that is. Cateline explained to him most candidly, "You see, I told you all along, this was not my song. All those songs I sang are on these CDs from the original artists." Cateline declared many truths as she handed over the CD player.

"What is this?"

"It is called a CD player and the shiny disc inside, look," she responded, taking it from him to stop the music and open the front while taking out the CD. "This is the CD, and they record songs onto this disc, then the player will play the music."

"Where did this come from?"

"This particular one was invented in the 1990s, Oscar."

He looked at her while pushing the buttons on the player, questioning, "1990s?"

"Yes, I was born in 1975. It is a very long story."

"So, they have learned how to send people back in time?"

"No, of course not. Do you remember your quote, where you said, *'I can believe anything, provided that it is quite incredible?'*[3]"

"Yes, that is one of my quotes. Did I share that one with you?"

"No, you did not. I knew it because I have read it in my time. I am here, Oscar, because God desired to send me here for you," she proclaimed with tears once again.

"If I believe you, I do not understand why—why would God send you to me?"

"Remember when I told you that I had dreamed of you most of my life and that I knew I was supposed to be with you. I have never loved anyone, but you, Oscar."

"Yes, I remember I also acknowledged that I had dreamt of you, as well—it was you, your face. I still do not understand."

"Oscar, God does work in mysterious ways. I am assuming that He was also preparing you for my coming here. I didn't come to change history, Oscar. Everything you will live through must happen; therefore, I cannot remain, and—I also cannot impart to you where your future lies. My purpose for being here was for two reasons. One—was for you to know how much God loves you and, with that said, for you to know there will also be a time in your life where you will feel like God has abandoned you. He hasn't, Oscar—He never will give up on you. Sometimes, it is in our darkest hour that we actually find Him and genuinely receive our forgiveness for any and all sins we commit in our lives. You will face those days, and you must remember that true Christianity is about seeking Jesus Christ one on one. No one, no pastor, no priest can save you. They may lead you to your Savior, but only you can find Him when you truly seek. Needless to say, it will be a time when you are absolutely ready to let go of your life here—letting go of everything that would keep you from entering into that narrow gate that few shall ever find."

Oscar sat looking out over the cliffs while he listened to her speak. After she had finished, it became quiet as both felt the despair, while reality started to creep over them, realizing that what they had was not forever, neither speaking but both feeling the emotions of loss. They felt the loss of the love they had come to appreciate in such a short time, the pain of knowing it was not forever, and realizing one day, this would all end. There was silence, complete silence for some time, and then, Oscar finally spoke, "—and, there was silence in the house of judgment, and the man came naked before God—"[4]

Cateline responding, in a broken voice with tears streaming down her face, "And, God opened the Book of the Life of the Man."[4]

Oscar, shaken, looked up into Cateline's eyes and then spoke softly, "And God said to the man, *'Evil hath been thy life...'* and God closed the Book of the Life of the man, and said, *'Surely, I will send thee into Hell—"*[4]

There was silence among them for a brief moment when Cateline spoke softly once again, "And the man cried out, *'Thou canst not... because in Hell, have I always lived—"*[4]

Oscar, with tears in his eyes, responded, "—and there was silence in the house of judgment, and after a space, God spake, and said to the man, *'Seeing that I may not send thee into Hell, surely, I will send thee unto Heaven.'*—and the man cried out, *'Thou canst not because never, and in no place, have I been able to imagine it.'*—and there was silence in the House of Judgment."[4] Finishing his words, he

465

looked over at Cateline while tears had begun to steadily stream down her face. "You knew my words?"

"Yes, I know many of your words. I love you, Oscar—God sees your heart. He discerns your inner self more so than you can comprehend. My being here is not just for you; it is also to make things right."

Oscar looked over at her and spoke, "Make things, right? Whatever do you mean?"

"That is something you will not understand right now, but one day, you will."

They both became very quiet, looking out at the water and marvelous scenery. Some time had passed before Oscar reached over to pick up the CD player and CDs, "I'm walking down to the beach; would you care to join me?"

"Yes, I would love to," she responded, carrying her bag while Oscar retrieved the blanket for them to have a place to sit.

They walked a short distance and came to an area one could safely tread down from the cliffs to the beach. It was quite beautiful, with unspoiled sand, whitecaps flowing to the shores, and the glimmering blue waters surrounded by the serene beauty of the white cliffs. Oscar spread out the blanket and sat back down as he opened up the compartment to the CD player, finding the section which held the batteries. Upon taking them out, he inquired, "What are these?"

"That would be the batteries, the devices which give the unit power to work."

"Batteries, how do they work—how are they made?"

"Well, I am not sure I can give you an answer that shall satisfy your curiosity. Batteries supply electric power to various electrical devices such as this player and many other items that were invented in the years to come. They do not last forever—well, these do not because they are not rechargeable. Once they have been used to some extent, they no longer work, and you must replace them with new ones. However, as I said, some batteries are rechargeable that can be used repeatedly, but there is a device that recharges them. I'm not sure exactly when they were invented, but I believe they actually initiated the process of experiments and research during this era. Oh, and they do come in multiple sizes as well."

He held one of the batteries in his hand while continuing to examine it in-depth, to include reading all the fine print. His attention then focused on the actual shiny CD. "I still cannot imagine how songs are somehow on this small disc which plays so wonderfully through this player, as you call it."

"The disc is actually a format to store data. In other words, it stores and plays audio recordings. All I can say is there have been many inventions over the years which have resulted in further developments in all fields, progressing science and technology forward. Every disc is copied from an original through equipment that uses laser beams to burn the songs or recordings of music to the original. Then the consumer can purchase the CDs to play the music in their players. Of course, there is the microphone, right here," Cateline pointed it out, continuing, "where you can hear the music or use the earphones, either way. Yes, things have swiftly changed over the last one hundred years, Oscar."

After a brief period, where Oscar continued to examine every aspect of the player, he then sifted through the assortment of CDs while intently listening to the newly discovered music of centuries yet to come. Cateline rummaged through her bag and pulled out her white gown, which was more like a nightshirt. "I brought this to swim in since we are in a secluded place. Do you think it will be alright?"

Oscar looked up briefly to address her, "I am sure it will be fine, my dear. We could have bought you a swim dress."

"Hmm, I believe those to be quite distasteful. Besides, it's just the two of us." She undressed and put the nightshirt on before going down to the water. "Would you like to come?"

"No, I need some time alone; I am not in a mood for talking right now," he responded without looking up at her.

While Oscar was busily sifting through the range of songs, Cateline took her hair down and then proceeded to the shoreline to enjoy the feel of the sun and wind on her body while experiencing the cool of the water. As she waded along the beach, Cateline could see Oscar was deep in thought, lost in the music, and decided it was best to allow him time to reflect on the whole situation. Cateline had dreaded this day many times over the last weeks, knowing their days were numbered all along. The pain felt inside was so unbearable at times, even though she would have never chosen not to have known him and shared in the love they felt. Cateline strolled along, looking out at the English Channel and the beauty of her surroundings while wondering what he was feeling at that moment. She knew that it had all come as a shock to him and wished there was some way to take away the pain, knowing the love they both felt was so genuine. Although, there was nothing that could easily stop the aching which burned deep within. Reflecting on her life over the last few months, Cateline was deep in thought herself of everything that had transpired.

Oscar, feeling as though his world had ended, was in awe of the music—songs he had never heard, instruments playing styles he had yet to experience. He stopped on a particular tune, where the words seemed to capture his spirit at that moment. While continuing to listen to the music, he watched Cateline in her white nightshirt, revealing her long slender legs, swaying with the sounds of nature— elegantly, while the waves rushed forth. She stood on her toes, barefoot, chasing the whitecaps back and forth with every prance of her graceful dominance while in deep thought. Breakers protruded with her bounce and her hair flowing freely, rendering a dancer in a burlesque, dancing to the sound of the waves, as if she were liberated—free as a bird flying over the seas. Cateline spun around, cascading along while her every step was light. She wisped besides spinning and prancing with such a charming smile. Twirling with the wind, making her own way and her own steps, Cateline frolicked with the waters as they crashed upon the sand. Unaware of his every gaze fixated on her beauty, her innocence, her gracefulness, she was as an angel sent to him—for him. Oscar knew that there was something about her, something different he had never known. With her shirt blowing in the wind, sweeping forth her nightgown persuasively, and her hair erotically, it was an image that he would not forget—forget— how could he ever forget her, this woman who had possessed his soul.

Cateline gazed out at sea, feeling the energy of the waves, the sun, and her surroundings, as it was such a magnificently beautiful day. She shut her eyes and held up both arms to the heavens in order to feel His presence—God's aura, knowing He was her reason—her existence. Daydreaming, she slowly moved while keeping her eyes closed. Within, Cateline dreamt of their times together, of the moments they had shared. Tears fell while she visualized future times, times without Oscar—without his love—without those moments, moments felt, those instances of the precious adoration, the tender love, the passion known, sensed and experienced.

Beckoned by her every move, the song he had come across, Oscar knew was meant for her—it spoke of her—the way she moved.

Briefly being able to hear the sound of the music amongst the resonances of the waves and wind, Cateline turned to smile at Oscar, where he lay watching her. She spoke loudly to be heard over the crashing breakers, "You look so serious; are you enjoying watching me?"

"Yes, I think I am most assuredly," he shouted back with a cordially handsome smile.

"I see you're still listening to music."

"The words and sound are all quite amazing. I believe if I had a choice of you or the CD player, I might have a hard time deciding," he spoke with a laugh.

"I find that hard to believe! I do not imagine the CD player can bring you the pleasures which I have," Cateline responded while walking a bit closer to the blanket before stopping.

He chuckled and quipped, "You are probably right, my love."

"Have you found any favorite songs?"

"Yes, several. But I believe I truly am enjoying this one."

"I can't hear it very well from the waves; what is it?"

"It is called *Something*."[5]

"Oh, by the Beatles. You like the song? I am assuming that it reminds you of me?"

"Truly it does—watching you, your movements—"

"You like the way I dance and sway with the waves, with nature?" Cateline probed as she resumed laughing while walking closer to him.

"Let's just say, I doubt I will ever meet anyone that mesmerizes me like you, my dear."

"Well, if you like what you see, why not come and dance with me?"

While standing, Oscar walked towards Cateline. Bending down, she picked up a handful of sand. Once he was close, she threw the sand at him before running towards the water, screaming, as Oscar yelled, "You are going to pay dearly for that."

"Perhaps—but first, I dare say you will have to catch me," shrieking loudly, she ran down to the beach at the edge of the water leaping over the crest of waves and whitecaps that cascaded over the sand. Catching up with her, Oscar took her in his arms as they both fell over into the water at the edge where the crest of waves broke on the shore. Cateline screaming while Oscar laughed as the whitecaps rushed over them, yet he continued to hold her in an intimate clasp.

469

They both lay laughing in between kisses with the waters and sand frolicking over their bodies. No longer caring, the sand continued to surge forth while they remained in an endless embrace, caressing deeply, knowing their days were numbered, and they realized these days would soon end.

Covered with sand, finally standing to walk out into the water, they washed all the grains off. Oscar taking her hand, led her back towards the blanket, where the music was still playing. He held her in his arms very gently, and romantically they slow danced, swaying to the music. He leaned over closer to her, where his lips gently touched hers as they kissed deeply. In between embraces, he spoke softly, tenderly, "Cateline, you do something to me—I can't explain it."

"I love you so deeply, Oscar."

"And I love you, my dear," he paused before continuing, "Cateline—you cannot leave me."

"I would not ever leave you if it were my choice. You do know that, don't you?"

"But—you cannot leave me! I do not want you to leave me. I cannot live without the atmosphere of Love: I must love and be loved, whatever price I pay for it.⁶"

"This is not my choice. Oscar, we have to trust that this is His plan—God's plan. I am only here because He sent me. We must be satisfied with the times we have had—our times together."

"But—it is not enough."

Cateline stopped dancing and stood back to look deeply into Oscar's eyes, speaking intensely, "If we could go back—if I could go back to the beginning before we ever met—and, I chose not to go through with His plan, where we never met, would you have wanted it that way? Would you have rather we had never met, where we did not have to go through the pain of losing each other? Would you have rather your heart never felt what it has for me if you had known it would have only been for such a short time?"

Forcefully, he replied, "How could I say that now? How could I have known this? No! Of course, I would not have ever chosen not to have known you—know this, this love that I feel. Erase these memories of knowing you and of the love we have shared, never—ever, my own one, my flesh, and my blood."

In a compelling voice, she replied to his comment, "I, too, would have chosen this all over again, Oscar. Please know, I, too, must live the rest of my life knowing you—knowing what we had and feeling the pain of losing that. If I am sent back to my time, I will spend my days looking out at the ocean—dreaming—reminiscing—holding you, forever in my heart. I will cherish every moment spent by your side. Why loving you and knowing you, my life is forever changed from the person I was, the person I am. I do hope that you, too, will never forget me."

"Forget you—how could you even think such a thing? Needless to say, I could never forget you! I could never stop loving you, not ever!"

There was a time of complete silence where neither said anything, as they continued to hold each other and dance to the song before Oscar spoke again, "My darling—"

"Yes, Oscar?"

"I have always said, hearts are made to be broken.[7] Yet, I have never realized the amount of pain it produces. I am quite sure that I have never met anyone like you, Cateline."

"I dare say, you probably never will again."

"But you, my dear, are entirely unlike anyone I know."

"Well, you are right in your assumptions, Oscar. I am somewhat unique."

"Yes, I had often wondered why you were so different, and now I know. The women, what are they like compared to this century?"

"Things have changed over the years for women. It's a completely altered world."

"In what ways have things changed?"

"Well, let's just say that all the efforts which your mother made and many others like her paid off."

"She would be pleased to hear this."

"Yes, I am sure she would. The modern woman, well, she has all the privileges of the man—at least in most countries. Women have the same advantages as men to attend college and become whatever they desire. Things definitely changed for women. They are no longer merely homemakers, and many have succeeded in remarkable things."

"You—your education and career?"

"Well, I do have an extensive college education, and like yourself, I love to write. Before coming here, I worked for a large newspaper firm in Chicago. I doubt I will return once I go back. I believe my life with you has impacted me where I do not think I could ever pick up where I left off."

471

"I can see you doing great things, but I am sure there are many distinguished men in your time; why would you have fallen in love with me?"

"Oscar," she spoke while looking into his eyes, "I do not think you realize precisely how brilliant you are. In fact, there are probably few in my time who could compare to your brilliance." After a brief silence, Cateline spoke once more, "Oscar, are you familiar with Ellen Huntington Gates?"

"Yes, I have heard of her. She is an American poet, is she not?"

"Yes, she was. Of course, born in your time. One of her poems comes to mind, for I, too, grieve deeply, knowing we will soon be torn apart, Oscar. My days at that point will continually cry out for you. Her words in *I Shall Not Cry Return*, they burn within my heart—

I shall not cry Return! Return!
—Nor weep my years away;
But just as long as sunsets burn,
—And dawns make no delay,
I shall be lonesome—I shall miss
Your hand, your voice, your smile, your kiss.[8]

Towards the end of the day, the chauffeur from the hotel had arrived. Quietly, riding towards Dover, they were consumed in deep thought. A bit later, having a fascinating dinner that evening, they retired to their room while Oscar shuffled through Cateline's bag, pulling out the book and articles. He sat down to study them closely, "Cateline, there is one picture here that I do not remember nor the scenery in the background. I believe it may be Paris, but we have not journeyed there."

Cateline walked over and picked up the photo before acknowledging to him that this was the only picture that had not been taken that she knew of. "I, too, assume that this was taken in France, darling. All these were the only known photos of myself during this timeframe that I knew of; however, there have been some which I did not know of, such as our wedding pictures. But I do know for history to repeat itself, all these must be taken. Of course, my dreams have been my guide. They have led me. With all the dreams over the years, I have also been given the vision of returning to my own time. That is the reason I do know this will end. And this being the only photo that I know of that has yet to be captured, I also knew I would still remain."

"Why then must we even go to Paris? If we can prevent this photo, would you not be sent back to your time?"

"Do you hear what you are asking? If we do anything that could change history, I possibly may have never even been born. Can't you understand that this is not about us? This is about His plan—God's plan, my love," Cateline stated while walking over to sit next to him. "I love you so much, Oscar—but honestly, I must trust His plan, which will be far greater in the end."

She stood and walked over to her bag to retrieve a small envelope before walking back to Oscar. Cateline sat down again and pulled out two identical photos that she had brought with her from America, pictures of them together. "Listen, I have spent much time thinking about these days before actually being here. Oh—don't get me wrong, I never knew for sure that His plan was to send me back to your timeframe. Despite everything, I must admit there were times I had dreams and visions of these days, but I never knew if it was my being hopeful or really His plan. Therefore, I had two copies made of this photo of us together," she related, handing him one of the pictures. "The other day, I wrote on the back of the one you are holding." Turning it over, Oscar read the words—

To Oscar,
My love— My life!
I will love you until the end of time!

"I do hope you will cherish this reminder of our times together, my love," she spoke softly, continuing, "I would also love for you to write an inscription on this other photo for me to treasure."

Oscar took the photo from her hand and walked over to the davenport, where he sat down to begin writing on the back. After finishing, he stood and walked over to hand it to her. She began to read his words while tears formed in her eyes—

Cateline, my own darling,
Ever since I looked upon your beauty
I have dared to love you,
Wildly, passionately, and hopelessly.[9]
If you are not too long, my own dear wife,
I will wait here for you, all my life![10]

"Oscar, that is so beautiful," Cateline spoke, wiping her tears away. "I will always cherish this, my love. It will remain close to my heart. Please keep your photo secure—it should never be found; you do understand?"

"I suppose I do. I will find a way where it remains with me always until the end of time—my time."

Getting ready to retire for the night, Cateline climbed into the bed while Oscar poured them a glass of champagne and sat down beside her. "There is something I must inquire," he began.

"Please, feel free to ask away. What would you like to know?"

"I'm just curious. Were you ever in love with anyone from your era?"

"No, Oscar, I was not. I have never loved anyone but you. If you will remember, before we were married, I told you that I had never been involved with anyone for any significant time. I found it rather hard to be able to connect."

"When you said that you had loved me your whole life—that you had dreamt of me, what were you implying? I mean, I have dreamed of you, but it was only within a few years of our actual meeting. It was not a prolonged period. Yet, it was a significant time before I laid eyes upon you. You said that you had dreamt of me your whole life."

"Well, my love, it has been a very long journey for me. You see, I had these dreams from the time I was a little girl. In the beginning, I would see some faces, but they really meant nothing to me because I didn't recognize any of them. As I got older, I still did not know who the faces were, but there was one—it was you. I truly did not comprehend any of this, but it did impact my life. I grew up believing there was something more to my dreams than I knew, but I did not understand what that meant. Then I found those pictures while searching for clues in the library. I was broken at that point because I knew—I knew it was you and knew that I had always loved you. I believe this was the reason that I was never able to connect to anyone else."

"And I—did I become famous?"

"Well, let's just say that many in this timeframe made a mark in history. All the same, as you have noted, many are never appreciated until they have passed away."

Thinking for a brief moment on her comment, Oscar resumed, "And now—what happens now? You will finally be free to love and to marry."

"I will never be free from you. My feelings that I have for you simply cannot be turned off."

"There is nothing left for us. You have fulfilled your quest."

"Perhaps, I do not know, really. I know nothing further than you. All I can distinguish is that this was—no, you—were my purpose, you are my purpose, and neither of us can foresee what the future holds."

"Yet, you have seen my future."

"Yes—I have, but I cannot reveal anything more to you which could change your course in life."

"Cateline, I am having a hard time understanding how a good God would bring us together, knowing how much we love each other and then merely take that away."

"It's not about us, Oscar. God holds the pieces to His miraculous puzzle, so to speak. And it's His puzzle and His pieces that fit into place according to the way that He planned. Yes, He already sees our ending, but every person who was ever born has their own tiny part. Everything we do in this life fills our own puzzles. But God has given every single person a chance for their small portion in this life to fit into His perfect plan, doing it His way, not our own. I know that we all miss it—all of us, and then our life goes a different way. While other times, we make it right. All I can tell you about your life—your future, you will miss it, like we all do. In your life, you will walk far away from the Lord, but you will make it right one day. You will live through a time of trials, and you will make it right between you and God. That is all that matters. It does not matter what we have done wrong in this world; all that matters is how we end this life. Do we choose to live in our wrong choices, or do we make it right with God in the end? My purpose was not to make sure you get it right with Him; every person today makes their own choices, and most of those choices are based on their own selfish desires, all of us. All the same, our focus should never be on our sin but instead on Him. We are all incapable of living a pure life; we all sin. Yet, in the end, what matters is if we turn from our choices, and we choose Him. It's all about choosing Him, loving Him. My reason for being here was to let you know how much He loves you, but—my purpose was also to enlighten the world to see that you got it right. Why? Because in

475

the end, many will be blinded and unable to see what is truly visible. I am merely making an example of your life, your life where it has been wronged by so many who are blind."

He looked at her and spoke, "I am not entirely sure what all this means, but if I understand correctly, your being here was purely to show others they were wrong about me."

"Your life is an example to many, Oscar. And, I am very much here for you now, for you to know that when you face uncertainties, God hears your pleas. Sometimes, we think that He is not listening to our cries, but I assure you, He listens to every one of our cries. Of course, His way of answering sometimes seems as if He is not there. He is there, but His ways are not our ways, and His thoughts are not our thoughts. He answers our prayers in ways we are unable to see. More often, our prayers are answered in our storms than when our life seems at peace. If you remember nothing else, remember that He hears you—He loves you, and in your deepest storm, He has not left you. His answer to your prayer will not be what you expect—but know, it is not through crying out to a priest or clergyman that you will find Him. It will be in your darkest moments that you will cry out to Him—in your alone time, and He will answer you." Cateline paused as neither spoke for several minutes; resuming, she stated a most earnest quote, "To err is human, but to rise above is simply divine, my love."

"Derived from Alexander Pope's "To err is human, to forgive is divine.""

"Yes, but in your case, you will rise above your circumstances, Oscar. Even Pope spoke of God's forgiveness. All mankind will make mistakes, and many will fall on this walk of life, yet it is not about the fall—it is about what follows. Do we choose to remain in our lowly state, or do we rise up and continue on the race in which we are called? And, it isn't just about rising; it is also about forgiving, forgiving ourselves, that's the hard part."

There was silence for some time while Oscar slid under the sheets to hold Cateline in his arms. They laid there peacefully, neither speaking, but both were in deep thought. Cateline finally shared with him once again, "Oscar, there was this man—famous in the early part of the twentieth century, a writer. His writings were very remarkable, but he died much too young, a most tragic death, as he was very gifted. There was something he wrote once. I suppose it was something I have always cherished. He said something to this effect,

'Youth is something that only young men have, and only old men know how to use.'[12] He referred to how those who are young waste their youth and later in life regret it, but wisdom doesn't come until we grow older. It is wasted youth that is not necessary but happens to all of us. There are always regrets about how we would have chosen to do things differently if we had only had the wisdom needed while young. I have tried to carry this with me in my life for many years now, but I am sure that I will also fail at some point. Often, we fail in our youth because it takes living our lives to some extent before we gain the wisdom to understand how we could have chosen to live life another way, ending life on a better note, so to speak. Nonetheless, life is life! But God is God and will always be there to clean up our lives and ultimately change our heart, where we find Him and desire Him once we begin to seek Him."

The following morning, Oscar arose before Cateline and went for a walk to smoke and think. Coming back to the room, Cateline was still asleep, and he lay down next to her, striving to awaken her from slumber. "Cateline, are you awake?"

She rolled over and opened her eyes to say, "I am now. Is it time to get ready to leave?"

"No, I merely wanted to let you know that I secured the room for another night. I am not in such a hurry to get to Paris, are you?"

With a sullen look, Cateline responded, "No, I'm not either, but you do know that we can't prolong God sending me back."

"I know. I just want to be sure that we have a little more time together," he responded while climbing back under the coverlet to hold her for a while.

After drifting back off to sleep, a few hours later, Cateline awoke to Oscar sitting next to her with a book. "What are you reading?"

Oscar smiled as he looked down where their eyes met, "I am reading some of Shelley's poems. Listen—I read this one which made me think of you," he stated while beginning to recite the lines—

I arise from dreams of thee
In the first sleep of night—
The winds are breathing low
And the stars are burning bright.

477

I arise from dreams of thee—
And a spirit in my feet
Has borne me—Who knows how?
To thy chamber window, sweet! —

The wandering airs they faint
On the dark silent stream—
The champak odors fail
Like sweet thoughts in a dream;
The nightingale's complaint—
It dies upon her heart—
As I must die on thine
O beloved as thou art!

O lift me from the grass!
I die, I faint, I fail!
Let thy love in kisses rain
On my lips and eyelids pale.
My cheek is cold and white, alas!
My heart beats loud and fast.[15]

"Most pleasing, to be sure," Cateline proclaimed while snuggling up next to him as he laid back down. They cuddled for some time before deciding to get out of bed to begin dressing for the day. It was a fine late morning with the most wonderful oceanic weather. While Cateline was still preparing for the day, Oscar decided to step out with the CD player and CDs to take a brief walk while listening to the music.

"You better be careful that no one hears you playing the music. Please be sure to use the headphones. It has not been invented as of yet."

"I know. I am going to see if I can find a quiet place where I can smoke and listen. If I cannot find a secluded place, I will use the headphones. I love this, you know?"

"I can see that. Perhaps, honesty was revealed when you said you would have a hard time choosing between the player and me."

He smiled and approached her, kissing her cheek before admonishing, "You know which I would choose, my dear."

"I believe I do," she replied while turning to face him with a most amiable smile.

"I will be back shortly," Oscar noted as he walked out of their room.

After some time, Oscar returned, "You look divine, Cateline."

"Merci, mon chéri."

"I have a request," he said.

"And, what would that be? Please do not tell me that you desire me right now; I have devoted too much time being beautiful for you."

Oscar laughed and replied, "That was not on my mind—but you could persuade me."

"No, we have plans today. Please tell me what you were going to say."

"When you leave and go back to your era, I want you to always remember me."

"I could never forget you; you know that. I doubt there will ever be anyone who could take your place for all time, Oscar."

"Would you promise me something?"

"Of course, if it is something I can do—anything."

"I found this song, and I rather like the words as they remind me of *us*. When I listen to it, I think only of you."

"What song is it?"

"*I Don't Want to Miss a Thing.*"

"Ah, Aerosmith! Yes, I am quite familiar with the song."

"I would like you to promise me, once you are back in your era, from time to time, you will listen to the song, and when you hear the words, you will know that this is my song to you for all times—that way, you will always know that my thoughts are with you, and I will always love you."

With tears welling up in her eyes, Cateline walked over close to him and spoke softly, "I will always, always play that song Oscar and will always think of this moment with you, knowing that we are both thinking of each other."

Leaving their hotel, they walked through the quaint town of Dover, stopping off at a café to enjoy a delightful breakfast before hiring a hackney carriage, or more accurately a taxi, to take them to Dover Castle. Cateline was enthralled with all the beauty of their surroundings during the short ride to where the chateau lay. Once arrived, they stepped out of the taxi to get a better view, even though

479

it was not open to the public. The castle was such a mighty fortress, dating back to the Iron Age, with an Anglo-Saxon church and Roman lighthouse on the grounds besides. The entirety was surrounded by walls where there were a few sections in which one could stand to get a glimpse.

Once back in town, the remainder of their day was spent doing a bit of shopping and sightseeing before retiring to the hotel relatively early to rest before their journey the following morning to Calais.

They arose early on Friday and ate a quick breakfast; afterward, the hotel porter assisted with their baggage and arrangement for a ride to the Port of Dover. Once dropped off at the wharves, Oscar secured a ferry to cross the Strait of Dover over to Calais. They swiftly boarded and were soon on their way with many other passengers, as the channel was already busy with numerous ships and ferries coming and going across the strait. On the initial journey, Oscar and Cateline devoted much of their energies in deep conversation as the ferry began the course across the English Channel into France.

CHAPTER
30

As time evolved, crossing the channel, Oscar and Cateline became somewhat composed, neither knowing what to say nor any desire to discuss the detrimental future which lay ahead. For the remainder of the journey across the channel, they sat motionless, striving to enjoy the genial views of the waters while silencing their fears. Both were experiencing feelings, unable to appreciate their day or days to come as life at this point was unsure. Time appeared to fly by as the ferry seared through the dark waters, where it seemed like such a short period before they were able to see land as they neared Calais. Arriving at the port, Oscar rapidly secured a clarence to assist with their baggage and take them to the Le Chariot Royal, located midway through town on Rue Edmond Roche.

Cateline viewed the hotel's architectural design, where it was evident that it must have been built sometime back in the eighteenth century. Deep in thought, she turned to walk with Oscar into the hotel, where they were soon assisted by a porter who secured their baggage. After acquiring a room for the night, they hurriedly followed the young man to their lodgings, where they unpacked sufficiently enough to manage. Oscar being somewhat fatigued from their journey and lack of sleep the night before, asked, "Cateline, we have a long trip ahead of us; perhaps, we should inquire if they have in-room dining, where we can just relax. If that suits you?"
"Yes, Oscar, that suits me quite well."

While very brief in Calais, their time was merely spent catching up on needed sleep, enjoying their dine-in service with iced champagne, naturally, and Oscar continually taking possession of the CD player.
"Oscar, I do believe it is conceivable if given a choice, you might very well choose that CD player over me, after all," Cateline laughed.
"Ah, you are jealous."
"Possibly, but I do declare that you should not be so attached; after all, it does leave with me."
"Unless it comes up missing, my dear."

"I do believe what came with me will leave with me, mon chéri."

"Ah—can you be certain on that front, my love?" Oscar finished with a smile, and of course, Cateline was not for sure.

While cuddling, they enjoyed each other's company in between eating, drinking, and napping, all the way up until it was time to go to sleep for the night. Oscar leaned over to kiss Cateline, speaking with words of assurance, "Goodnight, my love—pleasant dreams of me."

"Yes—they are only of you," she responded, and they soon drifted off in slumber.

The following morning, hurriedly, they arose, dressed for their extended journey, where they immediately headed for the hotel dining room to have a quick and delightful breakfast. Leaving for the train, the porter assisted them with their luggage, and they were thus off for the city of *Paree*.

It was a most dreary journey of seven hours or rather seven and a half with several stops along the way. Even so, traveling first-class made for a much better occasion. And being in better spirits than the day prior, they spent time talking, sipping champagne, sleeping a wink here and there, and, needless to say, enjoying a good meal in the dining car. The long journey provided the time needed where Cateline could journal in her diary from the last entry she had made. At the same time, Oscar worked effectively on his writings since his ambitions were to become that great playwright one day. It was only during their times of sleep that the day seemed to drift by much quicker. It was such an extensive and tiresome trip, but eventually, the whistle blew to announce their arrival in the grand city.

They hailed a hackney and were taken to the Hotel Voltaire located on la rive droite, in which he was very familiar. "You have stayed at this hotel, Oscar?"

"Many times, as it was, I resided here on my very first trip to Paris with my mother. The Voltaire was always her favorite. I was nineteen that first visit. In spite of this, after growing up and visiting Paris on my own, it has still remained my choice all these years."

"Your mother sounds somewhat sentimental; I suppose a quality you have assumed as well," she identified with an agreeable smile.

"Sentimental, yes! Truthfully, most would never admit to being such—the romantic, mawkish, indeed! Yet, I believe many to be sentimental, quite so. I do declare, I much prefer those who are."

Oscar securing a room for a fortnight, Cateline spoke up, "I may not be here for that long, Oscar."

"Yes, but you may be. Besides, I would not leave immediately, and it is entirely possible that you could be here longer than a fortnight."

"Yes, I suppose that may be so."

After settling into their room, they unpacked all their bags for the lengthy stay or at least their hope of being there for some time before Cateline's departure.

"I believe I would much rather just spend the remainder of the day and night in our room, Cateline. I would hate to explore the dining options only to wind up in some absurd establishment, not to our liking. It might be more romantic to dine in the room; do you not agree?"

"Ah! That does sound enchanting. Perhaps, a quiet evening in bed," she responded while finishing up sorting through her belongings before walking over to put her arms around Oscar's neck. "I believe I could simply stay in the room with you the whole time we are here."

"My thoughts precisely—at least that way, the last picture can be prolonged."

With a faint smile, she responded, "Oh, how tempting that would be, but honestly, I imagine we need to get out and do things together. I would hate to waste these last days where they were not filled with much enjoyment and memories made."

"I suppose you may be right, but I am confident that we could make memories in our room just the same."

Cateline giggled and responded, "Yes—but, Oscar, I don't want to spend the next two days nor the next two weeks where our thoughts are continually feeling the upcoming pain of loss. I want to live—really live, where our last days are filled with so much pleasure and new experiences—experiences together, enjoying the now and not worrying about tomorrow."

"I love you," he countered while pulling her closer to him, "I truly love you, and I will never, ever forget all our days together."

483

Room service came later that evening and delivered an attractive spread of French cuisine. They laid around enjoying their time collectively—talking, laughing, eating, and sharing stories of times in each of their lives, memorable moments they would always cherish. In between the laughter and tales, Cateline suddenly remembered, "Oh, I almost forgot," getting up from the bed, she walked over to her bag to pull out an envelope. "Oscar, I have something I have written that I need to give you. It is a letter to my family in Ireland. You will send this for me once I am gone—s'il vous plaît?"

"But of course, you know I will," he replied as Cateline handed it to him.

"I would like you to read it."

He opened the letter and commenced reading; upon finishing, Oscar responded, "I assume you believe this to be better?"

"I do. I don't want anyone wondering why I am no longer here. This is to protect you. It would pain me something fierce for anyone to believe my no longer being here was due to some action on your part. I prefer to take the blame for my actions, as it will be presumed, I went back to America on my own account. This way, my family will simply presume that I eventually chose America and never came back. You will be free—that way, you should be able to have the marriage annulled and begin your life once again. Please, do remember to have the marriage dissolved—you would have every right due to desertion on my part."

"You make it sound so final, but I would rather not speak about this. I know that look, Cateline, and it depresses me so. Your words speak of departing where we shall never see one another, but your eyes feel the same pain which I am feeling. These last days, let us spend them enjoying each other as husband and wife, not reflecting on what lies ahead."

"You are right. I, too, would much prefer to spend these times making wonderful memories, Oscar," she concluded. Leaning over to give him a kiss, he seized her arm, pulling her back down beside him. Kissing her intimately, once again, Cateline remembered, "Oh, there is something else that I would like to ask."

He propped himself up, once more, with a quizzical look, "As long as it is not depressing, ask away," he replied while steadily kissing her neck again and again.

"Will you promise me something? It is not a gloomy request, darling."

"In that case, I will promise you anything; how could I ever tell you no?"

"When you go to America, will you wear the blue necktie that I gave you before our wedding? It will mean a lot for you to have a part of me with you."

Oscar smiled while looking into her eyes, "You know I will, and I will think of you every time that I wear it. Is there anything else you need to ask?"

"Why, is that my cue to stop talking?"

"Yes, perhaps it is," he retorted as Cateline responded to his kisses.

The following morning, it was pleut à Paris. Cateline standing at the window in excitement, exclaimed, "Oh—Oscar, it is raining—raining in Paris. We must go for a walk."

"It is May ma chérie. It is always raining in May. However, I did bring my mackintosh and an umbrella, for it is one item never to leave behind when in Paris."

Cateline exclaimed in a relatively high tone while walking back over to sit next to him on the bed, "An umbrella? No—you may wear your mackintosh; I want to experience Paris while strolling the streets and viewing the sights with the rain cascading down my body. Surely, you are not afraid of a light drizzle of rain, are you?"

"Ah—you may experience Paris in the rain if you wish, but I need not experience that myself. I can remember many moments walking in the rain while in Paris."

"No, Oscar! I want you beside me sharing in the experience!"

"Ma chérie, we would be drenched. I would not want you to catch a cold."

"Why—a little water never hurt anyone, mon chéri—everyone must walk in the rain in Paris at least once. I have often dreamt of doing so. Would you dare prevent my dream from coming true?"

Oscar laughed while he pulled her back down on the bed, replying, "If it makes you happy, we will walk in the precipitation and become drenched with your light drizzle of rain, as you seem to refer."

"Yes, I want to experience Paris with you, mon chéri—a most romantic time in the rain."

They arose and dressed hastily in simple attire since Cateline desired them to experience Paris in the rain. Before leaving, Oscar declared, "There are many terraced-cafés in Paris. We could eat outdoors and still keep dry, if you would like or if you prefer to eat in the rain, we could do that as well, ma chérie."

"Don't be silly! No, I do not want my food soaked, but—yes, I would like to sit outside of the café."

"We will have to hail a fiacre. One I am thinking of, a café that is—is located on la rive gauche, not too far, but I dare say, too far to walk."

Oscar acquired the taxi. Wearing his mackintosh, he carried the umbrella just in case it would be needed in the event of a downpour. They rode along, crossing the Seine to la rive gauche while the rain gently pattered upon the carriage. Oscar opened the umbrella as he declared, "You said *walk in the rain*, which we are not at this moment—walking, that is."

Annoyed at his comment, Cateline declared firmly, "Once we get out of the fiacre, the umbrella goes away—please, we shall not melt due to the rain, mon chéri."

Oscar smiled ostensibly while trying to hold back laughter when Cateline inquired dryly, "Do you find my comment one to laugh about?"

"I find everything about you quite remarkable. You are determined to be wet; why not just get in the river where I can stay dry," he concluded with a most presumptuous laugh.

"I dare say, Oscar Wilde, it should be your duty to make me happy."

He realized his error and strived aimlessly to get back into her good graces, "I am sorry, ma chérie. If it makes you happy that we both get soaked today, then I will be most obliged. And, I assure you, I will endeavor to find much pleasure in walking in the rain while in Paris with you."

"That sounds better, but I will not be convinced until I see you revel in getting wet with me today."

"I would love to get wet with you today. I would love to see your lovely little body in your elegant dress dripping wet and your hair hanging down, dampened in streams of flowing water—your face moist with tiny droplets while I kiss each and every one of them away. And once back at the hotel, I will immensely relish helping you disrobe your soggy raiment away from your beautiful body," he finished while laughing.

"Hmm, it does amaze me that you can find much pleasure and humor in whatever I say."

"Not at all, ma chérie! I am only picturing what our day shall be and finding much joy in the results. You do want me to enjoy getting wet with you, I presume. And I dare say that I have been able to picture this day in a way that will bring me much satisfaction, which you desired of me, did you not?"

Amused at his wit, she responded, "I do believe this conversation needs to end. You are finding too much delight."

With the narrow streets packed with traffic, the chauffeur could not let them out directly in front of Café de Flore. Oscar folding up the umbrella, assisted Cateline down, running towards the terraced café together as the rain became more forceful.

"Why did you fold up the umbrella?"

"I thought that was what you wanted?"

"I do once we leave from breakfast, and if it is only drizzling, but at the moment, it is no longer light rain."

"You do not want to get wet, or you want to get wet? Your words are misleading; which do you prefer?"

"Oh—never mind, we are not too wet, I suppose."

Oscar acquired a table outdoors and initiated drying Cateline's face with a cloth napkin from the café. "You still look ravishing, even being wet."

"Merci, mon chéri. You look rather handsome yourself."

Pleased, he replied, "If anything, I believe you look most alluring with your hair down and, of course, with your attire quite damp."

With a slight glow, Cateline blushed at his remark.

After placing the order with le serveur, Oscar continued in small talk with Cateline until their hot tea and breakfast had arrived. A French Parisian style *petit dejeuner* was most enjoyed with delightful croissants, baguettes, pastries, and the like. While taking pleasure in another cup of elderflower tea, Cateline, in her most energetic voice, brimmed over with many inquisitive questions of Paris, as Oscar was more than eager to share his genius. While savoring their meal, the light rain started to diminish, as they say in

Paree—it comes and goes often. Soon, they left Café de Flore, walking toward the Île de la Cité, where they would saunter in the midst of Cathédrale Notre-Dame de Paris. It was a most pleasant walk as they cherished the views of Paris hand in hand—a young couple in love strolling about in the city of many lovers and stories of romance.

Oscar reveled in sharing the history of Notre Dame while having Cateline stand with her back to the façade, looking towards the tip of the Île de la Cité. "If you look to your right, you get a most awesome view across the Seine of la rive droite, and opposite, la rive gauche." Taking in all the beauty on the Île de la Cité, the medieval cathedral in its French Gothic style, and the river stretched out on both sides, Cateline thought about the Eiffel Tower. She envisioned the enormous structure which would be positioned far off in the distance, one day, several years to come, naturally. La tour Eiffel would become the tallest structure not only in Paris but also in the world for many generations. Yet, when Cateline stood looking off, she knew the towers of Notre Dame were undeniably the tallest structure in Paris for 1881. Cateline walking out into the lush grounds, looked up to view the glorious spire where the bronze rooster reliquary was perched on top, even though, from ground-level, it was hardly visible, or at least, one could not detect its nature.

"Oscar, can we tour inside? I would love to see Our Lady of Joy," Cateline inquired while remembering an article she had read in her timeframe.

"Of course, my dear," he replied while taking her hand to lead her into the cathedral to view Notre Dame de Liesse. They observed the shrine as both were very quiet. A sense of peace was felt while they walked among all the ancient artifacts viewing various historical relics, which included what was believed to be a crown of thorns worn by Jesus Christ. Many other such treasures were enjoyed, to name a few—the statue of the Virgin Child, Joan of Arc, many eminent paintings dating back hundreds of years, sculptures, bronze statuary, and quite a collection of other symbolic statues of Biblical nature. Gazing at the glorious rose windows stained beautifully in fascinating colors depicted many saints and prophets. Last but definitely not least, as they browsed through the various chambers, one could not fail to be enthused by the diverse stone creatures, referred to as gargoyles, not to mention the collection of sculptures referred to as chimera.

Oscar led Cateline towards the stairwell, where they climbed many, many steps ascending to the north tower until they were high above Paris. As they gazed out over the vastness of the ancient city, a 360-degree view, Cateline stood in awe, overtaken at that moment in the very place of inspirational beauty—renaissances erupting through her mind as she strived to capture every scene of brilliance. Gleaming down from where they stood gave a most splendid analysis of places they had recently walked, the many patrons going about, the lifestyle, history, scenic photographs all played in Cateline's mind as if visibly cherished. At the same time, she gazed out over the expanse of the Victorian era's existence, as it broadcast throughout every distinct observation—off in the distance, to be seen, Quartier Latin, Place du Châtelet, and Hôtel de Ville. Along the Parisian streets, overflowed with carriages, horse trams, men adorned in their top hats, and women with their Parisian style bonnets, headdresses, and parasols. Cateline strived to capture every sight where she could remember that day forever, as she stood breathless in her elation of 1881. Oh, how she could have stayed forever, how she could have relished in that lifestyle. She looked up at Oscar while he was also in his own world. Cateline smiled, knowing she was on top of the world right at that moment, standing next to him. A vision in her mind that would always remain.

Upon leaving, they walked along Rue Dante, while Cateline was in deep thought, "Oscar—"

"Yes?"

"You have read John Bunyan's, *The Pilgrim's Progress*?"

"I have, and you?"

"Yes, I believe it is one of the best books written to guide one to find the pathway which leads to heaven."

"Honestly, I have only read it once, quite some time ago."

"I see—Oscar, will you promise me something else?"

"I will promise you anything that I am able to do, Cateline."

"There will be a day when you will be faced with uncertainty. During this time, you will have John Bunyan's book with you; please promise me you will read it over and over again."

"If that will make you happy."

"I am sure when the time comes, you will remember this discussion. I merely want you to understand how important your life is, and nothing happens by chance. God will make sure you have that book beside you one day; please let it be to your advantage."

"I will, Cateline. And I am assuming you cannot tell me anything more."

"No, I really cannot. Just know God will always give us every opportunity in this life to choose Him. I believe you know what a pioneer is, based on Bunyan's book."

"Yes, I do."

Pleased, she resumed, "I know you are a pioneer because I am one. One who is unafraid to go forth in areas and places that are uninhibited by others—yes, that again is the rebel," Cateline finished with a slight laugh.

Oscar, speaking theoretically, inquired, "If you had been born in this timeframe, do you think we would have met and been together?"

"I'm not sure. Perhaps, but I am delighted we have been brought together, even if for a short time."

"So am I," he responded with a most affectionate smile.

They walked back to la rive gauche, stopping briefly at a small pub to have Oscar's pink champagne. "I think I could become accustomed to your pink blend, my love."

"I do say you seem to have enjoyed this more than your glass of wine."

"Well, I do enjoy a fine red wine from time to time, but this is most refreshing over ice," she acknowledged.

They continued on the left bank, enjoying brief stops at various shops before entering into a most quaint bookstore with many relics to be found—classic books of first editions by far thrilled Cateline. Even though she knew more than likely, they could not travel back in time with her. As they left the store, the rain came down once more, only very slightly. "Most certainly, I believe you shall have the pleasure of enjoying the light rain, after all," Oscar declared.

Cateline laughed while inquiring, "Yes—so I shall. Are you not pleased on this account?"

"What can I say—I am pleased if you are, ma chérie."

With the rain sprinkling down on the pavement, they held hands while strolling along—oh, how Cateline felt so alive in those moments shared with Oscar. Her enthusiasm seemed to overflow with her eyes capturing every part of the splendor, as could be portrayed on canvas.

"Oscar, the views are so lovely. While the rain dampens the streets with its glistening effects, everything seems to come to life. This is remarkable; can you not see how it is so natural? It is nature intertwined with everything in view—a clean and vibrant feel and the smell of the rain, so fresh, musky. It is most pleasant, is it not?"

"Petrichor," he stated.

"Petrichor?"

"A Greek term, the fluid which flows in the veins of the gods in Greek mythology. Petrichor is the earthy scent of rain."

She smiled and stated, "You charm me, you know? I love your brilliance on everything. I do believe I could spend hours listening to your thoughts and reasons."

With a slight laugh, his response was not with words, but rather, he stopped while they stood with the raindrops flowing down over their bodies and held her in his arms. Then, he leaned over and kissed her intimately.

Cateline, startled at his openness in public, casually pulled away, "Please, not in public, Oscar."

"Why not? You are my wife. I could care less what anyone thinks if I want to kiss my wife. Besides, what better memory walking in the rain in *Paree* than to be with the one you love—and a kiss in the rain is a most exquisite memory, is it not?"

"Yes, I suppose you are right."

"And I would think you would not object, for I believe you are just as much of a rebel as I, my dear."

"What makes you think so?"

"In truth, Cateline, every woman is a rebel and usually in wild revolt against herself. Remember, I have been with you every single day, almost every single waking moment, since we first met, except for the hunting trip spent with your uncle. I have watched you, listened to your theories, absorbed your thoughts and reasonings— you are far from following the ways of the majority. I do not see you swimming with the current, but I see you as somewhat of a fighter, one who would dare strive to swim against the current. You are too much like I, my dear. You see and feel things, as I do. You are willing to give everything one hundred percent if it is something you firmly believe or oppose. Tell me if I am wrong."

491

Cateline, smiling, concurred, "Yes, I suppose that may all be true."

"I assure you it is true; it is this character in you which would never have allowed you to be in any relationship. That is why you never were able to connect with anyone in your timeframe. Is this not the character of those first twelve disciples that followed Jesus Christ? Oh—do not think I have not devoted much time in the Scriptures, for I have. It may not be a topic I speak about often, but I assure you I have searched for answers many times in my life and continue to do so. Yes, his true disciples were willing to go against the religions and rules of that day; they were rebels like we both are. You have occupied a good part of your life dreaming about stepping out to do something extraordinary to impact lives. You were willing to go forth—unafraid to allow God to use you in some mighty way, and so, here you are. You knew I was a rebel. Despite this, you desired to be part of my life—why? You care more about your convictions than what others may think of you. You are willing to be like Paul and Silas, who turned the world upside down—just as I, only my rebellion has not been one to walk as a disciple. I have had strong convictions to do so, but I have yet to cross that line."

Cateline thought intently on his words spoken while they sustained walking in the enjoyment of the light rain. Finally, after some time, she replied, "Oscar, everything you said is true—maybe, I simply never looked at it that way. Yes, I would much rather be a rebel and make it right with God than miss my chance in this life. I only pray you will remember all our talks. And one day, my hope is that you make the right decision."

Oscar remained quiet while they strolled along until the rain became more intense, "Come—we are close to the catacombs. We must elude the rain while exploring. You will love it," Oscar spoke hastily as he took her hand and began to run along the street, with Cateline joyfully laughing. Oscar finding her extremely fascinating was bubbled over with delight and became intoxicated with her air of pleasure as he joined in her merriment.

Almost out of breath, they arrived at the entrance of Les Catacombs de Paris. He took her hand and led her inside as they descended to the underground tunnels that lay beneath the streets of Paris. "I can honestly say I have yet to ever go into a catacomb, Oscar?"

Only visible by faint lights scattered about, there were many tunnels in various directions which held human remains —skulls, bones, and such, embedded along the walls—a resting place for lost souls—many unknown. It was quite an eerie setting with remnants of skeletons in every direction, visible to those who dared venture into this remote place—buried under the earth. Oscar noted, "This tomb was built sometime in the eighteenth century to eliminate the overflow of the remains in the cemeteries. A considerable amount of time was spent transferring millions to their final resting place.

With his arm around Cateline to help warm her from the chill of the air within the tunnels, Oscar shared with her frightening stories of the dead. They ventured on their mile walk, where it was pretty dark with only slight illumination along the way in a number of places. With the despicable smell of dampness and the stillness of the air bestowing a most obscure presence—Oscar veered off in the distance, and with a shallow voice, he spoke, "Did you see that?"

"See what, Oscar?"

"The shadowy figure that darted on the other side of that rock."

"No, I didn't see anything, did you?"

"Yes, you know they say that the dead often walks among the tunnels—shh—listen—," he whispered.

"What is that sound?" Cateline nervously inquired.

"Obviously, we are not alone, be very quiet not to disturb the spirits," he muttered softly, and within a few seconds, Oscar started running and screaming, leaving Cateline behind.

"Oscar—do not leave me—please wait—," Cateline screamed, striving to catch up with him when suddenly, he stopped and burst out laughing—

"You should see your face," he spoke while snickering hysterically.

"It's NOT funny!" Cateline exclaimed in an upset tone as she persisted in walking down the tunnel while Oscar caught up with her.

"I'm sorry. I couldn't resist, but it was funny."

With a slight grin, she replied, "I suppose it was. Can we just get out of this most sinister place, now?"

"I believe the exit is not too much further," he said while putting his arm back around her to bring comfort.

"Thank you, Oscar."

"For what?"

493

"For merely being who you are. I did enjoy the catacombs with you," smiling, Cateline continued, "it seems the more I get to know you, the more there is to know. Tell me something unusual—anything which you have done that was extremely bizarre."

"Hmm, let me think a moment—," laughing, he resumed, "there was this one time where I decided to wear a live snake around my neck as a scarf; it was at an art exhibit. I believe it caused quite a stir."

Cateline, laughing intensely, was unable to speak when Oscar noted, "Yes, it was funny but probably not that funny!"

"No—no, you don't understand. I am laughing so hard because I did the same thing. Well, it was not an art exhibit but rather a store. I wore a live snake around my neck into this quaint little shop. It was so funny at how fast everyone seemed to flee the building."

Oscar laughed with her before speaking again, "Yes, it was the same effect at the exhibit. I do believe, my dear, we have far too much in common."

They continued venturing along while he shared with her more of the history of the catacombs. As they came close to the exit, light from above the tunnels finally became visible. They ascended back to the streets, where the rain had subsided, and the air was once again vibrant with the pure smell of the dampness and the glistening beauty of Paris in all its grandeur and charm.

The streets were lined with many businesses of all sorts—quaint shops, Parisian cafes, distinct bars, and cabarets. Carrying on in their adventures, in and out of several establishments, there were occasions where they would decide on a prominent place for needed refreshment. As it was, once again, a time to enjoy life in Paris, they stumbled upon La Closerie des Lilas, a French restaurant in which Oscar was quite familiar, where they quickly resolved to enjoy a Parisian style high tea along with a meal. They took a seat on the outdoor patio, after which Oscar placed their order. Momentarily, the tea arrived with Cateline elaborating to le serveur, "Je voudrais un peu de lait pour mon thé, s'il vous plait." Very soon, they were enthralled with a most incredible serving of baked fish and potatoes, a variety of bread, delectable desserts, and other delightful hors d'oeuvres. "I believe I could live in Paris and eat like this forever," Cateline expressed.

"Perhaps, one day, you will."

To complete their meal, Oscar ordered champagne—pink to his delight, even though Cateline found his creation utterly enjoyable.

They hailed a fiacre and rode along, enjoying the views crossing back over the Seine to la rive droite until they arrived at the Musée du Louvre. Oscar was anxious for Cateline to view the bust of Emperor Nero, one of his most favorite exhibits on display. Simultaneously, she was most excited to view all the wonderful paintings portrayed by artists of past centuries. Passing on through the various chambers, while appreciating all the history and the numerous works of art lined extensively throughout, they came upon a most impressive Italian painting, Saint Sebastian, by Mantegna—a very unique contrast of the protector against the plague which was widespread in the fifteenth century. "The techniques the artist used are very original, wouldn't you agree?"

"Ruskin said it this way, 'All great art is the expression of man's delight in God's work, not in his own.[2] All great art is to some degree didactic, all great art is praise to our God who created all.'"[2]

"Hmmm," Cateline thought, reflecting on his words before she answered, "I would have to agree. You are close to Ruskin, yes?"

"I admire John very much. I have learned much from his influence."

As they tread further into another room, Cateline's thoughts were on one particular French painter, Gustave Caillebotte. Caillebotte, a most remarkably talented artist, painted *Paris Street Rainy Day*, which hung in a Chicago museum. That painting had come alive to her while they ventured along the streets of Paris *dans la pluie*. Caillebotte was such a fine artist who had not really become known until much later. Yet, much of his work hung in museums, not only in America but throughout Europe. "Oscar, did you not adore Caillebotte's painting of Paris in the rain? His work speaks so to my heart."

"Yes, there are works of art which do speak to our heart, as you say. Yet, in its primary aspect, a painting has no more spiritual message than an exquisite fragment of Venetian glass. The channel by which all noble and imaginative work in painting should touch the soul are not those of the truths of lives."[3]

"Yes, I agree. However, I do believe that Venetian glass is just as artistic and beautiful as works of art on canvas. But I love the painting of Paris in the rain immensely, my dear."

In a resolute manner, Oscar disclosed, "Gustave, yes, I love his painting immensely, but I have loved walking with you, my dear—in the rain, more so."

Both were quite dry from their earlier meander through Paris in the rain when they left the Louvre, strolling along the quay of the Seine. Walking through Place du Carrousel, they soon came upon the Jardin des Tuileries, which had been relatively close to the Louvre. Sauntering through the gardens, they enjoyed the remarkable beauty of the plush lawn—shrubbery and flowers, along with the history shown forth in the astonishing sculptures and statues within the premises. The grounds were heightened in spectacular creations, artworks of grandeur—Le Serment de Spartacus, Thésée combatant le Minotaure, Mercury riding Pegasus, Nymphe sculpted by Louis Auguste Leveque, and numerous others. Before leaving the gardens, Oscar noted in excitement, "We are close to the boulevards! We must walk to rue Royale where we can promenade to the boulevard de la Madeleine and boulevard des Capucines—*the life of a boulevardier*, my love."

"A boulevardier—I have yet to hear that term. You will enlighten me?"

"It is the stroll of the boulevardier to leisurely walk the boulevards daily. Of course, stopping along the way to sip a drink and watch others who are also boulevardiers. One is recognized, as they are often seen—yes, the life of a boulevardier!"

Cateline smiling, thought to herself, "I wish America was as laid back as Paris—one could get used to this life if one had no need to make a living." They continued ambling along the boulevards at all the various shops, cafes, restaurants, and such—stopping at one point to have a delicious, refreshing drink before they had fulfilled the daily life of a true boulevardier.

Oscar and Cateline proceeded back towards the river, strolling hand in hand, arriving at the Seine, they wandered down the Quai du Louvre, which would one day be renamed the Quai François Mitterrand. Oscar and Cateline enjoyed the views which Paris presented with the clouds on the horizon and the sun's demise showcasing its brilliant rays of gallant streams bursting forth in colors of bright yellows, oranges, pinks, purples, and sultry greys and blues. The river was alive with its ripples mixed with hues of blues and greens. Life, shown from within the buildings which lay alongside, brought forth radiance as the vast explosions of bright lights sparkled over the river's surface, invigorating mysterious shades, brisk tones in golds and silvers. Paris, a truly vibrant setting with its twilight hours descending upon the most romantic city with its ancient buildings flourishing in the diverse architectural styles of Medieval, Roman, Baroque, Classical, Neo-Classical, Renaissance, Art Nouveau, and Contemporary. A supremely unique Parisian lifestyle with its love for art, history, and literature. It was the city of life, love, romance in all its grandeur, transcendence, fame, and prominence! Known as one of rich wealth and luxurious appeal and lure—its ornamental value and incredible magnetism! Celebrated for the antiquity of various classes—writers, painters, literary giants, intellects, and more. With the glorious landmarks and points of interest, all of which Paris afforded, the city of romance was known as the city of light. This, by far, was due to its leading role in the Age of Enlightenment and because it was also the first large city to use gas street lighting, *La Ville Lumière*. Paree stood grand among cities of its time—lost within the seas and rivers, the mountains and hills, and France's valleys and plateaus. Paris, a city known, adored, cherished which brought forth the life of those long-gone—memoirs of time felt, known, never to be lost to the artist, the painter, the writer, the poet. Eyes gazing towards the very existence of what those beyond also saw and cherished—Paris toujours vivant jamais oublié.

Days resumed while they enjoyed exploring the sights, spending countless hours alone with room service, relishing in their times together, their love for each other, and making the many memories to be cherished eternally. Thus far, there had been no photo taken nor any location which looked familiar based on the background in the picture Cateline beheld.

"Cateline," Oscar spoke while in the midst of such deep thought, "perhaps the time will not be so soon—perchance, it may not be for another year, or maybe, seeing how much we love each other, God will not send you back to your time after all."

"Oscar, I so wish that could be true, but I know it cannot. I know that I am not noted in history in your time. I am so very thankful that I am still here by your side. Yet, just the same, I do not want to regret any of our days together. I would much prefer our days continue as they have, with us making memories and being intimate, as long as we possibly can, without taking one day for granted, Oscar. None of us truly know when our lives will end. Let's just love each other for today, always."

"Yes, I do agree with you, but it has almost been two weeks. It may be feasible to presume we will be paying for another fortnight, or maybe we should travel to see another place."

Thinking about what he said, she responded, "Another place? Oh, Oscar, suppose it was not Paris—suppose the photo was taken in another place!"

"If it was, then let us not try to find it. We planned for Paris; let's remain in Paris." With these thoughts in mind, they both drifted off to sleep that night.

CHAPTER
31

Morning soon came, and their day drifted by while they enjoyed spending it lazily together, all cuddled up in their room with grand plans to ensue that evening. Mid-day, Cateline decided to begin getting herself prepared for their splendid night of entertainment. She stationed her hair up in a most magnificent *Gibson Girl* style, which would not become popular until towards the end of that century. It was a design in which she had worn in the twentieth as well as the twenty-first century on special occasions. Her long locks of hair, being as thick as it was, easily transformed into that most elegant style, which later became an Edwardian icon. Fashioned loosely in an elaborate mode, slight waves and curls dangling about secured with tiny jewels randomly to accentuate the work of art.

All dolled up in her splendid attire, ready to take in a theatrical performance followed by a late-night in Paris, Cateline walked out of the boudoir to where Oscar sat reading while awaiting her presence. She presented herself, festooned in the most spectacular soft white gown, an empire style gathered under the breasts with a low square shoulder and neckline, gorgeously portrayed. The soft, smooth fabric flowed down lightly and curved about her figure—a bold crimson band of velvet accented under the breasts added a bit of color, while around her neck dangled a lightweight necklace of small jewels which complemented those in her hair. Her complete costume and hairstyle drew attention to her feminine features of elegance in a most glamorous way, which seemed to leave Oscar in a state of awe while Cateline stood glimmering in ecstasy.

After a moment of silence, he was drawn to her exquisite beauty, entirely captivated, before he finally spoke, "My dear, you are always breathtaking, but I believe this time I feel speechless. You are astonishing; I am afraid that I will be forced to stand by your side every moment to protect you from the wolves," he concluded while Cateline laughed.

"Really, Oscar—wolves?"

"Well, of course. All men are wolves until they become tamed by the right woman."

"Oh, is that what happened to you?"

499

"I am not quite sure what has happened to me. I do know I have never been the same since I met you. Perhaps, I am so taken with you because of all that you possess. Undeniably, you are most different from any woman in this century, which I am sure has brought about the utmost attraction on my part. I am unsure a woman from this era could have had the effect you have had on my life, which by the way, has transformed my very existence."

"I am not sure that is a compliment. You believe that you would not have had as strong a connection if I had been born in the nineteenth century?"

"I can't say. Your beauty is extraordinary, but your intelligence far exceeds that of women in this century. Of course, no matter what century, if I had met you, more than likely I would have fallen in love."

Cateline, beaming, seemed to be pleased with his last statement. Walking over to Oscar, he ran his arms along her back while exclaiming, "No bustle, I could see, but no corset either?"

"I find them most uncomfortable and binding, to include the petticoat. Will this not be appropriate?"

"Ah—but remember, we are both rebels. I am flogged most often for my own dress; I find you terribly charming. I will say that I may have a hard time keeping my hands to myself."

With a bright smile, Cateline disclosed, "I am most delighted you desire me the way that you do, Oscar. I would not wish it any other way," she took his arm as they proceeded to leave.

Upon exiting the Hotel Voltaire, they took a fiacre to the Théâtre des Variétés, located on the Boulevard Montmartre. As they arrived, the crowds were flourishing about anticipating the opening of the doors. Trees were lined along the street, stretching tall and slender above the city, providing a canopy of branches and speckles of green leaves. The theatre's façade was graced with spectacular columns, where many a gentleman stood nearby smoking cigars and the like, while ladies gathered close, engaged in much dialogue. A rush of occasional laughter could be heard, mingled in with the other bystanders. In his excitement, Oscar declared, "Once the performance has come to an end, I shall introduce you to Sarah Bernhardt; she is most pleasant. I do believe you will enjoy her presentation in Sardou's *Fédora*."

When the time came near, the crowds filed in a few at a time; as Oscar and Cateline found their seats, they quietly sat down while gazing about—Oscar, desiring to see fellow chums, with Cateline's focus on the architecture of that period. The theatre itself, she found entirely to her liking.

Soon, the production commenced, and all were quiet throughout the performance, with much suspense, drama, and romance. Once the play ended, Oscar observed Cateline had tears in her eyes, "Were you crying, my darling?"

"I was. Ms. Bernhardt is such a remarkable actress. She was very dramatic as Princess Fedora, but the ending was too much. I was not expecting her to end her life, as she did."

He smiled and proclaimed, "I assure you, in person, you will positively adore her just as much as you have on stage. She is a genius! And my dear, the tears that we shed at a play are a type of the exquisite sterile emotions that it is the function of Art to awaken. We weep, but we are not wounded. We grieve, but our grief is not bitter."[1]

Backstage, they proceeded for Cateline to meet Ms. Bernhardt, where she was in awe of her very delicate beauty. Soon, they joined her and others employed in the theatrical realm to a favorite late-night club, Le Chat Noir, which provided for good company along with their famous shadow plays. The cabaret, located in the Montmartre district and having recently opened, was quite popular among the artist type, with its new mode of entertainment and bohemian atmosphere.

The group took pleasure in their surroundings as much dialogue evolved, intermittent laughter, and of course, there was undoubtedly great delight in the venue. As they enjoyed an occasional iced champagne along with Perrier Jouët, Cateline observed how Oscar truly admired Ms. Bernhardt and how she, in return, took pleasure in his company immensely.

As their late evening persisted, Cateline became much engaged in conversation with a few gentlemen at their table; it seemed that all were having a jolly good time. At first, they did not realize a photographer was going about snapping pictures of groups when suddenly, it happened! Both Oscar and Cateline glanced at each other, realizing this was the place, and that was the picture, which they had not observed because Ms. Bernhardt was not in the last snapshot in which Cateline had brought. As it was, Ms. Bernhardt was seated on the opposite side, and though there were photographs taken from different angles, there had only been one with her and Oscar. At this point, they knew it was just a matter of time before Cateline would be sent back to her era. Oscar leaned over to whisper in her ear, "Cateline, I am ready to leave."

"Yes, I am as well."

They proceeded to stand when Ms. Bernhardt spoke up, "Oscar, you are not calling it a night so early. It is rather unlike you," she finished while glancing up at Cateline, perceiving she was his reason for leaving somewhat hastily. Even though they had been told Cateline was merely a friend of his, Sarah was not blind to the glances and whispers shared amongst the two during the night.

Ms. Bernhardt continued, speaking once again, "I am sure Cateline is not ready to leave, are you, dear?"

Cateline looked over to Oscar, unsure what to say, starting to speak when he interrupted her. "I am sorry, Sarah, you know I would normally stay longer, but I am afraid that it is I who am ready to leave. In consequence of your wonderful performance this evening and my desire to celebrate among friends, I do not feel entirely myself tonight. I will surely see you before I leave Paris," he declared, leaning over to kiss both cheeks, which was the custom among the French.

Once all the conversations had ended, they finally left, hailing down a fiacre, which took them back to the hotel.

As they laid down across the bed, Oscar held Cateline close as she spoke first, "I know what you are feeling because I am feeling the same thing. But Oscar, the last thing I want is for our last night to be where we are miserable." Cateline stopped and turned to face him while resuming, "Look at me! We love each other; neither of us can stop this from happening. Please, let's not think about tomorrow; let's just enjoy each other for our last night, I beg you."

Oscar pulling her close while kissing her intimately, whispered, "I do want this night to be remembered, Cateline—my soul and my body, they both belong to you, my dear."

For much of the remaining hours of the night, they stayed awake, being fearful of falling asleep. They talked and laughed, had a few glasses of champagne, and found much pleasure in their lovemaking. One would doze off while the other would always say, "Are you asleep?"

"No—no, I am awake."

At one point, Oscar quipped, "I do not want to close my eyes and awaken where you are no longer by my side."

Cateline, seeing the tears in his eyes, turned over to hold him close, "Please—don't do this! Oscar, I will always be with you—always in your heart."

They both held each other close to the wee hours of the morning, but eventually, from total exhaustion, they drifted off to sleep.

It was mid-morning before Oscar awoke in a jolt, "Cateline—Cateline! Wake up, ma chérie! You have not left me."

She sat up from her slumber while tears streamed down her cheeks, "I'm still here, Oscar. Oh, but—I am still here!" She exclaimed in excitement.

As they lay holding each other in an embrace, both rejoiced with tears of happiness when Oscar questioned, "What do you think this means?"

"Well—I'm not sure unless perhaps there are other photos I know not of, Oscar. Although, I do know I will not remain forever. We must choose to live each day with gladness for the time we have left."

Over the next few days, Cateline awoke frightfully both nights having the most shocking nightmares of being pulled back into time, as she could see her body leaving and would watch Oscar in the distance trying to pull her back. While crying, in the midst of tears, she poured out her heart, "It was most dreadful, Oscar. I was awake, and I could see you, and I was reaching for you. You were trying so very hard to reach me with your hand—and then our hands touched, but just as soon as you touched me, you were unable to grasp hold. I was screaming and screaming for you! And—then I awoke," bursting into tears again, Oscar pulled her close to him.

After some time of silence, his thoughts were in preparation for a most clever statement, when finally, the words came to him as he quietly spoke, "In this world, there are only two tragedies, my love. One is not getting what one wants, and the other is getting it.[2] I know neither of us understands why we have met and loved, only to be separated. One day, perchance, we shall both understand more fully."

Cateline looked up at him and smiled while disclosing, "I know you said one time you would never meet anyone like me again. I, too, know that I shall never meet anyone like you."

"It's going to be alright, my dear. I am right here with you for now. Perhaps, it may be best if we leave Paris. I feel like we are merely waiting every single night for it to be our last. I can't do this night after night—please, we have been here a little over two weeks, let us leave. I know a place on the Normandy coast, Dieppe, a fishing port, or possibly, even Berneval. Both are quite beautiful; they sit on cliffs. The beaches are rather tranquil, with tiny pebbles. A very inspiring place, one where we can enjoy our days with refreshing walks and rejuvenating swims. Let me take you there, please."

She dried her tears in agreement, "I believe you are right; we should leave."

Oscar and Cateline enjoyed their breakfast that morning. Afterward, checking out of the hotel, a ride was secured to the train station. They rode back towards the English Channel to the Normandy coast. Dieppe being much closer than Calais, the distance was about a two-hour journey. After arriving in Dieppe, they ate a late lunch at the Café des Tribunaux before deciding to take the carriage ride to Berneval. This minor farming village, Oscar had mentioned, was more secluded.

Cateline enjoyed the views along the route, verdant terrains surrounded by graceful hills with luscious shrubbery and sporadic small trees. On occasion, wild daffodils dressed in glorious yellows stood proudly waving as a warm greeting to Normandy. Along the pathway, right outside of Berneval, a field thrived amongst the tree line. Cateline wondered and speculated in thought, "*Berneval Meadows, Morning,* Camille Pissarro's landscape impression." Undeniably, the picturesque scene was one on canvas, one she had esteemed.

Dandelion puffs and clovers were scattered about, inviting for all who toured the vastness of this glorious land. As they drew near, the village could be seen as it sat atop the cliffs, welcoming their arrival with many structures scattered about as they approached their lodgings.

They checked into the Hotel de la Plage, hurriedly unpacked, and changed their attire before wandering down to the beach, which was only a short distance. Holding hands, they walked along the promenade, a relatively wide divide between the cliffs where it gradually declined, unfolding gracefully to the shores. "Oh, yes, this is perfect, Oscar. I love it here," Cateline declared as they strolled down the rocky beach, looking out to the English Channel. It was late evening, yet the sun still shone in the sky, with the daylight hours being fairly extensive at that time of the year. The views which Berneval had to offer were much enjoyed in such a tiny community. Oscar and Cateline soon found themselves quite alone, watching the waves one by one scurrying up to shore, tumbling gently over their toes with a cloudy white tousle of water hurriedly rising inch by inch. The gusty breeze from the channel prickled about their faces, blowing strands of hair swirling. It was a breath of crisp air, a moist smell filled with a multitude of wildflowers mixed with the fragrance of apple trees in full blossom, a most pleasant tropical aroma mingled with the oceanic waters. Plush green grasses toppled the cliffs, coursing downward among the gouges which stretched throughout the declivity of the rigid vertical bluffs to the sea, forming the backdrop of the pebbly beach blended with sand, a serene setting. Simultaneously, the sounds stimulated their senses—the briskness, the rumble, and roar—splashing, lapping, and gushing of seawaters coming forth and rescinding.

As they sat down on the beach, looking out to the channel, Oscar pulled out his journal, where he kept much of his works along with several other writings of those he admired, one being Lord Byron. He began to read one of Byron's poems to Cateline—

"She walks in beauty, like the night
Of cloudless climes and starry skies;
And all that's best of dark and bright
Meet in her aspect and her eyes;
Thus, mellowed to that tender light
Which heaven to gaudy day denies.

One shade the more, one ray the less,
Had half impaired the nameless grace
Which waves in every raven tress,

505

Or softly lightens o'er her face;
Where thoughts serenely sweet express,
How pure, how dear their dwelling-place.

And on that cheek, and o'er that brow,
So soft, so calm, yet eloquent,
The smiles that win, the tints that glow,
But tell of days in goodness spent,
A mind at peace with all below,
A heart whose love is innocent![3]

There was a moment of solitude when Oscar spoke serenely, "I love it with you, Cateline. I believe this is what we needed—away from people, where we can just have slow days filled with each other, the beach, cliffs. This is much like the Cliffs of Moher, small and secluded, very tranquil, is it not?"

"Yes, we have made perfect memories in our times together, Oscar," she acknowledged lovingly as her features emitted radiance.

In a cheerful dialogue, he responded, "Wonderful memories, Cateline. I fear I shall never make such memoirs again."

"Oscar, there will be many remembrances. We all have memories that are good and then others that are not so good. Nevertheless, it really takes both the good and bad to mold us to be who we are meant to be."

"I was your first love, Cateline?"

"You were, and you are also my only love, Oscar."

"Men always want to be a woman's first love. That is their clumsy vanity. Women have a more subtle instinct about things. What they like is to be a man's last romance."[4] Cateline was silent before Oscar continued with his thought; turning to look her in the eyes, he finished, "If ever it is imaginable, I shall be your last romance, my dear."

After some moments, Cateline inquired, "Oscar, what will you do once I am gone?"

Thinking about her question for a brief period, he finally responded, "It is far too close to the social season ending in London. I shall have no reason to return, as many of my friends will come to France by the end of June. Dieppe and Berneval, after all, are an artist's paradise. If you are to leave soon, I would think I need this time alone to spend right here remembering everything about us," he finished with a solemn look.

"I am so sorry, for I know this will be hard for you. It will be hard for both of us."

"Yes, and you? Where will you go, back to Chicago?"

"Oh no, I cannot continue my life as it was. Remember, I told you I would more than likely buy a home on the east coast."

"I do remember, my dear. What was the place called again?"

"Wells, Maine."

"Yes, I will have to go there and see this place you speak of when I am in America—see if it is quite as beautiful as you say."

Pleased at his reply, Cateline spoke after a few moments, "What about our rings? What will you do with your wedding band, Oscar?"

"I am not sure; what about you?"

"Oh, I shall always keep your ring. Perhaps, I will wear it forever."

"I, too, my love—."

As he spoke those words, she knew there was no mention of that wedding ring in his possession. With this knowledge, Cateline inquired, "Oscar, can I keep your band instead? I would simply like to keep them together if that is alright with you."

He looked at her and responded hastily, "You gave me this ring, Cateline! It means far too much to me. I do not want to tell you no, but it really means the world to me."

She smiled and took his hand in hers, speaking softly, "I understand, truly I do. It's just there is no mention of this ring in your history. I do not know why. I thought, possibly, it would be better if the rings stayed with me and remained together, that's all."

With nothing further said about the rings from that point, lying in bed after a most delightful day spent at the beach, Oscar read Cateline a poem. "My love, this poem was written by Walt Whitman. When I read it, I thought of you. Whitman called it, *Out of the Rolling Ocean the Crowd*. Please, listen—

Out of the rolling ocean, the crowd came a drop gently to me,
Whispering I love you, before I die,
For I could not die till I once look'd on you,
For I fear'd I might afterward lose you.

507

Now we have met, we have look'd, we are safe,
Return in peace of that ocean, my love,
I, too, am part of that ocean, my love; we are not so much
separated,
Behold the great rondure, the cohesion of all, how perfect!
But as for me, for you, the irresistible sea is to separate us,
As for an hour carrying us diverse, yet cannot carry us diverse
forever;
Be not impatient—a little space—know you I salute the air, the
ocean, and the land,
Every day at sundown for your dear sake, my love.[5]

With tears in her eyes, she softly spoke, "Oh, Oscar, I do love you. Always remember me, and I will you. Perhaps, someday we will be together once again. And Oscar, when I stand on the beach in Wells at sundown, I will often gaze out at the waters and see you—feel your presence."

Oscar leaned over to wipe her tears, "My love, it pains me to see you cry." Kissing her goodnight, he spoke once again, "Remember, Cateline, though oceans and time may separate us, my love shall always remain!"

"I shall never forget, never! Oscar, do you remember when we first met, down at the lake at my uncle's, we recited that silly play?"

With a prominent smile, he addressed, "I shall never forget that time. It was a very memorable day, to say the least."

"I told you then that I could produce tears when needed by thinking on something sad."

"Yes, I remember that feat!"

"My thoughts to produce those tears were of these days which I knew would come. I had always loved you and knew our days would be few."

With those last words, Oscar reached over to take her in his arms, as they cuddled until they fell fast asleep.

It was that first night in Berneval, Oscar awakened around four that morning. He rolled over to watch her sleeping when he had a wonderful thought. Kissing her gently on her face over and over again and finally on her eyelids until Cateline stirred. In a most sleepy voice, she proclaimed, "Oscar—what is the matter? Could you not sleep?"

"No, I have been lying here watching you, my dear."

She smiled and cuddled up next to him, "Is it morning already?"

"It is four, early in the morning but dreadfully dark outside. I had a most brilliant thought."

"And what might that thought be?" Cateline asked while gazing into his eyes.

"I know you will laugh at me, but let us go out into the night while others are still sleeping. We could stroll down to the beach, lie amongst the sand and wait upon the sun to ascend in the sky."

Cateline pictured how romantic it would be and declared, "Oscar, why yes, that is a marvelous idea."

She climbed out of bed and dressed when Oscar exclaimed, "No, my dear! Let us be daring—in our nightgowns. I doubt we will be seen at this hour, and if we are, why should we care?"

Cateline laughed and replied, "Yes—in our rebel state, why should we?"

Hand in hand, both in their white nightgowns which covered down to mid-thighs, playfully ran down to the beach, barefoot, laughing in the very early morning with the moon overhead and darkness surrounding them, only the brief twilight of the moonbeams cast through the shadows along the waters to the rocky shores. Oscar watched her with awe, knowing he had never met anyone quite like her. Her looks, the way she moved and danced, her voice when she spoke or in song, her smile, and most of all, her demeanor, which portrayed her exotic, flamboyant, mysterious, and sensual style in a most eccentric yet discreet way. Everything Cateline possessed filled him with so much delight and kept him hostage by the unending love he felt for this woman. Cateline filled his senses with a tantalizing aura, and he knew it would be impossible to ever forget her.

Here they were, carefree—young lovers, knowing their days were limited, freely enjoying the feel of the air cascading down over their bodies, the touch of the sand as it gently obscured their bare feet. Holding hands, they walked along the pebbly beach with the wind from the sea breezily flowing through their hair and sweeping their nightgowns briskly against their bodies. They ran along the shores, laughing and frolicking, playfully kissing and taunting, enjoying the feel of the occasional gusts of wind as it howled through

509

the dark waters and the scent of the moist air, when all of a sudden, Oscar blurted out, "Sing to me, Cateline."

"What would you like me to sing?"

"Anything, but with words spoken to me."

"Well, let's see—," she responded while beginning to think about the perfect song. As she commenced to sing, they stood facing the waters with his arms wrapped around her body, where Oscar started kissing her neck gently, which was distracting. "Oscar—stop! I cannot focus. I cannot sing," Cateline giggled. Every time she began, he was adamant in disrupting her while laughing. With both joined in a most playful moment of giggles and merriment, Cateline broke free from his hold and ran down the beach, with Oscar dashing after her. Fabulous memories were being made—moonlight meanderings, frolicking through the waters at the shoreline, strolls through the lush green grass surrounding the beach, the feel and the fragrance of the tropical climate.

Oscar stopped at one point and wrapped her in his arms as they kissed and touched so very gently. With Cateline standing ever so close against his body, he held her tight, speaking in almost a whisper, "I will remember this night with you always, my own true love. At night, when I gaze at the moon, I will find comfort in knowing somewhere in time you are looking at the same moon as I."

Cateline, responding, seriously advocated, "Oscar, always remember, memories have a way of navigating our passage in this life, but love holds the key for our choices to stay on course."

They remained on the beach, lying among the sand and pebbles on a blanket brought from their room. Cateline was wrapped up in Oscar's arms while they watched the rising of the sun over the English Channel. It was a truly beautiful sight intertwined together with nature, only the sounds of the waters in their most serene melody. The beach, radiant from the far outstretched early morning sun as it briefly materialized with a glistening effect amongst the dampness along the shore, a smooth shine of grey mingling into the ripple of waters—greyish blue stretching forth to the horizon. Exploding into the surrounding sky, dribbling over into the clouds, traveling higher and higher into the atmosphere, an unformed circular sphere froze in its grandeur. It was most splendidly shaped in deep orange with the brilliant splash of a vast white tinge mixed with yellows, forming irregular shapes which faded out in various hues diluting into the white and then pallid blue sky as it rose overhead. Oscar, in a most serene expression, asserted, "Vue Sur la Mer."

With much delight in Cateline's heart, she countered, "Yes, my love—the sea view, it doesn't get any better."

Ending the tranquil setting, the beginning of dawn, hand in hand, they returned back to their room while Cateline walked over to pick up a sheet of paper, "Oscar, I wanted to leave you with a poem that I wrote just for you," she spoke serenely while he sat down on the bed as she approached. Cateline read—

Remember Me

Once we stood overlooking the cliffs, a serene place,
I by your side, feeling a love that I never knew.
The sun shone brightly upon your gentle face,
The waves crashed on the shores, and seagulls flew.

Holding my hand as you kissed my lips, again and again,
Our days were filled with countless laughs and play.
Lost in our world of many words spoken,
While in the gondola floating along the quay.

A love never known such as ours, unfailingly,
Feeling as though time has forever stood still.
Suddenly the clock moves forward eternally
Wondering and questioning was it ever real.

When you awaken, and I am no more,
Know that I loved you always and forever.
Hold me in your heart until your death, for
I, too, will be broken as I strive to endeavor.[6]

Oscar took Cateline's hand and pulled her down beside him as he held her in his arms. He kissed her lightly before speaking— "Every heart sings a song, incomplete until another heart whispers back. Those who wish to sing always find a song. At the touch of a lover, everyone becomes a poet."[7]

Pleased, she inquired in a soft tone, "You are calling me a poet?"

511

"Plato's words, not mine," he proclaimed while smiling back, "Mais, J'adore toi, Cateline. I will keep your poem forever close to my heart."

The following days were filled with much togetherness, an abundance of love exchanged, sharing, talking, laughing, and teasing. It was time spent significantly to reflect on their vows made to each other and to ponder the reasons they were brought together to begin with. Being thankful for the time they were given, they both felt resilient to face the uncertainty as one collectively, wherever their lives may lead them.

Upon Cateline awakening days after their arrival in Berneval, she realized her surroundings were very different. Startled, she stormed out of the bed, looking around the room with tears forming in her eyes—Oscar was no longer with her. Cateline screamed over and over again in her distress, "Jamais oublié—Jamais oublié—Jamais oublié—Jamais oublié!" She assumed by the décor of the room, once again, to be back in the hotel where her journey had begun. Cateline ran to the window, glancing out at the scenery. Yes, without a doubt, it was the Clontarf Castle Hotel in modern-day. It was pretty obvious, this was not the same room from the beginning of her journey several months past, but it was apparent, this was Dublin's famous Clontarf Castle Hotel. Distraught, she sat down on the end of the bed and sobbed hysterically. "Why—oh, why Lord—why did I have to leave? You know how much I love him, Lord. I cannot imagine my life without Oscar. Oh, Father, please protect him! Please, remind him daily of how much I loved him."

Cateline's sobs continued as she lay back on the bed in her sorrow. Even though this was inevitable to play out as it had, Cateline had dared to hope that God would have allowed her to remain. She tried to pull herself together, sitting up in the bed, wiping away the tears, when all of a sudden, she noticed the wedding band was still on her finger. She twirled it around and around, quickly remembering the locket as she reached to find it around her neck. Cateline pulled it out from her shirt, and the sobs came more and more, "Yes, Lord, I will be strong and trust you. I know you love him and will be with him through everything he must endure."

She stood and walked over to the phone to dial Mary's number. "Hello," the voice on the other end spoke.

"Mary—is that you?"

"Oh my gosh—Cateline! I have been so worried about you. Why haven't you called me?"

"I—I couldn't call you, Mary. I was—I was not where I could have called," she spoke in broken syllables from tears that had resurfaced.

"Where are you; are you okay?"

"I am back in Ireland. No, I am not okay."

"Where are you staying? I will take the first flight I can get to Ireland. Let me know where you are, and I will be there as quickly as I can."

"I am back at the Clontarf Castle Hotel; you will come?"

"Certainly, I will come. I will let you know when I can get a flight, alright?"

"Yes, please hurry, I need you," she sobbed with tears flowing.

"Of course, Cateline! I will call you back as soon as I can confirm a time and take care of being absent from work for a period."

"I will be waiting for your call, Mary."

"Do you have your cell phone?"

"I—I am not sure. I have not looked, but if I do, I am sure it needs to be charged."

"Okay, I will just call the hotel if I cannot get you on your phone."

After hanging up from Mary, Cateline walked around the room to see what belongings had accompanied her back through time, merely to find her original luggage. However, she did have the one bag she had carried with her throughout the journey, which still held her cell phone, CD player, and the photo in which Oscar had written the poem. She held the picture while tears persisted streaming down her face. Her thoughts were lost in his awakening to know that she was also gone—forever. The love they had shared and experienced—it was only a memory, a wonderful remembrance of love bestowed between two people lost together in a realm unknown, a time-spent but for a moment—one born too soon and the other too late. Cateline lay across the bed and wept uncontrollably, subdued in brokenness. Her life seemed as it had ended, feeling as if there was nothing further to live for. "Oh, Oscar, if we could have had more time. If only it never had to end, my love. Whatever shall my life be, for I

513

feel as I have died—nothing shall ever have meaning. Part of myself has forever been torn out of me, out of my heart—it is shattered, numb! I shall never feel whole again!" Grief seemed to have settled over her entire being. She was despondent, discouraged, and felt empty inside. "Oh, please, Lord—take this pain from me, make me feel alive once more." In the depths of her despair, the tears seemed to have stopped, for there was nothing left inside. She laid on top of the bedspread, lifeless—there were no sounds, no tears, no movement. Hours had passed where Cateline never moved nor spoke a sound. Sometime in the night, she rose from the bed and walked over to where her bag lay; opening it, she searched to determine if everything came back with her. Besides the CD player and phone, all her original clothing was present, all her IDs and assorted documents. Suddenly, Cateline became quite astonished when she realized the diary was among the book and articles which were originally packed. "Oh, yes, the diary and the photos of our marriage I had tucked inside," Cateline exclaimed while filming through the various pages and gazing at the memoirs of their wedding day. Feeling comforted in having a record of all their times together, once again, she dug deeper, looking through every single item within the bag. All of a sudden, she cried out in astonishment, "His wedding band—his wedding band!" Cateline repeated. "Oh my, did he decide to put this in my bag after all?" This was a question she would never know for sure, but his wedding band along with the chain was bound in a soft cloth, not just any cloth, but the handkerchief which had been given to her by her aunt on the day of their wedding. She hurriedly put his ring around her neck on the chain with the locket, where Cateline felt as if she carried a part of him with her.

Several days later, Mary had arrived to console her best friend. Cateline anxiously waited for her at the entrance of the hotel. Her excitement would rise with every taxi that pulled in, and disappointment followed when it was not Mary. At last, Mary exited a cab, and Cateline ran to hug her. With tears streaming down both of the girls' faces, neither could speak for some time. After depositing Mary's luggage in Cateline's room, they dined at the Fahrenheit Restaurant within the hotel while Mary was much engaged on all which had occurred in Cateline's life from the time she had arrived in the nineteenth century. In between Wildean Champagne, that Cateline had introduced to Mary—over ice, they both laughed and cried of all the spectacular roads she had been so fortunate to have traveled beside this remarkable man, Oscar Wilde.

The girls, finishing their scrumptious meal, to include the refreshing drinks, strolled down to the beach, where they sat to enjoy the feel of the breeze as it cascaded to the shores. Cateline showed Mary all the items she had gathered to bring with them, including the fabulous wedding photos. Finally, at one point, Mary recognized all the stories were actually true and understood how Cateline must have felt all these years. Having many of the memories to share, Mary was able to view several other pictures, which were never before seen nor published because they had left with Cateline. She was also able to share the poem in which Oscar had written on the back of the photograph taken of them together. Besides the snapshots and wedding rings, Cateline also held in her possession their marriage record. Thankful for all of these items, she secured the rings and locket close to her heart.

"Cateline—even though I saw all those pictures in the articles and the book, I was still very skeptical. When you left, I thought you would realize what you were feeling was irrational. I have to say, when I could not get in touch with you, I thought something dreadful had happened. There was no way for me to know or anything I could do. I kept telling myself that you had told me to not worry if I did not hear from you for a while. All I could do was wait. Until now, I honestly doubted your story and thought there had to be an explanation. But after seeing these photos and everything—you were right, and you knew all along there was something more to this. So, what now? What are your plans now, Cateline? Do you just go on with your life after all of this?"

Cateline, drying her eyes once more, spoke very softly, "I am not quite sure, Mary. I really loved him. I do not see myself ever being able to forget nor ever being able to fall in love with anyone else. I had thought about that question many times before you arrived," she continued looking out at the Irish Sea where they sat, "I know I cannot leave until I revisit all those places we went together. I was hoping that you would accompany me."

"Well, yes—I would love to, Cateline. How long do you plan for this to take? You pretty much traveled Ireland, much of England, and a part of France."

515

"I know, and I will understand if you cannot come. I do not want to stay in any particular location for a prolonged period. I simply must walk where I once walked with Oscar—take pictures of those places. I know we can go by train to most of the locations, which is much quicker today. I suppose we could fly from some areas to others—maybe a few months. Please, do not worry about the cost. I do plan to pay for everything."

"I'm not concerned about the cost, Cateline. I was merely thinking about the time away from work. But yes, I think I can manage that, and then we fly back home. You are coming back to Chicago?"

Cateline looked down while speaking faintly, "No, I mean—yes, I will fly there to make arrangements for my belongings eventually and to get my car. But I cannot do that again. After this journey, my life has changed. I can never be the same person, Mary. I plan to use the funds from my father's estate to purchase a house on the east coast. I really want to live in a small community, have a place on the beach. I was thinking of Wells, Maine."

That evening, before retiring to bed, Cateline picked up the diary and read some of her journal entries with tears flowing down her cheeks. Mary seeing her, asked, "What are you holding?"

"Oh, Mary—I had totally forgotten to tell you—look..." she stated, holding out the diary for her to take.

Mary, flipping through the pages, exclaimed, "Wow, every single day you were gone is filled in with all the particulars. Can I read it?"

"Of course, you can. I do not think I can read it just yet. I am so glad that my cousin talked me into logging my days in a diary. I would have never thought about it. Every single thing that happened to me is in this book by the day."

"You never forgot? You wrote every day?"

"Well, no. There were many days where our time was much filled, and there was no time to write. Even so, the days I could write, I would go back and catch up. Every single day is in here."

CHAPTER
32

Days and weeks seemed to go by while the two girls traveled to various locations—a month and then into the second month of their travels, as Cateline relived the times she had spent alongside Oscar, sharing all the wonderful moments and memories with Mary. They journeyed throughout Ireland, many stops in England up to London and then into France. At almost every place they went, there was a substantial amount of memorabilia pertaining to Oscar, which was heartbreaking. Still, in a way, those sights seemed to bring comfort, knowing he had made a mark on history. When in London, during their tour of Père Lachaise Cemetery, his final resting place, it had been very hard for Cateline to hold back the tears. It was not like they were alone; in fact, in order to even view the burial grounds, one had to be with a tour guide since there were so many famous laid to rest.

The last stop of their travels was Berneval in Normandy. This was the most heartbreaking of all, as it was the final place occupied by his side. To her, those remaining days with him had not seemed so very long ago because, in reality, it wasn't. Nonetheless, in 2000, Berneval had changed somewhat due to the bombing of World War II, where much of the original structures had been destroyed. However, the beach area was still vibrant and picturesque, not much different from 1881, except for more buildings constructed since that timeframe.

They arrived in Berneval about the time the sun was descending, but after checking into the hotel and getting settled, dusk had already begun to set in. Yet, Cateline insisted they take a stroll down to the pebbly beach. With the twilight hours beginning to loom, they were able to gaze at the wonders of the most stunning moon as it was stationed in the night sky, where streams of light cascaded over the deep waters. Cateline, with tears flowing down her cheeks, shared with Mary that final evening they had spent together.

"It was such a remarkable night. I do not believe I could ask for a more perfect memory than that of the remaining time shared in Berneval. Yes, it was right along here—on this same stretch of beach.

517

The memory will stay with me forever, Mary," she spoke solemnly while trying to stay composed enough to impart their last moments.

Mary, reaching over, put her hand on Cateline's shoulder, "Cateline, I would love to hear about that night if you think it will not be too painful."

Cheerfully, she responded, "It is painful, but it is a most amazing memory, Mary. Truly, it does me good to talk about it. We had actually gone back to the room, deciding to have dinner privately instead of going to a restaurant. I changed into something more comfortable while Oscar stepped out, telling me he would be right back. Upon returning, he handed me a bouquet of wildflowers," smiling at remembering that moment, Cateline resumed, "they grew along the bluffs and were most striking. Oh, I know it was already getting late when we arrived, Mary. Still, you must remember to look out at the cliffs in the morning before we leave. They were filled with color when we were here. I do hope it is the same. I have honestly come to love wildflowers so much from being in this country. They were quite lovely—Armeria Maritima, considered a sea thrift—a most gorgeous pink, well a cross between pink and purple, I would say. Long stems with a very delicate tiny petaled cluster of flowers stationed on the ends of each stalk. They grew beautifully throughout the precipices among the verdant grass, a pasture of color moving gracefully with the breeze from the sea, providing a slight fragrance. It was then that he told me he had a surprise." Lit up with a bright glow in her countenance, she stated, "I, naturally, was already wearing my white chemise and was barefoot." Spoken with a slight laugh, she persisted, "But Oscar, he insisted we walk along the shores, so he just wrapped a blanket around me, and we proceeded to the beach. Berneval, being such a quaint village at that time, I do see that it has grown, but it was much smaller in those days. There seldom was anyone at the beach or especially at this time of year, with London's social season in full swing. The elite would not leave for the country or other adventures until sometime in August, so there were not as many people at the resort in May. It was also somewhat insignificant compared to Dieppe and still is today, I presume," she pondered. Cateline continued with her story, "That evening, the sun had begun to go down, and it was not far until the moon would be ascending," she related. After a pause, in deep reflection, she laughed, "It wasn't enough for me to merely walk down to the beach—no, he had to blindfold me, needless to say. I protested profusely. I mean, it was not quite dark yet, and here I was in a nightshirt. But Oscar was set on blindfolding me, so I complied." They laughed most prominently as Cateline endured with the story, "We proceeded to stroll alongside each other while he led me down to the beach. Of course, it was not far from our room, and in no time, I felt the pebbles under my feet, being barefoot and all. Once we stopped, he took the blindfold off, and there to my surprise sat a table with two chairs, candles lay atop which were blocked by the wind—a remarkable feat that he constructed, and a most glorious spread of food—oysters, scallops, tripes à la mode de Caen, Camembert cheese de Normandie, brioche, and complemented with red wine— Alicante Bouschet, the boldest flavor of berries and cherries with a spicy, smoky taste along with tones of dark chocolate, spice, and— vanilla bean—,"

Mary, interrupting her, "What? With tones of chocolate AND vanilla bean?"

"Yes, it was truly a delight. We must try to find it."

"Undeniably, please do not forget!"

"Affirmative, Mary! We shall search until we find such a creature today," Cateline laughed. She resumed her story, "And so, he purchased the red wine, knowing how much I loved red. Even though I always drank his champagne concoction," smiling she maintained, "he even paid a very young boy to stand and watch over the table until we had arrived. Such a cute little guy, of about twelve, I would say."

"It sounded like such a romantic evening, Cateline."

"Oh, that wasn't all. Undoubtedly, I felt out of sorts in my chemise, even though I had the blanket around me. In due course, I insisted upon Oscar going back to the room to change, which he did, and soon returned with his own covering for warmth along with my CD player. We ate on the beach, observing the sun in all its magnificence as it continued to subside over the horizon. At the same time, the beauty of the moon rose high, illuminating the dark sky. Different songs were playing, but he had chosen very romantic music. After finishing off the bottle of wine, we ran down to the beach like a couple of children, barefoot with nothing but our nightshirts on, like that first day when we had arrived. Oh, Mary, it was so magnificent—the rushing shores cascading over the pebbly beach with only a tiny glimmer of light shining across the waters from the moon. There were a lot of clouds in the sky that night. The moon was so mysterious, almost a full moon, but clouds perpetually floated

519

about, obscuring the view. Yet, it shone so bright, so white with a pathway shining from the far distance of the channel all the way to shore. It was a rather dark night but so romantic. I felt alive, without any cares at all in the world, just the two of us, frolicking along the shoreline—running, jumping, and chasing the waves. I don't believe I have ever laughed so much. Oh my, Mary—," she began, but with laughter spilling forth profusely, Cateline was unable to continue with her story. Finally, gaining her composure, she reminisced once again, "I wish the whole scene could have been recorded. Like I said, we merely were like a couple of children playing about and with the music going. Oscar was so absorbed in all my tunes, well—you know me, I have a bit of the 50s all the way to current music—"

Mary laughed, interrupting her, "Knowing you and your music, Cateline—I am sure I would have been doubled over in amusement watching you two."

"Oh, please let me finish. There were certain songs he enjoyed very well and wanted to learn how to dance as they did in those distinct times—the 50s, 60s, and on into other decades." Cateline strived to continue sharing the story but was overcome with laughter thinking about that evening before she was able to resume. "I taught him how to dance like they did in the 60s. We danced to *Hang on Sloopy*[1] and several of The Beach Boy's songs. Oh, but it gets better, *Twist and Shout*,[2] by the Beatles came on." At this point, Cateline was laughing so hard that tears had formed in her eyes before she could go on. "I taught him how to do the twist; he loved it. I believe we had to play that song three times. I laughed so hard at him; he was so funny. But we had the time of our life, Mary. It was so wonderful, so many memories, and we danced nonstop to so many different songs—through the 70s and 80s. We were having such a good time. I don't think I have ever laughed so much in my life. And, then there were the slow songs—such a romantic, everything you could ever dream of in someone or desire. He was everything, the complete package." Feeling nostalgic, her words became soft, and tears slowly trickled upon her face. "It felt so serene, and we were both just so alive, no cares only love for each other. He had been listening to many of the songs and had begun to also know some of the words and would sing them softly in my ear while we danced in each other's arms," she paused to wipe away tears before continuing with the story. "I believe we were both damp from jumping about the waves rolling to the shore, but we were not wet. We never got in the water completely, but it was quite chilly at night. Yet, it never seemed to bother either of us. I don't believe we felt the cold at all. Once we were both reasonably worn out from the dancing and running around the beach, we came back to where the table was, and he put Ritchie Valens's song on, *We Belong Together.*[3] He then held me while we slow-danced, with him singing the words to me," she paused and laughed. "It wasn't like the other songs where he knew some of the words. He evidently had practiced learning that song at different times when he would sneak off with my player. He knew every word."

Mary smiled before speaking, "He sounds like a pretty awesome guy, Cateline."

"Yes, he was. Once the song stopped, we listened to music relentlessly while lying on the blanket he had spread out. It was so peaceful and dreamy. We merely talked, kissed, and watched the moon. I believe we were there for most of the night. I had fallen asleep in his arms—I'm not quite sure Oscar ever slept that night on the beach. I awoke sometime in the early part of the morning as the sun had begun to rise over the channel. Oh, how delightful it was, lying there in his arms. The sphere of the sunlight gleamed forth upon the pebbly beach while the dreamy blue waters awakened as the tide coursed along onto the shores. The daylight hours rekindled life among the seagulls; I believe Oscar said they were called black-backed gulls. They were rather larger than our seagulls, and there were several in the vastness of the sky, along with other sea life splashing and frolicking about as the breakers collided onto the beach. It gave a sense of belonging, one with nature, all awakening, coming to life, another day, one of elegance, beauty, arousing one's sensations and awareness of joy and happiness." She hesitated with a deep sigh, "I turned over to face him, and of course, he was awake. I truly believe he often laid awake watching me sleep those last days." Silence ensued while she looked out to the channel in deep thought. With tears flowing, she commenced most tenderly, "He spoke and said to me, 'Good morning, my princess.'"

Mary, seeing Cateline in a somber state, expressed to her with much concern, "It's going to be alright, Cate. He loved you. You had a most beautiful connection, and you will carry him with you forever."

"I realize that, Mary. It's just that, what we had, I will never have that again. That was my last memory. We came back to the room and decided to get some sleep. It was already morning, but I know I had not slept much and was not sure he did at all. And then, I must

521

have only been asleep briefly before I had one of those bizarre awakenings," she paused. "You do remember me sharing with you the illusions I started having many years ago."

"You mean the ones with the smoke?"

"Yes, but I do perceive it to be some type of foggy haze, Mary. Yet, they do frighten me something horribly."

"Those seem to be fairly consistent, Cateline, once a year or so."

"I have not kept track from the beginning, but I do believe you are correct. Even so, Oscar did not awaken when I jumped out of bed shaking, and then eventually, I was able to go back to sleep."

"Did you ever share with Oscar about your mirages?"

"Yes, very briefly. I did not want to go into detail, for I would not have been able to explain what I do not know myself. Despite this, afterward, drifting off to sleep, I perceived I would awaken later by his side. Neither of us realized that I wouldn't be there later that day." Tears streamed once more before she spoke gently, "I wouldn't have thought I would have left like that. I believed since it was morning when we returned from the beach and I was still there, I had at least one more day."

"It's going to be alright," Mary assured her with a hug.

The two girls remained on the beach, both silent, in deep thought as they enjoyed the solitude of the evening and the sound of the waves crashing over the shores. After time had elapsed, Cateline spoke once again, "I believe he went to heaven, Mary. I honestly do."

"What makes you say that?"

"Something God had shown me during his time in prison. You do understand it really is the *Davids of this world* who genuinely come to know God. David was a man after God's own heart, we are told, yet he sinned terribly. David struggled with sin, as do many before him and since to this day. The world looks at Oscar as this dreadful sinner who is now in hell—but David was a terrible sinner, too. Oscar did not commit murder—he struggled with sexual sins. Truthfully, Oscar was no different than others before him and after, as well. Man wants to categorize sin, but honestly, when man tries to live without God doing things his own way, he lives in sin. Let's face it, once man becomes of age, all struggle with the desires of finding pleasures in this world, whether it be through riches, comforts, or our deepest passions. It is part of our sinful nature, and only God truly knows man's heart. We all fall short of being good enough for heaven; Oscar was no different. Those who want to claim they do not have sin in their lives, well, Jesus did not die for them. Jesus himself said that He only came for those who were sick, not those who perceive themselves to be well. Those who think themselves not sinners believe themselves to be well and in no need of a savior. Oscar knew he was not right with God. That is why he continually searched for Him. In his time, Oscar wrote a collection of five poems, all were Biblically based. As a poet myself, I know that what one writes comes from within—from their heart. You can read his poems and tell that Oscar knew he wasn't right with God, but he believed there was a God, and there were times he sought to find Him. The world looks at the outward person to identify one's character, their actions—those things one has done seem to define who they are to the world. Nevertheless, in the Bible, we are told that God looks on the inward man. God sees what is on the inside, looks at the heart of man. Why, if we were to look at the thief on the cross, we would see nothing good, only that which was sin. It is what is on the inside of every person that defines who they are to God."

There was a pause while both girls were silent in deep thought. Once again, Cateline expounded, "I believe the world has missed something regarding Oscar. Even the thief on the cross next to Jesus knew he was a sinner and that he didn't deserve heaven. All the same, do any of us really deserve eternal bliss? The thief spent his whole life in sin, but in his last moment, this man spoke to Jesus and asked that He remember him when He came to His paradise. Jesus replied to the man that he would be with Him that same day. This man knew he was undeserving of Jesus, yet Jesus saved him. In those poems, Oscar knew he was unworthy. Oscar's time alone in prison, he diligently sought out the Lord and felt so undeserving of heaven. His remaining years, he pretty much lived out those days in poverty—yes, Oscar fell back into his way of life, but this is nothing new either. Many have—none of us can walk this life when we strive to do it alone. I think that Oscar never gained wealth and fame again in his life because God had another plan. I believe in his alone time, he continued to talk with God. People who are the *Davids* of this world have the fiercest storms, and it is evident that Oscar was truly a man of much sin and struggles in this life. Yet, God is continually at work in the lives of those who battle between good and evil in order to save them. Most of the world would disagree, but most of the world never studies the Bible. I cannot say that Oscar is in heaven, but I can say there is an excellent chance he is. Knowing him today, I would be more likely to think he made it. In his own words, Oscar said that he spent most of his life trying to even imagine what heaven looked like and never could. I honestly think that today, Oscar knows what heaven looks like—him spending his entire life not even being able to imagine it, that today, possibly he is living in paradise. After all, his whole life had been hell."

After a brief moment of thought, Mary replied, "But, the world will never believe you; they will not see it that way."

"I get that, but I feel like there is something more I am to do. I just don't feel like my sole purpose was to be sent back to his timeframe. I feel there has to be some way that I make things right for Oscar—something to give the world, where at least those who have looked at his life, feasibly would be able to see they may have misjudged him, not only Oscar but all the *Davids* of this world." She took a moment to reflect before continuing, "There's a famous quote—Mozart said, 'You should show the whole world that you are not afraid. Be silent, if you choose, but when it is necessary, speak—and speak in such a way that people will remember it.'⁴ Those words speak to me, Mary. I feel that it is necessary to not remain silent but to share what I know, what I see." Cateline paused for a few moments while she thought about something else Oscar had written while in prison. Cateline continued on the topic, relating, "Mary, there were so many things Oscar wrote about while in prison. I remember towards the end in *The Ballad of Reading Gaol*, he wrote this poem—

"Ah! happy they whose hearts can break
And peace of pardon win!
How else may man make straight his plan
And cleanse his soul from Sin?
How else but through a broken heart
May Lord Christ enter in?"⁵

Cateline finished with a most fervent look upon her face, "We must remember that God does not look at us through the same eyes as man does. We are often judged harshly by those in this world, yet God, he looks within. He looks at our heart, the core of our existence. In reading many of the works written by Oscar Wilde, I was amazed how far too often his writings revealed a heart that searched for God more than once.

There was a long silence as both girls were in deep thought. After some time, Mary spoke, "Perhaps, we should be getting back to the hotel?"

"You go ahead; I think I will stay here for a while if you don't mind. I just need some time to say goodbye."

Mary walked away while Cateline strolled along the shore, looking out at the channel, so beautiful and peaceful. To her, it was as if it had only been yesterday. With tears streaming down her cheeks, she spoke silently, "Au revoir, my love, until we meet again someday, you shall always remain a part of me."

The following morning, they traveled to Calais port for an excursion back to England, where they could book a flight from London to America to leave the next day. Saying goodbye to Europe was extremely hard for Cateline, knowing that somehow, she had to make sense of her life once again and find something which would soothe her pain and give her life and Oscar's purpose.

CHAPTER
33

Upon returning to America, Cateline soon made all the arrangements to move back to the New England states, as she decided not to go back to work in Chicago. Her experiences over the past months had drastically changed her life, where Cateline was unsure who she was or what road she desired to travel. She realized her life would never be the same due to all that had transpired, where she continued to be led back to her roots on the east coast. It somehow seemed to make sense to her to live close to the Atlantic Ocean, where she believed it at least brought her closer to Oscar's memory. Using the funds from the sale of the pubs, Cateline traveled along the coastal regions in Maine. She was in search of the perfect location, a place where she could somehow commence to rectify her life with a new beginning, a fresh start, even though she anticipated it would be quite hard.

Cateline's first day on the east coast, in her new home, she ventured down to the shoreline of the Atlantic Ocean. Time had seemed to continue, but her heart remained tied to the one man she would love forever. Walking along, in deep thought of the love she had left behind, Cateline gazed out to the vastness of the ocean and spoke in a most tranquil voice—

The solemn beauty of the sea, the deep blue waters caress
Rolling waves so peaceful, the whitecaps soon transgress
Streams of light peep through the clouds, across the waters flow
The warmth fills the air—as the breeze begins to blow
A trillion grains of sand, embrace one's feet so calm
Remembrances fill the mind, a sweet soothing balm
The tears I cry are many; the desires are so pure
I miss every part of you; my life cannot endure
I see you in each sunset; your presence fills my heart
I long to hold your memory, my love to impart.[1]

That evening, while unpacking many of her items, she picked up her novel of *Nana*. Yes, Cateline had purchased a third edition while in London but had soon found a first edition in which she bought upon returning home—quite old, it was indeed. She flipped through the pages while remembering what Oscar had shared with her on how many copies had sold the day it was released. "This book being a first edition," she thought, "may have been sold that very day, so long ago." As she sat reminiscing, Cateline reflected, "What a novel, one that took Europe by storm, written so many years ago, in a time not known except by those who lived in the nineteenth century. The novel itself was pretty explicit, yet it did give a narrative of those times in a day where the social elite lived by a different standard." As for the actual story, the novel, Cateline's thoughts continued, "What wonder and amazement of all the thousands who have read these pages throughout such a prolonged period—terms and expressions which portrayed that era, such wisdom to be gained of that decade. How great the mystery of Emile Zola and his writings, the admiration and wonder of all those over the last one hundred years, those who have turned these pages, the mysteries within, of those moments—generations gone by, lives lived and died—those who breathed and those who cried—past days, past times, spanned out over a century, years and years. The writings cherished by those well-known, many commoners, and just plain folks—traveling over Europe and then the Americas. How glorious to embrace this very book and imagine those who have held and touched this precise novel." Her thoughts drifted about with many notions and perceptions when she considered that possibly, there may have been some of those whom she had even met. Anticipating the likelihood of such, Cateline reflected, "Maybe, even Oscar had touched this very book. Oh, but if books could speak, would they proclaim the names of those who had held them? Or, of those who had laughed and cried? And, of those who loved and those who died—the secrecies, books of years gone by shall always hold. Is the mystery far greater for the words spoken so long ago or for the lives that have lived and breathed within the stories, lost in the prose of centuries past?" The spectacle and the bewilderment filled Cateline with so many inspirations. Perhaps, concepts she would never have perceived had she not touched that era.

From a distance, Mary had remained in close contact with Cateline, flying to see her when feasible. On one such occasion, several months following her time in Europe, Mary had flown in to celebrate the purchase of her new abode, Cateline having found the perfect location during her search. It was situated in a most tranquil community on a gorgeous stretch of the coast only a matter of steps from the beach. Immediately after acquiring the beach home, Cateline had driven into Boston to pick up Mary from the airport, where the two girls enjoyed conversation on the drive to Wells, Maine, for Mary to spend a few days at Cateline's new residence.

"I am so pleased to see you, Mary, and do hope that you will love my new home," Cateline shared with her best friend after leaving the airport and traveling towards her beach house.

"I told you I could have flown into Maine."

"Don't be silly; I always love an excuse to be in Boston. Besides, it is only a little over an hour away. On another note, I do believe you are going to love my place."

"From your description, it sounds wonderful. Have you decided if you are going to go back to work?"

"I have—or rather, I am working, but I am doing so from home. That is quite another surprise."

"Please, wait not a minute longer. I must have the details!"

"I am actually writing a column for The Boston Globe. So, you see, my editor is always thrilled when I drive into the city. I actually came in early before your arrival where I could meet with her."

"That sounds like the perfect job for you."

"It is, and it also gives me time to write in my manuscript."

"Your manuscript?"

Cateline smiled and replied, "I suppose that I am full of surprises for you; I started to write a book."

"And go on, please tell me more."

"Well, it is a story that will make things right for Oscar. Of course, it is fiction, so to speak," she stated with a sympathetic smile.

"Oh, so to speak—your story, huh?"

"Quite so. I couldn't just let this linger and never do anything to make his life right. I felt that I had a voice and had to use it for his sake. You do understand, don't you?"

"I do, and I do hope after this you will get on with your life."

"I promise, and I will."

"Well, you are not the only one with surprises," Mary expressed with a smile while holding up her left hand.

"Oh my gosh—you are engaged?"

"Yes," she proclaimed with such excitement, "Cateline, you will love him. He is absolutely wonderful."

"If he makes you glow like this, I already love him."

Both girls, filled with excitement, were looking forward to spending time together enjoying Cateline's first week in her most intricate beach home. Once they had pulled onto the beachfront road, rows of houses were adorned along the way, a quaint area in the township of Wells, known as the *Friendliest Town* in Maine. Turning into her driveway, Mary was already excited, "Cateline, I love it and the location. It is superb."

The front part of the residence, a quaint two-story, faced a small road lined with many of the same manner of houses, one by one, uniquely established with story-book facades, charming in detail. Cateline, replying to Mary's enthusiasm, "Wait—you haven't even seen inside nor the scenic aspect of the beach from the back patio, showcasing the elaborate panoramic views of the ocean—a most picturesque landscape. It is quite outstanding."

Mary touring the inside, the home itself was not that large, but more than sufficient with three bedrooms all on the second floor, two and a half baths, a substantial living area, dining, and kitchen. Towards the back of the home stood an amazing lanai, the entire length of the residence, enclosed with glass to provide a full view of the ocean. Off from the enclosed veranda, a door opened onto a distinct patio complete for barbecues, flowing out to the sandy beach, steps from the waters. The sights from within the lanai without leaving the room, one could take in all the landscapes of grandeur—the crest of the waves tumbling over the sandy shores along with the gallantry of the waters far out into the distance, linked together, at a remote place beyond, where the waters merged—the ocean to the sea.

Mary quickly settled into her room and then joined Cateline downstairs, where the girls soon walked down to the shores. Mary very promptly exclaimed, "Oh, Cateline, I believe I am so jealous. I am in such awe of your home and just look at the glorious views. This feels so perfect; I am so very happy for you."

They enjoyed their first day catching up on all the particulars in both of their lives and retired to bed relatively late.

Early the following morning, while Mary still slept, Cateline stepped out onto the patio. The aromatic air was fresh with its moistness from the waters, and the scent of the salt breeze mixed with the marsh plants as the ocean settled on the shore, the sand, with every element of its touch. Listening to the sounds of the seagulls, clamoring about in precise motion, swooping up and down over the waters drawing closer towards the shore, Cateline started to walk further towards the beach. The breeze could be felt gently on her body, bringing a sensation she once had known and once again revisited in her mind on those days and times in Oscar's arms. Memories of such days in his presence while at the shores in Ireland and once again in England, lastly their days in France. Slipping off her shoes, she strolled along barefoot, feeling the sand between her toes while envisioning those days, those times, encased in his arms, for a season—one which could never be forgotten. Cateline's mornings were always spent with her peaceful walk on the beach. These were times reminiscent of a life she had known, a love embraced, one which remained embedded in her very soul—the man, never to be forgotten, as Oscar had once declared, he, too, could never forget her. How could she ever truly forget him?

While Cateline stood alone on the beach on that particular morning, her thoughts drifted as they usually did. The landscapes in all their grandeur with the sunset bowering over the waters, her reflection at that very moment laid upon Oscar—joined together as one surrounded by nature. She could feel his presence encircling her, for his apparition was sensed in every breeze as it enveloped her form. She could see him in the dawn as the sun lifted radiantly in the folds of the sky. Emotions stirred her even at dusk as the brilliance of the sun would cascade into the horizon. In all she enjoyed, her thoughts were of him, persistently—only of him. In the midst of her inspirations, she quietly whispered, "Oh, love of my heart, it seems impossible to live away from you. Come back to me, my love—come back to me."

The weekend continued with the girls taking much pleasure in their days of sauntering along the beach, talking and reminiscing of old times, relishing in each other's company before Mary had to get back to Chicago. It felt like the days they had shared growing up in Boston while they enjoyed their time spent catching up on each other's lives. On their last night, they sat out on the sandy shores watching the waves tumble gently onto the beach and the occasional flickering light far out in the ocean from a passing vessel in the distance. Both girls sat appreciating the serenity of the moment—the peace, beauty, and the sensation of the brisk wind, as it blew ever so lightly to shore. In moments like these, Cateline felt as though Oscar was still with her somewhere in time.

In the quiet of the moment, Mary looked over at Cateline, who seemed lost in her own world, conveying quietly to her friend with concern, "You've barely mentioned him since I have been here. How are you?"

She smiled and beheld Mary closely before sharing, "I'm okay, really! I seem to have found a sense of peace, supposedly in my writings." As she made a slight laugh, Cateline continued while surveying the ocean, "I don't think I will ever get over him if that is what you want to know."

"No, I wouldn't think that you could. I simply believe that maybe, if you were to meet someone, it would help you to go on with your life."

"If you are asking me to get over him, Mary—I will never get over him. You are in love right now," Cateline voiced, as she looked into Mary's eyes, tears beginning to stream down her cheeks, "do you think that you could walk away and get over Patrick just like that?"

"Well, no, of course not, Cateline. But, if something happened where our relationship ended, and we didn't get married, eventually, yes, I would get on with my life. You are not the only one that has lost someone. Please, know that I love you very much, and I know that you loved him more than anyone, but I worry about you. I know there is someone out there for you."

With a warm smile, Cateline spoke softly, "I know you love me, and I am glad you care enough about me for this discussion. But really, I am okay, and I will make it through this."

"Well—okay then," Mary responded with a quick smile, "I will not worry about you. You are a big girl, and I am sure you will get through this but promise me one thing—"

"Sure, Mary—" Cateline answered.

"Promise me, if you ever feel that you cannot do this alone anymore, you will call me."

Cateline putting her hand on Mary's shoulder, responded, "Mary, I promise that you would be the person I call if I sense the need for someone to talk with."

Upon Mary's departure, time was sustained, and days were many; seasons came and passed. Cateline seemed to go through the motions very slowly for one who felt such loss. Her life was no longer her own as it was caught up in the memories she had left behind. Weeks turned into months and years. Cateline remained busy, working and writing, doing many of the things she loved. Even though the days drifted on and the years trickled by, her heart, she knew, would always remain connected to Oscar.

Yet, the day did arrive when Cateline had decided to take off her wedding band and put it on the same chain along with his, wearing both of them for quite some time around her neck. A year or so later, Cateline had decided to put the chain up in one of her small jewelry boxes for keep's sake, but there were times when she would take it out to wear, especially on the anniversary dates. It was on those special occasions—their marriage, his birthday, and the day he had died, she would spend a considerable amount of time laying out on the beach. The songs they had shared, hours were spent listening over and over, particularly Aerosmith's, *I Don't Want to Miss a Thing*. It was this one song he had dedicated to her. The words were so embedded within, knowing his thoughts remained on their times together, as did his love. With many tears during these times of reminiscing about the past, Cateline was so pleased that she lived by the shores, which somehow seemed to make her feel closer to his memory. Though a shadow seemed to alight over her, and in her most gloomy despair, this had become her life for many years. What remained, she clung to—the photos of their lives together, the poems, and above all, the poem he had written on the back of that photo during their last days. It was all the memorabilia in which she held close, celebrating their short life together even though it was but brief, on those gloomy days like today, Cateline would read the poem—

Cateline, my own darling,
Ever since I looked upon your beauty
I have dared to love you,
Wildly, passionately, and hopelessly.²
If you are not too long, my own dear wife,
I will wait here for you, all my life!³

Eventually, over the years, her walk had become more manageable, the aching lessened as her time became much enthralled with putting every effort into writing the book—the book of her life with him. Even so, some days and times were more challenging. Cateline had often thought that she would have been able to let go after a separation of time had passed, for some years were not as painful but forgetting that life spent with him no longer seemed possible. Her life alongside Oscar had consisted of so many memories where she was unable to let go. As time moved forward and grew closer to the year he would have died, Cateline often drifted into contemplating where she would be today if she had never left that period. She often found herself mornings and evenings at the beach, sitting and gazing out over the ocean, remembering their life together and how far apart they were—separated forever by oceans and time. Cateline had never stopped keeping track of the days and years, continually thinking to herself, "If I had never left, we would have been together for five years, ten years, fifteen years, and then some."

Mary had gone on with her life, married, and had two children—no longer working outside the home. The girls remained as close as they always had, with Mary flying in to see Cateline regularly, and at times, Patrick and their children joining her.

Cateline had slowly maintained writing in the book over many years but never completed it. It was as if she were afraid to completely finish the book. To her, it felt like she would have to let go once the book was finally finished, and somehow, the thought of moving forward without his memory seemed to frighten her. For the most part, the manuscript was completed, but she desired to not have it published just yet. Prior to the book being released, Cateline had worked on various other projects and had acquired a literary agent, being quite successful with her career. This had eventually become her avenue for wealth over the years and had filled the void in much of her life, where Cateline no longer felt she lacked that relationship she once would have given everything for. However, her deep thoughts resumed year after year, where Cateline would ponder on her life and where she would be if she had remained. She often wondered if they would have still been together—would he have unremittingly loved her to the end—would he not have ventured into the affairs which led to his fall, and if he had not, would they have had a good long life, as husband and wife. These became her dreams—her obsessions, where she would predict their life if she had never left. In that year, 2000, Cateline had met Oscar, two years younger, twenty-four to his being twenty-six. Although, it was the early part of the year, with neither celebrating a birthday until later on. However, Cateline calculated and calculated each year where it drove her to a place that held her captive with remorse and at the same time brought clarity to just how much she loved him, knowing that her love for him would never, ever cease. Cateline knew the time eventually would be right when she would decide to release the book, which would allow the world a different perspective on Oscar's life.

Time continued to progress, days upon days and year after year, with 2019 finally arriving. Fast-forward 19 years from 1881, for this was the dreaded year of his death. And here she was, in her timeframe, having already celebrated a birthday, at forty-four years old to his forty-six if she had remained by his side in that era. Oh, how Cateline was still a beautiful woman. She could have undoubtedly passed for thirty-five and had met many suitable gentlemen over the years who fought for her attention. Yet, Cateline had nothing to give. Her life had been so enveloped around Oscar's that she had nothing further she could offer to any relationship. Her days were devoted to writing, and many of her evenings were spent down at the beach, where she would sit and dream, remembering all the times they had enjoyed, reminiscing of days long gone, times past, and love left behind. The days lost in watching the sunset and awaiting the moon as it would shine down upon the ocean from the horizon to the shores reminiscent of those days consumed with him—in his arms, lost in time. On numerous sunsets, she would read inserts from her diary—a much-worn memoir, stained with many a tear. Sadness would fill her soul on those particular dates, especially their wedding anniversary, but also so many other times they shared together.

In the early part of 2019, Cateline had contacted her agent to advise her that this was the year. Knowing about the book all these years, the agent had been extremely excited for it to be released. So, here it was, and this was the year. The only thing that Cateline desired was that it be released on the anniversary date of his death, which was the thirtieth of November. Her agent had been working tirelessly with all the details, ads, publicity where everything was falling into place as the time was drawing near to its big release. Here Cateline was, 2019, forty-four years old, finally knowing that she would be able to find closure after so much time.

Towards the date of release, being excited, Mary had flown in close to that time to be there for Cateline. "Cateline, I have to say this is so very exciting," Mary exclaimed, continuing, "I read the manuscript you sent me, and I must say, reading your story, I found it most touching. I believe it will make many see Oscar from a different perspective. I know that was your desire."

"Yes, my love for him is hard to describe, but my hope is for readers to see the story as a didactic novel. Where, in turn, God's people look to His Word for direction in their lives, knowing there is only one God, and it is only through Him any and all can find salvation. The world must know, in reality, Oscar Wilde could have found heaven, for Jesus came for the broken, not for those who think they are good."

Cheerfully, Mary responded, "I must admit, I never saw this until I read your manuscript, Cateline. You are so right; I do believe that others will be able to see this truth you speak of instead of judging the world so harshly for their sins."

"Yes, for none of us are righteous, Mary. We all need a savior."

Mary rested her hand on Cateline's shoulder and added, "Now that you have finished this book, I do hope you will be able to let go and get closure in your own life after all these years."

Warmly, responding to her friend, "Yes, Mary, I plan to do just that. I know I have held on to that life for far too long, but at the same time, I now believe it is time for me to look ahead and not behind."

"I am delighted to hear you say that. You know you are still a very attractive woman and would make a lovely wife for any man."

"I know, Mary—I know, and I do believe maybe it is time for me to begin anew and perhaps, give some proper gentleman a chance," she finished with a laugh.

As the day of the book's release approached, Cateline started having odd dreams. She would be awakened at night and burst into tears. While climbing out of bed one night, she went to get their rings in order to feel some kind of solace, having a part of him close to her heart. Confiding in Mary the following morning, she replied, "Cateline, I clearly believe the dreams are because the book is bringing all of the reality back to you once again. I am sure once it is released, the dreams are going to subside."

Cateline, with tears in her eyes, responded, "I am sure you are right. After all these years, I simply do not understand why I have to suffer all of this over again in this capacity. I do hope it will all end before long."

535

The day finally came, and the book was released. Cateline had declined flying into New York for the release date, feeling that she could not compose herself to do this just yet. Having made an excuse to her agent, Cateline promised her that she would be in New York soon after the release. On that same day, in the midst of winter, bundled up with her lavish furry coat, she spent long hours down on the beach looking out at the waters in a world full of dreams, dreams of what could have been, dreams of times gone by—visions and thoughts of Oscar—reflections of them together, all the beautiful moments they had shared. Yes, this was her closure, this was the final triumph in her life, one of letting go of an image that she could never again hold—letting go of the only man she had ever loved—a time where she would be able to walk back into her life and feel once again, love once more. In spite of this, Cateline knew today was not that day. No, this day was one she basked in despair and great turmoil. This was her pain of letting go once and for all.

With the twilight hours fast approaching and Mary having flown back to Chicago, Cateline walked back to the beach as the moon started shining down over the horizon. It was such a cold evening, the wind billowing through the waters tumbling to shore, breakers off in the distance, even with her thick gloves on, winter coat, and furry knitted hat, the cold could still be felt. Numb from the chill in the air, her only thoughts were of those precious memories in which she had held onto for all those years. With tears flowing down her cheeks, Cateline cried and cried while alone on the beach at the end of the day. She used that time to talk to Oscar and to let him know in her own way, she no longer could hold onto a memory; she had to let him go. She dried her tears and walked back into her home for the night, curled up on the sofa with a hot cup of tea, where she eventually fell asleep.

Cateline awakened the following morning and took a soothing hot shower, dressing warm and comfortable for the day. Before taking her stroll in the early daylight hours down to the beach, she noticed her agent had left a message on her cell phone, where she called her back promptly. It was excellent news as she learned projections on sales for the book seemed to be at a perfect place. Cateline made arrangements for her arrival, letting her agent know she would fly into New York within a few days. Hanging up the phone,

Cateline knew she should have been excited about the projections, yet she could not shake that feeling of emptiness inside. "Was all this a means of letting go? Was I merely being hopeful in writing the manuscript that it would make it easier? I feel so withdrawn. I feel that I have truly ended what I had with Oscar. With the book now published, I deem there is nothing more to hold on to. It is finished. Yes, God, it is done, just like that." Consumed in thoughts, Cateline walked out her back door towards the beach, experiencing a sense of uneasiness. She could not breathe or focus as her mind was filled with a longing to spend time with God.

As she walked down to the shore, there was a deepfelt need to be surrounded by the beauty of the ocean to hear the serenity of the waves gently rolling up on the sand. Yes, Cateline needed the fresh air from the deep blue waters, to encounter the breeze and wind savoring over her body, to escape, to hear God's voice, and to savor in His comfort. She walked along, crying to the Lord while stopping to look out into the mysterious dark waters. "Why—why God? Why do I hurt as I do? You sent me back to him, and I loved him and still love him. Now it is clearly over. It has always been over, but my emotions and feelings have never subsided, Lord." Cateline fell down on her knees, yielding to the pain, while tears flowed as she sobbed, all the while continuing to talk to God, "I have completed everything you called me to do, Father. I finished the book. I did everything you wanted, yet, my life appears to be so incomplete. Please let Oscar know that I have always loved him," Cateline spoke softly with tears strolling down her cheeks. "It is done, Father! I have sacrificed my life to fulfill what you have called me to do. Nevertheless, the pain inside of me has never faltered; my pain is so great! It is much too painful. Why can't you just take my life; why do I have to continue being here? Please, God, I pray that you take this pain from me."

Sitting on the beach, looking out at the ocean again, the mass of waters seemed to bring back memories. Once more, it seemed to yield a sense of sadness, knowing she had to let go. With the sun rising in the sky, Cateline strived to say her last goodbyes to his memory, tears gently streaming down her cheeks with every word spoken. "My love, oh how I have loved thee always—lost in a time, a time where one lived and breathed—moments shared, intimacy—never shall they be artificial, for they were so real, so sublime. Know that you shall never be forgotten."

With her last words spoken, Cateline slightly raised her head as the tears sustained, coursing down her cheeks. Off in the distance, farther down the beach, a man seemed to be walking towards her path, "Was it her neighbor," she thought to herself, knowing that he often took walks. Not desiring for anyone to see her in her current state of turmoil, her brokenness, she turned her face to wipe away the tears. Cateline gazed back as she persisted in viewing the beautiful scenery of the sun shining down upon the waves as they cascaded towards the shore, remembering the good times they had shared, which seemed to help bring about a more pleasant countenance. She glanced once again towards where the man was walking. It looked as though he had continued in the course where she sat. As she stood, Cateline took another look in his direction, where he was now in very close proximity to where she was standing, realizing that it did not look like her neighbor. In fact, there was something familiar, "Was it the coat?" she thought to herself.

The man finally approaching, Cateline very soon grasped the realization that it was not her neighbor, after all. "But who was he," she thought silently. Suddenly, the man closed in, and Cateline felt as if she could not breathe. In a most earnest voice, she spoke quietly, "It's you."

"Were you expecting someone else?"

With a slight smile, Cateline responded, "I wasn't expecting you. I mean—I clearly thought, well—I've had these dreams, but I thought it didn't really mean anything. In my dreams, I was walking—entirely alone. It was so dark, but I could hear a voice, a quiet voice, even so, I thought it was you. I did not want to awaken, but I was afraid. There were different pathways, and I was unsure which to take. And yet, I thought perhaps it was the past, and I had already made that choice, so it was too late. I was so afraid of never knowing, and then I would always awaken, and there would be nothing. I felt as though God was telling me it was time to let go. It's just that it has been so long, and then yesterday, well—I thought if the dream meant anything, it would have been yesterday. It has been such a very long time, although what I feel deep inside and the love I have, has never faded," she concluded with tears slowly flowing down her cheeks.

"Yes, it has been a very long time," the man spoke softly, reaching out to take her hand. With his other hand, he gently wiped away her tears while he resumed speaking, "I have longed for this day. I thought it would never evolve; it was merely dreams. I, too, had feared never seeing you—never holding you or experiencing your heartbeat next to mine. I went on with my life, as you had encouraged, but you were somehow tucked deep inside. I tried to forget, but I could not. I seldom mentioned you to anyone because it was easier to believe it was not real than to suffer the thoughts of never seeing you again. You do know, I would have waited forever and ever if I had only known it possible."

As she took her hand and caressed his face, Cateline quoted his words with a smile,

"If you are not too long, my dear,
I will wait here for you, all my life!" [4]

With tears streaming down her cheeks, perpetually, Cateline gazed into his vividly light blue eyes, stating, "Nineteen years seem like forever, but time can never erase the love we shared so intimately. I have waited and waited, for I do not believe I could have ever loved another. I thought this would never be, and I wanted to give up. But there was something that would not let me erase you from my mind—the dreams and the smoke like cloud, they persisted and persisted. I would gaze out at sea, the ocean. I would see your face looking back at me. It was as if a force was telling me not to let go."

"I, too, stood at the shores, gazing far out to the horizon, and somehow, I knew you were there. Perhaps, in another time, but you were staring back at me. Cateline, you knew the pain I would endure and the shame that I brought to so many, yet you still loved me. You must know that I did cry out for forgiveness those two years, and I struggled. But I do know now that the Lord always loved me, and you were my angel."

With tears in her eyes, she responded, "I thought all these years were in vain and that I would never see you again, my love."

"We are together again, Cateline."

"But—for how long?"

Oscar held her in his arms while kissing her gently on her lips before responding, "Forever, ma chérie, forever."

Ending this fairy-tale love story, it must be noted, Oscar was Cateline's first love, and she, in turn, was his last romance!

Work Cited

Chapter One
1. *"Thou wouldst as soon go kindle fire with snow, as seek to quench the fire of love with words."* William Shakespeare, *The Two Gentlemen of Verona*, Act 2, Scene 7, Julia speaks to Lucetta.
2. *"Yes, I am a dreamer. For a dreamer is one who can only find his way by moonlight, and his punishment is that he sees the dawn before the rest of the world."* Oscar Wilde, *The Critic as Artist*, an essay by Oscar Wilde.
3. *"Parting is such sweet sorrow that I shall say goodnight till it be morrow."* William Shakespeare, *Romeo and Juliet*, Act 2, Scene 2, Juliet speaks to Romeo.

Chapter Three
1. *American Pie. The Day the Music Died.* Don McLean, artist and writer.
2. *"The very essence of romance is uncertainty. If I ever get married, I'll certainly try to forget the fact."* Oscar Wilde, *The Importance of Being Earnest*.

Chapter Four
1. *"After all, tomorrow is another day, Rhett dear."* *Gone with the Wind*, 1936 novel by Margaret Mitchell, 1939 American epic historical romance film produced by David O. Selznick of Selznick International Pictures, directed by Victor Fleming.

Chapter Seven
1. *"Life must be lived as play, playing certain games, making sacrifices, singing and dancing, and then a man will be able to propitiate the gods, and defend himself against his enemies, and win in the contest."* Plato, Quote.
2. *Thousand Stars*, Kathy Young and The Innocents. Writers: Leviston Joshua.

Chapter Eleven
1. *"Paris is a city which pleases me greatly. While in London one hides everything, in Paris one reveals everything. One can go where one likes, and no-one dreams of criticizing one"* Oscar Wilde: *Interviews and Recollections Volume I*, edited by E.H. Mikhail.
2. *"I have the simplest tastes; I am always satisfied with the best."* *The Epigrams of Oscar Wilde*, Edited by Alvin Redman, Introduction by Vyvyan Holland.
3. *"I wish I had a good Irish accent; my Irish accent was one of the many things I forgot at Oxford."* Oxford Alumni, When Oscar Wilde Came to Oxford, Michèle Mendelssohn.
https://www.alumni.ox.ac.uk/quad/article/when-oscar-wilde-came-oxford

4. *"Beholding beauty with the eye of the mind, he will be enabled to bring forth, not images of beauty, but realities (for he has hold not of an image but of a reality), and bringing forth and nourishing true virtue to become the friend of God and be immortal, if mortal man may."* Plato, Quote.

5. *The Tables Turned*, William Wordsworth, Poem. Poetry Foundation, *The Tables Turned.*

https://www.poetryfoundation.org/poems/45557/the-tables-turned

6. *"If we take nature to mean natural simple instinct as opposed to self-conscious culture, the work produced under this influence is always old-fashioned, antiquated, and out of date. One touch of nature may make the whole world kin, but two touches of nature will destroy any work of art. If, on the other hand, we regard nature as the collection of phenomena external to man, people only discover in her what they bring to her. She has no suggestions of her own. Wordsworth went to the lakes, but he was never a lake poet. He found in stones the sermons he had already hidden there. He went moralizing about the district, but his good work was produced when he returned, not to nature but to poetry. Poetry gave him 'Laodamia,' and the fine sonnets, and the great Ode, such as it is. Nature gave him 'Martha Ray' and 'Peter Bell,' and the address to Mr. Wilkinson's spade."* Oscar Wilde, *The Decay of Lying*, A Dialogue between Cyril and Vivian.

7. *"You knew what my Art was to me, the great primal note by which I had revealed, first myself to myself, and then myself to the world, the great passion of my life, the love to which all other loves were as marsh water to red wine, or the glowworm of the marsh to the magic mirror of the moon."* Oscar Wilde; His Life and Confessions, Frank Harris.

8. *"This is what I think art is and what I demand of it: that it pull everyone in, that it show one person another's most intimate thoughts and feelings, that it throw open the window of the soul."* Felix Mendelssohn, German Composer, Quote.

9. *"Life and art are not two different things."* Felix Mendelssohn, German Composer, Quote.

10. Art for Art's Sake spoken by Shakespeare; L'art pour l'art coined by Victor Cousin and others Samuel Coleridge, Edgar Allan Poe.

GUÉRARD, ALBERT. "Art for Art's Sake." *Southwest Review*, vol. 59, no. 4, 1974, pp. 522–536. JSTOR, www.jstor.org/stable/43468679. Accessed 31 May 2021.

https://www.jstor.org/stable/43468679?seq=1

Victorian Era, Art for Art's Sake.

http://victorian-era.org/art-for-arts-sake.html

11. *"Aestheticism is a search after the signs of the beautiful... it is, to speak more exactly, the search after the secret of life."* Oscar Wilde, *The Wit & Wisdom of Oscar Wilde*, Ralph Keyes.

12. *"Aesthetics are higher than ethics. They belong to a more spiritual sphere. To discern the beauty of a thing is the finest point to which one can arrive."* Oscar Wilde, *The Critic as Artist*, an essay by Oscar Wilde.

13. *"But, youth smiles without any reason. It is one of its chiefest [sic] charms."* Oscar Wilde, *The Picture of Dorian Gray.*

14. *"He rides in the row at ten o'clock in the morning, goes to the Opera three times a week, changes his clothes at least five times a day, and dines out every night of the season. You don't call that leading an idle life, do you?"* Oscar Wilde, *An Ideal Husband*, Act 1, Mabel speaking to Lord Caversham.

15. *"I have always been of the opinion that hard work is simply the refuge of people who have nothing whatever to do."* Oscar Wilde, *Complete Fairy Tales of Oscar Wilde.*

16. *The End of the World*, Brenda Lee/ Skeeter Davis. Writers: Kent Arthur, Dee Sylvia.

17. *In the Gold Room, A Harmony.* Oscar Wilde. Poem (1881).

17. *"Music is the bond that unites the life of the spirit to the life of the senses. Melody is the sensitive life of the poet."* Beethoven, Quote.

18. *"Music is capable of reproducing, in its real form, the pain that tears the soul and the smile that it inebriates."* Beethoven, Quote.

19. *"The only way to get rid of a temptation is to yield to it. Resist it, and your soul grows sick with longing for the things it has forbidden to itself, with desire for what its monstrous laws have made monstrous and unlawful."* Oscar Wilde, *The Picture of Dorian Gray.*

Chapter Twelve

1. *"O, beware my lord of jealousy! It is the green-eyed monster which doth mock the meat it feeds on."* William Shakespeare, *Othello*, Act 3, Scene 3, spoken by Iago to Othello.

2. *I Love How You Love Me*, The Paris Sisters. Writers: Larry Koldber, Barry Mann.

3. *"Ordinary people waited till life disclosed to them its secrets, but to the few, to the elect, the mysteries of life were revealed before the veil was drawn away. Sometimes this was the effect of art, and chiefly of the art of literature, which dealt immediately with the passions and the intellect."* Oscar Wilde, *The Picture of Dorian Gray.*

Chapter Thirteen

1. *"I suppose society is wonderfully delightful! To be in it is merely a bore. But to be out of it simply a tragedy. Society is a necessary thing."* Oscar Wilde, *A Woman of No Importance*, Act 3, conversation between Gerald and Lord Illingworth.

2. *"Paradox though it may seem—and paradoxes are always dangerous things—it is none the less true that life imitates Art far more than Art imitates Life."* Oscar Wilde, 1889 essay, *The Decay of Lying, A Dialogue* between Cyril and Vivian.

3. *"When I am... completely myself, entirely alone... or during the night when I cannot sleep, it is on such occasions that my ideas flow best and most*

abundantly. Whence and how these ideas come I know not nor can I force them." Wolfgang Amadeus Mozart, Quote.

4. "Straight-away the ideas flow in upon me, directly from God, and not only do I see distinct themes in my mind's eye, but they are clothed in the right forms, harmonies, and orchestration." Johannes Brahms, Quote.

5. "In my study I can lay my hand on the Bible in the pitch dark. All truly inspired ideas come from God. The powers from which all truly great composers like Mozart, Schubert, Bach and Beethoven drew their inspirations is the same power that enabled Jesus to do his miracles." Johannes Brahms, Quote.

6. "For the meaning of any beautiful created thing is, at least, as much in the soul of him who looks at it, as it was in his soul who wrought it." Oscar Wilde, The Critic as Artist, an essay by Oscar Wilde.

7. "Vice and virtue are to the artist materials for an art." Oscar Wilde. The Picture of Dorian Gray (Preface).

8. "Well, of the young artist who paints nothing but beautiful things, I say he misses one half of the world." Oscar Wilde, Lecture to art students.

9. "Indeed, the moment that an artist takes notice of what other people want, and tries to supply the demand, he ceases to be an artist, and becomes a dull or an amusing craftsman, an honest or dishonest tradesman." Oscar Wilde, The Artist as Critic: Critical Writings of Oscar Wilde, an essay; The Soul of Man Under Socialism, Oscar Wilde, 1891.

10. Can't Take My Eyes Off of You, Brenda Lee. Writers: Bob Crewe, Bob Gaudiio.

11. "Love looks not with the eyes, but with the mind, and therefore is winged Cupid painted blind." William Shakespeare, A Midsummer Night's Dream, Act 1, Scene 1, spoken by Helena says of Demetrius.

Chapter Fourteen

1. When Erin First Rose. William Drennan, Poem, 1884.

2. "Human behavior flows from three main sources: desire, emotion, and knowledge." Plato quoting Socrates.

3. "There is a boundary to men's passions when they act from feelings; but none when they are under the influence of imagination." Edmund Burke, Quote.

4. The most important act of creativity is the creation of one's own image. Wilde learned from Lady Jane Wilde that identity was a kind of fiction, and that being oneself was a form of playacting. Irish Central. How Oscar Wilde became the first celebrity "famous for being famous".
https://www.irishcentral.com/roots/history/how-oscar-wilde-become-the-first-celebrity-famous-for-being-famous#:~:text=According%20to%20Friedman%2C%20%E2%80%9Clt%20was,creation%20of%20one's%20own%20image.%E2%80%9D&text=Wilde%20was%20just%2022%20when%20he%20made%20his%20London%20debut.

5. *"Nothing is good in moderation. You cannot know the good in anything till you have torn the heart out of it by excess."* Oscar Wilde, *The Wit & Wisdom of Oscar Wilde,* Ralph Keyes. Quote Fancy, https://quotefancy.com/quote/882059/Oscar-Wilde-Nothing-is-good-in-moderation-You-cannot-know-good-in-anything-until-you-have#:~:text=Oscar%20Wilde%20Quote%3A%20%E2%80%9CNothing%20is,out%20of%20it%20by%20excess.%E2%80%9D)

6. *"Women love us for our defects. If we have enough of them, they will forgive us everything, even our intellects."* Oscar Wilde, *The Picture of Dorian Gray, A Woman of No Importance.*

7. *"Whatever my life may have been ethically, it has always been romantic."* *The Epigrams of Oscar Wilde,* Edited by Alvin Redman, Introduction by Vyvyan Holland.

8. Languages spoken by Oscar Wilde. Daily Genius, Untold Facts About the Famous Playwright Oscar Wilde Revealed. https://dailygenius.com/general/untold-facts-about-the-famous-playwright-oscar-wilde-revealed/

Chapter Fifteen

1. *Requiescat.* Oscar Wilde, Poem.

2. *"Had we not loved so well, not loved at all, none would have tolled the bell, none borne the pall. O bitter fate, when some long-strangled memory of sin, strikes with its poisoned knife into a heart, while she has slept at peace. Coffin-board, heavy stone, Lie on her breast, I vex my heart alone, she is at rest."* Oscar Wilde. Poem missing lyrics.

3. *"Education is an admirable thing, but it is well to remember from time to time that nothing that is worth knowing can be taught."* *The Artist as Critic: Critical Writings of Oscar Wilde; A Few Maxims for the Instruction of the Over-Educated,* by Oscar Wilde.

4. *"We spend our days, each one of us, in looking for the secret of life. Well, the secret of life is in art."* *The English Renaissance of Art,* by Oscar Wilde. Lecture delivered in the Chickering Hall, New York, on January 9, 1882.

5. *"Life under a good government is rarely dramatic; life under a bad government is always so."* Oscar Wilde, *The Wit & Wisdom of Oscar Wilde,* Ralph Keyes.

6. *"To be entirely free, and at the same time entirely dominated by law, is the eternal paradox of human life that we realize at every moment."* Oscar Wilde, *The letters of Oscar Wilde (ed. 1962) De Profundis (Letters 443)*

7. *"From the sixteenth century to our own day there is hardly any form of torture that has not been inflicted on girls, and endured by women, in obedience to the dictates of an unreasonable and monstrous Fashion."* Oscar Wilde, *Women's World* when he was editor 1,40. *The Wit & Wisdom of Oscar Wilde,* Ralph Keyes.

Chapter Sixteen

1. *"And I do think it so kind of him to tell us who he is imitating. It avoids discussion, doesn't it?"* Oscar Wilde: Interviews and Recollections by E.H. Mikhail, pp 285-286.

2. *"Ah! How sweet coffee tastes! Lovelier than a thousand kisses, sweeter far than muscatel wine!"* John Sebastian Bach, Quote.

3. *"Yes: I am a dreamer. For a dreamer is one who can only find his way by moonlight, and his punishment is that he sees the dawn before the rest of the world."* Oscar Wilde, The Critic as Artist, an essay by Oscar Wilde.

4. *"It is a marvel that those red-roseleaf lips of yours should be made no less for the madness of music and song than for the madness of kissing."* Oscar Wilde, letter to Lord Alfred Douglas, January 1893, Babbacombe Cliff.

5. In the Gold Room, A Harmony. Oscar Wilde. Poem (1881).

Chapter Seventeen

1. In the Forest, Oscar Wilde, Poem. First published in Lady's Pictorial, Christmas Number 1889.

2. There are mentions of Wilde's scarab ring by many who knew him, documented accounts by close friend Ada Leverson, poet Henri de Regnier, close friend and biographer Robert Sherard, Wilfred Hugh Chesson, Chris Healy, William Rothenstein, and some believed the ring to have been given to him by his mother, Jane Wilde. Eafitz Simons, Beside Every Man, Oscar Wilde and the Mystery of the Scarab Ring. https://eafitzsimons.wordpress.com/2017/10/03/oscar-wilde-and-the-mystery-of-the-scarab-ring/

3. *"Spontaneity is a meticulously prepared art."* Oscar Wilde, Quote. Quote Fancy. https://quotefancy.com/quote/881303/Oscar-Wilde-Spontaneity-is-a-meticulously-prepared-art

4. *"The English country gentlemen galloping after a fox—the unspeakable in full pursuit of the uneatable!"* Oscar Wilde, A Woman of No Importance.

Chapter Eighteen

1. *"You can produce tragic effects by introducing comedy. A laugh in an audience does not destroy terror but by relieving it aids it. Never be afraid that by raising a laugh you destroy tragedy. On the contrary, you intensify it."* The Epigrams of Oscar Wilde, Edited by Alvin Redman, Introduction by Vyvyan Holland.

2. *"Between men and women there is no friendship possible. There is passion, enmity, worship, love, but no friendship."* Oscar Wilde, Lady Windermere's Fan.

Chapter Nineteen

1. *"I never travel without my diary. One should always have something sensational to read in the train."* Oscar Wilde, *The Importance of Being Earnest*.

2. *"I keep a diary in order to enter the wonderful secrets of my life. If I didn't write them down, I should probably forget all about them. Memory, my dear Cecily, is the diary that we all carry about with us."* Oscar Wilde, *The Importance of Being Earnest*.

3. Wilde called white wine yellow because his friend Robert Sherard once pointed out to him that white wine was not really white. 1890s Writers in London, 100 Random Things about Oscar Wilde. http://1890swriters.blogspot.com/2013/12/100-random-things-about-oscar-wilde.html#:~:text=Wilde%20called%20white%20wine%20yellow,isn't%20white%20at%20all.

Chapter Twenty-One
1. *Pledging My Love*, Johnny Ace, writers: Robey Don D., Washington Ferdinand.

2. *"She is all the great heroines of the world in one. She is more than an individual. I love her, and I must make her love me. I want to make Romeo jealous. I want the dead lovers of the world to hear our laughter, and grow sad. I want a breath of our passion to stir dust into consciousness, to wake their ashes into pain."* Oscar Wilde, *The Picture of Dorian Gray*.

3. *"There is no such thing as a romantic experience; there are romantic memories, and there is the desire of romance—that is all. Our most fiery moments of ecstasy are merely shadows of what somewhere else we have felt, or what we long someday to feel."* Oscar Wilde in conversation, *The Epigrams of Oscar Wilde*, Edited by Alvin Redman, Introduction by Vyvyan Holland.

Chapter Twenty-Two
1. *"You know we poor artists have to show ourselves in society from time to time, just to remind the public that we are not savages."* Oscar Wilde, *The Picture of Dorian Gray*.

2. *"To recognize that the soul of a man is unknowable is the ultimate achievement of wisdom. The final mystery is oneself. When one has weighed the sun in a balance, and measured the steps of the moon, and mapped out the seven heavens star by star, there still remains oneself. Who can calculate the orbit of his own soul?"* Oscar Wilde, *De Profundis*.

Chapter Twenty-Three
1. *To Love Somebody*, Bee Gees, writers: Barry Gibb, Robin Gibb.

2. *There be None of Beauty's Daughters*, Lord Byron, Poem.

3. *"England never appreciates a poet until he is dead."* Oscar Wilde during his American lecture tour, quoted to reporters at the Alding Hotel in

Philadelphia referring to Whitman, the American poet he most admired. January 16, 1882.

Chapter Twenty-Four

1. *"I should be miserable if I thought I should ever be more serious than I am at the present moment."* Oscar Wilde, *The Picture of Dorian Gray.*
2. *The Long and Winding Road,* The Beatles, writers: John Lennon, Paul McCartney.
3. *"Beauty is a form of genius—is higher, indeed, than genius as it needs no explanation." The Epigrams of Oscar Wilde,* Edited by Alvin Redman, Introduction by Vyvyan Holland; Oscar Wilde, *The Picture of Dorian Gray.*
4. *"Always! That is a dreadful word. It makes me shudder when I hear it."* Oscar Wilde, *The Picture of Dorian Gray.*
5. *"There is only one thing in the world worse than being talked about, and that is not being talked about."* Oscar Wilde, *The Picture of Dorian Gray.*
6. *"It seemed to me that all my life had been narrowed to one perfect point of rose-coloured joy."* Oscar Wilde, *The Picture of Dorian Gray.*
7. *"Why, he is a demy who hails from Trinity College, Dublin, where he got medals and things. A most interesting chap: I'll get him to come up here and meet you. You ought to hear him talk!"* Hunter-Blair D. (1979) Oscar Wilde at Magdalen College Oxford. In: Mikhail E.H. (eds) Oscar Wilde. Palgrave Macmillan, London. https://doi.org/10.1007/978-1-349-03923-4_3
8. *"After the first glass of absinth you see things as you wish they were. After the second you see them as they are not. Finally, you see things as they really are, and that is the most horrible thing in the world. I mean disassociated. Take a top hat. You think you see it as it really is. But you don't because you associated it with other things and ideas. If you had never heard of one before, and suddenly saw it alone, you'd be frightened, or you'd laugh. That is the effect absinthe has, and that is why it drives men mad. Three nights I sat up all night drinking absinthe, and thinking that I was singularly clear-headed and sane. The waiter came in and began watering the sawdust. The most wonderful flowers, tulips, lilies and roses, sprang up, and made a garden in the café. 'Don't you see them?' I said to him. 'Mais non, monsieur, il n'y a rien.'"* Oscar Wilde, in-conversation with friends. Quote Investigator, Absinthe.
https://quoteinvestigator.com/2012/06/20/absinthe-wilde/
9. *Imagine,* John Lennon. Writers: John Lennon, Yoko Ono.
10. *Rhiannon,* Fleetwood Mac. Writers: Stephanie (Stevie) Nicks.
11. *We Belong Together,* Ritchie Valens. Writers: Robert Carr, Johnny Mitchell, Hy Weiss.
12. *At Last,* Etta James. Writers: Gordon Mack, Warren Harry.

Chapter Twenty-Five

1. *"How fond women are of doing dangerous things! It is one of the qualities in them that I admire most."* Oscar Wilde, *The Picture of Dorian Gray.*

2. *"A woman will flirt with anybody in the world as long as other people are looking on."* Oscar Wilde, *The Picture of Dorian Gray.*

3. *Where Be Ye Going, You Devon Maid?* John Keats, Poem.

4. *"Women are meant to be loved, not to be understood."* Oscar Wilde, *The Sphinx Without a Secret.*

5. *"The critic has to educate the public; the artist has to educate the critic."* Oscar Wilde, *The Wit & Wisdom of Oscar Wilde*, Ralph Keyes.

6. *"To live is the rarest thing in the world. Most people exist, that is all."* *The Soul of Man under Socialism*, Oscar Wilde, 1891.

Chapter Twenty-Six

1. *"To banish imperfection is to destroy expression, to check exertion, to paralyze vitality."* John Ruskin, *The Stones of Venice.*

2. *"If we are to have great men working at all, or less men doing their best, the work will be imperfect, however beautiful. Of human work none but what is bad can be perfect, in its own way."* John Ruskin, *The Stones of Venice.*

3. *"There is a good deal to be said for blushing, if one can do it at the proper moment."* Oscar Wilde, *A Woman of No Importance.*

4. *"The costume of the nineteenth century is detestable. It is so somber, so depressing."* Oscar Wilde, *The Picture of Dorian Gray.*

5. *"The only thing one never regrets are one's mistakes."* Oscar Wilde, *The Picture of Dorian Gray.*

6. *"I want to place her on a pedestal of gold and to see the world worship the woman who is mine. What is marriage? An irrevocable vow. It is an irrevocable vow that I want to take. Her trust makes me faithful; her belief makes me good."* Oscar Wilde, *The Picture of Dorian Gray.*

Chapter Twenty-Seven

1. *"To get into the best society, nowadays, one has either to feed people, amuse people, or shock people—that is all!"* Oscar Wilde, *A Woman of No Importance*, Act 3, conversation between Gerald and Lord Illingworth.

2. *"To the world I seem, by intention on my part, a dilettante and dandy merely—it is not wise to show one's heart to the world—and as seriousness of manner is the disguise of the fool, folly in its exquisite modes of triviality and indifference and lack of care is the robe of the wise man. In so vulgar an age as this we all need masks."* Oscar Wilde, *The Picture of Dorian Gray.*

3. *"For him Art has no marvel, and Beauty no meaning, and the past no message. He thinks that civilization began with the introduction of steam, and looks with contempt upon all centuries that had no hot-water apparatuses in their houses."* Oscar Wilde, *The American Man*, article American tour.
https://www.oscarwildeinamerica.org/Resources/The-American-Man.pdf

4. *"What has Oscar in common with Art? Except that he dines at our tables, and picks from our platters the plums for the pudding he peddles in the*

provinces." James McNeill Whistler. *The World,* 17 November 1886, in *The Gentle Art of Making Enemies* (1890); University of Glasgow, The Correspondence of James McNeill Whistler.

https://www.whistler.arts.gla.ac.uk/correspondence/recno/display/?cid=114 06

5. *"I have nothing to declare except my genius."* Oscar Wilde, Oscar Wilde in America by John Cooper.

https://www.oscarwildeinamerica.org/quotations/nothing-to-declare.html

The Epigrams of Oscar Wilde, Edited by Alvin Redman, Introduction by Vyvyan Holland.

6. *"Would you like to know the great drama of my life? It is that I put all my genius into my life; I put only my talent into my works." The Epigrams of Oscar Wilde,* Edited by Alvin Redman, Introduction by Vyvyan Holland.

7. *"Whistler is indeed one of the very greatest masters of painting, in my opinion. And I may add that in this opinion Mr. Whistler himself entirely concurs."* Oscar Wilde, *Pall Mall Gazette.*

8. *"When you and I are together we never talk about anything except ourselves."* Oscar Wilde, conversation with James Whistler, University of Glasgow, The Correspondence of James McNeill Whistler.

https://www.whistler.arts.gla.ac.uk/correspondence/freetext/display/?rs=23 41&q=&year1=&year2=1903

9. *"No, no, Oscar, you forget. When you and I are together, we never talk about anything except me."* James Whistler, conversation with Oscar Wilde, University of Glasgow, The Correspondence of James McNeill Whistler.

https://www.whistler.arts.gla.ac.uk/correspondence/recno/display/?cid=113 90

10. *"It is true, Jimmy, we were talking about you, but I was thinking of myself."* Oscar Wilde, conversation with James Whistler, University of Glasgow, The Correspondence of James McNeill Whistler.

https://www.whistler.arts.gla.ac.uk/correspondence/recno/display/?cid=110 24

11. *"If I were all alone, marooned on some desert island and had my things with me, I should dress for dinner every evening." The Epigrams of Oscar Wilde,* Edited by Alvin Redman, Introduction by Vyvyan Holland.

12. *"One's real life is so often the life that one does not lead."* Oscar Wilde, In Conversation, *The Epigrams of Oscar Wilde,* Edited by Alvin Redman, Introduction by Vyvyan Holland.

13. Publicity stunt for opening of his play, *Lady Windermere's Fan,* Wilde asked several friends to wear a green carnation in their button-holes with the mystery heightened by an actor wearing one as well. There are several accounts to this story not being actual where there were no accounts to this being done at *Lady Windermere's Fan.* However, there were accounts of Wilde and several men wearing carnations two weeks later at London's Royalty Theatre production of Banville's play, *The Kiss.* The carnation at that time had superseded the lily and the sunflower and was in fact dyed

green, blue, and heliotrope, which was called a "metallic blue carnation." The white lily was used to replace the carnation due to the controversy of actual events and the history that Wilde did from time to time carry a white lily at events in his hand. Oscar Wilde and the Green Carnation, Karl Beckson, *English Literature in Transition, 1880-1920*, ELT Press, Vol. 43, Number 4, 2000, pp. 387-397, Article
https://muse.jhu.edu/article/367465
Wilde, Society, and Society Drama by Cary M. Mazer
https://web.english.upenn.edu/~cmazer/imp.html#:~:text=Wilde%20spent%20most%20of%20the,chain%20hung%20from%20his%20white

14. Prior to the U.S. lecture tour, concerned he did not have talent for public speaking, he took elocution lessons from a friend where he was quoted saying, *"I want a natural style, with a touch of affection."* Oscar Wilde, *The Wit & Wisdom of Oscar Wilde*, Ralph Keyes.

15. *"He finds it difficult to live up to the level of his blue China."* Oscar Wilde, *A Lecture in America, The Epigrams of Oscar Wilde*, Edited by Alvin Redman, Introduction by Vyvyan Holland.

16. *Baby, I Love You*, The Ronettes. Writers: Jeff Barry, Ellie Greenwich, Phil Spector.

17. *"I quite agree with Dr. Nordau's assertion that all men of genius are insane, but Dr. Nordau forgets that all sane people are idiots."* Oscar Wilde, *The Wit & Wisdom of Oscar Wilde*, Ralph Keyes.

Chapter Twenty-Eight

1. *"There is no such thing as a good influence, Mr. Gray. All influence is immoral—immoral from the scientific point of view."* Oscar Wilde, *The Picture of Dorian Gray*.

2. *"A cigarette is the perfect type of a perfect pleasure. It is exquisite, and it leaves one unsatisfied. What more could one want?"* Oscar Wilde, *The Picture of Dorian Gray*.

3. *"The advantage of the emotions is that they lead us astray, and the advantage of science is that it is not emotional.* Oscar Wilde, *The Picture of Dorian Gray*.

4. *"Nowadays people know the price of everything and the value of nothing."* Oscar Wilde, *The Picture of Dorian Gray*.

5. *"M. Zola... is determined to show that, if he has not got genius, he can at least be dull."* Oscar Wilde, *The Decay of Lying*, A Dialogue between Cyril and Vivian.

6. *"Women represent the triumph of matter over mind, just as men represent the triumph of mind over morals."* Oscar Wilde, *The Picture of Dorian Gray*.

7. *"London is too full of fogs and serious people. Whether the fogs produce the serious people or whether the serious people produce the fogs, I don't know."* Oscar Wilde, *Lady Windermere's Fan*, Act 4, Mrs. Erlynne.

8. *"I was working on the proof of one of my poems all the morning, and took out a comma. In the afternoon I put it back again."* The Epigrams of Oscar Wilde, Edited by Alvin Redman, Introduction by Vyvyan Holland.

9. *Symphony in Yellow*, Oscar Wilde, Poem.

10. *"I often have long conversations with myself, and I am so clever that sometimes I don't understand a single word of what I am saying."* Oscar Wilde, *The Remarkable Rocket*, The Happy Prince and Other Stories.

11. *"Murder is always a mistake. One should never do anything that one cannot talk about after dinner."* Oscar Wilde, *The Picture of Dorian Gray.*

12. *"I adore them (London dinner parties). The clever people never listen, and the stupid people never talk."* Oscar Wilde, *A Woman of No Importance*, Act 1, Mrs. Allonby speaking to Hester of a London dinner-party.

13. *"Man is least himself when he talks in his own person. Give him a mask, and he will tell you the truth."* Oscar Wilde, *The Critic as Artist*, an essay by Oscar Wilde.

14. *"A mask tells us more than a face."* Oscar Wilde, *Pen, Pencil and Poison.*

15. *"A man who can dominate a London dinner table can dominate the world."* Oscar Wilde, *A Woman of No Importance*, conversation between Gerald and Lord Illingworth.

16. *"She behaves as if she was beautiful. Most American women do. It is the secret of their charm."* Oscar Wilde, *The Picture of Dorian Gray.*

Chapter Twenty-Nine

1. *"Sentiment is all very well for the buttonhole. But the essential thing for a necktie is style. A well-tied tie is the first serious step in life."* Oscar Wilde, *A Woman of No Importance*, Act 3, conversation between Gerald and Lord Illingworth.

2. *"Fashion is such an essential part of the mundus muliebris (woman's world) of our day, that it seems to me absolutely necessary that its growth, development, and phases should be duly chronicled."* Oscar Wilde, editor of Woman's World, Literary and Other Notes, repr. Wilde 104.

3. *"As for believing things, I can believe anything, provided that it is quite incredible."* Oscar Wilde, *The Picture of Dorian Gray.*

4. *The House of Judgment*, Oscar Wilde and Jane Francesca Wilde, Poems in Prose.

5. *Something*, The Beatles. Writers: George Harrison.

6. *"I cannot live without the atmosphere of Love: I must love and be loved, whatever price I pay for it."* Oscar Wilde, *The Wit & Wisdom of Oscar Wilde*, Ralph Keyes.

7. *"The most terrible thing about it is not that it breaks one's heart—hearts are made to be broken—but that it turns one's heart to stone."* Oscar Wilde, *De Profundis*. *"My desire to live is as intense as ever, and though my heart is broken, hearts are made to be broken: that is why God sends sorrow into the world."* Oscar Wilde, *The Complete Letters of Oscar Wilde.*

8. *I Shall Not Cry Return*, Ellen Huntington, Poem.

9. *"My own darling, ever since I first looked upon your wonderful and incomparable beauty, I have dared to love you wildly, passionately, devotedly, hopelessly."* Oscar Wilde, *The Importance of Being Earnest*.

10. *"If you are not too long, I will wait here for you all my life."* Oscar Wilde, *The Importance of Being Earnest*, conversation between Jack and Gwendolen.

11. *"To err is humane (human); to forgive, divine."* Alexander Pope, Quote.

12. *"Youth is something which only young men have, and which only old men know how to use."* Thomas Wolfe, *Of Time and the River*.

13. *I Arise from Dreams of Thee*, Percy Bysshe Shelley, Poem.

Chapter Thirty

1. *"Every woman is a rebel, and usually in wild revolt against herself."* Oscar Wilde, *A Woman of No Importance*, Act 3, conversation between Gerald and Lord Illingworth.

2. *"All great art is the expression of man's delight in God's work, not in his own."* John Ruskin, Quote. *"All great art is to some degree didactic; all great art is praise—to our God who created all."* John Ruskin, *Stones of Venice*,

3. *"In its primary aspect, a painting has no more spiritual message than an exquisite fragment of Venetian glass or a blue tile from the wall of Damascus: it is a beautifully coloured surface, nothing more. The channels by which all noble imaginative work in painting should touch, and do touch the soul, are not those of the truths of life, nor metaphysical truths."* Oscar Wilde, *The English Renaissance of Art*, by Oscar Wilde. Lecture delivered in the Chickering Hall, New York, on January 9, 1882.

Chapter Thirty-One

1. *"The tears that we shed at a play are a type of the exquisite sterile emotions that it is the function of Art to awaken. We weep, but we are not wounded. We grieve, but our grief is not bitter."* Oscar Wilde, *The Critic as Artist*, an essay by Oscar Wilde.

2. *"In this world there are only two tragedies. One is not getting what one wants, and the other is getting it. The last is much the worst, the last is a real tragedy!"* Oscar Wilde, *Lady Windermere's Fan*. Act 3, Mr. Dumby.

3. *She Walks in Beauty*, Lord Byron, Poem.

4. *"Men always want to be a woman's first love. That is their clumsy vanity. We women have a more subtle instinct about things. What we like is to be a man's last romance."* Oscar Wilde, *A Woman of No Importance*, Act 2, Mrs. Allonby.

5. *Out of the Rolling Ocean the Crowd*, Walt Whitman, Poem.

6. *Remember Me*, Jolene McCall, Poem.

7. *"Every heart sings a song, incomplete, until another heart whispers back. Those who wish to sing always find a song. At the touch of a lover, everyone becomes a poet."* Plato, Quote.

Chapter Thirty-Two

1. *Hang on Sloopy*, The McCoys. Writers: Wes Farrell, Bert Berns.
2. *Twist and Shout*, the Beatles. Writers: Phil Medley, Bert Berns.
3. *We Belong Together*, Ritchie Valens. Writers: Robert Carr, Johnny Mitchell, Hy Weiss.
4. *"All I insist on, and nothing else, is that you should show the whole world that you are not afraid. Be silent, if you choose; but when it is necessary, speak—and speak in such a way that people will remember it."* Wolfgang Amadeus Mozart, Quote.
5. *"Ah! happy they whose hearts can break, and peace of pardon win! How else may man make straight his plan, and cleanse his soul from Sin? How else but through a broken heart, may Lord Christ enter in?"* Oscar Wilde, *The Ballad of Reading Gaol.*

Chapter Thirty-Three

1. *Memories of You*, Jolene McCall, Poem.
2. *"My own darling, ever since I first looked upon your wonderful and incomparable beauty, I have dared to love you wildly, passionately, devotedly, hopelessly."* Oscar Wilde, *The Importance of Being Earnest.*
3. *"If you are not too long, I will wait here for you all my life."* Oscar Wilde, *The Importance of Being Earnest,* conversation between Jack and Gwendolen.
4. *"If you are not too long, I will wait here for you all my life."* Oscar Wilde, *The Importance of Being Earnest,* conversation between Jack and Gwendolen.

Sources

- *A Few Maxims for the Instruction of the Over-Educated*, Oscar Wilde
- *A Woman of No Importance*, Oscar Wilde
- *An Ideal Husband*, Oscar Wilde
- *De Profundis*, Oscar Wilde
- *Impressions of America*, Oscar Wilde
- *Lady Windermere's Fan*, Oscar Wilde
- *Lord Arthur Savile's Crime*, Oscar Wilde
- *Oscar Wilde A Life in Letters, Writings and Wit*, Juliet Gardiner
- *Oscar Wilde; His Life and Confessions*, Frank Harris
- *Oscar Wilde: Interviews and Recollections*, E.H. Mikhail
- *Oscar Wilde Selected Poems*, Robert Mighall
- *Pen, Pencil and Poison*, Oscar Wilde
- *Phrases and Philosophies for the Use of the Young (1894)*, Oscar Wilde
- *Poems in Prose*, Oscar Wilde and Jane Francesca Wilde
- *Salome*, Oscar Wilde
- *The American Man*, Oscar Wilde
- *The Artist as Critic: Critical Writings of Oscar Wilde*, an essay
- *The Ballad of Reading Gaol*, Oscar Wilde
- *The Canterville Ghost*, Oscar Wilde
- *The Complete Fairy Tales of Oscar Wilde*
- *The Complete Letters of Oscar Wilde*, Oscar Wilde
- *The Complete Short Stories of Oscar Wilde*, Oscar Wilde
- *The Critic as Artist*, Oscar Wilde. David Zwirner Books
- *The Decay of Lying*, Oscar Wilde
- *The Duchess of Padua*, Oscar Wilde
- *The English Renaissance of Art*, Oscar Wilde
- *The Epigrams of Oscar Wilde*, Edited by Alvin Redman, Introduction by Vyvyan Holland
- *The Happy Prince and Other Stories*, Oscar Wilde
- *The Importance of Being Earnest*, Oscar Wilde
- *The Model Millionaire*, Oscar Wilde
- *The Pall Mall Gazette*
- *The Picture of Dorian Gray*, Oscar Wilde
- *The Portrait of Mr. W. H.*, Oscar Wilde
- *The Remarkable Rocket*, Oscar Wilde
- *The Sphinx Without a Secret*, Oscar Wilde
- *The Soul of Man Under Socialism*, Oscar Wilde
- *The Truth of Masks, a Note on Illusion*, Oscar Wilde

- *The Unmasking of Oscar Wilde*, Joseph Pearce
- *The Wit & Wisdom of Oscar Wilde*, Ralph Keyes
- *Vera, or the Nihilists*, Oscar Wilde
- *Wilde's Women*, Eleanor Fitzsimmons

DISCREPANCIES & FACTS OF HISTORY

- Oscar Wilde's quotes were used to bring the character and style alive for the reader to better understand the famous icon and the greatest playwriter of the 1890s, and to give the reader a more accurate depiction of Wilde's life. The quotes used may or may not have been ones Wilde actually spoke during or before 1881.
- The American tour where Wilde traveled throughout the United States in 1882, was depicted within the story as Wilde aware of the tour the early part of 1881, when in fact, this was not known until after the premier of Patience. The actual premier was depicted within the novel accurately.
- Bewley's Café, 19th century, located on Grafton Street, Dublin, Ireland. Bewley's Café originally opened in the 1890s. Bewley's was one of the first cafes to bring many more to the city of Dublin and with its rich history, it was incorporated into the novel. Bewley's recently closed their doors in May of 2020. https://www.thejournal.ie/readme/bewleys-grafton-street-5094430-May2020/
- Dublin is noted as being part of the UK. From the Act of Union on 1 January 1801, until 6 December 1922, the island of Ireland was part of the United Kingdom of Great Britain and Ireland.

TRANSLATIONS & ODD WORDS

CHAPTER SEVEN

- Joie de vivre; Translation: Joy of living

CHAPER FOURTEEN

- Faiche Stiabhna (Irish); Translation: St. Stephen's Lawn

- Sa beauté est rare, n'est-ce pas; Translation: Her beauty is rare, isn't she?
  Talent de beauté intelligent, non; Translation: Clever, beauty, talent, no?
  Oui, tout un tresor; Translation: Yes, a whole treasure.
  Oui, messieurs. Je suis tout à fait le trésor et je fais bien de rendre mon homme heureux. Droit mon cheri? Translation: Yes gentlemen. I am quite the treasure and I do well to make my man happy. Right my darling?

CHAPTER FIFTEEN

- Donner & Blitzen (German); Translation: Thunder & Lightning
- Henry, Oscar's Friend, Horses
  Names: Ardan & Fionna
  Ardan, Irish, Meaning "High Aspiration."
  https://babynamesofireland.com/ardan#:~:text=MEANING%3A%20
  From%20ardanach%20meaning%20%E2%80%9C%E2%80%9D,%
  E2%80%9C%E2%80%9Dare%20%2B%20dawn%E2%80%9D%E2
  %80%9D
  Fionna or Fiona, Gaelic Word Fionn, Meaning "White, Fair."
  https://en.wikipedia.org/wiki/Fiona

CHAPTER SEVENTEEN

- Joie de vivre; Translation: Joy of living

CHAPTER TWENTY-ONE

- Sláinte chuig na fir, agus go mairfídh na mná go deo (Irish);
  Translation: Health to the men, and may the women live forever.

CHAPTER TWENTY-FOUR

- Musn't, slang used by Oscar Wilde in many of his plays.

CHAPTER TWENTY-FIVE

- Scammered Meaning

The Dictionary of Victorian Insults & Niceties, Victorian Drinking Words, Tinehreno
https://victoriandictionary.wordpress.com/2015/01/17/victorian-drinking-words/

- Prairie Oyster
  Cultura Colectiva, 6 Hangover Cures From the 19th Century, by Sairy Romero
  https://culturacolectiva.com/history/hangover-cure-from-the-nineteenth-century
- Katzenjammer, German screeching cats
  Discover Magazine, Why Don't Some People Seem to Get Hangovers? By Jesse Hawley
  https://www.discovermagazine.com/health/why-dont-some-people-seem-to-get-hangovers

CHAPTER TWENTY-SIX

- Eau de vie; Translation: Water of life
- Loge Seating
  Dictionary, Loge
  https://www.dictionary.com/browse/loge

CHAPTER TWENTY-SEVEN

- Cri de Coeur: A passionate appeal, complaint, or protest
- The Word Nice, a lady once told Oscar Wilde that something was 'awfully nice,' where he replied, 'But, nice is a nasty word.' The lady responded, 'But, is nasty such a nice word?'
- Trovi la Cateline più affascinante (Italian); Translation: Do you find Cateline most charming?
- Lo voglio— Lei è parlato per? (Italian); Translation: I do—she is spoken for?
  Credo che lei sia (Italian); Translation: I believe she is.

CHAPTER TWENTY-NINE

- Mundus Muliebris (Latin); Translation: Ornaments

CHAPTER THIRTY

- Petrichor (Greek)
  Met Office, Petrichor
  https://www.metoffice.gov.uk/weather/learn-about/weather/types-of-weather/rain/petrichor
- Paris toujours vivant jamais oublié; Translation: Paris still alive, never forget

CHAPTER THIRTY-ONE
- Vue Sur la Mer; Translation: Sea View
- Mais, J'adore toi; Translation: But, I love you
- Jamais Oublie; Translation: Never forget

HISTORICAL BACKGROUND AND RESEARCH
OSCAR WILLDE
OCEANS AND TIME BETWEEN US
Jolene McCall
Copyright © 2021 by Hori-Son Press

www.horisonpress.com

info@horisonpress.com

Hori-Son
PRESS